Wuthering Heights

Emily Brontë

ALMA CLASSICS

ALMA CLASSICS
an imprint of

ALMA BOOKS LTD
3 Castle Yard
Richmond
Surrey TW10 6TF
United Kingdom
www.almabooks.com

Wuthering Heights first published in 1847
This edition first published by Alma Classics in 2007. Reprinted 2009, 2010
This new edition first published in 2013. Reprinted 2014, 2017

Edited text, notes and background material © Alma Classics

Printed in Great Britain by CPI Group (UK) Ltd, Croydon, CR0 4YY

ISBN: 978-1-84749-321-7

Contents

Emily Brontë (1818–48)

Revd Patrick Brontë,
Emily's father

Maria Branwell,
Emily's mother

Charlotte Brontë

Anne Brontë

The Brontë Parsonage in Haworth (above) and
Haworth's parish church and cemetery (below)

High Sunderland, a seventeenth-century mansion near
Law Hill, Halifax, a possible inspiration for Wuthering Heights

Ponden Hall, near Stanbury, a possible inspiration for
Thrushcross Grange

WUTHERING HEIGHTS

1

1 801 – I HAVE JUST RETURNED FROM A VISIT to my landlord, the solitary neighbour that I shall be troubled with. This is certainly a beautiful country! In all England, I do not believe that I could have fixed on a situation so completely removed from the stir of society. A perfect misanthropist's heaven – and Mr Heathcliff and I are such a suitable pair to divide the desolation between us. A capital fellow! He little imagined how my heart warmed towards him when I beheld his black eyes withdraw so suspiciously under their brows, as I rode up, and when his fingers sheltered themselves, with a jealous resolution, still further in his waistcoat, as I announced my name.

"Mr Heathcliff?" I said.

A nod was the answer.

"Mr Lockwood, your new tenant, sir. I do myself the honour of calling as soon as possible after my arrival, to express the hope that I have not inconvenienced you by my perseverance in soliciting the occupation of Thrushcross Grange: I heard yesterday you had had some thoughts—"

"Thrushcross Grange is my own, sir," he interrupted, wincing. "I should not allow anyone to inconvenience me, if I could hinder it – walk in!"

The "walk in!" was uttered with closed teeth, and expressed the sentiment: "Go to the Deuce!" Even the gate over which he leant manifested no sympathizing movement to the words; and I think that circumstance determined me to accept the invitation: I felt interested in a man who seemed more exaggeratedly reserved than myself.

When he saw my horse's breast fairly pushing the barrier, he did pull out his hand to unchain it, and then sullenly preceded me up the causeway, calling, as we entered the court: "Joseph, take Mr Lockwood's horse – and bring up some wine."

"Here we have the whole establishment of domestics, I suppose," was the reflection suggested by this compound order. "No wonder the grass grows up between the flags, and cattle are the only hedge-cutters."

Joseph was an elderly, nay, an old man: very old, perhaps, though hale and sinewy.

"The Lord help us!" he soliloquized in an undertone of peevish displeasure, while relieving me of my horse: looking, meantime, in my face so sourly, that I charitably conjectured he must have need of divine aid to digest his dinner, and his pious ejaculation had no reference to my unexpected advent.

Wuthering Heights is the name of Mr Heathcliff's dwelling, "Wuthering" being a significant provincial adjective, descriptive of the atmospheric tumult to which its station is exposed in stormy weather. Pure, bracing ventilation they must have up there at all times, indeed: one may guess the power of the north wind blowing over the edge by the excessive slant of a few stunted firs at the end of the house; and by a range of gaunt thorns all stretching their limbs one way, as if craving alms of the sun. Happily, the architect had foresight to build it strong: the narrow windows are deeply set in the wall, and the corners defended with large jutting stones.

Before passing the threshold, I paused to admire a quantity of grotesque carving lavished over the front, and especially about the principal door, above which, among a wilderness of crumbling griffins and shameless little boys, I detected the date "1500" and the name "Hareton Earnshaw". I would have made a few comments and requested a short history of the place from the surly owner, but his attitude at the door appeared to demand my speedy entrance, or complete departure, and I had no desire to aggravate his impatience previous to inspecting the penetralium.*

One step brought us into the family sitting room, without any introductory lobby or passage: they call it here "the house" pre-eminently. It includes kitchen and parlour, generally, but I believe at Wuthering Heights the kitchen is forced to retreat altogether into another quarter: at least I distinguished a chatter of tongues, and a clatter of culinary utensils, deep within; and I observed no signs of roasting, boiling or baking about the huge fireplace; nor any glitter of copper saucepans and tin colanders on the walls. One end, indeed, reflected splendidly both light and heat from ranks of immense pewter dishes, interspersed with silver jugs and tankards, towering row after row, on a vast oak dresser, to the very roof. The latter had never been underdrawn: its entire anatomy lay bare to an enquiring eye, except where a frame of wood laden with oatcakes and clusters of legs of beef, mutton and ham concealed it. Above the chimney were sundry villainous old guns and a couple of horse pistols, and by way of ornament, three gaudily painted canisters disposed along its ledge. The floor was of smooth white stone; the chairs high-backed, primitive structures, painted green: one or two heavy black ones lurking in the shade. In an arch under the dresser reposed a huge liver-coloured bitch pointer, surrounded by a swarm of squealing puppies, and other dogs haunted other recesses.

The apartment and furniture would have been nothing extraordinary as belonging to a homely, northern farmer with a stubborn countenance and stalwart limbs set out to advantage in knee breeches and gaiters. Such an individual, seated in his armchair, his mug of ale frothing on the round table before him, is to be seen in any circuit of five or six miles among these hills, if you go at the right time after dinner. But Mr Heathcliff forms a singular contrast to his abode and style of living. He is a dark-skinned gypsy in aspect, in dress and manners a gentleman – that is, as much a gentleman as many a country squire: rather slovenly perhaps, yet not looking amiss with his negligence, because he has an erect and handsome figure – and rather morose. Possibly, some people might suspect him of a degree of underbred pride – I have a sympathetic chord within that tells me it is nothing of the sort; I know, by instinct, his reserve springs from an aversion to showy displays of feeling – to manifestations of mutual kindliness. He'll love and hate, equally under cover, and esteem it a species of impertinence to be loved or hated again. No, I'm running on too fast: I bestow my own attributes over-liberally on him. Mr Heathcliff may have entirely dissimilar reasons for keeping his hand out of the way, when he meets a would-be acquaintance, to those which actuate me. Let me hope my constitution is almost peculiar: my dear mother used to say I should never have a comfortable home, and only last summer I proved myself perfectly unworthy of one.

While enjoying a month of fine weather at the sea coast, I was thrown into the company of a most fascinating creature: a real goddess in my eyes, as long as she took no notice of me. I "never told my love"* vocally; still, if looks have language, the merest idiot might have guessed I was over head and ears: she understood me at last, and looked a return – the sweetest of all imaginable looks – and what did I do? I confess it with shame – shrunk icily into myself, like a snail; at every glance retired colder and further; till finally the poor innocent was led to doubt her own senses and, overwhelmed with confusion at her supposed mistake, persuaded her mama to decamp.

By this curious turn of disposition I have gained the reputation of deliberate heartlessness; how undeserved, I alone can appreciate.

I took a seat at the end of the hearthstone opposite that towards which my landlord advanced, and filled up an interval of silence by attempting to caress the canine mother, who had left her nursery and was sneaking wolfishly to the back of my legs, her lip curled up and her white teeth watering for a snatch. My caress provoked a long, guttural gnarl.*

"You'd better let the dog alone," growled Mr Heathcliff in unison, checking fiercer demonstrations with a punch of his foot. "She's not accustomed to be spoilt – not kept for a pet."

Then, striding to a side door, he shouted again:

"Joseph!"

Joseph mumbled indistinctly in the depths of the cellar, but gave no intimation of ascending; so his master dived down to him, leaving me vis-à-vis the ruffianly bitch and a pair of grim, shaggy sheep dogs, who shared with her a jealous guardianship over all my movements.

Not anxious to come in contact with their fangs, I sat still – but, imagining they would scarcely understand tacit insults, I unfortunately indulged in winking and making faces at the trio, and some turn of my physiognomy so irritated madam that she suddenly broke into a fury and leapt on my knees. I flung her back, and hastened to interpose the table between us. This proceeding aroused the whole hive: half a dozen four-footed fiends, of various sizes and ages, issued from hidden dens to the common centre. I felt my heels and coat laps peculiar subjects of assault; and, parrying off the larger combatants as effectually as I could with the poker, I was constrained to demand, aloud, assistance from some of the household in re-establishing peace.

Mr Heathcliff and his man climbed the cellar steps with vexatious phlegm. I don't think they moved one second faster than usual, though the hearth was an absolute tempest of worrying and yelping.

6

Happily, an inhabitant of the kitchen made more dispatch: a lusty dame, with tucked-up gown, bare arms and fire-flushed cheeks, rushed into the midst of us, flourishing a frying pan; and used that weapon, and her tongue, to such purpose that the storm subsided magically, and she only remained, heaving like a sea after a high wind, when her master entered on the scene.

"What the devil is the matter?" he asked, eyeing me in a manner that I could ill endure, after this inhospitable treatment.

"What the devil, indeed!" I muttered. "The herd of possessed swine* could have had no worse spirits in them than those animals of yours, sir. You might as well leave a stranger with a brood of tigers!"

"They won't meddle with persons who touch nothing," he remarked, putting the bottle before me and restoring the displaced table. "The dogs do right to be vigilant. Take a glass of wine?"

"No, thank you."

"Not bitten, are you?"

"If I had been, I would have set my signet on the biter." Heathcliff's countenance relaxed into a grin.

"Come, come," he said, "you are flurried, Mr Lockwood. Here, take a little wine. Guests are so exceedingly rare in this house that I and my dogs, I am willing to own, hardly know how to receive them. Your health, sir!"

I bowed and returned the pledge, beginning to perceive that it would be foolish to sit sulking for the misbehaviour of a pack of curs; besides, I felt loath to yield the fellow further amusement at my expense, since his humour took that turn. He – probably swayed by prudential consideration of the folly of offending a good tenant – relaxed a little in the laconic style of chipping off his pronouns and auxiliary verbs, and introduced what he supposed would be a subject of interest to me, a discourse on the advantages and disadvantages of my present place of retirement.

I found him very intelligent on the topics we touched, and before I went home I was encouraged so far as to volunteer another visit tomorrow.

He evidently wished no repetition of my intrusion. I shall go notwithstanding. It is astonishing how sociable I feel myself, compared with him.

2

YESTERDAY AFTERNOON SET IN, misty and cold. I had half a mind to spend it by my study fire, instead of wading through heath and mud to Wuthering Heights. On coming up from dinner, however (NB: I dine between twelve and one o'clock; the housekeeper, a matronly lady, taken as a fixture along with the house, could not, or would not, comprehend my request that I might be served at five), on mounting the stairs with this lazy intention, and stepping into the room, I saw a servant girl on her knees, surrounded by brushes and coal scuttles, and raising an infernal dust as she extinguished the flames with heaps of cinders. This spectacle drove me back immediately; I took my hat, and after a four-miles' walk, arrived at Heathcliff's garden gate just in time to escape the first feathery flakes of a snow shower.

On that bleak hilltop the earth was hard with a black frost, and the air made me shiver through every limb. Being unable to remove the chain, I jumped over and, running up the flagged causeway bordered with straggling gooseberry bushes, knocked vainly for admittance, till my knuckles tingled and the dogs howled.

"Wretched inmates!" I ejaculated mentally, "you deserve perpetual isolation from your species for your churlish inhospitality. At least, I would not keep my doors barred in the daytime. I don't care – I will get in!"

So resolved, I grasped the latch and shook it vehemently. Vinegar-faced Joseph projected his head from a round window of the barn.

"Whet are ye for?" he shouted. "T' maister's dahn i' t' fowld.* Goa rahnd by th' end ut' laith,* if yah went tuh spake tull him."

"Is there nobody inside to open the door?" I hallooed responsively.

"They's nobbut t' missis; and shoo'll not oppen 't an ye mak yer flaysome* dins till neeght."

"Why? Cannot you tell her who I am, eh, Joseph?"

"Nor-ne me! I'll hae no hend wi't," muttered the head, vanishing.

The snow began to drive thickly. I seized the handle to essay another trial, when a young man without coat, and shouldering a pitchfork, appeared in the yard behind. He hailed me to follow him, and after marching through a wash house and a paved area containing a coal shed, pump and pigeon cot, we at length arrived in the large, warm, cheerful apartment where I was formerly received.

It glowed delightfully in the radiance of an immense fire, compounded of coal, peat and wood; and near the table, laid for a plentiful evening meal, I was pleased to observe the "missis", an individual whose existence I had never previously suspected.

I bowed and waited, thinking she would bid me take a seat. She looked at me, leaning back in her chair, and remained motionless and mute.

"Rough weather!" I remarked. "I'm afraid, Mrs Heathcliff, the door must bear the consequence of your servants' leisure attendance: I had hard work to make them hear me."

She never opened her mouth. I stared – she stared also: at any rate, she kept her eyes on me in a cool, regardless manner, exceedingly embarrassing and disagreeable.

"Sit down," said the young man gruffly. "He'll be in soon."

I obeyed, and hemmed, and called the villain Juno, who deigned, at this second interview, to move the extreme tip of her tail, in token of owning my acquaintance.

"A beautiful animal!" I commenced again. "Do you intend parting with the little ones, madam?"

"They are not mine," said the amiable hostess, more repellingly than Heathcliff himself could have replied.

"Ah, your favourites are among these!" I continued, turning to an obscure cushion full of something like cats.

"A strange choice of favourites," she observed scornfully.

Unluckily, it was a heap of dead rabbits. I hemmed once more, and drew closer to the hearth, repeating my comment on the wildness of the evening.

"You should not have come out," she said, rising and reaching from the chimney piece two of the painted canisters.

Her position before was sheltered from the light; now I had a distinct view of her whole figure and countenance. She was slender, and apparently scarcely past girlhood: an admirable form, and the most exquisite little face that I have ever had the pleasure of beholding; small features, very fair; flaxen ringlets, or rather golden, hanging loose on her delicate neck; and eyes, had they been agreeable in expression, they would have been irresistible: fortunately for my susceptible heart, the only sentiment they evinced hovered between scorn and a kind of desperation singularly unnatural to be detected there.

The canisters were almost out of her reach; I made a motion to aid her; she turned upon me as a miser might turn if anyone attempted to assist him in counting his gold.

"I don't want your help," she snapped, "I can get them for myself."

"I beg your pardon," I hastened to reply.

"Were you asked to tea?" she demanded, tying an apron over her neat black frock and standing with a spoonful of the leaf poised over the pot.

"I shall be glad to have a cup," I answered.

"Were you asked?" she repeated.

"No," I said, half-smiling. "You are the proper person to ask me."

She flung the tea back, spoon and all, and resumed her chair in a pet, her forehead corrugated, and her red underlip pushed out, like a child's ready to cry.

Meanwhile, the young man had slung onto his person a decidedly shabby upper garment, and, erecting himself before the blaze, looked down on me from the corner of his eyes, for all the world as if there were some mortal feud unavenged between us. I began to doubt whether he were a servant or not: his dress and speech were both rude, entirely devoid of the superiority observable in Mr and Mrs Heathcliff; his thick brown curls were rough and uncultivated, his whiskers encroached bearishly over his cheeks, and his hands were embrowned like those of a common labourer: still his bearing was free, almost haughty, and he showed none of a domestic's assiduity in attending on the lady of the house.

In the absence of clear proofs of his condition, I deemed it best to abstain from noticing his curious conduct, and five minutes afterwards, the entrance of Heathcliff relieved me in some measure from my uncomfortable state.

"You see, sir, I am come, according to promise!" I exclaimed, assuming the cheerful, "and I fear I shall be weather-bound for half an hour, if you can afford me shelter during that space."

"Half an hour?" he said, shaking the white flakes from his clothes, "I wonder you should select the thick of a snowstorm to ramble about in. Do you know that you run a risk of being lost in the marshes? People familiar with these moors often miss their road on such evenings, and I can tell you there is no chance of a change at present."

"Perhaps I can get a guide among your lads, and he might stay at the Grange till morning – could you spare me one?"

"No, I could not."

"Oh, indeed! Well then, I must trust to my own sagacity."

"Umph!"

"Are you going to mak th' tea?" demanded he of the shabby coat, shifting his ferocious gaze from me to the young lady.

"Is *he* to have any?" she asked, appealing to Heathcliff.

"Get it ready, will you?" was the answer, uttered so savagely that I started. The tone in which the words were said revealed a genuine bad nature. I no longer felt inclined to call Heathcliff a capital fellow.

When the preparations were finished, he invited me with:

"Now, sir, bring forwards your chair." And we all, including the rustic youth, drew round the table, an austere silence prevailing while we discussed* our meal.

I thought if I had caused the cloud it was my duty to make an effort to dispel it. They could not every day sit so grim and taciturn, and it was impossible, however ill-tempered they might be, that the universal scowl they wore was their everyday countenance.

"It is strange," I began, in the interval of swallowing one cup of tea and receiving another, "it is strange how custom can mould our tastes and ideas: many could not imagine the existence of happiness in a life of such complete exile from the world as you spend, Mr Heathcliff; yet I'll venture to say that surrounded by your family, and with your amiable lady as the presiding genius over your home and heart—"

"My amiable lady!" he interrupted, with an almost diabolical sneer on his face. "Where is she – my amiable lady?"

"Mrs Heathcliff, your wife, I mean."

"Well, yes – Oh! You would intimate that her spirit has taken the post of ministering angel, and guards the fortunes of Wuthering Heights, even when her body is gone. Is that it?"

Perceiving myself in a blunder, I attempted to correct it. I might have seen there was too great a disparity between the ages of the parties to make it likely that they were man and wife. One was about forty, a period of mental vigour at which men seldom cherish the delusion of being married for love by girls: that dream is reserved for the solace of our declining years. The other did not look seventeen.

Then it flashed on me: "The clown at my elbow, who is drinking his tea out of a basin* and eating his bread with unwashed hands, may be her husband: Heathcliff junior, of course. Here is the consequence of

11

being buried alive: she has thrown herself away upon that boor, from sheer ignorance that better individuals existed! A sad pity – I must beware how I cause her to regret her choice."

The last reflection may seem conceited; it was not. My neighbour struck me as bordering on repulsive. I knew through experience that I was tolerably attractive.

"Mrs Heathcliff is my daughter-in-law," said Heathcliff, corroborating my surmise. He turned, as he spoke, a peculiar look in her direction: a look of hatred – unless he has a most perverse set of facial muscles that will not, like those of other people, interpret the language of his soul.

"Ah, certainly – I see now: you are the favoured possessor of the beneficent fairy," I remarked, turning to my neighbour.

This was worse than before: the youth grew crimson and clenched his fist, with every appearance of a meditated assault. But he seemed to recollect himself presently, and smothered the storm in a brutal curse, muttered on my behalf, which, however, I took care not to notice.

"Unhappy in your conjectures, sir!" observed my host, "we neither of us have the privilege of owning your good fairy; her mate is dead. I said she was my daughter-in-law, therefore, she must have married my son."

"And this young man is—"

"Not my son, assuredly!"

Heathcliff smiled again, as if it were rather too bold a jest to attribute the paternity of that bear to him.

"My name is Hareton Earnshaw," growled the other, "and I'd counsel you to respect it!"

"I've shown no disrespect," was my reply, laughing internally at the dignity with which he announced himself.

He fixed his eye on me longer than I cared to return the stare, for fear I might be tempted either to box his ears or render my hilarity audible. I began to feel unmistakably out of place in that pleasant family circle. The dismal spiritual atmosphere overcame and more than neutralized the glowing physical comforts round me, and I resolved to be cautious how I ventured under those rafters a third time.

The business of eating being concluded, and no one uttering a word of sociable conversation, I approached a window to examine the weather.

A sorrowful sight I saw: dark night coming down prematurely, and sky and hills mingled in one bitter whirl of wind and suffocating snow.

"I don't think it possible for me to get home now without a guide," I could not help exclaiming. "The roads will be buried already; and if they were bare I could scarcely distinguish a foot in advance."

"Hareton, drive those dozen sheep into the barn porch. They'll be covered if left in the fold all night; and put a plank before them," said Heathcliff.

"How must I do?" I continued, with rising irritation.

There was no reply to my question; and on looking round I saw only Joseph bringing in a pail of porridge for the dogs and Mrs Heathcliff leaning over the fire, diverting herself with burning a bundle of matches which had fallen from the chimney piece as she restored the tea canister to its place.

The former, when he had deposited his burden, took a critical survey of the room, and in cracked tones grated out:

"Aw woonder hagh yah can faishion tuh* stand thear i' idleness un' war,* when all on 'em's goan aght! Bud yah're a nowt, and it's no use talking – yah'll niver mend uh yer ill ways, bud goa raight tuh t' divil, like yer mother afore ye!"

I imagined for a moment that this piece of eloquence was addressed to me, and, sufficiently enraged, stepped towards the aged rascal with an intention of kicking him out of the door.

Mrs Heathcliff, however, checked me by her answer.

"You scandalous old hypocrite!" she replied. "Are you not afraid of being carried away bodily, whenever you mention the Devil's name? I warn you to refrain from provoking me, or I'll ask your abduction as a special favour! Stop, look here, Joseph," she continued, taking a long dark book from a shelf. "I'll show you how far I've progressed in the black art – I shall soon be competent to make a clear house of it. The red cow didn't die by chance, and your rheumatism can hardly be reckoned among providential visitations!"

"Oh, wicked, wicked!" gasped the elder, "may the Lord deliver us from evil!"

"No, reprobate! You are a castaway – be off, or I'll hurt you seriously! I'll have you all modelled in wax and clay, and the first who passes the limits I fix shall – I'll not say what he shall be done to* – but you'll see! Go, I'm looking at you!"

The little witch put a mock malignity into her beautiful eyes, and Joseph, trembling with sincere horror, hurried out, praying and ejaculating "wicked" as he went.

I thought her conduct must be prompted by a species of dreary fun, and now that we were alone I endeavoured to interest her in my distress.

"Mrs Heathcliff," I said earnestly, "you must excuse me for troubling you. I presume, because, with that face, I'm sure you cannot help being good-hearted. Do point out some landmarks by which I may know my way home – I have no more idea how to get there than you would have how to get to London!"

"Take the road you came," she answered, ensconcing herself in a chair, with a candle and the long book open before her. "It is brief advice, but as sound as I can give."

"Then, if you hear of me being discovered dead in a bog or a pit full of snow, your conscience won't whisper that it is partly your fault?"

"How so? I cannot escort you. They wouldn't let me go to the end of the garden wall."

"*You!* I should be sorry to ask you to cross the threshold for my convenience on such a night," I cried. "I want you to *tell* me my way, not to *show* it, or else to persuade Mr Heathcliff to give me a guide."

"Who? There is himself, Earnshaw, Zillah, Joseph and I. Which would you have?"

"Are there no boys at the farm?"

"No, those are all."

"Then it follows that I am compelled to stay."

"That you may settle with your host. I have nothing to do with it."

"I hope it will be a lesson to you to make no more rash journeys on these hills," cried Heathcliff's stern voice from the kitchen entrance. "As to staying here, I don't keep accommodations for visitors: you must share a bed with Hareton or Joseph if you do."

"I can sleep on a chair in this room," I replied.

"No, no! A stranger is a stranger, be he rich or poor – it will not suit me to permit anyone the range of the place while I am off guard!" said the unmannerly wretch.

With this insult my patience was at an end. I uttered an expression of disgust, and pushed past him into the yard, running against Earnshaw in my haste. It was so dark that I could not see the means of

14

exit; and as I wandered round I heard another specimen of their civil behaviour amongst each other.

At first the young man appeared about to befriend me.

"I'll go with him as far as the park," he said.

"You'll go with him to hell!" exclaimed his master, or whatever relation he bore. "And who is to look after the horses, eh?"

"A man's life is of more consequence than one evening's neglect of the horses: somebody must go," murmured Mrs Heathcliff, more kindly than I expected.

"Not at your command!" retorted Hareton. "If you set store on him, you'd better be quiet."

"Then I hope his ghost will haunt you; and I hope Mr Heathcliff will never get another tenant till the Grange is a ruin," she answered sharply.

"Hearken, hearken, shoo's cursing on 'em!" muttered Joseph, towards whom I had been steering.

He sat within earshot, milking the cows by the light of a lantern, which I seized unceremoniously, and, calling out that I would send it back on the morrow, rushed to the nearest postern.

"Maister, maister, he's staling t' lantern!" shouted the ancient, pursuing my retreat. "Hey Gnasher! Hey dog! Hey Wolf, holld him, holld him!"

On opening the little door, two hairy monsters flew at my throat, bearing me down, and extinguishing the light, while a mingled guffaw from Heathcliff and Hareton put the copestone on my rage and humiliation.

Fortunately, the beasts seemed more bent on stretching their paws and yawning and flourishing their tails than devouring me alive, but they would suffer no resurrection, and I was forced to lie till their malignant masters pleased to deliver me: then, hatless and trembling with wrath, I ordered the miscreants to let me out – on their peril to keep me one minute longer – with several incoherent threats of retaliation that, in their indefinite depth of virulency, smacked of King Lear.

The vehemence of my agitation brought on a copious bleeding at the nose, and still Heathcliff laughed, and still I scolded. I don't know what would have concluded the scene, had there not been one person at hand rather more rational than myself, and more benevolent than my entertainer. This was Zillah, the stout housewife, who at length issued forth to inquire into the nature of the uproar. She thought that some of them had been laying violent hands on me, and, not daring to attack her master, she turned her vocal artillery against the younger scoundrel.

"Well, Mr Earnshaw," she cried, "I wonder what you'll have agait* next? Are we going to murder folk on our very door stones? I see this house will never do for me – look at t' poor lad, he's fair choking! Whisht,* whisht, you munn't go on so… come in, and I'll cure that. There now, hold ye still."

With these words she suddenly splashed a pint of icy water down my neck, and pulled me into the kitchen. Mr Heathcliff followed, his accidental merriment expiring quickly in his habitual moroseness.

I was sick exceedingly, and dizzy and faint, and thus compelled perforce to accept lodgings under his roof. He told Zillah to give me a glass of brandy, and then passed on to the inner room, while she condoled with me on my sorry predicament, and, having obeyed his orders, whereby I was somewhat revived, ushered me to bed.

3

WHILE LEADING THE WAY UPSTAIRS, she recommended that I should hide the candle and not make a noise; for her master had an odd notion about the chamber she would put me in, and never let anybody lodge there willingly.

I asked the reason.

She did not know, she answered: she had only lived there a year or two, and they had so many queer goings-on she could not begin to be curious.

Too stupefied to be curious myself, I fastened my door and glanced round for the bed. The whole furniture consisted of a chair, a clothes press* and a large oak case, with squares cut out near the top resembling coach windows.

Having approached this structure, I looked inside, and perceived it to be a singular sort of old-fashioned couch, very conveniently designed to obviate the necessity for every member of the family having a room to himself. In fact, it formed a little closet, and the ledge of a window, which it enclosed, served as a table.

I slid back the panelled sides, got in with my light, pulled them together again, and felt secure against the vigilance of Heathcliff, and everyone else.

The ledge, where I placed my candle, had a few mildewed books piled up in one corner; and it was covered with writing scratched on the paint. This writing, however, was nothing but a name repeated in all kinds of characters, large and small – *Catherine Earnshaw*, here and there varied to *Catherine Heathcliff*, and then again to *Catherine Linton*.

In vapid listlessness I leant my head against the window, and continued spelling over Catherine Earnshaw – Heathcliff – Linton, till my eyes closed, but they had not rested five minutes when a glare of white letters started from the dark, as vivid as spectres – the air swarmed with Catherines, and, rousing myself to dispel the obtrusive name, I discovered my candlewick reclining on one of the antique volumes, and perfuming the place with an odour of roasted calfskin.

I snuffed it off, and, very ill at ease under the influence of cold and lingering nausea, sat up and spread open the injured tome on my knee. It was a testament, in lean type,* and smelling dreadfully musty: a fly-leaf bore the inscription "Catherine Earnshaw, her book" and a date some quarter of a century back.

I shut it, and took up another and another, till I had examined all. Catherine's library was select, and its state of dilapidation proved it to have been well-used, though not altogether for a legitimate purpose: scarcely one chapter had escaped, a pen-and-ink commentary – at least the appearance of one – covering every morsel of blank that the printer had left.

Some were detached sentences; other parts took the form of a regular diary, scrawled in an unformed, childish hand. At the top of an extra page – quite a treasure, probably, when first lighted on – I was greatly amused to behold an excellent caricature of my friend Joseph, rudely yet powerfully sketched.

An immediate interest kindled within me for the unknown Catherine, and I began forthwith to decipher her faded hieroglyphics.

"An awful Sunday," commenced the paragraph beneath. "I wish my father were back again. Hindley is a detestable substitute – his conduct to Heathcliff is atrocious – H. and I are going to rebel – we took our initiatory step this evening.

"All day had been flooding with rain; we could not go to church, so Joseph must needs get up a congregation in the garret; and while Hindley and his wife basked downstairs before a comfortable fire –

doing anything but reading their Bibles, I'll answer for it – Heathcliff, myself and the unhappy ploughboy were commanded to take our prayer books, and mount: we were ranged in a row, on a sack of corn, groaning and shivering, and hoping that Joseph would shiver too, so that he might give us a short homily for his own sake. A vain idea! The service lasted precisely three hours, and yet my brother had the face to exclaim, when he saw us descending, 'What, done already?'

"On Sunday evenings we used to be permitted to play, if we did not make much noise. Now a mere titter is sufficient to send us into corners!

"'You forget you have a master here,' says the tyrant. 'I'll demolish the first who puts me out of temper! I insist on perfect sobriety and silence. Oh, boy, was that you? Frances darling, pull his hair as you go by: I heard him snap his fingers.'

"Frances pulled his hair heartily, and then went and seated herself on her husband's knee, and there they were, like two babies, kissing and talking nonsense by the hour – foolish palaver that we should be ashamed of.

"We made ourselves as snug as our means allowed in the arch of the dresser. I had just fastened our pinafores together, and hung them up for a curtain, when in comes Joseph, on an errand from the stables. He tears down my handiwork, boxes my ears, and croaks:

"'T' maister nobbut just buried, and Sabbath nut o'ered, und t' sahnd o' t' gospel still i' yer lugs,* and yah darr be laiking!* Shame on ye! Sit ye dahn, ill childer! There's good books eneugh if ye'll read 'em: sit ye dahn, and think uh yer sowls!'

"Saying this, he compelled us so to square our positions that we might receive from the far-off fire a dull ray to show us the text of the lumber he thrust upon us.

"I could not bear the employment. I took my dingy volume by the scroop,* and hurled it into the dog kennel, vowing I hated a good book. Heathcliff kicked his to the same place. Then there was a hub-bub!

"'Maister Hindley!' shouted our chaplain. 'Maister, coom hither! Miss Cathy's riven th' back off "Th' Helmet o' Salvation", un' Heathcliff's pawsed his fit* into t' first part o' "T' Brooad Way to Destruction!" It's fair flaysome ut yah let 'em goa on this gait.* Ech! Th' owd man ud uh laced* 'em properly – but he's goan!'

"Hindley hurried up from his paradise on the hearth, and seizing one of us by the collar and the other by the arm, hurled both into the back kitchen, where Joseph asseverated 'owd Nick' would fetch us as sure as we were living, and, so comforted, we each sought a separate nook to await his advent.

"I reached this book and a pot of ink from a shelf, and pushed the house door ajar to give me light, and I have got the time on with writing for twenty minutes, but my companion is impatient, and proposes that we should appropriate the dairywoman's cloak and have a scamper on the moors under its shelter. A pleasant suggestion – and then, if the surly old man come in, he may believe his prophecy verified – we cannot be damper, or colder, in the rain than we are here."

* * *

I suppose Catherine fulfilled her project, for the next sentence took up another subject: she waxed lachrymose.

"How little did I dream that Hindley would ever make me cry so!" she wrote. "My head aches till I cannot keep it on the pillow, and still I can't give over. Poor Heathcliff! Hindley calls him a vagabond, and won't let him sit with us, nor eat with us any more, and he says he and I must not play together, and threatens to turn him out of the house if we break his orders.

He has been blaming our father (how dared he?) for treating H. too liberally, and swears he will reduce him to his right place…"

* * *

I began to nod drowsily over the dim page; my eye wandered from manuscript to print. I saw a red ornamented title: 'Seventy Times Seven,* and the First of the Seventy-First. A Pious Discourse Delivered by the Reverend Jabes Branderham,* in the Chapel of Gimmerden Sough'. And while I was half-consciously worrying my brain to guess what Jabes Branderham would make of his subject, I sank back in bed, and fell asleep.

Alas, for the effects of bad tea and bad temper! What else could it be that made me pass such a terrible night? I don't remember another that I can at all compare with it since I was capable of suffering.

I began to dream almost before I ceased to be sensible of my locality. I thought it was morning, and I had set out on my way home, with Joseph for a guide. The snow lay yards deep in our road, and as we floundered on, my companion wearied me with constant reproaches that I had not brought a pilgrim's staff; telling me that I could never get into the house without one, and boastfully flourishing a heavy-headed cudgel, which I understood to be so denominated.

For a moment I considered it absurd that I should need such a weapon to gain admittance into my own residence. Then a new idea flashed across me. I was not going there: we were journeying to hear the famous Jabes Branderham preach from the text – 'Seventy Times Seven' – and either Joseph, the preacher or I had committed the "First of the Seventy-First", and were to be publicly exposed and excommunicated.

We came to the chapel. I have passed it really in my walks twice or thrice: it lies in a hollow between two hills – an elevated hollow – near a swamp, whose peaty moisture is said to answer all the purposes of embalming on the few corpses deposited there. The roof has been kept whole hitherto, but as the clergyman's stipend is only twenty pounds per annum and a house with two rooms, threatening speedily to determine into one, no clergyman will undertake the duties of pastor, especially as it is currently reported that his flock would rather let him starve than increase the living by one penny from their own pockets. However, in my dream, Jabes had a full and attentive congregation, and he preached – good God! – what a sermon: divided into *four hundred and ninety* parts, each fully equal to an ordinary address from the pulpit, and each discussing a separate sin! Where he searched for them, I cannot tell; he had his private manner of interpreting the phrase, and it seemed necessary the brother should sin different sins on every occasion.

They were of the most curious character – odd transgressions that I never imagined previously.

Oh, how weary I grew. How I writhed and yawned and nodded and revived! How I pinched and pricked myself, and rubbed my eyes, and stood up, and sat down again, and nudged Joseph to inform me if he would *ever* have done!

I was condemned to hear all out. Finally, he reached the "*First of the Seventy-First*". At that crisis, a sudden inspiration descended on me; I was moved to rise and denounce Jabes Branderham as the sinner of the sin that no Christian need pardon.

"Sir," I exclaimed, "sitting here, within these four walls, at one stretch, I have endured and forgiven the four hundred and ninety heads of your discourse. Seventy times seven times have I plucked up my hat and been about to depart – seventy times seven times have you preposterously forced me to resume my seat. The four hundred and ninety-first is too much. Fellow martyrs, have at him! Drag him down, and crush him to atoms, that the place which knows him may know him no more!"*

"*Thou art the Man!*"* cried Jabes after a solemn pause, leaning over his cushion. "Seventy times seven times didst thou gapingly contort thy visage – seventy times seven did I take counsel with my soul – lo, this is human weakness; this also may be absolved! The First of the Seventy-First is come. Brethren, execute upon him the judgement written.* Such honour have all His saints!"

With that concluding word, the whole assembly, exalting their pilgrim's staves, rushed round me in a body, and I, having no weapon to raise in self-defence, commenced grappling with Joseph, my nearest and most ferocious assailant, for his. In the confluence of the multitude, several clubs crossed; blows, aimed at me, fell on other sconces. Presently the whole chapel resounded with rappings and counter-rappings. Every man's hand was against his neighbour,* and Branderham, unwilling to remain idle, poured forth his zeal in a shower of loud taps on the boards of the pulpit, which responded so smartly that, at last, to my unspeakable relief, they woke me.

And what was it that had suggested the tremendous tumult, what had played Jabes's part in the row? Merely the branch of a fir tree that touched my lattice as the blast wailed by, and rattled its dry cones against the panes!

I listened doubtingly an instant, detected the disturber, then turned and dozed, and dreamt again; if possible, still more disagreeably than before.

This time, I remembered I was lying in the oak closet, and I heard distinctly the gusty wind and the driving of the snow; I heard, also, the fir bough repeat its teasing sound, and ascribed it to the right cause, but it annoyed me so much that I resolved to silence it, if possible; and I thought I rose and endeavoured to unhasp the casement. The hook was soldered into the staple, a circumstance observed by me when awake, but forgotten.

"I must stop it, nevertheless!" I muttered, knocking my knuckles through the glass, and stretching an arm out to seize the importunate branch, instead of which, my fingers closed on the fingers of a little ice-cold hand!

The intense horror of nightmare came over me; I tried to draw back my arm, but the hand clung to it, and a most melancholy voice sobbed:

"Let me in... let me in!"

"Who are you?" I asked, struggling meanwhile to disengage myself.

"Catherine Linton," it replied shiveringly (why did I think of *Linton*? I had read *Earnshaw* twenty times for Linton). "I'm come home: I'd lost my way on the moor!"

As it spoke, I discerned, obscurely, a child's face looking through the window. Terror made me cruel, and, finding it useless to attempt shaking the creature off, I pulled its wrist onto the broken pane, and rubbed it to and fro till the blood ran down and soaked the bedclothes. Still it wailed, "Let me in!" and maintained its tenacious gripe, almost maddening me with fear.

"How can I?" I said at length. "Let *me* go, if you want me to let you in!"

The fingers relaxed, I snatched mine through the hole, hurriedly piled the books up in a pyramid against it, and stopped my ears to exclude the lamentable prayer.

I seemed to keep them closed above a quarter of an hour, yet the instant I listened again, there was the doleful cry moaning on!

"Begone!" I shouted, "I'll never let you in, not if you beg for twenty years!"

"It is twenty years," mourned the voice, "twenty years. I've been a waif for twenty years!"

Thereat began a feeble scratching outside, and the pile of books moved as if thrust forwards.

I tried to jump up, but could not stir a limb; and so yelled aloud in a frenzy of fright.

To my confusion, I discovered the yell was not ideal.* Hasty footsteps approached my chamber door; somebody pushed it open with a vigorous hand, and a light glimmered through the squares at the top of the bed. I sat shuddering yet, and wiping the perspiration from my forehead; the intruder appeared to hesitate, and muttered to himself.

At last he said in a half-whisper, plainly not expecting an answer:

"Is anyone here?"

I considered it best to confess my presence, for I knew Heathcliff's accents and feared he might search further if I kept quiet.

With this intention, I turned and opened the panels. I shall not soon forget the effect my action produced.

Heathcliff stood near the entrance, in his shirt and trousers, with a candle dripping over his fingers, and his face as white as the wall behind him. The first creak of the oak startled him like an electric shock: the light leapt from his hold to a distance of some feet, and his agitation was so extreme that he could hardly pick it up.

"It is only your guest, sir," I called out, desirous to spare him the humiliation of exposing his cowardice further. "I had the misfortune to scream in my sleep, owing to a frightful nightmare. I'm sorry I disturbed you."

"Oh, God confound you, Mr Lockwood! I wish you were at the…" commenced my host, setting the candle on a chair, because he found it impossible to hold it steady.

"And who showed you up to this room?" he continued, crushing his nails into his palms, and grinding his teeth to subdue the maxillary convulsions. "Who was it? I've a good mind to turn them out of the house this moment!"

"It was your servant Zillah," I replied, flinging myself onto the floor, and rapidly resuming my garments. "I should not care if you did, Mr Heathcliff; she richly deserves it. I suppose that she wanted to get another proof that the place was haunted, at my expense. Well, it is – swarming with ghosts and goblins! You have reason in shutting it up, I assure you. No one will thank you for a doze in such a den!"

"What do you mean?" asked Heathcliff, "and what are you doing? Lie down and finish out the night, since you *are* here, but, for Heaven's sake, don't repeat that horrid noise – nothing could excuse it, unless you were having your throat cut!"

"If the little fiend had got in at the window, she probably would have strangled me!" I returned. "I'm not going to endure the persecutions of your hospitable ancestors again. Was not the Reverend Jabes Branderham akin to you on the mother's side? And that minx, Catherine Linton, or Earnshaw, or however she was called – she must have been a changeling – wicked little soul! She told me she had been walking the earth these twenty years: a just punishment for her mortal transgressions, I've no doubt!"

Scarcely were these words uttered when I recollected the association of Heathcliff's with Catherine's name in the book, which had completely slipped from my memory till thus awakened. I blushed at my inconsideration, but, without showing further consciousness of the offence, I hastened to add:

"The truth is, sir, I passed the first part of the night in..." Here I stopped afresh – I was about to say "perusing those old volumes", then it would have revealed my knowledge of their written as well as their printed contents. So, correcting myself, I went on:

"In spelling over the name scratched on that window ledge. A monotonous occupation, calculated to set me asleep, like counting, or—"

"What *can* you mean by talking in this way to *me*!" thundered Heathcliff with savage vehemence. "How... how *dare* you, under my roof... God! He's mad to speak so!" And he struck his forehead with rage.

I did not know whether to resent this language or pursue my explanation, but he seemed so powerfully affected that I took pity and proceeded with my dreams, affirming I had never heard the appellation of "Catherine Linton" before, but reading it often overproduced an impression which personified itself when I had no longer my imagination under control.

Heathcliff gradually fell back into the shelter of the bed as I spoke, finally sitting down almost concealed behind it. I guessed, however, by his irregular and intercepted breathing, that he struggled to vanquish an excess of violent emotion.

Not liking to show him that I had heard the conflict, I continued my toilette rather noisily, looked at my watch, and soliloquized on the length of the night:

"Not three o'clock yet! I could have taken oath it had been six. Time stagnates here: we must surely have retired to rest at eight!"

"Always at nine in winter, and rise at four," said my host, suppressing a groan, and, as I fancied, by the motion of his arm's shadow, dashing a tear from his eyes.

"Mr Lockwood," he added, "you may go into my room: you'll only be in the way, coming downstairs so early, and your childish outcry has sent sleep to the devil for me."

"And for me too," I replied. "I'll walk in the yard till daylight, and then I'll be off, and you need not dread a repetition of my intrusion.

24

I'm now quite cured of seeking pleasure in society, be it country or town. A sensible man ought to find sufficient company in himself."

"Delightful company!" muttered Heathcliff. "Take the candle, and go where you please. I shall join you directly. Keep out of the yard, though, the dogs are unchained, and the house – Juno mounts sentinel there – and… nay, you can only ramble about the steps and passages. But, away with you! I'll come in two minutes!"

I obeyed, so far as to quit the chamber, when, ignorant where the narrow lobbies led, I stood still, and was witness involuntarily to a piece of superstition on the part of my landlord which belied oddly his apparent sense.

He got onto the bed, and wrenched open the lattice, bursting, as he pulled at it, into an uncontrollable passion of tears.

"Come in! Come in!" he sobbed. "Cathy, do come. Oh, do – *once* more! Oh, my heart's darling, hear me *this* time, Catherine, at last!"

The spectre showed a spectre's ordinary caprice: it gave no sign of being, but the snow and wind whirled wildly through, even reaching my station, and blowing out the light.

There was such anguish in the gush of grief that accompanied this raving that my compassion made me overlook its folly, and I drew off, half-angry to have listened at all, and vexed at having related my ridiculous nightmare, since it produced that agony, though *why* was beyond my comprehension. I descended cautiously to the lower regions, and landed in the back kitchen, where a gleam of fire, raked compactly together, enabled me to rekindle my candle.

Nothing was stirring except a brindled-grey cat, which crept from the ashes, and saluted me with a querulous mew.

Two benches, shaped in sections of a circle, nearly enclosed the hearth; on one of these I stretched myself, and Grimalkin mounted the other. We were both of us nodding ere anyone invaded our retreat, and then it was Joseph, shuffling down a wooden ladder that vanished in the roof through a trap: the ascent to his garret, I suppose.

He cast a sinister look at the little flame which I had enticed to play between the ribs, swept the cat from its elevation, and, bestowing himself in the vacancy, commenced the operation of stuffing a three-inch pipe with tobacco. My presence in his sanctum was evidently esteemed a piece of impudence too shameful for remark. He silently applied the tube to his lips, folded his arms, and puffed away.

I let him enjoy the luxury unannoyed, and after sucking out his last wreath, and heaving a profound sigh, he got up, and departed as solemnly as he came.

A more elastic footstep entered next, and now I opened my mouth for a "good morning", but closed it again, the salutation unachieved, for Hareton Earnshaw was performing his orison sotto voce, in a series of curses directed against every object he touched, while he rummaged a corner for a spade or shovel to dig through the drifts. He glanced over the back of the bench, dilating his nostrils, and thought as little of exchanging civilities with me as with my companion the cat.

I guessed by his preparations that egress was allowed, and, leaving my hard couch, made a movement to follow him. He noticed this, and thrust at an inner door with the end of his spade, intimating by an inarticulate sound that there was the place where I must go, if I changed my locality.

It opened into the house, where the females were already astir: Zillah urging flakes of flame up the chimney with a colossal bellows, and Mrs Heathcliff kneeling on the hearth, reading a book by the aid of the blaze.

She held her hand interposed between the furnace heat and her eyes, and seemed absorbed in her occupation, desisting from it only to chide the servant for covering her with sparks, or to push away a dog, now and then, that snoozled* its nose overforwardly into her face.

I was surprised to see Heathcliff there also. He stood by the fire, his back towards me, just finishing a stormy scene to poor Zillah, who ever and anon interrupted her labour to pluck up the corner of her apron and heave an indignant groan.

"And you, you worthless—" he broke out as I entered, turning to his daughter-in-law, and employing an epithet as harmless as duck, or sheep, but generally represented by a dash.

"There you are, at your idle tricks again! The rest of them do earn their bread – you live on my charity! Put your trash away, and find something to do. You shall pay me for the plague of having you eternally in my sight – do you hear, damnable jade?"

"I'll put my trash away, because you can make me if I refuse," answered the young lady, closing her book, and throwing it on a chair. "But I'll not do anything, though you should swear your tongue out, except what I please!"

Heathcliff lifted his hand, and the speaker sprang to a safer distance, obviously acquainted with its weight.

Having no desire to be entertained by a cat-and-dog combat, I stepped forwards briskly, as if eager to partake the warmth of the hearth, and innocent of any knowledge of the interrupted dispute. Each had enough decorum to suspend further hostilities: Heathcliff placed his fists, out of temptation, in his pockets; Mrs Heathcliff curled her lip, and walked to a seat far off, where she kept her word by playing the part of a statue during the remainder of my stay.

That was not long. I declined joining their breakfast and, at the first gleam of dawn, took an opportunity of escaping into the free air, now clear and still and cold as impalpable ice.

My landlord hallooed for me to stop ere I reached the bottom of the garden, and offered to accompany me across the moor. It was well he did, for the whole hill back was one billowy white ocean, the swells and falls not indicating corresponding rises and depressions in the ground: many pits, at least, were filled to a level, and entire ranges of mounds, the refuse of the quarries, blotted from the chart which my yesterday's walk left pictured in my mind.

I had remarked on one side of the road, at intervals of six or seven yards, a line of upright stones, continued through the whole length of the barren:* these were erected and daubed with lime on purpose to serve as guides in the dark, and also when a fall, like the present, confounded the deep swamps on either hand with the firmer path, but, excepting a dirty dot pointing up here and there, all traces of their existence had vanished, and my companion found it necessary to warn me frequently to steer to the right or left, when I imagined I was following correctly the windings of the road.

We exchanged little conversation, and he halted at the entrance of Thrushcross Park, saying I could make no error there. Our adieus were limited to a hasty bow, and then I pushed forwards, trusting to my own resources, for the porter's lodge is untenanted as yet.

The distance from the gate to the grange is two miles: I believe I managed to make it four, what with losing myself among the trees, and sinking up to the neck in snow, a predicament which only those who have experienced it can appreciate. At any rate, whatever were my wanderings, the clock chimed twelve as I entered the house, and that gave exactly an hour for every mile of the usual way from Wuthering Heights.

My human fixture and her satellites rushed to welcome me, exclaiming tumultuously, they had completely given me up: everybody conjectured that I perished last night, and they were wondering how they must set about the search for my remains.

I bid them be quiet, now that they saw me returned, and, benumbed to my very heart, I dragged upstairs, whence, after putting on dry clothes and pacing to and fro thirty or forty minutes to restore the animal heat, I adjourned to my study, feeble as a kitten, almost too much so to enjoy the cheerful fire and smoking coffee which the servant had prepared for my refreshment.

4

WHAT VAIN WEATHERCOCKS we are! I, who had determined to hold myself independent of all social intercourse and thanked my stars that, at length, I had lighted on a spot where it was next to impracticable – I, weak wretch, after maintaining till dusk a struggle with low spirits and solitude, was finally compelled to strike my colours, and, under pretence of gaining information concerning the necessities of my establishment, I desired Mrs Dean, when she brought in supper, to sit down while I ate it, hoping sincerely she would prove a regular gossip, and either rouse me to animation or lull me to sleep by her talk.

"You have lived here a considerable time," I commenced, "did you not say sixteen years?"

"Eighteen, sir: I came when the mistress was married, to wait on her; after she died, the master retained me for his housekeeper."

"Indeed."

There ensued a pause. She was not a gossip, I feared; unless about her own affairs, and those could hardly interest me. However, having studied for an interval, with a fist on either knee and a cloud of meditation over her ruddy countenance, she ejaculated:

"Ah, times are greatly changed since then!"

"Yes," I remarked, "you've seen a good many alterations, I suppose?"

"I have, and troubles too," she said.

"Oh, I'll turn the talk on my landlord's family!" I thought to myself. "A good subject to start! And that pretty girl-widow, I should like to know her history: whether she be a native of the country, or, as is more

28

probable, an exotic that the surly *indigenae** will not recognize for kin."

With this intention I asked Mrs Dean why Heathcliff let Thrushcross Grange, and preferred living in a situation and residence so much inferior. "Is he not rich enough to keep the estate in good order?" I enquired.

"Rich, sir!" she returned. "He has nobody knows what money, and every year it increases. Yes, yes, he's rich enough to live in a finer house than this, but he's very near... close-handed, and if he had meant to flit to Thrushcross Grange, as soon as he heard of a good tenant he could not have borne to miss the chance of getting a few hundreds more. It is strange people should be so greedy, when they are alone in the world!"

"He had a son, it seems?"

"Yes, he had one – he is dead."

"And that young lady, Mrs Heathcliff, is his widow?"

"Yes."

"Where did she come from originally?"

"Why, sir, she is my late master's daughter: Catherine Linton was her maiden name. I nursed her, poor thing! I did wish Mr Heathcliff would remove here, and then we might have been together again."

"What, Catherine Linton?" I exclaimed, astonished. But a minute's reflection convinced me it was not my ghostly Catherine. "Then," I continued, "my predecessor's name was Linton?"

"It was."

"And who is that Earnshaw, Hareton Earnshaw, who lives with Mr Heathcliff? Are they relations?"

"No, he is the late Mrs Linton's nephew."

"The young lady's cousin, then?"

"Yes, and her husband was her cousin also – one on the mother's, the other on the father's side – Heathcliff married Mr Linton's sister."

"I see the house at Wuthering Heights has 'Earnshaw' carved over the front door. Are they an old family?"

"Very old, sir, and Hareton is the last of them, as our Miss Cathy is of us... I mean, of the Lintons. Have you been to Wuthering Heights? I beg pardon for asking, but I should like to hear how she is!"

"Mrs Heathcliff? She looked very well, and very handsome; yet, I think, not very happy."

"Oh dear, I don't wonder! And how did you like the master?"

"A rough fellow, rather, Mrs Dean. Is not that his character?"

"Rough as a saw edge, and hard as whinstone! The less you meddle with him the better."

"He must have had some ups and downs in life to make him such a churl. Do you know anything of his history?"

"It's a cuckoo's, sir – I know all about it, except where he was born, and who were his parents, and how he got his money at first. And Hareton has been cast out like an unfledged dunnock! The unfortunate lad is the only one in all this parish that does not guess how he has been cheated."

"Well, Mrs Dean, it will be a charitable deed to tell me something of my neighbours: I feel I shall not rest if I go to bed, so be good enough to sit and chat an hour."

"Oh, certainly, sir! I'll just fetch a little sewing, and then I'll sit as long as you please. But you've caught cold: I saw you shivering, and you must have some gruel to drive it out."

The worthy woman bustled off, and I crouched nearer the fire: my head felt hot, and the rest of me chill; moreover, I was excited almost to a pitch of foolishness through my nerves and brain. This caused me to feel not uncomfortable, but rather fearful (as I am still) of serious effects from the incidents of today and yesterday.

She returned presently, bringing a smoking basin and a basket of work, and, having placed the former on the hob, drew in her seat, evidently pleased to find me so companionable.

Before I came to live here – she commenced, waiting no further invitation to her story – I was almost always at Wuthering Heights, because my mother had nursed Mr Hindley Earnshaw, that was Hareton's father, and I got used to playing with the children. I ran errands too, and helped to make hay, and hung about the farm ready for anything that anybody would set me to.

One fine summer morning – it was the beginning of harvest, I remember – Mr Earnshaw, the old master, came downstairs, dressed for a journey, and, after he had told Joseph what was to be done during the day, he turned to Hindley and Cathy and me – for I sat eating my porridge with them – and he said, speaking to his son:

"Now, my bonny man, I'm going to Liverpool today, what shall I bring you? You may choose what you like: only let it be little, for I shall walk there and back: sixty miles each way, that is a long spell!"

Hindley named a fiddle, and then he asked Miss Cathy; she was hardly six years old, but she could ride any horse in the stable, and she chose a whip.

He did not forget me, for he had a kind heart, though he was rather severe sometimes. He promised to bring me a pocketful of apples and pears, and then he kissed his children goodbye, and set off.

It seemed a long while to us all – the three days of his absence – and often did little Cathy ask when he would be home. Mrs Earnshaw expected him by supper time on the third evening, and she put the meal off hour after hour; there were no signs of his coming, however, and at last the children got tired of running down to the gate to look. Then it grew dark; she would have had them to bed, but they begged sadly to be allowed to stay up, and, just about eleven o'clock, the door latch was raised quietly, and in stepped the master. He threw himself into a chair, laughing and groaning, and bid them all stand off, for he was nearly killed – he would not have such another walk for the three kingdoms.

"And at the end of it to be flighted* to death!" he said, opening his greatcoat, which he held bundled up in his arms. "See here, wife: I was never so beaten* with anything in my life, but you must e'en take it as a gift of God, though it's as dark almost as if it came from the devil."

We crowded round, and over Miss Cathy's head I had a peep at a dirty, ragged, black-haired child, big enough both to walk and talk – indeed, its face looked older than Catherine's – yet when it was set on its feet, it only stared round, and repeated over and over again some gibberish that nobody could understand. I was frightened, and Mrs Earnshaw was ready to fling it out of doors: she did fly up, asking how he could fashion to bring that gypsy brat into the house, when they had their own bairns to feed and fend for? What he meant to do with it, and whether he were mad?

The master tried to explain the matter, but he was really half-dead with fatigue, and all that I could make out, amongst her scolding, was a tale of his seeing it starving, and houseless, and as good as dumb, in the streets of Liverpool, where he picked it up and enquired for its owner. Not a soul knew to whom it belonged, he said, and his money and time being both limited, he thought it better to take it home with him at once, than run into vain expenses there – because he was determined he would not leave it as he found it.

Well, the conclusion was that my mistress grumbled herself calm, and Mr Earnshaw told me to wash it, and give it clean things, and let it sleep with the children.

Hindley and Cathy contented themselves with looking and listening till peace was restored, then both began searching their father's pockets for the presents he had promised them. The former was a boy of fourteen, but when he drew out what had been a fiddle, crushed to morsels in the greatcoat, he blubbered aloud; and Cathy, when she learnt the master had lost her whip in attending on the stranger, showed her humour* by grinning and spitting at the stupid little thing, earning for her pains a sound blow from her father to teach her cleaner manners.

They entirely refused to have it in bed with them, or even in their room, and I had no more sense, so I put it on the landing of the stairs, hoping it might be gone on the morrow. By chance, or else attracted by hearing his voice, it crept to Mr Earnshaw's door, and there he found it on quitting his chamber. Inquiries were made as to how it got there; I was obliged to confess, and in recompense for my cowardice and inhumanity was sent out of the house.

This was Heathcliff's first introduction to the family. On coming back a few days afterwards – for I did not consider my banishment perpetual – I found they had christened him "Heathcliff": it was the name of a son who died in childhood, and it has served him ever since, both for Christian and surname.

Miss Cathy and he were now very thick, but Hindley hated him – and to say the truth I did the same – and we plagued and went on with him shamefully, for I wasn't reasonable enough to feel my injustice, and the mistress never put in a word on his behalf when she saw him wronged.

He seemed a sullen, patient child, hardened, perhaps, to ill-treatment: he would stand Hindley's blows without winking or shedding a tear, and my pinches moved him only to draw in a breath and open his eyes, as if he had hurt himself by accident, and nobody was to blame.

This endurance made old Earnshaw furious, when he discovered his son persecuting the poor fatherless child, as he called him. He took to Heathcliff strangely, believing all he said (for that matter, he said precious little, and generally the truth), and petting him up far above Cathy, who was too mischievous and wayward for a favourite.

So from the very beginning, he bred bad feeling in the house, and at Mrs Earnshaw's death, which happened in less than two years after, the young master had learnt to regard his father as an oppressor rather than a friend, and Heathcliff as a usurper of his parent's affections and his privileges, and he grew bitter with brooding over these injuries.

I sympathized awhile, but when the children fell ill of the measles, and I had to tend them and take on me the cares of a woman at once, I changed my idea. Heathcliff was dangerously sick, and while he lay at the worst he would have me constantly by his pillow: I suppose he felt I did a good deal for him, and he hadn't wit to guess that I was compelled to do it. However, I will say this, he was the quietest child that ever nurse watched over. The difference between him and the others forced me to be less partial. Cathy and her brother harassed me terribly: he was as uncomplaining as a lamb, though hardness, not gentleness, made him give little trouble.

He got through, and the doctor affirmed it was in a great measure owing to me, and praised me for my care. I was vain of his commendations, and softened towards the being by whose means I earned them, and thus Hindley lost his last ally. Still I couldn't dote on Heathcliff, and I wondered often what my master saw to admire so much in the sullen boy, who never, to my recollection, repaid his indulgence by any sign of gratitude. He was not insolent to his benefactor; he was simply insensible, though knowing perfectly the hold he had on his heart, and conscious he had only to speak and all the house would be obliged to bend to his wishes.

As an instance, I remember Mr Earnshaw once bought a couple of colts at the parish fair, and gave the lads each one. Heathcliff took the handsomest, but it soon fell lame, and when he discovered it, he said to Hindley:

"You must exchange horses with me: I don't like mine, and if you won't, I shall tell your father of the three thrashings you've given me this week, and show him my arm, which is black to the shoulder."

Hindley put out his tongue, and cuffed him over the ears.

"You'd better do it at once," he persisted, escaping to the porch (they were in the stable), "you will have to, and if I speak of these blows, you'll get them again with interest."

"Off, dog!" cried Hindley, threatening him with an iron weight used for weighing potatoes and hay.

"Throw it," he replied, standing still, "and then I'll tell how you boasted that you would turn me out of doors as soon as he died, and see whether he will not turn you out directly."

Hindley threw it, hitting him on the breast, and down he fell, but staggered up immediately, breathless and white, and had not I prevented it he would have gone just so to the master, and got full revenge by letting his condition plead for him, intimating who had caused it.

"Take my colt, gypsy, then!" said young Earnshaw. "And I pray that he may break your neck: take him, and be damned, you beggarly interloper! And wheedle my father out of all he has, only afterwards show him what you are, imp of Satan. And take that, I hope he'll kick out your brains!"

Heathcliff had gone to loose the beast, and shift it to his own stall. He was passing behind it, when Hindley finished his speech by knocking him under its feet, and without stopping to examine whether his hopes were fulfilled, ran away as fast as he could.

I was surprised to witness how coolly the child gathered himself up, and went on with his intention, exchanging saddles and all, and then sitting down on a bundle of hay to overcome the qualm which the violent blow occasioned, before he entered the house.

I persuaded him easily to let me lay the blame of his bruises on the horse: he minded little what tale was told since he had what he wanted. He complained so seldom, indeed, of such stirs as these, that I really thought him not vindictive – I was deceived completely, as you will hear.

5

IN THE COURSE OF TIME MR EARNSHAW began to fail. He had been active and healthy, yet his strength left him suddenly, and when he was confined to the chimney corner he grew grievously irritable. A nothing vexed him, and suspected slights of his authority nearly threw him into fits.

This was especially to be remarked if anyone attempted to impose upon, or domineer over, his favourite: he was painfully jealous lest a word should be spoken amiss to him, seeming to have got into his head the notion that, because he liked Heathcliff, all hated and longed to do him an ill turn.

It was a disadvantage to the lad, for the kinder among us did not wish to fret the master, so we humoured his partiality, and that humouring was rich nourishment to the child's pride and black tempers. Still it became in a manner necessary; twice, or thrice, Hindley's manifestation of scorn, while his father was near, roused the old man to a fury: he seized his stick to strike him, and shook with rage that he could not do it.

At last, our curate (we had a curate then who made the living answer by teaching the little Lintons and Earnshaws, and farming his bit of land himself) advised that the young man should be sent to college, and Mr Earnshaw agreed, though with a heavy spirit, for he said:

"Hindley was nought, and would never thrive as where he wandered."

I hoped heartily we should have peace now. It hurt me to think the master should be made uncomfortable by his own good deed. I fancied the discontent of age and disease arose from his family disagreements, as he would have it that it did – really, you know, sir, it was in his sinking frame.

We might have got on tolerably, notwithstanding, but for two people: Miss Cathy and Joseph, the servant – you saw him, I dare say, up yonder. He was, and is yet, most likely the wearisomest self-righteous Pharisee that ever ransacked a Bible to rake the promises to himself and fling the curses on his neighbours. By his knack of sermonizing and pious discoursing, he contrived to make a great impression on Mr Earnshaw, and the more feeble the master became, the more influence he gained.

He was relentless in worrying him about his soul's concerns, and about ruling his children rigidly. He encouraged him to regard Hindley as a reprobate, and night after night, he regularly grumbled out a long string of tales against Heathcliff and Catherine, always minding to flatter Earnshaw's weakness by heaping the heaviest blame on the latter.

Certainly she had ways with her such as I never saw a child take up before, and she put all of us past our patience fifty times and oftener in a day: from the hour she came downstairs till the hour she went to bed, we had not a minute's security that she wouldn't be in mischief. Her spirits were always at high water mark, her tongue always going – singing, laughing and plaguing everybody who would not do the same. A wild, wick* slip she was – but she had the bonniest eye, and sweetest smile, and lightest foot in the parish, and after all I believe she meant no harm, for when once she made you cry in good earnest, it seldom happened that she would not keep you company, and oblige you to be quiet that you might comfort her.

She was much too fond of Heathcliff. The greatest punishment we could invent for her was to keep her separate from him, yet she got chided more than any of us on his account.

In play, she liked exceedingly to act the little mistress, using her hands freely, and commanding her companions: she did so to me, but I would not bear slapping and ordering, and so I let her know.

Now Mr Earnshaw did not understand jokes from his children: he had always been strict and grave with them, and Catherine, on her part, had no idea why her father should be crosser and less patient in his ailing condition than he was in his prime.

His peevish reproofs wakened in her a naughty delight to provoke him: she was never so happy as when we were all scolding her at once, and she defying us with her bold, saucy look and her ready words, turning Joseph's religious curses into ridicule, baiting me, and doing just what her father hated most – showing how her pretended insolence, which he thought real, had more power over Heathcliff than his kindness; how the boy would do *her* bidding in anything, and *his* only when it suited his own inclination.

After behaving as badly as possible all day, she sometimes came fondling to make it up at night.

"Nay, Cathy," the old man would say, "I cannot love thee: thou'rt worse than thy brother. Go, say thy prayers, child, and ask God's pardon. I doubt thy mother and I must rue that we ever reared thee!"

That made her cry at first, and then being repulsed continually hardened her, and she laughed if I told her to say she was sorry for her faults, and beg to be forgiven.

But the hour came, at last, that ended Mr Earnshaw's troubles on earth. He died quietly in his chair one October evening, seated by the fireside.

A high wind blustered round the house, and roared in the chimney: it sounded wild and stormy, yet it was not cold, and we were all together – I, a little removed from the hearth, busy at my knitting, and Joseph reading his Bible near the table (for the servants generally sat in the house then, after their work was done). Miss Cathy had been sick, and that made her still; she leant against her father's knee, and Heathcliff was lying on the floor with his head in her lap.

I remember the master, before he fell into a doze, stroking her bonny hair – it pleased him rarely to see her gentle – and saying:

"Why canst thou not always be a good lass, Cathy?"

And she turned her face up to his, and laughed, and answered:

"Why cannot you always be a good man, Father?"

But as soon as she saw him vexed again, she kissed his hand, and said she would sing him to sleep. She began singing very low, till his fingers dropped from hers, and his head sank on his breast. Then I told her to hush, and not stir, for fear she should wake him. We all kept as mute as mice a full half-hour, and should have done so longer, only Joseph, having finished his chapter, got up and said that he must rouse the master for prayers and bed. He stepped forwards, and called him by name, and touched his shoulder, but he would not move – so he took the candle and looked at him.

I thought there was something wrong as he set down the light, and, seizing the children each by an arm, whispered them to frame* upstairs, and make little din – they might pray alone that evening – he had summut to do.

"I shall bid Father goodnight first," said Catherine, putting her arms round his neck, before we could hinder her.

The poor thing discovered her loss directly – she screamed out:
"Oh, he's dead, Heathcliff, he's dead!"

And they both set up a heartbreaking cry.

I joined my wail to theirs, loud and bitter, but Joseph asked what we could be thinking of, to roar in that way over a saint in heaven.

He told me to put on my cloak and run to Gimmerton for the doctor and the parson. I could not guess the use that either would be of then. However, I went, through wind and rain, and brought one, the doctor, back with me; the other said he would come in the morning.

Leaving Joseph to explain matters, I ran to the children's room: their door was ajar, I saw they had never laid down, though it was past midnight; but they were calmer, and did not need me to console them. The little souls were comforting each other with better thoughts than I could have hit on: no parson in the world ever pictured heaven so beautifully as they did in their innocent talk, and, while I sobbed and listened, I could not help wishing we were all there safe together.

6

M R HINDLEY CAME HOME TO THE FUNERAL, and – a thing that amazed us, and set the neighbours gossiping right and left – he brought a wife with him.

What she was, and where she was born, he never informed us: probably she had neither money nor name to recommend her, or he would scarcely have kept the union from his father.

She was not one that would have disturbed the house much on her own account. Every object she saw, the moment she crossed the threshold, appeared to delight her; and every circumstance that took place about her, except the preparing for the burial and the presence of the mourners.

I thought she was half-silly, from her behaviour while that went on; she ran into her chamber, and made me come with her, though I should have been dressing the children, and there she sat shivering and clasping her hands, and asking repeatedly:

"Are they gone yet?"

Then she began describing with hysterical emotion the effect it produced on her to see black, and started, and trembled, and at last fell a-weeping – and when I asked what was the matter, answered she didn't know, but she felt so afraid of dying!

I imagined her as little likely to die as myself. She was rather thin, but young and fresh-complexioned, and her eyes sparkled as bright as diamonds. I did remark, to be sure, that mounting the stairs made her breathe very quick, that the least sudden noise set her all in a quiver, and that she coughed troublesomely sometimes – but I knew nothing of what these symptoms portended, and had no impulse to sympathize with her. We don't in general take to foreigners here, Mr Lockwood, unless they take to us first.

Young Earnshaw was altered considerably in the three years of his absence. He had grown sparer, and lost his colour, and spoke and dressed quite differently; and on the very day of his return, he told Joseph and me we must thenceforth quarter ourselves in the back kitchen, and leave the house for him. Indeed, he would have carpeted and papered a small spare room for a parlour, but his wife expressed such pleasure at the white floor and huge glowing fireplace, at the pewter dishes and delf case,* and dog kennel, and the wide space there was to move about in where they usually sat, that he thought it unnecessary to her comfort, and so dropped the intention.

She expressed pleasure, too, at finding a sister among her new acquaintance, and she prattled to Catherine, and kissed her, and ran about with her, and gave her quantities of presents, at the beginning. Her affection tired very soon, however, and when she grew peevish, Hindley became tyrannical. A few words from her, evincing a dislike to Heathcliff, were enough to rouse in him all his old hatred of the boy. He drove him from their company to the servants, deprived him of the instructions of the curate, and insisted that he should labour out of doors instead, compelling him to do so as hard as any other lad on the farm.

Heathcliff bore his degradation pretty well at first, because Cathy taught him what she learnt, and worked or played with him in the fields. They both promised fair to grow up as rude as savages, the young master being entirely negligent how they behaved and what they did, so they kept clear of him. He would not even have seen after their going to church on Sundays, only Joseph and the curate reprimanded his carelessness when they absented themselves, and that reminded him to order Heathcliff a flogging, and Catherine a fast from dinner or supper.

But it was one of their chief amusements to run away to the moors in the morning and remain there all day, and the after-punishment grew a mere thing to laugh at. The curate might set as many chapters as he pleased for Catherine to get by heart, and Joseph might thrash Heathcliff till his arm ached; they forgot everything the minute they were together again – at least the minute they had contrived some naughty plan of revenge – and many a time I've cried to myself to watch them growing more reckless daily, and I not daring to speak a syllable, for fear of losing the small power I still retained over the unfriended creatures.

One Sunday evening, it chanced that they were banished from the sitting room for making a noise, or a light offence of the kind, and when I went to call them to supper, I could discover them nowhere.

We searched the house, above and below, and the yard and stables; they were invisible, and at last Hindley in a passion told us to bolt the doors, and swore nobody should let them in that night.

The household went to bed, and I, too anxious to lie down, opened my lattice and put my head out to hearken, though it rained, determined to admit them in spite of the prohibition should they return.

In a while, I distinguished steps coming up the road, and the light of a lantern glimmered through the gate.

I threw a shawl over my head and ran to prevent them from waking Mr Earnshaw by knocking. There was Heathcliff, by himself: it gave me a start to see him alone.

"Where is Miss Catherine?" I cried hurriedly. "No accident, I hope?"

"At Thrushcross Grange," he answered, "and I would have been there too, but they had not the manners to ask me to stay."

"Well, you will catch it!" I said, "you'll never be content till you're sent about your business. What in the world led you wandering to Thrushcross Grange?"

"Let me get off my wet clothes, and I'll tell you all about it, Nelly," he replied.

I bid him beware of rousing the master, and while he undressed and I waited to put out the candle he continued:

"Cathy and I escaped from the wash house to have a ramble at liberty, and getting a glimpse of the Grange lights, we thought we would just go and see whether the Lintons passed their Sunday evenings standing shivering in corners, while their father and mother sat eating and drinking, and singing and laughing, and burning their eyes out before the fire. Do you think they do? Or reading sermons, and being catechized by their manservant, and set to learn a column of Scripture names, if they don't answer properly?"

"Probably not," I responded. "They are good children, no doubt, and don't deserve the treatment you receive for your bad conduct."

"Don't cant, Nelly," he said, "nonsense! We ran from the top of the Heights to the park without stopping – Catherine completely beaten in the race, because she was barefoot. You'll have to seek for her shoes in the bog tomorrow. We crept through a broken hedge, groped our way up the path, and planted ourselves on a flower plot under the drawing-room window. The light came from thence; they had not put up the shutters, and the curtains were only half-closed. Both of us were able to look in by standing on the basement* and clinging to the ledge, and we saw – ah! It was beautiful – a splendid place carpeted with crimson, and crimson-covered chairs and tables, and a pure white ceiling bordered by gold, a shower of glass-drops hanging in silver chains from the centre, and shimmering with little soft tapers. Old Mr and Mrs Linton were not there. Edgar and his sisters had it entirely to themselves; shouldn't they have been happy? We should have thought ourselves in heaven! And now guess what your good children were doing? Isabella – I believe she is eleven, a year younger than Cathy – lay screaming at the further end of the room, shrieking as if witches were running red-hot needles into her. Edgar stood on the hearth weeping silently, and in the middle of the table sat a little dog, shaking its paw

40

and yelping, which, from their mutual accusations, we understood they had nearly pulled in two between them. The idiots! That was their pleasure! To quarrel who should hold a heap of warm hair, and each begin to cry because both, after struggling to get it, refused to take it. We laughed outright at the petted things, we did despise them! When would you catch me wishing to have what Catherine wanted? Or find us by ourselves, seeking entertainment in yelling and sobbing and rolling on the ground, divided by the whole room? I'd not exchange, for a thousand lives, my condition here for Edgar Linton's at Thrushcross Grange – not if I might have the privilege of flinging Joseph off the highest gable, and painting the house front with Hindley's blood!"

"Hush, hush!" I interrupted. "Still you have not told me, Heathcliff, how Catherine is left behind?"

"I told you we laughed," he answered. "The Lintons heard us, and with one accord they shot like arrows to the door; there was silence, and then a cry, 'Oh, Mama, Mama! Oh, Papa! Oh, Mama, come here. Oh, Papa, oh!' They really did howl out something in that way. We made frightful noises to terrify them still more, and then we dropped off the ledge, because somebody was drawing the bars, and we felt we had better flee. I had Cathy by the hand, and was urging her on, when all at once she fell down.

"'Run, Heathcliff, run!' she whispered. 'They have let the bulldog loose, and he holds me!'

"The devil had seized her ankle, Nelly: I heard his abominable snorting. She did not yell out – no! She would have scorned to do it if she had been spitted on the horns of a mad cow. I did, though: I vociferated curses enough to annihilate any fiend in Christendom, and I got a stone and thrust it between his jaws, and tried with all my might to cram it down his throat. A beast of a servant came up with a lantern at last, shouting:

"'Keep fast, Skulker, keep fast!'

"He changed his note, however, when he saw Skulker's game. The dog was throttled off, his huge purple tongue hanging half a foot out of his mouth, and his pendent lips streaming with bloody slaver.

"The man took Cathy up; she was sick, not from fear, I'm certain, but from pain. He carried her in; I followed, grumbling execrations and vengeance.

"'What prey, Robert?' hallooed Linton from the entrance.

41

"'Skulker has caught a little girl, sir,' he replied, 'and there's a lad here,' he added, making a clutch at me, 'who looks an out-and-outer!* Very like, the robbers were for putting them through the window, to open the doors to the gang after all were asleep, that they might murder us at their ease. Hold your tongue, you foul-mouthed thief, you! You shall go to the gallows for this. Mr Linton, sir, don't lay by your gun.'

"'No, no, Robert,' said the old fool. 'The rascals knew that yesterday was my rent day: they thought to have me cleverly. Come in; I'll furnish them a reception. There, John, fasten the chain. Give Skulker some water, Jenny. To beard a magistrate in his stronghold, and on the Sabbath, too! Where will their insolence stop? Oh, my dear Mary, look here! Don't be afraid, it is but a boy – yet the villain scowls so plainly in his face, would it not be a kindness to the country to hang him at once, before he shows his nature in acts as well as features?'

"He pulled me under the chandelier, and Mrs Linton placed her spectacles on her nose and raised her hands in horror. The cowardly children crept nearer also, Isabella lisping:

"'Frightful thing! Put him in the cellar, Papa. He's exactly like the son of the fortune-teller that stole my tame pheasant. Isn't he, Edgar?'

"While they examined me, Cathy came round; she heard the last speech, and laughed. Edgar Linton, after an inquisitive stare, collected sufficient wit to recognize her. They see us at church, you know, though we seldom meet them elsewhere.

"'That's Miss Earnshaw!' he whispered to his mother, 'and look how Skulker has bitten her – how her foot bleeds!'

"'Miss Earnshaw? Nonsense!' cried the dame, 'Miss Earnshaw scouring the country with a gypsy! And yet, my dear, the child is in mourning – surely it is – and she may be lamed for life!'

"'What culpable carelessness in her brother!' exclaimed Mr Linton, turning from me to Catherine. 'I've understood from Shielders'" – that was the curate, sir – "'that he lets her grow up in absolute heathenism. But who is this? Where did she pick up this companion? Oho! I declare he is that strange acquisition my late neighbour made in his journey to Liverpool – a little Lascar, or an American or Spanish castaway.'

"'A wicked boy, at all events,' remarked the old lady, 'and quite unfit for a decent house! Did you notice his language, Linton? I'm shocked that my children should have heard it.'

"I recommenced cursing – don't be angry, Nelly – and so Robert was ordered to take me off – I refused to go without Cathy – he dragged me into the garden, pushed the lantern into my hand, assured me that Mr Earnshaw should be informed of my behaviour, and, bidding me march directly, secured the door again.

"The curtains were still looped up at one corner, and I resumed my station as spy, because, if Catherine had wished to return, I intended shattering their great glass panes to a million fragments unless they let her out.

"She sat on the sofa quietly. Mrs Linton took off the grey cloak of the dairymaid which we had borrowed for our excursion, shaking her head and expostulating with her, I suppose: she was a young lady, and they made a distinction between her treatment and mine. Then the woman-servant brought a basin of warm water, and washed her feet, and Mr Linton mixed a tumbler of negus, and Isabella emptied a plateful of cakes into her lap, and Edgar stood gaping at a distance. Afterwards, they dried and combed her beautiful hair, and gave her a pair of enormous slippers, and wheeled her to the fire, and I left her, as merry as she could be, dividing her food between the little dog and Skulker, whose nose she pinched as he ate, and kindling a spark of spirit in the vacant blue eyes of the Lintons – a dim reflection from her own enchanting face. I saw they were full of stupid admiration; she is so immeasurably superior to them – to everybody on earth, is she not, Nelly?"

"There will more come of this business than you reckon on," I answered, covering him up and extinguishing the light. "You are incurable, Heathcliff, and Mr Hindley will have to proceed to extremities, see if he won't."

My words came truer than I desired. The luckless adventure made Earnshaw furious. And then Mr Linton, to mend matters, paid us a visit himself on the morrow, and read the young master such a lecture on the road he guided his family that he was stirred to look about him in earnest.

Heathcliff received no flogging, but he was told that the first word he spoke to Miss Catherine should ensure a dismissal, and Mrs Earnshaw undertook to keep her sister-in-law in due restraint when she returned home, employing art, not force – with force she would have found it impossible.

7

CATHY STAYED AT THRUSHCROSS GRANGE five weeks, till Christmas. By that time her ankle was thoroughly cured, and her manners much improved. The mistress visited her often in the interval, and commenced her plan of reform by trying to raise her self-respect with fine clothes and flattery, which she took readily, so that instead of a wild, hatless little savage jumping into the house and rushing to squeeze us all breathless, there lighted from a handsome black pony a very dignified person, with brown ringlets falling from the cover of a feathered beaver, and a long cloth habit, which she was obliged to hold up with both hands that she might sail in.

Hindley lifted her from her horse, exclaiming delightedly:

"Why, Cathy, you are quite a beauty! I should scarcely have known you: you look like a lady now. Isabella Linton is not to be compared with her, is she, Frances?"

"Isabella has not her natural advantages," replied his wife, "but she must mind and not grow wild again here. Ellen, help Miss Catherine off with her things – stay, dear, you will disarrange your curls – let me untie your hat."

I removed the habit, and there shone forth, beneath a grand plaid silk frock, white trousers and burnished shoes, and while her eyes sparkled joyfully when the dogs came bounding up to welcome her, she dared hardly touch them lest they should fawn upon her splendid garments.

She kissed me gently – I was all flour making the Christmas cake, and it would not have done to give me a hug – and then she looked round for Heathcliff. Mr and Mrs Earnshaw watched anxiously their meeting, thinking it would enable them to judge, in some measure, what grounds they had for hoping to succeed in separating the two friends.

Heathcliff was hard to discover at first. If he were careless, and uncared for, before Catherine's absence, he had been ten times more so since.

Nobody but I even did him the kindness to call him a dirty boy, and bid him wash himself once a week – and children of his age seldom have a natural pleasure in soap and water. Therefore, not to mention his clothes, which had seen three months' service in mire and dust, and his thick uncombed hair, the surface of his face and hands was dismally beclouded. He might well skulk behind the settle, on beholding such a bright, graceful damsel enter the house, instead of a rough-headed counterpart of himself, as he expected.

"Is Heathcliff not here?" she demanded, pulling off her gloves, and displaying fingers wonderfully whitened with doing nothing and staying indoors.

"Heathcliff, you may come forwards," cried Mr Hindley, enjoying his discomfiture, and gratified to see what a forbidding young blackguard he would be compelled to present himself. "You may come and wish Miss Catherine welcome, like the other servants."

Cathy, catching a glimpse of her friend in his concealment, flew to embrace him; she bestowed seven or eight kisses on his cheek within the second, and then stopped and, drawing back, burst into a laugh, exclaiming:

"Why, how very black and cross you look! And how... how funny and grim! But that's because I'm used to Edgar and Isabella Linton. Well, Heathcliff, have you forgotten me?"

She had some reason to put the question, for shame and pride threw double gloom over his countenance, and kept him immovable.

"Shake hands, Heathcliff," said Mr Earnshaw condescendingly, "once in a way, that is permitted."

"I shall not!" replied the boy, finding his tongue at last, "I shall not stand to be laughed at. I shall not bear it!" And he would have broken from the circle, but Miss Cathy seized him again.

"I did not mean to laugh at you," she said, "I could not hinder myself. Heathcliff, shake hands at least! What are you sulky for? It was only that you looked odd – if you wash your face and brush your hair, it will be all right. But you are so dirty!"

She gazed concernedly at the dusky fingers she held in her own, and also at her dress, which she feared had gained no embellishment from its contact with his.

"You needn't have touched me!" he answered, following her eye and snatching away his hand. "I shall be as dirty as I please, and I like to be dirty, and I will be dirty."

With that he dashed head foremost out of the room, amid the merriment of the master and mistress, and to the serious disturbance of

Catherine, who could not comprehend how her remarks should have produced such an exhibition of bad temper.

After playing lady's maid to the newcomer, and putting my cakes in the oven, and making the house and kitchen cheerful with great fires befitting Christmas Eve, I prepared to sit down and amuse myself by singing carols all alone, regardless of Joseph's affirmations that he considered the merry tunes I chose as next door to songs.

He had retired to private prayer in his chamber, and Mr and Mrs Earnshaw were engaging Missy's attention by sundry gay trifles bought for her to present to the little Lintons, as an acknowledgement of their kindness.

They had invited them to spend the morrow at Wuthering Heights, and the invitation had been accepted, on one condition: Mrs Linton begged that her darlings might be kept carefully apart from that "naughty, swearing boy".

Under these circumstances I remained solitary. I smelt the rich scent of the heating spices and admired the shining kitchen utensils, the polished clock, decked in holly, the silver mugs ranged on a tray ready to be filled with mulled ale for supper, and above all the speckless purity of my particular care – the scoured and well-swept floor.

I gave due inward applause to every object, and then I remembered how old Earnshaw used to come in when all was tidied, and call me a cant* lass, and slip a shilling into my hand as a Christmas box, and from that I went on to think of his fondness for Heathcliff, and his dread lest he should suffer neglect after death had removed him, and that naturally led me to consider the poor lad's situation now, and from singing I changed my mind to crying. It struck me soon, however, there would be more sense in endeavouring to repair some of his wrongs than shedding tears over them – I got up and walked into the court to seek him.

He was not far; I found him smoothing the glossy coat of the new pony in the stable, and feeding the other beasts, according to custom.

"Make haste, Heathcliff!" I said, "the kitchen is so comfortable – and Joseph is upstairs – make haste, and let me dress you smart before Miss Cathy comes out, and then you can sit together, with the whole hearth to yourselves, and have a long chatter till bedtime."

He proceeded with his task, and never turned his head towards me.

"Come... are you coming?" I continued. "There's a little cake for each of you, nearly enough, and you'll need half an hour's donning."*

I waited five minutes, but getting no answer, left him... Catherine supped with her brother and sister-in-law; Joseph and I joined at an unsociable meal, seasoned with reproofs on one side and sauciness on the other. His cake and cheese remained on the table all night for the fairies. He managed to continue work till nine o'clock, and then marched dumb and dour to his chamber.

Cathy sat up late, having a world of things to order for the reception of her new friends; she came into the kitchen once to speak to her old one, but he was gone, and she only stayed to ask what was the matter with him, and then went back.

In the morning he rose early and, as it was a holiday, carried his ill humour on to the moors, not reappearing till the family were departed for church. Fasting and reflection seemed to have brought him to a better spirit. He hung about me for a while, and having screwed up his courage, exclaimed abruptly:

"Nelly, make me decent, I'm going to be good."

"High time, Heathcliff," I said, "you *have* grieved Catherine; she's sorry she ever came home, I dare say! It looks as if you envied her, because she is more thought of than you."

The notion of *envying* Catherine was incomprehensible to him, but the notion of grieving her he understood clearly enough.

"Did she say she was grieved?" he enquired, looking very serious.

"She cried when I told her you were off again this morning."

"Well, *I* cried last night," he returned, "and I had more reason to cry than she."

"Yes, you had the reason of going to bed with a proud heart and an empty stomach," said I. "Proud people breed sad sorrows for themselves. But if you be ashamed of your touchiness, you must ask pardon, mind, when she comes in. You must go up and offer to kiss her, and say – you know best what to say – only, do it heartily, and not as if you thought her converted into a stranger by her grand dress. And now, though I have dinner to get ready, I'll steal time to arrange you so that Edgar Linton shall look quite a doll beside you, and that he does. You are younger, and yet, I'll be bound, you are taller and twice as broad across the shoulders – you could knock him down in a twinkling, don't you feel that you could?"

Heathcliff's face brightened a moment, then it was overcast afresh, and he sighed.

"But Nelly, if I knocked him down twenty times, that wouldn't make him less handsome or me more so. I wish I had light hair and a fair skin, and was dressed and behaved as well, and had a chance of being as rich as he will be!"

"And cried for Mama at every turn," I added, "and trembled if a country lad heaved his fist against you, and sat at home all day for a shower of rain. Oh, Heathcliff, you are showing a poor spirit! Come to the glass, and I'll let you see what you should wish. Do you mark those two lines between your eyes; and those thick brows, that instead of rising arched, sink in the middle; and that couple of black fiends, so deeply buried, who never open their windows boldly, but lurk glinting under them, like devil's spies? Wish and learn to smooth away the surly wrinkles, to raise your lids frankly, and change the fiends to confident, innocent angels, suspecting and doubting nothing, and always seeing friends where they are not sure of foes. Don't get the expression of a vicious cur that appears to know the kicks it gets are its desert, and yet hates all the world, as well as the kicker, for what it suffers."

"In other words, I must wish for Edgar Linton's great blue eyes and even forehead," he replied. "I do – and that won't help me to them."

"A good heart will help you to a bonny face, my lad," I continued, "if you were a regular black, and a bad one will turn the bonniest into something worse than ugly. And now that we've done washing and combing and sulking – tell me whether you don't think yourself rather handsome? I'll tell you, I do. You're fit for a prince in disguise. Who knows but your father was Emperor of China, and your mother an Indian queen, each of them able to buy up, with one week's income, Wuthering Heights and Thrushcross Grange together? And you were kidnapped by wicked sailors and brought to England. Were I in your place, I would frame* high notions of my birth, and the thoughts of what I was should give me courage and dignity to support the oppressions of a little farmer!"

So I chattered on, and Heathcliff gradually lost his frown and began to look quite pleasant, when all at once our conversation was interrupted by a rumbling sound moving up the road and entering the court. He ran to the window and I to the door, just in time to behold the two Lintons descend from the family carriage, smothered in cloaks and furs, and the Earnshaws dismount from their horses – they often rode to church in winter. Catherine took a hand of each of the children, and brought them into the house and set them before the fire, which quickly put colour into their white faces.

I urged my companion to hasten now and show his amiable humour, and he willingly obeyed, but ill luck would have it that as he opened the door leading from the kitchen on one side, Hindley opened it on the other. They met, and the master, irritated at seeing him clean and cheerful, or perhaps eager to keep his promise to Mrs Linton, shoved him back with a sudden thrust, and angrily bade Joseph, "Keep the fellow out of the room – send him into the garret till dinner is over. He'll be cramming his fingers in the tarts and stealing the fruit if left alone with them a minute."

"Nay, sir," I could not avoid answering, "he'll touch nothing, not he – and I suppose he must have his share of the dainties as well as we."

"He shall have his share of my hand, if I catch him downstairs again till dark," cried Hindley. "Begone, you vagabond! What, you are attempting the coxcomb, are you? Wait till I get hold of those elegant locks – see if I won't pull them a bit longer!"

"They are long enough already," observed Master Linton, peeping from the doorway, "I wonder they don't make his head ache. It's like a colt's mane over his eyes!"

He ventured this remark without any intention to insult, but Heathcliff's violent nature was not prepared to endure the appearance of impertinence from one whom he seemed to hate, even then, as a rival. He seized a tureen of hot apple sauce – the first thing that came under his gripe – and dashed it full against the speaker's face and neck, who instantly commenced a lament that brought Isabella and Catherine hurrying to the place.

Mr Earnshaw snatched up the culprit directly and conveyed him to his chamber, where, doubtless, he administered a rough remedy to cool the fit of passion, for he appeared red and breathless. I got the dishcloth, and rather spitefully scrubbed Edgar's nose and mouth, affirming it served him right for meddling. His sister began weeping to go home, and Cathy stood by confounded, blushing for all.

"You should not have spoken to him!" she expostulated with Master Linton. "He was in a bad temper, and now you've spoilt your visit and he'll be flogged – I hate him to be flogged! I can't eat my dinner. Why did you speak to him, Edgar?"

"I didn't," sobbed the youth, escaping from my hands and finishing the remainder of the purification with his cambric pocket handkerchief. "I promised Mama that I wouldn't say one word to him, and I didn't."

"Well, don't cry," replied Catherine contemptuously, "you're not killed – don't make more mischief – my brother is coming – be quiet! Hush, Isabella! Has anybody hurt *you*?"

"There, there, children – to your seats!" cried Hindley, bustling in. "That brute of a lad has warmed me nicely. Next time, Master Edgar, take the law into your own fists – it will give you an appetite!"

The little party recovered its equanimity at sight of the fragrant feast. They were hungry after their ride, and easily consoled, since no real harm had befallen them.

Mr Earnshaw carved bountiful platefuls, and the mistress made them merry with lively talk. I waited behind her chair, and was pained to behold Catherine, with dry eyes and an indifferent air, commence cutting up the wing of a goose before her.

"An unfeeling child," I thought to myself, "how lightly she dismisses her old playmate's troubles. I could not have imagined her to be so selfish."

She lifted a mouthful to her lips, then she set it down again, her cheeks flushed, and the tears gushed over them. She slipped her fork to the floor, and hastily dived under the cloth to conceal her emotion. I did not call her unfeeling long, for I perceived she was in purgatory throughout the day, and wearying to find an opportunity of getting by herself, or paying a visit to Heathcliff, who had been locked up by the master, as I discovered on endeavouring to introduce to him a private mess* of victuals.

In the evening we had a dance. Cathy begged that he might be liberated then, as Isabella Linton had no partner: her entreaties were vain, and I was appointed to supply the deficiency.

We got rid of all gloom in the excitement of the exercise, and our pleasure was increased by the arrival of the Gimmerton band, mustering fifteen strong: a trumpet, a trombone, clarionets, bassoons, French horns and a bass viol, besides singers. They go the rounds of all the respectable houses, and receive contributions every Christmas, and we esteemed it a first-rate treat to hear them.

After the usual carols had been sung, we set them to songs and glees. Mrs Earnshaw loved the music, and so they gave us plenty.

Catherine loved it too, but she said it sounded sweetest at the top of the steps, and she went up in the dark – I followed. They shut the house door below, never noting our absence, it was so full of people. She made no stay at the stairs' head, but mounted further, to the garret where Heathcliff was confined, and called him. He stubbornly declined answering for a while – she persevered, and finally persuaded him to hold communion with her through the boards.

I let the poor things converse unmolested, till I supposed the songs were going to cease, and the singers to get some refreshment, then I clambered up the ladder to warn her.

Instead of finding her outside, I heard her voice within. The little monkey had crept by the skylight of one garret, along the roof, into the skylight of the other, and it was with the utmost difficulty I could coax her out again.

When she did come, Heathcliff came with her, and she insisted that I should take him into the kitchen, as my fellow servant had gone to a neighbour's, to be removed from the sound of our "devil's psalmody", as it pleased him to call it.

I told them I intended by no means to encourage their tricks, but as the prisoner had never broken his fast since yesterday's dinner, I would wink at his cheating Mr Hindley that once.

He went down; I set him a stool by the fire, and offered him a quantity of good things, but he was sick and could eat little, and my attempts to entertain him were thrown away. He leant his two elbows on his knees, and his chin on his hands, and remained rapt in dumb meditation. On my enquiring the subject of his thoughts, he answered gravely:

"I'm trying to settle how I shall pay Hindley back. I don't care how long I wait, if I can only do it at last. I hope he will not die before I do!"

"For shame, Heathcliff!" said I. "It is for God to punish wicked people; we should learn to forgive."

"No, God won't have the satisfaction that I shall," he returned. "I only wish I knew the best way! Let me alone, and I'll plan it out: while I'm thinking of that I don't feel pain."

But Mr Lockwood, I forget these tales cannot divert you. I'm annoyed how I should dream of chattering on at such a rate, and your gruel cold, and you nodding for bed! I could have told Heathcliff's history, all that you need hear, in half-a-dozen words.

Thus interrupting herself, the housekeeper rose, and proceeded to lay aside her sewing, but I felt incapable of moving from the hearth, and I was very far from nodding.

"Sit still, Mrs Dean," I cried, "do sit still another half-hour! You've done just right to tell the story leisurely. That is the method I like, and you must finish it in the same style. I am interested in every character you have mentioned, more or less."

"The clock is on the stroke of eleven, sir."

"No matter – I'm not accustomed to go to bed in the long hours. One or two is early enough for a person who lies till ten."

"You shouldn't lie till ten. There's the very prime of the morning gone long before that time. A person who has not done one half his day's work by ten o'clock runs a chance of leaving the other half undone."

"Nevertheless, Mrs Dean, resume your chair; because tomorrow I intend lengthening the night till afternoon. I prognosticate for myself an obstinate cold, at least."

"I hope not, sir. Well, you must allow me to leap over some three years: during that space Mrs Earnshaw—"

"No, no, I'll allow nothing of the sort! Are you acquainted with the mood of mind in which, if you were seated alone, and the cat licking its kitten on the rug before you, you would watch the operation so intently that puss's neglect of one ear would put you seriously out of temper?"

"A terribly lazy mood, I should say."

"On the contrary, a tiresomely active one. It is mine at present, and therefore, continue minutely. I perceive that people in these regions acquire over people in towns the value that a spider in a dungeon does over a spider in a cottage, to their various occupants, and yet the deepened attraction is not entirely owing to the situation of the looker-on. They *do* live more in earnest, more in themselves, and less in surface, change and frivolous external things. I could fancy a love for life here almost possible – and I was a fixed unbeliever in any love of a year's standing. One state resembles setting a hungry man down to a single dish, on which he may concentrate his entire appetite and do it justice

– the other, introducing him to a table laid out by French cooks: he can perhaps extract as much enjoyment from the whole, but each part is a mere atom in his regard and remembrance."

"Oh! Here we are the same as anywhere else, when you get to know us," observed Mrs Dean, somewhat puzzled at my speech.

"Excuse me," I responded, "you, my good friend, are a striking evidence against that assertion. Excepting a few provincialisms of slight consequence, you have no marks of the manners which I am habituated to consider as peculiar to your class. I am sure you have thought a great deal more than the generality of servants think. You have been compelled to cultivate your reflective faculties for want of occasions for frittering your life away in silly trifles."

Mrs Dean laughed.

"I certainly esteem myself a steady, reasonable kind of body," she said, "not exactly from living among the hills and seeing one set of faces, and one series of actions, from year's end to year's end – but I have undergone sharp discipline, which has taught me wisdom, and then, I have read more than you would fancy, Mr Lockwood. You could not open a book in this library that I have not looked into, and got something out of also, unless it be that range of Greek and Latin, and that of French – and those I know one from another – it is as much as you can expect of a poor man's daughter.

"However, if I am to follow my story in true gossip's fashion, I had better go on, and instead of leaping three years, I will be content to pass to the next summer – the summer of 1778, that is nearly twenty-three years ago."

8

O N THE MORNING OF A FINE JUNE DAY, my first bonny little nursling, and the last of the ancient Earnshaw stock, was born.

We were busy with the hay in a faraway field, when the girl that usually brought our breakfasts came running an hour too soon across the meadow and up the lane, calling me as she ran.

"Oh, such a grand bairn!" she panted out. "The finest lad that ever breathed! But the doctor says Missis must go; he says she's been in a consumption these many months. I heard him tell Mr Hindley – and now she has nothing to keep her, and she'll be dead before winter. You must come home directly. You're to nurse it, Nelly – to feed it with sugar and milk, and take care of it day and night. I wish I were you, because it will be all yours when there is no Missis!"

"But is she very ill?" I asked, flinging down my rake and tying my bonnet.

"I guess she is, yet she looks bravely," replied the girl, "and she talks as if she thought of living to see it grow a man. She's out of her head for joy, it's such a beauty! If I were her I'm certain I should not die. I should get better at the bare sight of it, in spite of Kenneth. I was fairly mad at him. Dame Archer brought the cherub down to Master, in the house, and his face just began to light up, when the old croaker steps forwards, and says he: 'Earnshaw, it's a blessing your wife has been spared to leave you this son. When she came, I felt convinced we shouldn't keep her long, and now I must tell you the winter will probably finish her. Don't take on and fret about it too much, it can't be helped. And besides, you should have known better than to choose such a rush of a lass!'"

"And what did the master answer?" I enquired.

"I think he swore – but I didn't mind him, I was straining to see the bairn," and she began again to describe it rapturously. I, as zealous as herself, hurried eagerly home to admire, on my part; though I was very sad for Hindley's sake. He had room in his heart only for two idols – his wife and himself – he doted on both, and adored one, and I couldn't conceive how he would bear the loss.

When we got to Wuthering Heights, there he stood at the front door, and as I passed in, I asked how was the baby?

"Nearly ready to run about, Nell!" he replied, putting on a cheerful smile.

"And the mistress?" I ventured to enquire, "the doctor says she's—"

"Damn the doctor!" he interrupted, reddening. "Frances is quite right – she'll be perfectly well by this time next week. Are you going upstairs? Will you tell her that I'll come, if she'll promise not to talk. I left her because she would not hold her tongue, and she must – tell her Mr Kenneth says she must be quiet."

I delivered this message to Mrs Earnshaw; she seemed in flighty spirits, and replied merrily:

"I hardly spoke a word, Ellen, and there he has gone out twice, crying. Well, say I promise I won't speak, but that does not bind me not to laugh at him!"

Poor soul! Till within a week of her death that gay heart never failed her; and her husband persisted doggedly, nay, furiously, in affirming her health improved every day. When Kenneth warned him that his medicines were useless at that stage of the malady, and he needn't put him to further expense by attending her, he retorted:

"I know you need not – she's well – she does not want any more attendance from you! She never was in a consumption. It was a fever, and it is gone – her pulse is as slow as mine now, and her cheek as cool."

He told his wife the same story, and she seemed to believe him; but one night, while leaning on his shoulder, in the act of saying she thought she should be able to get up tomorrow, a fit of cough-ing took her – a very slight one – he raised her in his arms, she put her two hands about his neck, her face changed, and she was dead.

As the girl had anticipated, the child Hareton fell wholly into my hands. Mr Earnshaw, provided he saw him healthy and never heard him cry, was contented, as far as regarded him. For himself, he grew desperate: his sorrow was of that kind that will not lament. He neither wept nor prayed: he cursed and defied, execrated God and man, and gave himself up to reckless dissipation.

The servants could not bear his tyrannical and evil conduct long: Joseph and I were the only two that would stay. I had not the heart to leave my charge, and besides, you know, I had been his foster-sister, and excused his behaviour more readily than a stranger would.

Joseph remained to hector over tenants and labourers, and because it was his vocation to be where he had plenty of wickedness to reprove.

The master's bad ways and bad companions formed a pretty exam-ple for Catherine and Heathcliff. His treatment of the latter was enough to make a fiend of a saint. And truly it appeared as if the lad *were* possessed of something diabolical at that period. He delighted to witness Hindley degrading himself past redemption, and became daily more notable for savage sullenness and ferocity.

I could not half tell what an infernal house we had. The curate dropped calling, and nobody decent came near us at last, unless Edgar Linton's visits to Miss Cathy might be an exception. At fifteen she was the queen of the countryside, she had no peer – and she did turn out a haughty, headstrong creature! I own I did not like her, after infancy was past, and I vexed her frequently by trying to bring down her arrogance – she never took an aversion to me, though. She had a wondrous constancy to old attachments, even Heathcliff kept his hold on her affections unalterably, and young Linton, with all his superiority, found it difficult to make an equally deep impression.

He was my late master: that is his portrait over the fireplace. It used to hang on one side, and his wife's on the other, but hers has been removed, or else you might see something of what she was. Can you make that out?

Mrs Dean raised the candle, and I discerned a soft-featured face, exceedingly resembling the young lady at the Heights, but more pensive and amiable in expression. It formed a sweet picture. The long light hair curled slightly on the temples; the eyes were large and serious; the figure almost too graceful. I did not marvel how Catherine Earnshaw could forget her first friend for such an individual. I marvelled much how he, with a mind to correspond with his person, could fancy my idea of Catherine Earnshaw.

"A very agreeable portrait," I observed to the housekeeper. "Is it like?"

"Yes," she answered, "but he looked better when he was animated – that is his everyday countenance: he wanted spirit in general."

Catherine had kept up her acquaintance with the Lintons since her five weeks' residence among them, and as she had no temptation to show her rough side in their company, and had the sense to be ashamed of being rude where she experienced such invariable courtesy, she imposed unwittingly on the old lady and gentleman by her ingenious cordiality, gained the admiration of Isabella, and the heart and soul of her brother, acquisitions that flattered her from the first – for she was full of ambition – and led her to adopt a double character without exactly intending to deceive anyone.

In the place where she heard Heathcliff termed a "vulgar young ruffian", and "worse than a brute", she took care not to act like him, but at home she had small inclination to practise politeness that would only be laughed at, and restrain an unruly nature when it would bring her neither credit nor praise.

Mr Edgar seldom mustered courage to visit Wuthering Heights openly. He had a terror of Earnshaw's reputation, and shrunk from encountering him, and yet he was always received with our best attempts at civility: the master himself avoided offending him – knowing why he came – and if he could not be gracious, kept out of the way. I rather think his appearance there was distasteful to Catherine; she was not artful, never played the coquette, and had evidently an objection to her two friends meeting at all, for when Heathcliff expressed contempt of Linton in his presence, she could not half-coincide, as she did in his absence; and when Linton evinced disgust and antipathy to Heathcliff, she dared not treat his sentiments with indifference, as if depreciation of her playmate were of scarcely any consequence to her.

I've had many a laugh at her perplexities and untold troubles, which she vainly strove to hide from my mockery. That sounds ill-natured – but she was so proud it became really impossible to pity her distresses, till she should be chastened into more humility.

She did bring herself, finally, to confess, and to confide in me. There was not a soul else that she might fashion into an adviser.

Mr Hindley had gone from home one afternoon, and Heathcliff presumed to give himself a holiday on the strength of it. He had reached the age of sixteen then, I think, and, without having bad features or being deficient in intellect, he contrived to convey an impression of inward and outward repulsiveness that his present aspect retains no traces of.

In the first place, he had by that time lost the benefit of his early education: continual hard work, begun soon and concluded late, had extinguished any curiosity he once possessed in pursuit of knowledge, and any love for books or learning. His childhood's sense of superiority, instilled into him by the favours of old Mr Earnshaw, was faded away. He struggled long to keep up an equality with Catherine in her studies, and yielded with poignant though silent regret – but he yielded completely, and there was no prevailing on him to take a step in the way of moving upwards, when he found he must necessarily sink beneath his former level. Then personal appearance sympathized with mental deterioration: he acquired a slouching gait and ignoble look, his naturally reserved disposition was exaggerated into an almost idiotic excess of unsociable moroseness, and he took a grim pleasure, apparently, in exciting the aversion rather than the esteem of his few acquaintance.

Catherine and he were constant companions still at his seasons of respite from labour; but he had ceased to express his fondness for her in words, and recoiled with angry suspicion from her girlish caresses, as if conscious there could be no gratification in lavishing such marks of affection on him. On the before-named occasion he came into the house to announce his intention of doing nothing, while I was assisting Miss

Cathy to arrange her dress: she had not reckoned on his taking it into his head to be idle, and imagining she would have the whole place to herself, she managed by some means to inform Mr Edgar of her brother's absence, and was then preparing to receive him.

"Cathy, are you busy this afternoon?" asked Heathcliff. "Are you going anywhere?"

"No, it is raining," she answered.

"Why have you that silk frock on, then?" he said. "Nobody coming here, I hope?"

"Not that I know of," stammered Miss, "but you should be in the field now, Heathcliff. It is an hour past dinner time – I thought you were gone."

"Hindley does not often free us from his accursed presence," observed the boy. "I'll not work any more today, I'll stay with you."

"Oh, but Joseph will tell," she suggested, "you'd better go!"

"Joseph is loading lime on the further side of Pennistow Crags; it will take him till dark, and he'll never know."

So saying, he lounged to the fire, and sat down. Catherine reflected an instant, with knitted brows – she found it needful to smooth the way for an intrusion.

"Isabella and Edgar Linton talked of calling this afternoon," she said, at the conclusion of a minute's silence. "As it rains, I hardly expect them, but they may come, and if they do, you run the risk of being scolded for no good."

"Order Ellen to say you are engaged, Cathy," he persisted. "Don't turn me out for those pitiful, silly friends of yours! I'm on the point, sometimes, of complaining that they... but I'll not—"

"That they what?" cried Catherine, gazing at him with a troubled countenance. "Oh, Nelly!" she added petulantly, jerking her head away from my hands, "you've combed my hair quite out of curl! That's enough, let me alone. What are you on the point of complaining about, Heathcliff?"

"Nothing – only look at the almanac on that wall," he pointed to a framed sheet hanging near the window, and continued:

"The crosses are for the evenings you have spent with the Lintons, the dots for those spent with me – do you see? I've marked every day."

"Yes – very foolish, as if I took notice!" replied Catherine, in a peevish tone. "And where is the sense of that?"

"To show that I *do* take notice," said Heathcliff.

"And should I always be sitting with you?" she demanded, growing more irritated. "What good do I get? What do you talk about? You might be dumb, or a baby, for anything you say to amuse me, or for anything you do, either!"

"You never told me before that I talked too little, or that you disliked my company, Cathy!" exclaimed Heathcliff, in much agitation.

"It's no company at all, when people know nothing and say nothing," she muttered.

Her companion rose up, but he hadn't time to express his feelings further, for a horse's feet were heard on the flags, and, having knocked gently, young Linton entered, his face brilliant with delight at the unexpected summons he had received.

Doubtless Catherine marked the difference between her friends, as one came in and the other went out. The contrast resembled what you see in exchanging a bleak, hilly, coal country for a beautiful fertile valley, and his voice and greeting were as opposite as his aspect. He had a sweet, low manner of speaking, and pronounced his words as you do: that's less gruff than we talk here, and softer.

"I'm not come too soon, am I?" he said, casting a look at me. I had begun to wipe the plate, and tidy some drawers at the far end in the dresser.

"No," answered Catherine. "What are you doing there, Nelly?"

"My work, miss," I replied. (Mr Hindley had given me directions to make a third party in any private visits Linton chose to pay.)

She stepped behind me and whispered crossly, "Take yourself and your dusters off! When company are in the house, servants don't commence scouring and cleaning in the room where they are!"

"It's a good opportunity, now that Master is away," I answered aloud, "he hates me to be fidgeting over these things in his presence – I'm sure Mr Edgar will excuse me."

"I hate you to be fidgeting in *my* presence," exclaimed the young lady imperiously, not allowing her guest time to speak – she had failed to recover her equanimity since the little dispute with Heathcliff.

"I'm sorry for it, Miss Catherine," was my response, and I proceeded assiduously with my occupation.

She, supposing Edgar could not see her, snatched the cloth from my hand, and pinched me, with a prolonged wrench, very spitefully on the arm.

I've said I did not love her, and rather relished mortifying her vanity now and then – besides, she hurt me extremely – so I started up from my knees, and screamed out:

"Oh, miss, that's a nasty trick! You have no right to nip me, and I'm not going to bear it!"

"I didn't touch you, you lying creature!" cried she, her fingers tingling to repeat the act, and her ears red with rage. She never had power to conceal her passion, it always set her whole complexion in a blaze.

"What's that, then?" I retorted, showing a decided purple witness to refute her.

She stamped her foot, wavered a moment, and then, irresistibly impelled by the naughty spirit within her, slapped me on the cheek a stinging blow that filled both eyes with water.

"Catherine, love! Catherine!" interposed Linton, greatly shocked at the double fault of falsehood and violence which his idol had committed.

"Leave the room, Ellen!" she repeated, trembling all over.

Little Hareton, who followed me everywhere, and was sitting near me on the floor, at seeing my tears, commenced crying himself, and sobbed out complaints against "wicked aunt Cathy", which drew her fury on to his unlucky head: she seized his shoulders, and shook him till the poor child waxed livid, and Edgar thoughtlessly laid hold of her hands to deliver him. In an instant one was wrung free, and the astonished young man felt it applied over his own ear in a way that could not be mistaken for jest.

He drew back in consternation. I lifted Hareton in my arms, and walked off to the kitchen with him, leaving the door of communication open, for I was curious to watch how they would settle their disagreement.

The insulted visitor moved to the spot where he had laid his hat, pale and with a quivering lip.

"That's right!" I said to myself. "Take warning and begone! It's a kindness to let you have a glimpse of her genuine disposition."

"Where are you going?" demanded Catherine, advancing to the door.

He swerved aside, and attempted to pass.

"You must not go!" she exclaimed energetically.

"I must and shall!" he replied in a subdued voice.

"No," she persisted, grasping the handle, "not yet, Edgar Linton

– sit down, you shall not leave me in that temper. I should be miserable all night, and I won't be miserable for you!"

"Can I stay after you have struck me?" asked Linton.

Catherine was mute.

"You've made me afraid and ashamed of you," he continued, "I'll not come here again!"

Her eyes began to glisten and her lids to twinkle.

"And you told a deliberate untruth!" he said.

"I didn't!" she cried, recovering her speech, "I did nothing deliberately... Well, go, if you please – get away! And now I'll cry... I'll cry myself sick!"

She dropped down on her knees by a chair, and set to weeping in serious earnest. Edgar persevered in his resolution as far as the court; there he lingered. I resolved to encourage him.

"Miss is dreadfully wayward, sir," I called out. "As bad as any marred* child... you'd better be riding home, or else she will be sick, only to grieve us."

The soft thing looked askance through the window – he possessed the power to depart as much as a cat possesses the power to leave a mouse half-killed, or a bird half-eaten.

Ah, I thought, there will be no saving him: he's doomed, and flies to his fate!

And so it was: he turned abruptly, hastened into the house again, shut the door behind him, and when I went in a while after to inform them that Earnshaw had come home rabid drunk, ready to pull the whole place about our ears (his ordinary frame of mind in that condition), I saw the quarrel had merely effected a closer intimacy – had broken the outworks of youthful timidity, and enabled them to forsake the disguise of friendship, and confess themselves lovers.

Intelligence of Mr Hindley's arrival drove Linton speedily to his horse, and Catherine to her chamber. I went to hide little Hareton, and to take the shot out of the master's fowling piece, which he was fond of playing with in his insane excitement, to the hazard of the lives of any who provoked, or even attracted his notice too much, and I had hit upon the plan of removing it, that he might do less mischief, if he did go the length of firing the gun.

9

HE ENTERED, VOCIFERATING OATHS dreadful to hear, and caught me in the act of stowing his son away in the kitchen cupboard. Hareton was impressed with a wholesome terror of encountering either his wild beast's fondness or his madman's rage – for in one he ran a chance of being squeezed and kissed to death, and in the other of being flung into the fire, or dashed against the wall – and the poor thing remained perfectly quiet wherever I chose to put him.

"There, I've found it out at last!" cried Hindley, pulling me back by the skin of my neck, like a dog. "By heaven and hell, you've sworn between you to murder that child! I know how it is now, that he is always out of my way. But, with the help of Satan, I shall make you swallow the carving knife, Nelly! You needn't laugh, for I've just crammed Kenneth, head-downmost, in the Blackhorse marsh, and two is the same as one – and I want to kill some of you, I shall have no rest till I do!"

"But I don't like the carving knife, Mr Hindley," I answered, "it has been cutting red herrings... I'd rather be shot, if you please."

"You'd rather be damned!" he said, "and so you shall. No law in England can hinder a man from keeping his house decent, and mine's abominable! Open your mouth."

He held the knife in his hand, and pushed its point between my teeth, but for my part, I was never much afraid of his vagaries. I spat out, and affirmed it tasted detestably – I would not take it on any account.

"Oh!" said he, releasing me, "I see that hideous little villain is not Hareton – I beg your pardon, Nell. If it be, he deserves flaying alive for not running to welcome me, and for screaming as if I were a goblin. Unnatural cub, come hither! I'll teach thee to impose on a good-hearted, deluded father... Now, don't you think the lad would be handsomer cropped? It makes a dog fiercer, and I love something fierce – get me a scissors – something fierce and trim! Besides, it's infernal affectation – devilish conceit it is, to cherish our ears – we're asses enough without them. Hush, child, hush! Well then, it is my darling! Whisht,[14] dry thy eyes – there's a joy, kiss me. What! It won't? Kiss me, Hareton! Damn thee, kiss me! By God, as if I would rear such a monster! As sure as I'm living, I'll break the brat's neck."

Poor Hareton was squalling and kicking in his father's arms with all his might, and redoubled his yells when he carried him upstairs and lifted him over the banister. I cried out that he would frighten the child into fits, and ran to rescue him.

As I reached them, Hindley leant forwards on the rails to listen to a noise below, almost forgetting what he had in his hands.

"Who is that?" he asked, hearing someone approaching the stairs' foot.

I leant forwards also, for the purpose of signing to Heathcliff, whose step I recognized, not to come further, and at the instant when my eye quitted Hareton, he gave a sudden spring, delivered himself from the careless grasp that held him, and fell.

There was scarcely time to experience a thrill of horror before we saw that the little wretch was safe. Heathcliff arrived underneath just at the critical moment; by a natural impulse he arrested his descent, and setting him on his feet, looked up to discover the author of the accident.

A miser who has parted with a lucky lottery ticket for five shillings, and finds next day he has lost in the bargain five thousand pounds, could not show a blanker countenance than he did on beholding the figure of Mr Earnshaw above. It expressed, plainer than words could do, the intensest anguish at having made himself the instrument of thwarting his own revenge. Had it been dark, I dare say he would have tried to remedy the mistake by smashing Hareton's skull on the steps – but we witnessed his salvation – and I was presently below with my precious charge pressed to my heart.

Hindley descended more leisurely, sobered and abashed.

"It is your fault, Ellen," he said, "you should have kept him out of sight, you should have taken him from me! Is he injured anywhere?"

"Injured!" I cried angrily, "if he is not killed, he'll be an idiot! Oh! I wonder his mother does not rise from her grave to see how you use him. You're worse than a heathen – treating your own flesh and blood in that manner!"

He attempted to touch the child, who, on finding himself with me, sobbed off his terror directly. At the first finger his father laid on him, however, he shrieked again louder than before, and struggled as if he would go into convulsions.

"You shall not meddle with him!" I continued. "He hates you – they all hate you – that's the truth! A happy family you have, and a pretty state you're come to!"

"I shall come to a prettier yet, Nelly," laughed the misguided man, recovering his hardness. "At present, convey yourself and him away. And hark you, Heathcliff! Clear you too quite from my reach and hearing... I wouldn't murder you tonight – unless, perhaps, I set the house on fire – but that's as my fancy goes."

While saying this he took a pint bottle of brandy from the dresser, and poured some into a tumbler.

"Nay, don't!" I entreated, "Mr Hindley, do take warning. Have mercy on this unfortunate boy, if you care nothing for yourself!"

"Anyone will do better for him than I shall," he answered.

"Have mercy on your own soul!" I said, endeavouring to snatch the glass from his hand.

"Not I! On the contrary, I shall have great pleasure in sending it to perdition to punish its maker," exclaimed the blasphemer. "Here's to its hearty damnation!"

He drank the spirits and impatiently bade us go, terminating his command with a sequel of horrid imprecations too bad to repeat or remember.

"It's a pity he cannot kill himself with drink," observed Heathcliff, muttering an echo of curses back when the door was shut. "He's doing his very utmost, but his constitution defies him – Mr Kenneth says he would wager his mare that he'll outlive any man on this side Gimmerton, and go to the grave a hoary sinner, unless some happy chance out of the common course befall him."

I went into the kitchen, and sat down to lull my little lamb to sleep. Heathcliff, as I thought, walked through to the barn. It turned out afterwards that he only got as far as the other side the settle, when he flung himself on a bench by the wall removed from the fire, and remained silent.

I was rocking Hareton on my knee, and humming a song that began:

> It was far in the night, and the bairnies grat,
> The mither beneath the mools heard that—*

when Miss Cathy, who had listened to the hubbub from her room, put her head in, and whispered:

"Are you alone, Nelly?"

"Yes, miss," I replied.

She entered and approached the hearth. I, supposing she was going to say something, looked up. The expression of her face seemed disturbed and anxious. Her lips were half-asunder, as if she meant to speak, and she drew a breath, but it escaped in a sigh instead of a sentence.

I resumed my song, not having forgotten her recent behaviour.

"Where's Heathcliff?" she said, interrupting me.

"About his work in the stable," was my answer.

He did not contradict me, perhaps he had fallen into a doze.

There followed another long pause, during which I perceived a drop or two trickle from Catherine's cheek to the flags.

Is she sorry for her shameful conduct? I asked myself. That will be a novelty, but she may come to the point as she will – I shan't help her!

No, she felt small trouble regarding any subject, save her own concerns.

"Oh dear!" she cried at last. "I'm very unhappy!"

"A pity," observed I, "you're hard to please – so many friends and so few cares, and can't make yourself content!"

"Nelly, will you keep a secret for me?" she pursued, kneeling down by me, and lifting her winsome eyes to my face with that sort of look which turns off bad temper, even when one has all the right in the world to indulge it.

"Is it worth keeping?" I enquired, less sulkily.

"Yes, and it worries me, and I must let it out! I want to know what I should do. Today, Edgar Linton has asked me to marry him, and I've given him an answer. Now, before I tell you whether it was a consent or denial, you tell me which it ought to have been."

"Really, Miss Catherine, how can I know?" I replied. "To be sure, considering the exhibition you performed in his presence this afternoon, I might say it would be wise to refuse him – since he asked you after that, he must either be hopelessly stupid or a venturesome fool."

"If you talk so, I won't tell you any more," she returned, peevishly rising to her feet. "I accepted him, Nelly. Be quick, and say whether I was wrong!"

"You accepted him? Then what good is it discussing the matter? You have pledged your word and cannot retract."

"But say whether I should have done so – do!" she exclaimed in an irritated tone, chafing her hands together, and frowning.

"There are many things to be considered before that question can be answered properly," I said sententiously. "First and foremost, do you love Mr Edgar?"

"Who can help it? Of course I do," she answered.

Then I put her through the following catechism: for a girl of twenty-two it was not injudicious.

"Why do you love him, Miss Cathy?"

"Nonsense, I do – that's sufficient."

"By no means – you must say why?"

"Well, because he is handsome, and pleasant to be with."

"Bad," was my commentary.

"And because he is young and cheerful."

"Bad, still."

"And because he loves me."

"Indifferent, coming there."

"And he will be rich, and I shall like to be the greatest woman of the neighbourhood, and I shall be proud of having such a husband."

"Worst of all. And now say how you love him?"

"As everybody loves – you're silly, Nelly."

"Not at all – answer."

"I love the ground under his feet, and the air over his head, and everything he touches, and every word he says. I love all his looks, and all his actions, and him entirely and altogether. There now!"

"And why?"

"Nay – you are making a jest of it – it is exceedingly ill-natured! It's no jest to me!" said the young lady, scowling, and turning her face to the fire.

"I'm very far from jesting, Miss Catherine," I replied. "You love Mr Edgar because he is handsome, and young, and cheerful, and rich, and loves you. The last, however, goes for nothing – you would love him without that, probably – and with it you wouldn't, unless he possessed the four former attractions."

"No, to be sure not: I should only pity him – hate him, perhaps, if he were ugly and a clown."

"But there are several other handsome rich young men in the world – handsomer, possibly, and richer than he is. What should hinder you from loving them?"

"If there be any, they are out of my way – I've seen none like Edgar."

"You may see some – and he won't always be handsome, and young, and may not always be rich."

"He is now, and I have only to do with the present. I wish you would speak rationally."

"Well, that settles it – if you have only to do with the present, marry Mr Linton."

"I don't want your permission for that – I *shall* marry him – and yet you have not told me whether I'm right."

"Perfectly right, if people be right to marry only for the present. And now, let us hear what you are unhappy about. Your brother will be pleased, the old lady and gentleman will not object, I think, you will escape from a disorderly, comfortless home into a wealthy, respectable one, and you love Edgar, and Edgar loves you. All seems smooth and easy – where is the obstacle?"

"*Here*, and *here*!" replied Catherine, striking one hand on her forehead, and the other on her breast. "In whichever place the soul lives. In my soul and in my heart I'm convinced I'm wrong!"

"That's very strange! I cannot make it out."

"It's my secret, but if you will not mock at me, I'll explain it: I can't do it distinctly, but I'll give you a feeling of how I feel."

She seated herself by me again; her countenance grew sadder and graver, and her clasped hands trembled.

"Nelly, do you never dream queer dreams?" she said suddenly, after some minutes' reflection.

"Yes, now and then," I answered.

"And so do I. I've dreamt in my life dreams that have stayed with me ever after, and changed my ideas: they've gone through and through me, like wine through water, and altered the colour of my mind. And this is one – I'm going to tell it – but take care not to smile at any part of it."

"Oh, don't, Miss Catherine!" I cried. "We're dismal enough without conjuring up ghosts and visions to perplex us. Come, come, be merry and like yourself! Look at little Hareton! *He's* dreaming nothing dreary. How sweetly he smiles in his sleep!"

"Yes, and how sweetly his father curses in his solitude! You remember him, I dare say, when he was just such another as that chubby thing – nearly as young and innocent. However, Nelly, I shall oblige you to listen – it's not long, and I've no power to be merry tonight."

"I won't hear it, I won't hear it!" I repeated hastily.

I was superstitious about dreams then, and am still, and Catherine had an unusual gloom in her aspect that made me dread something from which I might shape a prophecy and foresee a fearful catastrophe.

She was vexed, but she did not proceed. Apparently taking up another subject, she recommenced in a short time.

"If I were in heaven, Nelly, I should be extremely miserable."

"Because you are not fit to go there," I answered. "All sinners would be miserable in heaven."

"But it is not for that. I dreamt once that I was there."

"I tell you I won't hearken to your dreams, Miss Catherine! I'll go to bed," I interrupted again.

She laughed, and held me down, for I made a motion to leave my chair.

"This is nothing," cried she, "I was only going to say that heaven did not seem to be my home, and I broke my heart with weeping to come back to earth, and the angels were so angry that they flung me out into the middle of the heath on the top of Wuthering Heights, where I woke, sobbing for joy. That will do to explain my secret, as well as the other. I've no more business to marry Edgar Linton than I have to be in heaven, and if the wicked man in there had not brought Heathcliff so low, I shouldn't have thought of it. It would degrade me to marry Heathcliff now; so he shall never know how I love him; and that, not because he's handsome, Nelly, but because he's more myself than I am. Whatever our souls are made of, his and mine are the same, and Linton's is as different as a moonbeam from lightning, or frost from fire."

Ere this speech ended I became sensible of Heathcliff's presence. Having noticed a slight movement, I turned my head, and saw him rise from the bench and steal out noiselessly. He had listened till he heard Catherine say it would degrade her to marry him, and then he stayed to hear no further.

My companion, sitting on the ground, was prevented by the back of the settle from remarking his presence or departure, but I started, and bade her hush!

"Why?" she asked, gazing nervously round.

"Joseph is here," I answered, catching opportunely the roll of his cartwheels up the road, "and Heathcliff will come in with him. I'm not sure whether he were not at the door this moment."

"Oh, he couldn't overhear me at the door!" said she. "Give me Hareton, while you get the supper, and when it is ready ask me to sup with you. I want to cheat my uncomfortable conscience, and be convinced that Heathcliff has no notion of these things – he has not, has he? He does not know what being in love is!"

"I see no reason that he should not know, as well as you," I returned, "and if *you* are his choice, he'll be the most unfortunate creature that ever was born! As soon as you become Mrs Linton, he loses friend, and love, and all! Have you considered how you'll bear the separation, and how he'll bear to be quite deserted in the world? Because, Miss Catherine—"

"He quite deserted! We separated!" she exclaimed with an accent of indignation. "Who is to separate us, pray? They'll meet the fate of Milo!* Not as long as I live, Ellen – for no mortal creature. Every Linton on the face of the earth might melt into nothing before I could consent to forsake Heathcliff. Oh, that's not what I intend – that's not what I mean! I shouldn't be Mrs Linton were such a price demanded! He'll be as much to me as he has been all his lifetime. Edgar must shake off his antipathy, and tolerate him at least. He will when he learns my true feelings towards him. Nelly, I see now you think me a selfish wretch, but did it never strike you that if Heathcliff and I married, we should be beggars? Whereas, if I marry Linton I can aid Heathcliff to rise, and place him out of my brother's power."

"With your husband's money, Miss Catherine?" I asked. "You'll find him not so pliable as you calculate upon, and though I'm hardly a judge, I think that's the worst motive you've given yet for being the wife of young Linton."

"It is not," retorted she, "it is the best! The others were the satisfaction of my whims, and for Edgar's sake too, to satisfy him. This is for the sake of one who comprehends in his person my feelings to Edgar and myself. I cannot express it, but surely you and everybody have a notion that there is or should be an existence of yours beyond you. What were the use of my creation, if I were entirely contained here? My great miseries in this world have been Heathcliff's miseries, and I watched and felt each from the beginning: my great thought in living is himself. If all else perished, and *he* remained, I should still continue to be; and if all else remained, and he were annihilated, the universe would turn to a mighty stranger. I should not seem a part of it. My love for Linton is like the foliage in the woods. Time will change it, I'm well aware, as winter changes the trees. My love for Heathcliff resembles the eternal rocks beneath: a source of little visible delight, but necessary. Nelly, I am Heathcliff! He's always, always in my mind – not as a pleasure, any more than I am always a pleasure to myself, but as my own being. So don't talk of our separation again – it is impracticable – and…"

She paused, and hid her face in the folds of my gown, but I jerked it forcibly away. I was out of patience with her folly!

"If I can make any sense of your nonsense, miss," I said, "it only goes to convince me that you are ignorant of the duties you undertake in marrying, or else that you are a wicked, unprincipled girl. But trouble me with no more secrets. I'll not promise to keep them."

"You'll keep that?" she asked eagerly.

"No, I'll not promise," I repeated.

She was about to insist, when the entrance of Joseph finished our conversation, and Catherine removed her seat to a corner, and nursed Hareton while I made the supper.

After it was cooked, my fellow servant and I began to quarrel who should carry some to Mr Hindley, and we didn't settle it till all was nearly cold. Then we came to the agreement that we would let him ask if he wanted any, for we feared particularly to go into his presence when he had been some time alone.

"Und hah isn't that nowt comed in frough th' field, be this time? What is he abaht? Girt idle seeght!"* demanded the old man, looking round for Heathcliff.

"I'll call him," I replied. "He's in the barn, I've no doubt."

I went and called, but got no answer. On returning, I whispered to Catherine that he had heard a good part of what she said, I was sure, and told how I saw him quit the kitchen just as she complained of her brother's conduct regarding him.

She jumped up in a fine fright, flung Hareton onto the settle, and ran to seek for her friend herself, not taking leisure to consider why she was so flurried, or how her talk would have affected him.

She was absent such a while that Joseph proposed we should wait no longer. He cunningly conjectured they were staying away in order to avoid hearing his protracted blessing. They were "ill eneugh for ony fahl* manners", he affirmed. And on their behalf he added that night a special prayer to the usual quarter-of-an-hour's supplication before meat, and would have tacked another to the end of the grace had not his young mistress broken in upon him with a hurried command that he must run down the road, and, wherever Heathcliff had rambled, find and make him re-enter directly!

"I want to speak to him, and I *must*, before I go upstairs," she said. "And the gate is open: he is somewhere out of hearing, for he would not reply, though I shouted at the top of the fold as loud as I could."

Joseph objected at first; she was too much in earnest, however, to suffer contradiction, and at last he placed his hat on his head, and walked grumbling forth.

Meantime Catherine paced up and down the floor, exclaiming:

"I wonder where he is – I wonder where he *can* be! What did I say, Nelly? I've forgotten. Was he vexed at my bad humour this afternoon? Dear, tell me what I've said to grieve him? I do wish he'd come. I do wish he would!"

"What a noise for nothing!" I cried, though rather uneasy myself. "What a trifle scares you! It's surely no great cause of alarm that Heathcliff should take a moonlight saunter on the moors, or even lie too sulky to speak to us in the hayloft. I'll engage he's lurking there. See if I don't ferret him out!"

I departed to renew my search; its result was disappointment, and Joseph's quest ended in the same.

"Yon lad gets war un' war!" observed he on re-entering. "He's left th' gate ut t' full swing, and Miss's pony has trodden dahn two rigs* uh corn, un' plottered* through, raight o'er intuh t' meadow! Hahsomdiver,* t' maister 'ull play t' divil tomorn, and he'll do weel. He's patience itsseln wi' sich careless, offald* craters – patience itsseln he is! Bud he'll nut be soa allus – yah's see, all on ye! Yah munn't drive him aht uf his heead for nowt!"

"Have you found Heathcliff, you ass?" interrupted Catherine. "Have you been looking for him as I ordered?"

"Aw sud more likker look for th' horse," he replied. "It 'ud be tuh more sense. Bud Aw can look for norther horse nur man of a neeght loike this – as black as t' chimbley! Und Heathcliff's noan t' chap tuh coom ut *maw* whistle – happen he'll be less hard uh hearing wi' *ye*!"

It *was* a very dark evening for summer: the clouds appeared inclined to thunder, and I said we had better all sit down; the approaching rain would be certain to bring him home without further trouble.

However, Catherine would not be persuaded into tranquillity. She kept wandering to and fro, from the gate to the door, in a state of agitation which permitted no repose, and at length took up a permanent situation on one side of the wall, near the road, where, heedless of my expostulations and the growling thunder, and the great drops that began to plash around her, she remained, calling at intervals, and then listening, and then crying outright. She beat Hareton, or any child, at a good passionate fit of crying.

About midnight, while we still sat up, the storm came rattling over the Heights in full fury. There was a violent wind, as well as thunder, and either one or the other split a tree off at the corner of the building: a huge bough fell across the roof, and knocked down a portion of the east chimney stack, sending a clatter of stones and soot into the kitchen fire.

We thought a bolt had fallen in the middle of us, and Joseph swung onto his knees, beseeching the Lord to remember the patriarchs Noah and Lot, and as in former times, spare the righteous,* though he smote the ungodly. I felt some sentiment that it must be a judgement on us also. The Jonah, in my mind, was Mr Earnshaw, and I shook the handle of his den that I might ascertain if he were yet living. He replied audibly enough, in a fashion which made my companion vociferate more clamorously than before that a wide distinction might be drawn between saints like himself and sinners like his master. But the uproar passed away in twenty minutes, leaving us all unharmed, excepting Cathy, who got thoroughly drenched for her obstinacy in refusing to take shelter, and standing bonnetless and shawl-less to catch as much water as she could with her hair and clothes.

She came in and lay down on the settle, all soaked as she was, turning her face to the back and putting her hands before it.

"Well, miss!" I exclaimed, touching her shoulder, "you are not bent on getting your death, are you? Do you know what o'clock it is? Half-past twelve. Come, come to bed! There's no use waiting any longer on that foolish boy – he'll be gone to Gimmerton, and he'll stay there now. He guesses we shouldn't wait for him till this late hour; at least he guesses that only Mr Hindley would be up, and he'd rather avoid having the door opened by the master."

"Nay, nay, he's noan at Gimmerton," said Joseph. "Aw's niver wonder bud he's at t' bothom of a bog hoile. This visitation worn't for nowt, and Aw wod hev ye tuh look aht, miss – yah muh be t' next. Thank

Hivin for all! All warks togither for gooid* tuh them as is chozzen, and piked aht froo' th' rubbidge! Yah knaw whet t' Scripture ses…"

And he began quoting several texts, referring us to chapters and verses where we might find them.

I, having vainly begged the wilful girl to rise and remove her wet things, left him preaching and her shivering, and betook myself to bed with little Hareton, who slept as fast as if everyone had been sleeping round him.

I heard Joseph read on a while afterwards, then I distinguished his slow step on the ladder, and then I dropped asleep.

Coming down somewhat later than usual, I saw, by the sunbeams piercing the chinks of the shutters, Miss Catherine still seated near the fireplace. The house door was ajar, too – light entered from its unclosed windows – Hindley had come out, and stood on the kitchen hearth, haggard and drowsy.

"What ails you, Cathy?" he was saying when I entered. "You look as dismal as a drowned whelp. Why are you so damp and pale, child?"

"I've been wet," she answered reluctantly, "and I'm cold, that's all."

"Oh, she is naughty!" I cried, perceiving the master to be tolerably sober. "She got steeped in the shower of yesterday evening, and there she has sat the night through, and I couldn't prevail on her to stir."

Mr Earnshaw stared at us in surprise. "The night through," he repeated. "What kept her up, not fear of the thunder, surely? That was over hours since."

Neither of us wished to mention Heathcliff's absence, as long as we could conceal it, so I replied I didn't know how she took it into her head to sit up, and she said nothing.

The morning was fresh and cool; I threw back the lattice, and presently the room filled with sweet scents from the garden, but Catherine called peevishly to me:

"Ellen, shut the window. I'm starving!"* And her teeth chattered as she shrank closer to the almost extinguished embers.

"She's ill," said Hindley, taking her wrist, "I suppose that's the reason she would not go to bed. Damn it! I don't want to be troubled with more sickness here. What took you into the rain?"

"Running after t' lads, as usuald!" croaked Joseph, catching an opportunity from our hesitation to thrust in his evil tongue. "If Aw wur yah, maister, Aw'd just slam t' boards* i' their faces all on 'em, gentle and simple!* Never a day ut yah're off, but yon cat uh Linton comes sneaking hither – and Miss Nelly, shoo's a fine lass! Shoo sits watching for ye i' t' kitchen, and as yah're in at one door, he's aht at t' other. Und then wer* grand lady goes a-coorting uf hor side! It's bonny behaviour, lurking amang t' fields, after twelve ut' night, wi' that fahl, flaysome divil uf a gypsy, Heathcliff! They think *Aw'm* blind, but Aw'm noan, nowt ut t' soart! Aw seed young Linton boath coming and going, and Aw seed *yah*," (directing his discourse to me), "yah gooid fur nowt, slattenly witch, nip up and bolt intuh th' hahs, t' minute yah heard t' maister's horse fit clatter up t' road."

"Silence, eavesdropper!" cried Catherine. "None of your insolence before me! Edgar Linton came yesterday by chance, Hindley, and it was I who told him to be off, because I knew you would not like to have met him as you were."

"You lie, Cathy, no doubt," answered her brother, "and you are a confounded simpleton! But never mind Linton at present – tell me, were you not with Heathcliff last night? Speak the truth now. You need not be afraid of harming him: though I hate him as much as ever, he did me a good turn a short time since that will make my conscience tender of breaking his neck. To prevent it, I shall send him about his business this very morning, and after he's gone I'd advise you all to look sharp: I shall only have the more humour for you."

"I never saw Heathcliff last night," answered Catherine, beginning to sob bitterly, "and if you do turn him out of doors, I'll go with him. But perhaps you'll never have an opportunity – perhaps he's gone." Here she burst into uncontrollable grief, and the remainder of her words were inarticulate.

Hindley lavished on her a torrent of scornful abuse, and bade her get to her room immediately, or she shouldn't cry for nothing! I obliged her to obey, and I shall never forget what a scene she acted when we reached her chamber. It terrified me – I thought she was going mad, and I begged Joseph to run for the doctor.

It proved the commencement of delirium: Mr Kenneth, as soon as he saw her, pronounced her dangerously ill; she had a fever.

He bled her, and he told me to let her live on whey and water gruel, and take care she did not throw herself downstairs or out of the window, and then he left, for he had enough to do in the parish, where two or three miles was the ordinary distance between cottage and cottage.

Though I cannot say I made a gentle nurse, and Joseph and the master were no better, and though our patient was as wearisome and headstrong as a patient could be, she weathered it through.

Old Mrs Linton paid us several visits, to be sure, and set things to rights, and scolded and ordered us all; and when Catherine was convalescent, she insisted on conveying her to Thrushcross Grange, for which deliverance we were very grateful. But the poor dame had reason to repent of her kindness: she and her husband both took the fever, and died within a few days of each other.

Our young lady returned to us saucier and more passionate, and haughtier than ever. Heathcliff had never been heard of since the evening of the thunderstorm, and one day I had the misfortune, when she had provoked me exceedingly, to lay the blame of his disappearance on her – where indeed it belonged, as she well knew. From that period, for several months, she ceased to hold any communication with me, save in the relation of a mere servant. Joseph fell under a ban also – he would speak his mind and lecture her all the same as if she were a little girl – and she esteemed herself a woman, and our mistress, and thought that her recent illness gave her a claim to be treated with consideration. Then the doctor had said that she would not bear crossing much, she ought to have her own way, and it was nothing less than murder in her eyes for anyone to presume to stand up and contradict her.

From Mr Earnshaw and his companions she kept aloof; and tutored by Kenneth, and serious threats of a fit that often attended her rages, her brother allowed her whatever she pleased to demand, and generally avoided aggravating her fiery temper. He was rather *too* indulgent in humouring her caprices, not from affection but from pride: he wished earnestly to see her bring honour to the family by an alliance with the Lintons, and as long as she let him alone she might trample on us like slaves, for aught he cared!

Edgar Linton, as multitudes have been before and will be after him, was infatuated, and believed himself the happiest man alive on the day he led her to Gimmerton Chapel, three years subsequent to his father's death.

Much against my inclination, I was persuaded to leave Wuthering Heights and accompany her here. Little Hareton was nearly five years old, and I had just begun to teach him his letters. We made a sad parting, but Catherine's tears were more powerful than ours. When I refused to go, and when she found her entreaties did not move me, she went lamenting to her husband and brother. The former offered me munificent wages; the latter ordered me to pack up – he wanted no women in the house, he said, now that there was no mistress, and as to Hareton, the curate should take him in hand, by and by. And so I had but one choice left: to do as I was ordered. I told the master he got rid of all decent people only to run to ruin a little faster, I kissed Hareton, said goodbye, and since then he has been a stranger – and it's very queer to think it, but I've no doubt he has completely forgotten all about Ellen Dean, and that he was ever more than all the world to her, and she to him!

At this point of the housekeeper's story she chanced to glance towards the timepiece over the chimney, and was in amazement on seeing the minute hand measure half-past one. She would not hear of staying a second longer – in truth, I felt rather disposed to defer the sequel of her narrative myself. And now that she is vanished to her rest, and I have meditated for another hour or two, I shall summon courage to go also, in spite of aching laziness of head and limbs.

10

A CHARMING INTRODUCTION TO A HERMIT'S LIFE! Four weeks' torture, tossing and sickness! Oh, these bleak winds and bitter northern skies, and impassable roads, and dilatory country surgeons! And oh, this dearth of the human physiognomy, and worse than all, the terrible intimation of Kenneth that I need not expect to be out of doors till spring!

Mr Heathcliff has just honoured me with a call. About seven days ago he sent me a brace of grouse – the last of the season. Scoundrel! He is not altogether guiltless in this illness of mine, and that I had a great mind to tell him. But alas, how could I offend a man who was charitable enough to sit at my bedside a good hour, and talk on some other subject than pills and draughts, blisters and leeches?

This is quite an easy interval. I am too weak to read, yet I feel as if I could enjoy something interesting. Why not have up Mrs Dean to finish her tale? I can recollect its chief incidents, as far as she had gone.

Yes, I remember her hero had run off, and never been heard of for three years, and the heroine was married. I'll ring: she'll be delighted to find me capable of talking cheerfully.

Mrs Dean came.

"It wants twenty minutes, sir, to taking the medicine," she commenced.

"Away, away with it!" I replied, "I desire to have——"

"The doctor says you must drop the powders."

"With all my heart! Don't interrupt me. Come and take your seat here. Keep your fingers from that bitter phalanx of vials. Draw your knitting out of your pocket – that will do – now continue the history of Mr Heathcliff, from where you left off to the present day. Did he finish his education on the Continent, and come back a gentleman? Or did he get a sizar's place at college? Or escape to America, and earn honours by drawing blood from his foster-country?* Or make a fortune more promptly on the English highways?"

"He may have done a little in all these vocations, Mr Lockwood, but I couldn't give my word for any. I stated before that I didn't know how he gained his money, neither am I aware of the means he took to raise his mind from the savage ignorance into which it was sunk, but, with your leave, I'll proceed in my own fashion, if you think it will amuse and not weary you. Are you feeling better this morning?"

"Much."

"That's good news."

I got Miss Catherine and myself to Thrushcross Grange, and to my agreeable disappointment, she behaved infinitely better than I dared to expect. She seemed almost overfond of Mr Linton, and even to his sister she showed plenty of affection. They were both very attentive to her comfort, certainly. It was not the thorn bending to the honeysuckles, but the honeysuckles embracing the thorn. There were no mutual concessions: one stood erect, and the others yielded, and who can be ill-natured and bad-tempered when they encounter neither opposition nor indifference?

I observed that Mr Edgar had a deep-rooted fear of ruffling her humour. He concealed it from her, but if ever he heard me answer sharply, or saw any other servant grow cloudy at some imperious order of hers, he would show his trouble by a frown of displeasure that never darkened on his own account. He many a time spoke sternly to me about my pertness, and averred that the stab of a knife could not inflict a worse pang than he suffered at seeing his lady vexed.

Not to grieve a kind master, I learnt to be less touchy, and for the space of half a year the gunpowder lay as harmless as sand, because no fire came near to explode it. Catherine had seasons of gloom and silence now and then: they were respected with sympathizing silence by her husband, who ascribed them to an alteration in her constitution, produced by her perilous illness, as she was never subject to depression of spirits before. The return of sunshine was welcomed by answering sunshine from him. I believe I may assert that they were really in possession of deep and growing happiness.

It ended. Well, we *must* be for ourselves in the long run – the mild and generous are only more justly selfish than the domineering – and it ended when circumstances caused each to feel that the one's interest was not the chief consideration in the other's thoughts.

On a mellow evening in September, I was coming from the garden with a heavy basket of apples which I had been gathering. It had got dusk, and the moon looked over the high wall of the court, causing undefined shadows to lurk in the corners of the numerous projecting portions of the building. I set my burden on the house steps by the kitchen door, and lingered to rest, and drew in a few more breaths of the soft, sweet air; my eyes were on the moon, and my back to the entrance, when I heard a voice behind me say:

"Nelly, is that you?"

It was a deep voice, and foreign in tone, yet there was something in the manner of pronouncing my name which made it sound familiar. I turned about to discover who spoke, fearfully, for the doors were shut, and I had seen nobody on approaching the steps.

Something stirred in the porch, and moving nearer I distinguished a tall man dressed in dark clothes, with dark face and hair. He leant against the side, and held his fingers on the latch as if intending to open for himself.

"Who can it be?" I thought. "Mr Earnshaw? Oh, no! The voice has no resemblance to his."

"I have waited here an hour," he resumed, while I continued staring, "and the whole of that time all round has been as still as death. I dared not enter. You do not know me? Look, I'm not a stranger!"

A ray fell on his features; the cheeks were sallow and half-covered with black whiskers, the brows lowering, the eyes deep-set and singular. I remembered the eyes.

"What!" I cried, uncertain whether to regard him as a worldly visitor, and I raised my hands in amazement. "What, you come back? Is it really you? Is it?"

"Yes, Heathcliff," he replied, glancing from me up to the windows, which reflected a score of glittering moons, but showed no lights from within. "Are they at home? Where is she? Nelly, you are not glad – you needn't be so disturbed. Is she here? Speak! I want to have one word with her – your mistress. Go and say some person from Gimmerton desires to see her."

"How will she take it?" I exclaimed. "What will she do? The surprise bewilders me – it will put her out of her head! And you *are* Heathcliff! But altered! Nay, there's no comprehending it. Have you been for a soldier?"

"Go and carry my message," he interrupted impatiently. "I'm in hell till you do!"

He lifted the latch, and I entered, but when I got to the parlour where Mr and Mrs Linton were, I could not persuade myself to proceed. At length I resolved on making an excuse to ask if they would have the candles lit, and I opened the door.

They sat together in a window whose lattice lay back against the wall, and displayed, beyond the garden trees and the wild green park, the valley of Gimmerton, with a long line of mist winding nearly to its top (for very soon after you pass the chapel, as you may have noticed, the sough* that runs from the marshes joins a beck which follows the bend of the glen). Wuthering Heights rose above this silvery vapour, but our old house was invisible – it rather dips down on the other side.

Both the room and its occupants, and the scene they gazed on, looked wondrously peaceful. I shrank reluctantly from performing my errand, and was actually going away leaving it unsaid, after having put my question about the candles, when a sense of my folly compelled me to return and mutter:

"A person from Gimmerton wishes to see you, ma'am."

"What does he want?" asked Mrs Linton.

"I did not question him," I answered.

"Well, close the curtains, Nelly," she said, "and bring up tea. I'll be back again directly."

She quitted the apartment; Mr Edgar enquired carelessly who it was.

"Someone Mistress does not expect," I replied. "That Heathcliff – you recollect him, sir – who used to live at Mr Earnshaw's."

"What, the gypsy – the ploughboy?" he cried. "Why did you not say so to Catherine?"

"Hush! You must not call him by those names, master," I said. "She'd be sadly grieved to hear you. She was nearly heartbroken when he ran off; I guess his return will make a jubilee* to her."

Mr Linton walked to a window on the other side of the room that overlooked the court. He unfastened it, and leant out. I suppose they were below, for he exclaimed quickly:

"Don't stand there, love! Bring the person in, if it be anyone particular."

Ere long, I heard the click of the latch, and Catherine flew upstairs, breathless and wild, too excited to show gladness: indeed, by her face, you would rather have surmised an awful calamity.

"Oh, Edgar, Edgar!" she panted, flinging her arms round his neck. "Oh, Edgar darling! Heathcliff's come back – he is!" And she tightened her embrace to a squeeze.

"Well, well," cried her husband crossly, "don't strangle me for that! He never struck me as such a marvellous treasure. There is no need to be frantic!"

"I know you didn't like him," she answered, repressing a little the intensity of her delight. "Yet for my sake you must be friends now. Shall I tell him to come up?"

"Here," he said, "into the parlour?"

"Where else?" she asked.

He looked vexed, and suggested the kitchen as a more suitable place for him.

Mrs Linton eyed him with a droll expression – half angry, half laughing at his fastidiousness.

"No," she added after a while, "I cannot sit in the kitchen. Set two tables here, Ellen: one for your master and Miss Isabella, being gentry; the other for Heathcliff and myself, being of the lower orders. Will that please you, dear? Or must I have a fire lit elsewhere? If so, give directions. I'll run down and secure my guest. I'm afraid the joy is too great to be real!"

She was about to dart off again, but Edgar arrested her.

"*You* bid him step up," he said, addressing me, "and Catherine, try to be glad without being absurd. The whole household need not witness the sight of your welcoming a runaway servant as a brother."

I descended, and found Heathcliff waiting under the porch, evidently anticipating an invitation to enter. He followed my guidance without waste of words, and I ushered him into the presence of the master and mistress, whose flushed cheeks betrayed signs of warm talking. But the lady's glowed with another feeling when her friend appeared at the door: she sprang forwards, took both his hands, and led him to Linton, and then she seized Linton's reluctant fingers and crushed them into his.

Now fully revealed by the fire and candlelight, I was amazed, more than ever, to behold the transformation of Heathcliff. He had grown a tall, athletic, well-formed man, beside whom my master seemed quite slender and youthlike. His upright carriage suggested the idea of his having been in the army. His countenance was much older in expression and decision of feature than Mr Linton's; it looked intelligent, and retained no marks of former degradation. A half-civilized ferocity lurked yet in the depressed brows and eyes full of black fire, but it was subdued, and his manner was even dignified, quite divested of roughness, though too stern for grace.

My master's surprise equalled or exceeded mine: he remained for a minute at a loss how to address the ploughboy, as he had called him. Heathcliff dropped his slight hand, and stood looking at him coolly till he chose to speak.

"Sit down, sir," he said at length. "Mrs Linton, recalling old times, would have me give you a cordial reception, and of course I am gratified when anything occurs to please her."

"And I also," answered Heathcliff, "especially if it be anything in which I have a part. I shall stay an hour or two willingly."

He took a seat opposite Catherine, who kept her gaze fixed on him as if she feared he would vanish were she to remove it. He did not raise his to her often – a quick glance now and then sufficed – but it flashed back, each time more confidently, the undisguised delight he drank from hers.

They were too much absorbed in their mutual joy to suffer embarrassment. Not so Mr Edgar: he grew pale with pure annoyance, a feeling that reached its climax when his lady rose and, stepping across the rug, seized Heathcliff's hands again, and laughed like one beside herself.

"I shall think it a dream tomorrow!" she cried. "I shall not be able to believe that I have seen, and touched, and spoken to you once more – and yet, cruel Heathcliff! you don't deserve this welcome. To be absent and silent for three years, and never to think of me!"

"A little more than you have thought of me!" he murmured. "I heard of your marriage, Cathy, not long since, and while waiting in the yard below I meditated this plan: just to have one glimpse of your face – a stare of surprise, perhaps, and pretended pleasure – afterwards settle my score with Hindley, and then prevent the law by doing execution on myself. Your welcome has put these ideas out of my mind, but beware of meeting me with another aspect next time! Nay, you'll not drive me off again – you were really sorry for me, were you? Well, there was cause. I've fought through a bitter life since I last heard your voice, and you must forgive me, for I struggled only for you!"

"Catherine, unless we are to have cold tea, please to come to the table," interrupted Linton, striving to preserve his ordinary tone, and a due measure of politeness. "Mr Heathcliff will have a long walk, wherever he may lodge tonight, and I'm thirsty."

She took her post before the urn, and Miss Isabella came, summoned by the bell; then, having handed their chairs forwards, I left the room.

The meal hardly endured ten minutes – Catherine's cup was never filled, she could neither eat nor drink. Edgar had made a slop in his saucer, and scarcely swallowed a mouthful.

Their guest did not protract his stay that evening above an hour longer. I asked, as he departed, if he went to Gimmerton?

"No, to Wuthering Heights," he answered: "Mr Earnshaw invited me when I called this morning."

Mr Earnshaw invited *him*! And *he* called on Mr Earnshaw! I pondered this sentence painfully, after he was gone. Is he turning out a bit of a hypocrite, and coming into the country to work mischief under a cloak? I mused – I had a presentiment in the bottom of my heart that he had better have remained away.

About the middle of the night, I was wakened from my first nap by Mrs Linton gliding into my chamber, taking a seat on my bedside and pulling me by the hair to rouse me.

"I cannot rest, Ellen," she said, by way of apology. "And I want some living creature to keep me company in my happiness! Edgar is sulky, because I'm glad of a thing that does not interest him. He refuses to open his mouth, except to utter pettish, silly speeches, and he affirmed I was cruel and selfish for wishing to talk when he was so sick and sleepy. He always contrives to be sick at the least cross! I gave a few sentences of commendation to Heathcliff, and he, either for a headache or a pang of envy, began to cry – so I got up and left him."

"What use is it praising Heathcliff to him?" I answered. "As lads they had an aversion to each other, and Heathcliff would hate just as much to hear him praised – it's human nature. Let Mr Linton alone about him, unless you would like an open quarrel between them."

"But does it not show great weakness?" pursued she. "I'm not envious, I never feel hurt at the brightness of Isabella's yellow hair and the whiteness of her skin; at her dainty elegance, and the fondness all the family exhibit for her. Even you, Nelly, if we have a dispute sometimes, you back Isabella at once, and I yield like a foolish mother – I call her a darling, and flatter her into a good temper. It pleases her brother to see us cordial, and that pleases me. But they are very much alike: they are spoilt children, and fancy the world was made for their accommodation, and though I humour both, I think a smart chastisement might improve them all the same."

"You're mistaken, Mrs Linton," said I. "They humour you – I know what there would be to do if they did not. You can well afford to indulge their passing whims, as long as their business is to anticipate all your desires. You may however fall out, at last, over something of equal consequence to both sides, and then those you term weak are very capable of being as obstinate as you."

"And then we shall fight to the death, shan't we, Nelly?" she returned, laughing. "No! I tell you, I have such faith in Linton's love that I believe I might kill him, and he wouldn't wish to retaliate."

I advised her to value him the more for his affection.

"I do," she answered, "but he needn't resort to whining for trifles. It is childish, and instead of melting into tears because I said that Heathcliff was now worthy of anyone's regard, and it would honour the first gentleman in the country to be his friend, he ought to have said it for me, and been delighted from sympathy. He must get accustomed to him, and he may as well like him – considering how Heathcliff has reason to object to him, I'm sure he behaved excellently!"

"What do you think of his going to Wuthering Heights?" I enquired. "He is reformed in every respect, apparently – quite a Christian, offering the right hand of fellowship to his enemies all around!"

"He explained it," she replied. "I wondered as much as you. He said he called to gather information concerning me from you, supposing you resided there still, and Joseph told Hindley, who came out and fell to questioning him of what he had been doing, and how he had been living, and finally desired him to walk in. There were some persons sitting at cards, Heathcliff joined them, my brother lost some money to him, and, finding him plentifully supplied, he requested that he would come again in the evening, to which he consented. Hindley is too reckless to select his acquaintance prudently, he doesn't trouble himself to reflect on the causes he might have for mistrusting one whom he has basely injured. But Heathcliff affirms his principal reason for resuming a connection with his ancient persecutor is a wish to install himself in quarters at walking distance from the Grange, and an attachment to the house where we lived together, and likewise a hope that I shall have more opportunities of seeing him there than I could have if he settled in Gimmerton. He means to offer liberal payment for permission to lodge at the Heights, and doubtless my brother's covetousness will prompt him to accept the terms; he was always greedy, though what he grasps with one hand he flings away with the other."

"It's a nice place for a young man to fix his dwelling in!" said I. "Have you no fear of the consequences, Mrs Linton?"

"None for my friend," she replied, "his strong head will keep him from danger – a little for Hindley, but he can't be made morally worse than he is, and I stand between him and bodily harm. The event of this evening has reconciled me to God and humanity! I had risen in angry rebellion against Providence – oh, I've endured very, very bitter misery, Nelly! If that creature knew how bitter, he'd be ashamed to cloud its removal with idle petulance. It was kindness for him which induced me to bear it alone: had I expressed the agony I frequently felt, he would have been taught to long for its alleviation as ardently as I... However, it's over, and I'll take no revenge on his folly – I can afford to suffer anything hereafter! Should the meanest thing alive slap me on the cheek, I'd not only turn the other, but I'd ask pardon for provoking it – and as a proof I'll go make my peace with Edgar instantly. Goodnight! I'm an angel!"

In this self-complacent conviction she departed, and the success of her fulfilled resolution was obvious on the morrow: Mr Linton had not only abjured his peevishness (though his spirits seemed still subdued by Catherine's exuberance of vivacity), but he ventured no objection to her taking Isabella with her to Wuthering Heights in the afternoon, and she rewarded him with such a summer of sweetness and affection in return as made the house a paradise for several days – both master and servants profiting from the perpetual sunshine.

Heathcliff – Mr Heathcliff I should say in future – used the liberty of visiting at Thrushcross Grange cautiously at first: he seemed estimating how far its owner would bear his intrusion. Catherine also deemed it judicious to moderate her expressions of pleasure in receiving him, and he gradually established his right to be expected.

He retained a great deal of the reserve for which his boyhood was remarkable, and that served to repress all startling demonstrations of feeling. My master's uneasiness experienced a lull, and further circumstances diverted it into another channel for a space.

His new source of trouble sprang from the not anticipated misfortune of Isabella Linton evincing a sudden and irresistible attraction towards the tolerated guest. She was at that time a charming young lady of eighteen, infantile in manners, though possessed of keen wit, keen feelings and a keen temper, too, if irritated. Her brother, who loved her tenderly, was appalled at this fantastic preference. Leaving aside the degradation of an alliance with a nameless man, and the possible fact that his property, in default of heirs male, might pass into such a one's power, he had sense to comprehend Heathcliff's disposition – to know that, though his exterior was altered, his mind was unchangeable and unchanged. And he dreaded that mind, it revolted him; he shrank forebodingly from the idea of committing Isabella to its keeping.

He would have recoiled still more had he been aware that her attachment rose unsolicited, and was bestowed where it awakened no reciprocation of sentiment, for the minute he discovered its existence he laid the blame on Heathcliff's deliberate designing.

We had all remarked during some time that Miss Linton fretted and pined over something. She grew cross and wearisome, snapping at and teasing Catherine continually, at the imminent risk of exhausting her limited patience. We excused her to a certain extent, on the plea of ill health – she was dwindling and fading before our eyes. But one day, when she had been peculiarly wayward, rejecting her breakfast, complaining that the servants did not do what she told them; that the mistress would allow her to be nothing in the house and Edgar neglected her; that she had caught a cold with the doors being left open, and we let the parlour fire go out on purpose to vex her – with a hundred yet more frivolous accusations – Mrs Linton peremptorily insisted that she should get to bed, and, having scolded her heartily, threatened to send for the doctor.

Mention of Kenneth caused her to exclaim instantly that her health was perfect, and it was only Catherine's harshness which made her unhappy.

"How can you say I am harsh, you naughty fondling?"* cried the mistress, amazed at the unreasonable assertion. "You are surely losing your reason. When have I been harsh, tell me?"

"Yesterday," sobbed Isabella, "and now!"

"Yesterday!" said her sister-in-law. "On what occasion?"

"In our walk along the moor: you told me to ramble where I pleased, while you sauntered on with Mr Heathcliff!"

"And that's your notion of harshness?" said Catherine, laughing. "It was no hint that your company was superfluous – we didn't care whether you kept with us or not – I merely thought Heathcliff's talk would have nothing entertaining for your ears."

"Oh no," wept the young lady, "you wished me away, because you knew I liked to be there!"

"Is she sane?" asked Mrs Linton, appealing to me. "I'll repeat our conversation, word for word, Isabella – and you point out any charm it could have had for you."

"I don't mind the conversation," she answered, "I wanted to be with…"

"Well?" said Catherine, perceiving her hesitate to complete the sentence.

"With him – and I won't be always sent off!" she continued, kindling up. "You are a dog in the manger, Cathy, and desire no one to be loved but yourself!"

"You are an impertinent little monkey!" exclaimed Mrs Linton in surprise. "But I'll not believe this idiocy! It is impossible that you can covet the admiration of Heathcliff – that you consider him an agreeable person! I hope I have misunderstood you, Isabella?"

"No, you have not," said the infatuated girl. "I love him more than ever you loved Edgar, and he might love me, if you would let him!"

"I wouldn't be you for a kingdom, then!" Catherine declared emphatically – and she seemed to speak sincerely. "Nelly, help me to convince her of her madness. Tell her what Heathcliff is: an unreclaimed creature, without refinement, without cultivation – an arid wilderness of furze and whinstone. I'd as soon put that little canary into the park on a winter's day, as recommend you to bestow your heart on him! It is deplorable ignorance of his character, child, and nothing else, which makes that dream enter your head. Pray, don't imagine that he conceals depths of benevolence and affection beneath a stern exterior! He's not a rough diamond, a pearl-containing oyster of a rustic: he's a fierce, pitiless, wolfish man. I never say to him, 'Let this or that enemy alone, because it would be ungenerous or cruel to harm them' – I say, 'Let them alone, because *I* should hate them to be wronged' – and he'd crush you like a sparrow's egg, Isabella, if he found you a troublesome charge. I know he couldn't love a Linton, and yet he'd be quite capable of marrying your fortune and expectations. Avarice is growing with him a besetting sin. There's my picture – and I'm his friend, so much so, that had he thought seriously to catch you, I should perhaps have held my tongue, and let you fall into his trap."

Miss Linton regarded her sister-in-law with indignation.

"For shame! For shame!" she repeated angrily. "You are worse than twenty foes, you poisonous friend!"

"Ah, you won't believe me then?" said Catherine. "You think I speak from wicked selfishness?"

"I'm certain you do," retorted Isabella, "and I shudder at you!"

"Good!" cried the other. "Try for yourself, if that be your spirit; I have done, and yield the argument to your saucy insolence."

"And I must suffer for her egotism!" she sobbed, as Mrs Linton left the room. "All, all is against me: she has blighted my single consolation. But she uttered falsehoods, didn't she? Mr Heathcliff is not a fiend: he has an honourable soul, and a true one, or how could he remember her?"

"Banish him from your thoughts, miss," I said. "He's a bird of bad omen – no mate for you. Mrs Linton spoke strongly, and yet I can't contradict her. She is better acquainted with his heart than I, or anyone besides, and she never would represent him as worse than he is. Honest people don't hide their deeds. How has he been living? How has he got rich? Why is he staying at Wuthering Heights, the house of a man whom he abhors? They say Mr Earnshaw is worse and worse since he came. They sit up all night together continually, and Hindley has been borrowing money on his land, and does nothing but play and drink, I heard only a week ago – it was Joseph who told me, I met him at Gimmerton.

"'Nelly,' he said, 'we's hae a crahnr's 'quest enah,* at ahr folks'. One on 'em's a'most getten his finger cut off wi'hauding* t' other froo' sticking* hisseln loike a cawlf. That's maister, yah knaw, ut's soa up uh going tuh t' grand 'sizes.* He's noan feard uh t' bench uh judges, norther Paul, nur Peter, nur John, nor Matthew, nor noan on 'em, nut he! He fair likes, he langs tuh set his brazened face agean 'em! And yon bonny lad Heathcliff, yah mind, he's a rare un! He can girn a laugh as weel 's onybody at a raight divil's jest. Does he niver say nowt of his fine living amang us, when he goas tuh t' Grange? This is t' way on 't: up at sundahn, dice, brandy, cloised shutters und can'lelight till next day at nooin; then, t' fooil gangs banning* un' raving tuh his cham'er, makking dacent fowks dig thur fingers i' thur lugs fur varry shame; un' the knave, wah he can cahnt his brass, un' ate, un' sleep, un' off tuh his neighbour's tuh gossip wi' t' wife. I' course, he tells Dame Catherine hah hor father's goold runs intuh his pocket, and her fathur's son gallops dahn t' broad road,* while he flees afore tuh oppen t' pikes!'* Now, Miss Linton, Joseph is an old rascal, but no liar, and if his account of Heathcliff's conduct be true, you would never think of desiring such a husband, would you?"

"You are leagued with the rest, Ellen!" she replied. "I'll not listen to your slanders. What malevolence you must have to wish to convince me that there is no happiness in the world!"

Whether she would have got over this fancy if left to herself, or persevered in nursing it perpetually, I cannot say: she had little time to reflect. The day after, there was a justice meeting* at the next town; my master was obliged to attend, and Mr Heathcliff, aware of his absence, called rather earlier than usual.

Catherine and Isabella were sitting in the library, on hostile terms, but silent: the latter alarmed at her recent indiscretion, and the disclosure she had made of her secret feelings in a transient fit of passion; the former, on mature consideration, really offended with her companion, and, if she laughed again at her pertness, inclined to make it no laughing matter to *her*.

88

She did laugh as she saw Heathcliff pass the window. I was sweeping the hearth, and I noticed a mischievous smile on her lips. Isabella, absorbed in her meditations, or a book, remained till the door opened, and it was too late to attempt an escape, which she would gladly have done had it been practicable.

"Come in, that's right!" exclaimed the mistress gaily, pulling a chair to the fire. "Here are two people sadly in need of a third to thaw the ice between them, and you are the very one we should both of us choose. Heathcliff, I'm proud to show you, at last, somebody that dotes on you more than myself. I expect you to feel flattered – nay, it's not Nelly, don't look at her! My poor little sister-in-law is breaking her heart by mere contemplation of your physical and moral beauty. It lies in your own power to be Edgar's brother! No, no, Isabella, you shan't run off," she continued, arresting, with feigned playfulness, the confounded girl, who had risen indignantly. "We were quarrelling like cats about you, Heathcliff, and I was fairly beaten in protestations of devotion and admiration, and moreover, I was informed that if I would but have the manners to stand aside, my rival, as she will have herself to be, would shoot a shaft into your soul that would fix you for ever, and send my image into eternal oblivion!"

"Catherine," said Isabella, calling up her dignity and disdaining to struggle from the tight grasp that held her, "I'd thank you to adhere to the truth and not slander me, even in joke! Mr Heathcliff, be kind enough to bid this friend of yours release me – she forgets that you and I are not intimate acquaintances, and what amuses her is painful to me beyond expression."

As the guest answered nothing, but took his seat and looked thoroughly indifferent what sentiments she cherished concerning him, she turned and whispered an earnest appeal for liberty to her tormentor.

"By no means!" cried Mrs Linton in answer. "I won't be named a dog in the manger again. You *shall* stay – now then! Heathcliff, why don't you evince satisfaction at my pleasant news? Isabella swears that the love Edgar has for me is nothing to that she entertains for you. I'm sure she made some speech of the kind, did she not, Ellen? And she has fasted ever since the day before yesterday's walk, from sorrow and rage that I dispatched her out of your society under the idea of its being unacceptable."

a very venomous species

"I think you belie her," said Heathcliff, twisting his chair to face them. "She wishes to be out of my society now, at any rate!"

And he stared hard at the object of discourse, as one might do at a strange repulsive animal – a centipede from the Indies* for instance, which curiosity leads one to examine in spite of the aversion it raises.

The poor thing couldn't bear that: she grew white and red in rapid succession, and while tears beaded her lashes, bent the strength of her small fingers to loosen the firm clutch of Catherine, and perceiving that as fast as she raised one finger off her arm another closed down, and she could not remove the whole together, she began to make use of her nails, and their sharpness presently ornamented the detainer's with crescents of red.

"There's a tigress!" exclaimed Mrs Linton, setting her free, and shaking her hand with pain. "Begone, for God's sake, and hide your vixen face! How foolish to reveal those talons to *him*. Can't you fancy the conclusions he'll draw? Look, Heathcliff! They are instruments that will do execution – you must beware of your eyes."

"I'd wrench them off her fingers if they ever menaced me," he answered brutally, when the door had closed after her. "But what did you mean by teasing the creature in that manner, Cathy? You were not speaking the truth, were you?"

"I assure you I was," she returned. "She has been pining for your sake several weeks, and raving about you this morning, and pouring forth a deluge of abuse, because I represented your failings in a plain light, for the purpose of mitigating her adoration. But don't notice it further. I wished to punish her sauciness, that's all. I like her too well, my dear Heathcliff, to let you absolutely seize and devour her up."

"And I like her too ill to attempt it," said he, "except in a very ghoulish fashion. You'd hear of odd things if I lived alone with that mawkish, waxen face: the most ordinary would be painting on its white the colours of the rainbow, and turning the blue eyes black, every day or two – they detestably resemble Linton's."

"Delectably!" observed Catherine. "They are dove's eyes... angel's!"

"She's her brother's heir, is she not?" he asked, after a brief silence.

"I should be sorry to think so," returned his companion. "Half a dozen nephews shall erase her title, please Heaven! Abstract your mind from the subject at present – you are too prone to covet your neighbour's goods: remember *this* neighbour's goods are mine."

CHAPTER 11

"If they were *mine*, they would be none the less that," said Heathcliff, "but though Isabella Linton may be silly, she is scarcely mad, and in short, we'll dismiss the matter, as you advise."

From their tongues they did dismiss it, and Catherine probably from her thoughts. The other, I felt certain, recalled it often in the course of the evening. I saw him smile to himself – grin rather – and lapse into ominous musing whenever Mrs Linton had occasion to be absent from the apartment.

I determined to watch his movements. My heart invariably cleaved to the master's, in preference to Catherine's side – with reason I imagined, for he was kind, and trustful, and honourable, and she – she could not be called *opposite*, yet she seemed to allow herself such wide latitude that I had little faith in her principles, and still less sympathy for her feelings. I wanted something to happen which might have the effect of freeing both Wuthering Heights and the Grange of Mr Heathcliff quietly, leaving us as we had been prior to his advent. His visits were a continual nightmare to me, and, I suspected, to my master also. His abode at the Heights was an oppression past explaining. I felt that God had forsaken the stray sheep there to its own wicked wanderings, and an evil beast prowled between it and the fold, waiting his time to spring and destroy.

11

SOMETIMES WHILE MEDITATING on these things in solitude, I've got up in a sudden terror and put on my bonnet to go see how all was at the farm. I've persuaded my conscience that it was a duty to warn him how people talked regarding his ways, and then I've recollected his confirmed bad habits, and, hopeless of benefiting him, have flinched from re-entering the dismal house, doubting if I could bear to be taken at my word.

One time I passed the old gate, going out of my way on a journey to Gimmerton. It was about the period that my narrative has reached – a bright frosty afternoon, the ground bare, and the road hard and dry.

I came to a stone where the highway branches off onto the moor at your left hand; a rough sand pillar,* with the letters W.H. cut on its north side, on the east, G., and on the south-west, T.G. It serves as a guidepost to the Grange, the Heights and village.

The sun shone yellow on its grey head, reminding me of summer, and I cannot say why, but all at once a gush of child's sensations flowed into my heart. Hindley and I held it a favourite spot twenty years before.

I gazed long at the weather-worn block, and, stooping down, perceived a hole near the bottom still full of snail shells and pebbles, which we were fond of storing there with more perishable things, and, as fresh as reality, it appeared that I beheld my early playmate seated on the withered turf, his dark, square head bent forwards, and his little hand scooping out the earth with a piece of slate.

"Poor Hindley!" I exclaimed involuntarily.

I started – my bodily eye was cheated into a momentary belief that the child lifted its face and stared straight into mine! It vanished in a twinkling, but immediately I felt an irresistible yearning to be at the Heights. Superstition urged me to comply with this impulse – supposing he should be dead! – I thought – or should die soon! Supposing it were a sign of death!

The nearer I got to the house the more agitated I grew, and on catching sight of it I trembled in every limb. The apparition had outstripped me: it stood looking through the gate. That was my first idea on observing an elf-locked, brown-eyed boy setting his ruddy countenance against the bars. Further reflection suggested this must be Hareton, *my* Hareton, not altered greatly since I left him ten months since.

"God bless thee, darling!" I cried, forgetting instantaneously my foolish fears. "Hareton, it's Nelly – Nelly, thy nurse."

He retreated out of arm's length, and picked up a large flint.

"I am come to see thy father, Hareton," I added, guessing from the action that Nelly, if she lived in his memory at all, was not recognized as one with me.

He raised his missile to hurl it; I commenced a soothing speech, but could not stay his hand. The stone struck my bonnet, and then ensued, from the stammering lips of the little fellow, a string of curses, which, whether he comprehended them or not, were delivered with practised emphasis and distorted his baby features into a shocking expression of malignity.

You may be certain this grieved more than angered me. Fit to cry, I took an orange from my pocket, and offered it to propitiate him.

He hesitated, and then snatched it from my hold, as if he fancied I only intended to tempt and disappoint him. I showed another, keeping it out of his reach.

"Who has taught you those fine words, my barn?"* I enquired. "The curate?"

"Damn the curate, and thee! Gie me that," he replied.

"Tell us where you got your lessons, and you shall have it," said I. "Who's your master?"

"Devil Daddy," was his answer.

"And what do you learn from Daddy?" I continued.

He jumped at the fruit; I raised it higher. "What does he teach you?" I asked.

"Naught," said he, "but to keep out of his gait. Daddy cannot bide me, because I swear at him."

"Ah! and the Devil teaches you to swear at Daddy?" I observed.

"Ay... nay," he drawled.

"Who, then?"

"Heathcliff."

I asked if he liked Mr Heathcliff?

"Ay!" he answered again.

Desiring to have his reasons for liking him, I could only gather the sentences: "I known't... He pays Dad back what he gies to me... He curses Daddy for cursing me... He says I mun do as I will."

"And the curate does not teach you to read and write, then?" I pursued.

"No, I was told the curate should have his *** teeth dashed down his *** throat, if he stepped over the threshold – Heathcliff had promised that!"

I put the orange in his hand, and bade him tell his father that a woman called Nelly Dean was waiting to speak with him by the garden gate.

He went up the walk, and entered the house, but instead of Hindley, Heathcliff appeared on the door stones, and I turned directly and ran down the road as hard as ever I could race, making no halt till I gained the guidepost, and feeling as scared as if I had raised a goblin.

This is not much connected with Miss Isabella's affair, except that it urged me to resolve further on mounting vigilant guard, and doing my utmost to check the spread of such bad influence at the Grange, even though I should wake a domestic storm by thwarting Mrs Linton's pleasure.

The next time Heathcliff came, my young lady chanced to be feeding some pigeons in the court. She had never spoken a word to her sister-in-law for three days, but she had likewise dropped her fretful complaining, and we found it a great comfort.

Heathcliff had not the habit of bestowing a single unnecessary civility on Miss Linton, I knew. Now, as soon as he beheld her, his first precaution was to take a sweeping survey of the house front. I was standing by the kitchen window, but I drew out of sight. He then stepped across the pavement to her, and said something: she seemed embarrassed, and desirous of getting away; to prevent it, he laid his hand on her arm: she averted her face; he apparently put some question which she had no mind to answer. There was another rapid glance at the house, and supposing himself unseen, the scoundrel had the impudence to embrace her.

"Judas! Traitor!" I ejaculated. "You are a hypocrite too, are you? A deliberate deceiver."

"Who is, Nelly?" said Catherine's voice at my elbow: I had been over-intent on watching the pair outside to mark her entrance.

"Your worthless friend!" I answered warmly, "the sneaking rascal yonder. Ah, he has caught a glimpse of us – he is coming in! I wonder will he have the art to find a plausible excuse for making love to Miss, when he told you he hated her?"

Mrs Linton saw Isabella tear herself free and run into the garden, and a minute after, Heathcliff opened the door.

I couldn't withhold giving some loose to my indignation, but Catherine angrily insisted on silence, and threatened to order me out of the kitchen, if I dared to be so presumptuous as to put in my insolent tongue.

"To hear you, people might think *you* were the mistress!" she cried. "You want setting down in your right place! Heathcliff, what are you about, raising this stir? I said you must let Isabella alone!... I beg you will, unless you are tired of being received here, and wish Linton to draw the bolts against you!"

"God forbid that he should try!" answered the black villain – I detested him just then. "God keep him meek and patient! Every day I grow madder after sending him to heaven!"

CHAPTER 11

"Hush!" said Catherine, shutting the inner door. "Don't vex me. Why have you disregarded my request? Did she come across you on purpose?"

"What is it to you?" he growled. "I have a right to kiss her, if she chooses, and you have no right to object. I am not *your* husband: *you* needn't be jealous of me!"

"I'm not jealous of you," replied the mistress, "I'm jealous *for* you. Clear your face, you shan't scowl at me! If you like Isabella, you shall marry her. But do you like her? Tell the truth, Heathcliff! There, you won't answer. I'm certain you don't."

"And would Mr Linton approve of his sister marrying that man?" I enquired.

"Mr Linton should approve," returned my lady decisively.

"He might spare himself the trouble," said Heathcliff, "I could do as well without his approbation... And as to you, Catherine, I have a mind to speak a few words now, while we are at it. I want you to be aware that I know you have treated me infernally – infernally! Do you hear? And if you flatter yourself that I don't perceive it, you are a fool; and if you think I can be consoled by sweet words, you are an idiot; and if you fancy I'll suffer unrevenged, I'll convince you of the contrary in a very little while! Meantime, thank you for telling me your sister-in-law's secret – I swear I'll make the most of it – and stand you aside!"

"What new phase of his character is this?" exclaimed Mrs Linton in amazement. "I've treated you infernally – and you'll take your revenge! How will you take it, ungrateful brute? How have I treated you infernally?"

"I seek no revenge on you," replied Heathcliff less vehemently. "That's not the plan... The tyrant grinds down his slaves and they don't turn against him: they crush those beneath them... You are welcome to torture me to death for your amusement, only allow me to amuse myself a little in the same style – and refrain from insult as much as you are able. Having levelled my palace, don't erect a hovel and complacently admire your own charity in giving me that for a home. If I imagined you really wished me to marry Isabella, I'd cut my throat!"

"Oh, the evil is that I am *not* jealous, is it?" cried Catherine. "Well, I won't repeat my offer of a wife – it is as bad as offering Satan a lost soul. Your bliss lies, like his, in inflicting misery – you prove it. Edgar is restored from the ill temper he gave way to at your coming, I begin to be secure and tranquil, and you, restless to know us at peace, appear resolved on exciting a quarrel. Quarrel with Edgar, if you please, Heathcliff, and deceive his sister: you'll hit on exactly the most efficient method of revenging yourself on me."

The conversation ceased. Mrs Linton sat down by the fire, flushed and gloomy. The spirit which served her was growing intractable, she could neither lay nor control it. He stood on the hearth with folded arms, brooding on his evil thoughts, and in this position I left them to seek the master, who was wondering what kept Catherine below so long.

"Ellen," said he, when I entered, "have you seen your mistress?"

"Yes, she's in the kitchen, sir," I answered. "She's sadly put out by Mr Heathcliff's behaviour, and indeed, I do think it's time to arrange his visits on another footing. There's harm in being too soft, and now it's come to this…" And I related the scene in the court and, as near as I dared, the whole subsequent dispute. I fancied it could not be very prejudicial to Mrs Linton, unless she made it so afterwards by assuming the defensive for her guest.

Edgar Linton had difficulty in hearing me to the close. His first words revealed that he did not clear his wife of blame.

"This is insufferable!" he exclaimed. "It is disgraceful that she should own him for a friend, and force his company on me! Call me two men out of the hall, Ellen. Catherine shall linger no longer to argue with the low ruffian – I have humoured her enough."

He descended, and, bidding the servants wait in the passage, went, followed by me, to the kitchen. Its occupants had recommenced their angry discussion – Mrs Linton, at least, was scolding with renewed vigour, Heathcliff had moved to the window and hung his head, somewhat cowed by her violent rating,* apparently.

He saw the master first, and made a hasty motion that she should be silent, which she obeyed abruptly, on discovering the reason of his intimation.

"How is this?" said Linton, addressing her, "what notion of propriety must you have to remain here, after the language which has been held to you by that blackguard? I suppose because it is his ordinary talk you think nothing of it – you are habituated to his baseness, and perhaps imagine I can get used to it too!"

"Have you been listening at the door, Edgar?" asked the mistress, in a tone particularly calculated to provoke her husband, implying both carelessness and contempt of his irritation.

Heathcliff, who had raised his eyes at the former speech, gave a sneering laugh at the latter, on purpose, it seemed, to draw Mr Linton's attention to him. He succeeded, but Edgar did not mean to entertain him with any high flights of passion.

"I've been so far forbearing with you, sir," he said quietly, "not that I was ignorant of your miserable, degraded character, but I felt you were only partly responsible for that, and Catherine wishing to keep up your acquaintance, I acquiesced – foolishly. Your presence is a moral poison that would contaminate the most virtuous – for that cause, and to prevent worse consequences, I shall deny you hereafter admission into this house, and give notice now that I require your instant departure. Three minutes' delay will render it involuntary and ignominious."

Heathcliff measured the height and breadth of the speaker with an eye full of derision.

"Cathy, this lamb of yours threatens like a bull!" he said. "It is in danger of splitting its skull against my knuckles. By God, Mr Linton, I'm mortally sorry that you are not worth knocking down!"

My master glanced towards the passage, and signed me to fetch the men – he had no intention of hazarding a personal encounter.

I obeyed the hint, but Mrs Linton, suspecting something, followed, and when I attempted to call them, she pulled me back, slammed the door to, and locked it.

"Fair means!" she said, in answer to her husband's look of angry surprise. "If you have not courage to attack him, make an apology, or allow yourself to be beaten. It will correct you of feigning more valour than you possess. No, I'll swallow the key before you shall get it! I'm delightfully rewarded for my kindness to each! After constant indulgence of one's weak nature, and the other's bad one, I earn for thanks two samples of blind ingratitude, stupid to absurdity! Edgar, I was defending you and yours, and I wish Heathcliff may flog you sick for daring to think an evil thought of me!"

It did not need the medium of a flogging to produce that effect on the master. He tried to wrest the key from Catherine's grasp, and for safety she flung it into the hottest part of the fire, whereupon Mr Edgar was taken with a nervous trembling, and his countenance grew deadly pale. For his life he could not avert that excess of emotion – mingled anguish and humiliation overcame him completely. He leant on the back of a chair, and covered his face.

"Oh Heavens! In old days this would win you knighthood!" exclaimed Mrs Linton. "We are vanquished! We are vanquished! Heathcliff would as soon lift a finger at you as the king would march his army against a colony of mice. Cheer up, you shan't be hurt! Your type is not a lamb, it's a sucking leveret."

"I wish you joy of the milk-blooded coward, Cathy!" said her friend. "I compliment you on your taste – and that is the slavering, shivering thing you preferred to me! I would not strike him with my fist, but I'd kick him with my foot, and experience considerable satisfaction. Is he weeping, or is he going to faint for fear?"

The fellow approached and gave the chair on which Linton rested a push. He'd better have kept his distance: my master quickly sprang erect, and struck him full on the throat a blow that would have levelled a slighter man.

It took his breath for a minute, and while he choked, Mr Linton walked out by the back door into the yard, and from thence to the front entrance.

"There! You've done with coming here," cried Catherine. "Get away now – he'll return with a brace of pistols and half-a-dozen assistants. If he did overhear us, of course he'd never forgive you. You've played me an ill turn, Heathcliff! But go – make haste! I'd rather see Edgar at bay than you."

"Do you suppose I'm going with that blow burning in my gullet?" he thundered. "By hell, no! I'll crush his ribs in like a rotten hazelnut before I cross the threshold! If I don't floor him now, I shall murder him some time, so, as you value his existence, let me get at him!"

"He is not coming," I interposed, framing* a bit of a lie. "There's the coachman and the two gardeners, you'll surely not wait to be thrust into the road by them! Each has a bludgeon, and Master will very likely be watching from the parlour windows to see that they fulfil his orders."

The gardeners and coachman *were* there, but Linton was with them. They had already entered the court. Heathcliff on second thoughts resolved to avoid a struggle against three underlings: he seized the poker, smashed the lock from the inner door, and made his escape as they tramped in.

Mrs Linton, who was very much excited, bade me accompany her upstairs. She did not know my share in contributing to the disturbance, and I was anxious to keep her in ignorance.

"I'm nearly distracted, Nelly!" she exclaimed, throwing herself on the sofa. "A thousand smiths' hammers are beating in my head! Tell Isabella to shun me – this uproar is owing to her – and should she or anyone else aggravate my anger at present, I shall get wild. And Nelly, say to Edgar, if you see him again tonight, that I'm in danger of being seriously ill – I wish it may prove true. He has startled and distressed me shockingly! I want to frighten him. Besides, he might come and begin a string of abuse or complainings – I'm certain I should recriminate, and God knows where we should end! Will you do so, my good Nelly? You are aware that I am no way blameable in this matter. What possessed him to turn listener? Heathcliff's talk was outrageous, after you left us, but I could soon have diverted him from Isabella, and the rest meant nothing. Now all is dashed wrong by the fool's craving to hear evil of self, that haunts some people like a demon! Had Edgar never gathered our conversation, he would never have been the worse for it. Really, when he opened on me in that unreasonable tone of displeasure after I had scolded Heathcliff till I was hoarse for *him*, I did not care hardly what they did to each other, especially as I felt that however the scene closed, we should all be driven asunder for nobody knows how long! Well, if I cannot keep Heathcliff for my friend, if Edgar will be mean and jealous, I'll try to break their hearts by breaking my own. That will be a prompt way of finishing all, when I am pushed to extremity! But it's a deed to be reserved for a forlorn hope – I'd not take Linton by surprise with it. To this point he has been discreet in dreading to provoke me; you must represent the peril of quitting that policy, and remind him of my passionate temper, verging, when kindled, on frenzy. I wish you could dismiss that apathy out of that countenance, and look rather more anxious about me."

The stolidity with which I received these instructions was no doubt rather exasperating, for they were delivered in perfect sincerity, but I believed a person who could plan the turning of her fits of passion to account beforehand might, by exerting her will, manage to control herself tolerably even while under their influence, and I did not wish to "frighten" her husband, as she said, and multiply his annoyances for the purpose of serving her selfishness.

Therefore I said nothing when I met the master coming towards the parlour, but I took the liberty of turning back to listen whether they would resume their quarrel together.

He began to speak first.

"Remain where you are, Catherine," he said, without any anger in his voice, but with much sorrowful despondency. "I shall not stay. I am neither come to wrangle nor be reconciled, but I wish just to learn whether, after this evening's events, you intend to continue your intimacy with—"

"Oh, for mercy's sake," interrupted the mistress, stamping her foot, "for mercy's sake, let us hear no more of it now! Your cold blood cannot be worked into a fever: your veins are full of ice water, but mine are boiling, and the sight of such chillness makes them dance."

"To get rid of me, answer my question," persevered Mr Linton. "You must answer it, and that violence does not alarm me. I have found that you can be as stoical as anyone when you please. Will you give up Heathcliff hereafter, or will you give up me? It is impossible for you to be *my* friend and *his* at the same time, and I absolutely *require* to know which you choose."

"I require to be let alone!" exclaimed Catherine furiously. "I demand it! Don't you see I can scarcely stand? Edgar, you... you leave me!"

She rang the bell till it broke with a twang; I entered leisurely. It was enough to try the temper of a saint, such senseless, wicked rages! There she lay dashing her head against the arm of the sofa and grinding her teeth, so that you might fancy she would crash them to splinters! Mr Linton stood looking at her in sudden compunction and fear. He told me to fetch some water. She had no breath for speaking.

I brought a glassful, and as she would not drink, I sprinkled it on her face. In a few seconds she stretched herself out stiff and turned up her eyes, while her cheeks, at once blanched and livid, assumed the aspect of death.

Linton looked terrified.

"There is nothing in the world the matter," I whispered. I did not want him to yield, though I could not help being afraid in my heart.

"She has blood on her lips!" he said, shuddering.

"Never mind!" I answered tartly. And I told him how she had resolved, previous to his coming, on exhibiting a fit of frenzy.

I incautiously gave the account aloud, and she heard me, for she started up – her hair flying over her shoulders, her eyes flashing, the muscles of her neck and arms standing out preternaturally. I made up my mind for broken bones at least, but she only glared about her for an instant, and then rushed from the room.

The master directed me to follow; I did, to her chamber door; she hindered me from going further by securing it against me.

As she never offered to descend to breakfast next morning, I went to ask whether she would have some carried up.

"No!" she replied peremptorily.

The same question was repeated at dinner and tea, and again on the morrow after, and received the same answer.

Mr Linton, on his part, spent his time in the library, and did not enquire concerning his wife's occupations. Isabella and he had had an hour's interview, during which he tried to elicit from her some senti-ment of proper horror for Heathcliff's advances, but he could make nothing of her evasive replies, and was obliged to close the examina-tion unsatisfactorily – adding however a solemn warning that if she were so insane as to encourage that worthless suitor, it would dissolve all bonds of relationship between herself and him.

12

WHILE MISS LINTON MOPED about the park and garden, always silent and almost always in tears, and her brother shut himself up among books that he never opened – wearying, I guessed, with a continual vague expectation that Catherine, repenting her conduct, would come of her own accord to ask pardon and seek a reconciliation – and *she* fasted per-tinaciously, under the idea, probably, that at every meal Edgar was ready to choke for her absence, and pride alone held him from running to cast himself at her feet; I went about my household duties, convinced that the Grange had but one sensible soul in its walls, and that lodged in my body.

I wasted no condolences on Miss, nor any expostulations on my mistress, nor did I pay much attention to the sighs of my master, who yearned to hear his lady's name, since he might not hear her voice.

I determined they should come about as they pleased for me, and though it was a tiresomely slow process, I began to rejoice at length in a faint dawn of its progress – as I thought at first.

Mrs Linton on the third day unbarred her door, and, having finished the water in her pitcher and decanter, desired a renewed supply, and a basin of gruel, for she believed she was dying. That I set down as a speech meant for Edgar's ears; I believed no such thing, so I kept it to myself and brought her some tea and dry toast.

She ate and drank eagerly, and sank back on her pillow again, clenching her hands and groaning.

"Oh, I will die," she exclaimed, "since no one cares anything about me. I wish I had not taken that."

Then a good while after I heard her murmur:

"No, I'll not die... he'd be glad... he does not love me at all... he would never miss me!"

"Did you want anything, ma'am?" I enquired, still preserving my external composure, in spite of her ghastly countenance and strange exaggerated manner.

"What is that apathetic being doing?" she demanded, pushing the thick entangled locks from her wasted face. "Has he fallen into a lethargy, or is he dead?"

"Neither," replied I, "if you mean Mr Linton. He's tolerably well, I think, though his studies occupy him rather more than they ought: he is continually among his books, since he has no other society."

I should not have spoken so if I had known her true condition, but I could not get rid of the notion that she acted a part of her disorder.

"Among his books!" she cried, confounded. "And I dying! I on the brink of the grave! My God! Does he know how I'm altered?" continued she, staring at her reflection in a mirror hanging against the opposite wall. "Is that Catherine Linton? He imagines me in a pet – in play, perhaps. Cannot you inform him that it is frightful earnest? Nelly, if it be not too late, as soon as I learn how he feels, I'll choose between these two: either to starve at once – that would be no punishment unless he had a heart – or to recover and leave the country. Are you speaking the truth about him now? Take care. Is he actually so utterly indifferent for my life?"

"Why, ma'am," I answered, "the master has no idea of your being deranged, and of course he does not fear that you will let yourself die of hunger."

"You think not? Cannot you tell him I will?" she returned. "Persuade him – speak of your own mind – say you are certain I will!"

"No, you forget, Mrs Linton," I suggested, "that you have eaten some food with a relish this evening, and tomorrow you will perceive its good effects."

"If I were only sure it would kill him," she interrupted, "I'd kill myself directly! These three awful nights I've never closed my lids – and oh, I've been tormented! I've been haunted, Nelly! But I begin to fancy you don't like me. How strange! I thought, though everybody hated and despised each other, they could not avoid loving me. And they have all turned to enemies in a few hours. *They* have, I'm positive, the people *here*. How dreary to meet death surrounded by their cold faces! Isabella, terrified and repelled, afraid to enter the room, it would be so dreadful to watch Catherine go. And Edgar standing solemnly by to see it over, then offering prayers of thanks to God for restoring peace to his house, and going back to his *books*! What in the name of all that feels has he to do with *books*, when I am dying?"

She could not bear the notion which I had put into her head of Mr Linton's philosophical resignation. Tossing about, she increased her feverish bewilderment to madness, and tore the pillow with her teeth, then raising herself up all burning, desired that I would open the window. We were in the middle of winter, the wind blew strong from the north-east, and I objected.

Both the expressions flitting over her face and the changes of her moods began to alarm me terribly, and brought to my recollection her former illness, and the doctor's injunction that she should not be crossed.

A minute previously she was violent; now, supported on one arm and not noticing my refusal to obey her, she seemed to find childish diversion in pulling the feathers from the rents she had just made, and ranging them on the sheet according to their different species: her mind had strayed to other associations.

"That's a turkey's," she murmured to herself, "and this is a wild duck's, and this is a pigeon's. Ah, they put pigeons' feathers in the pillows* – no wonder I couldn't die! Let me take care to throw it on the floor when I lie down. And here is a moorcock's, and this – I should know it among a thousand – it's a lapwing's. Bonny bird, wheeling over our heads in the middle of the moor. It wanted to get to its nest, for the clouds had touched the swells,* and it felt rain coming. This feather was picked up from the heath, the bird was not shot – we saw its nest in the winter, full of little skeletons. Heathcliff set a trap over it, and the old ones dared not come. I made him promise he'd never shoot a lapwing after that, and he didn't. Yes, here are more! Did he shoot my lapwings, Nelly? Are they red, any of them? Let me look."

"Give over with that baby work!" I interrupted, dragging the pillow away and turning the holes towards the mattress, for she was removing its contents by handfuls. "Lie down and shut your eyes – you're wandering. There's a mess! The down is flying about like snow."

I went here and there collecting it.

"I see in you, Nelly," she continued dreamily, "an aged woman: you have grey hair and bent shoulders. This bed is the fairy cave under Penistone Crag, and you are gathering elf bolts* to hurt our heifers, pretending, while I am near, that they are only locks of wool. That's what you'll come to fifty years hence: I know you are not so now. I'm not wandering, you're mistaken, or else I should believe you really *were* that withered hag, and I should think I *was* under Penistone Crag, and I'm conscious it's night, and there are two candles on the table making the black press* shine like jet."

"The black press? Where is that?" I asked. "You are talking in your sleep!"

"It's against the wall, as it always is," she replied. "It *does* appear odd… I see a face in it!"

"There's no press in the room, and never was," said I, resuming my seat, and looping up the curtain that I might watch her.

"Don't *you* see that face?" she enquired, gazing earnestly at the mirror.

And say what I could, I was incapable of making her comprehend it to be her own, so I rose and covered it with a shawl.

"It's behind there still!" she pursued anxiously. "And it stirred. Who is it? I hope it will not come out when you are gone! Oh, Nelly, the room is haunted! I'm afraid of being alone!"

I took her hand in mine, and bid her be composed, for a succession of shudders convulsed her frame, and she would keep straining her gaze towards the glass.

"There's nobody here!" I insisted. "It was *yourself*, Mrs Linton, you knew it a while since."

"Myself," she gasped, "and the clock is striking twelve! It's true then! That's dreadful!"

Her fingers clutched the clothes and gathered them over her eyes. I attempted to steal to the door with an intention of calling her husband, but I was summoned back by a piercing shriek – the shawl had dropped from the frame.

"Why, what *is* the matter?" cried I. "Who is coward now? Wake up! That is the glass – the mirror, Mrs Linton, and you see yourself in it, and there am I too by your side."

Trembling and bewildered, she held me fast, but the horror gradually passed from her countenance; its paleness gave place to a glow of shame.

"Oh dear! I thought I was at home," she sighed. "I thought I was lying in my chamber at Wuthering Heights. Because I'm weak, my brain got confused, and I screamed unconsciously. Don't say anything, but stay with me. I dread sleeping: my dreams appal me."

"A sound sleep would do you good, ma'am," I answered, "and I hope this suffering will prevent your trying starving again."

"Oh, if I were but in my own bed in the old house!" she went on bitterly, wringing her hands. "And that wind sounding in the firs by the lattice. Do let me feel it – it comes straight down the moor – do let me have one breath!"

To pacify her I held the casement ajar a few seconds. A cold blast rushed through; I closed it, and returned to my post.

She lay still now, her face bathed in tears. Exhaustion of body had entirely subdued her spirit; our fiery Catherine was no better than a wailing child!

"How long is it since I shut myself in here?" she asked, suddenly reviving.

"It was Monday evening," I replied, "and this is Thursday night, or rather Friday morning, at present."

"What, of the same week?" she exclaimed. "Only that brief time?"

"Long enough to live on nothing but cold water and ill temper," observed I.

"Well, it seems a weary number of hours," she muttered doubtfully, "it must be more… I remember being in the parlour after they had quarrelled, and Edgar being cruelly provoking, and me running into this room desperate. As soon as ever I had barred the door, utter blackness overwhelmed me, and I fell on the floor. I couldn't explain to Edgar how certain I felt of having a fit, or going raging mad, if he persisted in

105

teasing me! I had no command of tongue or brain, and he did not guess my agony, perhaps – it barely left me sense to try to escape from him and his voice. Before I recovered sufficiently to see and hear, it began to be dawn, and, Nelly, I'll tell you what I thought, and what has kept recurring and recurring till I feared for my reason. I thought as I lay there, with my head against that table leg and my eyes dimly discerning the grey square of the window, that I was enclosed in the oak-panelled bed at home, and my heart ached with some great grief which, just waking, I could not recollect. I pondered, and worried myself to discover what it could be, and, most strangely, the whole last seven years of my life grew a blank! I did not recall that they had been at all. I was a child, my father was just buried, and my misery arose from the separation that Hindley had ordered between me and Heathcliff. I was laid alone, for the first time, and, rousing from a dismal doze after a night of weeping, I lifted my hand to push the panels aside: it struck the tabletop! I swept it along the carpet, and then memory burst in – my late anguish was swallowed in a paroxysm of despair. I cannot say why I felt so wildly wretched – it must have been temporary derangement – for there is scarcely cause. But supposing at twelve years old I had been wrenched from the Heights and every early association, and my all in all, as Heathcliff was at that time, and been converted at a stroke into Mrs Linton, the lady of Thrushcross Grange, and the wife of a stranger – an exile and outcast thenceforth, from what had been my world. You may fancy a glimpse of the abyss where I grovelled! Shake your head as you will, Nelly, *you* have helped to unsettle me! You should have spoken to Edgar, indeed you should, and compelled him to leave me quiet! Oh, I'm burning! I wish I were out of doors – I wish I were a girl again, half-savage and hardy and free... and laughing at injuries, not maddening under them! Why am I so changed? Why does my blood rush into a hell of tumult at a few words? I'm sure I should be myself were I once among the heather on those hills... Open the window again wide, fasten it open! Quick, why don't you move?"

"Because I won't give you your death of cold," I answered.

"You won't give me a chance of life, you mean," she said sullenly. "However, I'm not helpless yet, I'll open it myself."

And, sliding from the bed before I could hinder her, she crossed the room, walking very uncertainly, threw it back, and bent out, careless of the frosty air that cut about her shoulders as keen as a knife.

I entreated, and finally attempted to force her to retire. But I soon found her delirious strength much surpassed mine (she was delirious, I became convinced by her subsequent actions and ravings).

There was no moon, and everything beneath lay in misty darkness, not a light gleamed from any house far or near, all had been extinguished long ago, and those at Wuthering Heights were never visible – still she asserted she caught their shining.

"Look!" she cried eagerly, "that's my room with the candle in it, and the trees swaying before it... and the other candle is in Joseph's garret... Joseph sits up late, doesn't he? He's waiting till I come home that he may lock the gate... Well, he'll wait a while yet. It's a rough journey, and a sad heart to travel it, and we must pass by Gimmerton Kirk to go that journey! We've braved its ghosts often together, and dared each other to stand among the graves and ask them to come... But Heathcliff, if I dare you now, will you venture? If you do, I'll keep you. I'll not lie there by myself – they may bury me twelve feet deep, and throw the church down over me, but I won't rest till you are with me... I never will!"

She paused, and resumed with a strange smile. "He's considering... he'd rather I'd come to him! Find a way then! Not through that kirkyard. You are slow! Be content, you always followed me!"

Perceiving it vain to argue against her insanity, I was planning how I could reach something to wrap about her, without quitting my hold of herself – for I could not trust her alone by the gaping lattice – when, to my consternation, I heard the rattle of the door handle, and Mr Linton entered. He had only then come from the library, and, in passing through the lobby, had noticed our talking and been attracted by curiosity, or fear, to examine what it signified at that late hour.

"Oh, sir!" I cried, checking the exclamation risen to his lips at the sight which met him and the bleak atmosphere of the chamber. "My poor mistress is ill, and she quite masters me – I cannot manage her at all – pray, come and persuade her to go to bed. Forget your anger, for she's hard to guide any way but her own."

"Catherine ill?" he said, hastening to us. "Shut the window, Ellen! Catherine, why..."

He was silent: the haggardness of Mrs Linton's appearance smote him speechless, and he could only glance from her to me in horrified astonishment.

107

"She's been fretting here," I continued, "and eating scarcely anything, and never complaining – she would admit none of us till this evening, and so we couldn't inform you of her state, as we were not aware of it ourselves – but it is nothing."

I felt I uttered my explanations awkwardly; the master frowned. "It is nothing, is it, Ellen Dean?" he said sternly. "You shall account more clearly for keeping me ignorant of this!" And he took his wife in his arms, and looked at her with anguish.

At first she gave him no glance of recognition: he was invisible to her abstracted gaze. The delirium was not fixed, however; having weaned her eyes from contemplating the outer darkness, by degrees she centred her attention on him, and discovered who it was that held her.

"Ah, you are come, are you, Edgar Linton?" she said with angry animation. "You are one of those things that are ever found when least wanted, and when you are wanted, never! I suppose we shall have plenty of lamentations now – I see we shall – but they can't keep me from my narrow home out yonder, my resting place, where I'm bound before spring is over! There it is: not among the Lintons, mind, under the chapel roof, but in the open air, with a headstone – and you may please yourself whether you go to them or come to me!"

"Catherine, what have you done?" commenced the master. "Am I nothing to you any more? Do you love that wretch Heath—"

"Hush!" cried Mrs Linton. "Hush, this moment! You mention that name and I end the matter instantly by a spring from the window! What you touch at present you may have, but my soul will be on that hilltop before you lay hands on me again. I don't want you, Edgar: I'm past wanting you. Return to your books – I'm glad you possess a consolation, for all you had in me is gone."

"Her mind wanders, sir," I interposed. "She has been talking nonsense the whole evening, but let her have quiet and proper attendance, and she'll rally. Hereafter, we must be cautious how we vex her."

"I desire no further advice from you," answered Mr Linton. "You knew your mistress's nature, and you encouraged me to harass her. And not to give me one hint of how she has been these three days! It was heartless! Months of sickness could not cause such a change!"

I began to defend myself, thinking it too bad to be blamed for another's wicked waywardness.

108

"I knew Mrs Linton's nature to be headstrong and domineering," cried I, "but I didn't know that you wished to foster her fierce temper! I didn't know that to humour her I should wink at Mr Heathcliff. I performed the duty of a faithful servant in telling you, and I have got a faithful servant's wages! Well, it will teach me to be careful next time. Next time you may gather intelligence for yourself!"

"The next time you bring a tale to me you shall quit my service, Ellen Dean," he replied.

"You'd rather hear nothing about it, I suppose then, Mr Linton?" said I. "Heathcliff has your permission to come a-courting to Miss, and to drop in at every opportunity your absence offers, on purpose to poison the mistress against you?"

Confused as Catherine was, her wits were alert at applying our conversation.

"Ah! Nelly has played traitor," she exclaimed passionately. "Nelly is my hidden enemy – you witch! So you do seek elf bolts to hurt us! Let me go, and I'll make her rue! I'll make her howl a recantation!"

A maniac's fury kindled under her brows; she struggled desperately to disengage herself from Linton's arms. I felt no inclination to tarry the event, and, resolving to seek medical aid on my own responsibility, I quitted the chamber.

In passing the garden to reach the road, at a place where a bridle hook is driven into the wall, I saw something white, moved irregularly, evidently by another agent than the wind. Notwithstanding my hurry, I stayed to examine it, lest ever after I should have the conviction impressed on my imagination that it was a creature of the other world.

My surprise and perplexity were great to discover, by touch more than vision, Miss Isabella's springer, Fanny, suspended by a handkerchief, and nearly at its last gasp.

I quickly released the animal and lifted it into the garden. I had seen it follow its mistress upstairs when she went to bed, and wondered much how it could have got out there, and what mischievous person had treated it so.

While untying the knot round the hook, it seemed to me that I repeatedly caught the beat of horses' feet galloping at some distance, but there were such a number of things to occupy my reflections that I hardly gave the circumstance a thought, though it was a strange sound, in that place, at two o'clock in the morning.

Mr Kenneth was fortunately just issuing from his house to see a patient in the village as I came up the street, and my account of Catherine Linton's malady induced him to accompany me back immediately.

He was a plain, rough man, and he made no scruple to speak his doubts of her surviving this second attack, unless she were more submissive to his directions than she had shown herself before.

"Nelly Dean," said he, "I can't help fancying there's an extra cause for this. What has there been to do at the Grange? We've odd reports up here. A stout, hearty lass like Catherine does not fall ill for a trifle; and that sort of people should not either. It's hard work bringing them through fevers and such things. How did it begin?"

"The master will inform you," I answered, "but you are acquainted with the Earnshaws' violent dispositions, and Mrs Linton caps them all. I may say this: it commenced in a quarrel. She was struck during a tempest of passion with a kind of fit. That's her account, at least: for she flew off in the height of it, and locked herself up. Afterwards she refused to eat, and now she alternately raves and remains in a half-dream, knowing those about her, but having her mind filled with all sorts of strange ideas and illusions."

"Mr Linton will be sorry?" observed Kenneth interrogatively.

"Sorry? He'll break his heart should anything happen!" I replied. "Don't alarm him more than necessary."

"Well, I told him to beware," said my companion, "and he must bide the consequences of neglecting my warning! Hasn't he been thick with Mr Heathcliff lately?"

"Heathcliff frequently visits at the Grange," answered I, "though more on the strength of the mistress having known him when a boy than because the master likes his company. At present he's discharged from the trouble of calling, owing to some presumptuous aspirations after Miss Linton which he manifested. I hardly think he'll be taken in again."

"And does Miss Linton turn a cold shoulder on him?" was the doctor's next question.

"I'm not in her confidence," returned I, reluctant to continue the subject.

"No, she's a sly one," he remarked, shaking his head. "She keeps her own counsel! But she's a real little fool. I have it from good authority that last night – and a pretty night it was! – she and Heathcliff were walking in the plantation at the back of your house above two hours, and he pressed her not to go in again, but just mount his horse and away with him! My informant said she could only put him off by pledging her word of honour to be prepared on their first meeting after that: when it was to be he didn't hear, but you urge Mr Linton to look sharp!"

This news filled me with fresh fears; I outstripped Kenneth and ran most of the way back. The little dog was yelping in the garden yet. I spared a minute to open the gate for it, but instead of going to the house door, it coursed up and down snuffing the grass, and would have escaped to the road had I not seized it and conveyed it in with me.

On ascending to Isabella's room my suspicions were confirmed: it was empty. Had I been a few hours sooner Mrs Linton's illness might have arrested her rash step. But what could be done now? There was a bare possibility of overtaking them if pursued instantly. *I* could not pursue them however, and I dared not rouse the family and fill the place with confusion; still less unfold the business to my master, absorbed as he was in his present calamity and having no heart to spare for a second grief!

I saw nothing for it but to hold my tongue and suffer matters to take their course, and Kenneth being arrived, I went with a badly composed countenance to announce him.

Catherine lay in a troubled sleep; her husband had succeeded in soothing the excess of frenzy; he now hung over her pillow, watching every shade and every change of her painfully expressive features.

The doctor, on examining the case for himself, spoke hopefully to him of its having a favourable termination if we could only preserve around her perfect and constant tranquillity. To me he signified the threatening danger was not so much death as permanent alienation of intellect.

I did not close my eyes that night, nor did Mr Linton – indeed we never went to bed – and the servants were all up long before the usual hour, moving through the house with stealthy tread and exchanging whispers as they encountered each other in their vocations. Everyone was active but Miss Isabella; and they began to remark how sound she slept – her brother, too, asked if she had risen, and seemed impatient for her presence, and hurt that she showed so little anxiety for her sister-in-law.

I trembled lest he should send me to call her, but I was spared the pain of being the first proclaimant* of her flight. One of the maids, a thoughtless girl who had been on an early errand to Gimmerton, came panting upstairs, open-mouthed, and dashed into the chamber, crying:

"Oh, dear, dear! What mun we have next? Master, master, our young lady—"

"Hold your noise!" cried I hastily, enraged at her clamorous manner.

"Speak lower, Mary. What is the matter?" said Mr Linton. "What ails your young lady?"

"She's gone, she's gone! Yon Heathcliff's run off wi' her!" gasped the girl.

"That is not true!" exclaimed Linton, rising in agitation. "It cannot be – how has the idea entered your head? Ellen Dean, go and seek her. It is incredible: it cannot be."

As he spoke he took the servant to the door, and then repeated his demand to know her reasons for such an assertion.

"Why, I met on the road a lad that fetches milk here," she stammered, "and he asked whether we wern't in trouble at the Grange. I thought he meant for Missis's sickness, so I answered yes. Then says he, 'There's somebody gone after 'em, I guess?' I stared. He saw I knew naught about it, and he told how a gentleman and lady had stopped to have a horse's shoe fastened at a blacksmith's shop, two miles out of Gimmerton, not very long after midnight! and how the blacksmith's lass had got up to spy who they were: she knew them both directly. And she noticed the man – Heathcliff it was, she felt certain: nob'dy could mistake him, besides – put a sovereign in her father's hand for payment. The lady had a cloak about her face, but, having desired a sup of water, while she drank it fell back, and she saw her very plain. Heathcliff held both bridles as they rode on, and they set their faces from the village, and went as fast as the rough roads would let them. The lass said nothing to her father, but she told it all over Gimmerton this morning."

I ran and peeped, for form's sake, into Isabella's room: confirming, when I returned, the servant's statement. Mr Linton had resumed his seat by the bed; on my re-entrance he raised his eyes, read the meaning of my blank aspect, and dropped them without giving an order or uttering a word.

"Are we to try any measures for overtaking and bringing her back?" I enquired. "How should we do?"

"She went of her own accord," answered the master. "She had a right to go if she pleased – trouble me no more about her. Hereafter she is only my sister in name: not because I disown her, but because she has disowned me."

And that was all he said on the subject: he did not make a single enquiry further, or mention her in any way, except directing me to send what property she had in the house to her fresh home, wherever it was, when I knew it.

13

FOR TWO MONTHS THE FUGITIVES remained absent; in those two months, Mrs Linton encountered and conquered the worst shock of what was denominated a brain fever. No mother could have nursed an only child more devotedly than Edgar tended her. Day and night he was watching, and patiently enduring all the annoyances that irritable nerves and a shaken reason could inflict, and though Kenneth remarked that what he saved from the grave would only recompense his care by forming the source of constant future anxiety – in fact, that his health and strength were being sacrificed to preserve a mere ruin of humanity – he knew no limits in gratitude and joy when Catherine's life was declared out of danger, and hour after hour he would sit beside her, tracing the gradual return to bodily health and flattering his too sanguine hopes with the illusion that her mind would settle back to its right balance also, and she would soon be entirely her former self.

The first time she left her chamber was at the commencement of the following March. Mr Linton had put on her pillow, in the morning, a handful of golden crocuses; her eye, long stranger to any gleam of pleasure, caught them in waking, and shone delighted as she gathered them eagerly together.

"These are the earliest flowers at the Heights!" she exclaimed. "They remind me of soft thaw winds and warm sunshine, and nearly melted snow. Edgar, is there not a south wind, and is not the snow almost gone?"

"The snow is quite gone down here, darling!" replied her husband, "and I only see two white spots on the whole range of moors: the sky is blue and the larks are singing, and the becks and brooks are all brimful. Catherine, last spring at this time, I was longing to have you under this roof – now I wish you were a mile or two up those hills: the air blows so sweetly, I feel that it would cure you."

"I shall never be there but once more," said the invalid, "and then you'll leave me, and I shall remain for ever. Next spring you'll long again to have me under this roof, and you'll look back and think you were happy today."

Linton lavished on her the kindest caresses, and tried to cheer her by the fondest words, but vaguely regarding the flowers, she let the tears collect on her lashes and stream down her cheeks unheeding.

We knew she was really better, and therefore decided that long confinement to a single place produced much of this despondency, and it might be partially removed by a change of scene.

The master told me to light a fire in the many-weeks-deserted parlour and to set an easy chair in the sunshine by the window, and then he brought her down, and she sat a long while enjoying the genial heat and, as we expected, revived by the objects round her, which, though familiar, were free from the dreary associations investing her hated sick chamber. By evening she seemed greatly exhausted, yet no arguments could persuade her to return to that apartment, and I had to arrange the parlour sofa for her bed, till another room could be prepared.

To obviate the fatigue of mounting and descending the stairs, we fitted up this – where you lie at present – on the same floor with the parlour, and she was soon strong enough to move from one to the other, leaning on Edgar's arm.

Ah, I thought myself, she might recover, so waited on as she was. And there was double cause to desire it, for on her existence depended that of another: we cherished the hope that in a little while Mr Linton's heart would be gladdened, and his lands secured from a stranger's gripe by the birth of an heir.

I should mention that Isabella sent to her brother, some six weeks from her departure, a short note, announcing her marriage with Heathcliff. It appeared dry and cold, but at the bottom was dotted in with pencil an obscure apology, and an entreaty for kind remembrance and reconciliation, if her proceeding had offended him, asserting that she could not help it then, and being done, she had now no power to repeal it.

Linton did not reply to this, I believe, and in a fortnight more I got a long letter, which I considered odd, coming from the pen of a bride just out of the honeymoon. I'll read it, for I keep it yet. Any relic of the dead is precious, if they were valued living.

Dear Ellen – it begins—

I came last night to Wuthering Heights, and heard for the first time that Catherine has been, and is yet, very ill. I must not write to her, I suppose, and my brother is either too angry or too distressed to answer what I send him. Still, I must write to somebody, and the only choice left me is you.

Inform Edgar that I'd give the world to see his face again – that my heart returned to Thrushcross Grange in twenty-four hours after I left it, and is there at this moment, full of warm feelings for him and Catherine! *I can't follow it though* – those words are underlined – they need not expect me, and they may draw what conclusions they please, taking care however to lay nothing at the door of my weak will or deficient affection.

The remainder of the letter is for yourself alone. I want to ask you two questions: the first is:

How did you contrive to preserve the common sympathies of human nature when you resided here? I cannot recognize any sentiment which those around share with me.

The second question I have great interest in – it is this:

Is Mr Heathcliff a man? If so, is he mad? And if not, is he a devil? I shan't tell my reasons for making this inquiry, but I beseech you to explain, if you can, what I have married – that is, when you call to see me, and you must call, Ellen, very soon. Don't write, but come, and bring me something from Edgar.

Now you shall hear how I have been received in my new home, as I am led to imagine the Heights will be. It is to amuse myself that I dwell on such subjects as the lack of external comforts: they never occupy my thoughts, except at the moment when I miss them. I should laugh and dance for joy, if I found their absence was the total of my miseries, and the rest was an unnatural dream!

The sun set behind the Grange as we turned on to the moors – by that I judged it to be six o'clock – and my companion halted half an hour to inspect the park and the gardens, and probably the place itself, as well as he could; so it was dark when we dismounted in the paved yard of the farmhouse, and your old fellow servant, Joseph, issued out to receive us by the light of a dip candle.* He did it with a courtesy that redounded to his credit. His first act was to elevate his torch to a level with my face, squint malignantly, project his underlip, and turn away.

Then he took the two horses and led them into the stables, reappearing for the purpose of locking the outer gate, as if we lived in an ancient castle.

Heathcliff stayed to speak to him, and I entered the kitchen – a dingy, untidy hole; I dare say you would not know it, it is so changed since it was in your charge.

By the fire stood a ruffianly child, strong in limb and dirty in garb, with a look of Catherine in his eyes and about his mouth.

"This is Edgar's legal nephew," I reflected, "mine in a manner; I must shake hands, and... yes... I must kiss him. It is right to establish a good understanding at the beginning."

I approached, and, attempting to take his chubby fist, said:

"How do you do, my dear?"

He replied in a jargon I did not comprehend.

"Shall you and I be friends, Hareton?" was my next essay at conversation.

An oath and a threat to set Throttler on me if I did not "frame off" rewarded my perseverance.

"Hey, Throttler, lad!" whispered the little wretch, rousing a half-bred bulldog from its lair in a corner. "Now, wilt tuh be ganging?" he asked authoritatively.

Love for my life urged a compliance: I stepped over the threshold to wait till the others should enter. Mr Heathcliff was nowhere visible, and Joseph, whom I followed to the stables and requested to accompany me in, after staring and muttering to himself, screwed up his nose and replied:

"Mim! Mim! Mim!* Did iver Christian body hear owt like it? Minching un' munching!* Hah can Aw tell whet ye say?"

"I say, I wish you to come with me into the house!" I cried, thinking him deaf, yet highly disgusted at his rudeness.

"Nor nuh me!* Aw getten summut else to do," he answered, and continued his work, moving his lantern jaws meanwhile, and surveying my dress and countenance (the former a great deal too fine, but the latter, I'm sure, as sad* as he could desire) with sovereign contempt.

I walked round the yard and through a wicket to another door, at which I took the liberty of knocking, in hopes some more civil servant might show himself.

After a short suspense, it was opened by a tall, gaunt man, without neckerchief and otherwise extremely slovenly; his features were lost in masses of shaggy hair that hung on his shoulders, and *his* eyes, too, were like a ghostly Catherine's, with all their beauty annihilated.

"What's your business here?" he demanded grimly. "Who are you?"

"My name *was* Isabella Linton," I replied. "You've seen me before, sir. I'm lately married to Mr Heathcliff, and he has brought me here – I suppose by your permission."

"Is he come back then?" asked the hermit, glaring like a hungry wolf.

"Yes. We came just now," I said, "but he left me by the kitchen door, and when I would have gone in, your little boy played sentinel over the place, and frightened me off by the help of a bulldog."

"It's well the hellish villain has kept his word!" growled my future host, searching the darkness beyond me in expectation of discovering Heathcliff, and then he indulged in a soliloquy of execrations, and threats of what he would have done had the "fiend" deceived him.

I repented having tried this second entrance, and was almost inclined to slip away before he finished cursing, but ere I could execute that intention, he ordered me in, and shut and refastened the door.

There was a great fire, and that was all the light in the huge apartment, whose floor had grown a uniform grey; and the once brilliant pewter dishes which used to attract my gaze when I was a girl partook of a similar obscurity, created by tarnish and dust.

I enquired whether I might call the maid and be conducted to a bedroom? Mr Earnshaw vouchsafed no answer. He walked up and down with his hands in his pockets, apparently quite forgetting my presence, and his abstraction was evidently so deep, and his whole aspect so misanthropical, that I shrank from disturbing him again.

You'll not be surprised, Ellen, at my feeling particularly cheerless, seated in worse than solitude on that inhospitable hearth, and remembering that four miles distant lay my delightful home, containing the only people I loved on earth – and there might as well be the Atlantic to part us, instead of those four miles, I could not overpass them!

I questioned with myself – where must I turn for comfort? And mind you don't tell Edgar or Catherine – above every sorrow beside, this rose pre-eminent: despair at finding nobody who could or would be my ally against Heathcliff!

I had sought shelter at Wuthering Heights almost gladly, because I was secured by that arrangement from living alone with him, but he knew the people we were coming amongst, and he did not fear their intermeddling.

I sat and thought a doleful time; the clock struck eight, and nine, and still my companion paced to and fro, his head bent on his breast, and perfectly silent, unless a groan or a bitter ejaculation forced itself out at intervals.

I listened to detect a woman's voice in the house, and filled the interim with wild regrets and dismal anticipations, which at last spoke audibly in irrepressible sighing and weeping.

I was not aware how openly I grieved, till Earnshaw halted opposite, in his measured walk, and gave me a stare of newly awakened surprise. Taking advantage of his recovered attention, I exclaimed:

"I'm tired with my journey, and I want to go to bed! Where is the maidservant? Direct me to her, as she won't come to me!"

"We have none," he answered, "you must wait on yourself!"

"Where must I sleep then?" I sobbed – I was beyond regarding self-respect, weighed down by fatigue and wretchedness.

"Joseph will show you Heathcliff's chamber," said he. "Open that door – he's in there."

I was going to obey, but he suddenly arrested me, and added in the strangest tone:

"Be so good as to turn your lock, and draw your bolt – don't omit it!"

"Well!" I said. "But why, Mr Earnshaw?" I did not relish the notion of deliberately fastening myself in with Heathcliff.

"Look here!" he replied, pulling from his waistcoat a curiously constructed pistol, having a double-edged spring knife attached to the barrel. "That's a great tempter to a desperate man, is it not? I cannot resist going up with this every night and trying his door. If once I find it open he's done for! I do it invariably, even though the minute before I have been recalling a hundred reasons that should make me refrain: it is some devil that urges me to thwart my own schemes by killing him. You fight against that devil for love as long as you may; when the time comes, not all the angels in heaven shall save him!"

CHAPTER 13

I surveyed the weapon inquisitively; a <u>hideous</u> notion struck me. How powerful I should be possessing such an instrument! I took it from his hand, and touched the blade. He looked astonished at the expression my face assumed during a brief second: it was not horror, it was covetousness. He snatched the pistol back jealously, shut the knife and returned it to its concealment.

"I don't care if you tell him," said he. "Put him on his guard and watch for him. You know the terms we are on, I see; his danger does not shock you."

"What has Heathcliff done to you?" I asked. "In what has he wronged you, to warrant this appalling hatred? Wouldn't it be wiser to bid him quit the house?"

"No," thundered Earnshaw, "should he offer to leave me, he's a dead man: persuade him to attempt it, and you are a murderess! Am I to lose *all*, without a chance of retrieval? Is Hareton to be a beggar? Oh, damnation! I *will* have it back, and I'll have *his* gold too, and then his blood, and hell shall have his soul! It will be ten times blacker with that guest than ever it was before!"

You've acquainted me, Ellen, with your old master's habits. He is clearly on the verge of madness – he was so last night at least. I shuddered to be near him, and thought on the servant's ill-bred moroseness as comparatively agreeable.

He now recommenced his moody walk, and I raised the latch, and escaped into the kitchen.

Joseph was bending over the fire, peering into a large pan that swung above it, and a wooden bowl of oatmeal stood on the settle close by. The contents of the pan began to boil, and he turned to plunge his hand into the bowl; I conjectured that this preparation was probably for our supper, and, being hungry, I resolved it should be eatable – so, crying out sharply, "*I'll* make the porridge!" I removed the vessel out of his reach, and proceeded to take off my hat and riding habit. "Mr Earnshaw," I continued, "directs me to wait on myself – I will. I'm not going to act the lady among you, for fear I should starve."

"Gooid Lord!" he muttered, sitting down and stroking his ribbed stockings from the knee to the ankle. "If they's tuh be fresh ortherings* – just when Aw getten used to two maisters – if Aw mun hev a *mistress* set o'er my heead, it's loike time tuh be flitting. Aw niver *did* think tuh say t' day ut Aw mud lave th' owld place – but Aw daht* it's nigh at hend!"

This lamentation drew no notice from me: I went briskly to work, sighing to remember a period when it would have been all merry fun, but compelled speedily to drive off the remembrance. It racked me to recall past happiness, and the greater peril there was of conjuring up its apparition, the quicker the thible* ran round, and the faster the handfuls of meal fell into the water.

Joseph beheld my style of cookery with growing indignation.

"Thear!" he ejaculated. "Hareton, thah willn't sup thy porridge tuhneeght; they'll be nowt bud lumps as big as maw nave.* Thear, agean! Aw'd fling in bowl un' all, if Aw wer yah! Thear, pale t' guilp off,* un' then yah'll hae done wi't. Bang, bang. It's a marcy t' bothom isn't deaved aht!"*

It *was* rather a rough mess, I own, when poured into the basins; four had been provided, and a gallon pitcher of new milk was brought from the dairy, which Hareton seized and commenced drinking and spilling from the expansive lip.

I expostulated, and desired that he should have his in a mug, affirming that I could not taste the liquid treated so dirtily. The old cynic chose to be vastly offended at this nicety, assuring me repeatedly that "the barn was every bit as gooid" as I, "and every bit as wollsome", and wondering how I could fashion to be so conceited. Meanwhile the infant ruffian continued sucking, and glowered up at me defyingly, as he slavered into the jug.

"I shall have my supper in another room," I said. "Have you no place you call a parlour?"

"*Parlour!*" he echoed sneeringly, "*Parlour!* Nay, we've noa *parlours.* If yah dunnut loike wer company, they's maister's; un' if yah dunnut loike maister, they's us."

"Then I shall go upstairs," I answered, "show me a chamber!"

I put my basin on a tray, and went myself to fetch some more milk. With great grumblings, the fellow rose, and preceded me in my ascent: we mounted to the garrets; he opened a door, now and then, to look into the apartments we passed.

"Here's a rahm," he said at last, flinging back a cranky* board on hinges. "It's weel eneugh tuh ate a few porridge in. There's a pack uh corn i' t' corner, thear, meeterly clane;* if ye're feared uh muckying yer grand silk cloes, spread yer hankerchir ut t' top on't."

The "rahm" was a kind of lumber hole smelling strong of malt and

120

grain, various sacks of which articles were piled around, leaving a wide, bare space in the middle.

"Why, man!" I exclaimed, facing him angrily, "this is not a place to sleep in. I wish to see my bedroom."

"*Bed-rume*!" he repeated, in a tone of mockery. "Yah's see all t' *bed-rumes* thear is – yon's mine."

He pointed into the second garret, only differing from the first in being more naked about the walls, and having a large, low, curtainless bed, with an indigo-coloured quilt at one end.

"What do I want with yours?" I retorted. "I suppose Mr Heathcliff does not lodge at the top of the house, does he?"

"Oh, it's Maister *Hathecliff's* yah're wenting?" cried he, as if making a new discovery. "Couldn't ye uh said soa at onst? Un' then, Aw mud uh telled ye, baht all this wark,* uh that's just one yah cannut see – he allas keeps it locked, un' nob'dy iver mells on't* but hisseln."

"You've a nice house, Joseph," I could not refrain from observing, "and pleasant inmates, and I think the concentrated essence of all the madness in the world took up its abode in my brain the day I linked my fate with theirs! However, that is not to the present purpose – there are other rooms. For Heaven's sake be quick, and let me settle somewhere!"

He made no reply to this adjuration, only plodding doggedly down the wooden steps and halting before an apartment which, from that halt and the superior quality of its furniture, I conjectured to be the best one. There was a carpet – a good one, but the pattern was obliterated by dust – a fireplace hung with cut paper, dropping to pieces; a handsome oak bedstead with ample crimson curtains of rather expensive material and modern make. But they had evidently experienced rough usage: the vallances hung in festoons, wrenched from their rings, and the iron rod supporting them was bent in an arc on one side, causing the drapery to trail upon the floor. The chairs were also damaged, many of them severely, and deep indentations deformed the panels of the walls.

I was endeavouring to gather resolution for entering and taking possession, when my fool of a guide announced:

"This here is t' maister's."

My supper by this time was cold, my appetite gone, and my patience exhausted. I insisted on being provided instantly with a place of refuge and means of repose.

"Whear the Divil?" began the religious elder. "The Lord bless us! The Lord forgie us! Whear the *hell* wold ye gang? ye marred, wearisome nowt! Yah seen all but Hareton's bit of a cham'er. They's nut another hoile tuh lig* dahn in i' th' hahse!"

I was so vexed I flung my tray and its contents on the ground, and then seated myself at the stairs' head, hid my face in my hands, and cried.

"Ech! Ech!" exclaimed Joseph. "Weel done, Miss Cathy! Weel done, Miss Cathy! Hahsiver, t' maister sall just tum'le o'er them brocken pots, un' then we's hear summut; we's hear hah it's tuh be. Gooid-furnowt madling!* Yah desarve pining* froo this tuh Churstmas, flinging t' precious gifts uh God under fooit i' yer flaysome rages! Bud Aw'm mista'en if yah shew yer sperrit lang. Will Hathecliff bide sich bonny ways, think ye? Aw nobbut wish he may catch ye i' that plisky.* Aw nobbut wish he may."

And so he went on scolding to his den beneath, taking the candle with him, and I remained in the dark.

The period of reflection succeeding this silly action compelled me to admit the necessity of smothering my pride and choking my wrath, and bestirring myself to remove its effects.

An unexpected aid presently appeared in the shape of Throttler, whom I now recognized as a son of our old Skulker; it had spent its whelphood at the Grange, and was given by my father to Mr Hindley. I fancy it knew me: it pushed its nose against mine by way of salute, and then hastened to devour the porridge, while I groped from step to step, collecting the shattered earthenware and drying the spatters of milk from the banister with my pocket handkerchief.

Our labours were scarcely over when I heard Earnshaw's tread in the passage; my assistant tucked in his tail, and pressed to the wall; I stole into the nearest doorway. The dog's endeavour to avoid him was unsuccessful – as I guessed by a scutter downstairs and a prolonged, piteous yelping. I had better luck: he passed on, entered his chamber, and shut the door.

Directly after, Joseph came up with Hareton, to put him to bed. I had found shelter in Hareton's room, and the old man, on seeing me, said:

"They's rahm fur boath yah un' yer pride nah, Aw sud think, i' the hahse. It's empty: yah muh hev it all to yerseln, un' Him* as allas maks a third, i' sich ill company!"

Gladly did I take advantage of this intimation, and the minute I flung myself into a chair by the fire, I nodded, and slept.

My slumber was deep and sweet, though over far too soon. Mr Heathcliff awoke me; he had just come in, and demanded, in his loving manner, what I was doing there?

I told him the cause of my staying up so late – that he had the key of our room in his pocket.

The adjective "our" gave mortal offence. He swore it was not, nor ever should be mine, and he'd – but I'll not repeat his language, nor describe his habitual conduct: he is ingenious and unresting in seeking to gain my abhorrence! I sometimes wonder at him with an intensity that deadens my fear, yet I assure you, a tiger or a venomous serpent could not rouse terror in me equal to that which he wakens. He told me of Catherine's illness, and accused my brother of causing it, promising that I should be Edgar's proxy in suffering, till he could get hold of him.

I do hate him – I am wretched – I have been a fool! Beware of uttering one breath of this to anyone at the Grange. I shall expect you every day – don't disappoint me!

Isabella

14

A S SOON AS I HAD PERUSED THIS EPISTLE I went to the master and informed him that his sister had arrived at the Heights, and sent me a letter expressing her sorrow for Mrs Linton's situation, and her ardent desire to see him, with a wish that he would transmit to her as early as possible some token of forgiveness by me.

"Forgiveness?" said Linton. "I have nothing to forgive her, Ellen – you may call at Wuthering Heights this afternoon if you like, and say that I am not *angry*, but I'm *sorry* to have lost her, especially as I can never think she'll be happy. It is out of the question my going to see her, however: we are eternally divided – and should she really wish to oblige me, let her persuade the villain she has married to leave the country."

"And you won't write her a little note, sir?" I asked imploringly.

"No," he answered. "It is needless. My communication with Heathcliff's family shall be as sparing as his with mine. It shall not exist!"

Mr Edgar's coldness depressed me exceedingly, and all the way from the Grange I puzzled my brains how to put more heart into what he said when I repeated it; and how to soften his refusal of even a few lines to console Isabella.

I dare say she had been on the watch for me since morning: I saw her looking through the lattice as I came up the garden causeway, and I nodded to her, but she drew back as if afraid of being observed.

I entered without knocking. There never was such a dreary, dismal scene as the formerly cheerful house presented! I must confess that if I had been in the young lady's place I would at least have swept the hearth and wiped the tables with a duster. But she already partook of the pervading spirit of neglect which encompassed her. Her pretty face was wan and listless; her hair uncurled, some locks hanging lankly down, and some carelessly twisted round her head. Probably she had not touched her dress since yester-evening.

Hindley was not there. Mr Heathcliff sat at a table, turning over some papers in his pocketbook, but he rose when I appeared, asked me how I did, quite friendly, and offered me a chair.

He was the only thing there that seemed decent, and I thought he never looked better. So much had circumstances altered their positions, that he would certainly have struck a stranger as a born and bred gentleman; and his wife as a thorough little slattern!

She came forwards eagerly to greet me, and held out one hand to take the expected letter.

I shook my head. She wouldn't understand the hint, but followed me to a sideboard, where I went to lay my bonnet, and importuned me in a whisper to give her directly what I had brought.

Heathcliff guessed the meaning of her manoeuvres, and said:

"If you have got anything for Isabella – as no doubt you have, Nelly – give it to her. You needn't make a secret of it: we have no secrets between us."

"Oh, I have nothing," I replied, thinking it best to speak the truth at once. "My master bid me tell his sister that she must not expect either a letter or a visit from him at present. He sends his love, ma'am, and his wishes for your happiness, and his pardon for the grief you have occasioned, but he thinks that after this time his household and the household here should drop intercommunication, as nothing could come of keeping it up."

Mrs Heathcliff's lip quivered slightly, and she returned to her seat in the window. Her husband took his stand on the hearthstone, near me, and began to put questions concerning Catherine.

I told him as much as I thought proper of her illness, and he extorted from me by cross-examination most of the facts connected with its origin.

I blamed her, as she deserved, for bringing it all on herself, and ended by hoping that he would follow Mr Linton's example and avoid future interference with his family, for good or evil.

"Mrs Linton is now just recovering," I said, "she'll never be like she was, but her life is spared, and if you really have a regard for her, you'll shun crossing her way again. Nay, you'll move out of this country entirely; and that you may not regret it, I'll inform you Catherine Linton is as different now from your old friend Catherine Earnshaw as that young lady is different from me. Her appearance is changed greatly, her character much more so; and the person who is compelled of necessity to be her companion will only sustain his affection hereafter by the remembrance of what she once was, by common humanity and a sense of duty!"

"That is quite possible," remarked Heathcliff, forcing himself to seem calm, "quite possible that your master should have nothing but common humanity and a sense of duty to fall back upon. But do you imagine that I shall leave Catherine to his *duty* and *humanity*? And can you compare my feelings respecting Catherine to his? Before you leave this house, I must exact a promise from you that you'll get me an interview with her – consent or refuse, I *will* see her! What do you say?"

"I say, Mr Heathcliff," I replied, "you must not – you never shall through my means. Another encounter between you and the master would kill her altogether!"

"With your aid that may be avoided," he continued, "and should there be danger of such an event – should he be the cause of adding a single trouble more to her existence – why, I think I shall be justified in going to extremes! I wish you had sincerity enough to tell me whether Catherine would suffer greatly from his loss: the fear that she would restrains me. And there you see the distinction between our feelings: had he been in my place, and I in his, though I hated him with a hatred that turned my life to gall, I never would have raised a hand against him. You may look incredulous if you please! I never would have banished him from her society as long as she desired his. The moment her regard ceased, I would have torn his heart out, and drunk his blood! But till then – if you don't believe me, you don't know me – till then, I would have died by inches before I touched a single hair of his head!"

"And yet," I interrupted, "you have no scruples in completely ruining all hopes of her perfect restoration, by thrusting yourself into her remembrance now, when she has nearly forgotten you, and involving her in a new tumult of discord and distress."

"You suppose she has nearly forgotten me?" he said. "Oh Nelly! You know she has not! You know as well as I do, that for every thought she spends on Linton she spends a thousand on me! At a most miserable period of my life, I had a notion of the kind: it haunted me on my return to the neighbourhood last summer, but only her own assurance could make me admit the horrible idea again. And then Linton would be nothing, nor Hindley, nor all the dreams that ever I dreamt. Two words would comprehend my future: *death* and *hell* – existence, after losing her, would be hell.

"Yet I was a fool to fancy for a moment that she valued Edgar Linton's attachment more than mine. If he loved with all the powers of his puny being, he couldn't love as much in eighty years as I could in a day. And Catherine has a heart as deep as I have; the sea could be as readily contained in that horse trough as her whole affection be monopolized by him. Tush! He is scarcely a degree dearer to her than her dog or her horse.* It is not in him to be loved like me: how can she love in him what he has not?"

"Catherine and Edgar are as fond of each other as any two people can be!" cried Isabella with sudden vivacity. "No one has a right to talk in that manner, and I won't hear my brother depreciated in silence!"

"Your brother is wondrous fond of you too, isn't he?" observed Heathcliff scornfully. "He turns you adrift on the world with surprising alacrity."

"He is not aware of what I suffer," she replied. "I didn't tell him that."

"You have been telling him something then – you have written, have you?"

"To say that I was married, I did write – you saw the note."

"And nothing since?"

"No."

"My young lady is looking sadly the worse for her change of condition," I remarked. "Somebody's love comes short in her case, obviously – whose, I may guess, but perhaps I shouldn't say."

"I should guess it was her own," said Heathcliff. "She degenerates into a mere slut! She is tired of trying to please me uncommonly early. You'd hardly credit it, but the very morrow of our wedding she was weeping to go home. However, she'll suit this house so much the better for not being overnice, and I'll take care she does not disgrace me by rambling abroad."

"Well, sir," returned I, "I hope you'll consider that Mrs Heathcliff is accustomed to be looked after and waited on, and that she has been brought up like an only daughter, whom everyone was ready to serve. You must let her have a maid to keep things tidy about her, and you must treat her kindly. Whatever be your notion of Mr Edgar, you cannot doubt that she has a capacity for strong attachments, or she wouldn't have abandoned the elegancies and comforts and friends of her former home to fix contentedly in such a wilderness as this with you."

"She abandoned them under a delusion," he answered, "picturing in me a hero of romance, and expecting unlimited indulgences from my chivalrous devotion. I can hardly regard her in the light of a rational creature, so obstinately has she persisted in forming a fabulous notion of my character and acting on the false impressions she cherished. But at last I think she begins to know me: I don't perceive the silly smiles and grimaces that provoked me at first, and the senseless incapability of discerning that I was in earnest when I gave her my opinion of her infatuation and herself. It was a marvellous effort of perspicacity to discover that I did not love her. I believed, at one time, no lessons could teach her that! And yet it is poorly learnt, for this morning she announced, as a piece of appalling intelligence, that I had actually succeeded in making her hate me! A positive labour of Hercules, I assure you! If it be achieved, I have cause to return thanks. Can I trust your assertion, Isabella; are you sure you hate me? If I let you alone for half a day, won't you come sighing and wheedling to me again? I dare say she would rather I had seemed all tenderness before you: it wounds her vanity to have the truth exposed. But I don't care who knows that the passion was wholly on one side, and I never told her a lie about it. She cannot accuse me of showing one bit of deceitful softness. The first thing she saw me do on coming out of the Grange was to hang up her little dog, and when she pleaded for it, the first words I uttered were a wish that I had the hanging of every being belonging to her, except one – possibly she took that exception for herself. But no brutality disgusted her: I suppose she has an innate admiration of it, if only her precious person were secure from injury! Now was it not the depth of absurdity – of genuine idiocy – for that pitiful, slavish, mean-minded brach* to dream that I could love her? Tell your master, Nelly, that I never in all my life met with such an abject thing as she is. She even disgraces the name of Linton; and I've sometimes relented, from pure lack of invention in my experiments on what she could endure and still creep shamefully cringing back! But tell him also to set his fraternal and magisterial heart at ease, that I keep strictly within the limits of the law. I have avoided, up to this period, giving her the slightest right to claim a separation; and what's more, she'd thank nobody for dividing us – if she desired to go, she might – the nuisance of her presence outweighs the gratification to be derived from tormenting her!"

"Mr Heathcliff," said I, "this is the talk of a madman, and your wife, most likely, is convinced you are mad, and for that reason she has borne with you hitherto, but now that you say she may go, she'll doubtless avail herself of the permission. You are not so bewitched, ma'am, are you, as to remain with him of your own accord?"

"Take care, Ellen!" answered Isabella, her eyes sparkling irefully – there was no misdoubting by their expression the full success of her partner's endeavours to make himself detested. "Don't put faith in a single word he speaks. He's a lying fiend, a monster, and not a human being! I've been told I might leave him before – and I've made the attempt, but I dare not repeat it! Only, Ellen, promise you'll not mention a syllable of his infamous conversation to my brother or Catherine. Whatever he may pretend, he wishes to provoke Edgar to desperation: he says he has married me on purpose to obtain power over him; and he shan't obtain it – I'll die first! I just hope, I pray, that he may forget his diabolical prudence and kill me! The single pleasure I can imagine is to die, or to see him dead!"

"There – that will do for the present!" said Heathcliff. "If you are called upon in a court of law, you'll remember her language, Nelly! And take a good look at that countenance – she's near the point which would suit me. No, you're not fit to be your own guardian, Isabella, now; and I, being your legal protector, must retain you in my custody, however distasteful the obligation may be. Go upstairs; I have something to say to Ellen Dean in private. That's not the way – upstairs, I tell you! Why, this is the road upstairs, child!"

He seized and thrust her from the room, and returned muttering:

"I have no pity! I have no pity! The more the worms writhe, the more I yearn to crush out their entrails! It is a moral teething, and I grind with greater energy in proportion to the increase of pain."

"Do you understand what the word pity means?" I said, hastening to resume my bonnet. "Did you ever feel a touch of it in your life?"

"Put that down!" he interrupted, perceiving my intention to depart. "You are not going yet... Come here now, Nelly... I must either persuade or compel you to aid me in fulfilling my determination to see Catherine, and that without delay. I swear that I meditate no harm; I don't desire to cause any disturbance, or to exasperate or insult Mr Linton: I only wish to hear from herself how she is, and why she has been ill, and to ask if anything that I could do would be of use to her. Last night I was in the Grange garden six hours, and I'll return there tonight; and every night I'll haunt the place, and every day, till I find an opportunity of entering. If Edgar Linton meets me, I shall not hesitate to knock him down, and give him enough to insure his quiescence while I stay. If his servants oppose me, I shall threaten them off with these pistols... But wouldn't it be better to prevent my coming in contact with them or their master? And you could do it so easily! I'd warn you when I came, and then you might let me in unobserved as soon as she was alone, and watch till I departed, your conscience quite calm – you would be hindering mischief."

I protested against playing that treacherous part in my employer's house, and besides, I urged the cruelty and selfishness of his destroying Mrs Linton's tranquillity for his satisfaction.

"The commonest occurrence startles her painfully," I said. "She's all nerves, and she couldn't bear the surprise, I'm positive. Don't persist, sir! or else I shall be obliged to inform my master of your designs, and he'll take measures to secure his house and its inmates from any such unwarrantable intrusions!"

"In that case I'll take measures to secure you, woman!" exclaimed Heathcliff, "you shall not leave Wuthering Heights till tomorrow morning. It is a foolish story to assert that Catherine could not bear to see

129

me – and as to surprising her, I don't desire it: you must prepare her, ask her if I may come. You say she never mentions my name, and that I am never mentioned to her. To whom should she mention me if I am a forbidden topic in the house? She thinks you are all spies for her husband... Oh, I've no doubt she's in hell among you! I guess, by her silence as much as anything, what she feels. You say she is often restless, and anxious-looking – is that a proof of tranquillity? You talk of her mind being unsettled – how the devil could it be otherwise in her frightful isolation? And that insipid, paltry creature attending her from *duty* and *humanity*! From *pity* and *charity*! He might as well plant an oak in a flowerpot and expect it to thrive, as imagine he can restore her to vigour in the soil of his shallow cares! Let us settle it at once: will you stay here, and am I to fight my way to Catherine over Linton and his footman? Or will you be my friend, as you have been hitherto, and do what I request? Decide! because there is no reason for my lingering another minute, if you persist in your stubborn ill nature!"

Well, Mr Lockwood, I argued and complained, and flatly refused him fifty times, but in the long run he forced me to an agreement: I engaged to carry a letter from him to my mistress; and should she consent, I promised to let him have intelligence of Linton's next absence from home, when he might come, and get in as he was able – I wouldn't be there, and my fellow servants should be equally out of the way.

Was it right or wrong? I fear it was wrong, though expedient. I thought I prevented another explosion by my compliance, and I thought, too, it might create a favourable crisis in Catherine's mental illness – and then I remembered Mr Edgar's stern rebuke of my carrying tales, and I tried to smooth away all disquietude on the subject by affirming, with frequent iteration, that that betrayal of trust, if it merited so harsh an appellation, should be the last.

Notwithstanding, my journey homewards was sadder than my journey thither, and many misgivings I had ere I could prevail on myself to put the missive into Mrs Linton's hand.

But here is Kenneth – I'll go down and tell him how much better you are. My history is *dree*,* as we say, and will serve to while away another morning.

Dree, and dreary! I reflected as the good woman descended to receive the doctor, and not exactly of the kind which I should have chosen to amuse me, but never mind! I'll extract wholesome medicines from Mrs Dean's bitter herbs; and firstly, let me beware of the fascination that lurks in Catherine Heathcliff's brilliant eyes. I should be in a curious taking if I surrendered my heart to that young person, and the daughter turned out a second edition of the mother.

15

A NOTHER WEEK OVER – and I am so many days nearer health, and spring! I have now heard all my neighbour's history, at different sittings, as the housekeeper could spare time from more important occupations. I'll continue it in her own words, only a little condensed. She is on the whole a very fair narrator, and I don't think I could improve her style.

In the evening – she said – the evening of my visit to the Heights, I knew, as well as if I saw him, that Mr Heathcliff was about the place, and I shunned going out, because I still carried his letter in my pocket and didn't want to be threatened or teased any more.

I had made up my mind not to give it till my master went somewhere, as I could not guess how its receipt would affect Catherine. The consequence was that it did not reach her before the lapse of three days. The fourth was Sunday, and I brought it into her room after the family were gone to church.

There was a manservant left to keep the house with me, and we generally made a practice of locking the doors during the hours of service, but on that occasion the weather was so warm and pleasant that I set them wide open, and to fulfil my engagement, as I knew who would be coming, I told my companion that the mistress wished very much for some oranges, and he must run over to the village and get a few, to be paid for on the morrow. He departed, and I went upstairs.

Mrs Linton sat in a loose white dress, with a light shawl over her shoulders, in the recess of the open window, as usual. Her thick, long hair had been partly removed at the beginning of her illness, and now she wore it simply combed in its natural tresses over her temples and neck. Her appearance was altered, as I had told Heathcliff, but when she was calm, there seemed unearthly beauty in the change.

The flash of her eyes had been succeeded by a dreamy and melancholy softness; they no longer gave the impression of looking at the objects around her: they appeared always to gaze beyond, and far beyond – you would have said out of this world. Then the paleness of her face – its haggard aspect having vanished as she recovered flesh – and the peculiar expression arising from her mental state, though painfully suggestive of their causes, added to the touching interest which she wakened, and – invariably to me, I know, and to any person who saw her, I should think – refuted more tangible proofs of convalescence and stamped her as one doomed to decay.

A book lay spread on the sill before her, and the scarcely perceptible wind fluttered its leaves at intervals. I believe Linton had laid it there, for she never endeavoured to divert herself with reading, or occupation of any kind, and he would spend many an hour in trying to entice her attention to some subject which had formerly been her amusement.

She was conscious of his aim, and in her better moods endured his efforts placidly, only showing their uselessness by now and then suppressing a wearied sigh, and checking him at last with the saddest of smiles and kisses. At other times, she would turn petulantly away, and hide her face in her hands, or even push him off angrily, and then he took care to let her alone, for he was certain of doing no good.

Gimmerton chapel bells were still ringing, and the full, mellow flow of the beck in the valley came soothingly on the ear. It was a sweet substitute for the yet absent murmur of the summer foliage, which drowned that music about the Grange when the trees were in leaf. At Wuthering Heights it always sounded on quiet days following a great thaw or a season of steady rain – and of Wuthering Heights Catherine was thinking as she listened – that is, if she thought or listened at all – but she had the vague, distant look I mentioned before, which expressed no recognition of material things either by ear or eye.

"There's a letter for you, Mrs Linton," I said, gently inserting it in one hand that rested on her knee. "You must read it immediately, because it wants an answer. Shall I break the seal?"

"Yes," she answered, without altering the direction of her eyes. I opened it – it was very short.

"Now," I continued, "read it."

She drew away her hand and let it fall. I replaced it in her lap and stood waiting till it should please her to glance down, but that movement was so long delayed that at last I resumed:

"Must I read it, ma'am? It is from Mr Heathcliff."

There was a start and a troubled gleam of recollection, and a struggle to arrange her ideas. She lifted the letter, and seemed to peruse it, and when she came to the signature she sighed; yet still I found she had not gathered its import, for upon my desiring to hear her reply she merely pointed to the name and gazed at me with mournful and questioning eagerness.

"Well, he wishes to see you," said I, guessing her need of an interpreter. "He's in the garden by this time, and impatient to know what answer I shall bring."

As I spoke, I observed a large dog, lying on the sunny grass beneath, raise its ears as if about to bark, and then, smoothing them back, announce by a wag of the tail that someone approached whom it did not consider a stranger.

Mrs Linton bent forwards, and listened breathlessly. The minute after, a step traversed the hall: the open house was too tempting for Heathcliff to resist walking in, most likely he supposed that I was inclined to shirk my promise, and so resolved to trust to his own audacity.

With straining eagerness Catherine gazed towards the entrance of her chamber. He did not hit the right room directly; she motioned me to admit him, but he found it out ere I could reach the door, and in a stride or two was at her side, and had her grasped in his arms.

He neither spoke nor loosed his hold for some five minutes, during which period he bestowed more kisses than ever he gave in his life before, I dare say – but then my mistress had kissed him first, and I plainly saw that he could hardly bear, for downright agony, to look into her face! The same conviction had stricken him as me, from the instant he beheld her, that there was no prospect of ultimate recovery there – she was fated, sure to die.

"Oh Cathy! Oh my life! How can I bear it?" was the first sentence he uttered, in a tone that did not seek to disguise his despair.

And now he stared at her so earnestly that I thought the very intensity of his gaze would bring tears into his eyes, but they burned with anguish, they did not melt.

"What now?" said Catherine, leaning back and returning his look with a suddenly clouded brow – her humour was a mere vane for constantly varying caprices. "You and Edgar have broken my heart, Heathcliff! And you both come to bewail the deed to me, as if you were the people to be pitied! I shall not pity you, not I. You have killed me – and thriven on it, I think. How strong you are! How many years do you mean to live after I am gone?"

Heathcliff had knelt on one knee to embrace her; he attempted to rise, but she seized his hair, and kept him down.

"I wish I could hold you," she continued bitterly, "till we were both dead! I shouldn't care what you suffered. I care nothing for your sufferings. Why shouldn't you suffer? I do! Will you forget me? Will you be happy when I am in the earth? Will you say twenty years hence, 'That's the grave of Catherine Earnshaw. I loved her long ago, and was wretched to lose her, but it is past. I've loved many others since; my children are dearer to me than she was, and at death I shall not rejoice that I am going to her: I shall be sorry that I must leave them!' Will you say so, Heathcliff?"

"Don't torture me till I'm as mad as yourself," cried he, wrenching his head free and grinding his teeth.

The two, to a cool spectator, made a strange and fearful picture. Well might Catherine deem that heaven would be a land of exile to her, unless with her mortal body she cast away her moral character also. Her present countenance had a wild vindictiveness in its white cheek, and a bloodless lip and scintillating eye; and she retained in her closed fingers a portion of the locks she had been grasping. As to her companion, while raising himself with one hand, he had taken her arm with the other; and so inadequate was his stock of gentleness to the requirements of her condition, that on his letting go I saw four distinct impressions left blue in the colourless skin.

"Are you possessed with a devil," he pursued savagely, "to talk in that manner to me, when you are dying? Do you reflect that all those words will be branded in my memory, and eating deeper eternally after you have left me? You know you lie to say I have killed you, and Catherine, you know that I could as soon forget you as my existence! Is it not sufficient for your infernal selfishness, that while you are at peace I shall writhe in the torments of hell?"

"I shall not be at peace," moaned Catherine, recalled to a sense of physical weakness by the violent, unequal throbbing of her heart, which beat visibly and audibly under this excess of agitation.

She said nothing further till the paroxysm was over, then she continued, more kindly:

CHAPTER 15

"I'm not wishing you greater torment than I have, Heathcliff. I only wish us never to be parted – and should a word of mine distress you hereafter, think I feel the same distress underground, and for my own sake, forgive me! Come here and kneel down again! You never harmed me in your life. Nay, if you nurse anger, that will be worse to remember than my harsh words! Won't you come here again? Do!"

Heathcliff went to the back of her chair and leant over, but not so far as to let her see his face, which was livid with emotion. She bent round to look at him; he would not permit it: turning abruptly, he walked to the fireplace, where he stood silent, with his back towards us.

Mrs Linton's glance followed him suspiciously: every movement woke a new sentiment in her. After a pause and a prolonged gaze, she resumed, addressing me in accents of indignant disappointment.

"Oh, you see, Nelly, he would not relent a moment to keep me out of the grave! *That* is how I'm loved! Well, never mind. That is not *my* Heathcliff. I shall love mine yet, and take him with me: he's in my soul. And," added she musingly, "the thing that irks me most is this shattered prison, after all. I'm tired, tired of being enclosed here. I'm wearying to escape into that glorious world, and to be always there, not seeing it dimly through tears, and yearning for it through the walls of an aching heart, but really with it, and in it. Nelly, you think you are better and more fortunate than I, in full health and strength – you are sorry for me – very soon that will be altered. I shall be sorry for *you*. I shall be incomparably beyond and above you all. I *wonder* he won't be near me!" She went on to herself. "I thought he wished it. Heathcliff, dear! you should not be sullen now. Do come to me, Heathcliff."

In her eagerness she rose, and supported herself on the arm of the chair. At that earnest appeal he turned to her, looking absolutely desperate. His eyes, wide and wet, at last flashed fiercely on her; his breast heaved convulsively. An instant they held asunder, and then how they met I hardly saw, but Catherine made a spring, and he caught her, and they were locked in an embrace from which I thought my mistress would never be released alive. In fact, to my eyes, she seemed directly insensible. He flung himself into the nearest seat, and on my approaching hurriedly to ascertain if she had fainted, he gnashed at me and foamed like a mad dog, and gathered her to him with greedy jealousy. I did not feel as if I were in the company of a creature of my own species – it appeared that he would not

135

understand, though I spoke to him – so I stood off, and held my tongue in great perplexity.

A movement of Catherine's relieved me a little presently: she put up her hand to clasp his neck and bring her cheek to his as he held her, while he, in return, covering her with frantic caresses, said wildly:

"You teach me now how cruel you've been – cruel and false. *Why* did you despise me? *Why* did you betray your own heart, Cathy? I have not one word of comfort – you deserve this. You have killed yourself. Yes, you may kiss me, and cry, and wring out my kisses and tears. They'll blight you – they'll damn you. You loved me – then what *right* had you to leave me? What right – answer me – for the poor fancy you felt for Linton? Because misery and degradation and death, and nothing that God or Satan could inflict would have parted us, *you*, of your own will, did it. I have not broken your heart – *you* have broken it – and in breaking it, you have broken mine. So much the worse for me that I am strong. Do I want to live? What kind of living will it be when you... oh, God! Would *you* like to live with your soul in the grave?"

"Let me alone. Let me alone," sobbed Catherine. "If I've done wrong, I'm dying for it. It is enough! You left me too, but I won't upbraid you! I forgive you. Forgive me!"

"It is hard to forgive, and to look at those eyes, and feel those wasted hands," he answered. "Kiss me again, and don't let me see your eyes! I forgive what you have done to me. I love *my* murderer – but *yours*! How can I?"

They were silent – their faces hid against each other, and washed by each other's tears. At least I suppose the weeping was on both sides, as it seemed Heathcliff *could* weep on a great occasion like this.

I grew very uncomfortable meanwhile, for the afternoon wore fast away, the man whom I had sent off returned from his errand, and I could distinguish, by the shine of the western sun up the valley, a concourse thickening outside Gimmerton chapel porch.

"Service is over," I announced. "My master will be here in half an hour."

Heathcliff groaned a curse, and strained Catherine closer – she never moved.

Ere long I perceived a group of the servants passing up the road towards the kitchen wing. Mr Linton was not far behind; he opened the gate himself and sauntered slowly up, probably enjoying the lovely afternoon that breathed as soft as summer.

"Now he is here," I exclaimed. "For Heaven's sake, hurry down! You'll not meet anyone on the front stairs. Do be quick, and stay among the trees till he is fairly in."

"I must go, Cathy," said Heathcliff, seeking to extricate himself from his companion's arms. "But if I live, I'll see you again before you are asleep. I won't stray five yards from your window."

"You must not go!" she answered, holding him as firmly as her strength allowed. "You *shall* not, I tell you."

"For one hour," he pleaded earnestly.

"Not for one minute," she replied.

"I *must* – Linton will be up immediately," persisted the alarmed intruder.

He would have risen, and unfixed her fingers by the act – she clung fast, gasping: there was mad resolution in her face.

"No!" she shrieked. "Oh, don't, don't go. It is the last time! Edgar will not hurt us. Heathcliff, I shall die! I shall die!"

"Damn the fool! There he is," cried Heathcliff, sinking back into his seat. "Hush, my darling! Hush, hush, Catherine! I'll stay. If he shot me so, I'd expire with a blessing on my lips."

And there they were fast again. I heard my master mounting the stairs – the cold sweat ran from my forehead; I was horrified.

"Are you going to listen to her ravings?" I said passionately. "She does not know what she says. Will you ruin her, because she has not wit to help herself? Get up! You could be free instantly. That is the most diabolical deed that ever you did. We are all done for – master, mistress and servant."

I wrung my hands and cried out, and Mr Linton hastened his step at the noise. In the midst of my agitation, I was sincerely glad to observe that Catherine's arms had fallen relaxed, and her head hung down.

"She's fainted or dead," I thought, "so much the better. Far better that she should be dead, than lingering a burden and a misery-maker to all about her."

Edgar sprang to his unbidden guest, blanched with astonishment and rage. What he meant to do I cannot tell, however, the other stopped all demonstrations at once by placing the lifeless-looking form in his arms.

"Look there!" he said. "Unless you be a fiend, help her first... then you shall speak to me!"

He walked into the parlour and sat down. Mr Linton summoned me, and with great difficulty, and after resorting to many means, we managed to restore her to sensation, but she was all bewildered; she sighed, and moaned, and knew nobody. Edgar, in his anxiety for her, forgot her hated friend. I did not. I went at the earliest opportunity and besought him to depart, affirming that Catherine was better, and he should hear from me in the morning how she passed the night.

"I shall not refuse to go out of doors," he answered, "but I shall stay in the garden – and Nelly, mind you keep your word tomorrow. I shall be under those larch trees. Mind! or I pay another visit, whether Linton be in or not."

He sent a rapid glance through the half-open door of the chamber, and, ascertaining that what I stated was apparently true, delivered the house of his luckless* presence.

16

ABOUT TWELVE O'CLOCK THAT NIGHT was born the Catherine you saw at Wuthering Heights – a puny, seven-months' child – and two hours after the mother died, having never recovered sufficient consciousness to miss Heathcliff, or know Edgar.

The latter's distraction at his bereavement is a subject too painful to be dwelt on; its after-effects showed how deep the sorrow sunk.

A great addition, in my eyes, was his being left without an heir. I bemoaned that, as I gazed on the feeble orphan, and I mentally abused old Linton for – what was only natural partiality – the securing his estate to his own daughter, instead of his son's.

An unwelcomed infant it was, poor thing! It might have wailed out of life, and nobody cared a morsel, during those first hours of existence. We redeemed the neglect afterwards, but its beginning was as friendless as its end is likely to be.

Next morning – bright and cheerful out of doors – stole softened in through the blinds of the silent room, and suffused the couch and its occupant with a mellow, tender glow.

Edgar Linton had his head laid on the pillow, and his eyes shut. His young and fair features were almost as deathlike as those of the form beside him, and almost as fixed, but *his* was the hush of exhausted anguish, and *hers* of perfect peace. Her brow smooth, her lids closed, her lips wearing the expression of a smile; no angel in heaven could be more beautiful than she appeared, and I partook of the infinite calm in which she lay. My mind was never in a holier frame than while I gazed on that untroubled image of divine rest. I instinctively echoed the words she had uttered a few hours before: "Incomparably beyond and above us all! Whether still on earth or now in heaven, her spirit is at home with God!"

I don't know if it be a peculiarity in me, but I am seldom otherwise than happy while watching in the chamber of death, should no frenzied or despairing mourner share the duty with me. I see a repose that neither earth nor hell can break, and I feel an assurance of the endless and shadowless hereafter – the Eternity they have entered – where life is boundless in its duration, and love in its sympathy, and joy in its fullness. I noticed on that occasion how much selfishness there is even in a love like Mr Linton's, when he so regretted Catherine's blessed release!

To be sure, one might have doubted, after the wayward and impatient existence she had led, whether she merited a haven of peace at last. One might doubt in seasons of cold reflection, but not then, in the presence of her corpse. It asserted its own tranquillity, which seemed a pledge of equal quiet to its former inhabitant.

Do you believe such people *are* happy in the other world, sir? I'd give a great deal to know.

I declined answering Mrs Dean's question, which struck me as something heterodox. She proceeded:

"Retracing the course of Catherine Linton, I fear we have no right to think she is; but we'll leave her with her Maker."

The master looked asleep, and I ventured soon after sunrise to quit the room and steal out to the pure, refreshing air. The servants thought me gone to shake off the drowsiness of my protracted watch; in reality, my chief motive was seeing Mr Heathcliff. If he had remained among the larches all night, he would have heard nothing of the stir at the Grange, unless, perhaps, he might catch the gallop of the messenger going to Gimmerton. If he had come nearer, he would probably be aware, from the lights flitting to and fro, and the opening and shutting of the outer doors, that all was not right within.

I wished, yet feared, to find him. I felt the terrible news must be told, and I longed to get it over, but *how* to do it I did not know.

He was there, at least a few yards further in the park, leant against an old ash tree, his hat off and his hair soaked with the dew that had gathered on the budded branches, and fell pattering round him. He had been standing a long time in that position, for I saw a pair of ouzels passing and repassing scarcely three feet from him, busy in building their nest and regarding his proximity no more than that of a piece of timber. They flew off at my approach, and he raised his eyes and spoke:

"She's dead!" he said, "I've not waited for you to learn that. Put your handkerchief away – don't snivel before me. Damn you all! She wants none of *your* tears!"

I was weeping as much for him as her – we do sometimes pity creatures that have none of the feeling either for themselves or others – and when I first looked into his face, I perceived that he had got intelligence of the catastrophe, and a foolish notion struck me that his heart was quelled and he prayed, because his lips moved and his gaze was bent on the ground.

"Yes, she's dead!" I answered, checking my sobs and drying my cheeks. "Gone to heaven, I hope, where we may everyone join her, if we take due warning and leave our evil ways to follow good!"

"Did *she* take due warning, then?" asked Heathcliff, attempting a sneer. "Did she die like a saint? Come, give me a true history of the event. How did…"

He endeavoured to pronounce the name, but could not manage it, and compressing his mouth he held a silent combat with his inward agony, defying, meanwhile, my sympathy with an unflinching, ferocious stare.

"How did she die?" he resumed at last – fain, notwithstanding his hardihood, to have a support behind him, for after the struggle he trembled, in spite of himself, to his very finger ends.

"Poor wretch!" I thought, "you have a heart and nerves the same as your brother men! Why should you be so anxious to conceal them? Your pride cannot blind God! You tempt Him to wring them till He forces a cry of humiliation."

"Quietly as a lamb!" I answered aloud. "She drew a sigh and stretched herself, like a child reviving and sinking again to sleep, and five minutes after I felt one little pulse at her heart, and nothing more!"

"And… and did she ever mention me?" he asked, hesitating, as if he dreaded the answer to his question would introduce details that he could not bear to hear.

"Her senses never returned – she recognized nobody from the time you left her," I said. "She lies with a sweet smile on her face, and her latest ideas wandered back to pleasant early days. Her life closed in a gentle dream – may she wake as kindly in the other world!"

"May she wake in torment!" he cried with frightful vehemence, stamping his foot and groaning in a sudden paroxysm of ungovernable passion. "Why, she's a liar to the end! Where is she? Not *there* – not in heaven – not perished – where? Oh, you said you cared nothing for my sufferings! And I pray one prayer – I repeat it till my tongue stiffens – Catherine Earnshaw, may you not rest as long as I am living; you said I killed you – haunt me then! The murdered *do* haunt their murderers. I believe… I know that ghosts *have* wandered on earth. Be with me always – take any form – drive me mad! Only *do* not leave me in this abyss, where I cannot find you! Oh God, it is unutterable! I *cannot* live without my life! I *cannot* live without my soul!"

He dashed his head against the knotted trunk, and, lifting up his eyes, howled, not like a man, but like a savage beast being goaded to death with knives and spears.

I observed several splashes of blood about the bark of the tree, and his hand and forehead were both stained; probably the scene I witnessed was a repetition of others acted during the night. It hardly moved my compassion – it appalled me – still I felt reluctant to quit him so. But the moment he recollected himself enough to notice me watching, he thundered a command for me to go, and I obeyed. He was beyond my skill to quiet or console!

Mrs Linton's funeral was appointed to take place on the Friday following her decease, and till then her coffin remained, uncovered and strewn with flowers and scented leaves, in the great drawing room. Linton spent his days and nights there, a sleepless guardian, and – a circumstance concealed from all but me – Heathcliff spent his nights, at least, outside, equally a stranger to repose.

I held no communication with him; still I was conscious of his design to enter, if he could; and on the Tuesday, a little after dark, when my master, from sheer fatigue, had been compelled to retire a couple of hours, I went and opened one of the windows, moved by his

141

perseverance to give him a chance of bestowing on the faded image of his idol one final adieu.

He did not omit to avail himself of the opportunity, cautiously and briefly – too cautiously to betray his presence by the slightest noise. Indeed, I shouldn't have discovered that he had been there, except for the disarrangement of the drapery about the corpse's face, and for observing on the floor a curl of light hair, fastened with a silver thread, which on examination I ascertained to have been taken from a locket hung round Catherine's neck. Heathcliff had opened the trinket and cast out its contents, replacing them by a black lock of his own. I twisted the two, and enclosed them together.

Mr Earnshaw was of course invited to attend the remains of his sister to the grave, and he sent no excuse, but he never came, so that besides her husband, the mourners were wholly composed of tenants and servants. Isabella was not asked.

The place of Catherine's interment, to the surprise of the villagers, was neither in the chapel, under the carved monument of the Lintons, nor yet by the tombs of her own relations outside. It was dug on a green slope in a corner of the kirkyard, where the wall is so low that heath and bilberry plants have climbed over it from the moor, and peat mould almost buries it. Her husband lies in the same spot now, and they have each a simple headstone above and a plain grey block at their feet, to mark the graves.

17

THAT FRIDAY MADE THE LAST of our fine days for a month. In the evening the weather broke: the wind shifted from south to north-east, and brought rain first, and then sleet and snow.

On the morrow one could hardly imagine that there had been three weeks of summer: the primroses and crocuses were hidden under wintry drifts, the larks were silent, the young leaves of the early trees smitten and blackened. And dreary and chill and dismal that morrow did creep over! My master kept his room; I took possession of the lonely parlour, converting it into a nursery: and there I was, sitting with the moaning doll of a child laid on my knee, rocking it to and fro, and watching, meanwhile, the still-driving flakes build up the uncurtained window, when the door opened and some person entered, out of breath and laughing!

My anger was greater than my astonishment for a minute. I supposed it one of the maids, and I cried:

"Have done! How dare you show your giddiness here? What would Mr Linton say if he heard you?"

"Excuse me!" answered a familiar voice, "but I know Edgar is in bed, and I cannot stop myself."

With that the speaker came forwards to the fire, panting and holding her hand to her side.

"I have run the whole way from Wuthering Heights!" she continued, after a pause. "Except where I've flown – I couldn't count the number of falls I've had... Oh, I'm aching all over! Don't be alarmed... There shall be an explanation as soon as I can give it – only just have the goodness to step out and order the carriage to take me on to Gimmerton, and tell a servant to seek up a few clothes in my wardrobe."

The intruder was Mrs Heathcliff. She certainly seemed in no laughing predicament: her hair streamed on her shoulders, dripping with snow and water; she was dressed in the girlish dress she commonly wore, befitting her age more than her position: a low frock with short sleeves, and nothing on either head or neck. The frock was of light silk, and clung to her with wet, and her feet were protected merely by thin slippers; add to this a deep cut under one ear, which only the cold prevented from bleeding profusely, a white face scratched and bruised, and a frame hardly able to support itself through fatigue, and you may fancy my first fright was not much allayed when I had leisure to examine her.

"My dear young lady," I exclaimed, "I'll stir nowhere, and hear nothing, till you have removed every article of your clothes and put on dry things – and certainly you shall not go to Gimmerton tonight, so it is needless to order the carriage."

"Certainly I shall," she said, "walking or riding – yet I've no objection to dress myself decently, and... ah, see how it flows down my neck now! The fire does make it smart."

She insisted on my fulfilling her directions before she would let me touch her; and not till after the coachman had been instructed to get ready, and a maid set to pack up some necessary attire, did I obtain her consent for binding the wound and helping to change her garments.

"Now, Ellen," she said, when my task was finished and she was seated in an easy chair on the hearth, with a cup of tea before her, "you sit down opposite me, and put poor Catherine's baby away – I don't like to see it! You mustn't think I care little for Catherine because I behaved so foolishly on entering: I've cried too, bitterly – yes, more than anyone else has reason to cry. We parted unreconciled, you remember, and I shan't forgive myself. But, for all that, I was not going to sympathize with him – the brute beast! Oh, give me the poker! This is the last thing of his I have about me" – she slipped the gold ring from her third finger, and threw it on the floor. "I'll smash it!" she continued, striking it with childish spite, "and then I'll burn it!" and she took and dropped the misused article among the coals. "There! He shall buy another, if he gets me back again. He'd be capable of coming to seek me, to tease Edgar – I dare not stay, lest that notion should possess his wicked head! And besides, Edgar has not been kind, has he? And I won't come suing for his assistance, nor will I bring him into more trouble. Necessity compelled me to seek shelter here; though if I had not learnt he was out of the way, I'd have halted at the kitchen, washed my face, warmed myself, got you to bring what I wanted, and departed again to anywhere out of the reach of my accursed... of that incarnate goblin! Ah, he was in such a fury! If he had caught me!... It's a pity Earnshaw is not his match in strength – I wouldn't have run till I'd seen him all but demolished, had Hindley been able to do it!"

"Well, don't talk so fast, miss!" I interrupted, "you'll disorder the handkerchief I have tied round your face, and make the cut bleed again. Drink your tea, and take breath, and give over laughing – laughter is sadly out of place under this roof, and in your condition!"

"An undeniable truth," she replied. "Listen to that child! It maintains a constant wail – send it out of my hearing for an hour; I shan't stay any longer."

I rang the bell, and committed it to a servant's care, and then I enquired what had urged her to escape from Wuthering Heights in such an unlikely plight, and where she meant to go, as she refused remaining with us?

"I ought, and I wish to remain," answered she, "to cheer Edgar and take care of the baby, for two things, and because the Grange is my right home – but I tell you he wouldn't let me! Do you think he could bear to see me grow fat and merry, and could bear to think that we were tranquil, and not resolve on poisoning our comfort? Now I have the satisfaction of being sure that he detests me, to the point of its annoying him seriously to have me within earshot or eyesight – I notice, when I enter his presence, the muscles of his countenance are involuntarily distorted into an expression of hatred, partly arising from his knowledge of the good causes I have to feel that sentiment for him, and partly from original aversion. It is strong enough to make me feel pretty certain that he would not chase me over England, supposing I contrived a clear escape, and therefore I must get quite away. I've recovered from my first desire to be killed by him: I'd rather he'd kill himself! He has extinguished my love effectually, and so I'm at my ease. I can recollect yet how I loved him, and can dimly imagine that I could still be loving him, if... No, no! Even if he had doted on me, the devilish nature would have revealed its existence somehow. Catherine had an awfully perverted taste to esteem him so dearly, knowing him so well... Monster! Would that he could be blotted out of creation, and out of my memory!"

"Hush, hush! He's a human being," I said. "Be more charitable: there are worse men than he is yet!"

"He's not a human being," she retorted, "and he has no claim on my charity. I gave him my heart, and he took and pinched it to death, and flung it back to me. People feel with their hearts, Ellen, and since he has destroyed mine, I have not power to feel for him – and I would not, though he groaned from this to his dying day, and wept tears of blood for Catherine! No indeed, indeed I wouldn't!" And here Isabella began to cry, but, immediately dashing the water from her lashes, she recommenced.

"You asked what has driven me to flight at last? I was compelled to attempt it because I had succeeded in rousing his rage a pitch above his malignity. Pulling out the nerves with red-hot pincers requires more coolness than knocking on the head. He was worked up to forget the fiendish prudence he boasted of, and proceeding to murderous violence. I experienced pleasure in being able to exasperate him – the sense of pleasure woke my instinct of self-preservation – so I fairly broke free, and if ever I come into his hands again he is welcome to a signal revenge.

"Yesterday, you know, Mr Earnshaw should have been at the funeral. He kept himself sober for the purpose – tolerably sober: not going to bed mad at six o'clock and getting up drunk at twelve. Consequently, he rose in suicidal low spirits, as fit for the church as for a dance, and instead he sat down by the fire and swallowed gin or brandy by tumblerfuls.

"Heathcliff – I shudder to name him! – has been a stranger in the house from last Sunday till today. Whether the angels have fed him, or his kin beneath, I cannot tell, but he has not eaten a meal with us for nearly a week. He has just come home at dawn, and gone upstairs to his chamber, locking himself in – as if anybody dreamt of coveting his company! There he has continued, praying like a Methodist – only the deity he implored is senseless dust and ashes; and God, when addressed, was curiously confounded with his own black father! After concluding these precious orisons – and they lasted generally till he grew hoarse and his voice was strangled in his throat – he would be off again, always straight down to the Grange! I wonder Edgar did not send for a constable, and give him into custody! For me, grieved as I was about Catherine, it was impossible to avoid regarding this season of deliverance from degrading oppression as a holiday.

"I recovered spirits sufficient to hear Joseph's eternal lectures without weeping, and to move up and down the house, less with the foot of a frightened thief than formerly. You wouldn't think that I should cry at anything Joseph could say, but he and Hareton are detestable companions. I'd rather sit with Hindley, and hear his awful talk, than with 't' little maister' and his staunch supporter, that odious old man!

"When Heathcliff is in, I'm often obliged to seek the kitchen and their society, or starve among the damp uninhabited chambers; when he is not, as was the case this week, I establish a table and chair at one corner of the house fire, and never mind how Mr Earnshaw may occupy himself – and he does not interfere with my arrangements. He is quieter now than he used to be, if no one provokes him: more sullen and depressed, and less furious. Joseph affirms he's sure he's an altered man; that the Lord has touched his heart, and he is saved 'so as by fire'.* I'm puzzled to detect signs of the favourable change – but it is not my business.

"Yester-evening I sat in my nook reading some old books till late on towards twelve. It seemed so dismal to go upstairs, with the wild snow blowing outside and my thoughts continually reverting to the kirkyard and the new-made grave! I dared hardly lift my eyes from the page before me: that melancholy scene so instantly usurped its place.

"Hindley sat opposite, his head leant on his hand, perhaps meditating on the same subject. He had ceased drinking at a point below irrationality, and had neither stirred nor spoken during two or three hours. There was no sound through the house but the moaning wind, which shook the windows every now and then, the faint crackling of the coals, and the click of my snuffers as I removed at intervals the long wick of the candle. Hareton and Joseph were probably fast asleep in bed. It was very, very sad, and while I read I sighed, for it seemed as if all joy had vanished from the world, never to be restored.

"The doleful silence was broken at length by the sound of the kitchen latch: Heathcliff had returned from his watch earlier than usual, owing, I suppose, to the sudden storm.

"That entrance was fastened, and we heard him coming round to get in by the other. I rose with an irrepressible expression of what I felt on my lips, which induced my companion, who had been staring towards the door, to turn and look at me.

"'I'll keep him out five minutes,' he exclaimed. 'You won't object?'

"'No, you may keep him out the whole night for me,' I answered. 'Do! Put the key in the lock and draw the bolts.'

"Earnshaw accomplished this ere his guest reached the front; he then came and brought his chair to the other side of my table, leaning over it and searching in my eyes for a sympathy with the burning hate that gleamed from his: as he both looked and felt like an assassin, he couldn't exactly find that, but he discovered enough to encourage him to speak.

"'You and I,' he said, 'have each a great debt to settle with the man out yonder! If we were neither of us cowards, we might combine to discharge it. Are you as soft as your brother? Are you willing to endure to the last, and not once attempt a repayment?'

"'I'm weary of enduring now,' I replied, 'and I'd be glad of a retaliation that wouldn't recoil on myself, but treachery and violence are spears pointed at both ends: they wound those who resort to them worse than their enemies.'

"'Treachery and violence are a just return for treachery and violence!' cried Hindley. 'Mrs Heathcliff, I'll ask you to do nothing but sit still and be dumb – tell me now, can you? I'm sure you would have as much pleasure as I in witnessing the conclusion of the fiend's existence; he'll be *your* death unless you overreach him – and he'll be *my* ruin... Damn the hellish villain! He knocks at the door as if he were

147

master here already! Promise to hold your tongue, and before that clock strikes – it wants three minutes of one – you're a free woman!'

"He took the implements which I described to you in my letter from his breast, and would have turned down the candle – I snatched it away, however, and seized his arm.

"'I'll not hold my tongue!' I said, 'you mustn't touch him... Let the door remain shut and be quiet!'

"'No! I've formed my resolution, and by God I'll execute it!' cried the desperate being. 'I'll do you a kindness in spite of yourself, and Hareton justice! And you needn't trouble your head to screen me, Catherine is gone – nobody alive would regret me or be ashamed, though I cut my throat this minute – and it's time to make an end!'

"I might as well have struggled with a bear, or reasoned with a lunatic. The only resource left me was to run to a lattice and warn his intended victim of the fate which awaited him.

"'You'd better seek shelter somewhere else tonight!' I exclaimed in rather a triumphant tone. 'Mr Earnshaw has a mind to shoot you if you persist in endeavouring to enter.'

"'You'd better open the door, you ***' he answered, addressing me by some elegant term that I don't care to repeat.

"'I shall not meddle in the matter,' I retorted again. 'Come in and get shot, if you please. I've done my duty.'

"With that I shut the window and returned to my place by the fire, having too small a stock of hypocrisy at my command to pretend any anxiety for the danger that menaced him.

"Earnshaw swore passionately at me, affirming that I loved the villain yet, and calling me all sorts of names for the base spirit I evinced. And I, in my secret heart (and conscience never reproached me) thought what a blessing it would be for *him*, should Heathcliff put him out of misery, and what a blessing for *me*, should he send Heathcliff to his right abode! As I sat nursing these reflections, the casement behind me was banged onto the floor by a blow from the latter individual, and his black countenance looked blightingly through. The stanchions stood too close to suffer his shoulders to follow, and I smiled, exulting in my fancied security. His hair and clothes were whitened with snow, and his sharp cannibal teeth, revealed by cold and wrath, gleamed through the dark.

"'Isabella, let me in, or I'll make you repent!' he 'girned',* as Joseph calls it.

148

"'I cannot commit murder,' I replied. 'Mr Hindley stands sentinel with a knife and loaded pistol.'

"'Let me in by the kitchen door,' he said.

"'Hindley will be there before me,' I answered, 'and that's a poor love of yours that cannot bear a shower of snow! We were left at peace in our beds as long as the summer moon shone, but the moment a blast of winter returns, you must run for shelter! Heathcliff, if I were you I'd go stretch myself over her grave and die like a faithful dog... The world is surely not worth living in now, is it? You had distinctly impressed on me the idea that Catherine was the whole joy of your life: I can't imagine how you think of surviving her loss.'

"'He's there, is he?' exclaimed my companion, rushing to the gap. 'If I can get my arm out I can hit him!'

"I'm afraid, Ellen, you'll set me down as really wicked – but you don't know all, so don't judge! I wouldn't have aided or abetted an attempt on even *his* life for anything. Wish that he were dead, I must, and therefore I was fearfully disappointed and unnerved by terror for the consequences of my taunting speech, when he flung himself on Earnshaw's weapon and wrenched it from his grasp.

"The charge exploded, and the knife, in springing back, closed into its owner's wrist. Heathcliff pulled it away by main force, slitting up the flesh as it passed on, and thrust it dripping into his pocket. He then took a stone, struck down the division between two windows, and sprang in. His adversary had fallen senseless with excessive pain and the flow of blood that gushed from an artery or a large vein.

"The ruffian kicked and trampled on him, and dashed his head repeatedly against the flags, holding me with one hand, meantime, to prevent me summoning Joseph.

"He exerted preter-human self-denial in abstaining from finishing him completely, but getting out of breath, he finally desisted, and dragged the apparently inanimate body onto the settle.

"There he tore off the sleeve of Earnshaw's coat, and bound up the wound with brutal roughness, spitting and cursing during the operation as energetically as he had kicked before.

"Being at liberty, I lost no time in seeking the old servant, who, having gathered by degrees the purport of my hasty tale, hurried below, gasping as he descended the steps two at once.

"'Whet is thur tuh do nah? Whet is thur tuh do nah?'

"'There's this to do,' thundered Heathcliff, 'that your master's mad, and should he last another month, I'll have him to an asylum. And how the devil did you come to fasten me out, you toothless hound? Don't stand muttering and mumbling there. Come, I'm not going to nurse him. Wash that stuff away, and mind the sparks of your candle – it is more than half brandy!'

"'Und soa yah been murthering on him?' exclaimed Joseph, lifting his hands and eyes in horror. 'If iver Aw seed a seeght loike this! May the Lord—'

"Heathcliff gave him a push onto his knees in the middle of the blood, and flung a towel to him, but instead of proceeding to dry it up, he joined his hands and began a prayer, which excited my laughter from its odd phraseology. I was in the condition of mind to be shocked at nothing; in fact I was as reckless as some malefactors show themselves at the foot of the gallows.

"'Oh, I forgot you,' said the tyrant. 'You shall do that. Down with you. And you conspire with him against me, do you, viper? There, that is work fit for you!'

"He shook me till my teeth rattled, and pitched me beside Joseph, who steadily concluded his supplications, and then rose, vowing he would set off for the Grange directly. Mr Linton was a magistrate, and though he had fifty wives dead he should inquire into this.

"He was so obstinate in his resolution that Heathcliff deemed it expedient to compel from my lips a recapitulation of what had taken place, standing over me, heaving with malevolence, as I reluctantly delivered the account in answer to his questions.

"It required a great deal of labour to satisfy the old man that Heathcliff was not the aggressor, especially with my hardly wrung replies. However, Mr Earnshaw soon convinced him that he was alive still; Joseph hastened to administer a dose of spirits, and by their succour, his master presently regained motion and consciousness.

"Heathcliff, aware that his opponent was ignorant of the treatment received while insensible, called him deliriously intoxicated, and said he should not notice his atrocious conduct further, but advised him to get to bed. To my joy, he left us after giving this judicious counsel, and Hindley stretched himself on the hearthstone. I departed to my own room, marvelling that I had escaped so easily.

"This morning, when I came down about half an hour before noon, Mr Earnshaw was sitting by the fire, deadly sick; his evil genius, almost as gaunt and ghastly, leant against the chimney. Neither appeared inclined to dine, and having waited till all was cold on the table, I commenced alone.

"Nothing hindered me from eating heartily, and I experienced a certain sense of satisfaction and superiority, as at intervals I cast a look towards my silent companions, and felt the comfort of a quiet conscience within me.

"After I had done, I ventured on the unusual liberty of drawing near the fire, going round Earnshaw's seat and kneeling in the corner beside him.

"Heathcliff did not glance my way, and I gazed up and contemplated his features almost as confidently as if they had been turned to stone. His forehead, that I once thought so manly, and that I now think so diabolical, was shaded with a heavy cloud; his basilisk eyes were nearly quenched by sleeplessness – and weeping perhaps, for the lashes were wet then – his lips devoid of their ferocious sneer and sealed in an expression of unspeakable sadness. Had it been another I would have covered my face in the presence of such grief. In *his* case, I was gratified, and ignoble as it seems to insult a fallen enemy, I couldn't miss this chance of sticking in a dart – his weakness was the only time when I could taste the delight of paying wrong for wrong."

"Fie, fie, miss!" I interrupted. "One might suppose you had never opened a Bible in your life. If God afflict your enemies, surely that ought to suffice you. It is both mean and presumptuous to add your torture to his!"

"In general I'll allow that it would be, Ellen," she continued, "but what misery laid on Heathcliff could content me, unless I have a hand in it? I'd rather he suffered *less*, if I might cause his sufferings and he might *know* that I was the cause. Oh, I owe him so much. On only one condition can I hope to forgive him. It is if I may take an eye for an eye, a tooth for a tooth, for every wrench of agony return a wrench, reduce him to my level. As he was the first to injure, make him the first to implore pardon, and then... why then, Ellen, I might show you some generosity. But it is utterly impossible I can ever be revenged, and therefore I cannot forgive him. Hindley wanted some water, and I handed him a glass, and asked him how he was.

"'Not as ill as I wish,' he replied. 'But leaving out my arm, every inch of me is as sore as if I had been fighting with a legion of imps!'

"'Yes, no wonder,' was my next remark. 'Catherine used to boast that she stood between you and bodily harm: she meant that certain persons would not hurt you for fear of offending her. It's well people don't *really* rise from their grave, or last night she might have witnessed a repulsive scene! Are not you bruised, and cut over your chest and shoulders?'

"'I can't say,' he answered, 'but what do you mean? Did he dare to strike me when I was down?'

"'He trampled on and kicked you, and dashed you on the ground,' I whispered. 'And his mouth watered to tear you with his teeth, because he's only half a man – not so much.'*

"Mr Earnshaw looked up, like me, to the countenance of our mutual foe, who, absorbed in his anguish, seemed insensible to anything around him; the longer he stood, the plainer his reflections revealed their blackness through his features.

"'Oh, if God would but give me strength to strangle him in my last agony, I'd go to hell with joy,' groaned the impatient man, writhing to rise and sinking back in despair, convinced of his inadequacy for the struggle.

"'Nay, it's enough that he has murdered one of you,' I observed aloud. 'At the Grange everyone knows your sister would have been living now, had it not been for Mr Heathcliff. After all, it is preferable to be hated than loved by him. When I recollect how happy we were – how happy Catherine was before he came – I'm fit to curse the day.'

"Most likely Heathcliff noticed more the truth of what was said than the spirit of the person who said it. His attention was roused, I saw, for his eyes rained down tears among the ashes, and he drew his breath in suffocating sighs.

"I stared full at him and laughed scornfully. The clouded windows of hell flashed a moment towards me; the fiend which usually looked out, however, was so dimmed and drowned that I did not fear to hazard another sound of derision.

"'Get up, and begone out of my sight,' said the mourner.

"I guessed he uttered those words at least, though his voice was hardly intelligible.

"'I beg your pardon,' I replied. 'But I loved Catherine too, and her brother requires attendance, which for her sake I shall supply. Now that she's dead, I see her in Hindley: Hindley has exactly her eyes, if you had not tried to gouge them out and made them black and red, and her—'

"'Get up, wretched idiot, before I stamp you to death!' he cried, making a movement that caused me to make one also.

"'But then,' I continued, holding myself ready to flee, 'if poor Catherine had trusted you, and assumed the ridiculous, contemptible, degrading title of Mrs Heathcliff, she would soon have presented a similar picture! *She* wouldn't have borne your abominable behaviour quietly: her detestation and disgust must have found voice.'

"The back of the settle and Earnshaw's person interposed between me and him; so instead of endeavouring to reach me, he snatched a dinner knife from the table and flung it at my head. It struck beneath my ear and stopped the sentence I was uttering, but, pulling it out, I sprang to the door and delivered another; which I hope went a little deeper than his missile.

"The last glimpse I caught of him was a furious rush on his part, checked by the embrace of his host, and both fell locked together on the hearth.

"In my flight through the kitchen I bid Joseph speed to his master; I knocked over Hareton, who was hanging a litter of puppies from a chair back in the doorway, and, blessed as a soul escaped from Purgatory, I bounded, leapt and flew down the steep road, then, quitting its windings, shot direct across the moor, rolling over banks, and wading through marshes, precipitating myself, in fact, towards the beacon light of the Grange. And far rather would I be condemned to a perpetual dwelling in the infernal regions than even for one night abide beneath the roof of Wuthering Heights again."

Isabella ceased speaking, and took a drink of tea; then she rose, and bidding me put on her bonnet and a great shawl I had brought, and turning a deaf ear to my entreaties for her to remain another hour, she stepped onto a chair, kissed Edgar's and Catherine's portraits, bestowed a similar salute on me, and descended to the carriage, accompanied by Fanny, who yelped, wild with joy at recovering her mistress. She was driven away, never to revisit this neighbourhood, but a regular correspondence was established between her and my master when things were more settled.

I believe her new abode was in the south, near London; there she had a son born a few months subsequent to her escape. He was christened

Linton, and from the first she reported him to be an ailing, peevish creature.

Mr Heathcliff, meeting me one day in the village, enquired where she lived. I refused to tell. He remarked that it was not of any moment, only she must beware of coming to her brother: she should not be with him, if he had to keep her himself.

Though I would give no information, he discovered, through some of the other servants, both her place of residence and the existence of the child. Still, he didn't molest her, for which forbearance she might thank his aversion, I suppose.

He often asked about the infant when he saw me, and on hearing its name, smiled grimly, and observed: "They wish me to hate it too, do they?"

"I don't think they wish you to know anything about it," I answered.

"But I'll have it," he said, "when I want it. They may reckon on that!"

Fortunately its mother died before the time arrived, some thirteen years after the decease of Catherine, when Linton was twelve, or a little more.

On the day succeeding Isabella's unexpected visit I had no opportunity of speaking to my master: he shunned conversation, and was fit for discussing nothing. When I could get him to listen, I saw it pleased him that his sister had left her husband, whom he abhorred with an intensity which the mildness of his nature would scarcely seem to allow. So deep and sensitive was his aversion that he refrained from going anywhere where he was likely to see or hear of Heathcliff. Grief and that together transformed him into a complete hermit: he threw up his office of magistrate, ceased even to attend church, avoided the village on all occasions, and spent a life of entire seclusion within the limits of his park and grounds, only varied by solitary rambles on the moors and visits to the grave of his wife, mostly at evening, or early morning before other wanderers were abroad.

But he was too good to be thoroughly unhappy long. *He* didn't pray for Catherine's soul to haunt him. Time brought resignation, and a melancholy sweeter than common joy. He recalled her memory with ardent, tender love and hopeful aspiring to the better world, where he doubted not she was gone.

And he had earthly consolation and affections also. For a few days, I said, he seemed regardless of the puny successor to the departed: that coldness melted as fast as snow in April, and ere the tiny thing could stammer a word or totter a step, it wielded a despot's sceptre in his heart.

It was named Catherine, but he never called it the name in full, as he had never called the first Catherine short, probably because Heathcliff had a habit of doing so. The little one was always Cathy: it formed to him a distinction from the mother, and yet a connection with her, and his attachment sprang from its relation to her, far more than from its being his own.

I used to draw a comparison between him and Hindley Earnshaw, and perplex myself to explain satisfactorily why their conduct was so opposite in similar circumstances. They had both been fond husbands, and were both attached to their children, and I could not see how they shouldn't both have taken the same road, for good or evil. But, I thought in my mind, Hindley, with apparently the stronger head, has shown himself sadly the worse and the weaker man. When his ship struck, the captain abandoned his post; and the crew, instead of trying to save her, rushed into riot and confusion, leaving no hope for their luckless vessel. Linton, on the contrary, displayed the true courage of a loyal and faithful soul: he trusted God, and God comforted him. One hoped and the other despaired: they chose their own lots, and were righteously doomed to endure them.

But you'll not want to hear my moralizing, Mr Lockwood; you'll judge, as well as I can, all these things, at least you'll think you will, and that's the same.

The end of Earnshaw was what might have been expected: it followed fast on his sister's, there were scarcely six months between them. We at the Grange never got a very succinct account of his state preceding it; all that I did learn was on occasion of going to aid in the preparations for the funeral. Mr Kenneth came to announce the event to my master.

"Well, Nelly," said he, riding into the yard one morning, too early not to alarm me with an instant presentiment of bad news, "it's yours and my turn to go into mourning at present. Who's given us the slip now, do you think?"

"Who?" I asked in a flurry.

"Why, guess!" he returned, dismounting and slinging his bridle on a hook by the door. "And nip up the corner of your apron; I'm certain you'll need it."

"Not Mr Heathcliff, surely?" I exclaimed.

"What! Would you have tears for him?" said the doctor. "No, Heathcliff's a tough young fellow: he looks blooming today. I've just seen him. He's rapidly regaining flesh since he lost his better half."

"Who is it then, Mr Kenneth?" I repeated impatiently.

"Hindley Earnshaw! Your old friend Hindley..." he replied, "and my wicked gossip – though he's been too wild for me this long while. There! I said we should draw water... But cheer up! He died true to his character, drunk as a lord... Poor lad! I'm sorry too. One can't help missing an old companion, though he had the worst tricks with him that ever man imagined, and has done me many a rascally turn... He's barely twenty-seven, it seems; that's your own age – who would have thought you were born in one year?"

I confess this blow was greater to me than the shock of Mrs Linton's death: ancient associations lingered round my heart; I sat down in the porch and wept as for a blood relation, desiring Mr Kenneth to get another servant to introduce him to the master.

I could not hinder myself from pondering on the question: "Had he had fair play?" Whatever I did, that idea would bother me: it was so tiresomely pertinacious that I resolved on requesting leave to go to Wuthering Heights and assist in the last duties to the dead. Mr Linton was extremely reluctant to consent, but I pleaded eloquently for the friendless condition in which he lay, and I said my old master and foster-brother had a claim on my services as strong as his own. Besides, I reminded him that the child Hareton was his wife's nephew, and in the absence of nearer kin he ought to act as its guardian – and he ought to and must enquire how the property was left, and look over the concerns of his brother-in-law.

He was unfit for attending to such matters then, but he bid me speak to his lawyer, and at length permitted me to go. His lawyer had been Earnshaw's also; I called at the village and asked him to accompany me. He shook his head, and advised that Heathcliff should be let alone, affirming, if the truth were known, Hareton would be found little else than a beggar.

"His father died in debt," he said, "the whole property is mortgaged, and the sole chance for the natural heir is to allow him an opportunity of creating some interest in the creditor's heart, that he may be inclined to deal leniently towards him."

When I reached the Heights, I explained that I had come to see everything carried on decently, and Joseph, who appeared in sufficient distress, expressed satisfaction at my presence. Mr Heathcliff said he did not perceive that I was wanted, but I might stay and order the arrangements for the funeral if I chose.

"Correctly," he remarked, "that fool's body should he buried at the crossroads,* without ceremony of any kind... I happened to leave him ten minutes yesterday afternoon, and in that interval he fastened the two doors of the house against me, and he has spent the night in drinking himself to death deliberately! We broke in this morning, for we heard him sporting like a horse, and there he was, laid over the settle, flaying and scalping would not have wakened him... I sent for Kenneth, and he came, but not till the beast had changed into carrion – he was both dead and cold, and stark – and so you'll allow it was useless making more stir about him!"

The old servant confirmed this statement, but muttered:

"Aw'd rayther he'd goan hisseln fur t' doctor! Aw sud uh taen tent* uh t' maister better nur him... un' he warn't deead when Aw left, nowt uh t' soart!"

I insisted on the funeral being respectable. Mr Heathcliff said I might have my own way there too; only he desired me to remember that the money for the whole affair came out of his pocket.

He maintained a hard, careless deportment, indicative of neither joy nor sorrow – if anything, it expressed a flinty gratification at a piece of difficult work successfully executed. I observed once indeed something like exultation in his aspect: it was just when the people were bearing the coffin from the house. He had the hypocrisy to represent a mourner, and previous to following with Hareton he lifted the unfortunate child onto the table and muttered with peculiar gusto:

"Now, my bonny lad, you are *mine*! And we'll see if one tree won't grow as crooked as another, with the same wind to twist it!"

The unsuspecting thing was pleased at this speech; he played with Heathcliff's whiskers and stroked his cheek; but I divined its meaning and observed tartly:

"That boy must go back with me to Thrushcross Grange, sir. There is nothing in the world less yours than he is!"

"Does Linton say so?" he demanded.

"Of course – he has ordered me to take him," I replied.

"Well," said the scoundrel, "we'll not argue the subject now, but I have a fancy to try my hand at rearing a young one, so intimate to your master that I must supply the place of this with my own, if he attempt to remove it. I don't engage to let Hareton go undisputed, but I'll be pretty sure to make the other come! Remember to tell him."

This hint was enough to bind our hands. I repeated its substance on my return, and Edgar Linton, little interested at the commencement, spoke no more of interfering. I'm not aware that he could have done it to any purpose, had he been ever so willing.

The guest was now the master of Wuthering Heights: he held firm possession, and proved to the attorney – who in his turn proved it to Mr Linton – that Earnshaw had mortgaged every yard of land he owned for cash to supply his mania for gaming – and he, Heathcliff, was the mortgagee.

In that manner Hareton, who should now be the first gentleman in the neighbourhood, was reduced to a state of complete dependence on his father's inveterate enemy, and lives in his own house as a servant, deprived of the advantage of wages, and quite unable to right himself, because of his friendlessness and his ignorance that he has been wronged.

18

THE TWELVE YEARS – continued Mrs Dean – following that dismal period were the happiest of my life: my greatest troubles in their passage rose from our little lady's trifling illnesses, which she had to experience in common with all children, rich and poor.

For the rest, after the first six months, she grew like a larch, and could walk and talk too, in her own way, before the heath blossomed a second time over Mrs Linton's dust.

She was the most winning thing that ever brought sunshine into a desolate house: a real beauty in face, with the Earnshaws' handsome dark eyes, but the Lintons' fair skin and small features and yellow curling hair. Her spirit was high, though not rough, and qualified by a heart sensitive and lively to excess in its affections. That capacity for intense attachments reminded me of her mother – still she did not resemble her, for she could be soft and mild as a dove, and she had a gentle voice and pensive expression: her anger was never furious; her love never fierce: it was deep and tender.

However it must be acknowledged she had faults to foil her gifts. A propensity to be saucy was one, and a perverse will that indulged children invariably acquire, whether they be good-tempered or cross. If a servant chanced to vex her, it was always: "I shall tell Papa!" And if he reproved her, even by a look, you would have thought it a heartbreaking business: I don't believe he ever did speak a harsh word to her.

He took her education entirely on himself, and made it an amusement. Fortunately, curiosity and a quick intellect made her an apt scholar: she learnt rapidly and eagerly, and did honour to his teaching.

Till she reached the age of thirteen she had not once been beyond the range of the park by herself. Mr Linton would take her with him a mile or so outside on rare occasions, but he trusted her to no one else. Gimmerton was an unsubstantial name in her ears; the chapel, the only building she had approached or entered, except her own home; Wuthering Heights and Mr Heathcliff did not exist for her: she was a perfect recluse, and apparently perfectly contented. Sometimes, indeed, while surveying the country from her nursery window, she would observe:

"Ellen, how long will it be before I can walk to the top of those hills? I wonder what lies on the other side... is it the sea?"

"No, Miss Cathy," I would answer, "it is hills again, just like these."

"And what are those golden rocks like when you stand under them?" she once asked.

The abrupt descent of Penistone Crags particularly attracted her notice, especially when the setting sun shone on it and the topmost heights, and the whole extent of landscape besides lay in shadow.

I explained that they were bare masses of stone with hardly enough earth in their clefts to nourish a stunted tree.

"And why are they bright so long after it is evening here?" she pursued.

"Because they are a great deal higher up than we are," replied I, "you could not climb them, they are too high and steep. In winter the frost is always there before it comes to us, and deep into summer I have found snow under that black hollow on the north-east side!"

159

"Oh, you have been on them!" she cried gleefully. "Then I can go too, when I am a woman. Has Papa been, Ellen?"

"Papa would tell you, miss," I answered hastily, "that they are not worth the trouble of visiting. The moors where you ramble with him are much nicer, and Thrushcross Park is the finest place in the world."

"But I know the park and I don't know those," she murmured to herself. "And I should delight to look round me from the brow of that tallest point... my little pony Minny shall take me some time."

One of the maids mentioning the fairy cave quite turned her head with a desire to fulfil this project; she teased Mr Linton about it, and he promised she should have the journey when she got older, but Miss Catherine measured her age by months, and "Now am I old enough to go to Penistone Crags?" was the constant question in her mouth.

The road thither wound close by Wuthering Heights. Edgar had not the heart to pass it, so she received as constantly the answer:

"Not yet, love, not yet."

I said Mrs Heathcliff lived above a dozen years after quitting her husband. Her family were of a delicate constitution: she and Edgar both lacked the ruddy health that you will generally meet in these parts. What her last illness was, I am not certain; I conjecture they died of the same thing, a kind of fever, slow at its commencement, but incurable, and rapidly consuming life towards the close.

She wrote to inform her brother of the probable conclusion of a four-months' indisposition under which she had suffered, and entreated him to come to her, if possible, for she had much to settle, and she wished to bid him adieu and deliver Linton safely into his hands. Her hope was that Linton might be left with him, as he had been with her – his father, she would fain convince herself, had no desire to assume the burden of his maintenance or education.

My master hesitated not a moment in complying with her request: reluctant as he was to leave home at ordinary calls, he flew to answer this, commanding Catherine to my peculiar vigilance in his absence, with reiterated orders that she must not wander out of the park, even under my escort – he did not calculate on her going unaccompanied.

He was away three weeks. The first day or two my charge sat in a corner of the library, too sad for either reading or playing: in that quiet state she caused me little trouble, but it was succeeded by an interval of impatient, fretful weariness; and being too busy, and too old then, to run up and down amusing her, I hit on a method by which she might entertain herself.

I used to send her on her travels round the grounds – now on foot, and now on a pony – indulging her with a patient audience of all her real and imaginary adventures when she returned.

The summer shone in full prime, and she took such a taste for this solitary rambling that she often contrived to remain out from breakfast till tea, and then the evenings were spent in recounting her fanciful tales. I did not fear her breaking bounds, because the gates were generally locked, and I thought she would scarcely venture forth alone if they had stood wide open.

Unluckily my confidence proved misplaced. Catherine came to me one morning at eight o'clock, and said she was that day an Arabian merchant, going to cross the desert with his caravan, and I must give her plenty of provision for herself and beasts: a horse and three camels, personated by a large hound and a couple of pointers.

I got together good store of dainties and slung them in a basket on one side of the saddle, and she sprang up as gay as a fairy, sheltered by her wide-brimmed hat and gauze veil from the July sun, and trotted off with a merry laugh, mocking my cautious counsel to avoid galloping and come back early.

The naughty thing never made her appearance at tea. One traveller, the hound, being an old dog and fond of its ease, returned, but neither Cathy nor the pony nor the two pointers were visible in any direction, and I dispatched emissaries down this path and that path, and at last went wandering in search of her myself.

There was a labourer working at a fence round a plantation, on the borders of the grounds. I enquired of him if he had seen our young lady?

"I saw her at morn," he replied, "she would have me to cut her a hazel switch, and then she leapt her galloway* over the hedge yonder, where it is lowest, and galloped out of sight."

You may guess how I felt at hearing this news. It struck me directly she must have started for Penistone Crags.

"What will become of her?" I ejaculated, pushing through a gap which the man was repairing, and making straight to the high road.

I walked as if for a wager, mile after mile, till a turn brought me in view of the Heights, but no Catherine could I detect, far or near.

161

The Crags lie about a mile and a half beyond Mr Heathcliff's place – and that is four from the Grange – so I began to fear night would fall ere I could reach them.

"And what if she should have slipped in clambering among them," I reflected, "and been killed, or broken some of her bones?"

My suspense was truly painful, and at first it gave me delightful relief to observe, in hurrying by the farmhouse, Charlie, the fiercest of the pointers, lying under a window, with swelled head and bleeding ear.

I opened the wicket and ran to the door, knocking vehemently for admittance. A woman whom I knew, and who formerly lived at Gimmerton, answered – she had been servant there since the death of Mr Earnshaw.

"Ah," said she, "you are come a-seeking your little mistress! Don't be frightened. She's here safe – but I'm glad it isn't the master."

"He is not at home then, is he?" I panted, quite breathless with quick walking and alarm.

"No, no," she replied: "both he and Joseph are off, and I think they won't return this hour or more. Step in and rest you a bit."

I entered, and beheld my stray lamb seated on the hearth, rocking herself in a little chair that had been her mother's when a child. Her hat was hung against the wall, and she seemed perfectly at home, laughing and chattering, in the best spirits imaginable, to Hareton – now a great strong lad of eighteen – who stared at her with considerable curiosity and astonishment, comprehending precious little of the fluent succession of remarks and questions which her tongue never ceased pouring forth.

"Very well, miss!" I exclaimed, concealing my joy under an angry countenance. "This is your last ride till Papa comes back. I'll not trust you over the threshold again, you naughty, naughty girl!"

"Aha, Ellen!" she cried gaily, jumping up and running to my side. "I shall have a pretty story to tell tonight – and so you've found me out. Have you ever been here in your life before?"

"Put that hat on, and home at once," said I. "I'm dreadfully grieved at you, Miss Cathy, you've done extremely wrong! It's no use pouting and crying: that won't repay the trouble I've had, scouring the country after you. To think how Mr Linton charged me to keep you in – and you stealing off so! It shows you are a cunning little fox, and nobody will put faith in you any more."

"What have I done?" sobbed she, instantly checked. "Papa charged me nothing – he'll not scold me, Ellen – he's never cross like you!"

"Come, come!" I repeated. "I'll tie the riband. Now let us have no petulance. Oh, for shame! You thirteen years old and such a baby!"

This exclamation was caused by her pushing the hat from her head and retreating to the chimney out of my reach.

"Nay," said the servant, "don't be hard on the bonny lass, Mrs Dean. We made her stop: she'd fain have ridden forwards, afeard you should be uneasy. Hareton offered to go with her, and I thought he should: it's a wild road over the hills."

Hareton, during the discussion, stood with his hands in his pockets, too awkward to speak, though he looked as if he did not relish my intrusion.

"How long am I to wait?" I continued, disregarding the woman's interference. "It will be dark in ten minutes. Where is the pony, Miss Cathy? And where is Phoenix? I shall leave you, unless you be quick; so please yourself."

"The pony is in the yard," she replied, "and Phoenix is shut in there. He's bitten... and so is Charlie. I was going to tell you all about it, but you are in a bad temper and don't deserve to hear."

I picked up her hat and approached to reinstate it, but, perceiving that the people of the house took her part, she commenced capering round the room, and on my giving chase, ran like a mouse over and under and behind the furniture, rendering it ridiculous for me to pursue.

Hareton and the woman laughed, and she joined them and waxed more impertinent still, till I cried in great irritation:

"Well, Miss Cathy, if you were aware whose house this is you'd be glad enough to get out."

"It's *your* father's, isn't it?" said she, turning to Hareton.

"Nay," he replied, looking down and blushing bashfully.

He could not stand a steady gaze from her eyes, though they were just his own.

"Whose then – your master's?" she asked.

He coloured deeper, with a different feeling, muttered an oath, and turned away.

"Who is his master?" continued the tiresome girl, appealing to me. "He talked about 'our house' and 'our folk'. I thought he had been the owner's son. And he never said 'miss': he should have done, shouldn't he, if he's a servant?"

Hareton grew black as a thundercloud at this childish speech. I silently shook my questioner, and at last succeeded in equipping her for departure.

"Now get my horse," she said, addressing her unknown kinsman as she would one of the stable boys at the Grange. "And you may come with me. I want to see where the goblin-hunter rises in the marsh, and to hear about the *fairishes*,* as you call them... but make haste! What's the matter? Get my horse, I say."

"I'll see thee damned before I be *thy* servant!" growled the lad.

"You'll see me *what*?" asked Catherine in surprise.

"Damned – thou saucy witch!" he replied.

"There, Miss Cathy, you see you have got into pretty company," I interposed. "Nice words to be used to a young lady! Pray don't begin to dispute with him... Come, let us seek for Minny ourselves, and begone."

"But Ellen," cried she, staring fixed in astonishment, "how dare he speak so to me? Mustn't he be made to do as I ask him? You wicked creature, I shall tell Papa what you said... Now then!"

Hareton did not appear to feel this threat, so the tears sprang into her eyes with indignation. "You bring the pony," she exclaimed, turning to the woman, "and let my dog free this moment!"

"Softly, miss," answered the addressed, "you'll lose nothing by being civil. Though Mr Hareton there be not the master's son, he's your cousin – and I was never hired to serve you."

"*He* my cousin!" cried Cathy, with a scornful laugh.

"Yes, indeed," responded her reprover.

"Oh Ellen, don't let them say such things!" she pursued in great trouble. "Papa is gone to fetch my cousin from London – my cousin is a gentleman's son – that my..." she stopped, and wept outright, upset at the bare notion of relationship with such a clown.

"Hush, hush!" I whispered. "People can have many cousins and of all sorts, Miss Cathy, without being any the worse for it; only they needn't keep their company, if they be disagreeable and bad."

"He's not... he's not my cousin, Ellen!" she went on, gathering fresh grief from reflection and flinging herself into my arms for refuge from the idea.

I was much vexed at her and the servant for their mutual revelations, having no doubt of Linton's approaching arrival – communicated by the former – being reported to Mr Heathcliff, and feeling as confident that Catherine's first thought on her father's return would be to seek an explanation of the latter's assertion concerning her rude-bred kindred.

Hareton, recovering from his disgust at being taken for a servant, seemed moved by her distress, and, having fetched the pony round to the door, he took, to propitiate her, a fine crooked-legged terrier whelp from the kennel, and putting it into her hand, bid her whisht,[14] for he meant naught.

Pausing in her lamentations, she surveyed him with a glance of awe and horror, then burst forth anew.

I could scarcely refrain from smiling at this antipathy to the poor fellow, who was a well-made, athletic youth, good-looking in features, and stout and healthy, but attired in garments befitting his daily occupations of working on the farm and lounging among the moors after rabbits and game. Still I thought I could detect in his physiognomy a mind owning better qualities than his father ever possessed. Good things lost amid a wilderness of weeds, to be sure, whose rankness far overtopped their neglected growth, yet notwithstanding evidence of a wealthy soil that might yield luxuriant crops under other and favourable circumstances. Mr Heathcliff, I believe, had not treated him physically ill, thanks to his fearless nature, which offered no temptation to that course of oppression; it had none of the timid susceptibility that would have given zest to ill-treatment in Heathcliff's judgement. He appeared to have bent his malevolence on making him a brute: he was never taught to read or write; never rebuked for any bad habit which did not annoy his keeper; never led a single step towards virtue or guarded by a single precept against vice. And from what I heard, Joseph contributed much to his deterioration, by a narrow-minded partiality which prompted him to flatter and pet him as a boy, because he was the head of the old family. And as he had been in the habit of accusing Catherine Earnshaw and Heathcliff, when children, of putting the master past his patience, and compelling him to seek solace in drink by what he termed their "offalld* ways", so at present he laid the whole burden of Hareton's faults on the shoulders of the usurper of his property.

If the lad swore, he wouldn't correct him, nor however culpably he behaved. It gave Joseph satisfaction, apparently, to watch him go the worst lengths. He allowed that the lad was ruined; that his soul was abandoned to perdition, but then he reflected that Heathcliff must answer for it. Hareton's blood would be required at his hands, and there lay immense consolation in that thought.

Joseph had instilled into him a pride of name and of his lineage; he would, had he dared, have fostered hate between him and the present owner of the Heights, but his dread of that owner amounted to superstition, and he confined his feelings regarding him to muttered innuendoes and private comminations.

I don't pretend to be intimately acquainted with the mode of living customary in those days at Wuthering Heights. I only speak from hearsay, for I saw little. The villagers affirmed Mr Heathcliff was *near*,* and a cruel hard landlord to his tenants, but the house inside had regained its ancient aspect of comfort under female management, and the scenes of riot common in Hindley's time were not now enacted within its walls. The master was too gloomy to seek companionship with any people, good or bad, and he is yet...

This, however, is not making progress with my story. Miss Cathy rejected the peace offering of the terrier and demanded her own dogs, Charlie and Phoenix. They came limping and hanging their heads; and we set out for home, sadly out of sorts, every one of us.

I could not wring from my little lady how she had spent the day, except that, as I supposed, the goal of her pilgrimage was Penistone Crags, and she arrived without adventure to the gate of the farmhouse, when Hareton happened to issue forth, attended by some canine followers, who attacked her train.

They had a smart battle, before their owners could separate them: that formed an introduction. Catherine told Hareton who she was and where she was going, and asked him to show her the way, finally beguiling him to accompany her.

He opened the mysteries of the fairy cave and twenty other queer places, but, being in disgrace, I was not favoured with a description of the interesting objects she saw.

I could gather, however, that her guide had been a favourite till she hurt his feelings by addressing him as a servant, and Heathcliff's housekeeper hurt hers by calling him her cousin.

Then the language he had held to her rankled in her heart; she who was always "love" and "darling" and "queen" and "angel" with everybody at the Grange, to be insulted so shockingly by a stranger! She did not comprehend it, and hard work I had to obtain a promise that she would not lay the grievance before her father.

I explained how he objected to the whole household at the Heights, and how sorry he would be to find she had been there, but I insisted most on the fact that if she revealed my negligence of his orders, he would perhaps be so angry that I should have to leave, and Cathy couldn't bear that prospect: she pledged her word and kept it for my sake. After all, she was a sweet little girl.

19

A LETTER, EDGED WITH BLACK, announced the day of my master's return. Isabella was dead, and he wrote to bid me get mourning for his daughter, and arrange a room and other accommodations for his youthful nephew.

Catherine ran wild with joy at the idea of welcoming her father back, and indulged most sanguine anticipations of the innumerable excellencies of her "real" cousin.

The evening of their expected arrival came. Since early morning she had been busy ordering her own small affairs, and now attired in her new black frock – poor thing! Her aunt's death impressed her with no definite sorrow – she obliged me, by constant worrying, to walk with her down through the grounds to meet them.

"Linton is just six months younger than I am," she chattered, as we strolled leisurely over the swells and hollows of mossy turf, under shadow of the trees. "How delightful it will be to have him for a playfellow! Aunt Isabella sent Papa a beautiful lock of his hair; it was lighter than mine – more flaxen and quite as fine. I have it carefully preserved in a little glass box, and I've often thought what a pleasure it would be to see its owner… Oh! I am happy… and Papa, dear, dear Papa! Come, Ellen, let us run! Come run!"

She ran, and returned and ran again many times before my sober footsteps reached the gate, and then she seated herself on the grassy bank beside the path, and tried to wait patiently, but that was impossible: she couldn't be still a minute.

"How long they are!" she exclaimed. "Ah, I see, some dust on the road... they are coming! No! When will they be here? May we not go a little way... half a mile, Ellen, only just half a mile? Do say yes – to that clump of birches at the turn!"

I refused staunchly, and at length her suspense was ended: the travelling carriage rolled in sight.

Miss Cathy shrieked and stretched out her arms as soon as she caught her father's face looking from the window. He descended, nearly as eager as herself, and a considerable interval elapsed ere they had a thought to spare for any but themselves.

While they exchanged caresses I took a peep in to see after Linton. He was asleep in a corner, wrapped in a warm, fur-lined cloak, as if it had been winter. A pale, delicate, effeminate boy, who might have been taken for my master's younger brother, so strong was the resemblance, but there was a sickly peevishness in his aspect that Edgar Linton never had.

The latter saw me looking, and, having shaken hands, advised me to close the door and leave him undisturbed, for the journey had fatigued him. Cathy would fain have taken one glance, but her father told her to come, and they walked together up the park, while I hastened before to prepare the servants.

"Now, darling," said Mr Linton, addressing his daughter, as they halted at the bottom of the front steps, "your cousin is not so strong or so merry as you are, and he has lost his mother, remember, a very short time since; therefore don't expect him to play and run about with you directly. And don't harass him much by talking: let him be quiet this evening at least, will you?"

"Yes, yes, Papa," answered Catherine, "but I do want to see him, and he hasn't once looked out."

The carriage stopped, and the sleeper, being roused, was lifted to the ground by his uncle.

"This is your cousin Cathy, Linton," he said, putting their little hands together. "She's fond of you already, and mind you don't grieve her by crying tonight. Try to be cheerful now; the travelling is at an end, and you have nothing to do but rest and amuse yourself as you please."

"Let me go to bed then," answered the boy, shrinking from Catherine's salute, and he put his fingers to remove incipient tears.

"Come, come, there's a good child," I whispered, leading him in. "You'll make her weep too... see how sorry she is for you!"

I do not know whether it was sorrow for him, but his cousin put on as sad a countenance as himself, and returned to her father. All three entered, and mounted to the library, where tea was laid ready.

I proceeded to remove Linton's cap and mantle, and placed him on a chair by the table, but he was no sooner seated than he began to cry afresh. My master enquired what was the matter.

"I can't sit on a chair," sobbed the boy.

"Go to the sofa then, and Ellen shall bring you some tea," answered his uncle patiently.

He had been greatly tried during the journey, I felt convinced, by his fretful, ailing charge.

Linton slowly trailed himself off and lay down. Cathy carried a footstool and her cup to his side.

At first she sat silent, but that could not last; she had resolved to make a pet of her little cousin, as she would have him to be, and she commenced stroking his curls and kissing his cheek, and offering him tea in her saucer, like a baby. This pleased him, for he was not much better; he dried his eyes and lightened into a faint smile.

"Oh, he'll do very well," said the master to me, after watching them a minute. "Very well, if we can keep him, Ellen. The company of a child of his own age will instil new spirit into him soon, and by wishing for strength he'll gain it."

"Ay, if we can keep him!" I mused to myself, and sore misgivings came over me that there was slight hope of that. And then, I thought, how ever will that weakling live at Wuthering Heights, between his father and Hareton? What playmates and instructors they'll be.

Our doubts were presently decided – even earlier than I expected. I had just taken the children upstairs, after tea was finished, and seen Linton asleep – he would not suffer me to leave him till that was the case – I had come down, and was standing by the table in the hall, lighting a bedroom candle for Mr Edgar, when a maid stepped out of the kitchen and informed me that Mr Heathcliff's servant Joseph was at the door, and wished to speak with the master.

"I shall ask him what he wants first," I said in considerable trepidation. "A very unlikely* hour to be troubling people, and the instant they have returned from a long journey. I don't think the master can see him."

Joseph had advanced through the kitchen as I uttered these words, and now presented himself in the hall. He was donned in his Sunday garments, with his most sanctimonious and sourest face, and, holding his hat in one hand and his stick in the other, he proceeded to clean his shoes on the mat.

"Good evening, Joseph," I said coldly. "What business brings you here tonight?"

"It's Maister Linton Aw mun spake to," he answered, waving me disdainfully aside.

"Mr Linton is going to bed; unless you have something particular to say, I'm sure he won't hear it now," I continued. "You had better sit down in there and entrust your message to me."

"Which is his rahm?" pursued the fellow, surveying the range of closed doors.

I perceived he was bent on refusing my mediation, so very reluctantly I went up to the library and announced the unseasonable visitor, advising that he should be dismissed till next day.

Mr Linton had no time to empower me to do so, for Joseph mounted close at my heels, and, pushing into the apartment, planted himself at the far side of the table, with his two fists clapped on the head of his stick, and began in an elevated tone, as if anticipating opposition:

"Hathecliff has send me for his lad, un' Aw munn't goa back baht him."

Edgar Linton was silent a minute – an expression of exceeding sorrow overcast his features – he would have pitied the child on his own account, but, recalling Isabella's hopes and fears and anxious wishes for her son, and her commendations of him to his care, he grieved bitterly at the prospect of yielding him up, and searched in his heart how it might be avoided. No plan offered itself – the very exhibition of any desire to keep him would have rendered the claimant more peremptory – there was nothing left but to resign him. However, he was not going to rouse him from his sleep.

"Tell Mr Heathcliff," he answered calmly, "that his son shall come to Wuthering Heights tomorrow. He is in bed and too tired to go the distance now. You may also tell him that the mother of Linton desired him to remain under my guardianship, and at present his health is very precarious."

"Noa!" said Joseph, giving a thud with his prop on the floor, and assuming an authoritative air. "Noa! That manes nowt. Hathecliff maks noa 'cahnt* uh t' mother, nur yah norther*... bud he'll hev his lad, und Aw mun tak him... soa nah yah knaw!"

"You shall not tonight!" answered Linton decisively. "Walk downstairs at once, and repeat to your master what I have said. Ellen, show him down. Go..."

And, aiding the indignant elder with a lift by the arm, he rid the room of him, and closed the door.

"Varrah weell!" shouted Joseph, as he slowly drew off. "Tuhmorn, he's come hisseln, un' thrust *him* aht, if yah darr!"

20

To OBVIATE THE DANGER OF THIS THREAT being fulfilled, Mr Linton commissioned me to take the boy home early on Catherine's pony, and said he:

"As we shall now have no influence over his destiny, good or bad, you must say nothing of where he is gone to my daughter: she cannot associate with him hereafter, and it is better for her to remain in ignorance of his proximity, lest she should be restless, and anxious to visit the Heights. Merely tell her his father sent for him suddenly, and he has been obliged to leave us."

Linton was very reluctant to be roused from his bed at five o'clock, and astonished to be informed that he must prepare for further travelling, but I softened off the matter by stating that he was going to spend some time with his father, Mr Heathcliff, who wished to see him so much he did not like to defer the pleasure till he should recover from his late journey.

"My father?" he cried in strange perplexity. "Mama never told me I had a father. Where does he live? I'd rather stay with Uncle."

"He lives a little distance from the Grange," I replied, "just beyond those hills, not so far, but you may walk over here when you get hearty. And you should be glad to go home and to see him. You must try to love him as you did your mother, and then he will love you."

"But why have I not heard of him before?" asked Linton. "Why didn't Mama and he live together, as other people do?"

"He had business to keep him in the north," I answered, "and your mother's health required her to reside in the south."

"And why didn't Mama speak to me about him?" persevered the child. "She often talked of Uncle, and I learnt to love him long ago. How am I to love Papa? I don't know him."

"Oh, all children love their parents," I said. "Your mother perhaps thought you would want to be with him if she mentioned him often to you. Let us make haste. An early ride on such a beautiful morning is much preferable to an hour's more sleep."

"Is *she* to go with us," he demanded, "the little girl I saw yesterday?"

"Not now," replied I.

"Is Uncle?" he continued.

"No, I shall be your companion there," I said.

Linton sank back on his pillow, and fell into a brown study.

"I won't go without Uncle," he cried at length. "I can't tell where you mean to take me."

I attempted to persuade him of the naughtiness of showing reluctance to meet his father, still he obstinately resisted any progress towards dressing, and I had to call for my master's assistance in coaxing him out of bed.

The poor thing was finally got off, with several delusive assurances that his absence should be short; that Mr Edgar and Cathy would visit him, and other promises equally ill-founded, which I invented and reiterated at intervals throughout the way.

The pure heather-scented air, the bright sunshine and the gentle canter of Minny relieved his despondency after a while. He began to put questions concerning his new home and its inhabitants with greater interest and liveliness.

"Is Wuthering Heights as pleasant a place as Thrushcross Grange?" he enquired, turning to take a last glance into the valley, whence a light mist mounted and formed a fleecy cloud on the skirts of the blue.

"It is not so buried in trees," I replied, "and it is not quite so large, but you can see the country beautifully all round, and the air is healthier for you – fresher and drier. You will perhaps think the building old and dark at first, though it is a respectable house, the next best in the neighbourhood. And you will have such nice rambles on the moors. Hareton Earnshaw – that is Miss Cathy's other cousin, and so yours in a manner – will show you all the sweetest spots, and you can bring a book in fine weather and make a green hollow your study, and now and then your uncle may join you in a walk; he does frequently walk out on the hills."

"And what is my father like?" he asked. "Is he as young and handsome as Uncle?"

"He's as young," said I, "but he has black hair and eyes, and looks sterner, and he is taller and bigger altogether. He'll not seem to you so gentle and kind at first, perhaps, because it is not his way... still, mind you be frank and cordial with him, and naturally he'll be fonder of you than any uncle, for you are his own."

"Black hair and eyes!" mused Linton. "I can't fancy him. Then I am not like him, am I?"

"Not much," I answered – not a morsel, I thought, surveying with regret the white complexion and slim frame of my companion, and his large languid eyes – his mother's eyes, save that, unless a morbid touchiness kindled them a moment, they had not a vestige of her sparkling spirit.

"How strange that he should never come to see Mama and me!" he murmured. "Has he ever seen me? If he has, I must have been a baby. I remember not a single thing about him!"

"Why, Master Linton," said I, "three hundred miles is a great distance, and ten years seem very different in length to a grown-up person compared with what they do to you. It is probable Mr Heathcliff proposed going from summer to summer, but never found a convenient opportunity – and now it is too late. Don't trouble him with questions on the subject: it will disturb him for no good."

The boy was fully occupied with his own cogitations for the remainder of the ride, till we halted before the farmhouse garden gate. I watched to catch his impressions in his countenance. He surveyed the carved front and low-browed lattices, the straggling gooseberry bushes and crooked firs with solemn intentness, and then shook his head: his private feelings entirely disapproved of the exterior of his new abode, but he had sense to postpone complaining – there might be compensation within.

Before he dismounted, I went and opened the door. It was half-past six; the family had just finished breakfast: the servant was clearing and wiping down the table. Joseph stood by his master's chair telling some tale concerning a lame horse, and Hareton was preparing for the hayfield.

"Hallo, Nelly!" said Mr Heathcliff when he saw me. "I feared I should have to come down and fetch my property myself. You've brought it, have you? Let us see what we can make of it."

He got up and strode to the door: Hareton and Joseph followed in gaping curiosity. Poor Linton ran a frightened eye over the faces of the three.

"Sure-ly," said Joseph, after a grave inspection, "he's swopped wi' ye, Maister, an' yon's his lass!"

Heathcliff, having stared his son into an ague of confusion, uttered a scornful laugh.

"God! What a beauty! What a lovely, charming thing!" he exclaimed. "Haven't they reared it on snails and sour milk, Nelly? Oh damn my soul! But that's worse than I expected – and the devil knows I was not sanguine!"

I bid the trembling and bewildered child get down and enter. He did not thoroughly comprehend the meaning of his father's speech, or whether it were intended for him: indeed, he was not yet certain that the grim, sneering stranger was his father. But he clung to me with growing trepidation, and on Mr Heathcliff's taking a seat and bidding him "come hither" he hid his face on my shoulder and wept.

"Tut, tut!" said Heathcliff, stretching out a hand and dragging him roughly between his knees, and then holding up his head by the chin. "None of that nonsense! We're not going to hurt thee, Linton – isn't that thy name? Thou art thy mother's child entirely! Where is my share in thee, puling chicken?"

He took off the boy's cap and pushed back his thick flaxen curls, felt his slender arms and his small fingers, during which examination Linton ceased crying and lifted his great blue eyes to inspect the inspector.

"Do you know me?" asked Heathcliff, having satisfied himself that the limbs were all equally frail and feeble.

"No," said Linton, with a gaze of vacant fear.

"You've heard of me, I dare say?"

"No," he replied again.

"No! What a shame of your mother, never to waken your filial regard for me! You are my son then, I'll tell you, and your mother was a wicked slut to leave you in ignorance of the sort of father you possessed... Now don't wince, and colour up! Though it *is* something to

174

see you have not white blood... Be a good lad, and I'll do for you...
Nelly, if you be tired you may sit down; if not, get home again. I guess
you'll report what you hear and see to the cipher at the Grange, and
this thing won't be settled while you linger about it."

"Well," replied I, "I hope you'll be kind to the boy, Mr Heathcliff, or
you'll not keep him long, and he's all you have akin in the wide world
that you will ever know – remember."

"I'll be *very* kind to him, you needn't fear!" he said, laughing. "Only
nobody else must be kind to him: I'm jealous of monopolizing his affection. And to begin my kindness, Joseph, bring the lad some breakfast...
Hareton, you infernal calf, begone to your work. Yes, Nell," he added
when they had departed, "my son is prospective owner of your place,
and I should not wish him to die till I was certain of being his successor. Besides, he's *mine*, and I want the triumph of seeing *my* descendant
fairly lord of their estates; my child hiring their children to till their
fathers' lands for wages... That is the sole consideration which can
make me endure the whelp: I despise him for himself and hate him for
the memories he revives! But that consideration is sufficient: he's as safe
with me and shall be tended as carefully as your master tends his own. I
have a room upstairs, furnished for him in handsome style; I've engaged
a tutor, also, to come three times a week, from twenty miles' distance,
to teach him what he pleases to learn. I've ordered Hareton to obey
him, and in fact I've arranged everything with a view to preserve the
superior and the gentleman in him, above his associates... I do regret,
however, that he so little deserves the trouble – if I wished any blessing
in the world, it was to find him a worthy object of pride; and I'm bitterly
disappointed with the whey-faced whining wretch!"

While he was speaking, Joseph returned bearing a basin of milk porridge, and placed it before Linton, who stirred round the homely mess
with a look of aversion, and affirmed he could not eat it.

I saw the old manservant shared largely in his master's scorn of
the child, though he was compelled to retain the sentiment in his
heart, because Heathcliff plainly meant his underlings to hold him
in honour.

"Cannot ate it?" repeated he, peering in Linton's face and subduing
his voice to a whisper for fear of being overheard. "But Maister Hareton
nivir ate nowt else, when he wer a little un, und what wer gooid eneugh
fur him's gooid eneugh fur yah, Aw's rayther think!"

"I *shan't* eat it!" answered Linton snappishly. "Take it away."

Joseph snatched up the food indignantly, and brought it to us.

"Is there owt ails th' victuals?" he asked, thrusting the tray under Heathcliff's nose.

"What should ail them?" he said.

"Wah!" answered Joseph, "yon dainty chap says he cannut ate 'em. Bud Aw guess it's raight! His mother wer just soa– we wer a'most too mucky tuh sow t' corn for makking her breead."

"Don't mention his mother to me," said the master angrily. "Get him something that he can eat, that's all. What is his usual food, Nelly?"

I suggested boiled milk or tea, and the housekeeper received instructions to prepare some.

Come, I reflected, his father's selfishness may contribute to his comfort. He perceives his delicate constitution and the necessity of treating him tolerably. I'll console Mr Edgar by acquainting him with the turn Heathcliff's humour has taken.

Having no excuse for lingering longer, I slipped out, while Linton was engaged in timidly rebuffing the advances of a friendly sheepdog. But he was too much on the alert to be cheated: as I closed the door I heard a cry and a frantic repetition of the words:

"Don't leave me! I'll not stay here! I'll not stay here!"

Then the latch was raised and fell – they did not suffer him to come forth. I mounted Minny, and urged her to a trot, and so my brief guardianship ended.

21

WE HAD SAD WORK WITH LITTLE CATHY that day: she rose in high glee, eager to join her cousin, and such passionate tears and lamentations followed the news of his departure that Edgar himself was obliged to soothe her by affirming he should come back soon – he added, however, "if I can get him," and there were no hopes of that.

This promise poorly pacified her, but time was more potent, and though still at intervals she enquired of her father when Linton would return, before she did see him again his features had waxed so dim in her memory that she did not recognize him.

When I chanced to encounter the housekeeper of Wuthering Heights, in paying business visits to Gimmerton, I used to ask how the young master got on, for he lived almost as secluded as Catherine herself, and was never to be seen. I could gather from her that he continued in weak health and was a tiresome inmate. She said Mr Heathcliff seemed to dislike him ever longer and worse, though he took some trouble to conceal it. He had an antipathy to the sound of his voice, and could not do at all with his sitting in the same room with him many minutes together.

There seldom passed much talk between them: Linton learnt his lessons and spent his evenings in a small apartment they called the parlour, or else lay in bed all day, for he was constantly getting coughs and colds, and aches and pains of some sort.

"And I never knew such a faint-hearted creature," added the woman, "nor one so careful of hisseln. He *will* go on, if I leave the window open a bit late in the evening. Oh, it's killing, a breath of night air! And he must have a fire in the middle of summer, and Joseph's 'bacca pipe is poison, and he must always have sweets and dainties, and always milk, milk forever – heeding naught how the rest of us are pinched in winter – and there he'll sit, wrapped in his furred cloak in his chair by the fire, with some toast and water or other slop on the hob to sip at, and if Hareton for pity comes to amuse him – Hareton is not bad-natured, though he's rough – they're sure to part, one swearing and the other crying. I believe the master would relish Earnshaw's thrashing him to a mummy if he were not his son, and I'm certain he would be fit to turn him out of doors if he knew half the nursing he gives hisseln. But then he won't go into danger of temptation: he never enters the parlour, and should Linton show those ways in the house where he is, he sends him upstairs directly."

I divined from this account that utter lack of sympathy had rendered young Heathcliff selfish and disagreeable, if he were not so originally, and my interest in him consequently decayed, though still I was moved with a sense of grief at his lot, and a wish that he had been left with us.

Mr Edgar encouraged me to gain information; he thought a great deal about him, I fancy, and would have run some risk to see him, and he told me once to ask the housekeeper whether he ever came into the village?

She said he had only been twice, on horseback, accompanying his father, and both times he pretended to be quite knocked up for three or four days afterwards.

That housekeeper left, if I recollect rightly, two years after he came, and another, whom I did not know, was her successor – she lives there still.

Time wore on at the Grange in its former pleasant way till Miss Cathy reached sixteen. On the anniversary of her birth we never manifested any signs of rejoicing, because it was also the anniversary of my late mistress's death. Her father invariably spent that day alone in the library, and walked, at dusk, as far as Gimmerton kirkyard, where he would frequently prolong his stay beyond midnight. Therefore Catherine was thrown on her own resources for amusement.

This twentieth of March was a beautiful spring day, and when her father had retired, my young lady came down dressed for going out, and said she asked to have a ramble on the edge of the moor with me, and Mr Linton had given her leave, if we went only a short distance and were back within the hour.

"So make haste, Ellen!" she cried. "I know where I wish to go: where a colony of moor game* are settled; I want to see whether they have made their nests yet."

"That must be a good distance up," I answered, "they don't breed on the edge of the moor."

"No, it's not," she said. "I've gone very near with Papa."

I put on my bonnet and sallied out, thinking nothing more of the matter. She bounded before me, and returned to my side, and was off again like a young greyhound, and at first I found plenty of entertainment in listening to the larks singing far and near, and enjoying the sweet warm sunshine; and watching her, my pet and my delight, with her golden ringlets flying loose behind and her bright cheek, as soft and pure in its bloom as a wild rose, and her eyes radiant with cloudless pleasure. She was a happy creature, and an angel, in those days. It's a pity she could not be content.

"Well," said I, "where are your moor game, Miss Cathy? We should be at them... the Grange park fence is a great way off now."

"Oh, a little further... only a little further, Ellen," was her answer continually. "Climb to that hillock, pass that bank, and by the time you reach the other side I shall have raised the birds."

But there were so many hillocks and banks to climb and pass, that at length I began to be weary, and told her we must halt and retrace our steps.

I shouted to her, as she had outstripped me a long way; she either did not hear or did not regard, for she still sprang on, and I was compelled to follow. Finally she dived into a hollow, and before I came in sight of her again, she was two miles nearer Wuthering Heights than her own home, and I beheld a couple of persons arrest her, one of whom I felt convinced was Mr Heathcliff himself.

Cathy had been caught in the fact of plundering, or at least hunting out the nests of the grouse.

The Heights were Heathcliff's land, and he was reproving the poacher.

"I've neither taken any nor found any," she said as I toiled to them, expanding her hands in corroboration of the statement. "I didn't mean to take them, but Papa told me there were quantities up here, and I wished to see the eggs."

Heathcliff glanced at me with an ill-meaning smile, expressing his acquaintance with the party, and consequently his malevolence towards it, and demanded who "Papa" was?

"Mr Linton of Thrushcross Grange," she replied. "I thought you did not know me, or you wouldn't have spoken in that way."

"You suppose Papa is highly esteemed and respected then?" he said sarcastically.

"And what are you?" enquired Catherine, gazing curiously on the speaker. "That man I've seen before. Is he your son?"

She pointed to Hareton, the other individual, who had gained nothing but increased bulk and strength by the addition of two years to his age: he seemed as awkward and rough as ever.

"Miss Cathy," I interrupted, "it will be three hours instead of one that we are out presently. We really must go back."

"No, that man is not my son," answered Heathcliff, pushing me aside. "But I have one, and you have seen him before too, and though your nurse is in a hurry, I think both you and she would be the better for a little rest. Will you just turn this nab* of heath and walk into my house? You'll get home earlier for the ease, and you shall receive a kind welcome."

I whispered Catherine that she mustn't on any account accede to the proposal; it was entirely out of the question.

"Why?" she asked aloud. "I'm tired of running, and the ground is dewy... I can't sit here. Let us go, Ellen. Besides, he says I have seen his son. He's mistaken, I think, but I guess where he lives: at the farmhouse I visited in coming from Penistone Crags. Don't you?"

"I do. Come, Nelly, hold your tongue... it will be a treat for her to look in on us. Hareton, get forwards with the lass. You shall walk with me, Nelly."

"No, she's not going to any such place," I cried, struggling to release my arm, which he had seized, but she was almost at the doorstones already, scampering round the brow at full speed. Her appointed companion did not pretend to escort her: he shied off by the roadside and vanished.

"Mr Heathcliff, it's very wrong," I continued, "you know you mean no good. And there she'll see Linton, and all will be told as soon as ever we return – and I shall have the blame."

"I want her to see Linton," he answered, "he's looking better these few days; it's not often he's fit to be seen. And we'll soon persuade her to keep the visit secret – where is the harm of it?"

"The harm of it is that her father would hate me if he found I suffered her to enter your house, and I am convinced you have a bad design in encouraging her to do so," I replied.

"My design is as honest as possible. I'll inform you of its whole scope," he said. "That the two cousins may fall in love and get married. I'm acting generously to your master: his young chit has no expectations, and should she second my wishes, she'll be provided for at once as joint successor with Linton."

"If Linton died," I answered, "and his life is quite uncertain, Catherine would be the heir."

"No, she would not," he said. "There is no clause in the will to secure it so: his property would go to me, but to prevent disputes I desire their union, and am resolved to bring it about."

"And I'm resolved she shall never approach your house with me again," I returned, as we reached the gate, where Miss Cathy waited our coming.

Heathcliff bade me be quiet, and, preceding us up the path, hastened to open the door. My young lady gave him several looks, as if she could not exactly make up her mind what to think of him, but now he smiled when he met her eye and softened his voice in addressing her, and I was foolish enough to imagine the memory of her mother might disarm him from desiring her injury.

Linton stood on the hearth. He had been out walking in the fields, for his cap was on and he was calling to Joseph to bring him dry shoes.

He had grown tall of his age, still wanting some months of sixteen. His features were pretty yet, and his eye and complexion brighter than I remembered them, though with merely temporary lustre borrowed from the salubrious air and genial sun.

"Now who is that?" asked Mr Heathcliff, turning to Cathy. "Can you tell?"

"Your son?" she said, having doubtfully surveyed first one and then the other.

"Yes, yes," answered he, "but is this the only time you have beheld him? Think! Ah, you have a short memory. Linton, don't you recall your cousin, that you used to tease us so with wishing to see?"

"What, Linton!" cried Cathy, kindling into joyful surprise at the name. "Is that little Linton? He's taller than I am! Are you Linton?"

The youth stepped forwards and acknowledged himself; she kissed him fervently, and they gazed with wonder at the change time had wrought in the appearance of each.

Catherine had reached her full height; her figure was both plump and slender, elastic as steel, and her whole aspect sparkling with health and spirits. Linton's looks and movements were very languid, and his form extremely slight, but there was a grace in his manner that mitigated these defects and rendered him not unpleasing.

After exchanging numerous marks of fondness with him, his cousin went to Mr Heathcliff, who lingered by the door, dividing his attention between the objects inside and those that lay without, pretending, that is, to observe the latter and really noting the former alone.

"And you are my uncle then!" she cried, reaching up to salute him. "I thought I liked you, though you were cross at first. Why don't you visit at the Grange with Linton? To live all these years such close neighbours and never see us is odd – what have you done so for?"

"I visited it once or twice too often before you were born," he answered. "There – damn it! If you have any kisses to spare, give them to Linton – they are thrown away on me."

"Naughty Ellen!" exclaimed Catherine, flying to attack me next with her lavish caresses. "Wicked Ellen, to try to hinder me from entering. But I'll take this walk every morning in future – may I, Uncle? – and sometimes bring Papa. Won't you be glad to see us?"

"Of course!" replied the uncle, with a hardly suppressed grimace, resulting from his deep aversion to both the proposed visitors. "But stay," he continued, turning towards the young lady. "Now I think of it, I'd better tell you. Mr Linton has a prejudice against me: we quarrelled at one time of our lives with unchristian ferocity, and if you mention coming here to him he'll put a veto on your visits altogether. Therefore you must not mention it, unless you be careless of seeing your cousin hereafter – you may come if you will, but you must not mention it."

"Why did you quarrel?" asked Catherine, considerably crestfallen.

"He thought me too poor to wed his sister," answered Heathcliff, "and was grieved that I got her – his pride was hurt, and he'll never forgive it."

"That's wrong!" said the young lady, "sometime I'll tell him so. But Linton and I have no share in your quarrel. I'll not come here, then – he shall come to the Grange."

"It will be too far for me," murmured her cousin, "to walk four miles would kill me. No, come here, Miss Catherine, now and then, not every morning, but once or twice a week."

The father launched towards his son a glance of bitter contempt.

"I am afraid, Nelly, I shall lose my labour," he muttered to me. "Miss Catherine, as the ninny calls her, will discover his value and send him to the devil. Now if it had been Hareton – do you know that twenty times a day I covet Hareton, with all his degradation? I'd have loved the lad had he been someone else. But I think he's safe from *her* love. I'll pit him against that paltry creature, unless it bestir itself briskly. We calculate it will scarcely last till it is eighteen. Oh, confound the vapid thing! He's absorbed in drying his feet, and never looks at her... Linton!"

"Yes, Father," answered the boy.

"Have you nothing to show your cousin anywhere about, not even a rabbit or a weasel's nest? Take her into the garden, before you change your shoes, and into the stable to see your horse."

"Wouldn't you rather sit here?" asked Linton, addressing Cathy in a tone which expressed reluctance to move again.

"I don't know," she replied, casting a longing look to the door, and evidently eager to be active.

He kept his seat and shrank closer to the fire.

Heathcliff rose and went into the kitchen, and from thence to the yard, calling out for Hareton.

Hareton responded, and presently the two re-entered. The young man had been washing himself, as was visible by the glow on his cheeks and his wetted hair.

"Oh, I'll ask *you*, Uncle," cried Miss Cathy, recollecting the housekeeper's assertion. "That is not my cousin, is he?"

"Yes," he replied, "your mother's nephew. Don't you like him?"

Catherine looked queer.

"Is he not a handsome lad?" he continued.

The uncivil little thing stood on tiptoe and whispered a sentence in Heathcliff's ear.

He laughed; Hareton darkened – I perceived he was very sensitive to suspected slights, and had obviously a dim notion of his inferiority. But his master or guardian chased the frown by exclaiming:

"You'll be the favourite among us, Hareton! She says you are a... what was it? Well, something very flattering... Here! You go with her round the farm. And behave like a gentleman, mind! Don't use any bad words, and don't stare when the young lady is not looking at you, and be ready to hide your face when she is, and when you speak, say your words slowly, and keep your hands out of your pockets. Be off, and entertain her as nicely as you can."

He watched the couple walking past the window. Earnshaw had his countenance completely averted from his companion. He seemed studying the familiar landscape with a stranger's and an artist's interest.

Catherine took a sly look at him, expressing small admiration. She then turned her attention to seeking out objects of amusement for herself, and tripped merrily on, lilting a tune to supply the lack of conversation.

"I've tied his tongue," observed Heathcliff. "He'll not venture a single syllable all the time! Nelly, you recollect me at his age – nay, some years younger – did I ever look so stupid, so 'gaumless',* as Joseph calls it?"

"Worse," I replied, "because more sullen with it."

"I've a pleasure in him," he continued, reflecting aloud. "He has satisfied my expectations... If he were a born fool I should not enjoy

183

it half so much – but he's no fool, and I can sympathize with all his feelings, having felt them myself... I know what he suffers now, for instance, exactly: it is merely a beginning of what he shall suffer, though. And he'll never be able to emerge from his bathos* of coarseness and ignorance. I've got him faster than his scoundrel of a father secured me, and lower, for he takes a pride in his brutishness. I've taught him to scorn everything extra-animal as silly and weak. Don't you think Hindley would be proud of his son if he could see him? Almost as proud as I am of mine... But there's this difference: one is gold put to the use of paving stones, and the other is tin polished to ape a service of silver. *Mine* has nothing valuable about it, yet I shall have the merit of making it go as far as such poor stuff can go. *His* had first-rate qualities, and they are lost, rendered worse than unavailing... I have nothing to regret; he would have more than any but I are aware of... And the best of it is, Hareton is damnably fond of me! You'll own that I've outmatched Hindley there. If the dead villain could rise from his grave to abuse me for his offspring's wrongs, I should have the fun of seeing the said offspring fight him back again, indignant that he should dare to rail at the one friend he has in the world!"

Heathcliff chuckled a fiendish laugh at the idea. I made no reply, because I saw that he expected none.

Meantime our young companion, who sat too removed from us to hear what was said, began to evince symptoms of uneasiness, probably repenting that he had denied himself the treat of Catherine's society for fear of a little fatigue.

His father remarked the restless glances wandering to the window and the hand irresolutely extended towards his cap.

"Get up, you idle boy!" he exclaimed with assumed heartiness. "Away after them – they are just at the corner, by the stand of hives."

Linton gathered his energies and left the hearth. The lattice was open, and as he stepped out I heard Cathy enquiring of her unsociable attendant, what was that inscription over the door? Hareton stared up and scratched his head like a true clown.

"It's some damnable writing," he answered. "I cannot read it."

"Can't read it?" cried Catherine, "I can read it... it's English – but I want to know why it is there."

Linton giggled – the first appearance of mirth he had exhibited.

184

"He does not know his letters," he said to his cousin. "Could you believe in the existence of such a colossal dunce?"

"Is he all as he should be?" asked Miss Cathy seriously, "or is he simple – not right? I've questioned him twice now, and each time he looked so stupid I think he does not understand me. I can hardly understand *him*, I'm sure!"

Linton repeated his laugh and glanced at Hareton tauntingly, who certainly did not seem quite clear of comprehension at that moment.

"There's nothing the matter but laziness, is there, Earnshaw?" he said. "My cousin fancies you are an idiot. There you experience the consequence of scorning 'book larning', as you would say. Have you noticed, Catherine, his frightful Yorkshire pronunciation?"

"Why, where the devil is the use on't?" growled Hareton, more ready in answering his daily companion. He was about to enlarge further, but the two youngsters broke into a noisy fit of merriment, my giddy Miss being delighted to discover that she might turn his strange talk to matter of amusement.

"Where is the use of the devil in that sentence?" tittered Linton. "Papa told you not to say any bad words, and you can't open your mouth without one… Do try to behave like a gentleman, now do!"

"If thou weren't more a lass than a lad, I'd fell thee this minute, I would, pitiful lath* of a crater!"* retorted the angry boor, retreating, while his face burned with mingled rage and mortification, for he was conscious of being insulted, and embarrassed how to resent it.

Mr Heathcliff, having overheard the conversation as well as I, smiled when he saw him go, but immediately afterwards cast a look of singular aversion on the flippant pair, who remained chattering in the doorway: the boy finding animation enough while discussing Hareton's faults and deficiencies, and relating anecdotes of his goings-on; and the girl relishing his pert and spiteful sayings without considering the ill nature they evinced. I began to dislike more than to compassionate Linton, and to excuse his father in some measure for holding him cheap.

We stayed till afternoon – I could not tear Miss Cathy away sooner – but happily my master had not quitted his apartment and remained ignorant of our prolonged absence.

As we walked home, I would fain have enlightened my charge on the characters of the people we had quitted, but she got it into her head that I was prejudiced against them.

"Aha!" she cried, "you take Papa's side, Ellen – you are partial... I know, or else you wouldn't have cheated me so many years into the notion that Linton lived a long way from here. I'm really extremely angry, only I'm so pleased I can't show it! But you must hold your tongue about my uncle – he's *my* uncle, remember, and I'll scold Papa for quarrelling with him."

And so she ran on, till I dropped endeavouring to convince her of her mistake.

She did not mention the visit that night, because she did not see Mr Linton. Next day it all came out, sadly to my chagrin – and still I was not altogether sorry: I thought the burden of directing and warning would be more efficiently borne by him than me, but he was too timid in giving satisfactory reasons for his wish that she should shun connection with the household of the Heights, and Catherine liked good reasons for every restraint that harassed her petted will.

"Papa!" she exclaimed after the morning's salutations, "guess whom I saw yesterday in my walk on the moors... Ah, Papa, you started! You've not done right, have you, now? I saw... but listen, and you shall hear how I found you out, and Ellen, who is in league with you and yet pretended to pity me so, when I kept hoping and was always disappointed about Linton's coming back!"

She gave a faithful account of her excursion and its consequences, and my master, though he cast more than one reproachful look at me, said nothing till she had concluded. Then he drew her to him and asked if she knew why he had concealed Linton's near neighbourhood from her? Could she think it was to deny her a pleasure that she might harmlessly enjoy?

"It was because you disliked Mr Heathcliff," she answered.

"Then you believe I care more for my own feelings than yours, Cathy?" he said. "No, it was not because I disliked Mr Heathcliff, but because Mr Heathcliff dislikes me, and is a most diabolical man, delighting to wrong and ruin those he hates, if they give him the slightest opportunity. I knew that you could not keep up an acquaintance with your cousin without being brought into contact with him, and I knew he would detest you on my account, so for your own good, and nothing else, I took precautions that you should not see Linton again – I meant to explain this some time as you grew older, and I'm sorry I delayed it."

"But Mr Heathcliff was quite cordial, Papa," observed Catherine, not at all convinced, "and *he* didn't object to our seeing each other: he said I might come to his house when I pleased, only I must not tell you, because you had quarrelled with him and would not forgive him for marrying Aunt Isabella. And you won't – *you* are the one to be blamed – he is willing to let us be friends at least – Linton and I – and you are not."

My master, perceiving that she would not take his word for her uncle-in-law's evil disposition, gave a hasty sketch of his conduct to Isabella and the manner in which Wuthering Heights became his property. He could not bear to discourse long upon the topic, for though he spoke little of it he still felt the same horror and detestation of his ancient enemy that had occupied his heart ever since Mrs Linton's death. "She might have been living yet, if it had not been for him!" was his constant bitter reflection, and in his eyes Heathcliff seemed a murderer.

Miss Cathy – conversant with no bad deeds except her own slight acts of disobedience, injustice and passion, arising from hot temper and thoughtlessness and repented of on the day they were committed – was amazed at the blackness of spirit that could brood on and cover* revenge for years, and deliberately prosecute its plans without a visitation of remorse. She appeared so deeply impressed and shocked at this new view of human nature – excluded from all her studies and all her ideas till now – that Mr Edgar deemed it unnecessary to pursue the subject. He merely added:

"You will know hereafter, darling, why I wish you to avoid his house and family – now return to your old employments and amusements, and think no more about them."

Catherine kissed her father, and sat down quietly to her lessons for a couple of hours, according to custom; then she accompanied him into the grounds, and the whole day passed as usual; but in the evening, when she had retired to her room, and I went to help her to undress, I found her crying on her knees by the bedside.

"Oh, fie, silly child!" I exclaimed. "If you had any real griefs, you'd be ashamed to waste a tear on this little contrariety. You never had one shadow of substantial sorrow, Miss Catherine. Suppose, for a minute, that master and I were dead, and you were by yourself in the world – how would you feel, then? Compare the present occasion with such an affliction as that, and be thankful for the friends you have, instead of coveting more."

"I'm not crying for myself, Ellen," she answered, "it's for him... He expected to see me again tomorrow, and there he'll be so disappointed – and he'll wait for me, and I shan't come!"

"Nonsense!" said I, "do you imagine he has thought as much of you as you have of him? Hasn't he Hareton for a companion? Not one in a hundred would weep at losing a relation they had just seen twice, for two afternoons... Linton will conjecture how it is, and trouble himself no further about you."

"But may I not write a note to tell him why I cannot come?" she asked, rising to her feet. "And just send those books I promised to lend him? His books are not as nice as mine, and he wanted to have them extremely, when I told him how interesting they were... May I not, Ellen?"

"No indeed! No indeed!" replied I with decision. "Then he would write to you, and there'd never be an end of it... No, Miss Catherine, the acquaintance must be dropped entirely – so Papa expects, and I shall see that it is done."

"But how can one little note—" she recommenced, putting on an imploring countenance.

"Silence!" I interrupted. "We'll not begin with your little notes. Get into bed."

She threw at me a very naughty look, so naughty that I would not kiss her goodnight at first: I covered her up and shut her door, in great displeasure, but repenting halfway, I returned softly, and lo! there was Miss standing at the table with a bit of blank paper before her and a pencil in her hand, which she guiltily slipped out of sight on my re-entrance.

"You'll get nobody to take that, Catherine," I said, "if you write it, and at present I shall put out your candle."

I set the extinguisher on the flame, receiving as I did so a slap on my hand and a petulant "cross thing!" – I then quitted her again, and she drew the bolt in one of her worst, most peevish humours.

The letter was finished and forwarded to its destination by a milk-fetcher who came from the village, but that I didn't learn till some time afterwards. Weeks passed on and Cathy recovered her temper, though she grew wondrous fond of stealing off to corners by herself, and often, if I came near her suddenly while reading, she would start and bend over the book, evidently desirous to hide it, and I detected edges of loose paper sticking out beyond the leaves.

She also got a trick of coming down early in the morning and lingering about the kitchen, as if she were expecting the arrival of something, and she had a small drawer in a cabinet in the library, which she would trifle over for hours, and whose key she took special care to remove when she left it.

One day, as she inspected this drawer, I observed that the playthings and trinkets which recently formed its contents were transmuted into bits of folded paper.

My curiosity and suspicions were roused; I determined to take a peep at her mysterious treasures, so at night, as soon as she and my master were safe upstairs, I searched and readily found among my house keys one that would fit the lock. Having opened, I emptied the whole contents into my apron and took them with me to examine at leisure in my own chamber.

Though I could not but suspect, I was still surprised to discover that they were a mass of correspondence – daily almost, it must have been – from Linton Heathcliff: answers to documents forwarded by her. The earlier dated were embarrassed and short; gradually, however, they expanded into copious love letters, foolish, as the age of the writer rendered natural, yet with touches here and there which I thought were borrowed from a more experienced source.

Some of them struck me as singularly odd compounds of ardour and flatness, commencing in strong feeling and concluding in the affected, wordy style that a schoolboy might use to a fancied, incorporeal sweetheart.

Whether they satisfied Cathy I don't know, but they appeared very worthless trash to me.

After turning over as many as I thought proper, I tied them in a handkerchief and set them aside, relocking the vacant drawer.

Following her habit, my young lady descended early and visited the kitchen: I watched her go to the door, on the arrival of a certain little boy, and while the dairymaid filled his can, she tucked something into his jacket pocket, and plucked something out.

I went round by the garden and laid wait for the messenger, who fought valorously to defend his trust, and we spilt the milk between us, but I succeeded in abstracting the epistle, and, threatening serious consequences if he did not look sharp home, I remained under the wall and perused Miss Cathy's affectionate composition. It was more simple and more eloquent than her cousin's, very pretty and very silly. I shook my head, and went meditating into the house.

The day being wet, she could not divert herself with rambling about the park; so, at the conclusion of her morning studies, she resorted to the solace of the drawer. Her father sat reading at the table, and I, on purpose, had sought a bit of work in some unripped fringes of the window curtain, keeping my eye steadily fixed on her proceedings.

Never did any bird flying back to a plundered nest, which it had left brimful of chirping young ones, express more complete despair in its anguished cries and flutterings than she by her single "Oh!" and the change that transfigured her late happy countenance. Mr Linton looked up.

"What is the matter, love? Have you hurt yourself?" he said.

His tone and look assured her *he* had not been the discoverer of the hoard.

"No, Papa!" she gasped. "Ellen! Ellen! Come upstairs – I'm sick!"

I obeyed her summons and accompanied her out.

"Oh, Ellen! You have got them," she commenced immediately, dropping on her knees, when we were enclosed alone. "Oh, give them to me, and I'll never, never do so again! Don't tell Papa… You have not told Papa, Ellen? Say you have not! I've been exceedingly naughty, but I won't do it any more!"

With a grave severity in my manner I bade her stand up.

"So," I exclaimed, "Miss Catherine, you are tolerably far on, it seems – you may well be ashamed of them! A fine bundle of trash you study in your leisure hours, to be sure – why, it's good enough to be printed! And what do you suppose the master will think when I display it before him? I haven't shown it yet, but you needn't imagine I shall keep your ridiculous secrets… For shame! And you must have led the way in writing such absurdities: he would not have thought of beginning, I'm certain."

"I didn't! I didn't!" sobbed Cathy, fit to break her heart. "I didn't once think of loving him till—"

"*Loving*!" cried I, as scornfully as I could utter the word. "*Loving*! Did anybody ever hear the like! I might just as well talk of loving the miller who comes once a year to buy our corn. Pretty loving indeed, and both times together you have seen Linton hardly four hours in your life! Now here is the babyish trash. I'm going with it to the library, and we'll see what your father says to such *loving*."

She sprang at her precious epistles, but I held them above my head, and then she poured out further frantic entreaties that I would burn them – do anything rather than show them. And being really fully as much inclined to laugh as scold – for I esteemed it all girlish vanity – I at length relented in a measure and asked:

"If I consent to burn them, will you promise faithfully neither to send nor receive a letter again, nor a book – for I perceive you have sent him books – nor locks of hair, nor rings, nor playthings?"

"We don't send playthings!" cried Catherine, her pride overcoming her shame.

"Nor anything at all then, my lady?" I said. "Unless you will, here I go."

"I promise, Ellen!" she cried, catching my dress. "Oh, put them in the fire, do, do!"

But when I proceeded to open a place with the poker, the sacrifice was too painful to be borne. She earnestly supplicated that I would spare her one or two.

"One or two, Ellen, to keep for Linton's sake!"

I unknotted the handkerchief, and commenced dropping them in from an angle, and the flame curled up the chimney.

"I will have one, you cruel wretch!" she screamed, darting her hand into the fire and drawing forth some half-consumed fragments at the expense of her fingers.

"Very well – and I will have some to exhibit to Papa!" I answered, shaking back the rest into the bundle, and turning anew to the door.

She emptied her blackened pieces into the flames and motioned me to finish the immolation. It was done; I stirred up the ashes and interred them under a shovelful of coals; and she mutely, and with a sense of intense injury, retired to her private apartment. I descended to tell my master that the young lady's qualm of sickness was almost gone, but I judged it best for her to lie down awhile.

She wouldn't dine, but she reappeared at tea, pale, and red about the eyes, and marvellously subdued in outward aspect.

Next morning I answered the letter by a slip of paper, inscribed "Master Heathcliff is requested to send no more notes to Miss Linton, as she will not receive them". And thenceforth the little boy came with vacant pockets.

22

SUMMER DREW TO AN END, and early autumn: it was past Michaelmas, but the harvest was late that year, and a few of our fields were still uncleared.

Mr Linton and his daughter would frequently walk out among the reapers: at the carrying of the last sheaves they stayed till dusk, and the evening happening to be chill and damp, my master caught a bad cold that settled obstinately on his lungs and confined him indoors throughout the whole of the winter, nearly without intermission.

Poor Cathy, frightened from her little romance, had been considerably sadder and duller since its abandonment, and her father insisted on her reading less and taking more exercise. She had his companionship no longer; I esteemed it a duty to supply its lack as much as possible with mine – an inefficient substitute, for I could only spare two or three hours from my numerous diurnal occupations to follow her footsteps, and then my society was obviously less desirable than his.

On an afternoon in October, or the beginning of November, a fresh, watery afternoon, when the turf and paths were rustling with moist, withered leaves, and the cold blue sky was half-hidden by clouds – dark grey streamers, rapidly mounting from the west and boding abundant rain – I requested my young lady to forgo her ramble, because I was certain of showers. She refused, and I unwillingly donned a cloak and took my umbrella to accompany her on a stroll to the bottom of the park, a formal walk which she generally affected if low-spirited – and that she invariably was when Mr Edgar had been worse than ordinary, a thing never known from his confession, but guessed both by her and me from his increased silence and the melancholy of his countenance.

She went sadly on; there was no running or bounding now, though the chill wind might well have tempted her to a race. And often, from the side of my eye, I could detect her raising a hand, and brushing something off her cheek. I gazed round for a means of diverting her thoughts. On one side of the road rose a high, rough bank, where hazels and stunted oaks, with their roots half-exposed, held uncertain tenure: the soil was too loose for the latter, and strong winds had blown some nearly horizontal. In summer Miss Catherine delighted to climb along these trunks and sit in the branches, swinging twenty feet above the ground; and I, pleased with her agility and her light, childish heart, still considered it proper to scold every time I caught her at such an elevation, but so that she knew there was no necessity for descending. From dinner to tea she would lie in her breeze-rocked cradle, doing nothing except singing old songs – my nursery lore – to herself, or watching the birds, joint tenants, feed and entice their young ones to fly: or nestling with closed lids, half-thinking, half-dreaming, happier than words can express.

"Look, miss!" I exclaimed, pointing to a nook under the roots of one twisted tree. "Winter is not here yet. There's a little flower up yonder, the last bud from the multitude of bluebells that clouded those turf steps in July with a lilac mist. Will you clamber up and pluck it to show to Papa?"

Cathy stared a long time at the lonely blossom trembling in its earthy shelter, and replied at length:

"No, I'll not touch it… but it looks melancholy, does it not, Ellen?"

"Yes," I observed, "about as starved and sackless* as you – your cheeks are bloodless; let us take hold of hands and run. You're so low I dare say I shall keep up with you."

"No," she repeated, and continued sauntering on, pausing at intervals to muse over a bit of moss, or a tuft of blanched grass, or a fungus spreading its bright orange among the heaps of brown foliage, and ever and anon her hand was lifted to her averted face.

"Catherine, why are you crying, love?" I asked, approaching and putting my arm over her shoulder. "You mustn't cry because Papa has a cold; be thankful it is nothing worse."

She now put no further restraint on her tears; her breath was stifled by sobs.

"Oh, it *will* be something worse," she said. "And what shall I do when Papa and you leave me, and I am by myself? I can't forget your words, Ellen; they are always in my ear. How life will be changed, how dreary the world will be, when Papa and you are dead."

193

"None can tell whether you won't die before us," I replied. "It's wrong to anticipate evil. We'll hope there are years and years to come before any of us go: Master is young, and I am strong and hardly forty-five. My mother lived till eighty, a canty* dame to the last. And suppose Mr Linton were spared till he saw sixty: that would be more years than you have counted, miss. And would it not be foolish to mourn a calamity above twenty years beforehand?"

"But Aunt Isabella was younger than Papa," she remarked, gazing up with timid hope to seek further consolation.

"Aunt Isabella had not you and me to nurse her," I replied. "She wasn't as happy as Master; she hadn't as much to live for. All you need do is to wait well on your father, and cheer him by letting him see you cheerful, and avoid giving him anxiety on any subject – mind that, Cathy! I'll not disguise but you might kill him if you were wild and reckless, and cherished a foolish, fanciful affection for the son of a person who would be glad to have him in his grave, and allowed him to discover that you fretted over the separation he has judged it expedient to make."

"I fret about nothing on earth except Papa's illness," answered my companion. "I care for nothing in comparison with Papa. And I'll never – never – oh, never, while I have my senses, do an act or say a word to vex him. I love him better than myself, Ellen, and I know it by this: I pray every night that I may live after him, because I would rather be miserable than that he should be – that proves I love him better than myself."

"Good words," I replied. "But deeds must prove it also, and after he is well, remember you don't forget resolutions formed in the hour of fear."

As we talked, we neared a door that opened on the road, and my young lady, lightening into sunshine again, climbed up and seated herself on the top of the wall, reaching over to gather some hips that bloomed scarlet on the summit branches of the wild-rose trees shadowing the highway side: the lower fruit had disappeared, but only birds could touch the upper, except from Cathy's present station.

In stretching to pull them her hat fell off, and as the door was locked, she proposed scrambling down to recover it. I bid her be cautious lest she got a fall, and she nimbly disappeared.

But the return was no such easy matter: the stones were smooth and neatly cemented, and the rose bushes and blackberry stragglers could yield no assistance in re-ascending. I, like a fool, didn't recollect that, till I heard her laughing and exclaiming:

"Ellen! You'll have to fetch the key, or else I must run round to the porter's lodge. I can't scale the ramparts on this side!"

"Stay where you are," I answered, "I have my bundle of keys in my pocket; perhaps I may manage to open it – if not, I'll go."

Catherine amused herself with dancing to and fro before the door, while I tried all the large keys in succession. I had applied the last, and found that none would do; so, repeating my desire that she would remain there, I was about to hurry home as fast as I could, when an approaching sound arrested me. It was the trot of a horse; Cathy's dance stopped; and in a minute the horse stopped also.

"Who is that?" I whispered.

"Ellen, I wish you could open the door," whispered back my companion anxiously.

"Ho, Miss Linton!" cried a deep voice (the rider's). "I'm glad to meet you. Don't be in haste to enter, for I have an explanation to ask and obtain."

"I shan't speak to you, Mr Heathcliff!" answered Catherine. "Papa says you are a wicked man and you hate both him and me, and Ellen says the same."

"That is nothing to the purpose," said Heathcliff. (He it was.) "I don't hate my son, I suppose, and it is concerning him that I demand your attention. Yes, you have cause to blush. Two or three months since, were you not in the habit of writing to Linton? Making love in play, eh? You deserved, both of you, flogging for that! You especially, the elder – and less sensitive, as it turns out. I've got your letters, and if you give me any pertness I'll send them to your father. I presume you grew weary of the amusement and dropped it, didn't you? Well, you dropped Linton with it into a Slough of Despond.* He was in earnest – in love – really. As true as I live, he's dying for you, breaking his heart at your fickleness – not figuratively but actually. Though Hareton has made him a standing jest for six weeks, and I have used more serious measures and attempted to frighten him out of his idiocy, he gets worse daily, and he'll be under the sod before summer, unless you restore him!"

"How can you lie so glaringly to the poor child?" I called from the inside. "Pray ride on! How can you deliberately get up such paltry falsehoods? Miss Cathy, I'll knock the lock off with a stone: you won't believe that vile nonsense. You can feel in yourself it is impossible that a person should die for love of a stranger."

"I was not aware there were eavesdroppers," muttered the detected villain. "Worthy Mrs Dean, I like you, but I don't like your double-dealing," he added aloud. "How could *you* lie so glaringly as to affirm I hated the 'poor child'? And invent bugbear stories to terrify her from my doorstones? Catherine Linton – the very name warms me – my bonny lass, I shall be from home all this week; go and see if I have not spoken truth: do, there's a darling! Just imagine your father in my place, and Linton in yours; then think how you would value your careless lover if he refused to stir a step to comfort you, when your father himself entreated him; and don't, from pure stupidity, fall into the same error. I swear on my salvation, he's going to his grave, and none but you can save him!"

The lock gave way and I issued out.

"I swear Linton is dying," repeated Heathcliff, looking hard at me. "And grief and disappointment are hastening his death. Nelly, if you won't let her go, you can walk over yourself. But I shall not return till this time next week, and I think your master himself would scarcely object to her visiting her cousin."

"Come in," said I, taking Cathy by the arm and half-forcing her to re-enter, for she lingered, viewing with troubled eyes the features of the speaker, too stern to express his inward deceit.

He pushed his horse close, and bending down, observed:

"Miss Catherine, I'll own to you that I have little patience with Linton – and Hareton and Joseph have less. I'll own that he's with a harsh set. He pines for kindness as well as love, and a kind word from you would be his best medicine. Don't mind Mrs Dean's cruel cautions, but be generous and contrive to see him. He dreams of you day and night, and cannot be persuaded that you don't hate him, since you neither write nor call."

I closed the door and rolled a stone to assist the loosened lock in holding it, and, spreading my umbrella, I drew my charge underneath, for the rain began to drive through the moaning branches of the trees, and warned us to avoid delay.

Our hurry prevented any comment on the encounter with Heathcliff, as we stretched* towards home, but I divined instinctively that Catherine's heart was clouded now in double darkness. Her features were so sad, they did not seem hers: she evidently regarded what she had heard as every syllable true.

The master had retired to rest before we came in. Cathy stole to his room to enquire how he was; he had fallen asleep. She returned and asked me to sit with her in the library. We took our tea together, and afterwards she lay down on the rug and told me not to talk, for she was weary.

I got a book and pretended to read. As soon as she supposed me absorbed in my occupation, she recommenced her silent weeping: it appeared, at present, her favourite diversion. I suffered her to enjoy it awhile; then I expostulated, deriding and ridiculing all Mr Heathcliff's assertions about his son, as if I were certain she would coincide. Alas! I hadn't skill to counteract the effect his account had produced: it was just what he intended.

"You may be right, Ellen," she answered, "but I shall never feel at ease till I know – and I must tell Linton it is not my fault that I don't write, and convince him that I shall not change."

What use were anger and protestations against her silly credulity? We parted that night – hostile – but next day beheld me on the road to Wuthering Heights, by the side of my wilful young mistress's pony. I couldn't bear to witness her sorrow, to see her pale, dejected countenance and heavy eyes; and I yielded, in the faint hope that Linton himself might prove, by his reception of us, how little of the tale was founded on fact.

23

THE RAINY NIGHT HAD USHERED IN a misty morning – half frost, half drizzle – and temporary brooks crossed our path, gurgling from the uplands. My feet were thoroughly wetted; I was cross and low, exactly the humour suited for making the most of these disagreeable things.

We entered the farmhouse by the kitchen way, to ascertain whether Mr Heathcliff were really absent, because I put slight faith in his own affirmation.

Joseph seemed sitting in a sort of Elysium alone, beside a roaring fire, a quart of ale on the table near him, bristling with large pieces of toasted oatcake, and his black, short pipe in his mouth.

Catherine ran to the hearth to warm herself. I asked if the master was in? My question remained so long unanswered that I thought the old man had grown deaf, and repeated it louder.

"Na-ay!" he snarled, or rather screamed through his nose. "Na-ay! Yah muh goa back whear yah coom frough."

"Joseph!" cried a peevish voice, simultaneously with me, from the inner room. "How often am I to call you? There are only a few red ashes now. Joseph! Come this moment."

Vigorous puffs, and a resolute stare into the grate, declared he had no ear for this appeal. The housekeeper and Hareton were invisible; one gone on an errand, and the other at his work, probably. We knew Linton's tones, and entered.

"Oh, I hope you'll die in a garret, starved to death!" said the boy, mistaking our approach for that of his negligent attendant.

He stopped on observing his error; his cousin flew to him.

"Is that you, Miss Linton?" he said, raising his head from the arm of the great chair in which he reclined. "No – don't kiss me: it takes my breath – dear me! Papa said you would call," continued he, after recovering a little from Catherine's embrace, while she stood by looking very contrite. "Will you shut the door, if you please? You left it open, and those... those *detestable* creatures won't bring coals to the fire. It's so cold!"

I stirred up the cinders, and fetched a scuttleful myself. The invalid complained of being covered with ashes, but he had a tiresome cough, and looked feverish and ill, so I did not rebuke his temper.

"Well, Linton," murmured Catherine, when his corrugated brow relaxed, "are you glad to see me? Can I do you any good?"

"Why didn't you come before?" he asked. "You should have come, instead of writing. It tired me dreadfully writing those long letters. I'd far rather have talked to you. Now I can neither bear to talk, nor anything else. I wonder where Zillah is! Will you" – looking at me – "step into the kitchen and see?"

I had received no thanks for my other service, and, being unwilling to run to and fro at his behest, I replied:

"Nobody is out there but Joseph."

"I want to drink," he exclaimed fretfully, turning away. "Zillah is constantly gadding off to Gimmerton since Papa went. It's miserable! And I'm obliged to come down here – they resolved never to hear me upstairs."

"Is your father attentive to you, Master Heathcliff?" I asked, perceiving Catherine to be checked in her friendly advances.

"Attentive? He makes *them* a little more attentive at least," he cried. "The wretches! Do you know, Miss Linton, that brute Hareton laughs at me! I hate him! Indeed, I hate them all – they are odious beings."

Cathy began searching for some water; she lighted on a pitcher in the dresser, filled a tumbler, and brought it. He bid her add a spoonful of wine from a bottle on the table; and having swallowed a small portion, appeared more tranquil, and said she was very kind.

"And are you glad to see me?" asked she, reiterating her former question, and pleased to detect the faint dawn of a smile.

"Yes, I am. It's something new to hear a voice like yours!" he replied. "But I *have* been vexed because you wouldn't come... And Papa swore it was owing to me: he called me a pitiful, shuffling, worthless thing, and said you despised me; and if he had been in my place, he would be more the master of the Grange than your father by this time. But you don't despise me, do you, Miss—"

"I wish you would say Catherine, or Cathy!" interrupted my young lady. "Despise you? No! Next to Papa and Ellen, I love you better than anybody living. I don't love Mr Heathcliff, though – and I dare not come when he returns – will he stay away many days?"

"Not many," answered Linton, "but he goes onto the moors frequently, since the shooting season commenced, and you might spend an hour or two with me in his absence – do! Say you will! I think I should not be peevish with you; you'd not provoke me, and you'd always be ready to help me, wouldn't you?"

"Yes" said Catherine, stroking his long soft hair, "if I could only get Papa's consent, I'd spend half my time with you. Pretty Linton! I wish you were my brother!"

"And then you would like me as well as your father?" observed he more cheerfully. "But Papa says you would love me better than him and all the world, if you were my wife – so I'd rather you were that."

"No, I should never love anybody better than Papa," she returned gravely. "And people hate their wives sometimes, but not their sisters and brothers, and if you were the latter, you would live with us, and Papa would be as fond of you as he is of me."

Linton denied that people ever hated their wives, but Cathy affirmed they did, and in her wisdom instanced his own father's aversion to her aunt.

I endeavoured to stop her thoughtless tongue. I couldn't succeed till everything she knew was out. Master Heathcliff, much irritated, asserted her relation was false.

"Papa told me… and Papa does not tell falsehoods," she answered pertly.

"*My* papa scorns yours!" cried Linton. "He calls him a sneaking fool."

"Yours is a wicked man," retorted Catherine, "and you are very naughty to dare to repeat what he says. He must be wicked to have made Aunt Isabella leave him as she did."

"She didn't leave him," said the boy, "you shan't contradict me."

"She did," cried my young lady.

"Well, I'll tell *you* something!" said Linton. "Your mother hated your father, now then."

"Oh!" exclaimed Catherine, too enraged to continue.

"And she loved mine," added he.

"You little liar! I hate you now!" she panted, and her face grew red with passion.

"She did! She did!" sang Linton, sinking into the recess of his chair, and leaning back his head to enjoy the agitation of the other disputant, who stood behind.

"Hush, Master Heathcliff!" I said, "that's your father's tale too, I suppose."

"It isn't – you hold your tongue!" he answered. "She did, she did, Catherine, she did, she did!"

Cathy, beside herself, gave the chair a violent push, and caused him to fall against one arm. He was immediately seized by a suffocating cough that soon ended his triumph.

It lasted so long that it frightened even me. As to his cousin, she wept with all her might, aghast at the mischief she had done, though she said nothing. I held him till the fit exhausted itself. Then he thrust me away, and leant his head down silently. Catherine quelled her lamentations also, took a seat opposite, and looked solemnly into the fire.

"How do you feel now, Master Heathcliff?" I enquired, after waiting ten minutes.

"I wish *she* felt as I do," he replied, "spiteful, cruel thing! Hareton never touches me, he never struck me in his life… And I was better today, and there…" his voice died in a whimper.

"*I* didn't strike you!" muttered Cathy, chewing her lip to prevent another burst of emotion.

He sighed and moaned like one under great suffering, and kept it up for a quarter of an hour, on purpose to distress his cousin apparently, for whenever he caught a stifled sob from her, he put renewed pain and pathos into the inflections of his voice.

"I'm sorry I hurt you, Linton!" she said at length, racked beyond endurance. "But *I* couldn't have been hurt by that little push, and I had no idea that you could either: you're not much, are you, Linton? Don't let me go home thinking I've done you harm. Answer, speak to me."

"I can't speak to you," he murmured, "you've hurt me so that I shall lie awake all night choking with this cough! If you had it you'd know what it was, but *you'll* be comfortably asleep while I'm in agony, and nobody near me. I wonder how you would like to pass those fearful nights!" And he began to wail aloud for very pity of himself.

"Since you are in the habit of passing dreadful nights," I said, "it won't be Miss who spoils your ease: you'd be the same had she never come. However, she shall not disturb you again, and perhaps you'll get quieter when we leave you."

"Must I go?" asked Catherine dolefully, bending over him. "Do you want me to go, Linton?"

"You can't alter what you've done," he replied pettishly, shrinking from her, "unless you alter it for the worse by teasing me into a fever."

"Well, then I must go?" she repeated.

"Let me alone at least," said he, "I can't bear your talking."

She lingered, and resisted my persuasions to departure a tiresome while, but as he neither looked up nor spoke, she finally made a movement to the door, and I followed.

We were recalled by a scream: Linton had slid from his seat onto the hearthstone, and lay writhing in the mere perverseness of an indulged plague of a child determined to be as grievous and harassing as it can.

I thoroughly gauged his disposition from his behaviour, and saw at once it would be folly to attempt humouring him. Not so my companion: she ran back in terror, knelt down, and cried and soothed and entreated till he grew quiet from lack of breath, by no means from compunction at distressing her.

"I shall lift him onto the settle," I said, "and he may roll about as he pleases; we can't stop to watch him. I hope you are satisfied, Miss

Cathy, that *you* are not the person to benefit him, and that his condition of health is not occasioned by attachment to you. Now then, there he is! Come away – as soon as he knows there is nobody by to care for his nonsense, he'll be glad to lie still."

She placed a cushion under his head and offered him some water; he rejected the latter and tossed uneasily on the former, as if it were a stone or a block of wood.

She tried to put it more comfortably.

"I can't do with that," he said, "it's not high enough!"

Catherine brought another to lay above it.

"That's *too* high," murmured the provoking thing.

"How must I arrange it then?" she asked despairingly.

He twined himself up to her, as she half-knelt by the settle and converted her shoulder into a support.

"No, that won't do!" I said. "You'll be content with the cushion, Master Heathcliff! Miss has wasted too much time on you already; we cannot remain five minutes longer."

"Yes, yes, we can!" replied Cathy. "He's good and patient now… He's beginning to think I shall have far greater misery than he will tonight, if I believe he is the worse for my visit – and then I dare not come again. Tell the truth about it, Linton, for I musn't come, if I have hurt you."

"You must come, to cure me," he answered. "You ought to come, because you have hurt me – you know you have extremely! I was not as ill when you entered as I am at present – was I?"

"But you've made yourself ill by crying and being in a passion. I didn't do it all," said his cousin. "However, we'll be friends now. And you want me – you would wish to see me sometimes, really?"

"I told you I did!" he replied impatiently. "Sit on the settle and let me lean on your knee. That's as Mama used to do, whole afternoons together… Sit quite still and don't talk, but you may sing a song if you can sing, or you may say a nice long interesting ballad – one of those you promised to teach me, or a story. I'd rather have a ballad, though: begin."

Catherine repeated the longest she could remember. The employment pleased both mightily. Linton would have another, and after that another, notwithstanding my strenuous objections, and so they went on until the clock struck twelve and we heard Hareton in the court returning for his dinner.

"And tomorrow, Catherine, will you be here tomorrow?" asked young Heathcliff, holding her frock as she rose reluctantly.

"No," I answered, "nor next day neither." She however gave a different response evidently, for his forehead cleared as she stooped and whispered in his ear.

"You won't go tomorrow, recollect, miss!" I commenced, when we were out of the house. "You are not dreaming of it, are you?"

She smiled.

"Oh, I'll take good care," I continued, "I'll have that lock mended, and you can escape by no way else."

"I can get over the wall," she said, laughing. "The Grange is not a prison, Ellen, and you are not my jailer. And besides, I'm almost seventeen: I'm a woman. And I'm certain Linton would recover quickly if he had me to look after him. I'm older than he is, you know, and wiser, less childish, am I not? And he'll soon do as I direct him, with some slight coaxing. He's a pretty little darling when he's good. I'd make such a pet of him, if he were mine. We should never quarrel, should we, after we were used to each other? Don't you like him, Ellen?"

"Like him?" I exclaimed. "The worst-tempered bit of a sickly slip that ever struggled into its teens! Happily, as Mr Heathcliff conjectured, he'll not win* twenty. I doubt whether he'll see spring, indeed – and small loss to his family whenever he drops off. And lucky it is for us that his father took him: the kinder he was treated, the more tedious and selfish he'd be. I'm glad you have no chance of having him for a husband, Miss Catherine."

My companion waxed serious at hearing this speech. To speak of his death so regardlessly wounded her feelings.

"He's younger than I," she answered, after a protracted pause of meditation, "and he ought to live the longest: he will... he must live as long as I do. He's as strong now as when he first came into the north, I'm positive of that. It's only a cold that ails him, the same as Papa has. You say Papa will get better, and why shouldn't he?"

"Well, well," I cried, "after all, we needn't trouble ourselves; for listen, miss – and mind, I'll keep my word – if you attempt going to Wuthering Heights again, with or without me, I shall inform Mr Linton, and unless he allow it, the intimacy with your cousin must not be revived."

"It has been revived," muttered Cathy sulkily.

"Must not be continued then!" I said.

"We'll see!" was her reply, and she set off at a gallop, leaving me to toil in the rear.

We both reached home before our dinner time; my master supposed we had been wandering through the park, and therefore he demanded no explanation of our absence. As soon as I entered I hastened to change my soaked shoes and stockings, but sitting such a while at the Heights had done the mischief. On the succeeding morning I was laid up, and during three weeks I remained incapacitated for attending to my duties: a calamity never experienced prior to that period, and never, I am thankful to say, since.

My little mistress behaved like an angel in coming to wait on me and cheer my solitude; the confinement brought me exceedingly low. It is wearisome to a stirring active body, but few have slighter reasons for complaint than I had. The moment Catherine left Mr Linton's room, she appeared at my bedside. Her day was divided between us; no amusement usurped a minute: she neglected her meals, her studies and her play, and she was the fondest nurse that ever watched. She must have had a warm heart, when she loved her father so, to give so much to me! I said her days were divided between us, but the master retired early, and I generally needed nothing after six o'clock, thus the evening was her own.

Poor thing, I never considered what she did with herself after tea. And though frequently, when she looked in to bid me goodnight, I remarked a fresh colour in her cheeks and a pinkness over her slender fingers; instead of fancying the hue borrowed from a cold ride across the moors, I laid it to the charge of a hot fire in the library.

24

AT THE CLOSE OF THREE WEEKS I WAS ABLE to quit my chamber and move about the house. And on the first occasion of my sitting up in the evening I asked Catherine to read to me, because my eyes were weak. We were in the library, the master having gone to bed: she consented rather unwillingly, I fancied, and imagining my sort of books did not suit her, I bid her please herself in the choice of what she perused.

She selected one of her own favourites, and got forwards steadily about an hour; then came frequent questions.

"Ellen, are not you tired? Hadn't you better lie down now? You'll be sick, keeping up so long, Ellen."

"No, no, dear, I'm not tired," I returned continually.

Perceiving me immovable, she essayed another method of showing her disrelish for her occupation. It changed to yawning and stretching and:

"Ellen, I'm tired."

"Give over then and talk," I answered.

That was worse: she fretted and sighed and looked at her watch till eight, and finally went to her room, completely overdone with sleep, judging by her peevish, heavy look and the constant rubbing she inflicted on her eyes.

The following night she seemed more impatient still, and on the third from recovering my company, she complained of a headache and left me.

I thought her conduct odd, and, having remained alone a long while, I resolved on going and enquiring whether she were better, and asking her to come and lie on the sofa, instead of upstairs in the dark.

No Catherine could I discover upstairs, and none below. The servants affirmed they had not seen her. I listened at Mr Edgar's door: all was silence. I returned to her apartment, extinguished my candle, and seated myself in the window.

The moon shone bright; a sprinkling of snow covered the ground, and I reflected that she might possibly have taken it into her head to walk about the garden for refreshment. I did detect a figure creeping along the inner fence of the park, but it was not my young mistress: on its emerging into the light I recognized one of the grooms.

He stood a considerable period, viewing the carriage road through the grounds, then started off at a brisk pace, as if he had detected something, and reappeared presently, leading Miss's pony, and there she was, just dismounted, and walking by its side.

The man took his charge stealthily across the grass towards the stable. Cathy entered by the casement window of the drawing room, and glided noiselessly up to where I awaited her.

She put the door gently to, slipped off her snowy shoes, untied her hat, and was proceeding, unconscious of my espionage, to lay aside her mantle, when I suddenly rose and revealed myself. The surprise petrified her an instant: she uttered an inarticulate exclamation and stood fixed.

"My dear Miss Catherine," I began, too vividly impressed by her recent kindness to break into a scold, "where have you been riding out at this hour? And why should you try to deceive me by telling a tale? Where have you been? Speak!"

"To the bottom of the park," she stammered. "I didn't tell a tale."

"And nowhere else?" I demanded.

"No," was the muttered reply.

"Oh, Catherine!" I cried sorrowfully. "You know you have been doing wrong, or you wouldn't be driven to uttering an untruth to me. That does grieve me. I'd rather be three months ill than hear you frame a deliberate lie."

She sprang forwards and, bursting into tears, threw her arms round my neck.

"Well, Ellen, I'm so afraid of you being angry," she said. "Promise not to be angry, and you shall know the very truth. I hate to hide it."

We sat down in the window seat; I assured her I would not scold, whatever her secret might be, and I guessed it, of course; so she commenced:

"I've been to Wuthering Heights, Ellen, and I've never missed going a day since you fell ill, except thrice before and twice after you left your room. I gave Michael books and pictures to prepare Minny every evening, and to put her back in the stable – you mustn't scold him either, mind. I was at the Heights by half-past six, and generally stayed till half-past eight, and then galloped home. It was not to amuse myself that I went: I was often wretched all the time. Now and then I was happy, once in a week perhaps. At first, I expected there would be sad work persuading you to let me keep my word to Linton, for I had engaged to call again next day, when we quitted him, but as you stayed upstairs on the morrow, I escaped that trouble. While Michael was refastening the lock of the park door in the afternoon, I got possession of the key, and told him how my cousin wished me to visit him, because he was sick and couldn't come to the Grange; and how Papa would object to my going: and then I negotiated with him about the pony. He is fond of reading, and he thinks of leaving soon to get married; so he offered, if I would lend him books out of the library, to do what I wished, but I preferred giving him my own, and that satisfied him better.

"On my second visit Linton seemed in lively spirits, and Zillah – that is their housekeeper – made us a clean room and a good fire, and told us that, as Joseph was out at a prayer meeting and Hareton Earnshaw was off with his dogs – robbing our woods of pheasants, as I heard afterwards – we might do what we liked.

"She brought me some warm wine and gingerbread, and appeared exceedingly good-natured, and Linton sat in the armchair, and I in the little rocking chair on the hearthstone, and we laughed and talked so merrily, and found so much to say: we planned where we would go, and what we would do in summer. I needn't repeat that, because you would call it silly.

"One time, however, we were near quarrelling. He said the pleasantest manner of spending a hot July day was lying from morning till evening on a bank of heath in the middle of the moors, with the bees humming dreamily about among the bloom, and the larks singing high up overhead, and the blue sky and bright sun shining steadily and cloudlessly. That was his most perfect idea of heaven's happiness – mine was rocking in a rustling green tree, with a west wind blowing, and bright white clouds flitting rapidly above, and not only larks, but throstles, and blackbirds, and linnets, and cuckoos, pouring out music on every side, and the moors seen at a distance, broken into cool dusky dells, but close by, great swells of long grass undulating in waves to the breeze, and woods and sounding water, and the whole world awake and wild with joy. He wanted all to lie in an ecstasy of peace – I wanted all to sparkle and dance in a glorious jubilee.

"I said his heaven would be only half-alive, and he said mine would be drunk; I said I should fall asleep in his, and he said he could not breathe in mine, and began to grow very snappish. At last we agreed to try both, as soon as the right weather came, and then we kissed each other and were friends. After sitting still an hour, I looked at the great room with its smooth, uncarpeted floor, and thought how nice it would be to play in, if we removed the table, and I asked Linton to call Zillah in to help us, and we'd have a game at blind man's buff; she should try to catch us – you used to, you know, Ellen. He wouldn't; there was no pleasure in it, he said, but he consented to play at ball with me. We found two in a cupboard, among a heap of old toys, tops and hoops, and battledores and shuttlecocks. One was marked C. and the other H. – I wished to have the C., because that stood for

Catherine, and the H. might be for Heathcliff, his name, but the bran came out of H., and Linton didn't like it.

"I beat him constantly, and he got cross again and coughed, and returned to his chair. That night, though, he easily recovered his good humour; he was charmed with two or three pretty songs – *your* songs, Ellen – and when I was obliged to go, he begged and entreated me to come the following evening, and I promised.

"Minny and I went flying home as light as air, and I dreamt of Wuthering Heights and my sweet, darling cousin till morning.

"On the morrow I was sad, partly because you were poorly, and partly that I wished my father knew and approved of my excursions, but it was beautiful moonlight after tea, and as I rode on, the gloom cleared.

"I shall have another happy evening, I thought to myself, and what delights me more, my pretty Linton will.

"I trotted up their garden, and was turning round to the back, when that fellow Earnshaw met me, took my bridle, and bid me go in by the front entrance. He patted Minny's neck, and said she was a bonny beast, and appeared as if he wanted me to speak to him. I only told him to leave my horse alone, or else it would kick him.

"He answered in his vulgar accent:

"'It wouldn't do mitch hurt if it did,' and surveyed its legs with a smile.

"I was half-inclined to make it try; however, he moved off to open the door, and as he raised the latch, he looked up to the inscription above, and said, with a stupid mixture of awkwardness and elation:

"'Miss Catherine! I can read yon, nah.'

"'Wonderful,' I exclaimed. 'Pray let us hear you... you *are* grown clever!'

"He spelt, and drawled over by syllables, the name 'Hareton Earnshaw'.

"'And the figures?' I cried encouragingly, perceiving that he came to a dead halt.

"'I cannot tell them yet,' he answered.

"'Oh, you dunce!' I said, laughing heartily at his failure.

"The fool stared, with a grin hovering about his lips, and a scowl gathering over his eyes, as if uncertain whether he might not join in my mirth; whether it were not pleasant familiarity, or what it really was, contempt.

"I settled his doubts by suddenly retrieving my gravity and desiring him to walk away, for I came to see Linton, not him.

"He reddened – I saw that by the moonlight – dropped his hand from the latch, and skulked off, a picture of mortified vanity. He imagined himself to be as accomplished as Linton, I suppose, because he could spell his own name, and was marvellously discomfited that I didn't think the same."

"Stop, Miss Catherine, dear!" I interrupted. "I shall not scold, but I don't like your conduct there. If you had remembered that Hareton was your cousin as much as Master Heathcliff, you would have felt how improper it was to behave in that way. At least it was praiseworthy ambition for him to desire to be as accomplished as Linton, and probably he did not learn merely to show off: you had made him ashamed of his ignorance before, I have no doubt, and he wished to remedy it and please you. To sneer at his imperfect attempt was very bad breeding. Had *you* been brought up in his circumstances, would you be less rude? He was as quick and as intelligent a child as ever you were, and I'm hurt that he should be despised now, because that base Heathcliff has treated him so unjustly."

"Well, Ellen, you won't cry about it, will you?" she exclaimed, surprised at my earnestness. "But wait, and you shall hear if he conned his ABC to please me, and if it were worthwhile being civil to the brute. I entered; Linton was lying on the settle, and half-got up to welcome me.

"'I'm ill tonight, Catherine, love,' he said, 'and you must have all the talk, and let me listen. Come and sit by me... I was sure you wouldn't break your word, and I'll make you promise again before you go.'

"I knew now that I mustn't tease him, as he was ill, and I spoke softly and put no questions, and avoided irritating him in any way. I had brought some of my nicest books for him; he asked me to read a little of one, and I was about to comply, when Earnshaw burst the door open, having gathered venom with reflection. He advanced direct to us, seized Linton by the arm, and swung him off the seat.

"'Get to thy own room!' he said in a voice almost inarticulate with passion, and his face looked swelled and furious. 'Take her there if she comes to see thee: thou shalln't keep me out of this. Begone wi' ye both!'

"He swore at us, and left Linton no time to answer, nearly throwing him into the kitchen, and he clenched his fist as I followed, seemingly longing to knock me down. I was afraid for a moment, and I let one volume fall; he kicked it after me, and shut us out.

"I heard a malignant, crackly laugh by the fire, and turning, beheld that odious Joseph, standing, rubbing his bony hands and quivering.

"'Aw wer sure he'd sarve ye aht!* He's a grand lad! He's getten t' raight sperrit in him! *He* knaws… ay, he knaws, as weel as Aw do, who sud be t' maister yonder… Ech, ech, ech! He mad ye skift* properly! Ech, ech, ech!'

"'Where must we go?' I asked of my cousin, disregarding the old wretch's mockery.

"Linton was white and trembling. He was not pretty then, Ellen – oh, no! He looked frightful, for his thin face and large eyes were wrought into an expression of frantic, powerless fury. He grasped the handle of the door and shook it: it was fastened inside.

"'If you don't let me in, I'll kill you! If you don't let me in, I'll kill you!' he rather shrieked than said. 'Devil! Devil! I'll kill you, I'll kill you!'

"Joseph uttered his croaking laugh again.

"'Thear, that's t' father!' he cried. 'That's father! We've allas summut uh orther* side in us… Niver heed, Hareton, lad – dunnut be 'feard – he cannot get at thee!'

"I took hold of Linton's hands and tried to pull him away, but he shrieked so shockingly that I dared not proceed. At last his cries were choked by a dreadful fit of coughing; blood gushed from his mouth, and he fell on the ground.

"I ran into the yard, sick with terror, and called for Zillah as loud as I could. She soon heard me; she was milking the cows in a shed behind the barn, and, hurrying from her work, she enquired what there was to do?

"I hadn't breath to explain; dragging her in, I looked about for Linton. Earnshaw had come out to examine the mischief he had caused, and he was then conveying the poor thing upstairs. Zillah and I ascended after him, but he stopped me at the top of the steps and said I shouldn't go in; I must go home.

"I exclaimed that he had killed Linton, and I *would* enter.

"Joseph locked the door and declared I should do 'no sich stuff', and asked me whether I were 'bahn* to be as mad as him'.

"I stood crying till the housekeeper reappeared. She affirmed he would be better in a bit, but he couldn't do with that shrieking and din, and she took me and nearly carried me into the house.

"Ellen, I was ready to tear my hair off my head! I sobbed and wept so that my eyes were almost blind, and the ruffian you have such sympathy with stood opposite, presuming every now and then to bid me 'whisht',[14] and denying that it was his fault, and, finally frightened by my assertions that I would tell Papa, and that he should be put in prison and hanged, he commenced blubbering himself, and hurried out to hide his cowardly agitation.

"Still I was not rid of him: when at length they compelled me to depart, and I had got some hundred yards off the premises, he suddenly issued from the shadow of the roadside, and checked Minny and took hold of me.

"'Miss Catherine, I'm ill-grieved,' he began, 'but it's rayther too bad—'

"I gave him a cut with my whip, thinking perhaps he would murder me. He let go, thundering one of his horrid curses, and I galloped home more than half out of my senses.

"I didn't bid you goodnight that evening, and I didn't go to Wuthering Heights the next: I wished to go exceedingly, but I was strangely excited, and dreaded to hear that Linton was dead sometimes, and sometimes shuddered at the thought of encountering Hareton.

"On the third day I took courage: at least, I couldn't bear longer suspense, and stole off once more. I went at five o'clock, and walked, fancying I might manage to creep into the house and up to Linton's room unobserved. However, the dogs gave notice of my approach. Zillah received me, and saying 'the lad was mending nicely', showed me into a small, tidy, carpeted apartment, where to my inexpressible joy I beheld Linton laid on a little sofa, reading one of my books. But he would neither speak to me nor look at me through a whole hour, Ellen… He has such an unhappy temper. And what quite confounded me, when he did open his mouth, it was to utter the falsehood that I had occasioned the uproar, and Hareton was not to blame!

"Unable to reply except passionately, I got up and walked from the room. He sent after me a faint 'Catherine!' He did not reckon on being answered so – but I wouldn't turn back, and the morrow was the second day on which I stayed at home, nearly determined to visit him no more.

"But it was so miserable going to bed, and getting up, and never hearing anything about him, that my resolution melted into air before it was properly formed. It *had* appeared wrong to take the journey once; now it seemed wrong to refrain. Michael came to ask if he must saddle Minny; I said yes, and considered myself doing a duty as she bore me over the hills.

"I was forced to pass the front windows to get to the court: it was no use trying to conceal my presence.

"'Young master is in the house,' said Zillah, as she saw me making for the parlour.

"I went in; Earnshaw was there also, but he quitted the room directly. Linton sat in the great armchair half-asleep; walking up to the fire, I began in a serious tone, partly meaning it to be true:

"'As you don't like me, Linton, and as you think I come on purpose to hurt you, and pretend that I do so every time, this is our last meeting – let us say goodbye, and tell Mr Heathcliff that you have no wish to see me, and that he mustn't invent any more falsehoods on the subject.'

"'Sit down and take your hat off, Catherine,' he answered. 'You are so much happier than I am, you ought to be better. Papa talks enough of my defects, and shows enough scorn of me, to make it natural I should doubt myself... I doubt whether I am not altogether as worthless as he calls me frequently, and then I feel so cross and bitter I hate everybody! I *am* worthless, and bad in temper and bad in spirit, almost always, and if you choose, you may say goodbye: you'll get rid of an annoyance. Only, Catherine, do me this justice: believe that if I might be as sweet, and as kind, and as good as you are, I would be, as willingly, and more so than as happy and as healthy. And believe that your kindness has made me love you deeper than if I deserved your love, and though I couldn't, and cannot help showing my nature to you, I regret it and repent it, and shall regret and repent it till I die!'

"I felt he spoke the truth, and I felt I must forgive him, and though we should quarrel the next moment, I must forgive him again. We were reconciled, but we cried, both of us, the whole time I stayed – not entirely for sorrow, yet I *was* sorry Linton had that distorted nature. He'll never let his friends be at ease, and he'll never be at ease himself!

"I have always gone to his little parlour since that night, because his father returned the day after. About three times, I think, we have been merry and hopeful, as we were the first evening; the rest of my visits were dreary and troubled – now with his selfishness and spite, and now with his sufferings – but I've learnt to endure the former with nearly as little resentment as the latter.

"Mr Heathcliff purposely avoids me. I have hardly seen him at all. Last Sunday, indeed, coming earlier than usual, I heard him abusing poor Linton cruelly for his conduct of the night before. I can't tell how he knew of it, unless he listened. Linton had certainly behaved provokingly; however, it was the business of nobody but me, and I interrupted Mr Heathcliff's lecture by entering and telling him so. He burst into a laugh and went away, saying he was glad I took that view of the matter. Since then, I've told Linton he must whisper his bitter things.

"Now, Ellen, you have heard all. I can't be prevented from going to Wuthering Heights, except by inflicting misery on two people, whereas, if you'll only not tell Papa, my going need disturb the tranquillity of none. You'll not tell, will you? It will be very heartless, if you do."

"I'll make up my mind on that point by tomorrow, Miss Catherine," I replied. "It requires some study, and so I'll leave you to your rest and go think it over."

I thought it over aloud in my master's presence, walking straight from her room to his, and relating the whole story, with the exception of her conversations with her cousin, and any mention of Hareton.

Mr Linton was alarmed and distressed more than he would acknowledge to me. In the morning, Catherine learnt my betrayal of her confidence, and she learnt also that her secret visits were to end.

In vain she wept and writhed against the interdict, and implored her father to have pity on Linton: all she got to comfort her was a promise that he would write and give him leave to come to the Grange when he pleased, but explaining that he must no longer expect to see Catherine at Wuthering Heights. Perhaps, had he been aware of his nephew's disposition and state of health, he would have seen fit to withhold even that slight consolation.

25

"THESE THINGS HAPPENED last winter, sir," said Mrs Dean, "hardly more than a year ago. Last winter I did not think, at another twelve months' end, I should be amusing a stranger to the family with relating them! Yet who knows how long you'll be a stranger? You're too young to rest always contented living by yourself, and I some way fancy no one could see Catherine Linton and not love her. You smile, but why do you look so lively and interested when I talk about her? And why have you asked me to hang her picture over your fireplace? And why—"

"Stop, my good friend!" I cried. "It may be very possible that I should love her, but would she love me? I doubt it too much to venture my tranquillity by running into temptation, and then my home is not here. I'm of the busy world, and to its arms I must return. Go on. Was Catherine obedient to her father's commands?"

"She was," continued the housekeeper. "Her affection for him was still the chief sentiment in her heart, and he spoke without anger; he spoke in the deep tenderness of one about to leave his treasure amid perils and foes, where his remembered words would be the only aid that he could bequeath to guide her.

He said to me a few days afterwards:

"I wish my nephew would write, Ellen, or call. Tell me sincerely what you think of him: is he changed for the better, or is there a prospect of improvement, as he grows a man?"

"He's very delicate, sir," I replied, "and scarcely likely to reach manhood; but this I can say: he does not resemble his father, and if Miss Catherine had the misfortune to marry him, he would not be beyond her control, unless she were extremely and foolishly indulgent. However, master, you'll have plenty of time to get acquainted with him and see whether he would suit her: it wants four years and more to his being of age."

Edgar sighed and, walking to the window, looked out towards Gimmerton Kirk. It was a misty afternoon, but the February sun shone dimly, and we could just distinguish the two fir trees in the yard, and the sparely scattered gravestones.

"I've prayed often," he half-soliloquized, "for the approach of what is coming, and now I begin to shrink, and fear it. I thought the memory of the hour I came down that glen a bridegroom would be less sweet than the anticipation that I was soon, in a few months, or possibly weeks, to be carried up, and laid in its lonely hollow! Ellen, I've been very happy with my little Cathy: through winter nights and summer days she was a living hope at my side. But I've been as happy musing by myself among those stones, under that old church, lying, through

214

the long June evenings, on the green mound of her mother's grave, and wishing, yearning for the time when I might lie beneath it. What can I do for Cathy? How must I quit her? I'd not care one moment for Linton being Heathcliff's son, nor for his taking her from me, if he could console her for my loss. I'd not care that Heathcliff gained his ends and triumphed in robbing me of my last blessing! But should Linton be unworthy – only a feeble tool to his father – I cannot abandon her to him! And, hard though it be to crush her buoyant spirit, I must persevere in making her sad while I live, and leaving her solitary when I die. Darling! I'd rather resign her to God and lay her in the earth before me."

"Resign her to God as it is, sir," I answered, "and if we should lose you – which may He forbid under His providence – I'll stand her friend and counsellor to the last. Miss Catherine is a good girl: I don't fear that she will go wilfully wrong, and people who do their duty are always finally rewarded."

Spring advanced, yet my master gathered no real strength, though he resumed his walks in the grounds with his daughter. To her inexperienced notions, this itself was a sign of convalescence, and then his cheek was often flushed, and his eyes were bright; she felt sure of his recovering.

On her seventeenth birthday he did not visit the churchyard: it was raining, and I observed:

"You'll surely not go out tonight, sir?"

He answered:

"No, I'll defer it this year a little longer."

He wrote again to Linton, expressing his great desire to see him, and had the invalid been presentable, I've no doubt his father would have permitted him to come. As it was, being instructed, he returned an answer, intimating that Mr Heathcliff objected to his calling at the Grange, but his uncle's kind remembrance delighted him, and he hoped to meet him sometimes in his rambles, and personally to petition that his cousin and he might not remain long so utterly divided.

That part of his letter was simple, and probably his own. Heathcliff knew he could plead eloquently for Catherine's company, then:

"I do not ask," he said, "that she may visit here, but am I never to see her, because my father forbids me to go to her home, and you forbid her to come to mine? Do, now and then, ride with her towards the Heights, and let us exchange a few words in your presence! We have done nothing to deserve this separation, and you are not angry with me: you have no reason to dislike me, you allow yourself. Dear Uncle! Send me a kind note tomorrow, and leave to join you anywhere you please, except at Thrushcross Grange. I believe an interview would convince you that my father's character is not mine; he affirms I am more your nephew than his son, and though I have faults which render me unworthy of Catherine, she has excused them, and for her sake you should also. You enquire after my health – it is better; but while I remain cut off from all hope and doomed to solitude, or the society of those who never did and never will like me, how can I be cheerful and well?"

Edgar, though he felt for the boy, could not consent to grant his request, because he could not accompany Catherine.

He said in summer perhaps they might meet; meantime he wished him to continue writing at intervals, and engaged to give him what advice and comfort he was able by letter, being well aware of his hard position in his family.

Linton complied, and had he been unrestrained, would probably have spoilt all by filling his epistles with complaints and lamentations, but his father kept a sharp watch over him, and of course insisted on every line that my master sent being shown, so instead of penning his peculiar personal sufferings and distresses – the themes constantly uppermost in his thoughts – he harped on the cruel obligation of being held asunder from his friend and love, and gently intimated that Mr Linton must allow an interview soon, or he should fear he was purposely deceiving him with empty promises.

Cathy was a powerful ally at home, and between them they at length persuaded my master to acquiesce in their having a ride or a walk together about once a week under my guardianship, and on the moors nearest the Grange, for June found him still declining. Though he had set aside yearly a portion of his income for my young lady's fortune, he had a natural desire that she might retain – or at least return in a short time to – the house of her ancestors, and he considered her only prospect of doing that was by a union with his heir: he had no idea that the latter was failing almost as fast as himself; nor had anyone, I believe: no doctor visited the Heights, and no one saw Master Heathcliff to make report of his condition among us.

CHAPTER 26

I for my part began to fancy my forebodings were false, and that he must be actually rallying, when he mentioned riding and walking on the moors, and seemed so earnest in pursuing his object.

I could not picture a father treating a dying child as tyrannically and wickedly as I afterwards learnt Heathcliff had treated him, to compel this apparent eagerness, his efforts redoubling the more imminently his avaricious and unfeeling plans were threatened with defeat by death.

26

SUMMER WAS ALREADY PAST ITS PRIME when Edgar reluctantly yielded his assent to their entreaties, and Catherine and I set out on our first ride to join her cousin.

It was a close, sultry day, devoid of sunshine, but with a sky too dappled and hazy to threaten rain, and our place of meeting had been fixed at the guide stone by the crossroads. On arriving there, however, a little herdboy, dispatched as a messenger, told us that:

"Maister Linton wer just ut this side th' Heights, and he'd be mitch obleeged to us to gang on a bit further."

"Then Master Linton has forgot the first injunction of his uncle," I observed, "he bid us keep on the Grange land, and here we are off at once."

"Well, we'll turn our horses' heads round when we reach him," answered my companion, "our excursion shall lie towards home."

But when we reached him, and that was scarcely a quarter of a mile from his own door, we found he had no horse, and we were forced to dismount and leave ours to graze.

He lay on the heath awaiting our approach, and did not rise till we came within a few yards. Then he walked so feebly, and looked so pale, that I immediately exclaimed:

"Why, Master Heathcliff, you are not fit for enjoying a ramble this morning. How ill you do look!"

Catherine surveyed him with grief and astonishment, and changed the ejaculation of joy on her lips to one of alarm; and the congratulation on their long-postponed meeting to an anxious enquiry whether he were worse than usual?

"No – better – better!" he panted, trembling, and retaining her hand as if he needed its support, while his large blue eyes wandered timidly over her, the hollowness round them transforming to haggard wildness the languid expression they once possessed.

"But you have been worse," persisted his cousin, "worse than when I saw you last – you are thinner, and—"

"I'm tired," he interrupted hurriedly. "It is too hot for walking, let us rest here. And in the morning I often feel sick… Papa says I grow so fast."

Badly satisfied, Cathy sat down, and he reclined beside her.

"This is something like your paradise," said she, making an effort at cheerfulness. "You recollect the two days we agreed to spend in the place and way each thought pleasantest? This is nearly yours, only there are clouds, but then they are so soft and mellow: it is nicer than sunshine. Next week, if you can, we'll ride down to the Grange Park and try mine."

Linton did not appear to remember what she talked of, and he had evidently great difficulty in sustaining any kind of conversation. His lack of interest in the subjects she started, and his equal incapacity to contribute to her entertainment, were so obvious that she could not conceal her disappointment. An indefinite alteration had come over his whole person and manner. The pettishness that might be caressed into fondness had yielded to a listless apathy; there was less of the peevish temper of a child which frets and teases on purpose to be soothed, and more of the self-absorbed moroseness of a confirmed invalid, repelling consolation and ready to regard the good-humoured mirth of others as an insult.

Catherine perceived as well as I did that he held it rather a punishment than a gratification to endure our company, and she made no scruple of proposing presently to depart.

That proposal unexpectedly roused Linton from his lethargy, and threw him into a strange state of agitation. He glanced fearfully towards the Heights, begging she would remain another half-hour at least.

"But I think," said Cathy, "you'd be more comfortable at home than sitting here, and I cannot amuse you today, I see, by my tales and songs and chatter: you have grown wiser than I in these six months; you have little taste for my diversions now, or else, if I could amuse you, I'd willingly stay."

"Stay to rest yourself," he replied. "And Catherine, don't think or say that I'm *very* unwell: it is the heavy weather and heat that make me dull, and I walked about, before you came, a great deal for me. Tell Uncle I'm in tolerable health, will you?"

"I'll tell him that *you* say so, Linton. I couldn't affirm that you are," observed my young lady, wondering at his pertinacious assertion of what was evidently an untruth.

"And be here again next Thursday," continued he, shunning her puzzled gaze. "And give him my thanks for permitting you to come – my best thanks, Catherine. And… and if you *did* meet my father, and he asked you about me, don't lead him to suppose that I've been extremely silent and stupid – don't look sad and downcast as you *are* doing – he'll be angry."

"I care nothing for his anger," exclaimed Cathy, imagining she would be its object.

"But I do," said her cousin, shuddering. "*Don't* provoke him against me, Catherine, for he is very hard."

"Is he severe to you, Master Heathcliff?" I enquired. "Has he grown weary of indulgence, and passed from passive to active hatred?"

Linton looked at me, but did not answer, and after keeping her seat by his side another ten minutes, during which his head fell drowsily on his breast and he uttered nothing except suppressed moans of exhaustion or pain, Cathy began to seek solace in looking for bilberries, and sharing the produce of her researches with me – she did not offer them to him, for she saw further notice would only weary and annoy.

"Is it half an hour now, Ellen?" she whispered in my ear at last. "I can't tell why we should stay. He's asleep, and Papa will be wanting us back."

"Well, we must not leave him asleep," I answered, "wait till he wakes, and be patient. You were mighty eager to set off, but your longing to see poor Linton has soon evaporated!"

"Why did *he* wish to see me?" returned Catherine. "In his crossest humours, formerly, I liked him better than I do in his present curious mood. It's just as if it were a task he was compelled to perform – this interview – for fear his father should scold him. But I'm hardly going to come to give Mr Heathcliff pleasure, whatever reason he may have for ordering Linton to undergo this penance. And though I'm glad he's better in health, I'm sorry he's so much less pleasant, and so much less affectionate to me."

"You think *he is* better in health then?" I said.

"Yes," she answered, "because he always made such a great deal of his sufferings, you know. He is not tolerably well, as he told me to tell Papa, but he's better, very likely."

"There you differ with me, Miss Cathy," I remarked, "I should conjecture him to be far worse."

Linton here started from his slumber in bewildered terror, and asked if anyone had called his name.

"No," said Catherine, "unless in dreams. I cannot conceive how you manage to doze out of doors in the morning."

"I thought I heard my father," he gasped, glancing up to the frowning nab above us. "You are sure nobody spoke?"

"Quite sure," replied his cousin. "Only Ellen and I were disputing concerning your health. Are you truly stronger, Linton, than when we separated in winter? If you be, I'm certain one thing is not stronger – your regard for me – speak, are you?"

The tears gushed from Linton's eyes as he answered:

"Yes, yes, I am!"

And still under the spell of the imaginary voice, his gaze wandered up and down to detect its owner.

Cathy rose.

"For today we must part," she said. "And I won't conceal that I have been sadly disappointed with our meeting, though I'll mention it to nobody but you – not that I stand in awe of Mr Heathcliff!"

"Hush," murmured Linton, "for God's sake, hush! He's coming." And he clung to Catherine's arm, striving to detain her, but at that announcement she hastily disengaged herself and whistled to Minny, who obeyed her like a dog.

"I'll be here next Thursday," she cried, springing to the saddle. "Goodbye. Quick, Ellen!"

And so we left him, scarcely conscious of our departure, so absorbed was he in anticipating his father's approach.

Before we reached home, Catherine's displeasure softened into a perplexed sensation of pity and regret, largely blended with vague, uneasy doubts about Linton's actual circumstances, physical and social – in which I partook, though I counselled her not to say much, for a second journey would make us better judges.

My master requested an account of our ongoings. His nephew's offering of thanks was duly delivered, Miss Cathy gently touching on the rest; I also threw little light on his enquiries, for I hardly knew what to hide and what to reveal.

27

SEVEN DAYS GLIDED AWAY, every one marking its course by the henceforth rapid alteration of Edgar Linton's state. The havoc that months had previously wrought was now emulated by the inroads of hours.

Catherine we would fain have deluded yet, but her own quick spirit refused to delude her: it divined in secret, and brooded on the dreadful probability, gradually ripening into certainty.

She had not the heart to mention her ride, when Thursday came round; I mentioned it for her, and obtained permission to order her out of doors: for the library, where her father stopped a short time daily – the brief period he could bear to sit up – and his chamber, had become her whole world. She grudged each moment that did not find her bending over his pillow, or seated by his side. Her countenance grew wan with watching and sorrow, and my master gladly dismissed her to what he flattered himself would be a happy change of scene and society, drawing comfort from the hope that she would not now be left entirely alone after his death.

He had a fixed idea, I guessed by several observations he let fall, that as his nephew resembled him in person he would resemble him in mind, for Linton's letters bore few or no indications of his defective character. And I through pardonable weakness refrained from correcting the error, asking myself what good there would be in disturbing his last moments with information that he had neither power nor opportunity to turn to account.

We deferred our excursion till the afternoon, a golden afternoon of August – every breath from the hills so full of life that it seemed whoever respired it, though dying, might revive.

Catherine's face was just like the landscape – shadows and sunshine flitting over it in rapid succession, but the shadows rested longer and the sunshine was more transient, and her poor little heart reproached itself for even that passing forgetfulness of its cares.

We discerned Linton watching at the same spot he had selected before. My young mistress alighted and told me that, as she was resolved to stay a very little while, I had better hold the pony and remain on horseback, but I dissented: I wouldn't risk losing sight of the charge committed to me a minute, so we climbed the slope of heath together.

Master Heathcliff received us with greater animation on this occasion – not the animation of high spirits though, nor yet of joy; it looked more like fear.

"It is late!" he said, speaking short and with difficulty. "Is not your father very ill? I thought you wouldn't come."

"*Why* won't you be candid?" cried Catherine, swallowing her greeting. "Why cannot you say at once you don't want me? It is strange, Linton, that for the second time you have brought me here on purpose, apparently to distress us both, and for no reason besides!"

Linton shivered and glanced at her, half-supplicating, half-ashamed, but his cousin's patience was not sufficient to endure this enigmatical behaviour.

"My father *is* very ill," she said, "and why am I called from his bedside? Why didn't you send to absolve me from my promise, when you wished I wouldn't keep it? Come! I desire an explanation – playing and trifling are completely banished out of my mind, and I can't dance attendance on your affections now!"

"My affections!" he murmured, "what are they? For Heaven's sake, Catherine, don't look so angry! Despise me as much as you please; I am a worthless, cowardly wretch – I can't be scorned enough, but I'm too mean for your anger – hate my father, and spare me for contempt."

"Nonsense!" cried Catherine in a passion. "Foolish, silly boy! And there he trembles, as if I were really going to touch him! You needn't bespeak contempt, Linton: anybody will have it spontaneously at your service. Get off! I shall return home – it is folly dragging you from the hearthstone, and pretending... what do we pretend? Let go my frock! If I pitied you for crying and looking so very frightened, you should spurn such pity! Ellen, tell him how disgraceful this conduct is. Rise, and don't degrade yourself into an abject reptile – *don't*."

With streaming face and an expression of agony, Linton had thrown his nerveless frame along the ground: he seemed convulsed with exquisite terror.

"Oh!" he sobbed, "I cannot bear it! Catherine, Catherine, I'm a traitor too, and I dare not tell you! But leave me and I shall be killed! *Dear* Catherine, my life is in your hands, and you have said you loved me, and if you did, it wouldn't harm you. You'll not go, then? Kind, sweet, good Catherine! And perhaps you *will* consent – and he'll let me die with you!"

My young lady, on witnessing his intense anguish, stooped to raise him. The old feeling of indulgent tenderness overcame her vexation, and she grew thoroughly moved and alarmed.

"Consent to what?" she asked. "To stay? Tell me the meaning of this strange talk, and I will. You contradict your own words and distract me! Be calm and frank, and confess at once all that weighs on your heart. You wouldn't injure me, Linton, would you? You wouldn't let any enemy hurt me, if you could prevent it? I'll believe you are a coward for yourself, but not a cowardly betrayer of your best friend."

"But my father threatened me," gasped the boy, clasping his attenuated fingers, "and I dread him – I dread him! I *dare* not tell!"

"Oh well!" said Catherine with scornful compassion. "Keep your secret: *I'm* no coward. Save yourself; I'm not afraid!"

Her magnanimity provoked his tears: he wept wildly, kissing her supporting hands, and yet could not summon courage to speak out.

I was cogitating what the mystery might be, and determined Catherine should never suffer to benefit him, or anyone else, by my goodwill, when, hearing a rustle among the ling,* I looked up and saw Mr Heathcliff almost close upon us, descending the Heights. He didn't cast a glance towards my companions, though they were sufficiently near for Linton's sobs to be audible, but, hailing me in the almost hearty tone he assumed to none besides – and the sincerity of which I couldn't avoid doubting – he said:

"It is something to see you so near to my house, Nelly! How are you at the Grange? Let us hear! The rumour goes," he added in a lower tone, "that Edgar Linton is on his deathbed – perhaps they exaggerate his illness?"

"No, my master is dying," I replied, "it is true enough. A sad thing it will be for us all, but a blessing for him!"

"How long will he last, do you think?" he asked.

"I don't know," I said.

"Because," he continued, looking at the two young people, who were fixed under his eye – Linton appeared as if he could not venture to stir or raise his head, and Catherine could not move on his account – "because that lad yonder seems determined to beat me; and I'd thank his uncle to be quick, and go before him... Hallo! Has the whelp been playing that game long? I *did* give him some lessons about snivelling. Is he pretty lively with Miss Linton generally?"

"Lively? No – he has shown the greatest distress," I answered. "To see him, I should say that instead of rambling with his sweetheart on the hills, he ought to be in bed, under the hands of a doctor."

"He shall be, in a day or two," muttered Heathcliff. "But first – get up, Linton! Get up!" he shouted. "Don't grovel on the ground there – up, this moment!"

Linton had sunk prostrate again in another paroxysm of helpless fear, caused by his father's glance towards him, I suppose: there was nothing else to produce such humiliation. He made several efforts to obey, but his little strength was annihilated for the time, and he fell back again with a moan.

Mr Heathcliff advanced, and lifted him to lean against a ridge of turf.

"Now," said he, with curbed ferocity, "I'm getting angry – and if you don't command that paltry spirit of yours... *Damn* you! Get up directly!"

"I will, Father!" he panted. "Only, let me alone, or I shall faint. I've done as you wished, I'm sure. Catherine will tell you that I... that I... have been cheerful. Ah! Keep by me, Catherine; give me your hand."

"Take mine," said his father; "stand on your feet. There now – she'll lend you her arm – that's right, look at *her*. You would imagine I was the Devil himself, Miss Linton, to excite such horror. Be so kind as to walk home with him, will you? He shudders if I touch him."

"Linton dear!" whispered Catherine, "I can't go to Wuthering Heights... Papa has forbidden me... He'll not harm you: why are you so afraid?"

"I can never re-enter that house," he answered. "I'm *not* to re-enter it without you!"

"Stop!" cried his father. "We'll respect Catherine's filial scruples. Nelly, take him in, and I'll follow your advice concerning the doctor without delay."

"You'll do well," replied I, "but I must remain with my mistress. To mind your son is not my business."

"You are very stiff!" said Heathcliff. "I know that – but you'll force me to pinch the baby and make it scream before it moves your charity. Come then, my hero. Are you willing to return, escorted by me?"

He approached once more, and made as if he would seize the fragile being, but, shrinking back, Linton clung to his cousin and implored her to accompany him with a frantic importunity that admitted no denial.

However I disapproved, I couldn't hinder her; indeed, how could she have refused him herself? What was filling him with dread we had no means of discerning, but there he was, powerless under its gripe, and any addition seemed capable of shocking him into idiocy.

We reached the threshold; Catherine walked in, and I stood waiting till she had conducted the invalid to a chair, expecting her out immediately, when Mr Heathcliff, pushing me forwards, exclaimed:

"My house is not stricken with the plague, Nelly, and I have a mind to be hospitable today – sit down, and allow me to shut the door."

He shut and locked it also. I started.

"You shall have tea before you go home," he added. "I am by myself. Hareton is gone with some cattle to the lees,* and Zillah and Joseph are off on a journey of pleasure, and though I'm used to being alone, I'd rather have some interesting company if I can get it. Miss Linton, take your seat by *him*. I give you what I have: the present is hardly worth accepting, but I have nothing else to offer. It is Linton, I mean. How she does stare! It's odd what a savage feeling I have to anything that seems afraid of me! Had I been born where laws are less strict and tastes less dainty, I should treat myself to a slow vivisection of those two as an evening's amusement."

He drew in his breath, struck the table, and swore to himself:

"By hell! I hate them."

"I'm not afraid of you!" exclaimed Catherine, who could not hear the latter part of his speech.

She stepped close up, her black eyes flashing with passion and resolution. "Give me that key – I will have it!" she said. "I wouldn't eat or drink here if I were starving."

Heathcliff had the key in his hand that remained on the table. He looked up, seized with a sort of surprise at her boldness, or possibly reminded by her voice and glance of the person from whom she inherited it.

She snatched at the instrument, and half-succeeded in getting it out of his loosened fingers, but her action recalled him to the present; he recovered it speedily.

"Now, Catherine Linton," he said, "stand off, or I shall knock you down, and that will make Mrs Dean mad."

Regardless of this warning, she captured his closed hand and its contents again.

"We *will* go!" she repeated, exerting her utmost efforts to cause the iron muscles to relax, and, finding that her nails made no impression, she applied her teeth pretty sharply.

Heathcliff glanced at me a glance that kept me from interfering a moment. Catherine was too intent on his fingers to notice his face. He opened them suddenly, and resigned the object of dispute, but ere she had well secured it, he seized her with the liberated hand, and, pulling her on his knee, administered with the other a shower of terrific slaps on both sides of the head, each sufficient to have fulfilled his threat, had she been able to fall.

At this diabolical violence I rushed on him furiously.

"You villain!" I began to cry. "You villain!"

A touch on the chest silenced me – I am stout, and soon put out of breath – and what with that and the rage, I staggered dizzily back, and felt ready to suffocate, or to burst a blood vessel.

The scene was over in two minutes; Catherine, released, put her two hands to her temples and looked just as if she were not sure whether her ears were off or on. She trembled like a reed, poor thing, and leant against the table perfectly bewildered.

"I know how to chastise children, you see," said the scoundrel grimly, as he stooped to repossess himself of the key, which had dropped to the floor. "Go to Linton now, as I told you, and cry at your ease! I shall be your father tomorrow – all the father you'll have in a few days – and you shall have plenty of that. You can bear plenty – you're no weakling – you shall have a daily taste, if I catch such a devil of a temper in your eyes again!"

Cathy ran to me instead of Linton, and knelt down, and put her burning cheek on my lap, weeping aloud. Her cousin had shrunk into a corner of the settle, as quiet as a mouse, congratulating himself, I dare say, that the correction had alighted on another than him.

Mr Heathcliff, perceiving us all confounded, rose and expeditiously made the tea himself. The cups and saucers were laid ready. He poured it out and handed me a cup.

"Wash away your spleen," he said. "And help your own naughty pet and mine. It is not poisoned, though I prepared it. I'm going out to seek your horses."

Our first thought, on his departure, was to force an exit somewhere. We tried the kitchen door, but that was fastened outside; we looked at the windows: they were too narrow for even Cathy's little figure.

"Master Linton," I cried, seeing we were regularly imprisoned, "you know what your diabolical father is after, and you shall tell us or I'll box your ears, as he has done your cousin's."

"Yes, Linton, you must tell," said Catherine. "It was for your sake I came, and it will be wickedly ungrateful if you refuse."

"Give me some tea – I'm thirsty – and then I'll tell you," he answered. "Mrs Dean, go away. I don't like you standing over me. Now, Catherine, you are letting your tears fall into my cup! I won't drink that. Give me another."

Catherine pushed another to him and wiped her face. I felt disgusted at the little wretch's composure, since he was no longer in terror for himself. The anguish he had exhibited on the moor subsided as soon as ever he entered Wuthering Heights, so I guessed he had been menaced with an awful visitation of wrath if he failed in decoying us there, and that accomplished, he had no further immediate fears.

"Papa wants us to be married," he continued, after sipping some of the liquid. "And he knows your papa wouldn't let us marry now, and he's afraid of my dying if we wait; so we are to be married in the morning, and you are to stay here all night, and if you do as he wishes, you shall return home next day and take me with you."

"Take you with her, pitiful changeling?" I exclaimed. "*You* marry? Why, the man is mad, or he thinks us fools, every one. And do you imagine that beautiful young lady, that healthy, hearty girl, will tie herself to a little perishing monkey like you? Are you cherishing the notion that *anybody*, let alone Miss Catherine Linton, would have you for a husband? You want whipping for bringing us in here at all, with your dastardly puling tricks, and… don't look so silly, now! I've a very good mind to shake you severely for your contemptible treachery and your imbecile conceit."

I did give him a slight shaking, but it brought on the cough, and he took to his ordinary resource of moaning and weeping, and Catherine rebuked me.

"Stay all night? No!" she said, looking slowly round. "Ellen, I'll burn that door down, but I'll get out."

And she would have commenced the execution of her threat directly, but Linton was up in alarm for his dear self again. He clasped her in his two feeble arms, sobbing:

"Won't you have me, and save me? Not let me come to the Grange? Oh darling Catherine! You mustn't go and leave me, after all. You *must* obey my father, you *must*!"

"I must obey my own," she replied, "and relieve him from this cruel suspense. The whole night! What would he think? He'll be distressed already. I'll either break or burn a way out of the house. Be quiet! You're in no danger, but if you hinder me... Linton, I love Papa better than you!"

The mortal terror he felt of Mr Heathcliff's anger restored to the boy his coward's eloquence. Catherine was near distraught; still she persisted that she must go home, and tried entreaty in her turn, persuading him to subdue his selfish agony.

While they were thus occupied, our jailer re-entered.

"Your beasts have trotted off," he said, "and... now, Linton! Snivelling again? What has she been doing to you? Come, come – have done, and get to bed. In a month or two, my lad, you'll be able to pay her back her present tyrannies with a vigorous hand. You're pining for pure love, are you not? Nothing else in the world – and she shall have you! There, to bed! Zillah won't be here tonight: you must undress yourself. Hush! Hold your noise! Once in your own room, I'll not come near you, you needn't fear. By chance, you've managed tolerably. I'll look to the rest."

He spoke these words, holding the door open for his son to pass, and the latter achieved his exit exactly as a spaniel might which suspected the person who attended on it of designing a spiteful squeeze.

The lock was resecured. Heathcliff approached the fire, where my mistress and I stood silent. Catherine looked up and instinctively raised her hand to her cheek – his neighbourhood revived a painful sensation.

Anybody else would have been incapable of regarding the childish act with sternness, but he scowled on her and muttered:

"Oh, you are not afraid of me? Your courage is well-disguised: you *seem* damnably afraid!"

"I *am* afraid now," she replied, "because if I stay, Papa will be miserable, and how can I endure making him miserable... when he... when he... Mr Heathcliff, *let* me go home! I promise to marry Linton: Papa would like me to, and I love him – and why should you wish to force me to do what I'll willingly do of myself?"

"Let him dare to force you!" I cried. "There's law in the land – thank God there is! – though we be in an out-of-the-way place. I'd inform if he were my own son, and it's felony without benefit of clergy!"*

"Silence!" said the ruffian. "To the devil with your clamour! I don't want *you* to speak. Miss Linton, I shall enjoy myself remarkably in thinking your father will be miserable; I shall not sleep for satisfaction. You could have hit on no surer way of fixing your residence under my roof for the next twenty-four hours than informing me that such an event would follow. As to your promise to marry Linton, I'll take care you shall keep it, for you shall not quit this place till it is fulfilled."

"Send Ellen then, to let Papa know I'm safe!" exclaimed Catherine, weeping bitterly. "Or marry me now. Poor Papa! Ellen, he'll think we're lost. What shall we do?"

"Not he! He'll think you are tired of waiting on him, and run off for a little amusement," answered Heathcliff. "You cannot deny that you entered my house of your own accord, in contempt of his injunctions to the contrary. And it is quite natural that you should desire amusement at your age, and that you would weary of nursing a sick man, and that man *only* your father. Catherine, his happiest days were over when your days began. He cursed you, I dare say, for coming into the world (I did, at least), and it would just do if he cursed you as *he* went out of it. I'd join him. I don't love you! How should I? Weep away. As far as I can see, it will be your chief diversion hereafter, unless Linton make amends for other losses, and your provident parent appears to fancy he may. His letters of advice and consolation entertained me vastly. In his last he recommended my jewel to be careful of his, and kind to her when he got her. Careful and kind – that's paternal! But Linton requires his whole stock of care and kindness for himself.

Linton can play the little tyrant well. He'll undertake to torture any number of cats, if their teeth be drawn and their claws pared. You'll be able to tell his uncle fine tales of his *kindness* when you get home again, I assure you."

"You're right there!" I said. "Explain your son's character. Show his resemblance to yourself, and then I hope Miss Cathy will think twice before she takes the cockatrice!"

"I don't much mind speaking of his amiable qualities now," he answered, "because she must either accept him or remain a prisoner, and you along with her, till your master dies. I can detain you both, quite concealed, here. If you doubt, encourage her to retract her word, and you'll have an opportunity of judging!"

"I'll not retract my word," said Catherine. "I'll marry him within this hour if I may go to Thrushcross Grange afterwards. Mr Heathcliff, you're a cruel man, but you're not a fiend, and you won't, from *mere* malice, destroy irrevocably all my happiness. If Papa thought I had left him on purpose, and if he died before I returned, could I bear to live? I've given over crying, but I'm going to kneel here at your knee, and I'll not get up, and I'll not take my eyes from your face, till you look back at me! No, don't turn away! *Do* look! You'll see nothing to provoke you. I don't hate you. I'm not angry that you struck me. Have you never loved *anybody* in all your life, Uncle? *Never?* Ah! You must look once – I'm so wretched – you can't help being sorry and pitying me."

"Keep your eft's fingers off and move, or I'll kick you!" cried Heathcliff, brutally repulsing her. "I'd rather be hugged by a snake. How the devil can you dream of fawning on me? I *detest* you!"

He shrugged his shoulders – shook himself, indeed, as if his flesh crept with aversion – and thrust back his chair, while I got up and opened my mouth to commence a downright torrent of abuse. But I was rendered dumb in the middle of the first sentence by a threat that I should be shown into a room by myself the very next syllable I uttered.

It was growing dark – we heard a sound of voices at the garden gate. Our host hurried out instantly: *he* had his wits about him; *we* had not. There was a talk of two or three minutes, and he returned alone.

"I thought it had been your cousin Hareton," I observed to Catherine. "I wish he would arrive! Who knows but he might take our part?"

230

"It was three servants sent to seek you from the Grange," said Heathcliff, overhearing me. "You should have opened a lattice and called out, but I could swear that chit is glad you didn't. She's glad to be obliged to stay, I'm certain."

At learning the chance we had missed, we both gave vent to our grief without control, and he allowed us to wail on till nine o'clock. Then he bid us go upstairs, through the kitchen, to Zillah's chamber, and I whispered my companion to obey – perhaps we might contrive to get through the window there, or into a garret and out by its skylight.

The window, however, was narrow, like those below, and the garret trap was safe from our attempts, for we were fastened in as before.

We neither of us lay down: Catherine took her station by the lattice and watched anxiously for morning, a deep sigh being the only answer I could obtain to my frequent entreaties that she would try to rest.

I seated myself in a chair and rocked to and fro, passing harsh judgement on my many derelictions of duty, from which, it struck me then, all the misfortunes of my employers sprang. It was not the case in reality, I am aware, but it was in my imagination, that dismal night, and I thought Heathcliff himself less guilty than I.

At seven o'clock he came and enquired if Miss Linton had risen. She ran to the door immediately, and answered:

"Yes."

"Here, then," he said, opening it and pulling her out.

I rose to follow, but he turned the lock again. I demanded my release.

"Be patient," he replied, "I'll send up your breakfast in a while."

I thumped on the panels and rattled the latch angrily, and Catherine asked why I was still shut up? He answered I must try to endure it another hour, and they went away.

I endured it two or three hours; at length I heard a footstep – not Heathcliff's.

"I've brought you something to eat," said a voice, "oppen t' door!"

Complying eagerly, I beheld Hareton, laden with food enough to last me all day.

"Tak it!" he added, thrusting the tray into my hand.

"Stay one minute," I began.

"Nay!" cried he, and retired, regardless of any prayers I could pour forth to detain him.

And there I remained enclosed the whole day, and the whole of the next night, and another, and another. Five nights and four days I remained altogether, seeing nobody but Hareton once every morning, and he was a model of a jailer: surly, and dumb, and deaf to every attempt at moving his sense of justice or compassion.

28

O N THE FIFTH MORNING, or rather afternoon, a different step approached – lighter and shorter – and this time the person entered the room. It was Zillah, donned in her scarlet shawl, with a black silk bonnet on her head, and a willow basket swung to her arm.

"Eh, dear! Mrs Dean!" she exclaimed. "Well! There is a talk about you at Gimmerton. I never thought but you were sunk in the Blackhorse marsh, and Missy with you, till Master told me you'd been found and he'd lodged you here! What, and you must have got on an island, sure? And how long were you in the hole? Did Master save you, Mrs Dean? But you're not so thin... you've not been so poorly, have you?"

"Your master is a true scoundrel!" I replied. "But he shall answer for it. He needn't have raised that tale – it shall all be laid bare!"

"What do you mean?" asked Zillah. "It's not his tale: they tell that in the village – about your being lost in the marsh – and I calls to Earnshaw, when I come in:

"'Eh, they's queer things, Mr Hareton, happened since I went off. It's a sad pity of that likely young lass and cant[41] Nelly Dean.'

"He stared. I thought he had not heard aught, so I told him the rumour.

"The master listened, and he just smiled to himself and said:

"'If they have been in the marsh, they are out now, Zillah. Nelly Dean is lodged, at this minute, in your room. You can tell her to flit, when you go up – here is the key. The bog water got into her head, and she would have run home quite flighty, but I fixed her till she came round to her senses. You can bid her go to the Grange at once, if she be able, and carry a message from me that her young lady will follow in time to attend the squire's funeral.'"

"Mr Edgar is not dead?" I gasped. "Oh! Zillah, Zillah!"

"No, no, sit you down, my good mistress," she replied, "you're right sickly yet. He's not dead: Doctor Kenneth thinks he may last another day. I met him on the road and asked."

Instead of sitting down, I snatched my outdoor things and hastened below, for the way was free.

On entering the house, I looked about for someone to give information of Catherine.

The place was filled with sunshine, and the door stood wide open, but nobody seemed at hand.

As I hesitated whether to go off at once or return and seek my mistress, a slight cough drew my attention to the hearth.

Linton lay on the settle, sole tenant, sucking a stick of sugar candy and pursuing my movements with apathetic eyes.

"Where is Miss Catherine?" I demanded sternly, supposing I could frighten him into giving intelligence by catching him thus alone.

He sucked on like an innocent.

"Is she gone?" I said.

"No," he replied, "she's upstairs; she's not to go – we won't let her."

"You won't let her, little idiot!" I exclaimed. "Direct me to her room immediately, or I'll make you sing out sharply."

"Papa would make you sing out, if you attempted to get there," he answered. "He says I'm not to be soft with Catherine: she's my wife, and it's shameful that she should wish to leave me! He says she hates me and wants me to die, that she may have my money; but she shan't have it – and she shan't go home! She never shall! She may cry, and be sick as much as she pleases!"

He resumed his former occupation, closing his lids as if he meant to drop asleep.

"Master Heathcliff," I resumed, "have you forgotten all Catherine's kindness to you last winter, when you affirmed you loved her, and when she brought you books and sung you songs, and came many a time through wind and snow to see you? She wept to miss one evening, because you would be disappointed, and you felt then that she was a hundred times too good to you – and now you believe the lies your father tells, though you know he detests you both. And you join him against her. That's fine gratitude, is it not?"

The corner of Linton's mouth fell, and he took the sugar candy from his lips.

"Did she come to Wuthering Heights because she hated you?" I continued. "Think for yourself! As to your money, she does not even know that you will have any. And you say she's sick, and yet you leave her alone up there in a strange house! *You* who have felt what it is to be so neglected! You could pity your own sufferings, and she pitied them, too, but you won't pity hers! I shed tears, Master Heathcliff, you see – an elderly woman, and a servant merely – and you, after pretending such affection, and having reason to worship her almost, store every tear you have for yourself, and lie there quite at ease. Ah, you're a heartless, selfish boy!"

"I can't stay with her," he answered crossly. "I'll not stay by myself. She cries so I can't bear it. And she won't give over, though I say I'll call my father. I did call him once, and he threatened to strangle her if she was not quiet, but she began again the instant he left the room, moaning and grieving all night long, though I screamed for vexation that I couldn't sleep."

"Is Mr Heathcliff out?" I enquired, perceiving that the wretched creature had no power to sympathize with his cousin's mental tortures.

"He's in the court," he replied, "talking to Doctor Kenneth, who says Uncle is dying, truly, at last. I'm glad, for I shall be master of the Grange after him – and Catherine always spoke of it as *her* house. It isn't hers! It's mine: Papa says everything she has is mine. All her nice books are mine; she offered to give me them, and her pretty birds, and her pony Minny, if I would get the key of our room and let her out, but I told her she had nothing to give: they were all, all mine. And then she cried, and took a little picture from her neck, and said I should have that: two pictures in a gold case, on one side her mother, and on the other Uncle, when they were young. That was yesterday – I said they were mine too, and tried to get them from her. The spiteful thing wouldn't let me: she pushed me off and hurt me. I shrieked out – that frightens her – she heard Papa coming, and she broke the hinges and divided the case, and gave me her mother's portrait; the other she attempted to hide, but Papa asked what was the matter, and I explained it. He took the one I had away, and ordered her to resign hers to me; she refused, and he... he struck her down and wrenched it off the chain, and crushed it with his foot."

"And were you pleased to see her struck?" I asked, having my designs in encouraging his talk.

"I winked," he answered. "I wink to see my father strike a dog or a horse; he does it so hard. Yet I was glad at first – she deserved punishing for pushing me – but when Papa was gone, she made me come to the window and showed me her cheek cut on the inside against her teeth, and her mouth filling with blood, and then she gathered up the bits of the picture, and went and sat down with her face to the wall – and she has never spoken to me since, and I sometimes think she can't speak for pain. I don't like to think so, but she's a naughty thing for crying continually, and she looks so pale and wild, I'm afraid of her."

"And you can get the key if you choose?" I said.

"Yes, when I am upstairs," he answered, "but I can't walk upstairs now."

"In what apartment is it?" I asked.

"Oh," he cried, "I shan't tell *you* where it is! It is our secret. Nobody, neither Hareton nor Zillah, is to know. There! You've tired me – go away, go away!" And he turned his face onto his arm, and shut his eyes again.

I considered it best to depart without seeing Mr Heathcliff, and bring a rescue for my young lady from the Grange.

On reaching it, the astonishment of my fellow servants to see me, and their joy also, was intense, and when they heard that their little mistress was safe, two or three were about to hurry up and shout the news at Mr Edgar's door, but I bespoke the announcement of it myself.

How changed I found him, even in those few days! He lay an image of sadness and resignation waiting his death. Very young he looked: though his actual age was thirty-nine, one would have called him ten years younger at least. He thought of Catherine, for he murmured her name. I touched his hand and spoke.

"Catherine is coming, dear master!" I whispered. "She is alive and well, and will be here, I hope, tonight."

I trembled at the first effects of this intelligence: he half rose up, looked eagerly round the apartment, and then sank back in a swoon.

As soon as he recovered, I related our compulsory visit and detention at the Heights. I said Heathcliff forced me to go in, which was not quite true. I uttered as little as possible against Linton, nor did I describe all his father's brutal conduct – my intentions being to add no bitterness, if I could help it, to his already overflowing cup.

He divined that one of his enemy's purposes was to secure the personal property, as well as the estate, to his son – or rather himself – yet why he did not wait till his decease was a puzzle to my master, because ignorant how nearly he and his nephew would quit the world together.

However, he felt that his will had better be altered: instead of leaving Catherine's fortune at her own disposal, he determined to put it in the hands of trustees for her use during life, and for her children, if she had any, after her. By that means, it could not fall to Mr Heathcliff should Linton die.

Having received his orders, I dispatched a man to fetch the attorney, and four more, provided with serviceable weapons, to demand my young lady of her jailer. Both parties were delayed very late. The single servant returned first.

He said Mr Green, the lawyer, was out when he arrived at his house, and he had to wait two hours for his re-entrance, and then Mr Green told him he had a little business in the village that must be done, but he would be at Thrushcross Grange before morning.

The four men came back unaccompanied also. They brought word that Catherine was ill – too ill to quit her room – and Heathcliff would not suffer them to see her.

I scolded the stupid fellows well for listening to that tale, which I would not carry to my master, resolving to take a whole bevy up to the Heights at daylight, and storm it, literally, unless the prisoner were quietly surrendered to us.

Her father *shall* see her, I vowed, and vowed again, if that devil be killed on his own door stones in trying to prevent it!

Happily I was spared the journey and the trouble.

I had gone downstairs at three o'clock to fetch a jug of water, and was passing through the hall with it in my hand, when a sharp knock at the front door made me jump. "Oh! It is Green," I said, recollecting myself, "only Green," and I went on, intending to send somebody else to open it, but the knock was repeated, not loud, but still importunately.

I put the jug on the banister and hastened to admit him myself.

The harvest moon shone clear outside. It was not the attorney. My own sweet little mistress sprang on my neck, sobbing:

"Ellen, Ellen! Is Papa alive?"

"Yes!" I cried. "Yes, my angel, he is! God be thanked, you are safe with us again!"

She wanted to run, breathless as she was, upstairs to Mr Linton's room, but I compelled her to sit down on a chair, and made her drink, and washed her pale face, chafing it into a faint colour with my apron. Then I said I must go first, and tell of her arrival, imploring her to say she should be happy with young Heathcliff. She stared, but, soon comprehending why I counselled her to utter the falsehood, she assured me she would not complain.

I couldn't abide to be present at their meeting. I stood outside the chamber door a quarter of an hour, and hardly ventured near the bed then.

All was composed, however: Catherine's despair was as silent as her father's joy. She supported him calmly, in appearance, and he fixed on her features his raised eyes, that seemed dilating with ecstasy.

He died blissfully, Mr Lockwood; he died so. Kissing her cheek, he murmured:

"I am going to her, and you, darling child, shall come to us," and never stirred or spoke again, but continued that rapt, radiant gaze, till his pulse imperceptibly stopped and his soul departed. None could have noticed the exact minute of his death, it was so entirely without a struggle.

Whether Catherine had spent her tears, or whether the grief were too weighty to let them flow, she sat there dry-eyed till the sun rose – she sat till noon, and would still have remained brooding over that deathbed, but I insisted on her coming away and taking some repose.

It was well I succeeded in removing her, for at dinner time appeared the lawyer, having called at Wuthering Heights to get his instructions how to behave. He had sold himself to Mr Heathcliff: that was the cause of his delay in obeying my master's summons. Fortunately, no thought of worldly affairs crossed the latter's mind to disturb him after his daughter's arrival.

Mr Green took upon himself to order everything and everybody about the place. He gave all the servants but me notice to quit. He would have carried his delegated authority to the point of insisting that Edgar Linton should not be buried beside his wife, but in the chapel with his family. There was the will, however, to hinder that, and my loud protestations against any infringement of its directions.

The funeral was hurried over; Catherine – Mrs Linton Heathcliff now – was suffered to stay at the Grange till her father's corpse had quitted it.

She told me that her anguish had at last spurred Linton to incur the risk of liberating her. She heard the men I sent disputing at the door, and she gathered the sense of Heathcliff's answer. It drove her desperate. Linton, who had been conveyed up to the little parlour soon after I left, was terrified into fetching the key before his father re-ascended.

He had the cunning to unlock and relock the door without shutting it, and when he should have gone to bed, he begged to sleep with Hareton, and his petition was granted for once.

Catherine stole out before break of day. She dared not try the doors lest the dogs should raise an alarm; she visited the empty chambers and examined their windows, and, luckily lighting on her mother's, she got easily out of its lattice and onto the ground, by means of the fir tree close by. Her accomplice suffered for his share in the escape, notwithstanding his timid contrivances.

29

THE EVENING AFTER THE FUNERAL, my young lady and I were seated in the library, now musing mournfully – one of us despairingly – on our loss, now venturing conjectures as to the gloomy future.

We had just agreed the best destiny which could await Catherine would be a permission to continue resident at the Grange, at least during Linton's life – he being allowed to join her there, and I to remain as housekeeper. That seemed rather too favourable an arrangement to be hoped for, and yet I did hope, and began to cheer up under the prospect of retaining my home and my employment, and above all, my beloved young mistress, when a servant – one of the discarded ones not yet departed – rushed hastily in, and said "that devil Heathcliff" was coming through the court: should he fasten the door in his face?

If we had been mad enough to order that proceeding, we had not time. He made no ceremony of knocking or announcing his name: he was master, and availed himself of the master's privilege to walk straight in without saying a word.

The sound of our informant's voice directed him to the library; he entered and, motioning him out, shut the door.

It was the same room into which he had been ushered as a guest, eighteen years before; the same moon shone through the window, and the same autumn landscape lay outside. We had not yet lighted a candle, but all the apartment was visible, even to the portraits on the wall: the splendid head of Mrs Linton, and the graceful one of her husband.

Heathcliff advanced to the hearth. Time had little altered his person either. There was the same man, his dark face rather sallower and more composed, his frame a stone or two heavier, perhaps, and no other difference.

Catherine had risen with an impulse to dash out when she saw him.

"Stop!" he said, arresting her by the arm. "No more runnings away! Where would you go? I'm come to fetch you home, and I hope you'll be a dutiful daughter and not encourage my son to further disobedience. I was embarrassed how to punish him when I discovered his part in the business – he's such a cobweb, a pinch would annihilate him – but you'll see by his look that he has received his due! I brought him down one evening, the day before yesterday, and just set him in a chair, and never touched him afterwards. I sent Hareton out, and we had the room to ourselves. In two hours, I called Joseph to carry him up again, and since then my presence is as potent on his nerves as a ghost, and I fancy he sees me often, though I am not near. Hareton says he wakes and shrieks in the night by the hour together, and calls you to protect him from me; and whether you like your precious mate or not, you must come: he's your concern now; I yield all my interest in him to you."

"Why not let Catherine continue here?" I pleaded, "and send Master Linton to her? As you hate them both, you'd not miss them: they *can* only be a daily plague to your unnatural heart."

"I'm seeking a tenant for the Grange," he answered, "and I want my children about me, to be sure. Besides, that lass owes me her services for her bread; I'm not going to nurture her in luxury and idleness after Linton is gone. Make haste and get ready now, and don't oblige me to compel you."

"I shall," said Catherine. "Linton is all I have to love in the world, and though you have done what you could to make him hateful to me, and me to him, you *cannot* make us hate each other. And I defy you to hurt him when I am by, and I defy you to frighten me!"

"You are a boastful champion," replied Heathcliff, "but I don't like you well enough to hurt him: you shall get the full benefit of the torment as long as it lasts. It is not I who will make him hateful to you: it is his own sweet spirit. He's as bitter as gall at your desertion and its consequences – don't expect thanks for this noble devotion. I heard him draw a pleasant picture to Zillah of what he would do if he were as strong as I – the inclination is there, and his very weakness will sharpen his wits to find a substitute for strength."

"I know he has a bad nature," said Catherine, "he's your son. But I'm glad I've a better, to forgive it, and I know he loves me, and for that reason I love him. Mr Heathcliff, *you* have *nobody* to love you, and however miserable you make us, we shall still have the revenge of thinking that your cruelty arises from your greater misery. You *are* miserable, are you not? Lonely like the devil, and envious like him? *Nobody* loves you… *nobody* will cry for you when you die!* I wouldn't be you!"

Catherine spoke with a kind of dreary triumph: she seemed to have made up her mind to enter into the spirit of her future family and draw pleasure from the griefs of her enemies.

"You shall be sorry to be yourself presently," said her father-in-law, "if you stand there another minute. Begone, witch, and get your things!"

She scornfully withdrew.

In her absence I began to beg for Zillah's place at the Heights, offering to resign mine to her, but he would suffer it on no account. He bid me be silent, and then for the first time allowed himself a glance round the room and a look at the pictures. Having studied Mrs Linton's, he said:

"I shall have that at home. Not because I need it, but…"

He turned abruptly to the fire and continued with what, for lack of a better word, I must call a smile:

"I'll tell you what I did yesterday! I got the sexton who was digging Linton's grave to remove the earth off her coffin lid, and I opened it. I thought, once, I would have stayed there, when I saw her face again – it is hers yet! – he had hard work to stir me, but he said it would change if the air blew on it, and so I struck one side of the coffin loose and covered it up – not Linton's side, damn him! I wish he'd been soldered in lead – and I bribed the sexton to pull it away when I'm laid there, and slide mine out too – I'll have it made so – and then by the time Linton gets to us he'll not know which is which!"

"You were very wicked, Mr Heathcliff!" I exclaimed. "Were you not ashamed to disturb the dead?"

"I disturbed nobody, Nelly," he replied, "and I gave some ease to myself. I shall be a great deal more comfortable now, and you'll have a better chance of keeping me underground when I get there. Disturbed her? No! She has disturbed me, night and day, through eighteen years – incessantly – remorselessly – till yesternight, and yesternight I was tranquil. I dreamt I was sleeping the last sleep by that sleeper, with my heart stopped and my cheek frozen against hers."

"And if she had been dissolved into earth, or worse, what would you have dreamt of then?" I said.

"Of dissolving with her, and being more happy still!" he answered. "Do you suppose I dread any change of that sort? I expected such a transformation on raising the lid, but I'm better pleased that it should not commence till I share it. Besides, unless I had received a distinct impression of her passionless features, that strange feeling would hardly have been removed. It began oddly. You know, I was wild after she died, and eternally, from dawn to dawn, praying her to return to me her spirit! I have a strong faith in ghosts; I have a conviction that they can, and do, exist among us!

"The day she was buried, there came a fall of snow. In the evening I went to the churchyard. It blew bleak as winter – all round was solitary. I didn't fear that her fool of a husband would wander up the den* so late, and no one else had business to bring them there.

"Being alone, and conscious two yards of loose earth was the sole barrier between us, I said to myself:

"'I'll have her in my arms again! If she be cold, I'll think it is this north wind that chills *me*, and if she be motionless, it is sleep.'

"I got a spade from the tool house, and began to delve with all my might – it scraped the coffin. I fell to work with my hands; the wood commenced cracking about the screws. I was on the point of attaining my object, when it seemed that I heard a sigh from someone above, close at the edge of the grave, and bending down. 'If I can only get this off,' I muttered, 'I wish they may shovel in the earth over us both!' and I wrenched at it more desperately still. There was another sigh, close at my ear. I appeared to feel the warm breath of it displacing the sleet-laden wind. I knew no living thing in flesh and blood was by, but, as certainly as you perceive the approach to some substantial body in the dark, though it cannot be discerned, so certainly I felt that Cathy was there, not under me, but on the earth.

"A sudden sense of relief flowed from my heart through every limb. I relinquished my labour of agony, and turned, consoled at once – unspeakably consoled. Her presence was with me: it remained while I refilled the grave and led me home. You may laugh if you will, but I was sure I should see her there. I was sure she was with me, and I could not help talking to her.

"Having reached the Heights, I rushed eagerly to the door. It was fastened, and I remember that accursed Earnshaw and my wife opposed my entrance. I remember stopping to kick the breath out of him, and then hurrying upstairs to my room and hers. I looked round impatiently – I felt her by me – I could *almost* see her, and yet I *could not*! I ought to have sweat blood then, from the anguish of my yearning, from the fervour of my supplications to have but one glimpse! I had not one. She showed herself, as she often was in life, a devil to me! And since then, sometimes more and sometimes less, I've been the sport of that intolerable torture! Infernal! Keeping my nerves at such a stretch that, if they had not resembled catgut, they would long ago have relaxed to the feebleness of Linton's.

"When I sat in the house with Hareton, it seemed that on going out, I should meet her; when I walked on the moors I should meet her coming in. When I went from home I hastened to return: she *must* be somewhere at the Heights, I was certain! And when I slept in her chamber, I was beaten out of that.* I couldn't lie there, for the moment I closed my eyes, she was either outside the window, or sliding back the panels, or entering the room, or even resting her darling head on the same pillow as she did when a child – and I must open my lids to see. And so I opened and closed them a hundred times a night – to be always disappointed! It racked me! I've often groaned aloud, till that old rascal Joseph no doubt believed that my conscience was playing the fiend inside of me.

"Now, since I've seen her, I'm pacified – a little. It was a strange way of killing – not by inches but by fractions of hairbreadths – to beguile me with the spectre of a hope through eighteen years!"

Mr Heathcliff paused and wiped his forehead; his hair clung to it, wet with perspiration; his eyes were fixed on the red embers of the fire, the brows not contracted, but raised next the temples, diminishing the grim aspect of his countenance, but imparting a peculiar look of trouble, and a painful appearance of mental tension towards one absorbing subject. He only half-addressed me, and I maintained silence. I didn't like to hear him talk!

After a short period he resumed his meditation on the picture, took it down and leant it against the sofa to contemplate it at better advantage, and while so occupied, Catherine entered, announcing that she was ready when her pony should be saddled.

"Send that over tomorrow," said Heathcliff to me, then, turning to her, he added, "You may do without your pony: it is a fine evening, and you'll need no ponies at Wuthering Heights; for what journeys you take, your own feet will serve you – come along."

"Goodbye, Ellen!" whispered my dear little mistress.

As she kissed me, her lips felt like ice. "Come and see me, Ellen, don't forget."

"Take care you do no such thing, Mrs Dean!" said her new father. "When I wish to speak to you I'll come here. I want none of your prying at my house!"

He signed her to precede him, and, casting back a look that cut my heart, she obeyed. I watched them, from the window, walk down the garden. Heathcliff fixed Catherine's arm under his – though she disputed the act at first evidently – and with rapid strides he hurried her into the alley, whose trees concealed them.

30

I HAVE PAID A VISIT TO THE HEIGHTS, but I have not seen her since she left: Joseph held the door in his hand when I called to ask after her, and wouldn't let me pass. He said Mrs Linton was "thrang",* and the master was not in. Zillah has told me something of the way they go on, otherwise I should hardly know who was dead and who living.

She thinks Catherine haughty and does not like her, I can guess by her talk. My young lady asked some aid of her when she first came, but Mr Heathcliff told her to follow her own business, and let his daughter-in-law look after herself, and Zillah willingly acquiesced, being a narrow-minded, selfish woman. Catherine evinced a child's annoyance at this neglect, repaid it with contempt, and thus enlisted my informant among her enemies as securely as if she had done her some great wrong.

I had a long talk with Zillah about six weeks ago, a little before you came, one day when we foregathered on the moor, and this is what she told me.

"The first thing Mrs Linton did," she said, "on her arrival at the Heights, was to run upstairs without even wishing good evening to me and Joseph; she shut herself into Linton's room and remained till morning. Then, while the master and Earnshaw were at breakfast, she entered the house, and asked all in a quiver if the doctor might be sent for? Her cousin was very ill.

"'We know that!' answered Heathcliff, 'but his life is not worth a farthing, and I won't spend a farthing on him.'

"'But I cannot tell how to do,' she said, 'and if nobody will help me, he'll die!'

"'Walk out of the room,' cried the master, 'and let me never hear a word more about him! None here care what becomes of him; if you do, act the nurse; if you do not, lock him up and leave him.'

"Then she began to bother me, and I said I'd had enough plague with the tiresome thing; we each had our tasks, and hers was to wait on Linton – Mr Heathcliff bid me leave that labour to her.

"How they managed together, I can't tell. I fancy he fretted a great deal, and moaned hisseln* night and day, and she had precious little rest – one could guess by her white face and heavy eyes. She sometimes came into the kitchen all wildered like, and looked as if she would fain beg assistance, but I was not going to disobey the master – I never dare disobey him, Mrs Dean – and though I thought it wrong that Kenneth should not be sent for, it was no concern of mine either to advise or complain, and I always refused to meddle.

"Once or twice, after we had gone to bed, I've happened to open my door again and seen her sitting, crying on the stairs' top, and then I've shut myself in quick, for fear of being moved to interfere. I did pity her then, I'm sure; still I didn't wish to lose my place, you know.

"At last one night she came boldly into my chamber, and frightened me out of my wits by saying:

"'Tell Mr Heathcliff that his son is dying – I'm sure he is this time. Get up instantly and tell him!'

"Having uttered this speech, she vanished again. I lay a quarter of an hour listening and trembling... Nothing stirred... the house was quiet.

"'She's mistaken,' I said to myself. 'He's got over it. I needn't disturb them.' And I began to doze. But my sleep was marred a second time by a sharp ringing of the bell – the only bell we have, put up on purpose for Linton – and the master called to me to see what was the matter, and inform them that he wouldn't have that noise repeated.

"I delivered Catherine's message. He cursed to himself, and in a few minutes came out with a lit candle, and proceeded to their room. I followed. Mrs Heathcliff was seated by the bedside, with her hands folded on her knees. Her father-in-law went up, held the light to Linton's face, looked at him, and touched him; afterwards he turned to her.

"'Now – Catherine,' he said, 'how do you feel?'

"She was dumb.

"'How do you feel, Catherine?' he repeated.

"'He's safe, and I'm free,' she answered, 'I should feel well – but,' she continued, with a bitterness she couldn't conceal, 'you have left me so long to struggle against death alone, that I feel and see only death! I feel like death!'

"And she looked like it too! I gave her a little wine. Hareton and Joseph, who had been wakened by the ringing and the sound of feet, and heard our talk from outside, now entered. Joseph was fain, I believe, of* the lad's removal; Hareton seemed a thought* bothered, though he was more taken up with staring at Catherine than thinking of Linton. But the master bid him get off to bed again – we didn't want his help. He afterwards made Joseph remove the body to his chamber, and told me to return to mine, and Mrs Heathcliff remained by herself.

"In the morning, he sent me to tell her she must come down to breakfast: she had undressed, and appeared going to sleep, and said she was ill – at which I hardly wondered. I informed Mr Heathcliff, and he replied:

"'Well, let her be till after the funeral, and go up now and then to get her what is needful, and as soon as she seems better, tell me.'"

Cathy stayed upstairs a fortnight, according to Zillah, who visited her twice a day, and would have been rather more friendly, but her attempts at increasing kindness were proudly and promptly repelled.

Heathcliff went up once, to show her Linton's will. He had bequeathed the whole of his – and what had been her – movable property to his father: the poor creature was threatened, or coaxed, into that act during her week's absence, when his uncle died. The lands, being a minor, he could not meddle with. However, Mr Heathcliff has claimed and kept them in his wife's right and his also – I suppose legally – at any rate, Catherine, destitute of cash and friends, cannot disturb his possession.

"Nobody," said Zillah, "ever approached her door, except that once, but I... and nobody asked anything about her. The first occasion of her coming down into the house was on a Sunday afternoon.

"She had cried out, when I carried up her dinner, that she couldn't bear any longer being in the cold, and I told her the master was going to Thrushcross Grange, and Earnshaw and I needn't hinder her from descending; so as soon as she heard Heathcliff's horse trot off, she made her appearance, donned in black, and her yellow curls combed back behind her ears as plain as a Quaker: she couldn't comb them out.

"Joseph and I generally go to chapel on Sundays" – the kirk, you know, has no minister now, explained Mrs Dean, and they call the Methodists' or Baptists' place (I can't say which it is) at Gimmerton a chapel – "Joseph had gone," she continued, "but I thought proper to bide at home. Young folks are always the better for an elder's over-looking,* and Hareton, with all his bashfulness, isn't a model of nice behaviour. I let him know that his cousin would very likely sit with us, and she had been always used to see the Sabbath respected, so he had as good leave his guns and bits of indoor work alone while she stayed.

"He coloured up at the news, and cast his eyes over his hands and clothes. The train oil and gunpowder were shoved out of sight in a minute. I saw he meant to give her his company, and I guessed, by his way, he wanted to be presentable; so, laughing as I durst not laugh when the master is by, I offered to help him, if he would, and joked at his confusion. He grew sullen, and began to swear.

"Now, Mrs Dean," Zillah went on, seeing me not pleased by her manner, "you happen think your young lady too fine for Mr Hareton – and happen you're right – but I own I should love well to bring her pride a peg lower. And what will all her learning and her daintiness do for her now? She's as poor as you or I – poorer, I'll be bound: you're saving, and I'm doing my little all that road."

Hareton allowed Zillah to give him her aid, and she flattered him into a good humour, so when Catherine came, half-forgetting her former insults, he tried to make himself agreeable, by the housekeeper's account.

"Missis walked in," she said, "as chill as an icicle and as high as a princess. I got up and offered her my seat in the armchair. No, she turned up her nose at my civility. Earnshaw rose too, and bid her come to the settle, and sit close by the fire; he was sure she was starved.

"'I've been starved a month and more,' she answered, resting on the word as scornful as she could.

"And she got a chair for herself, and placed it at a distance from both of us.

"Having sat till she was warm, she began to look round and discovered a number of books on the dresser: she was instantly upon her feet again, stretching to reach them, but they were too high up.

"Her cousin, after watching her endeavours awhile, at last summoned courage to help her; she held her frock, and he filled it with the first that came to hand.

"That was a great advance for the lad. She didn't thank him; still he felt gratified that she had accepted his assistance, and ventured to stand behind as she examined them, and even to stoop and point out what struck his fancy in certain old pictures which they contained; nor was he daunted by the saucy style in which she jerked the page from his finger: he contented himself with going a bit further back and looking at her instead of the book.

"She continued reading, or seeking for something to read. His attention became by degrees quite centred in the study of her thick silky curls – her face he couldn't see, and she couldn't see him. And perhaps not quite awake to what he did, but attracted like a child to a candle, at last he proceeded from staring to touching: he put out his hand and stroked one curl, as gently as if it were a bird. He might have stuck a knife into her neck, she started round in such a taking.*

"'Get away this moment! How dare you touch me? Why are you stopping there?" she cried in a tone of disgust. "I can't endure you! I'll go upstairs again, if you come near me.'

"Mr Hareton recoiled, looking as foolish as he could do; he sat down in the settle very quiet, and she continued turning over her volumes another half-hour; finally, Earnshaw crossed over and whispered to me:

"'Will you ask her to read to us, Zillah? I'm stalled* of doing naught, and I do like... I could like to hear her! Dunnot say I wanted it, but ask of yourseln.'

"'Mr Hareton wishes you would read to us, ma'am,' I said immediately. 'He'd take it very kind – he'd be much obliged.'

"She frowned, and looking up, answered:

"'Mr Hareton, and the whole set of you, will be good enough to understand that I reject any pretence at kindness you have the hypocrisy to offer! I despise you, and will have nothing to say to any of you! When I would have given my life for one kind word, even to see one of your faces, you all kept off. But I won't complain to you! I'm driven down here by the cold, not either to amuse you or enjoy your society.'

"'What could I ha' done?' began Earnshaw. 'How was I to blame?'

"'Oh, you are an exception,' answered Mrs Heathcliff. 'I never missed such a concern as you.'

"'But I offered more than once, and asked,' he said, kindling up at her pertness, 'I asked Mr Heathcliff to let me wake for you—'

"'Be silent! I'll go out of doors, or anywhere, rather than have your disagreeable voice in my ear!' said my lady.

"Hareton muttered she might go to hell for him! and unslinging his gun, restrained himself from his Sunday occupations no longer.

"He talked now freely enough, and she presently saw fit to retreat to her solitude, but the frost had set in, and in spite of her pride, she was forced to condescend to our company more and more. However, I took care there should be no further scorning at my good nature: ever since, I've been as stiff as herself, and she has no lover or liker among us – and she does not deserve one, for let them say the least word to her and she'll curl back* without respect of anyone! She'll snap at the master himself, and as good as dares him to thrash her, and the more hurt she gets, the more venomous she grows."

At first, on hearing this account from Zillah, I determined to leave my situation, take a cottage, and get Catherine to come and live with me, but Mr Heathcliff would as soon permit that as he would set up Hareton in an independent house, and I can see no remedy at present, unless she could marry again – and that scheme it does not come within my province to arrange.

* * *

248

Thus ended Mrs Dean's story. Notwithstanding the doctor's prophecy, I am rapidly recovering strength, and though it be only the second week in January, I propose getting out on horseback in a day or two, and riding over to Wuthering Heights, to inform my landlord that I shall spend the next six months in London; and, if he likes, he may look out for another tenant to take the place after October. I would not pass another winter here for much.

31

YESTERDAY WAS BRIGHT, calm and frosty. I went to the Heights as I proposed; my housekeeper entreated me to bear a little note from her to her young lady, and I did not refuse, for the worthy woman was not conscious of anything odd in her request.

The front door stood open, but the jealous gate was fastened, as at my last visit; I knocked and invoked Earnshaw from among the garden beds; he unchained it, and I entered. The fellow is as handsome a rustic as need be seen. I took particular notice of him this time, but then he does his best apparently to make the least of his advantages.

I asked if Mr Heathcliff were at home? He answered no, but he would be in at dinner time. It was eleven o'clock, and I announced my intention of going in and waiting for him, at which he immediately flung down his tools and accompanied me, in the office of watchdog, not as a substitute for the host.

We entered together; Catherine was there, making herself useful in preparing some vegetables for the approaching meal: she looked more sulky and less spirited than when I had seen her first. She hardly raised her eyes to notice me, and continued her employment with the same disregard to common forms of politeness as before, never returning my bow and good morning by the slightest acknowledgement.

"She does not seem so amiable," I thought, "as Mrs Dean would persuade me to believe. She's a beauty, it is true – but not an angel."

Earnshaw surlily bid her remove her things to the kitchen.

"Remove them yourself," she said, pushing them from her as soon as she had done, and retiring to a stool by the window, where she began to carve figures of birds and beasts out of the turnip parings in her lap.

I approached her, pretending to desire a view of the garden; and, as

I fancied, adroitly dropped Mrs Dean's note onto her knee, unnoticed by Hareton – but she asked aloud:

"What is that?" And chucked it off.

"A letter from your old acquaintance, the housekeeper at the Grange," I answered, annoyed at her exposing my kind deed, and fearful lest it should be imagined a missive of my own.

She would gladly have gathered it up at this information, but Hareton beat her; he seized and put it in his waistcoat, saying Mr Heathcliff should look at it first.

Thereat, Catherine silently turned her face from us, and very stealthily drew out her pocket handkerchief and applied it to her eyes; and her cousin, after struggling awhile to keep down his softer feelings, pulled out the letter and flung it on the floor beside her as ungraciously as he could.

Catherine caught and perused it eagerly; then she put a few questions to me concerning the inmates, rational and irrational, of her former home, and gazing towards the hills, murmured in soliloquy:

"I should like to be riding Minny down there! I should like to be climbing up there! Oh, I'm tired... I'm *stalled*, Hareton!"

And she leant her pretty head back against the sill with half a yawn and half a sigh, and lapsed into an aspect of abstracted sadness, neither caring nor knowing whether we remarked her.

"Mrs Heathcliff," I said, after sitting some time mute, "you are not aware that I am an acquaintance of yours? So intimate that I think it strange you won't come and speak to me. My housekeeper never wearies of talking about and praising you, and she'll be greatly disappointed if I return with no news of or from you, except that you received her letter and said nothing!"

She appeared to wonder at this speech, and asked:

"Does Ellen like you?"

"Yes, very well," I replied unhesitatingly.*

"You must tell her," she continued, "that I would answer her letter, but I have no materials for writing, not even a book from which I might tear a leaf."

"No books!" I exclaimed. "How do you contrive to live here without them? – if I may take the liberty to enquire... Though provided with a large library, I'm frequently very dull at the Grange – take my books away, and I should be desperate!"

"I was always reading when I had them," said Catherine, "and Mr Heathcliff never reads, so he took it into his head to destroy my books. I have not had a glimpse of one for weeks. Only once, I searched through Joseph's store of theology, to his great irritation; and once, Hareton, I came upon a secret stock in your room – some Latin and Greek, and some tales and poetry: all old friends. I brought the last here – and you gathered them, as a magpie gathers silver spoons, for the mere love of stealing! They are of no use to you – or else you concealed them in the bad spirit that, as you cannot enjoy them, nobody else shall. Perhaps *your* envy counselled Mr Heathcliff to rob me of my treasures? But I've most of them written on my brain and printed in my heart, and you cannot deprive me of those!"

Earnshaw blushed crimson when his cousin made this revelation of his private literary accumulations, and stammered an indignant denial of her accusations.

"Mr Hareton is desirous of increasing his amount of knowledge," I said, coming to his rescue. "He is not *envious* but *emulous* of your attainments. He'll be a clever scholar in a few years!"

"And he wants *me* to sink into a dunce meantime," answered Catherine. "Yes, I hear him trying to spell and read to himself, and pretty blunders he makes! I wish you would repeat 'Chevy Chase'* as you did yesterday: it was extremely funny. I heard you... and I heard you turning over the dictionary to seek out the hard words, and then cursing because you couldn't read their explanations!"

The young man evidently thought it too bad that he should be laughed at for his ignorance, and then laughed at for trying to remove it. I had a similar notion, and, remembering Mrs Dean's anecdote of his first attempt at enlightening the darkness in which he had been reared, I observed:

"But, Mrs Heathcliff, we have each had a commencement, and each stumbled and tottered on the threshold, and had our teachers scorned instead of aiding us, we should stumble and totter yet."

"Oh!" she replied, "I don't wish to limit his acquirements: still, he has no right to appropriate what is mine, and make it ridiculous to me with his vile mistakes and mispronunciations! Those books, both prose and verse, are consecrated to me by other associations, and I hate to have them debased and profaned in his mouth! Besides, of all, he has selected my favourite pieces that I love the most to repeat, as if out of deliberate malice!"

Hareton's chest heaved in silence a minute: he laboured under a severe sense of mortification and wrath, which it was no easy task to suppress.

I rose, and, from a gentlemanly idea of relieving his embarrassment, took up my station in the doorway, surveying the external prospect as I stood.

He followed my example, and left the room, but presently reappeared bearing half a dozen volumes in his hands, which he threw into Catherine's lap, exclaiming:

"Take them! I never want to hear or read or think of them again!"

"I won't have them now!" she answered. "I shall connect them with you, and hate them!"

She opened one that had obviously been often turned over and read a portion in the drawling tone of a beginner, then laughed and threw it from her.

"And listen!" she continued provokingly, commencing a verse of an old ballad in the same fashion.

But his self-love would endure no further torment: I heard, and not altogether disapprovingly, a manual check given to her saucy tongue. The little wretch had done her utmost to hurt her cousin's sensitive though uncultivated feelings, and a physical argument was the only mode he had of balancing the account, and repaying its effects on the inflicter.

He afterwards gathered the books and hurled them on the fire. I read in his countenance what anguish it was to offer that sacrifice to spleen. I fancied that as they consumed, he recalled the pleasure they had already imparted, and the triumph and ever-increasing pleasure he had anticipated from them – and I fancied I guessed the incitement to his secret studies also. He had been content with daily labour and rough animal enjoyments, till Catherine crossed his path. Shame at her scorn, and hope of her approval, were his first prompters to higher pursuits, and instead of guarding him from one and winning him to the other, his endeavours to raise himself had produced just the contrary result.

"Yes, that's all the good that such a brute as you can get from them!" cried Catherine, sucking her damaged lip and watching the conflagration with indignant eyes.

"You'd *better* hold your tongue now," he answered fiercely.

And his agitation precluded further speech; he advanced hastily to the entrance, where I made way for him to pass. But ere he had crossed the door stones, Mr Heathcliff, coming up the causeway, encountered him, and laying hold of his shoulder asked:

"What's to do now, my lad?"

"Naught, naught!" he said, and broke away to enjoy his grief and anger in solitude.

Heathcliff gazed after him, and sighed.

"It will be odd if I thwart myself," he muttered, unconscious that I was behind him. "But when I look for his father in his face, I find *her* every day more! How the devil is he so like? I can hardly bear to see him."

He bent his eyes to the ground and walked moodily in. There was a restless, anxious expression in his countenance I had never remarked there before, and he looked sparer in person.

His daughter-in-law, on perceiving him through the window, immediately escaped to the kitchen, so that I remained alone.

"I'm glad to see you out of doors again, Mr Lockwood," he said, in reply to my greeting, "from selfish motives partly: I don't think I could readily supply your loss in this desolation. I've wondered more than once what brought you here."

"An idle whim, I fear, sir," was my answer, "or else an idle whim is going to spirit me away. I shall set out for London next week, and I must give you warning that I feel no disposition to retain Thrushcross Grange beyond the twelve months I agreed to rent it. I believe I shall not live there any more."

"Oh, indeed, you're tired of being banished from the world, are you?" he said. "But if you be coming to plead off paying for a place you won't occupy, your journey is useless – I never relent in exacting my due from anyone."

"I'm coming to plead off nothing about it!" I exclaimed, considerably irritated. "Should you wish it, I'll settle with you now," and I drew my notebook from my pocket.

"No, no," he replied coolly, "you'll leave sufficient behind to cover your debts, if you fail to return – I'm not in such a hurry. Sit down and take your dinner with us: a guest that is safe from repeating his visit can generally be made welcome. Catherine, bring the things in... where are you?"

Catherine reappeared, bearing a tray of knives and forks.

"You may get your dinner with Joseph," muttered Heathcliff aside, "and remain in the kitchen till he is gone."

She obeyed his directions very punctually: perhaps she had no temptation to transgress. Living among clowns and misanthropists, she probably cannot appreciate a better class of people when she meets them.

With Mr Heathcliff, grim and saturnine, on the one hand, and Hareton, absolutely dumb, on the other, I made a somewhat cheerless meal, and bade adieu early. I would have departed by the back way, to get a last glimpse of Catherine and annoy old Joseph, but Hareton received orders to lead up my horse, and my host himself escorted me to the door, so I could not fulfil my wish.

"How dreary life gets over in that house!" I reflected, while riding down the road. "What a realization of something more romantic than a fairy tale it would have been for Mrs Linton Heathcliff, had she and I struck up an attachment, as her good nurse desired, and migrated together into the stirring atmosphere of the town!"

32

1802 – THIS SEPTEMBER I WAS INVITED to devastate the moors of a friend in the north, and on my journey to his abode, I unexpectedly came within fifteen miles of Gimmerton. The ostler at a roadside public house was holding a pail of water to refresh my horses, when a cart of very green oats, newly reaped, passed by, and he remarked:

"Yon's frough Gimmerton, nah! They're allas three wick* after other folk wi' ther harvest."

"Gimmerton?" I repeated – my residence in that locality had already grown dim and dreamy. "Ah! I know! How far is it from this?"

"Happen fourteen mile o'er th' hills, and a rough road," he answered.

A sudden impulse seized me to visit Thrushcross Grange. It was scarcely noon, and I conceived that I might as well pass the night under my own roof as in an inn. Besides, I could spare a day easily to arrange matters with my landlord, and thus save myself the trouble of invading the neighbourhood again.

Having rested awhile, I directed my servant to enquire the way to the village, and, with great fatigue to our beasts, we managed the distance in some three hours.

I left him there and proceeded down the valley alone. The grey church looked greyer and the lonely churchyard lonelier. I distinguished a moor sheep cropping the short turf on the graves. It was sweet, warm weather – too warm for travelling – but the heat did not hinder me from enjoying the delightful scenery above and below; had I seen it nearer August, I'm sure it would have tempted me to waste a month among its solitudes. In winter nothing more dreary, in summer nothing more divine than those glens shut in by hills, and those bluff, bold swells of heath.

I reached the Grange before sunset and knocked for admittance, but the family had retreated into the back premises, I judged, by one thin blue wreath curling from the kitchen chimney, and they did not hear.

I rode into the court. Under the porch, a girl of nine or ten sat knitting, and an old woman reclined on the horse steps, smoking a meditative pipe.

"Is Mrs Dean within?" I demanded of the dame.

"Mistress Dean? Nay!" she answered. "Shoo doesn't bide here: shoo's up at th' Heights."

"Are you the housekeeper then?" I continued.

"Eea, Aw keep th' hahse," she replied.

"Well, I'm Mr Lockwood, the master. Are there any rooms to lodge me in, I wonder? I wish to stay here all night."

"T' maister!" she cried in astonishment. "Whet, whoiver knew yah wur coming? Yah sud ha' send word. They's nowt norther dry nor mensful* abaht t' place – nowt there isn't!"

She threw down her pipe and bustled in; the girl followed, and I entered too, soon perceiving that her report was true, and, moreover, that I had almost upset her wits by my unwelcome apparition.

I bade her be composed – I would go out for a walk, and meantime she must try to prepare a corner of a sitting room for me to sup in, and a bedroom to sleep in. No sweeping and dusting, only good fire and dry sheets were necessary.

She seemed willing to do her best, though she thrust the hearth brush into the grates in mistake for the poker, and malappropriated several other articles of her craft, but I retired, confiding in her energy for a resting place against my return.

Wuthering Heights was the goal of my proposed excursion. An afterthought brought me back when I had quitted the court.

"All well at the Heights?" I enquired of the woman.

"Eea, f'r owt Ee knaw!"* she answered, scurrying away with a pan of hot cinders.

I would have asked why Mrs Dean had deserted the Grange, but it was impossible to delay her at such a crisis, so I turned away and made my exit, rambling leisurely along, with the glow of a sinking sun behind, and the mild glory of a rising moon in front – one fading and the other brightening – as I quitted the park, and climbed the stony byroad branching off to Mr Heathcliff's dwelling.

Before I arrived in sight of it, all that remained of day was a beamless amber light along the west, but I could see every pebble on the path and every blade of grass by that splendid moon.

I had neither to climb the gate nor to knock – it yielded to my hand.

That is an improvement! I thought. And I noticed another, by the aid of my nostrils: a fragrance of stocks and wallflowers wafted on the air from amongst the homely fruit trees.

Both doors and lattices were open, and yet, as is usually the case in a coal district, a fine red fire illumined the chimney – the comfort which the eye derives from it renders the extra heat endurable. But the house of Wuthering Heights is so large that the inmates have plenty of space for withdrawing out of its influence, and accordingly, what inmates there were had stationed themselves not far from one of the windows. I could both see them and hear them talk before I entered, and looked and listened in consequence, being moved thereto by a mingled sense of curiosity and envy, that grew as I lingered.

"Con-*trary*!" said a voice as sweet as a silver bell. "That for the third time, you dunce! I'm not going to tell you again. Recollect, or I'll pull your hair!"

"Contrary, then," answered another, in deep but softened tones. "And now kiss me for minding so well."

"No, read it over first correctly, without a single mistake."

The male speaker began to read: he was a young man, respectably dressed and seated at a table, having a book before him. His handsome features glowed with pleasure, and his eyes kept impatiently wandering from the page to a small white hand over his shoulder, which recalled him by a smart slap on the cheek whenever its owner detected such signs of inattention.

Its owner stood behind, her light, shining ringlets blending at intervals with his brown locks as she bent to superintend his studies, and her face – it was lucky he could not see her face, or he would never have been so steady. I could – and I bit my lip in spite at having thrown away the chance I might have had of doing something besides staring at its smiting beauty.

The task was done, not free from further blunders, but the pupil claimed a reward, and received at least five kisses, which, however, he generously returned. Then they came to the door, and from their conversation I judged they were about to issue out and have a walk on the moors. I supposed I should be condemned in Hareton Earnshaw's heart, if not by his mouth, to the lowest pit in the infernal regions, if I showed my unfortunate person in his neighbourhood then, and feeling very mean and malignant, I skulked round to seek refuge in the kitchen.

There was unobstructed admittance on that side also, and at the door sat my old friend Nelly Dean, sewing and singing a song, which was often interrupted from within by harsh words of scorn and intolerance, uttered in far from musical accents.

"Aw'd rayther, by th' haulf,* hev' 'em swearing i' my lugs frough morn to neeght, nur hearken yah hahsiver!"* said the tenant of the kitchen, in answer to an unheard speech of Nelly's. "It's a blazing shaime, ut Aw cannut oppen t' blessed Book, bud yah set up them glories tuh Sattan,* un' all t' flaysome wickednesses ut iver wer born intuh th' warld! Oh! Yah're a raight nowt; un' shoo's another; un' that poor lad 'ull be lost atween ye. Poor lad!" he added, with a groan. "He's witched: Aw'm sartin on't. O Lord, judge 'em, fur they's norther law nur justice amang wer rullers!"

"No! or we should be sitting in flaming faggots, I suppose," retorted the singer. "But whisht, old man, and read your Bible like a Christian and never mind me. This is 'Fairy Annie's Wedding'* – a bonny tune – it goes to a dance."

Mrs Dean was about to recommence, when I advanced, and recognizing me directly, she jumped to her feet, crying:

"Why bless you, Mr Lockwood! How could you think of returning in this way? All's shut up at Thrushcross Grange. You should have given us notice!"

"I've arranged to be accommodated there, for as long as I shall stay," I answered. "I depart again tomorrow. And how are you transplanted here, Mrs Dean? Tell me that."

"Zillah left, and Mr Heathcliff wished me to come, soon after you went to London, and stay till you returned. But step in, pray! Have you walked from Gimmerton this evening?"

"From the Grange," I replied, "and while they make me lodging room there, I want to finish my business with your master, because I don't think of having another opportunity in a hurry."

"What business, sir?" said Nelly, conducting me into the house. "He's gone out at present, and won't return soon."

"About the rent," I answered.

"Oh, then it is with Mrs Heathcliff you must settle," she observed, "or rather with me. She has not learnt to manage her affairs yet, and I act for her: there's nobody else."

I looked surprised.

"Ah, you have not heard of Heathcliff's death, I see," she continued.

"Heathcliff dead?" I exclaimed, astonished. "How long ago?"

"Three months since – but sit down, and let me take your hat, and I'll tell you all about it. Stop, you have had nothing to eat, have you?"

"I want nothing: I have ordered supper at home. You sit down too. I never dreamt of his dying! Let me hear how it came to pass. You say you don't expect them back for some time – the young people?"

"No, I have to scold them every evening for their late rambles, but they don't care for me. At least have a drink of our old ale – it will do you good: you seem weary."

She hastened to fetch it before I could refuse, and I heard Joseph asking whether "it warn't a crying scandal that she should have fellies* at her time of life? And then to get them jocks* out uh t' maister's cellar! He fair shaamed to bide still and see it."

She did not stay to retaliate, but re-entered in a minute, bearing a reaming* silver pint, whose contents I lauded with becoming earnestness. And afterwards she furnished me with the sequel of Heathcliff's history. He had a "queer" end, as she expressed it.

I was summoned to Wuthering Heights within a fortnight of your leaving us – she said – and I obeyed joyfully, for Catherine's sake.

My first interview with her grieved and shocked me: she had altered so much since our separation! Mr Heathcliff did not explain his reasons for taking a new mind about my coming here; he only told me he wanted me, and he was tired of seeing Catherine: I must make the little parlour my sitting room, and keep her with me. It was enough if he were obliged to see her once or twice a day.

She seemed pleased at this arrangement, and, by degrees, I smuggled over a great number of books and other articles that had formed her amusement at the Grange, and flattered myself we should get on in tolerable comfort.

The delusion did not last long. Catherine, contented at first, in a brief space grew irritable and restless. For one thing, she was forbidden to move out of the garden, and it fretted her sadly to be confined to its narrow bounds as spring drew on; for another, in following the house,* I was forced to quit her frequently, and she complained of loneliness: she preferred quarrelling with Joseph in the kitchen to sitting at peace in her solitude.

I did not mind their skirmishes, but Hareton was often obliged to seek the kitchen also, when the master wanted to have the house to himself, and though in the beginning she either left it at his approach, or quietly joined in my occupations, and shunned remarking or addressing him – and though he was always as sullen and silent as possible – after a while, she changed her behaviour, and became incapable of letting him alone: talking at him, commenting on his stupidity and idleness, expressing her wonder how he could endure the life he lived – how he could sit a whole evening staring into the fire and dozing.

"He's just like a dog, is he not, Ellen?" she once observed, "or a carthorse? He does his work, eats his food and sleeps eternally! What a blank, dreary mind he must have! Do you ever dream, Hareton? And if you do, what is it about? But you can't speak to me!"

Then she looked at him, but he would neither open his mouth nor look again.

"He's perhaps dreaming now," she continued. "He twitched his shoulder as Juno twitches hers. Ask him, Ellen."

"Mr Hareton will ask the master to send you upstairs, if you don't behave!" I said. He had not only twitched his shoulder but clenched his fist, as if tempted to use it.

"I know why Hareton never speaks when I am in the kitchen," she exclaimed on another occasion. "He is afraid I shall laugh at him. Ellen, what do you think? He began to teach himself to read once, and because I laughed, he burned his books and dropped it – was he not a fool?"

"Were not you naughty?" I said. "Answer me that."

"Perhaps I was," she went on, "but I did not expect him to be so silly. Hareton, if I gave you a book, would you take it now? I'll try!"

She placed one she had been perusing on his hand; he flung it off and muttered – if she did not give over, he would break her neck.

"Well I shall put it here," she said, "in the table drawer, and I'm going to bed."

Then she whispered me to watch whether he touched it, and departed. But he would not come near it, and so I informed her in the morning, to her great disappointment. I saw she was sorry for his persevering sulkiness and indolence – her conscience reproved her for frightening him off improving himself: she had done it effectually.

But her ingenuity was at work to remedy the injury: while I ironed or pursued other such stationary employments I could not well do in the parlour, she would bring some pleasant volume and read it aloud to me. When Hareton was there, she generally paused in an interesting part, and left the book lying about – that she did repeatedly – but he was as obstinate as a mule, and instead of snatching at her bait, in wet weather he took to smoking with Joseph, and they sat like automatons, one on each side of the fire, the elder happily too deaf to understand her wicked nonsense, as he would have called it, the younger doing his best to seem to disregard it. On fine evenings the latter followed his shooting expeditions, and Catherine yawned and sighed, and teased me to talk to her, and ran off into the court or garden the moment I began, and as a last resource cried and said she was tired of living, her life was useless.

Mr Heathcliff, who grew more and more disinclined to society, had almost banished Earnshaw out of his apartment. Owing to an accident at the commencement of March, he became for some days a fixture in the kitchen. His gun burst while out on the hills by himself; a splinter cut his arm, and he lost a good deal of blood before he could reach home. The consequence was that, perforce, he was condemned to the fireside and tranquillity till he made it up again.

It suited Catherine to have him there: at any rate, it made her hate her room upstairs more than ever, and she would compel me to find out business below, that she might accompany me.

On Easter Monday, Joseph went to Gimmerton fair with some cattle, and in the afternoon I was busy getting up* linen in the kitchen.

Earnshaw sat, morose as usual, at the chimney corner, and my little mistress was beguiling an idle hour with drawing pictures on the window panes, varying her amusement by smothered bursts of songs and whispered ejaculations, and quick glances of annoyance and impatience in the direction of her cousin, who steadfastly smoked and looked into the grate.

At a notice that I could do with her no longer intercepting my light, she removed to the hearthstone. I bestowed little attention on her proceedings, but presently I heard her begin:

"I've found out, Hareton, that I want... that I'm glad... that I should like you to be my cousin now, if you had not grown so cross to me, and so rough."

Hareton returned no answer.

"Hareton, Hareton, Hareton! Do you hear?" she continued.

"Get off wi' ye!" he growled with uncompromising gruffness.

"Let me take that pipe," she said, cautiously advancing her hand and abstracting it from his mouth.

Before he could attempt to recover it, it was broken and behind the fire. He swore at her and seized another.

"Stop!" she cried, "you must listen to me first, and I can't speak while those clouds are floating in my face."

"Will you go to the devil!" he exclaimed ferociously, "and let me be!"

"No," she persisted, "I won't; I can't tell what to do to make you talk to me, and you are determined not to understand. When I call you stupid, I don't mean anything: I don't mean that I despise you. Come, you shall take notice of me, Hareton: you are my cousin, and you shall own me."

"I shall have naught to do wi' you and your mucky pride, and your damned mocking tricks!" he answered. "I'll go to hell, body and soul, before I look sideways after you again. Side out of t' gait* now, this minute!"

Catherine frowned and retreated to the window seat, chewing her lip and endeavouring, by humming an eccentric tune, to conceal a growing tendency to sob.

"You should be friends with your cousin, Mr Hareton," I interrupted, "since she repents of her sauciness! It would do you a great deal of good – it would make you another man to have her for a companion."

"A companion?" he cried, "when she hates me, and does not think me fit to wipe her shoon! Nay, if it made me a king, I'd not be scorned for seeking her goodwill any more."

"It is not I who hate you, it is you who hate me!" wept Cathy, no longer disguising her trouble. "You hate me as much as Mr Heathcliff does, and more."

"You're a damned liar," began Earnshaw, "why have I made him angry, by taking your part, then, a hundred times? And that when you sneered at and despised me, and... Go on plaguing me, and I'll step in yonder, and say you worried me out of the kitchen!"

"I didn't know you took my part," she answered, drying her eyes, "and I was miserable and bitter at everybody, but now I thank you and beg you to forgive me – what can I do besides?"

She returned to the hearth and frankly extended her hand.

He blackened and scowled like a thundercloud, and kept his fists resolutely clenched, and his gaze fixed on the ground.

Catherine, by instinct, must have divined it was obdurate perversity, and not dislike, that prompted this dogged conduct, for after remaining an instant undecided, she stooped and impressed on his cheek a gentle kiss.

The little rogue thought I had not seen her, and, drawing back, she took her former station by the window quite demurely.

I shook my head reprovingly, and then she blushed and whispered:

"Well! what should I have done, Ellen? He wouldn't shake hands, and he wouldn't look... I must show him some way that I like him, that I want to be friends."

Whether the kiss convinced Hareton, I cannot tell: he was very careful, for some minutes, that his face should not be seen, and when he did raise it, he was sadly puzzled where to turn his eyes.

Catherine employed herself in wrapping a handsome book neatly in white paper, and having tied it with a bit of ribbon and addressed it to "Mr Hareton Earnshaw", she desired me to be her ambassadress, and convey the present to its destined recipient.

"And tell him, if he'll take it, I'll come and teach him to read it right," she said, "and if he refuse it, I'll go upstairs, and never tease him again."

I carried it and repeated the message, anxiously watched by my employer. Hareton would not open his fingers, so I laid it on his knee.

He did not strike it off either. I returned to my work; Catherine leant her head and arms on the table, till she heard the slight rustle of the covering being removed; then she stole away and quietly seated herself beside her cousin. He trembled, and his face glowed – all his rudeness and all his surly harshness had deserted him: he could not summon courage, at first, to utter a syllable in reply to her questioning look and her murmured petition.

"Say you forgive me, Hareton, do! You can make me so happy by speaking that little word."

He muttered something inaudible.

"And you'll be my friend?" added Catherine interrogatively.

"Nay, you'll be ashamed of me every day of your life!" he answered. "And the more, the more you know me – and I cannot bide it."

"So you won't be my friend?" she said, smiling as sweet as honey, and creeping close up.

I overheard no further distinguishable talk, but on looking round again, I perceived two such radiant countenances bent over the page of the accepted book, that I did not doubt the treaty had been ratified on both sides, and the enemies were, thenceforth, sworn allies.

The work they studied was full of costly pictures, and those and their position had charm enough to keep them unmoved till Joseph came home. He, poor man, was perfectly aghast at the spectacle of Catherine seated on the same bench with Hareton Earnshaw, leaning her hand on his shoulder, and confounded at his favourite's endurance of her proximity. It affected him too deeply to allow an observation on the subject that night. His emotion was only revealed by the immense sighs he drew, as he solemnly spread his large Bible on the table, and overlaid it with dirty banknotes from his pocketbook, the produce of the day's transactions. At length he summoned Hareton from his seat.

"Tak these in tuh t' maister, lad," he said, "un' bide there. Aw's gang up tuh my awn rahm. This hoile's norther mensful nor seemly* fur us: we mun side aht and seearch another!"

"Come, Catherine," I said, "we must 'side out' too. I've done my ironing, are you ready to go?"

"It is not eight o'clock!" she answered, rising unwillingly, "Hareton, I'll leave this book upon the chimney piece, and I'll bring some more tomorrow."

"Ony books ut yah leave Aw sall tak intuh th' hahse," said Joseph, "un' it 'ull be mitch if yah find 'em agean, soa yah muh plase yourseln!"

Cathy threatened that his library should pay for hers, and, smiling as she passed Hareton, went singing upstairs – lighter of heart, I venture to say, than ever she had been under that roof before, except perhaps during her earliest visits to Linton.

The intimacy thus commenced grew rapidly, though it encountered temporary interruptions. Earnshaw was not to be civilized with a wish, and my young lady was no philosopher and no paragon of patience, but both their minds tending to the same point – one loving and desiring to esteem, and the other loving and desiring to be esteemed – they contrived in the end to reach it.

You see, Mr Lockwood, it was easy enough to win Mrs Heathcliff's heart. But now I'm glad you did not try. The crown of all my wishes will be the union of those two. I shall envy no one on their wedding day – there won't be a happier woman than myself in England!

33

O N THE MORROW OF THAT MONDAY, Earnshaw being still unable to follow his ordinary employments, and therefore remaining about the house, I speedily found it would be impracticable to retain my charge beside me as heretofore.

She got downstairs before me, and out into the garden, where she had seen her cousin performing some easy work, and when I went to bid them come to breakfast, I saw she had persuaded him to clear a large space of ground from currant and gooseberry bushes, and they were busy planning together an importation of plants from the Grange.

I was terrified at the devastation which had been accomplished in a brief half-hour; the blackcurrant trees were the apple of Joseph's eye, and she had just fixed her choice of a flower bed in the midst of them!

"There! That will be all shown to the master," I exclaimed, "the minute it is discovered. And what excuse have you to offer for taking such liberties with the garden? We shall have a fine explosion on the head of it,* see if we don't! Mr Hareton, I wonder you should have no more wit than to go and make that mess at her bidding!"

"I'd forgotten they were Joseph's," answered Earnshaw, rather puzzled, "but I'll tell him I did it."

We always ate our meals with Mr Heathcliff. I held the mistress's post in making tea and carving, so I was indispensable at table. Catherine usually sat by me, but today she stole nearer to Hareton, and I presently saw she would have no more discretion in her friendship than she had in her hostility.

"Now mind you don't talk with and notice your cousin too much," were my whispered instructions as we entered the room. "It will certainly annoy Mr Heathcliff, and he'll be mad at you both."

"I'm not going to," she answered.

The minute after, she had sidled to him, and was sticking primroses in his plate of porridge.

He dared not speak to her there – he dared hardly look – and yet she went on teasing, till he was twice on the point of being provoked to laugh, and I frowned, and then she glanced towards the master, whose mind was occupied on other subjects than his company, as his countenance evinced, and she grew serious for an instant, scrutinizing him with deep gravity. Afterwards she turned and recommenced her nonsense; at last, Hareton uttered a smothered laugh.

Mr Heathcliff started; his eye rapidly surveyed our faces. Catherine met it with her accustomed look of nervousness and yet defiance, which he abhorred.

"It is well you are out of my reach," he exclaimed. "What fiend possesses you to stare back at me continually with those infernal eyes? Down with them! And don't remind me of your existence again. I thought I had cured you of laughing."

"It was me," muttered Hareton.

"What do you say?" demanded the master.

Hareton looked at his plate, and did not repeat the confession.

Mr Heathcliff looked at him a bit, and then silently resumed his breakfast and his interrupted musing.

We had nearly finished, and the two young people prudently shifted wider asunder, so I anticipated no further disturbance during that sitting, when Joseph appeared at the door, revealing by his quivering lip and furious eyes that the outrage committed on his precious shrubs was detected.

He must have seen Cathy and her cousin about the spot before he examined it, for while his jaws worked like those of a cow chewing its cud, and rendered his speech difficult to understand, he began:

"Aw mun hev my wage, and Aw mun goa! I *hed* aimed tuh dee wheare Aw'd sarved fur sixty year, un' Aw thowt Aw'd lug my books up intuh t' garret, un' all my bits uh stuff, un' they sud hev t' kitchen tuh theirseln, fur t' sake uh quietness. It wur hard tuh gie up my awn hearthstun, bud Aw thowt Aw *could* do that! Bud nah, shoo's taan my garden frough me, un' by th' heart, maister, Aw cannot stand it! Yah muh bend tuh th' yoak, an ye will – *Aw'm* noan used to 't, and an ow'd man doesn't sooin get used tuh new barthens.* Aw'd rayther arn my bite an' my sup wi' a hammer in th' road!"

"Now, now, idiot!" interrupted Heathcliff, "cut it short! What's your grievance? I'll interfere in no quarrels between you and Nelly. She may thrust you into the coal hole for anything I care."

"It's noan Nelly!" answered Joseph. "Aw sudn't shift for Nelly – nasty ill nowt as shoo is. Thank God! *Shoo* cannot stale t' sowl* uh nob'dy! Shoo wer niver soa handsome, bud whet a body mud look at her baht winking. It's yon flaysome, graceless quean, ut's witched ahr lad wi' her bold een un' her forrard ways, till… Nay! It fair brusts my heart! He's forgetten all E done for him, un' made on him, un' goan un' riven up a whole row ut t' grandest currant trees i' t' garden!" and here he lamented outright, unmanned by a sense of his bitter injuries, and Earnshaw's ingratitude and dangerous condition.

"Is the fool drunk?" asked Mr Heathcliff. "Hareton, is it you he's finding fault with?"

"I've pulled up two or three bushes," replied the young man, "but I'm going to set* 'em again."

"And why have you pulled them up?" said the master.

Catherine wisely put in her tongue.

"We wanted to plant some flowers there," she cried. "I'm the only person to blame, for I wished him to do it."

"And who the devil gave *you* leave to touch a stick about the place?" demanded her father-in-law, much surprised. "And who ordered *you* to obey her?" he added, turning to Hareton.

The latter was speechless; his cousin replied:

"You shouldn't grudge a few yards of earth for me to ornament, when you have taken all my land!"

"Your land, insolent slut? You never had any!" said Heathcliff.

"And my money," she continued, returning his angry glare, and meantime biting a piece of crust, the remnant of her breakfast.

"Silence!" he exclaimed. "Get done, and begone!"

"And Hareton's land, and his money," pursued the reckless thing. "Hareton and I are friends now, and I shall tell him all about you!"

The master seemed confounded a moment: he grew pale, and rose up, eyeing her all the while with an expression of mortal hate.

"If you strike me, Hareton will strike you," she said, "so you may as well sit down."

"If Hareton does not turn you out of the room, I'll strike him to hell," thundered Heathcliff. "Damnable witch! Dare you pretend to rouse him against me? Off with her! Do you hear? Fling her into the kitchen! I'll kill her, Ellen Dean, if you let her come into my sight again!"

Hareton tried, under his breath, to persuade her to go.

"Drag her away!" he cried savagely. "Are you staying to talk?" And he approached to execute his own command.

"He'll not obey you, wicked man, any more!" said Catherine, "and he'll soon detest you as much as I do!"

"Whisht! Whisht!"[14] muttered the young man reproachfully, "I will not hear you speak so to him. Have done!"

"But you won't let him strike me?" she cried.

"Come then!" he whispered earnestly.

It was too late: Heathcliff had caught hold of her.

"Now *you* go!" he said to Earnshaw. "Accursed witch! This time she has provoked me when I could not bear it, and I'll make her repent it for ever!"

He had his hand in her hair; Hareton attempted to release the locks, entreating him not to hurt her that once. Heathcliff's black eyes flashed; he seemed ready to tear Catherine in pieces, and I was just worked up to risk coming to the rescue, when of a sudden his fingers relaxed, he shifted his grasp from her head to her arm, and gazed intently in her face. Then he drew his hand over his eyes, stood a moment to collect himself, apparently, and, turning anew to Catherine, said with assumed calmness:

"You must learn to avoid putting me in a passion, or I shall really murder you some time! Go with Mrs Dean and keep with her, and confine your insolence to her ears. As to Hareton Earnshaw, if I see him listen to you, I'll send him seeking his bread where he can get it! Your love will make him an outcast and a beggar. Nelly, take her; and leave me, all of you! Leave me!"

I led my young lady out – she was too glad of her escape to resist – the other followed, and Mr Heathcliff had the room to himself till dinner.

I had counselled Catherine to get hers upstairs, but as soon as he perceived her vacant seat, he sent me to call her. He spoke to none of us, ate very little, and went out directly afterwards, intimating that he should not return before evening.

The two new friends established themselves in the house during his absence, where I heard Hareton sternly check his cousin, on her offering a revelation of her father-in-law's conduct to his father.

He said he wouldn't suffer a word to be uttered in his disparagement: if he were the devil, it didn't signify; he would stand by him, and he'd rather she would abuse himself, as she used to, than begin on Mr Heathcliff.

Catherine was waxing cross at this, but he found means to make her hold her tongue by asking how she would like *him* to speak ill of her father? And then she comprehended that Earnshaw took the master's reputation home to himself, and was attached by ties stronger than reason could break – chains, forged by habit, which it would be cruel to attempt to loosen.

She showed a good heart, thenceforth, in avoiding both complaints and expressions of antipathy concerning Heathcliff, and confessed to me her sorrow that she had endeavoured to raise a bad spirit between him and Hareton – indeed, I don't believe she has ever breathed a syllable in the latter's hearing against her oppressor since.

When this slight disagreement was over, they were thick again, and as busy as possible in their several occupations of pupil and teacher. I came in to sit with them, after I had done my work, and I felt so soothed and comforted to watch them, that I did not notice how time got on. You know, they both appeared in a measure my children: I had long been proud of one, and now I was sure the other would be a source of equal satisfaction. His honest, warm and intelligent nature shook off rapidly the clouds of ignorance and degradation in which it had been bred, and Catherine's sincere commendations acted as a spur to his industry. His brightening mind brightened his features and added spirit and nobility to their aspect – I could hardly fancy it the same individual I had beheld on the day I discovered my little lady at Wuthering Heights, after her expedition to the Crags.

While I admired and they laboured, dusk drew on, and with it returned the master. He came upon us quite unexpectedly, entering by the front way, and had a full view of the whole three, ere we could raise our heads to glance at him.

Well, I reflected, there was never a pleasanter, or more harmless sight, and it will be a burning shame to scold them. The red firelight glowed on their two bonny heads, and revealed their faces animated with the eager interest of children, for though he was twenty-three and she eighteen, each had so much of novelty to feel and learn, that neither experienced nor evinced the sentiments of sober disenchanted maturity.

They lifted their eyes together, to encounter Mr Heathcliff – perhaps you have never remarked that their eyes are precisely similar, and they are those of Catherine Earnshaw. The present Catherine has no other likeness to her, except a breadth of forehead, and a certain arch of the nostril that makes her appear rather haughty, whether she will or not. With Hareton the resemblance is carried further: it is singular at all times, *then* it was particularly striking, because his senses were alert, and his mental faculties wakened to unwonted activity.

I suppose this resemblance disarmed Mr Heathcliff: he walked to the hearth in evident agitation, but it quickly subsided as he looked at the young man, or, I should say, altered its character; for it was there yet.

He took the book from his hand, and glanced at the open page, then returned it without any observation, merely signing Catherine away – her companion lingered very little behind her, and I was about to depart also, but he bid me sit still.

"It is a poor conclusion, is it not?" he observed, having brooded awhile on the scene he had just witnessed, "an absurd termination to my violent exertions? I get levers and mattocks to demolish the two houses, and train myself to be capable of working like Hercules, and when everything is ready and in my power, I find the will to lift a slate off either roof has vanished! My old enemies have not beaten me – now would be the precise time to revenge myself on their representatives – I could do it, and none could hinder me. But where is the use? I don't care for striking; I can't take the trouble to raise my hand!

That sounds as if I had been labouring the whole time only to exhibit a fine trait of magnanimity. It is far from being the case: I have lost the faculty of enjoying their destruction, and I am too idle to destroy for nothing.

"Nelly, there is a strange change approaching; I'm in its shadow at present. I take so little interest in my daily life that I hardly remember to eat and drink... Those two who have left the room are the only objects which retain a distinct material appearance to me, and that appearance causes me pain amounting to agony. About *her* I won't speak and I don't desire to think, but I earnestly wish she were invisible: her presence invokes only maddening sensations. *He* moves me differently, and yet if I could do it without seeming insane, I'd never see him again! You'll perhaps think me rather inclined to become so," he added, making an effort to smile, "if I try to describe the thousand forms of past associations and ideas he awakens or embodies... But you'll not talk of what I tell you, and my mind is so eternally secluded in itself, it is tempting at last to turn it out to another.

"Five minutes ago Hareton seemed a personification of my youth, not a human being – I felt to him in such a variety of ways, that it would have been impossible to have accosted him rationally.

"In the first place, his startling likeness to Catherine connected him fearfully with her. That, however, which you may suppose the most potent to arrest my imagination, is actually the least – for what is not connected with her to me? And what does not recall her? I cannot look down to this floor, but her features are shaped in the flags! In every cloud, in every tree – filling the air at night, and caught by glimpses in every object by day – I am surrounded with her image! The most ordinary faces of men and women – my own features – mock me with a resemblance. The entire world is a dreadful collection of memoranda that she did exist, and that I have lost her!

"Well, Hareton's aspect was the ghost of my immortal love, of my wild endeavours to hold my right; my degradation, my pride, my happiness, and my anguish...

"But it is frenzy to repeat these thoughts to you; only it will let you know why, with a reluctance to be always alone, his society is no benefit – rather an aggravation of the constant torment I suffer – and it partly contributes to render me regardless how he and his cousin go on together. I can give them no attention any more."

"But what do you mean by a *change*, Mr Heathcliff?" I said, alarmed at his manner, though he was neither in danger of losing his senses, nor dying, according to my judgement: he was quite strong and healthy; and as to his reason, from childhood he had a delight in dwelling on dark things, and entertaining odd fancies. He might have had a mono-mania on the subject of his departed idol, but on every other point his wits were as sound as mine.

"I shall not know that till it comes," he said, "I'm only half-conscious of it now."

"You have no feeling of illness, have you?" I asked.

"No, Nelly, I have not," he answered.

"Then you are not afraid of death?" I pursued.

"Afraid? No!" he replied. "I have neither a fear, nor a presentiment, nor a hope of death – why should I? With my hard constitution and temperate mode of living, and unperilous occupations, I ought to and probably *shall* remain above ground till there is scarcely a black hair on my head. And yet I cannot continue in this condition! I have to remind myself to breathe – almost to remind my heart to beat! And it is like bending back a stiff spring: it is by compulsion that I do the slightest act not prompted by one thought; and by compulsion that I notice anything alive or dead, which is not associated with one uni-versal idea... I have a single wish, and my whole being and faculties are yearning to attain it. They have yearned towards it so long, and so unwaveringly, that I'm convinced it *will* be reached – and *soon* – because it has devoured my existence: I am swallowed up in the anticipation of its fulfilment.

"My confessions have not relieved me, but they may account for some otherwise unaccountable phases of humour which I show. O God! It is a long fight; I wish it were over!"

He began to pace the room, muttering terrible things to himself, till I was inclined to believe, as he said Joseph did, that conscience had turned his heart to an earthly hell. I wondered greatly how it would end.

Though he seldom before had revealed this state of mind, even by looks, it was his habitual mood, I had no doubt – he asserted it himself – but not a soul, from his general bearing, would have conjectured the fact. You did not when you saw him, Mr Lockwood, and at the period of which I speak, he was just the same as then, only fonder of contin-ued solitude, and perhaps still more laconic in company.

271

34

FOR SOME DAYS AFTER THAT EVENING, Mr Heathcliff shunned meeting us at meals; yet he would not consent formally to exclude Hareton and Cathy. He had an aversion to yielding so completely to his feelings, choosing rather to absent himself – and eating once in twenty-four hours seemed sufficient sustenance for him.

One night, after the family were in bed, I heard him go downstairs, and out at the front door. I did not hear him re-enter, and in the morning I found he was still away.

We were in April then: the weather was sweet and warm, the grass as green as showers and sun could make it, and the two dwarf apple trees near the southern wall in full bloom.

After breakfast, Catherine insisted on my bringing a chair and sitting with my work under the fir trees at the end of the house, and she beguiled Hareton, who had perfectly recovered from his accident, to dig and arrange her little garden, which was shifted to that corner by the influence of Joseph's complaints.

I was comfortably revelling in the spring fragrance around, and the beautiful soft blue overhead, when my young lady, who had run down near the gate to procure some primrose roots for a border, returned only half-laden, and informed us that Mr Heathcliff was coming in. "And he spoke to me," she added, with a perplexed countenance.

"What did he say?" asked Hareton.

"He told me to begone as fast as I could," she answered. "But he looked so different from his usual look that I stopped a moment to stare at him."

"How?" he enquired.

"Why, almost bright and cheerful – no, *almost* nothing – *very much* excited, and wild and glad!" she replied.

"Night-walking amuses him then," I remarked, affecting a careless manner – in reality as surprised as she was, and anxious to ascertain the truth of her statement, for to see the master looking glad would not be an everyday spectacle. I framed an excuse to go in.

Heathcliff stood at the open door; he was pale, and he trembled, yet certainly he had a strange joyful glitter in his eyes, that altered the aspect of his whole face.

"Will you have some breakfast?" I said. "You must be hungry, rambling about all night!"

I wanted to discover where he had been, but I did not like to ask directly.

"No, I'm not hungry," he answered, averting his head, and speaking rather contemptuously, as if he guessed I was trying to divine the occasion of his good humour.

I felt perplexed: I didn't know whether it were not a proper opportunity to offer a bit of admonition.

"I don't think it right to wander out of doors," I observed, "instead of being in bed: it is not wise, at any rate, this moist season. I dare say you'll catch a bad cold or a fever: you have something the matter with you now!"

"Nothing but what I can bear," he replied, "and with the greatest pleasure, provided you'll leave me alone – get in, and don't annoy me."

I obeyed, and in passing, I noticed he breathed as fast as a cat.

"Yes!" I reflected to myself, "we shall have a fit of illness. I cannot conceive what he has been doing."

That noon he sat down to dinner with us, and received a heaped-up plate from my hands, as if he intended to make amends for previous fasting.

"I've neither cold nor fever, Nelly," he remarked, in allusion to my morning's speech, "and I'm ready to do justice to the food you give me."

He took his knife and fork, and was going to commence eating, when the inclination appeared to become suddenly extinct. He laid them on the table, looked eagerly towards the window, then rose and went out.

We saw him walking to and fro in the garden while we concluded our meal, and Earnshaw said he'd go and ask why he would not dine – he thought we had grieved him some way.

"Well, is he coming?" cried Catherine when her cousin returned.

"Nay," he answered, "but he's not angry: he seemed rare and pleased* indeed; only I made him impatient by speaking to him twice, and then he bid me be off to you – he wondered how I could want the company of anybody else."

I set his plate to keep warm on the fender, and after an hour or two he re-entered, when the room was clear, in no degree calmer: the same unnatural – it was unnatural – appearance of joy under his black brows; the same bloodless hue, and his teeth visible now and then in a kind of smile; his frame shivering, not as one shivers with chill or weakness, but as a tight-stretched cord vibrates – a strong thrilling, rather than trembling.

I will ask what is the matter, I thought, or who should? And I exclaimed:

"Have you heard any good news, Mr Heathcliff? You look uncommonly animated."

"Where should good news come from to me?" he said. "I'm animated with hunger, and, seemingly, I must not eat."

"Your dinner is here," I returned, "why won't you get it?"

"I don't want it now," he muttered hastily, "I'll wait till supper. And Nelly, once for all, let me beg you to warn Hareton and the other away from me. I wish to be troubled by nobody – I wish to have this place to myself."

"Is there some new reason for this banishment?" I enquired. "Tell me why you are so queer, Mr Heathcliff? Where were you last night? I'm not putting the question through idle curiosity, but—"

"You are putting the question through very idle curiosity," he interrupted, with a laugh. "Yet I'll answer it. Last night I was on the threshold of hell. Today, I am within sight of my heaven – I have my eyes on it – hardly three feet to sever me! And now you'd better go… You'll neither see nor hear anything to frighten you, if you refrain from prying."

Having swept the hearth and wiped the table, I departed, more perplexed than ever.

He did not quit the house again that afternoon, and no one intruded on his solitude, till at eight o'clock I deemed it proper, though unsummoned, to carry a candle and his supper to him.

He was leaning against the ledge of an open lattice, but not looking out; his face was turned to the interior gloom. The fire had smouldered to ashes; the room was filled with the damp, mild air of the cloudy evening, and so still, that not only the murmur of the beck down Gimmerton was distinguishable, but its ripples and its gurgling over the pebbles, or through the large stones which it could not cover.

I uttered an ejaculation of discontent at seeing the dismal grate, and commenced shutting the casements, one after another, till I came to his.

"Must I close this?" I asked, in order to rouse him – for he would not stir.

The light flashed on his features as I spoke. Oh, Mr Lockwood, I cannot express what a terrible start I got by the momentary view! Those deep black eyes! That smile and ghastly paleness! It appeared to me, not Mr Heathcliff, but a goblin, and in my terror I let the candle bend towards the wall, and it left me in darkness.

"Yes, close it," he replied, in his familiar voice. "There, that is pure awkwardness! Why did you hold the candle horizontally? Be quick and bring another."

I hurried out in a foolish state of dread, and said to Joseph:

"The master wishes you to take him a light and rekindle the fire." For I dared not go in myself again just then.

Joseph rattled some fire into the shovel and went, but he brought it back immediately, with the supper tray in his other hand, explaining that Mr Heathcliff was going to bed and he wanted nothing to eat till morning.

We heard him mount the stairs directly; he did not proceed to his ordinary chamber, but turned into that with the panelled bed – its window, as I mentioned before, is wide enough for anybody to get through – and it struck me that he plotted another midnight excursion, which he had rather we had no suspicion of.

"Is he a ghoul or a vampire?" I mused. I had read of such hideous incarnate demons. And then I set myself to reflect how I had tended him in infancy, and watched him grow to youth, and followed him almost through his whole course, and what absurd nonsense it was to yield to that sense of horror.

"But where did he come from, the little dark thing, harboured by a good man to his bane?" muttered superstition, as I dozed into unconsciousness. And I began, half-dreaming, to weary myself with imagining some fit parentage for him, and, repeating my waking meditations, I tracked his existence over again, with grim variations; at last picturing his death and funeral; of which all I can remember is being exceedingly vexed at having the task of dictating an inscription for his monument, and consulting the sexton about it; and as he had no surname, and we could not tell his age, we were obliged to content ourselves with the single word "Heathcliff". That came true: we were. If you enter the kirkyard, you'll read on his headstone only that, and the date of his death.

Dawn restored me to common sense. I rose, and went into the garden as soon as I could see, to ascertain if there were any footmarks under his window. There were none.

"He has stayed at home," I thought, "and he'll be all right today!"

I prepared breakfast for the household, as was my usual custom, but told Hareton and Catherine to get theirs ere the master came down, for he lay late. They preferred taking it out of doors, under the trees, and I set a little table to accommodate them.

On my re-entrance I found Mr Heathcliff below. He and Joseph were conversing about some farming business; he gave clear, minute directions concerning the matter discussed, but he spoke rapidly and turned his head continually aside, and had the same excited expression, even more exaggerated.

When Joseph quitted the room, he took his seat in the place he generally chose, and I put a basin of coffee before him. He drew it nearer, and then rested his arms on the table and looked at the opposite wall, as I supposed, surveying one particular portion up and down with glittering, restless eyes, and with such eager interest that he stopped breathing during half a minute together.

"Come now," I exclaimed, pushing some bread against his hand, "eat and drink that, while it is hot. It has been waiting near an hour."

He didn't notice me, and yet he smiled. I'd rather have seen him gnash his teeth than smile so.

"Mr Heathcliff! Master!" I cried, "don't, for God's sake, stare as if you saw an unearthly vision."

"Don't, for God's sake, shout so loud," he replied. "Turn round and tell me, are we by ourselves?"

"Of course," was my answer, "of course we are."

Still I involuntarily obeyed him, as if I were not quite sure. With a sweep of his hand he cleared a vacant space in front among the breakfast things, and leant forwards to gaze more at his ease.

Now I perceived he was not looking at the wall, for when I regarded him alone, it seemed exactly that he gazed at something within two yards' distance. And whatever it was, it communicated, apparently, both pleasure and pain in exquisite extremes – at least the anguished yet raptured expression of his countenance suggested that idea.

The fancied object was not fixed either: his eyes pursued it with unwearied diligence, and, even in speaking to me, were never weaned away.

I vainly reminded him of his protracted abstinence from food: if he stirred to touch anything in compliance with my entreaties, if he stretched his hand out to get a piece of bread, his fingers clenched before they reached it and remained on the table, forgetful of their aim.

I sat, a model of patience, trying to attract his absorbed attention from its engrossing speculation – till he grew irritable and got up, asking why I would not allow him to have his own time in taking his meals? and saying that on the next occasion I needn't wait: I might set the things down and go.

Having uttered these words he left the house, slowly sauntered down the garden path, and disappeared through the gate.

The hours crept anxiously by; another evening came. I did not retire to rest till late, and when I did, I could not sleep. He returned after midnight, and instead of going to bed, shut himself into the room beneath. I listened and tossed about, and finally dressed and descended. It was too irksome to lie there, harassing my brain with a hundred idle misgivings.

I distinguished Mr Heathcliff's step, restlessly measuring the floor, and he frequently broke the silence by a deep inspiration, resembling a groan. He muttered detached words also – the only one I could catch was the name of Catherine, coupled with some wild term of endearment or suffering, and spoken as one would speak to a person present: low and earnest, and wrung from the depth of his soul.

I had not courage to walk straight into the apartment, but I desired to divert him from his reverie, and therefore fell foul of the kitchen fire, stirred it, and began to scrape the cinders. It drew him forth sooner than I expected. He opened the door immediately, and said:

"Nelly, come here... is it morning? Come in with your light."

"It is striking four," I answered. "You want a candle to take upstairs – you might have lit one at this fire."

"No, I don't wish to go upstairs," he said. "Come in, and kindle *me* a fire, and do anything there is to do about the room."

"I must blow the coals red first, before I can carry any," I replied, getting a chair and the bellows.

He roamed to and fro meantime in a state approaching distraction – his heavy sighs succeeding each other so thick as to leave no space for common breathing between.

"When day breaks I'll send for Green," he said, "I wish to make some legal enquiries of him while I can bestow a thought on those matters, and while I can act calmly. I have not written my will yet, and how to leave my property I cannot determine! I wish I could annihilate it from the face of the earth."

"I would not talk so, Mr Heathcliff," I interposed. "Let your will be a while – you'll be spared to repent of your many injustices yet! I never expected that your nerves would be disordered: they are at present marvellously so, however, and almost entirely through your own fault. The way you've passed these three last days might knock up a Titan. Do take some food and some repose. You need only look at yourself in a glass to see how you require both. Your cheeks are hollow, and your eyes bloodshot, like a person starving with hunger and going blind with loss of sleep."

"It is not my fault that I cannot eat or rest," he replied. "I assure you it is through no settled designs. I'll do both as soon as I possibly can. But you might as well bid a man struggling in the water rest within arm's length of the shore! I must reach it first, and then I'll rest. Well, never mind Mr Green – as to repenting of my injustices, I've done no injustice, and I repent of nothing. I'm too happy, and yet I'm not happy enough. My soul's bliss kills my body, but does not satisfy itself."

"Happy, master?" I cried. "Strange happiness! If you would hear me without being angry, I might offer some advice that would make you happier."

"What is that?" he asked. "Give it."

"You are aware, Mr Heathcliff," I said, "that from the time you were thirteen years old you have lived a selfish, unchristian life – and probably hardly had a Bible in your hands during all that period. You must have forgotten the contents of the book, and you may not have space to search it now. Could it be hurtful to send for someone – some minister of any denomination, it does not matter which – to explain it, and show you how very far you have erred from its precepts, and how unfit you will be for its heaven, unless a change takes place before you die?"

"I'm rather obliged than angry, Nelly," he said, "for you remind me of the manner that I desire to be buried in. It is to be carried to the church-yard in the evening. You and Hareton may, if you please, accompany me – and mind particularly to notice that the sexton obeys my directions concerning the two coffins! No minister need come; nor need anything be said over me... I tell you I have nearly attained *my* heaven, and that of others is altogether unvalued and uncoveted by me."

278

"And supposing you persevered in your obstinate fast, and died by that means, and they refused to bury you in the precincts of the kirk?" I said, shocked at his godless indifference. "How would you like it?"

"They won't do that," he replied, "if they did, you must have me removed secretly; and if you neglect it, you shall prove practically that the dead are not annihilated!"

As soon as he heard the other members of the family stirring, he retired to his den, and I breathed freer. But in the afternoon, while Joseph and Hareton were at their work, he came into the kitchen again, and, with a wild look, bid me come and sit in the house – he wanted somebody with him.

I declined, telling him plainly that his strange talk and manner frightened me, and I had neither the nerve nor the will to be his companion alone.

"I believe you think me a fiend," he said, with his dismal laugh, "something too horrible to live under a decent roof!"

Then turning to Catherine, who was there, and who drew behind me at his approach, he added half-sneeringly:

"Will *you* come, chuck? I'll not hurt you. No! To you I've made myself worse than the devil. Well, there is *one* who won't shrink from my company! By God! She's relentless. Oh, damn it! It's unutterably too much for flesh and blood to bear – even mine."

He solicited the society of no one more. At dusk he went into his chamber. Through the whole night, and far into the morning, we heard him groaning and murmuring to himself. Hareton was anxious to enter, but I bid him fetch Mr Kenneth, and he should go in and see him.

When he came, and I requested admittance and tried to open the door, I found it locked, and Heathcliff bid us be damned.

He was better, and would be left alone, so the doctor went away.

The following evening was very wet: indeed, it poured down till day-dawn, and as I took my morning walk round the house, I observed the master's window swinging open, and the rain driving straight in.

He cannot be in bed, I thought, those showers would drench him through! He must either be up or out. But I'll make no more ado, I'll go boldly and look!

Having succeeded in obtaining entrance with another key, I ran to unclose the panels, for the chamber was vacant; quickly pushing them aside, I peeped in. Mr Heathcliff was there – laid on his back. His eyes met mine so keen and fierce, I started, and then he seemed to smile.

I could not think him dead, but his face and throat were washed with rain; the bedclothes dripped, and he was perfectly still. The lattice, flapping to and fro,* had grazed one hand that rested on the sill – no blood trickled from the broken skin, and when I put my fingers to it, I could doubt no more – he was dead and stark!

I hasped the window; I combed his black long hair from his forehead; I tried to close his eyes – to extinguish, if possible, that frightful, lifelike gaze of exultation before anyone else beheld it. They would not shut – they seemed to sneer at my attempts, and his parted lips and sharp white teeth sneered too! Taken with another fit of cowardice, I cried out for Joseph. Joseph shuffled up and made a noise, but resolutely refused to meddle with him.

"Th' divil's harried* off his soul," he cried, "and he muh hev his carcass intuh t' bargin, for owt Aw care! Ech! What a wicked un he looks, gurning at death!" and the old sinner grinned in mockery.

I thought he intended to cut a caper round the bed, but suddenly composing himself, he fell on his knees, and raised his hands, and returned thanks that the lawful master and the ancient stock were restored to their rights.

I felt stunned by the awful event, and my memory unavoidably recurred to former times with a sort of oppressive sadness. But poor Hareton, the most wronged, was the only one who really suffered much. He sat by the corpse all night, weeping in bitter earnest. He pressed its hand, and kissed the sarcastic, savage face that everyone else shrank from contemplating, and bemoaned him with that strong grief which springs naturally from a generous heart, though it be tough as tempered steel.

Mr Kenneth was perplexed to pronounce of what disorder the master died. I concealed the fact of his having swallowed nothing for four days, fearing it might lead to trouble, and then, I am persuaded, he did not abstain on purpose: it was the consequence of his strange illness, not the cause.

We buried him, to the scandal of the whole neighbourhood, as he wished. Earnshaw and I, the sexton and six men to carry the coffin, comprehended the whole attendance.

The six men departed when they had let it down into the grave – we stayed to see it covered. Hareton, with a streaming face, dug green sods, and laid them over the brown mould himself: at present it is as smooth and verdant as its companion mounds – and I hope its tenant sleeps as soundly. But the country folks, if you ask them, would swear on the Bible that he *walks*. There are those who speak to having met him near the church, and on the moor, and even within this house. Idle tales, you'll say, and so say I. Yet that old man by the kitchen fire affirms he has seen two on 'em* looking out of his chamber window on every rainy night since his death – and an odd thing happened to me about a month ago.

I was going to the Grange one evening – a dark evening, threatening thunder – and just at the turn of the Heights, I encountered a little boy with a sheep and two lambs before him; he was crying terribly, and I supposed the lambs were skittish, and would not be guided.

"What is the matter, my little man?" I asked.

"There's Heathcliff and a woman yonder, under t' nab," he blubbered, "un' I darnut* pass 'em."

I saw nothing, but neither the sheep nor he would go on, so I bid him take the road lower down.

He probably raised the phantoms from thinking, as he traversed the moors alone, on the nonsense he had heard his parents and companions repeat. Yet still I don't like being out in the dark now, and I don't like being left by myself in this grim house – I cannot help it – I shall be glad when they leave it, and shift to the Grange!"

"They are going to the Grange then?" I said.

"Yes," answered Mrs Dean, "as soon as they are married, and that will be on New Year's Day."

"And who will live here then?"

"Why, Joseph will take care of the house, and perhaps a lad to keep him company. They will live in the kitchen, and the rest will be shut up."

"For the use of such ghosts as choose to inhabit it," I observed.

"No, Mr Lockwood," said Nelly, shaking her head. "I believe the dead are at peace – but it is not right to speak of them with levity."

At that moment the garden gate swung to: the ramblers were returning.

"*They* are afraid of nothing," I grumbled, watching their approach through the window. "Together, they would brave Satan and all his legions."

As they stepped onto the door stones, and halted to take a last look at the moon – or more correctly, at each other by her light – I felt irresistibly impelled to escape them again, and, pressing a remembrance into the hand of Mrs Dean, and disregarding her expostulations at my rudeness, I vanished through the kitchen as they opened the house door, and so should have confirmed Joseph in his opinion of his fellow servant's gay indiscretions, had he not fortunately recognized me for a respectable character by the sweet ring of a sovereign at his feet.

My walk home was lengthened by a diversion in the direction of the kirk. When beneath its walls, I perceived decay had made progress, even in seven months: many a window showed black gaps deprived of glass, and slates jutted off here and there, beyond the right line of the roof, to be gradually worked off in coming autumn storms.

I sought, and soon discovered, the three headstones on the slope next the moor: the middle one grey and half-buried in the heath; Edgar Linton's only harmonized by the turf and moss creeping up its foot; Heathcliff's still bare.

I lingered round them, under that benign sky; watched the moths fluttering among the heath and harebells; listened to the soft wind breathing through the grass, and wondered how anyone could ever imagine unquiet slumbers for the sleepers in that quiet earth.

Note on the Text and Illustrations

The text in the present edition is based on the first edition of *Wuthering Heights* (1847), collated with the second edition (1850). Several readings from the 1850 edition have been silently incorporated for the sake of clarity. The spelling and punctuation have been standardized, modernized and made consistent throughout.

The portrait of Maria Branwell and the photographs of the Haworth Parsonage and the Haworth Church are reproduced courtesy of the Brontë Society. The photograph of High Sunderland is by G. Bernard Wood.

Notes

p. 4, *penetralium*: The inner recesses of a building. A common yet incorrect singular form of "penetralia".

p. 5, *"never told my love"*: "She never told her love / But let concealment, like a worm i' the bud, / Feed on her damask cheek" – See *Twelfth Night*, Act II, Sc. 4, ll. 109–11.

p. 6, *gnarl*: Snarl.

p. 7, *possessed swine*: See Luke 8:33: "Then went the devils out of the man, and entered into the swine: and the herd ran violently down a steep place into the lake, and were choked."

p. 8, *fowld*: Sheep fold.

p. 8, *laith*: Barn.

p. 8, *flaysome*: Frightful.

p. 11, *discussed*: Consumed.

p. 11, *basin*: Handleless cup.

p. 13, *faishion tuh*: Have the nerve to.

p. 13, *un' war*: And worse.

p. 13, *I'll not say what he shall be done to*: Perhaps a reminiscence of *King Lear*, Act II, Sc. 4, ll. 278–80: "I will do such things, / What they are, yet I know not, but they shall be / The terrors of the earth."

p. 16, *agait*: Afoot, going on.

p. 16, *Whisht*: Hush.

p. 16, *clothes press*: Cupboard or chest in which clothes were kept folded.

p. 17, *lean type*: Faint type.

p. 18, *lugs*: Ears.

p. 18, *laiking*: Playing, fooling around.

p. 18, *scroop*: Spine.

p. 18, *pawsed his fit*: Kicked his feet.

p. 18, *gait*: Way.

p. 18, *laced*: Beaten.

p. 19, *Seventy Times Seven*: See Matthew 18:22.

p. 19, *Jabes Branderham*: Probably based on the popular Wesleyan preacher Jabez Bunting (1779–1858).

p. 21, *place which knows him may know him no more*: See Job 7:10.

p. 21, *Thou art the Man!*: See John 19:5.

p. 21, *the judgement written*: See Psalm 149:9.

p. 21, *Every man's... neighbour*: See Genesis 16:12, Isaiah 19:2 and Zechariah 8:10.

p. 22, *ideal*: Imaginary.

p. 26, *snoozled*: Nuzzled.

p. 27, *barren*: Stretch of barren land.

p. 29, *indigenae*: Natives.

p. 31, *flighted*: *OED* mentions this example and claims it means "frightened", but from the context it would seem that it means something along the lines of "beaten", as in Scots usage.

p. 31, *beaten*: Exhausted.

p. 32, *humour*: Ill disposition.

p. 35, *wick*: Quick.

p. 37, *frame*: Hurry.

p. 38, *delf case*: A cupboard for delf or delft, a type of glazed earthenware originally produced in Delft in Holland, but which was manufactured also in Britain.

p. 40, *basement*: Probably a ledge above the basement window.

p. 42, *out-and-outer*: "Bold scoundrel".

p. 46, *cant*: Cheerful. Also "canty" later on.

p. 47, *donning*: Dressing.

p. 48, *frame*: Imagine.

p. 50, *mess*: Serving.

p. 61, *marred*: Spoilt.

p. 64, *It was far in the night... mools heard that*: This is slightly misquoted from 'The Ghaist's Warning' a ballad translated from the Danish, which Scott included in his work *The Lady of the Lake*. "Grat", "mither" and "mools" mean "wept", "mother" and "earth" respectively.

p. 69, *fate of Milo*: This is a reference to the sixth-century BC athlete Milo of Croton, who attempted to tear apart a tree, only for the tree to close down on his hand. Thus trapped, he was devoured by wolves.

p. 70, *Girt idle seeght*: Great idle sight.

p. 70, *fahl*: Foul.

p. 71, *rigs*: Ridges.

p. 71, *plottered*: Splashed.

p. 71, *Hahsomdiver*: Howsoever.

p. 71, *offald*: Worthless.

p. 72, *spare the righteous*: See 2 Peter 2:5 and 7.

p. 73, *All warks togither for gooid*: See Romans 8:28.

p. 73, *starving*: Freezing.

p. 73, *boards*: Doors.

p. 73, *gentle and simple*: Of all walks of life.

p. 74, *wer*: Our.

p. 77, *escape to America... foster-country*: Heathcliff returns in 1783, just as the American War of Independence has ended.

p. 79, *sough*: Ditch.

p. 80, *jubilee*: "Jubilee" just means celebration in general in this context.

p. 86, *fondling*: Little fool.

p. 88, *crahnr's 'quest enah*: Coroner's inquest very soon (or immediately).

p. 88, *wi'hauding*: Restraining.

p. 88, *sticking*: Killing.

p. 88, *ut's soa up uh going tuh t' grand 'sizes*: Who's so intent on going to the grand assizes.

p. 88, *gangs banning*: Goes swearing.

p. 88, *broad road*: Matthew 7:13.

p. 88, *pikes*: Toll gates.

p. 88, *justice meeting*: Quarter sessions.

p. 90, *centipede from the Indies*: A very venomous species.

p. 91, *sand pillar*: Used in former times as milestones.

p. 93, *barn*: Bairn.

p. 96, *rating*: An angry reprimand.

p. 98, *framing*: Inventing.

p. 103, *they put pigeons' feathers in the pillows*: According to regional superstition, the soul could be temporarily prevented from leaving the body of the deceased by placing pigeon feathers inside the pillow.

p. 103, *swells*: Hills.

p. 104, *elf bolts*: Prehistoric arrowheads, which were superstitiously believed to be projectiles thrown by mischievous fairies.

p. 104, *press*: A clothes press, see third note to p. 16.

p. 112, *proclaimant*: Proclaimer.

p. 116, *dip candle*: A candle that is produced by dipping a wick into melted wax or tallow.

p. 116, *Mim*: Prim.

p. 116, *Minching un' munching*: Mincing: Joseph is mocking Isabella's southern, upper-class manner of speech.

p. 116, *Nor nuh me!*: Not I!

p. 117, *sad*: Sombre, conservative.

p. 119, *fresh ortherings*: New instructions.

p. 119, *Aw daht*: I don't doubt.

p. 120, *thible*: A thivel, or wooden spoon or stick used for stirring.

p. 120, *nave*: Fist.

p. 120, *pale t' guilp off*: There has been no definitive interpretation of this expression. It could either mean something along the lines of "scrape the froth off" or "pull the guilpot off" – the guilpot being a large cooking pot.

p. 120, *deaved aht*: Knocked out.

p. 120, *cranky*: Shaky.

p. 120, *meeterly clane*: Tolerably clean.

p. 121, *baht all this wark*: Without all this work.

p. 121, *mells on't*: Meddles with it.

p. 122, *lig*: Lie.

p. 122, *madling*: Fool.

p. 122, *pining*: Starving.

p. 122, *plisky*: Tantrum.

p. 122, *Him*: Presumably the Devil.

p. 126, *dearer to her than her dog or her horse*: It has been suggested that this is a reminiscence of Tennyson's 'Locksley Hall', l. 50: "Something better than his dog, a little dearer than his horse".

p. 128, *brach*: Bitch hound.

p. 130, *dree*: Tedious, dreary.

p. 138, *luckless*: Bearing bad luck.

p. 146, *so as by fire*: See 1 Corinthians 3:15.

p. 148, *girned*: Snarled.

p. 152, *not so much*: The 1850 edition, edited by Charlotte Brontë, reads: "he's only half a man – not so much – and the rest fiend."

p. 157, *buried at the crossroads*: Suicides were usually buried at cross-roads.

p. 157, *taen tent*: Taken care.

p. 161, *galloway*: In this case, a small breed of riding horse, originating from Galloway in Scotland.

p. 164, *fairishes*: Fairies.

p. 165, *offalld*: Wicked, awful.

p. 166, *near*: Miserly.

p. 169, *unlikely*: Unseemly.

p. 171, *maks noa 'cahnt*: Takes no account.

p. 171, *norther*: Neither.

p. 178, *moor game*: Grouse.

p. 179, *nab*: Promontory.

p. 183, *gaumless*: Gormless, awkward.

p. 184, *bathos*: Depth.

p. 185, *lath*: Weakling.

p. 185, *crater*: Creature.

p. 187, *cover*: Cover up, conceal.

p. 193, *starved and sackless*: Cold and demoralized.

p. 194, *canty*: See first note to p. 46 above.

p. 195, *Slough of Despond*: An allegorical bog in John Bunyan's *The Pilgrim's Progress* (1768), into which the protagonist Christian sinks under the burden of his sins.

p. 196, *stretched*: Hurried.

p. 203, *win*: Reach.

p. 210, *sarve you aht*: Have his revenge on you.

p. 210, *skift*: Shift, move away.

p. 210, *orther*: Other.

p. 210, *bahn*: Going, bound.

p. 223, *ling*: Heather.

p. 225, *lees*: Grazing ground.

p. 229, *benefit of clergy*: Exemption from the jurisdiction of secular courts for members of the clergy, abolished in 1827.

p. 240, *Nobody loves… you die*: Reminiscent of Shakespeare's *Richard III* Act v, Sc. 3, 200–1: "There is no creature loves me; / And if I die, no soul shall pity me".

p. 241, *den*: Hollow.

p. 242, *beaten out of that*: Thwarted in that endeavour.

p. 243, *thrang*: Busy.

p. 244, *hisseln*: At himself.

p. 245, *fain… of*: Pleased about.

p. 245, *a thought*: Rather.

p. 246, *overlooking*: Supervision.

p. 247, *taking*: State.

p. 248, *stalled*: Weary.

p. 248, *curl back*: Recoil.

p. 250, *unhesitatingly*: The 1850 edition reads "hesitatingly" instead.

p. 251, *Chevy Chase*: A sixteenth-century ballad.

p. 254, *wick*: Weeks.

p. 255, *mensful*: Clean, decent.

p. 256, *Eea, f'r owt Ee knaw*: Yes, for all I know.

p. 257, *by th' haulf*: Much.

p. 257, *nur hearken yah hahsiver*: Than listen to you in any case.

p. 257, *yah set up them glories tuh Sattan*: You burst into hymns to Satan.

p. 257, *Fairy Annie's Wedding*: The correct title of this seventeenth-century folk song is 'Fair Annie'.

p. 258, *fellies*: Fellows, suitors.

p. 258, *jocks*: Victuals.

p. 258, *reaming*: Frothing, brimful.

p. 259, *following the house*: Carrying out domestic duties.

p. 260, *getting up*: Preparing.

p. 261, *Side out of t' gait*: Get out of the way.

p. 263, *This hoile's norther mensful nor seemly*: This hole (room) is neither decent nor seemly.

p. 264, *on the head of it*: On that count.

p. 266, *barthens*: Burdens.

p. 266, *stale t' sowl*: Steal the soul.

p. 266, *set*: Plant.

p. 273, *rare and pleased*: Very pleased.

p. 280, *The lattice, flapping to and fro*: It has been suggested that the window, in accordance with superstition, has been opened in order to let the soul of the deceased depart.

p. 280, *harried*: Carried.

p. 281, *two on 'em*: Two of them.

p. 281, *darnut*: Dare not.

Extra Material

on

Emily Brontë's

Wuthering Heights

Emily Brontë's Life

Emily Jane Brontë was born on 30th July 1818 in her father's Birth and Early Years parsonage in Thornton, Yorkshire. She was the fifth child of Revd Patrick Brontë and Maria, née Branwell. Her older siblings were Maria, Elizabeth, Charlotte and Branwell Brontë. After the birth of her sister Anne in 1820, her father took up an appointment at Haworth, near Bradford, a place where Emily would spend most of her life and which would become one of the main inspirations for her writing.

Patrick Brontë was a Cambridge-educated Irish expatriate and Anglican clergyman who published several volumes of poems and prose, but later devoted most of his energies to his parishioners and to various aspects of public and religious life. This left little time for getting involved with his family, and the way he has been described varies between an eccentric, negligent tyrant and a tolerant, enlightened parent.

After the death of her mother in September 1821, Emily's maternal aunt Elizabeth Branwell moved from Cornwall to live with the family in Haworth on a permanent basis, acting as a mother figure to the Brontë children and teaching them the values of discipline and good housekeeping. Emily and her siblings were educated mainly at home, where they studied a broad range of subjects and enjoyed access to a wealth of books and newspapers.

In November 1824, Emily joined her sisters Maria, Elizabeth and Charlotte at the Clergy Daughters' School at Cowan Bridge under a subsidized scheme to aid the children of impecunious clergymen. This experience proved to be a difficult one for the sisters, with squalid living conditions and a severe teaching regime – the Lowood school described by Charlotte Brontë in *Jane Eyre* is largely based on this – although there is evidence to suggest that Emily, being the youngest, enjoyed a more favourable treatment. Their stay at the school came to a tragic and abrupt end as first Maria and then Elizabeth contracted tuberculosis, dying shortly after returning home. Their father removed Charlotte and Emily from the school in June 1825, when Elizabeth was in her final days.

Fantasy World   The remaining Brontë sisters resumed their education from home, along with Branwell. The following years were marked not only by their diligent learning and fervent curiosity, but by an abundance of creativity and imagination in the children's daily pursuits. Led by Charlotte and Branwell, the Brontë children acted out various self-made "plays". Charlotte and Branwell wrote journal articles modelled on those they were reading in contemporary publications such as *Blackwood's Magazine*, and went on to create their own fantasy worlds called Glasstown and Angria, which they chronicled in verse and prose. As well as participating in their elders' creations, Emily and Anne developed their own imaginary realm parallel to Angria, named Gondal, which also generated a wealth of material, written down in tiny, almost undecipherable letters in handmade booklets. Unfortunately none of the Gondal writings – with the exception of some of the poems – have survived.

Enigmatic Character   Not much is known about Emily's life: only three letters by her have been preserved – as opposed to the almost 700 letters which her sister Charlotte left behind. This relative lack of information has given licence to much speculation, and she has often, perhaps unjustly, been portrayed as a misanthrope and a mystic removed from the real world.

It is clear from first-hand sources that she was withdrawn and quiet, both as a child and as an adult, content with her immediate surroundings and family circle, and possessing a singularly vivid imagination. Charlotte Brontë described her sister as "not a person of demonstrative character, nor one on the recesses of whose mind and feelings even those nearest and dearest to her could, with impunity, intrude unlicensed", and Elizabeth Gaskell depicted her as "a tall, long-armed girl, more fully grown than her elder sister; extremely reserved in manner".

But Emily was also known for her acute reasoning skills, willpower and stoicism. One of the few anecdotes that we know about her – and which Charlotte later used in her novel *Shirley* – illustrates her fortitude: bitten in the arm by a stray dog when she was fifteen, she immediately cauterized the wound herself with a hot iron; when her arm began to show signs of infection and caused her to be ill, she refused to complain or tell anyone, for fear of raising alarm. Charlotte, probably the best authority on her sister's character, wrote of her: "I have never seen her parallel in anything. Stronger than a man, simpler than a child, her nature stood alone."

Emily's attachment to her Haworth home and its surroundings and lifestyle proved so strong that it was almost
impossible for her to pursue any form of education or
employment elsewhere. In July 1835 Emily left Haworth to
attend Roe Head School, some twenty miles from her home,
where Charlotte had secured a teaching position after having
been a pupil there herself. Her time at Roe Head was deeply
unhappy, as she had never – apart from a few months at
Cowan Bridge as a six-year-old – lived away from home, and
could not adapt to the constraints that the school's routine
and discipline placed on her freedom and imagination. Her
extremely reserved nature also made it difficult to gain social
acceptance among her peers. This homesickness led to physical illness, and she returned home in October of the same
year, her younger sister Anne taking her place at the school
three months later. *(margin: Attachment to Haworth)*

Emily was again jolted out of her Haworth routine in
September 1838, when she obtained a teaching post at Law
Hill, a girls' school in the village of Southowram, near
Halifax. But yet again the fetters of a constant workload
and a rigid lifestyle were an impediment to her happiness. In
the words of her sister Charlotte, "Liberty was the breath of
Emily's nostril – without it, she perished." At first it seemed
that she still found time to escape into her fantasy world, as
some of her best poems appear to have been written during
that period, but later on, having returned to Law Hill after her
Christmas holidays, her health and spirits deteriorated, forcing her to return to Haworth in the spring of 1839.

After these unsuccessful experiences away from home,
Emily relished her time back in her father's parsonage, where
she diligently combined housekeeping duties with writ-
ing about her fantasy world of Gondal. When in July 1841
Charlotte presented the idea of setting up their own school,
Emily responded enthusiastically. The two sisters decided it *(margin: Brussels)*

was best for them to attend a school on the Continent for at least six months, in order to gain experience and learn French before launching into the highly competitive school market in England. Charlotte persuaded their Aunt Branwell to fund their scheme and, in February 1842, the two sisters left for Brussels to stay at the Pensionnat Heger.

The sisters' experience at the Hegers' boarding school seems to have been a very demanding but generally pleasant one. Emily, whose knowledge of French was much more rudimentary than Charlotte's, clearly experienced difficulties learning in an environment of native speakers, but her application and hard work produced quick results and earned her praise from the teaching staff. As well as her French, she greatly improved her musical skills – being already an accomplished pianist – and her German – which gave her access to German literature, later a strong influence on the writing of *Wuthering Heights*. Being foreign and considerably older than the other pupils, the sisters did not fit in or make many friends among their peers. Emily's reserved and introspective temperament would, in any case, scarcely have facilitated this. After the agreed six months had elapsed, Charlotte obtained teaching posts for both of them at the school in exchange for board and tuition.

Return to Haworth   Unfortunately their stay was cut short by the sudden death of Aunt Branwell in October 1842, which precipitated the girls' immediate return to Haworth. Unlike Charlotte, who went back to the Pensionnat Heger to teach for another year, Emily chose to stay at home and take over her aunt's housekeeping role. She continued to read extensively – "anyone passing by the kitchen door might have seen her studying German out of an open book, propped up before her, as she kneaded the dough", Elizabeth Gaskell wrote – and her fascination with Gondal remained undiminished. Emily's absorption into her world of fantasy is said to have at times blinded her to her surroundings and to the sufferings and unhappiness of those around her – especially Charlotte and Anne, who often showed signs of frustration and despondency at their situation in life. An example of Emily's absent-mindedness is recorded in one of her extant diary entries about a trip to York with Anne in the summer of 1845: in it she mentions only what is happening in the dream land of Gondal, without a single mention of her impressions of York.

A turning point in the life of Emily and her sisters came in *Birth of a Literary Career* the autumn of 1845, when Charlotte chanced upon a book of Emily's poems and was greatly impressed by their quality, to the point of envisaging their publication: "Of course, I was not surprised, knowing that she could and did write verse: I looked it over, and something more than surprise seized me – a deep conviction that these were not common effusions, nor at all like the poetry women generally write. I thought them condensed and terse, vigorous and genuine. To my ear, they had also a peculiar music – wild, melancholy and elevating." Emily was initially incensed by this perceived intrusion on her privacy, since Gondal and all the related poems were a creation that she had shared only with Anne, just as Charlotte and Branwell had done with Angria material. But thanks to the insistence of Charlotte and Anne's mediation, Emily gradually warmed to the idea of publishing some of her verse jointly with her sisters', under the condition that they use pseudonyms and keep their identities secret. After spending the end of 1845 collating their various poems into one manuscript and editing out all the explicit Gondal and Angria references, Charlotte obtained a positive reply from the small London publisher Alyott & Jones in January 1846 – with the proviso that they must pay for publication themselves – and in May of the same year the sisters received the advance copies of *Poems by Currer, Ellis and Acton Bell*. Although there were some favourable reviews, they managed to sell only two copies of the book.

Still, seeing their work in print must have acted as a strong *Wuthering Heights* incentive to the Brontë sisters, as they devoted all their energies to writing their first novels: Emily's *Wuthering Heights*, Anne's *Agnes Grey* and Charlotte's *The Professor* were soon completed and submitted pseudonymously to London publishers. *Agnes Grey* and *Wuthering Heights* were accepted in July 1847 by Thomas Cautley Newby of 72 Mortimer Street, Cavendish Square, on condition that the authors pay a deposit of fifty pounds. However, it was only after Charlotte's *Jane Eyre* was published in October 1847 (under the pseudonym of Currer Bell) and achieved instant critical and commercial success that *Wuthering Heights* and *Agnes Grey* were rushed into publication by Newby in December, amidst rumours that the three novels might have been written by the same author.

Wuthering Heights was greeted by a mixture of bewilderment and hostility, but was generally applauded for its originality and imaginative powers. The sales were encouraging, and her publisher renewed Emily's contract for a second novel.

Illness and Death Unfortunately there was little time for Emily to dwell on her achievements, as 1848 brought death and tragedy into the Brontë household. On 24th September, Branwell, who had been leading a life of debt-ridden debauchery and alcohol and drug addiction, died suddenly, probably from a combination of tuberculosis and delirium tremens. Emily, who had been tirelessly caring for her dying brother, also showed symptoms of tuberculosis soon after his funeral. She refused to rest or see a doctor, and died on 19th December. She was buried three days later in the family vault.

Emily Brontë's Works

Although Emily Brontë's œuvre is not extensive – consisting of only one novel and about two hundred poems – it must be remembered that she was a relatively prolific writer during her short lifetime. Unfortunately very little of what she wrote survives, especially her prose. It is possible that she destroyed her Gondal manuscripts herself or that Charlotte did so after Emily's death – perhaps because she believed them to be unsuitable for the public eye or a taint on her sister's reputation.

Gondal Ever since she was a child, Emily – together with her sister Anne – had written tales revolving around the fantasy world of Gondal, a realm of adventure and romance, inspired in part by their Yorkshire surroundings and the works of Sir Walter Scott. Even though the prose writings have been lost, there are references to Gondal events in several of Emily and Anne's diary entries – the earliest mention dating back to 1834. There has been inconclusive debate over whether the Gondal writings formed a coherent whole and over which characters were the most central to the narrative. Fannie Ratchford's *Gondal Queen: A Novel in Verse*, published in 1955, based on Emily's and Anne's extant Gondal verse and a substantial amount of conjecture, was an attempt to recreate a sense of coherence and unity in the Gondal saga, which may have misled some commentators into accepting as fact a merely hypothetical arrangement.

296

What can safely be affirmed in relation to the broader context of Emily Brontë's literary achievements is that this fantasy writing led to an extensive body of written work and enabled her to find her poetic voice and imaginative powers. Indeed, all of her surviving poems and to some extent *Wuthering Heights* can be read within the Gondal context.

The only surviving literary material by Emily Brontë apart from *Wuthering Heights* is therefore her poetry, which amounts to approximately 200 poems of varying length – twenty-one published during her lifetime and eighteen posthumously by her sister Charlotte. It has been difficult to establish an exhaustive and authoritative edition of her verse, since many of her poems – transcribed from notebooks and manuscripts – are undated, partly illegible or of uncertain authorship. Moreover, her sister Charlotte made some questionable editorial interventions in the poems that she published and transcribed after her sister's death.   *Poems*

Some of the poems explicitly mention their Gondal setting, while others read more as general contemplations, but it is evident that Emily's poetic output was originally a by-product of Gondal. However, when it came to publishing her poetry, Emily felt the need to remove any traces of her fantasy world from her verse, and her contribution to *Poems by Currer, Ellis and Acton Bell* (1846) – twenty-one poems in total – was judged in her time – and still is to this day – as the one which showed the greatest poetic talent. According to one of her contemporary reviewers, Emily's poetry displayed "an evident power of wing that may reach heights not here attempted".

It is unclear when exactly and in what circumstances Emily Brontë wrote *Wuthering Heights*, as there is no existing manuscript: it has been claimed that it may have been composed as early as 1837 or 1843. In all probability, however, the bulk of it was not written until 1845–46, although many of the characters, events and motifs are adapted from Gondal material. There has also been speculation as to the authorship of the novel, notably the now discredited theory that her brother Branwell may have written it.   *Wuthering Heights*

In any case, the manuscript was being sent around to publishers pseudonymously from July 1846, along with Currer Bell's *The Professor* and Acton Bell's *Agnes Grey*. Charlotte had been hoping to have all three published in one three-volume edition, but *Wuthering Heights* was far too long for this to be possible.

An agreement with a publisher, Thomas Cautley Newby, was finally secured, around July 1847, for *Wuthering Heights* and *Agnes Grey* to be published at the sisters' expense, on terms "somewhat impoverishing to the two authors", as Charlotte wrote. Indeed, they had to pay a deposit of fifty pounds, which would be recouped through the sales of the books.

After the initial agreement with the publisher, Emily and Anne found it rather difficult to elicit any form of response from Mr Newby as to when publication would take place, and grew increasingly frustrated at his lack of commitment. They received the final proof sheets only in mid-November: it seems that Newby's interest in the project had been suddenly reawakened by the phenomenal success of Currer Bell's *Jane Eyre* – which had appeared in October – and the opportunity to capitalize on the Bell name. When their six publication copies arrived at Haworth, Emily and Anne finally obtained confirmation that their books had been published, but to their great dismay they discovered that the corrections they had made to the proofs had not found their way into the final version of their novels.

Wuthering Heights is set in the wild and windswept moors of Yorkshire and depicts events from the late eighteenth century to the early nineteenth century. The novel opens in 1801, with the main narrator, the urbane Mr Lockwood, moving to the remote Thrushcross Grange in order to escape city life. He recounts his first meeting with his landlord, Mr Heathcliff, who lives on the isolated estate of Wuthering Heights two miles away. Heathcliff is a dark, rugged, misanthropic figure with an irascible and violent temperament. After his first visit to Wuthering Heights, Lockwood returns the following afternoon and, forced to spend the night there because of the adverse weather, is lodged in a bedroom which he discovers to have been formerly occupied by a certain Catherine Earnshaw. Lockwood drowsily reads extracts from Catherine's childhood journal, falls asleep and has dreadful nightmares. Back at Thrushcross Grange, intrigued by the previous night's occurrences, Lockwood questions his housekeeper Ellen Dean – who had previously been employed as a servant at Wuthering Heights – about Heathcliff and Catherine Earnshaw, and she obliges him by recounting the history of Wuthering Heights and its inhabitants – a narrative which forms the bulk of the novel.

Mrs Dean's story begins with the former master of Wuthering Heights, Mr Earnshaw, returning from a trip to Liverpool and bringing back a foundling to live with his two children Catherine and Hindley. The adopted child is given the name Heathcliff, and forms an intense childhood bond with Catherine. Unfortunately this idyll comes to an end when, years later, following the death of Mr Earnshaw, Hindley returns from university with his new wife Frances, takes over as master of the house and mistreats Heathcliff – beating him and forcing him to do menial work. Catherine becomes friendly with the Linton children of Thrushcross Grange, Edgar and Isabella, after having spent several weeks at their home recovering from a dog bite, and ends up marrying the respectable though weak Edgar. Heathcliff, jealous of this union and convinced that the new Mrs Linton has developed a disdain for him, flees Wuthering Heights and returns only after three years, having in the meantime mysteriously acquired a considerable fortune and refined manners.

Heathcliff begins exacting his revenge on his former tormentors and, taking advantage of Hindley's drunken, dissolute and debt-ridden state – the latter having turned to alcohol after his wife Frances died giving birth to their son Hareton – dispossesses him of his Wuthering Heights estate by paying off his gambling debts. He also renews his acquaintance with Catherine – who is overjoyed to see him – much to the displeasure of her husband, with whom he has a violent altercation.

Out of spite and calculation, Heathcliff elopes with Isabella Linton and marries her, despite her brother Edgar's opposition. Isabella ends up fleeing her brutal, abusive husband and moving to the south, finally giving birth to their son Linton. Meanwhile Heathcliff's beloved Catherine dies while delivering her daughter, also named Catherine.

Hindley dies a few months after his sister, and Heathcliff becomes the effective owner of Wuthering Heights and the guardian of Hareton, whom he brings up neglectfully. Upon the death of his wife Isabella, Heathcliff also takes in his son Linton – a sickly, effeminate, sullen child who inspires his father's contempt. He encourages Linton to befriend the young Catherine, who had hitherto been growing up in Thrushcross Grange blissfully unaware of Wuthering Heights and its inhabitants. Edgar objects to this relationship, but, falling gravely ill, he gradually relents. To complete his revenge, Heathcliff forces Linton and Catherine into marriage. Edgar and Linton die soon after that, leaving Heathcliff in full control over Wuthering Heights and Thrushcross Grange.

At this point, Ellen Dean finishes her narrative, having related events up to the present day. Shortly afterwards, Lockwood decides to move back to London, returning to visit the area in September 1802. Mrs Dean relates to him what has happened during his absence: Heathcliff, still haunted by the memory of Catherine, has died and is now buried next to his beloved, while Hareton and the younger Catherine are planning to marry and move from Wuthering Heights to Thrushcross Grange.

Early reviews of *Wuthering Heights* were not entirely favourable. Most of the Victorian critics did grudgingly accept the originality and the raw passion of the novel – the *Britannia* describing it as "proceeding from a mind of limited experience, but of original energy, and of a singular and distinctive cast". *Douglas Jerrold's Weekly Newspaper* declared that *"Wuthering Heights* is a strange sort of book – baffling all regular criticism – yet it is impossible to begin and not finish it", assuring the reader that "they have never read anything like it before". An almost identical reaction came from the *Literary World*, but with greater emphasis on the novel's supposed negative effects: "Fascinated by strange magic we read what we dislike, we become interested in characters which are most revolting to our feelings, and are made subject to the immense power of the book".

The characters' immoral behaviour was indeed the focus of most of the critics' objections. The *Atlas* claimed that "There is not in the entire dramatis personae a single character which is not thoroughly hateful or thoroughly contemptible". Although some reviewers saw some purpose to it – "It strongly shows the brutalizing influence of unchecked passion" (*Britannia*) – the subject matter was generally seen as unsuitable. In this, *Wuthering Heights* resembled, in their eyes, *Jane Eyre* and *Agnes Grey* – the *Spectator* lamenting the authors' "injudicious selection of theme and matter".

It was only after Emily's death that the reviews became more laudatory and encouraging. In 1850 Sydney Dobell, speculating that *Wuthering Heights* was in fact an early novel by "Currer Bell", wrote anonymously in the *Palladium* that it was "the unformed writing of a giant's hand; the 'large utterance' of a baby god", recognizing in it "the stamp of high genius". This rekindled some interest in the novel, especially on the part of Charlotte, who edited and revised it for a new edition of *Wuthering Heights* and *Agnes Grey* to be published by Smith, Elder & Co. In her preface to the books, Charlotte clarified the identities of Ellis and Acton Bell and the circumstances of their composition. Charlotte also included some of her sisters' poems – eighteen of them by Emily – which she edited heavily, not only removing any Gondal reference and correcting what she perceived as errors in the metre, but controversially making substantial changes to some of the content.

Wuthering Heights' literary standing vastly improved throughout the nineteenth century, when writers and critics such as Algernon Swinburne started to champion the novel and its merits. Swinburne even went so far as comparing it to Shakespeare. In 1883, the poet A. Mary F. Robinson wrote the first biography of its author, reinforcing her romantic image. This rehabilitation process continued in the twentieth century, and the novel now ranks as one of the best-selling and most enduringly popular English classics.

Spin-offs and Adaptations

Such is the popular appeal of *Wuthering Heights* that it has prompted countless adaptations and literary spin-offs.

Literary Spin-offs

Jeffrey Caine's *Heathcliff* (1977) imagines the story of Heathcliff during his mysterious three years' absence from Wuthering Heights and takes the character to London, where he frequents the capital's underworld and eventually prospers in it. Lin Haire-Sargeant's *H: The Story of Heathcliff's Journey back to Wuthering Heights* (1992) also deals with Heathcliff's life during this period, but has the protagonist travelling to Liverpool in search of his roots and meeting a mysterious benefactor who promises to give him a gentleman's education. Rather than describing what happened during Heathcliff's mysterious lost years, *The Return to Wuthering Heights* (1977) by Anna L'Estrange (a pseudonym for the South African writer Rosemary Ellerback, who later republished the novel under yet another pseudonym, Nicola Thorne) is an attempt to write a straight sequel, picking up the narrative where the original ended and recounting the lives of Catherine and Hareton.

In *Windward Heights* (1998), the Guadeloupian writer Maryse Condé transposes the tale of *Wuthering Heights* to Guadeloupe and Cuba. The novel is considered a refreshing take on the original, as well as an insightful observation of Caribbean society. In 2005 Emma Tennant, the author of many popular literary spin-offs, published *Heathcliff's Tale*, which was not a straightforward retelling or continuation of the story, but rather a postmodern blend of fact and fiction. In it, the young lawyer Henry Newby, nephew of T.C. Newby, the original publisher of *Wuthering Heights*, pays a visit to the Haworth Parsonage after Emily Brontë's death to retrieve the manuscript of her second novel, only to find himself haunted by a ghostly Heathcliff-like figure.

Screen Adaptations   The dramatic intensity and haunting location of *Wuthering Heights* has inspired many film-makers to produce screen adaptations of the novel. The first one is believed to be a 1920 silent movie directed by A.V. Bramble, starring Ann Trevor and Milton Rosmer, of which unfortunately no copy survives. This was followed by William Wyler's *Wuthering Heights* (1939), starring Laurence Olivier and Merle Oberon, which is seen as a classic and definitive adaptation, even though it only relates events up to Chapter 17 of the novel. In 1948, the first feature-length television adaptation was screened in the UK, directed by George More O'Ferrall. Two more full-length versions appeared on the small screen, the first one – part of BBC *Sunday Night Theatre* – in 1953, and the second one in 1961, directed by Rudolph Cartier. Peter Sasdy's TV miniseries was aired in 1967, followed eleven years later by Peter Hammond's version, commonly seen as the best television serialization of *Wuthering Heights*.

The two most recent big-screen adaptations in English are Robert Fuest's *Wuthering Heights* (1970), starring Timothy Dalton as Heathcliff, and Peter Kosminsky's *Emily Brontë's Wuthering Heights* (1992), starring Ralph Fiennes and Juliette Binoche. Since then there have been two more English-language television adaptations of the novel – screened in 1998 and 2003 respectively – one directed by David Skinner and starring Robert Cavanah, and the other, a modern musical retelling of the story, directed by Suri Krishnamma.

Wuthering Heights has also had successful foreign adaptations, such as Luis Buñuel's *Abismos de pasión* (1954), Jacques Rivette's *Hurlevent* (1985) and Yoshishige Yoshida's

Arashi ga oka (1988). There have also been many popular European television adaptations of the novel, such as Mario Landi's *Cime tempestose* (1956) and Jean-Pierre Carrère's *Les Hauts de Hurlevent* (1968).

Select Bibliography

Standard Edition:
The Clarendon Edition, edited by Hilary Marsden and Ian Jack (Oxford: Oxford University Press, 1976), with extensive notes and all the variants between the 1847 and 1850 editions, is the most authoritative edition to date.

Biographies:
Bentley, Phyllis, *The Brontës* (London: Thames and Hudson, 1969)

Chitham, Edward, *A Life of Emily Brontë* (Oxford: Blackwell, 1992)

Barker, Juliet, *The Brontës* (London: Weidenfeld and Nicolson, 1994)

Frank, Katherine, *Chainless Soul: A Life of Emily Brontë* (Boston: Houghton Mufflin, 1990)

Gérin, Winifred, *Emily Brontë: A Biography* (Oxford: Oxford University Press, 1978)

Simpson, Charles, *Emily Brontë* (London: Country Life, 1929)

Spark, Muriel and Derek Stanford, *Emily Brontë: Her Life and Her Work* (London: Peter Owen, 1953)

Additional Recommended Background Material:
Barker, Juliet, *The Brontës: A Life in Letters* (London: Penguin, 1997)

Gaskell, Elizabeth, *The Life of Charlotte Brontë*, Everyman edition (London: Everyman, 1997)

Glen, Heather, ed., *The Cambridge Companion to the Brontës* (Cambridge: Cambridge University Press, 2002)

Winnifrith, Tom, *The Brontës and Their Background* (London: Macmillan, 1988)

Biographical Notice of Ellis and Acton Bell

This notice and the following preface were written by Charlotte Brontë for the second edition of Wuthering Heights *and* Agnes Grey, *published by Smith, Elder & Co. in 1850.*

It has been thought that all the works published under the names of Currer, Ellis and Acton Bell were, in reality, the production of one person. This mistake I endeavoured to rectify by a few words of disclaimer prefixed to the third edition of *Jane Eyre*. These too, it appears, failed to gain a general credence, and now, on the occasion of a reprint of *Wuthering Heights* and *Agnes Grey*, I am advised distinctly to state how the case really stands.

Indeed, I feel myself that it is time the obscurity attending those two names – Ellis and Acton – was done away. The little mystery, which formerly yielded some harmless pleasure, has lost its interest; circumstances are changed. It becomes then my duty to explain briefly the origin and authorship of the books written by Currer, Ellis and Acton Bell.

About five years ago, my two sisters and myself, after a somewhat prolonged period of separation, found ourselves reunited and at home. Resident in a remote district, where education had made little progress, and where, consequently, there was no inducement to seek social intercourse beyond our own domestic circle, we were wholly dependent on ourselves and each other, on books and study, for the enjoyments and occupations of life. The highest stimulus, as well as the liveliest pleasure we had known from childhood upwards, lay in attempts at literary composition; formerly we used to show each other what we wrote, but of late years, this habit of communication and consultation had been discontinued; hence, it ensued that we were mutually ignorant of the progress we might respectively have made.

One day, in the autumn of 1845, I accidentally lighted on a MS volume of verse in my sister Emily's handwriting. Of course I was not surprised, knowing that she could and did write verse: I looked it over, and something more than surprise seized me – a deep conviction that these were not common effusions, nor at all like the poetry women generally write. I thought them condensed and terse, vigorous and genuine. To my ear, they had also a peculiar music – wild, melancholy and elevating.

My sister Emily was not a person of demonstrative character, nor one on the recesses of whose mind and feelings even those nearest and dearest to her could, with impunity, intrude unlicensed; it took hours to reconcile her to the discovery I had made, and days to persuade her that such poems merited publication. I knew, however, that a mind like hers could not be without some latent spark of honourable ambition, and refused to be discouraged in my attempts to fan that spark to flame.

Meantime, my younger sister quietly produced some of her own compositions, intimating that since Emily's had given me pleasure, I might like to look at hers. I could not but be a partial judge, yet I thought that those verses too had a sweet sincere pathos of their own.

We had very early established the dream of one day becoming authors. This dream, never relinquished even when distance divided and absorbing tasks occupied us, now suddenly acquired strength and consistency: it took the character of a resolve. We agreed to arrange a small selection of our poems, and, if possible, get them printed. Averse to personal publicity, we veiled our own names under those of Currer, Ellis and Acton Bell; the ambiguous choice being dictated by a sort of conscientious scruple at assuming Christian names positively masculine, while we did not like to declare ourselves women, because – without at that time suspecting that our mode of writing and thinking was not what is called "feminine" – we had a vague impression that authoresses are liable to be looked on with prejudice; we had noticed how critics sometimes use for their chastisement the weapon of personality, and for their reward a flattery, which is not true praise.

The bringing out of our little book was hard work. As was to be expected, neither we nor our poems were at all wanted, but for this we had been prepared at the outset; though inexperienced ourselves, we had read the experience of others. The great puzzle lay in the difficulty of getting answers of any kind from the publishers to whom we applied. Being greatly harassed by this obstacle I ventured to apply to the Messrs Chambers of Edinburgh for a word of advice; they may have forgotten the circumstance, but I have not, for from them I received a brief and business-like but civil and sensible reply, on which we acted, and at last made a way.

The book was printed: it is scarcely known, and all of it that merits to be known are the poems of Ellis Bell. The fixed conviction I held, and hold, of the worth of these poems has not indeed received the confirmation of much favourable criticism, but I must retain it notwithstanding.

Ill success failed to crush us: the mere effort to succeed had given a wonderful zest to existence; it must be pursued. We each set to work on a prose tale; Ellis Bell produced *Wuthering Heights*, Acton Bell *Agnes Grey*, and Currer Bell also wrote a narrative in one volume. These MSS were perseveringly obtruded upon various publishers for the space of a year and a half; usually their fate was an ignominious and abrupt dismissal.

At last *Wuthering Heights* and *Agnes Grey* were accepted on terms somewhat impoverishing to the two authors; Currer Bell's book found acceptance nowhere, nor any acknowledgement of merit, so that something like the chill of despair began to invade his heart. As a forlorn hope, he tried one publishing house more – Messrs Smith, Elder. Ere long – in a much shorter space than that on which experience had taught him to calculate – there came a letter, which he opened in the dreary expectation of finding two hard, hopeless lines, intimating that Messrs Smith, Elder and Co. "were not disposed to publish the MS", and instead he took out of the envelope a letter of two pages. He read it trembling. It declined indeed to publish that tale for business reasons, but it discussed its merits and demerits so courteously, so considerately, in a spirit so rational, with a discrimination so enlightened, that this very refusal cheered the author better than a vulgarly expressed acceptance would have done. It was added that a work in three volumes would meet with careful attention.

I was then just completing *Jane Eyre*, at which I had been working while the one-volume tale was plodding its weary round in London: in three weeks I sent it off; friendly and skilful hands took it in. This was in the commencement of September 1847; it came out before the close of October following, while *Wuthering Heights* and *Agnes Grey*, my sisters' works, which had already been in the press for months, still lingered under a different management.

They appeared at last. Critics failed to do them justice. The immature but very real powers revealed in *Wuthering Heights* were scarcely recognized; its import and nature were misunderstood; the identity of its author was misrepresented; it was said that this was an earlier and ruder attempt of the same pen which had produced *Jane Eyre*. Unjust and grievous error! We laughed at it at first, but I deeply lament it now. Hence, I fear, arose a prejudice against the book. That writer who could attempt to palm off an inferior and immature production under cover of one successful effort must indeed be unduly eager after the secondary and sordid result of authorship, and pitiably indifferent to its true and honourable meed. If reviewers and the public truly believed this, no wonder that they looked darkly on the cheat.

Yet I must not be understood to make these things subject for reproach or complaint; I dare not do so: respect for my sister's memory forbids me. By her any such querulous manifestation would have been regarded as an unworthy and offensive weakness.

It is my duty, as well as my pleasure, to acknowledge one exception to the general rule of criticism. One writer, endowed with the keen vision and fine sympathies of genius, has discerned the real nature of *Wuthering Heights*, and has, with equal accuracy, noted its beauties and touched on its faults. Too often do reviewers remind us of the mob of astrologers, Chaldeans and soothsayers gathered before the "writing on the wall", and unable to read the characters or make known the interpretation. We have a right to rejoice when a true seer comes at last, some man in whom is an excellent spirit, to whom have been given light, wisdom and under-standing; who can accurately read the "Mene, Mene, Tekel, Upharsin" of an original mind (however unique, however inefficiently cultured and partially expanded that mind may be) and who can say with confidence, "This is the interpretation thereof."

Yet even the writer to whom I allude shares the mistake about the authorship, and does me the injustice to suppose that there was equivoque in my former rejection of this honour (as an honour I regard it). May I assure him that I would scorn in this and in every other case to deal in equivoque; I believe language to have been given us to make our meaning clear, and not to wrap it in dishonest doubt.

The Tenant of Wildfell Hall, by Acton Bell, had likewise an unfavourable reception. At this I cannot wonder. The choice of subject was an entire mis-take. Nothing less congruous with the writer's nature could be conceived. The motives which dictated this choice were pure, but, I think, slightly mor-bid. She had in the course of her life been called on to contemplate, near at hand and for a long time, the terrible effects of talents misused and faculties abused; hers was naturally a sensitive, reserved and dejected nature; what she saw sank very deeply into her mind; it did her harm. She brooded over it till she believed it to be a duty to reproduce every detail (of course with fictitious characters, incidents and situations) as a warning to others. She hated her work, but would pursue it. When reasoned with on the subject, she regarded such reasonings as a temptation to self-indulgence. She must be honest; she must not varnish, soften or conceal. This well-meant resolu-tion brought on her misconstruction, and some abuse which she bore, as it was her custom to bear whatever was unpleasant with mild, steady patience.

She was a very sincere and practical Christian, but the tinge of religious melancholy communicated a sad shade to her brief, blameless life.

Neither Ellis nor Acton allowed herself for one moment to sink under want of encouragement; energy nerved the one, and endurance upheld the other. They were both prepared to try again; I would fain think that hope and the sense of power was yet strong within them. But a great change approached: affliction came in that shape which to anticipate is dread; to look back on, grief. In the very heat and burden of the day, the labourers failed over their work.

My sister Emily first declined. The details of her illness are deep-branded in my memory, but to dwell on them, either in thought or narrative, is not in my power. Never in all her life had she lingered over any task that lay before her, and she did not linger now. She sank rapidly. She made haste to leave us. Yet, while physically she perished, mentally she grew stronger than we had yet known her. Day by day, when I saw with what a front she met suffering, I looked on her with an anguish of wonder and love. I have seen nothing like it – but indeed I have never seen her parallel in anything. Stronger than a man, simpler than a child, her nature stood alone. The awful point was that, while full of ruth for others, on herself she had no pity; the spirit was inexorable to the flesh; from the trembling hand, the unnerved limbs, the faded eyes, the same service was exacted as they had rendered in health. To stand by and witness this, and not dare to remonstrate, was a pain no words can render.

Two cruel months of hope and fear passed painfully by, and the day came at last when the terrors and pains of death were to be undergone by this treasure, which had grown dearer and dearer to our hearts as it wasted before our eyes. Towards the decline of that day, we had nothing of Emily but her mortal remains as consumption left them. She died December 19th 1848.

We thought this enough, but we were utterly and presumptuously wrong. She was not buried ere Anne fell ill. She had not been committed to the grave a fortnight before we received distinct intimation that it was necessary to prepare our minds to see the younger sister go after the elder. Accordingly, she followed in the same path with slower step, and with a patience that equalled the other's fortitude. I have said that she was religious, and it was by leaning on these Christian doctrines which she firmly believed that she found support through her most painful journey. I witnessed their efficacy in her latest hour and greatest trial, and must bear my testimony to the calm triumph with which they brought her through. She died May 28th 1849.

What more shall I say about them? I cannot and need not say much more. In externals, they were two unobtrusive women; a perfectly secluded life gave them retiring manners and habits. In Emily's nature the extremes of vigour and simplicity seemed to meet. Under an unsophisticated culture, inartificial tastes and an unpretending outside lay a secret power and fire that might have informed the brain and kindled the veins of a hero – but she had no worldly wisdom; her powers were unadapted to the practical business of life; she would fail to defend her most manifest rights, to consult her most legitimate advantage. An interpreter ought always to have stood between her and the world. Her will was not very flexible, and it generally opposed her interest. Her temper was magnanimous, but warm and sudden; her spirit altogether unbending.

Anne's character was milder and more subdued; she wanted the power, the fire, the originality of her sister, but was well endowed with quiet virtues of her own. Long-suffering, self-denying, reflective and intelligent, a constitutional reserve and taciturnity placed and kept her in the shade and covered her mind, and especially her feelings, with a sort of nunlike veil, which was rarely lifted. Neither Emily nor Anne was learned; they had no thought of filling their pitchers at the wellspring of other minds; they always wrote from the impulse of nature, the dictates of intuition, and from such stores of observation as their limited experience had enabled them to amass. I may sum up all by saying that for strangers they were nothing, but for those who had known them all their lives in the intimacy of close relationship, they were genuinely good and truly great.

This notice has been written because I felt it a sacred duty to wipe the dust off their gravestones, and leave their dear names free from soil.

– Currer Bell
September 19th, 1850

Editor's Preface to the
New Edition of *Wuthering Heights*

I have just read over *Wuthering Heights*, and for the first time have obtained a clear glimpse of what are termed (and perhaps really are) its faults; have gained a definite notion of how it appears to other people – to strangers who knew nothing of the author; who are unacquainted with the locality where the scenes of the story are laid; to whom the inhabitants, the customs, the natural characteristics of the outlying hills and hamlets in the West Riding of Yorkshire are things alien and unfamiliar.

To all such *Wuthering Heights* must appear a rude and strange production. The wild moors of the north of England can for them have no interest: the language, the manners, the very dwellings and household customs of the scattered inhabitants of those districts must be to such readers in a great measure unintelligible, and – where intelligible – repulsive. Men and women who – perhaps naturally very calm and with feelings moderate in degree and little marked in kind – have been trained from their cradle to observe the utmost evenness of manner and guardedness of language will hardly know what to make of the rough, strong utterance, the harshly manifested passions, the unbridled aversions and headlong partialities of unlettered moorland hinds and rugged moorland squires who have grown up untaught and unchecked, except by mentors as harsh as themselves. A large class of readers, likewise, will suffer greatly from the introduction into the pages of this work of words printed with all their letters, which it has become the custom to represent by the initial and final letter only – a blank line filling the interval. I may as well say at once that, for this circumstance, it is out of my power to apologize, deeming it myself a rational plan to write words at full length. The practice of hinting by single letters those expletives with which profane and violent persons are wont to garnish their discourse strikes me as a proceeding which, however well meant, is weak and futile. I cannot tell what good it does – what feeling it spares – what horror it conceals.

With regard to the rusticity of *Wuthering Heights* I admit the charge, for I feel the quality. It is rustic all through. It is moorish and wild and knotty as a root of heath. Nor was it natural that it should be otherwise

– the author being herself a native and nursling of the moors. Doubtless, had her lot been cast in a town, her writings, if she had written at all, would have possessed another character. Even had chance or taste led her to choose a similar subject, she would have treated it otherwise. Had Ellis Bell been a lady or a gentleman accustomed to what is called "the world", her view of a remote and unreclaimed region – as well as of the dwellers therein – would have differed greatly from that actually taken by the home-bred country girl. Doubtless it would have been wider – more comprehensive – whether it would have been more original or more truthful is not so certain. As far as the scenery and locality are concerned, it could scarcely have been so sympathetic: Ellis Bell did not describe as one whose eye and taste alone found pleasure in the prospect; her native hills were far more to her than a spectacle; they were what she lived in and by, as much as the wild birds, their tenants, or as the heather, their produce. Her descriptions, then, of natural scenery are what they should be, and all they should be.

Where delineation of human character is concerned, the case is different. I am bound to avow that she had scarcely more practical knowledge of the peasantry amongst whom she lived than a nun has of the country people who sometimes pass her convent gates. My sister's disposition was not naturally gregarious; circumstances favoured and fostered her tendency to seclusion, except to go to church or take a walk on the hills, she rarely crossed the threshold of home. Though her feeling for the people round was benevolent, intercourse with them she never sought – nor, with very few exceptions, ever experienced. And yet she knew them: knew their ways, their language, their family histories; she could hear of them with interest and talk of them with detail – minute, graphic and accurate – but *with* them she rarely exchanged a word. Hence it ensued that what her mind had gathered of the real concerning them was too exclusively confined to those tragic and terrible traits of which, in listening to the secret annals of every rude vicinage, the memory is sometimes compelled to receive the impress. Her imagination, which was a spirit more sombre than sunny, more powerful than sportive, found in such traits material whence it wrought creations like Heathcliff, like Earnshaw, like Catherine. Having formed these beings, she did not know what she had done. If the auditor of her work, when read in manuscript, shuddered under the grinding influence of natures so relentless and implacable, of spirits so lost and fallen; if it was complained that the mere hearing of certain vivid and fearful scenes banished sleep by night and disturbed mental peace by day, Ellis Bell would wonder what was meant, and suspect the complainant of affectation. Had she but lived, her mind would of itself have grown like a strong tree, loftier, straighter, wider-spreading, and its matured fruits would have attained a mellower ripeness and sunnier bloom – but on that mind time and experience alone could work: to the influence of other intellects it was not amenable.

Having avowed that over much of *Wuthering Heights* there broods "a horror of great darkness"; that, in its storm-heated and electrical atmosphere, we seem at times to breathe lightning, let me point to those spots where clouded daylight and the eclipsed sun still attest their existence. For a specimen of true benevolence and homely fidelity, look at the character of Nelly Dean; for an example of constancy and tenderness, remark that of Edgar Linton. (Some people will think these qualities do not shine so well incarnate in a man as they would do in a woman, but Ellis Bell could never be brought to comprehend this notion: nothing moved her more than any insinuation that the faithfulness and clemency, the long suffering and loving kindness which are esteemed virtues in the daughters of Eve become foibles in the sons of Adam. She held that mercy and forgiveness are the divinest attributes of the Great Being who made both man and woman, and that what clothes the Godhead in glory can disgrace no form of feeble humanity.) There is a dry saturnine humour in the delineation of old Joseph, and some glimpses of grace and gaiety animate the younger Catherine. Nor is even the first heroine of the name destitute of a certain strange beauty in her fierceness, or of honesty in the midst of perverted passion and passionate perversity.

Heathcliff, indeed, stands unredeemed; never once swerving in his arrow-straight course to perdition, from the time when "the little black-haired swarthy thing, as dark as if it came from the Devil", was first unrolled out of the bundle and set on its feet in the farmhouse kitchen, to the hour when Nelly Dean found the grim, stalwart corpse laid on its back in the panel-enclosed bed, with wide-gazing eyes that seemed "to sneer at her attempt to close them, and parted lips and sharp white teeth that sneered too".

Heathcliff betrays one solitary human feeling, and that is *not* his love for Catherine, which is a sentiment fierce and inhuman: a passion such as might boil and glow in the bad essence of some evil genius; a fire that might form the tormented centre – the ever-suffering soul of a magnate of the infernal world – and by its quenchless and ceaseless ravage effect the execution of the decree which dooms him to carry hell with him wherever he wanders. No, the single link that connects Heathcliff with humanity is his rudely confessed regard for Hareton Earnshaw – the young man whom he has ruined – and then his half-implied esteem for Nelly Dean. These solitary traits omitted, we should say he was child neither of Lascar nor gypsy, but a man's shape animated by demon life – a ghoul – an afreet.

Whether it is right or advisable to create beings like Heathcliff, I do not know – I scarcely think it is. But this I know: the writer who possesses the creative gift owns something of which he is not always master – something that, at times, strangely wills and works for itself. He may lay down rules and devise principles – and to rules and principles it will perhaps for years lie in subjection – and then, haply without any warning of revolt, there comes a time when it will no longer consent to "harrow the valleys or be bound with a band in the furrow" – when it "laughs at the multitude of the city and regards not the crying of the driver" – when, refusing absolutely to make ropes out of sea sand any longer, it sets to work on statue-hewing, and you have a Pluto or a Jove, a Tisiphone or a Psyche, a mermaid or a madonna, as fate or inspiration direct. Be the work grim or glorious, dread or divine, you have little choice left but quiescent adoption. As for you – the nominal artist – your share in it has been to work passively under dictates you neither delivered nor could question – that would not be uttered at your prayer, nor suppressed nor changed at your caprice. If the result be attractive, the world will praise you, who little deserve praise; if it be repulsive, the same world will blame you, who almost as little deserve blame.

Wuthering Heights was hewn in a wild workshop, with simple tools, out of homely materials. The statuary found a granite block on a solitary moor; gazing thereon, he saw how from the crag might be elicited a head, savage, swart, sinister; a form moulded with at least one element of grandeur – power. He wrought with a rude chisel, and from no model but the vision of his meditations. With time and labour, the crag took human shape, and there it stands colossal, dark and frowning, half statue, half rock – in the former sense, terrible and goblin-like; in the latter, almost beautiful, for its colouring is of mellow grey and moorland moss clothes it – and heath, with its blooming bells and balmy fragrance, grows faithfully close to the giant's foot.

– Currer Bell

ALMA CLASSICS

ALMA CLASSICS aims to publish mainstream and lesser-known European classics in an innovative and striking way, while employing the highest editorial and production standards. By way of a unique approach the range offers much more, both visually and textually, than readers have come to expect from contemporary classics publishing.

LATEST TITLES PUBLISHED BY ALMA CLASSICS

THERE'S A
GOD
on the
MIC

THE TRUE 50 GREATEST MCs

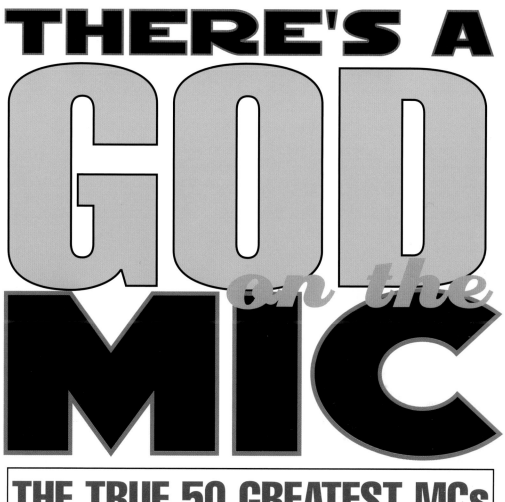

THERE'S A GOD on the MIC

THE TRUE 50 GREATEST MCs

KOOL MO DEE

FOREWORD BY CHUCK D
PHOTOGRAPHS BY ERNIE PANICCIOLI

THUNDER'S MOUTH PRESS • NEW YORK

There's a God on the Mic: The True 50 Greatest MCs

Published by
Thunder's Mouth Press
An Imprint of Avalon Publishing Group Incorporated
161 William St., 16th Floor
New York, NY 10038

ISBN: 1-56025-533-1

9 8 7 6 5 4 3 2 1

Designed by Paul 'Prizzmatik' Paddock
Printed in China
Distributed by Publishers Group West

FOREWORD

IN THE RECORDED HISTORY OF BLACK MUSIC, and we're talking about 80 some-odd years since jazzcat Freddie Keppard refused to be recorded because he thought that those listening would steal his licks, myth and folklore often loom above and beyond actual fact. Sounds and styles, fights and games have been re-ignited within the hallowed halls, walls, and floors of the unofficial meeting centers of the hood, i.e., the street corners, poolrooms, and barber shops. The music debates have run a distant second or third to the sports debates there, but in the last twenty years rap music and Hip-Hop have given the sports debates a good run for their money. Out of the element that often combined the skill of the fast-talking pimp with the power of the preacher and the wit of the comedian diggin' deep into the dozens, the rappers initially commanded the attention of a distracted black male public. Nothing against the ladies, but they almost always preferred to be sung to, and if a so-called emcee got her attention, it was because he played the popular singer's song as a DJ , or most likely carefully rhymed across it so as to not turn the girls off. Still, this perceived bragging and boasting out of the box, in essence, was the black male cry that positioned itself parallel to the testosterone fueled sonics them heavy metal white cats were doing in rock music. By rap music's first recorded era from 1979–1984, a flood of rhymers set off across music snatching up every sonic bed available on record to put their thing over.

From this period, innovators either shaped their ideas off the party thing that was closely connected to the DJ aspect of the music, or set upon new paths that redefined on a steady basis what this art form could potentially do. Kool Mo Dee is an example of the latter. Besides being a Hall of Fame rapper (whilst there's no hall of fame, yet . . . help), he introduced to the genre the first rap scientist. A scientist in the same way that in sports Ted Williams broke down the science of hitting, or Jordan the art of basketball, Kool Mo Dee dissected this art form when most were questioning what it was or how long it would be around. As debuted on Harlem record legend Bobby Robinson's 12-inch Enjoy Records label as a b-side to fellow Harlemite Spoony Gee's "Love Rap" A-side, his group, The Treacherous Three, cut a psycho, double-speed, rap classic called "A New Rap Language." This record served as testament to the analysis of cohorts Special K and LA Sunshine, raising the verbal bar, and simply doing what no one else would've thought of. Contrary to folklore, a lot of emcees were wack back then too, even more so than today because many didn't have a blueprint to build their thing off of. As the T3 ripped through their unparalleled period, 1980–83, moving eventually to Sugarhill Records, their skill legacy rivaled them as Rolling Stonish to Grandmaster Flash and the Furious Five's Beatlesque Hip Hop dominance. Back then the streets had no name, and nobody was measuring the cred after the radio stopped playing the uptown sounds as much as the next new thing that was coming out of Whodini's Brooklyn and Run-DMC's Queens. Mo Dee was keeping track of this. And while this new sound came in, it was also the unofficial word that four years rapping records and twenty-two years of age would signify being set out to a rap pasture, so to speak. Mo challenged this by wrapping up his college degree at the State University of Old Westbury in Long Island, New York—another first that Mo and I shared in 1984, the year that rappers graduated from college.

I first met Kool Mo Dee in the beginning of what was an unprecedented first, a Hip-Hop comeback. It was as an act added on to a southern run of the 1987 Def Jam tour with Whodini, Doug E Fresh , Eric B and Rakim, and LL Cool J, the headliner. We had chatted briefly in Columbus, Georgia, where I befriended his DJ, a cool cat by the name of Easy Lee. Later we kicked it and ate lunch in the back of a hot limo while doing some radio promotion for the Mid-South Coliseum gig in Memphis. Mo Dee had just released his first album on Jive Records and was four years past his roasting of fellow New Yorker Busy Bee in a battle that was recorded and sold as one of the areas most famous Hip-Hop tapes ever. By this time rap was starting to be watched by major record labels as album-viable, and artists were building on diversity as opposed to the battle thing that required directed skills. Plus, the real fact is that no rapper wanted to rub Kool Mo Dee's legend the wrong way, no one. This didn't stop KMD from doing a scientific analysis of the rhyme terrain he was re-entering. Behind those super rap-hero shades was a calculating mind stirring the pot he was gonna dip into. Mo Dee's album inner sleeve consisted of a rapper's report card, listing skill breakdowns, and calculating a final grade from A to F. This was two to three years before *The Source*. He was saying that you might be signed by a big record company, you may have millions of adoring fans, cats might dig you in the streets, but now we gonna break it down plain and simple . . . JUST HOW GOOD CAN

YOU RAP? I was just glad that PE made the list. I was very happy to get a B-and work hard from there. I was just honored he took the time to listen.

Fast forward to post millennium 2004, past the classic Kool Mo Dee–LL Cool J battles, a third comeback in records and film, Kool Mo takes the obvious next step after what his report card initiated in the mid-eighties: he's full-blown-out as an author, which should serve his vast mind as a playing field for many works to come. (Hello? Television and DVDs?) The research is twenty-five years thick now. Hip-Hop and rap music being so worldwide has the bottom line of it said and signed by many cats who never rhymed the game. In sports, former players become coaches and managers, sportscasters and writers. In Hip-Hop the comparison of Hip-Hop contributors and say-soers to the art is akin to the rings of the planet Saturn. You think the rings are a part of it, but the closer you get, you find out that they're not really a part of it at all, just debris floating around it. I can't bite this analogy because this too comes from Mo Dee's analytical mind. Its about time the masters write some of the script about this thing called rap. We talked many a night on the phone about the state of the rap game, and how the unknowing can perceive these calls as Wilt Chamberlainish–hating on the new game. Oh so far from the truth, indeed. This is an introduction to recognize the beauty of the genre, from the past twenty-five years, so . . . ladies and gentlemen—the True 50 Greatest MCs ever—coming from one of the best that ever rhymed it.

Chuck D
Public Enemy

A WORD FROM THE AUTHOR

ASK A HIP HOP FAN, "Who's the best emcee?", and immediately they begin naming the hottest rappers of the day. Some start naming their favorite records, and maybe quoting a few or more simplistic one-liners or popular hooks that they can sing-a-long with. But if asked the difference between a rapper and an emcee suddenly there's a look of confusion. Or if you ask the difference between a rapper, an emcee and a Hip Hop artist they won't know what to say. The difference between a lyricist and a flower? A rhymer and a poet? Or any combination of the above and forget it. Rarely what you here is expertise. I hear a lot of passion and a lot of emotion but no expertise.

Of course music is an emotional vehicle, and it is about emotion and passion and feeling, but it will take a trained ear to be able to hear the emcee. Like in the NBA, the fans get to vote on the All-Star game which is about the favorites, but that's not necessarily who is the best in the league. When it comes to the MVP's and the All-Time greats that's beyond the fans voting. That's where it takes expertise to break down the nuances of the game.

One might ask, "What about the journalists?" For the journalists or scribes of the Hip Hop industry there are major problems, three in particular. One is the payoffs and the labels contribution. A lot of fans don't really understand how much money it takes to run a magazine. They may not understand how much money labels, publicists and publicity departments contribute to the writers and what they're paying for. They're literally being paid for their opinions. Usually, as we say in the industry, they're the best opinions money can buy. When you see a favorable opinion it's usually based on who's being marketed or promoted at the time, rarely are these journalists honest. Once in a while the KRS-One's, the Rakim's, the Cool G Rap's, and similar emcees will come along that are so lyrical and so great in their prowess that you get some form of honesty, but it's usually not the case. Usually it is definitely about how much money is being spent to make sure that the artist receives a favorable opinion. The second problem I have is the voting by committee, after all the money is spent creating the images and personae and in many cases record sales these same writers vote on who's the best of these creations. It is amazing tome to see when people spend money to promote an artist as if he's one thing even though his image and his lyrical skill level may not have anything other than you spent money to promote him. People will start to buy into these very highly promoted personas and start to treat the artist as if the personae are an actual real fact. There are a few emcees that mandate the respect based on their skills, but more times than not based on the money spent and image created people are voting on the personas. A lot of journalists don't have the heart to go against the grain of the popular artist at the time. I call this the Godzilla syndrome. You create a fake monster, and then respond as if the monster is real. Welcome to the music industry. The final problem I have has to do with credentials and credibility. What reference point does the journalist use when forming these opinions? How far back did they go? Usually, if you do the numbers and the math you'd see that the average journalist writing on Hip Hop is somewhere between twenty, twenty-five, maybe thirty. Which means if you go back ten years ago that person is somewhere between 10-15. So if you were 10 in 1993 that means you've missed 14 years of recorded Hip Hop and another nine years of unrecorded Hip Hop. So your opinion has to be formed on a combination of other writings and other opinions that you've seen over the years, or the short window of information that you may have on Hip Hop based on how old you were when you were able to experience it and comprehend what was going on. This is a very big problem in the industry because this is how you see a situation where an icon in Hip Hop like Afrika Bambaataa or DJ Hollywood goes unrecognized for his contribution because the person who is ten years old in '93 is born in 1983, he doesn't really know.

Finally, like rap fans, there are few experts, and of the few experts that are even fewer that go beyond hit records and hot artists. So then one would ask, "Why me?" What makes me so different? What separates me from the pack? What separates me from the pack of opinionated fans, artists and scribes — allow me to count the ways.

First off I have extended experience. I've been rhyming at a high level since 1977, and at an elite level since 1979. I'm one of the few artists who was able to make the transition from the street era before there was records, to when they finally made records, to when it became a full out business. I have hits as a group, I have hits as a soloist, and a writer. I've been making hits since 1980 to 1992. I've been undefeated in all Hip Hop battles. I'm the first rapper to win an NAACP

Image Award, and also a multi-Grammy nominated and Grammy winner. Number two, there's no payola, no one can buy my opinion. My integrity will not be compromised by popularity. I have nothing vested in this other than the passion for clarity, and to give acknowledgement and recognition to those who usually don't get it. Finally, no one to my knowledge has comprised a more extensive list with the intricacies of breaking down so many aspects of emceeing. Because of my experience or intimate understanding of the aspects of emceeing that are usually overlooked when determining whose the best emcee in the game, I can break down emcees from the past to present with a clear understanding of the different job requirements of each era of emcees. I absolutely know the difference of what a storytelling emcee is going for as opposed to what a braggadocios emcee is going for, as opposed to what an emcee with a potent, powerful, Afro centric message is going for. I can thoroughly explain why Missy Misdemeanor Elliott is not a great emcee, but absolutely one of the greatest Hip Hop artists of all time. Or how an emcee as lyrical as Cannibus can be relatively unknown because he hasn't had a hit record, yet he's still one of the best rhymers in the game today.

I understand this is a business and emcees, rappers, and artists all have to make hits to survive, but as with most big business it is always solely about the money, and whenever that's the case then usually the art is compromised. So big respect and much love to all of the successful rappers and Hip Hop artists, but this book is about the emcee.

Let's get crackin'.

50

JUST-ICE
THE ORIGINAL GANGSTER

"I'm twice as nice
My grip is vice
Precise Just-Ice
Rockin' parties nine years of my life
It's a new conceptual
Highly intellectual
Only for me cause it is genetical"

I'M ALWAYS FRUSTRATED WHEN I SEE lists of the greatest emcees and Just-Ice is not included. This is one of the many reasons I decided to write this book. If Just-Ice isn't on your list of emcee greats, you don't know what an emcee is!!! Just-Ice, aka Sir Vicious, is one of Hip-Hop's first AUTHENTIC intellectual thugs on wax. He is also one of the first emcees to mix the reggae style of rhyming into Hip-Hop. He is also one of the first emcees to infuse the doctrine of the Five Percent Nation's science and mathematics on wax.

"Presenting my wisdom in a different form
We can spit high science makin' knowledge born
When I approach my advisory I'm comin' strong
From knowledge to cipher then releasing my bomb"

Like many emcees, Just-Ice had the unfortunate task of trying to stay true to the root laws of emceeing, while trying to sustain a successful career in the music industry. As usual, when trying to bring an unfamiliar art form to the masses, success relies heavily on the taste buds of ignorant consumers. The principles of business always force the hand of the artist to make certain compromises. Just-Ice made none. Outside of KRS-One, one would be hard pressed to find another emcee that fed fans a strict diet of beats and rhymes. If you search the seven albums of Just-Ice, you'll find an emcee whose only focus is to rock the mic. By no means does this mean that he wasn't trying to make hits. In fact, "Latoya," "Cold Gettin' Dumb," and "Way Back (We're Going)" are hits in the world of Hip-Hop circles.

However he, like many other true emcees, did not have the fortune of mainstream radio success. Unfortunately, from the mid- to late '80s (Just-Ice's reign) black radio and pop radio had major campaigns against rap music. This, in conjunction with his being on a small independent label, Sleeping Bag/Fresh Records, made it almost impossible for a hard-core emcee like Just-Ice to see any light. Only the love of the true Hip-Hop fans, combined with Just-Ice's love for the art of emceeing, made it possible for him to have the level of success he achieved.

Strength: Aggressive. Just-Ice always attacks a track. One of the few emcees that is never subordinate to the track.

Weakness: Overaggressive. Sometimes he's so hyped, and so attacking, that he becomes inaudible.

Favorite Record: "Cold Gettin' Dumb" and "The Hip-Hop Gangster"

Favorite LP: *Cool and Deadly*

#50: JUST-ICE

I call Just-Ice the original gangster because he's the first one, to my knowledge, that used the term before gangster rap came out.

ORIGINALITY: 90

He came from an era where you created your persona and it had nothing to do with anyone else's persona other than the fact that maybe everybody was rhyming a certain way and the cadences may have been the same. But Just-Ice created his own cadence, he created the gruff voice attack of the mic.

CONCEPTS: 80

Just-Ice was a pretty conceptual emcee. He didn't have a one-note song selection, so by the time he started making music, he was pretty conceptual.

VERSATILITY: 85

He could use multiple flows, he could take it high speed or slow it down. Records like "Latoya" and "Cold Gettin' Dumb" were coming from two totally different planes. One was a story about a girl and the other was just straight rhyming. He was a versatile emcee, based on what versatility meant at that time.

VOCABULARY: 90

Just-Ice was the first guy I heard use a *haiku*. He used the word *haiku*. I didn't even know what a *haiku* was.

SUBSTANCE: 80

He talked about street issues. He didn't go as hard as a Melle Mel or a Chuck D with it, but Just-Ice always did have a substantive edge to him. He wasn't frivolous in terms of his rhyme style and what he chose to talk about.

FLOW: 70

Just-Ice came straight at you, straight ahead. You knew what you were getting, he didn't particularly care for shifting gears or getting into colorful flows, even though he did play with it a little bit.

FLAVOR: 70

Straight at you. Just-Ice did not play around on the mic. It wasn't about trying to be funny, he went right at you.

FREESTYLE ABILITY: 60

Just-Ice said to me one time he doesn't freestyle. He was one of the lyrical emcees that prided himself on writing rhymes. In a lot of cases, a lot of old-school cats didn't freestyle the same way. There are a few, but for the most part, most don't really get down with the freestyle too tough.

VOCAL PRESENCE: 85

As soon as Just-Ice hit the mic you knew who it was. A lot of times you might not hear it, it would be a little inaudible if he got really, really excited and got on a roll, but for the most part his voice absolutely had some resonance to it, and you knew it was him.

LIVE PERFORMANCE: 75

The focus truthfully was about rocking the crowd, not too much on the call-and-response side. Hip-Hop got into a transitional position where it went from just rocking parties to having records, and having records meant having hits, and sometimes not having a lot of hit records could make your show not go so well. But Just-Ice did his thing in spite of whatever was going on in the climate.

POETIC VALUE: 70

Just-Ice was much more rhyme than poetry. He used the word *haiku* and he talked about things being poetic, but he basically was a rhymer. He rhymed straight at you, straight forward, straight ahead, and it was more about the rhyme than the poetry.

BODY OF WORK: 75

Just-Ice has a more extensive body of work than most people know about. He has six or seven albums. His more popular albums are the earlier albums, and then his record company, Select, went out of business. Even with the small label that he had, he still managed to have hit records and still managed to do his thing on the rhyme side, record after record.

INDUSTRY IMPACT: 60

Unfortunately when you're on a small label, it's very hard to make any kind of impact in terms of getting accolades, Grammys, or any of the awards, and except for real authentic Hip-Hop fans, most people don't even know who Just-Ice was.

SOCIAL IMPACT: 60

Once again, Just-Ice didn't get a chance to make that much of a social impact because a lot of us at the time were just looked at as rappers, and people didn't respect us, they didn't know what we were talking about, or where we came from. So it was very, very hard to make a social impact in those circumstances.

LONGEVITY: 50*

Just-Ice actually lasted longer than people understand, but he did have at least five years of strong notoriety. Once again, because of the small label, and the lack of marketing and promotion, it's really hard to see the longevity for what it's worth.

LYRICS: 85

Just-Ice is absolutely a lyrical emcee. There is no argument. If there is one thing that is his strong point, it is his lyrics, along with his vocabulary.

BATTLE SKILLS: 60

Most people wouldn't even test Just-Ice. There was a little situation where he dissed Kurtis Blow on the remix of "Cold Gettin' Dumb," and I guess that was based on Kurtis Blow using his beat or something to that effect, but for the most part Just-Ice is not a battler—he'd probably punch you in the face or beat you down before he'd actually battle you on the mic. That doesn't mean he couldn't do it, he just didn't do it.

TOTAL SCORE: 1245

AVERAGE SCORE: 73.2

* Asterisks are used throughout to note where low scores might have more connotation and denotation. In Just-Ice's case he is actually still recording today.

49

MACK 10
GANGSTER BOOGIE

"Now tell me
Is it the duce ones on the Bentley
The low riders, the mansions
Is that why you resent me
You smile in my face and act so friendly
Walk away with hate and a heart full of envy
Say bro what part of the game is that
You got ways like a dame and how lame is that
Acting like a groupie around famous cats
And it's strange you don't have no shame in that!"

THIS IS A PERFECT EXAMPLE OF what makes Hip-Hop so dichotomously diverse. Many of my peer group of Hip-Hop conscious, intellectual icons did not understand or agree with the selection of Mack 10 as one of the fifty greatest emcees. Their biggest knock was "his content is always sex, money, and murder." While I couldn't disagree, I reminded them of the many emcees they respect who have similar content. Suddenly there was silence! As I stated earlier, I'm not voting by committee. An emcee doesn't have to suit my taste buds for me to see his skill level. Like I said, I can see beyond the beat. What I see in Mack 10 is focus. He has a clear understanding of where the rap game is right now. He has figured out where the niche market is that best suits him. He is a hustler, and gangster rap is his hustle.

Of course I understand the arguments of the Hip-Hop fundamentalist, but I would argue that there are many so-called gangsta rappers who don't do it as well as Mack 10. If nothing else, when you listen to his body of work, you'll see consistency. You always know where he's coming from, but you might not know how he's coming. My opinion is he has a keen sense of how to make records that move people. He writes songs where other emcees write rhymes. Some emcees are very scattered. Their rhymes have nothing to do with their hooks, and sometimes nothing to do with any of the other rhymes in the song. You never hear Mack 10 do this. And in today's climate, this is a breath of fresh air.

As far as his lyrical prowess, he is not one of the most intricate emcees, but he is one of the most articulate. You never have to struggle to hear what he's saying.

As he says in the song, "Hate In Yo Eyes":

Stay real about my scrill
You know what I mean
I'm like a leprechaun
I want nuttin' but green

That's it in a nutshell; he's here to get money! Say what you want, but from his first hit "Foe Life" off his self-titled LP, through all of his work on the Westside Connection projects, and right up to "Bang or Ball" with the Cash Money Crew, Mack 10 has been consistently making his presence felt. He might not be lyrically profound, but sometimes the mastery is in the simplicity!!!

Strength: Delivery! He has the ability to come across with power and clarity.

Weakness: Wordplay. He doesn't seem to be interested in wowing the Hip-Hop fan that is interested in the rhyme skills part of the game.

Favorite Record: "Foe Life," "Hate In Yo Eyes"

Favorite LP: *Bang or Ball*

#49: MACK 10

ORIGINALITY: 80

He definitely came in doing his own thing, but the West Coast style of rap was already in full swing. He brought a little something extra to the game, but it wasn't anything in particular that we hadn't heard before.

CONCEPTS: 75

For the most part, Mack 10 kept it simple and plain, straight ahead. He didn't get too elaborate with the concepts or the lyrics; he basically let you know what he represented, where he was from, and what he was about.

VERSATILITY: 70

Mack 10 basically kept it really, really straight gangsta. He didn't go into too many other themes or subjects. You knew what it was about. Money, getting money, getting your cap peeled if you got too close or had bad intentions, and as many ladies as they could have. Putting it down, having fun.

VOCABULARY: 70

He keeps it very simple. He's like an efficient basketball player, nothing fancy, no behind-the-back passes, no no-look passing—just straight fundamentals going to the hole and getting the points. Mack 10 is just scoring.

SUBSTANCE: 75

This area is a little enigmatic to judge, because a lot of people would say that the gangsta style of rap isn't substantive. I think on some level it is of some substance because it is talking about a section or slice of real life that a lot of Black American youth in urban areas have to go through. If nothing else, the theme is consistent.

FLOW: 80

Mack 10 followed the West Coast cadence. As soon as you hear him spit, you know exactly where he's coming from.

FLAVOR: 70

He doesn't do a lot of fluctuating with his voice. He doesn't play with it too much. He is coming right at you down the lane with a hard dunk.

FREESTYLE ABILITY: 60

I think I heard Mack 10 say one time there is no such thing as freestyle; everything for him is about being paid. I don't think he's even interested in freestyling.

VOCAL PRESENCE: 80

For Hip-Hop fans that pay attention to the music, you definitely know who he is. I don't know if anybody outside of Hip-Hop would recognize his voice immediately once they heard it, but there's still enough presence there for the Hip-Hop fan to tell who he is. He also projects very well on the mic.

LIVE PERFORMANCE: 75

This category is a little strange to judge also because a lot of times emcees are on stage and they have a bunch of guys on stage with them, and they're going after an effect that's a little different from region to region. A lot of times the way the West Coast rappers put it down on stage is more about the party posse type of atmosphere. So they're on stage with the crew, and sometimes the guys will have mics and their job is to get the crowd up. But Mack 10's style is gangsta, and his music is gangsta, and a lot of times gangsta music is not about dancing and partying. So when he's live it's like you're getting to listen, if you know the songs you're definitely going to sing along. He's one of the few in the gangsta rap section that does focus on the "gangsta boogie."

POETIC VALUE: 70

Mack 10, like a lot of rappers, is more about the rhymes than the poetic value. There's a lot more to poetry than rhymes. That doesn't mean that poetry is better than rhymes, because a lot of times rhymes are better than poems. But poems are usually about evoking different types of thought, different types of emotions or moods. For the most part, Mack 10 just uses straight rhyming.

BODY OF WORK: 80

You can't overlook the work that he's done, not only on his own, but also with the Westside Connection. He's definitely made some hit records and has made an impact with that. For a lot of people that don't know, or don't understand, or don't see enough "hit singles," sometimes you have to get the album to see what a brother is really doing, and you have to pay attention to see how much he's putting into his work. Mack 10 is putting in work.

INDUSTRY IMPACT: 70

He came at a time when gangsta rap was in full bloom. It was already in stride, so he didn't get a chance to make too much of an industry impact because he was after the fact. NWA, Ice Cube, Dre, Snoop, all of that had already happened, and the industry is very fickled. They're very, very reluctant to give awards, accolades, or a lot of press; they'll jump on the negative press, but they don't jump on the positive side. So he didn't get a chance to make that much of an industry impact because of the timing.

SOCIAL IMPACT: 70

This goes hand in hand. On the one hand, the social impact is probably more personal than global for him. He's definitely put not only his 'hood, but his crew on the map. A lot of people are eating better because of him, so he does make some kind of social impact, although it's not really a nationwide thing. You can look at rappers like Chuck D of Public Enemy or KRS-One, and you can see a social impact in terms of the uplifting of people psychologically or consciously, but I would say Mack 10 is more about personal uplifting as opposed to a social one.

LONGEVITY: 70

He dropped with the "Foe Life" single and self-titled album in 1995, and he's still going strong. He's now with the Cash Money Crew and he's still putting out records. That's seven years in, and ten points for every year. I'm sure he's not going anywhere, so in three years, he'll probably get the hundred like anyone else that's lasted ten years or longer.

LYRICS: 80

One of the biggest things with rappers is people like to attack people for their lyrical skills. I do it a little differently. I try to figure out what the emcee is going for, and then break down how well he's delivering what he's going for. Mack 10 is not really about the braggadocio style of rap; he comes at it like a hustler or a banger, and for what he's doing with that, he's pretty lyrical.

BATTLE SKILLS: 75

Once again the intangibles of battling are very,

very elusive; it's really hard to put a finger on it. I can tell by his style that he has some kind of battle acumen, but at the end of the day, he doesn't seem like he's interested in battling. Similar to Just-Ice, I hear aggression in his energy, but I think Mack 10 might want to bring it to you on a physical level as opposed to a lyrical level, in a lot of cases. I don't think he would want to waste any time battling. That's what I get from his personality.

TOTAL SCORE: 1,250

AVERAGE SCORE: 73.5

48

FOXY BROWN

UNDERRATED LYRICAL LADY

I dream filthy
My moms and pops mixed me
With the trinny rum and whiskey
Proper set off six sped off gats let off
I speak calm
Gangsta and pulls off like
Screachy Don
Who y'all know rock Prada like Fox
Pop bottles in the back of the cellar
Wit Donna tella
Cartier wrist wear
Posha cage face
Y'all nickas stand in just to get a sneak taste

IF YOU THINK THE HIP-HOP PUNDITS are tough on the materialist rhyme styles and content of the men, wait until a female spits bars of blingin'! I can't recall ever seeing an emcee as reviled as Foxy Brown was on her sophomore LP, *Chyna Doll*. She was as reviled as Tupac was revered. It was almost like they were waiting for her to fail. Well of course, some of this can be attributed to the fickle finger of Hip-Hop heat, but a lot of it has to do with sexism in Hip-Hop. Foxy Brown is like a female version of Jay-Z, a skilled emcee, whose subject matter is money, clothes, killing, and hoes. The only difference is that Foxy Brown is almost exclusively rated-X.

Here is where the sexism comes in. Whenever a woman speaks on the inadequacies of men's sexual prowess or financial status in Hip-Hop, you hit a trifecta of problems: 1) Men will always root against you; 2) Because of the superficial nature of the content, the public begins to dissect you in areas that have nothing to do with your music or rhyme skills, i.e., what you look like, are you worthy of the things you talk about, do you have real money, who are you sleeping with, etc., etc.; and 3) Finally, women begin to nitpick at you because they perceive you as thinking you're better than them. Foxy Brown is a victim of all of the above. However, don't get it twisted, Foxy Brown does have fans. *Ill Na Na* is a platinum LP. She has hit singles and guest appearances with LL Cool J, Jay-Z, DMX, Cormega, and others where she absolutely shines.

When Foxy Brown first hit, she was instantly compared to Lil' Kim. This was unfortunate because fans were psyched into choosing one or the other. This also set up a bad climate for her sophomore LP, *Chyna Doll*. However, Foxy Brown weathered the storm and came through with her next project, *Broken Silence*. This I think is her best work. Not as commercial as *Ill Na Na*, and not as raunchy as *Chyna Doll*. I think it was a great balance of the two. You could clearly hear her lyrical prowess and confidence coming across better than ever. Ironically, the critics of Foxy became supporters. Many industry heads spoke openly about how they felt this LP was overlooked. For me, that's it in a nutshell. Too much hype in the beginning created over expectations, and after the letdown of her sophomore project, there was no hype and no expectations for the last. All in all, Foxy Brown has had public opinion swayed based on industry politics, and because of that she lost a little bit of momentum. However, I have never been influenced by the industry foolery. I was always focused on the emcee. Foxy Brown has always delivered razor-sharp, rated-X rhymes. She's definitely one of the dopest emcees I've heard!

Strength: She always matches the energy of her male partners on the collaborations. There is never a drop-off, no matter who she follows. Because of her voice, delivery, and content, many times she outshines her collaborators.

Weakness: Her content is one note! Sex and materialism. I understand that this is her choice, but as good as she rhymes, she could talk about anything and make it hot. Diversifying the subject matter would shut down a lot of the haters and naysayers.

Favorite Record: "China White," "Oh Yeah"

Favorite LP: *Broken Silence*

#48: FOXY BROWN

ORIGINALITY: 80

What's harder for the newer artists in this area is coming up with something that we haven't heard before, and being able to do something that hasn't been done before. It's much harder on the newer artists to get the higher points in originality. However, I gave Foxy Brown an 80 because her and Lil' Kim came out about the same time with the same type of subject matter, but I don't think that was intentional. I think it was organic: that's where they lived, that's what they did. They get originality points for being who they are. The table had already been set way back as far as Roxanne Shanté getting down with the raunchiest rhyme styles, even though in the '80s it was more about dissing lyrically as opposed to dissing financially and materialistically.

CONCEPTS: 75

Once in a while she'll dabble in a concept zone, but her rhymes basically are really straightforward—she's here to get paid, she's here to be pleased by men, and she's here to do her thing the way she does it. She doesn't get that conceptual.

VERSATILITY: 80

The versatility doesn't have to weigh heavily in the subject matter; I think her versatility has to do with which types of tracks she chooses to rhyme on. I've heard her on up-tempo, I've heard her on down-tempo, and on her first album, *Ill Na Na*, she did some great R&B type records. She strayed away from that on the next two albums, but she's a hard-core artist and in the beginning when you're first coming out, people direct you the way they think they need to direct you to make hits. I'm sure she brought her own flavor to it.

VOCABULARY: 70

Like a lot of emcees that rhyme in the zone that she rhymes in, they don't get too intricate on the vocabulary. That's not their premium order, that's not at the top of the list.

SUBSTANCE: 70

The same thing I said about Mack 10. A lot of people don't feel when you're talking about sex, money, robbing, stealing, and killing that it's substantive. The substance with her is simply her being who she is and bringing it the way she brings it. I do understand how people look at substance, and even how I rank substance. What are the artists doing for the consciousness of the fans? Is there a movement behind it? Is it motivating people in any realms other than materialism?

FLOW: 90

No matter what's she's saying, she always brings it across with a passion and with an aggression that a lot of female emcees had a problem with. Back in the '80s, one of the reasons a lot of female emcees couldn't break through until Salt-'N-Pepa, MC Lyte, and Queen Latifah was because a lot of female emcees didn't have a flow or cadence that people could really get with. Sha Rock was one of the first that had the cadence that men could grab onto because there is sexism in this business. I think Foxy Brown brings it across with a force and a confidence that can't be denied.

FLAVOR: 80

Foxy has, especially in her later records, exhibited a lot more flavor in her flow. It seems like she's having a little more fun with it this time around. If you look at what she's done on all three albums, and what she does live, it's basically straight at you.

FREESTYLE ABILITY: 80

I heard Foxy live a couple of times and I don't know if it was actually freestyle but it seemed like she got caught up in the moment of what was happening with the crowd. She would walk on stage and create excitement, and sometimes I would see her get caught up in the excitement and lose the rhyme, but I saw her come off the top of the head nicely in those scenarios.

VOCAL PRESENCE: 75

A lot of times people who are not into Hip-Hop would be confused about who she is. Vocal presence has more to do with the identifiability of your voice. Of course, people who follow Hip-Hop may be able to tell, but outside of Hip-Hop I don't know how distinct her voice actually is.

LIVE PERFORMANCE: 75

The few times that I've seen her she seems to get very, very caught up in the energy onstage. Sometimes you can get so hyped that you can lose the focus, and I think that's where the freestyle situation was born. She's certainly not scared on stage and she gives back to the audience what they give to her, and usually they're giving her so much energy. I've seen her actually start yelling in a rhyme flow while she was on stage.

POETIC VALUE: 60

Her rhymes have very little to do with poetry. They're definitely hard rhymes, but poetic value has more to do with structure and how the phrases are put together.

BODY OF WORK: 70

I see what she's trying to do. The *Ill Na Na* album was a very R&B, hit-laden, raunchy album. It had the best of both worlds in that sense. She received a lot of bad reviews on the *Chyna Doll* album, which I didn't think was that bad, personally. Then came *Broken Silence*, which I think is her best work; neither of the follow-up albums had the same level of hit power or prowess that *Ill Na Na* had, and unfortunately, the business is about making hits. I don't think she's failing at all in the body of work.

INDUSTRY IMPACT: 70

This is also a matter of timing. Foxy came in the mid-'90s and the industry was very slow to give accolades. She did get a platinum album out of *Ill Na Na*, and she did cause a stir, but as far as Grammys, Image Awards, and all of the accolades that come, the industry didn't vibe that way with Foxy.

SOCIAL IMPACT: 65

Even though she made a big dent when she hit, a lot of the press was very negative and attacking. There's something to be said for it being positive or at least the blow-back of it being positive, and Foxy had a lot of negative press, but she still did make enough of an impact on the street that you can't overlook it.

LONGEVITY: 70

She came out in '95, *Broken Silence* came out in 2002, so that's seven years in the game, ten points per year.

LYRICS: 80

Foxy is lyrical, she does rhyme. A lot of times we get caught up in the content and we miss the fact that she's putting these words together and she's flowing and rhyming.

BATTLE SKILLS: 80

Foxy is aggressive and, even in the rhyme skills, she puts innuendo inside of her rhymes like she's challenging people. She hasn't been tested in an actual battle yet, but you can tell by how she rhymes and by the way she rhymes that she definitely has battle skills.

TOTAL SCORE: 1,270

AVERAGE SCORE: 74.7

47

SPOONIE GEE

THE COLD CRUSHIN LOVER

I'm the cold crushin lover
World's woman supreme
And when it comes to fine girls
I'm like a lovin' machine
When it comes to makin' love
I do the best that I can
And I'm known from coast to coast
As the sixty minute man
I don't drink I don't smoke
I don't gamble neither
And most people call me the woman pleaser
I'm the man's threat, the woman's pet
Better known as the man of joy
A man who fights on the microphone
Who all the people enjoy!!!

THIS IS WHY YOU HAVE TO disregard the MTV, VH1, and BET list of emcees. They can't go back far enough. Spoonie Gee is to Hip-Hop as Barry White and Teddy Pendergrass are to soul and R&B. Spoonie is Hip-Hop's true troubadour. Not only a pioneer, but Spoonie Gee is the first and last of his kind. Sure there have been many emcees who have made love songs, sexually explicit songs, and songs dealing with male and female relationships, but there has never been another emcee who dealt solely with love and sex. Furthermore, Spoonie did it with simplicity and class. He never got intricate lyrically, and he never got vulgar or explicit in his expression. He kept it simple, smooth, and sexual. He always referred to himself as a lover, and referred to the act as making love. Between 1978 and 1983 where the lyrical landscape was more about rocking parties and braggadocios' bravado, about how great our rhymes were, Spoonie Gee decided to focus on the ladies.

You would never know how courageous this was if you weren't there to feel the climate. This could have been career suicide. It's the equivalent of, although not as significant as, Ali bragging about being "the greatest" in the openly racist South at a time when black fighters humbly let their promoters speak for them. Spoonie Gee was running the risk of being booed and run out of town after every performance—and believe me some nights didn't go so well. However, ultimately Hip-Hop became a part of the record industry, and this style of rhyme translated very well on wax. Spoonie developed a strong cult following that is still strong today. Many people are constantly asking me for old tapes and records of the great Spoonie Gee.

As a group member of Spoonie Gee and The Treacherous Three (Special K, LA Sunshine and Kool Moe Dee), Spoonie always felt like he was destined to go solo. We could have a routine designed to talk about breakfast, sausages, and somehow when it was Spoonie's time to rhyme, the sausage would have nothing to do with breakfast, and a woman would have something interesting to do with it. He was obsessed. Ultimately, he went solo, made some hit records, and cemented his legacy as one of the greatest emcees ever, using the lost art of love rhyming.

Strength: One of the smoothest voices on wax. Spoonie's voice automatically changes the party mood.

Weakness: Nervous energy. Whenever Spoonie gets nervous, he can't rhyme. He gets flustered and mumbles just about anything. He was nervous on his first record, "Spoonin' Rap."

Favorite Record: "Love Rap," "Take It Off"

Favorite LP: *The Godfather of Rap*

#47: SPOONIE GEE

ORIGINALITY: 100

This is what I meant when I said it's harder for newer acts to get originality points because after all of these years you have to be doing something so unique, it's just entropy. We've seen so much that it's hard to get originality points. Of course, Spoonie doesn't have that problem. Spoonie Gee is absolutely, without a doubt, a pioneer of emcees, coming up with the whole love rap style and sticking to that style. It's a style that has yet to be mastered. People have dabbled in it, people have made love songs, but nobody has done it the way Spoonie did it consistently, throughout his whole career. He's associated strictly as the "love rhymer."

CONCEPTS: 85

His whole style is conceptual. His whole rhyme style is a concept focusing on love. It's constantly about love. He does write things and it's almost like painting a picture in some of those records. He's got a lot of records that aren't hits, but they're very high in the concept world.

VERSATILITY: 70

He didn't stray outside of the love area. He got a little bit on the braggadocio side with his "Godfather" record, but for the most part,

Spoonie stayed in the one zone that he was in, and that was about being a lover.

VOCABULARY: 70

Spoonie kept it very, very simple. There aren't too many words that you can use to supplement the word love, so *love* is the word he used a lot, *love* and *sex*.

SUBSTANCE: 80

Sex and love can be substantive. It's not necessarily changing the world, even though they say it's what makes the world go round. He tried to keep it as positive as he positively could. I don't think he ever used any profanity in his songs, which is substantive in that sense.

FLOW: 70

He was one of the old-school artists that was more about getting the message across. He didn't get real intricate or colorful with the flows; he kept it basic and went straight at you.

FLAVOR: 70

In the later years, he started to get a little more flavorful, but in the beginning, in the first records, you'd hear he was very nervous, and I know this because I know him personally. He was very nervous, so his delivery wasn't that tight in the first two records that he made, "Spoonin' Rap" and "Love Rap." By the time he got the monster jam with "Sequence" you started to hear him loosening up and you could hear him melting into the track, and he started adding more flavor into the equation. But for the most part, he kept it simple and not real flavorful.

FREESTYLE ABILITY: 60

Spoonie's another one of the old-school artists that prided himself on writing his rhymes. He definitely didn't like coming off the top of his head. He'd do it, but a lot of the old-school artists didn't even respect what's being called freestyle now. Back in the day it was called coming off the top of the head.

VOCAL PRESENCE: 80

He had a very smooth, silky voice. He's like the Barry White or Teddy Pendergrass of Hip-Hop. He's what they are to R&B. He didn't have the deep voice like Barry White, more like Smokey Robinson.

LIVE PERFORMANCE: 75

The one thing about Spoonie was he always wanted somebody on stage with him. He had a very shy personality, so sometimes he wouldn't pull it off live, but once he started getting the confidence and he got the hit records, he got better as he went along.

POETIC VALUE: 70

Very simplified. More rhyme than poetry, straight at you, and he didn't really put a lot of thought into the poetic value of the equation; it was more about the rhyme.

BODY OF WORK: 80

Once again, he had three or four hits, but at the time that he was making records, there were no albums to be made, it was only singles. I'm not going to penalize any group. I'm not going to penalize the newer group for not being able to do what they have to do 'cause their job is their job now, but the older emcees I'm not going to penalize them for not having the opportunities that the new cats have. So all you can do is judge a cat for what he had to do. So every year, Spoonie put a record out and it hit and made an impact, and he did that all the way up to 1987.

INDUSTRY IMPACT: 75

At the time that he came, there just weren't too many accolades to be given. However, he does get points from the fact that in pioneering something when it's brand new, people don't know what to make of it, so what happens is

you grasp on to whatever little there is and then you start building from whatever that was. A lot of people built on where Spoonie came from.

SOCIAL IMPACT: 65

Just for being there. At that time, there was nothing else to do, so a lot of others were heralded as kings or queens of the neighborhood. We served as a motivational force as far as that goes, but that was localized in its social impact. We didn't have the global effect and the global timing that later artists could have.

LONGEVITY: 90

A lot of people don't know it, but Spoonie was rhyming in 1977. He was my partner, actually. So rhyming from '78 to '87, that's nine years at ten points per year.

LYRICS: 75

Spoonie never was a true lyricist. He was an excellent song and rhyme writer, but he wasn't a true lyricist. Being a lyricist has more to do with how you come across with a lot of the braggadocio, the intricacy of the rhyme. Spoonie wasn't really a lyricist.

BATTLE SKILLS: 60

Spoonie never had conflicts with anybody. He could battle if pushed, but he just wasn't that kind of emcee. Spoonie would rather have peace and talk love to women than battle somebody.

TOTAL SCORE: 1,275

AVERAGE SCORE: 75

50 GREATEST RAPPERS

This is specifically about how the MC sounds on records. Their dynamics, lyrics, flow, articulation and rhythmic pocket. (One does not have to be an MC in order to be a rapper. This is about how good you are on wax, and the wax doesn't necessarily have to translate to any other part of the game. These are some of the greatest on wax.)

1) Rakim (Rakim is the greatest MC on wax)
2) KRS-One
3) Notorious B.I.G.
4) Big Daddy Kane
5) LL Cool J
6) Tupac
7) Slick Rick
8) DMX
9) Eminem
10) Jay-Z
11) Melle Mel
12) Lauryn Hill
13) Chuck D
14) Mc Lyte
15) Nas
16) Method Man
17) Kool Mo Dee
18) Queen Latifah
19) Ice Cube
20) Kool G Rap
21) Grandmaster Caz
22) Treach
23) Busta Rhymes
24) Redman
25) Run

26) Snoop Dogg
27) Heavy D
28) Kurtis Blow
29) Will Smith
30) Lil' Kim
31) Guru
32) MC Shan
33) Eve
34) Black Thought
35) Xzibit
36) Keith Murray
37) Craig Mack
38) Foxy Brown
39) Doug E Fresh
40) Ras Kass
41) Kurupt
42) Common
43) Mystikal
44) Dana Dane
45) Fat Joe
46) Scarface
47) Ice-T
48) D-Nice
49) Special Ed
50) The D.O.C.

46

FAT JOE

THE PUERTO
RICAN RHYME
SUN

Everybody talk gats
Really don't pack 'em
98 percent of these rappers is all actors
Stay frontin'
Like you wild out and spray somethin'
Come to find out
You ain't never slayed nothin'
Think it's a game, gone lose the sport
I seen dudes get bruised through fought
Then choose the court
The news report
They just pursued the course
If you even think of bustin' their ass
They'd sue ya thoughts

BELIEVE IT OR NOT, FAT JOE is a pioneer. No, he's not the first successful Puerto Rican emcee. That would be Ruby Dee of the Fantastic Romantic Five. He's also not even the first highly acclaimed Puerto Rican emcee. That would be the devastating Tito of the Fearless Four. And yes, Gerardo had pop success, Kid Frost had the streets in the West, and B-Real of Cypress Hill is an icon in the Mexican and Latino Hip-Hop communities. But Fat Joe is the first true Puerto Rican soloist to cross over into the predominantly African-American world of Hip-Hop. Fat Joe, aka Joey Crack, aka Don Cartagena, is accepted as a lyricist, an emcee, and a hard-core artist in the tightly knit underground level of the Hip-Hop world. He's respected on the streets for the credibility of his lyrical content. He's the essence of "keep it real." When he first hit the scene in the early to mid-'90s, the same credibility that he is now respected for was viewed as problematic. The press was just beginning to turn the heat up on gangsta rap and the practitioners of its music. Add to the equation Joe's uncompromising rhyme style, and small scale independent label relativity, and you had a prescription for failure. However, with shoestring album and video budgets, Joe persevered. With marginal underground hits and guerilla style management via Mick Benzo, Fat Joe was able to maintain a street presence that would ultimately pay off for him in the long run.

Ironically, in the beginning, Fat Joe wasn't really that good of an emcee. I can honestly say he's one of the emcees who worked his way up lyrically. With each LP you could see clear growth. He hit his stride in the late '90s with the Terror Squad and Big Pun. Soon Fat Joe was on multiple collaborations and shining every time out. At the end of the millennium he signed with Atlantic/Big Beat and finally had some real money behind him. Suddenly Fat Joe had the breakthrough "Bet Ya Man Can't." This was the beginning of Fat Joe showing his diversity as an emcee. On his earlier works, 1993's *Represent*, and 1995's *Jealous Ones Envy*, Joe seemed to only be concerned with keeping it gangsta. However, as all emcees find out, no matter how lofty our dreams of being a real emcee may be, nine times out of ten, one cannot survive the game without hit records. This is one of the hardest jobs that the newer emcees have to face. Keeping your deal is job one. Fat Joe had figured it out. In 2001, he dropped *J.O.S.E.*, the cleverly self-titled acronym "Jealous Ones Still Envy." The single "We Thuggin" with R. Kelly transitioned Joe from a respected emcee into a Hip-Hop star.

What's great about this situation is that because of Joe's lyrical abilities, he never had to sacrifice his reputation, or compromise his lyrical integrity to make the hits. Many times emcees take a total departure from everything they represent, as they attempt to chase that elusive hit. Not only did Joe not do that, but he enhanced his image. He added the player persona to the thug persona and upgraded his lyrical skills. He followed the formula that Puffy created with Notorious B.I.G., gave the radio a couple of Spoony G–type love songs, played up the player energy for the ladies, and kept the rest of his LP gully and hard-core. Fat Joe followed this formula again on the 2002 release of *Loyalty*, and once again he delivered.

There was once a skeptical school of thought about Joe's ability to succeed without the help of Big Pun. Sometimes the pundits are too cynical. Not only did Fat Joe succeed, but he superseded all expectations. DEFINITELY ONE OF THE FIFTY GREATEST EMCEES.

Strength: Rhyme pitch. Fat Joe always seems to be able to stay right in the energy range of wherever the music is. He never sounds like he's pressing.

Weakness: Excess profanity. Sometimes he uses profanity just to fill in the rhyme or the rhymes rhythm.

Favorite Record: "We Thuggin," "John Blaze"

Favorite LP: *J.O.S.E.*

#46: FAT JOE

ORIGINALITY: 80

Another emcee based on the timing, though the ground work had been laid way, way back with Tito from the Fearless Four and Ruby Dee from the Fantastic Romantic, with Gerardo Rico Suave in the equation. It wasn't until Fat Joe that the Puerto Rican rapper hit at that level again. Fat Joe mastered the New York cadence and brought the energy off, so that he was respected as an emcee, as opposed to a novelty act. It's harder to give newer acts more for originality, but he put his flavor and his slant on the rhyme styles and the rhymes that he was using, even though we had heard these styles before.

CONCEPTS: 80

Joey Crack. A lot of people don't know this, but Fat Joe was the architect of the posse records he made with Pun, Jada Kiss, and Nory. That has something to do with concepts also, because you're putting a record together without knowing what anybody else is going to rhyme about, so you give them the theme and that's a concept in itself.

VERSATILITY: 80

When he first came out, Fat Joe seemed to be only concerned with coming off as a thug and coming off hard-core, so those are the types of records that he made. Then later, doing the joint with R. Kelly and doing the record with Genuine, you could tell that Joe was diversifying his game, and making bigger and stronger records, and he's starting to have a lot more impact in that sense. He still keeps the albums as hard-core as ever, but he is now making records in another zone.

VOCABULARY: 75

Joe doesn't use an extensive vocabulary; he keeps it simple, like a lot of emcees. Once in a while, he'll throw in a few words that seem to come out of nowhere, and being Puerto Rican, he had two languages anyway.

SUBSTANCE: 75

Joe keeps it street, keeps it gutter, keeps it real in the stories he brings across. A lot of critics will say it's one note, with the violence or the subject matter, but there's something to be said about street life still being substantive.

FLOW: 80

Fat Joe is like a power forward going to the hole strong. Nothing fancy, just going right at you.

FLAVOR: 70

Joe isn't playing on the mic, he just comes at you. He has his own flavor, he puts his inflections on it.

FREESTYLE ABILITY: 75!

I'm assuming Joe can freestyle on some level, but he's a writer, you can hear it in his rhymes. A lot of times writers, like me, are better writers than we are freestylers.

VOCAL PRESENCE: 80

Joe definitely attacks the mic with dominant energy. We definitely know who he is when he comes on. Usually it's when he's on a posse record; he's right in pocket and right on point with the energy of the record.

LIVE PERFORMANCE: 75

Similar to Pun, a bunch of people onstage and too many people have mics sometimes. The show is pretty cool, but it seems like he's still working out whatever kinks he has to master on that side of the game.

POETIC VALUE: 60

Fat Joe is definitely more rhymes than poetry. That's just the way it is.

BODY OF WORK: 80

Out of all the emcees on this list, I haven't seen too many that have grown at the rate that I see Fat Joe growing. I mean, he's literally getting better each album. When I hear the body of work, I can hear the growth.

INDUSTRY IMPACT: 65

When you decide to make hard-core records, you know the accolades won't come. He understood that and the industry basically didn't do any type of acknowledgement. His presence was still felt, and he was able to sustain without any industry impact.

SOCIAL IMPACT: 70

He came at a time when Hip-Hop was in full bloom and he had to fight for attention because of the type of records that he made. I think he opened the door and set the table for Big Pun to come in and be able to do what he did.

LONGEVITY: 80

Joe goes back to '94 and he's still here in 2003.

LYRICS: 80

Joe is absolutely a lyrical emcee. He focuses on the rhyme and the lyrics.

BATTLE SKILLS: 75

I heard Joe say once that he was a troublemaker. I remember one time when the East Coast and West Coast hype was going on, Joe was ready to set it off. So on some level I think he would battle, but I think he meant taking it to another level. Joe has some kind of battle skills within him, but I don't know if he would be putting in any kind of time into battling anybody.

TOTAL SCORE: 1,280

AVERAGE SCORE: 75.2

45

JERU THE DAMAJA

I snatch fake gangsta emcees
And make em faggot flambet
Your nines spray, my mind spray
Malignant mist that'll leave cart de funk
The results your remains stuffed in a car trunk
You couldn't come to the jungles of the
East poppin' that yang
You won't survive get live
Catchin' wreck is our thang
I don't gang bang
Or shoot out bang bang
The relentless lyrics
The only dope I sling
I'm a true master, you can check my credential
Cause I choose to use my infinite potential

JERU THE DAMAJA IS ONE OF the first emcees that openly and literally went on record with the East Coast's discontent with West Coast gangsta rap. This feud had been brewing since 1989 when N.W.A. was coming into prominence. The media sensationalized it, and took away its substance, turning it into a frivolous, mudslinging, death trap. In 1994, Jeru's single "Come Clean" crystallized the essence of the problem. Late '80s New York, thanks in part to Hip-Hop, was fifteen to twenty years removed from any real gang activity. But by 1994 suddenly we had Bloods and Crips in Brooklyn. The elder emcees were disgusted. We felt like we worked so hard to get away from where gangsta rap was taking us. Jeru the Damaja was among the conscious fraternity of emcees who touched on this musically.

Real rough and rugged shine like a gold nugget
Everytime I pick up the microphone I drug it
Unplug it on chumps with the gangsta battle
Leave ya nines at home
And bring ya skills to the battle
Ya rattling on and on and ain't sayin' nothin'!

This is truly what the substance of the beef was about. Jeru the Damaja is that unique emcee that uses the classic braggadocio rhyme style infused with positive messages. The best example of this is heard on his cartoon-like, superhero song, "The Prophet." This is one of the best concept records in Hip-Hop history. Only Common's "I Used to Love H.E.R.," and a short list of others, comes close. The Prophet's archenemy is Ignorance, and his henchmen are Jealousy, Hatred, and Envy. You get the picture.

Jeru, like many of the real emcees pre–Jay-Z, did not see a lot of commercial mainstream success. Part of this was by design. With music done by DJ Premier, one of Hip-Hop's elite producers, musically and lyrically Jeru was only concerned about the streets. Contrary to popular belief, the streets of Hip-Hop are multidimensional. The Hip-Hop media portrays the streets as a one-dimensional entity of drugs, sex, and violence spawning emcees that convey the attitudes of the streets through nonproductive, profane, profanity-laden lyrics. Jeru obliterates this stereotype. He personifies what I call "the other side of the street." It's more like a conscious thug, or better yet, not a thug at all. Jeru consistently represents the best of the street emcee, choosing to use his voice and his talent to inspire and enlighten his listeners. In this era of excess materialism, it's hard to get a feel for how the Hip-Hop fan regards Jeru. His absence on all of the lists of great emcees indicates to me he's not regarded highly enough. I know what this brother is working with, and he is definitely one of the fifty greatest emcees.

Strength: Positive concepts. One of the most conceptual emcees ever.

Weakness: Vocal presence and cadence. Jeru chooses to use a monotone delivery, which can underwhelm the listener.

Favorite Record: "Ya Playin' Ya Self"

Favorite LP: *The Sun Rises in the East*

#45: JERU THE DAMAJA

ORIGINALITY: 85

He brought who he is into the equation. He sounded a little bit similar to Guru, but I guess that has to do with proximity, who you're around, your production team, and a Guru executive who produces your first album.

CONCEPTS: 100

I have never heard a more conceptual record than "The Prophet," and that's just that one record.

VERSATILITY: 70

As some people get locked into bringing in gangsta, I think Jeru was locked into bringing in consciousness. Now that's not bad, but it didn't seem like he had too many aspects to his game. He definitely is an emcee, so he had the lyrical side to the game. He just seemed to be on the one vibe that he's on.

VOCABULARY: 80

He uses words that a lot of people wouldn't use.

SUBSTANCE: 90

It seems like Jeru is definitely trying to touch people. He's trying to make a difference and all of his stuff basically comes up with substance.

FLOW: 80

He defiantly knew how to spit to make his style of rhyme come across.

FLAVOR: 60

He absolutely has been one of the more monotone emcees and a lot of people aren't compelled to listen because of the tone of his voice. He is more involved in the substance of the equation rather than the flavor of it.

FREESTYLE ABILITY: 70

I saw him in the Blaze battle situation and I couldn't believe that he did the whole battle in freestyle, and that's one of the cardinal sins in my book. You need to be able to freestyle, but if you only have freestyle unprepared then you're gonna catch a bad one.

VOCAL PRESENCE: 70

Like the flavor, he keeps it very monotone, and he is straightforward. If you're not really into him, then his voice won't really grab you.

LIVE PERFORMANCE: 70

Unfortunately, cerebral emcees have a hard time translating live because it's really about listening to them as opposed to partying with them. I understand what he is doing, so he's not failing, but I can't give him much more of a score because of the tones of his style.

POETIC VALUE: 85

He approaches it poetically. He doesn't just rhyme, he's actually doing it in a poetic format, and the way he's posing and phrasing the rhyme has a lot to do with his score in this area.

BODY OF WORK: 80

Though there have only been two albums of his own, he's done guest appearances on some others. It's his voice on the record "Blasé, Blasé the East Is in the House." The albums that he's done are of high quality, high substance, high motivation, and high concepts.

INDUSTRY IMPACT: 60

With the style of records that he made, and being on a small label, there were no industry accolades coming. The industry has a hard time recognizing emcees that bring it the way he brings it.

SOCIAL IMPACT: 70

With a small label, and the subject matter, sometimes your social impact is a local impact. Even though he sold a few records, his impact was more personal and local. If you were into him you got into the records based on who he was and what he was about.

LONGEVITY: 60

I don't know what he's doing right now, but he came in '94, came back with "You're Playin' Yourself" in '96. He has six strong years in the game.

LYRICS: 85

He's conceptual, he's poetic, but he's also a lyricist. He's like a quintessential emcee. He understands how to put a rhyme together.

BATTLE SKILLS: 70

Just based on what I saw at the Blaze battle, I don't know if he was caught off guard or if he was overconfident, but in order to battle you definitely have to come with more than freestyle. Jeru is so into being positive that maybe it's not in his nature to really break somebody down like you must in a battle.

TOTAL SCORE: 1,285

AVERAGE SCORE: 75.5

50 GREATEST SOLO ARTISTS

(As an artist, this has to do with MC's and rappers' overall creative artistic impact, videos, movies, TV shows, television appearances, live performances and other personas.)

1) Tupac	26) Melle Mel
2) Will Smith	27) Kurtis Blow
3) LL Cool J	28) Big Daddy Kane
4) Queen Latifah	29) Ja Rule
5) Notorious BIG	30) Mc Lyte
6) Jay-Z	31) Coolio
7) Lauryn Hill	32) Tone Loc
8) Ice Cube	33) Speech
9) Eminem	34) Doug E Fresh
10) Snoop Dogg	35) Slick Rick
11) Missy Elliott	36) Nelly
12) Hammer	37) Lil Kim
13) Wyclef Jean	38) Kool G Rap
14) Busta Rhymes	39) Eve
15) Chuck D	40) Master P
16) Ice T	41) Guru
17) Nas	42) Da Brat
18) Rakim	43) Luke Sywalker
19) KRS-One	44) Black Thought
20) Puffy	45) Common
21) Method Man	46) Scarface
22) Redman	47) Young MC
23) Treach	48) Baby
24) Heavy D	49) Eazy-E
25) Kool Mo Dee	50) Too Short

44

CRAIG MACK

I'm gone rain
Rain forever
Rain like bad weather
Rain like whoever never
You can't bite my style
Cause my style ain't a style that is a style
So I can go buck wild
Bet you figured you got more
Funk for flow
It ain't so
Flava in ya ear let you know
Now I'm about a second from the hook dook
Scrap ya rap book
Before you get ya wet style shook!

CRAIG MACK IS INCREDIBLE. IF YOU read this book and are left not understanding the category for flavor, then pick up Craig Mack's 1994 LP *Project Funk Da World*. Right from the first song you'll hear an emcee playing with multi-flows, flippin' and fluctuating inflections, and backing himself up with the most incredible flavor-filled ad-libs in Hip-Hop history. Craig Mack is the benchmark for flavor. After hearing Craig Mack, I said that if an emcee had Kool Moe Dee's lyrics, Chuck D's voice, and Craig Mack's flavor, that emcee would be unseeable! Craig Mack is at the top of his game on the 1994 singles "Flava in Ya Ear" and "Get Down." To the common listener, it may sound like frivolous rhyming about rocking mics and outshining other emcees. And that's correct. However, in this case, it's not about the what, it's about the how! Hundreds of emcees, including myself, have talked about rocking other emcees. This is one of the fundamental elements of true emceeing. But Craig Mack shifted the cadence and flowed in such a unique way that from the point that record dropped until today, an emcee's flow became the most important element to his game. Nowadays if an emcee can't flow, he can't blow. There is no more success for the rhymer without flow. Not only does an emcee have to flow, but he or she has to have flavor in the delivery. Craig Mack almost single-handedly raised the bar. Method Man had a hand in this also, but while his influence was subtler, Craig Mack's shift was overtly overstated. Craig Mack also put rhythmic song like inflections in his rhymes, combined with wordplay unseen again until Jay-Z and Eminem.

Because of the business/game, Craig Mack has never matched the success of 1994. He also had the misfortune of coming out at the same time as his label-mate Notorious B.I.G. The impact of Biggie was too powerful for Craig Mack to be anything other than second. It's like Clyde Drexler coming into the NBA at the same time as Michael Jordan. We all know how that turned out. However, like Drexler, Craig Mack got his championship in '94 (Drexler in '95) and both ended up on the Top Fifty lists in their professions. Unfortunately, Hip-Hop isn't as organized as the NBA. So I have to let the world know that Craig Mack is a Top Fifty emcee.

Strength: Flavor. One of the few emcees that can make the listener have fun.

Weakness: Too much flavor. Because he's so colorful, it's hard to take him seriously on the songs where he's trying to deliver a message.

Favorite Record: "Flava in Ya Ear," "Get Down"

Favorite LP: *Project Funk Da World*

#44: CRAIG MACK

ORIGINALITY: 100

To come into the game in '94 with a brand new style that hadn't been heard or done before, and as he said, "my style is a style that ain't a style so I can go buck wild." There was no way to really put your finger on what he was doing. You just knew that he was doing something new and original, and he's what I call an "impact player."

CONCEPTS: 85

He's only done two albums because of the politics in the industry and losing his deal with Bad Boy, or whatever that was about. In the two albums, you could definitely hear that he was a conceptual emcee. There was another song, "So What You Gonna Do When God Comes for You." He did his thing on the concept side.

VERSATILITY: 75

He seemed to approach every record in the same way, and even though he dabbled in different subject matters, he didn't do a lot more than what he gave you with "Flava in Ya Ear" and "Can I Get Down."

VOCABULARY: 65

He kept it really simple, almost comically simple on some levels.

SUBSTANCE: 70

Craig Mack is one of the few emcees that understand the fun aspect of the game. He keeps it in a fun zone. He rhymes to have a good time; he's trying to make you have a good time. It's not a lot of substance and heavy subjects there.

FLOW: 95

His flow is incredible. It works in conjunction with originality. The way he was bringing the rhymes across had not been done before. I don't think people understood or appreciated the level of ingenuity that Craig Mack brought to the flow aspect of the game.

FLAVOR: 100

That says it all. The name of the song is "Flava in Ya Ear." I can't think of anybody more flavorful in the history of the game. He got on the mic and just played with the rhymes and played with the style. He flipped it on a level that I hadn't seen before and haven't seen since.

FREESTYLE ABILITY: 75

Based on the subject matter, the rhyme style, and the lack of vocabulary, doesn't mean he can't come off the top of the head, but when you come off the top of the head a lot of people grade you on a curve because it's just about finishing the rhymes.

VOCAL PRESENCE: 90

Before Jah Rule and DMX, but after Just-Ice, Craig Mack was the raspy voice, and because of the flavor it made him stand out.

LIVE PERFORMANCE: 80

Hit records make the show go. "Flava in Ya Ear" was a winner. I don't know if he ever got a chance to do more than what he was doing. I think there were a lot of timing issues, coming out at the same time as Biggie on Bad Boy.

POETIC VALUE: 60

More rhyme, more flow, more flavor, more color, but not a lot of poetic value.

BODY OF WORK: 70

The first album was incredible, the second album, whether it was production problems or label problems, didn't come off that well.

INDUSTRY IMPACT: 70

Craig Mack hit very hard with "Flava in Ya Ear," but the follow up after "Get Down" and the album, he didn't get a chance to make a real industry impact because he came simultaneously with Biggie. Which was a good strategy for the label, but not as good for the artist.

SOCIAL IMPACT: 65

The social impact was even less than the industry impact, really, because of Biggie. Once Biggie dropped his album, all of the attention went to Biggie, and Craig Mack got caught in a quagmire or in the shadow of that energy. After his first single, it's almost like people didn't know what he was doing, or where he was at, or what was happening. Then when he left the label, nobody knew what happened.

LONGEVITY: 55

He came in '94 with "Flava in Ya Ear," then he returned at the end of '98–early '99 with his second album, which didn't really hit, but he did make his presence known. Five-and-a-half years gets you 55.

LYRICS: 70

He's more of a colorful emcee. He wasn't a true lyricist, but he brought the flavor with the style and made the rhymes sing.

BATTLE SKILLS: 65

If your rhyme style and lyrical style isn't attacking and challenging, it doesn't mean that you can't battle. But battling is probably not your forte, based on what you'd be using in the battle, based on the indication of your style that precedes the battle zone.

TOTAL SCORE: 1,290

AVERAGE SCORE: 75.8

SPORTS EQUIVALENT

		Boxing	Basketball	Football	Baseball
1.)	Melle Mel	Joe Louis	Bill Russell	Jim Brown	Jackie Robinson
2.)	Rakim	Sugar Ray Leonard	Michael Jordan	Barry Sanders	Hank Aaron
3.)	KRS-One	Marvin Haggler	Kareem Abdul-Jabbar	Emmit Smith	Frank Thomas
4.)	Big Daddy Kane	Tommy Hearns	Dominique Wilkins	Thurman Thomas	Reggie Jackson
5.)	Kool Mo Dee	Sugar Ray Robinson	Julius Irving	Walter Payton	Willie Mays
6.)	Grandmaster Caz	Archie Moore	Wilt Chamberlain	Eric Dickerson	Josh Gibson
7.)	LL Cool J	Evander Holyfield	Magic Johnson	Jerry Rice	Mark McGwire
8.)	Chuck D	Muhammad Ali	Charles Barkley	Lawrence Taylor	Curt Flood
9.)	Notorious B.I.G.	Mike Tyson	Patrick Ewing	Bo Jackson	Bo Jackson
10.)	Lauryn Hill		Lisa Leslie		
11.)	Nas	Roy Jones	Kobe Bryant	Marshall Faulk	Sammy Sosa
12.)	Queen Latifah		Sheryl Swoops		
13.)	Tupac	Oscar De Lahoya	Allen Iverson	Deion Sanders	Ken Griffey, Jr.
14.)	Kool G Rap	Pernel Whittaker	Bernard King	Tony Dorsett	Dave Winfield
15.)	Jay-Z	Lenox Lewis	Shaq	Donovan McNabb	Barry Bonds
16.)	Treach	James Toney	Chris Webber	Curtis Martin	Gary Sheffield
17.)	Method Man	Vernon Forrest	Tracey McGrady	Randy Moss	Derek Jeter
18.)	Ice Cube	David Tua	KarlL Malone	Franco Harris	Mo Vaughn
19.)	Mc Lyte		Teresa Weatherspoon		
20.)	Redman	Bernard Hopkins	Scottie Pippin	Jerome Bettis	Bernie Williams
21.)	Ras Kass		Jason Kidd		
22.)	GZA		Kevin Garnett		
23.)	Will Smith				Ricky Henderson
24.)	Busta Rhymes		Latrell Spreewell		
25.)	Heavy D		Isaiah Thomas		
26.)	Xzibit		Steve Frances		
27.)	Common		Eddie Jones		
28.)	Pharoahe Monch		Vince Carter		
29.)	Black Thought		Jerry Stackhouse		
30.)	Scarface		Robert Horry		
31.)	Kurtis Blow		Walt Frazier		
32.)	Run		Larry Bird		
33.)	Snoop Dogg		Lamar Odom		
34.)	Guru		Ray Allen		
35.)	Ice-T		Dennis Rodman		
36.)	Doug E Fresh		Reggie Miller		
37.)	Keith Murray		Jalen Rose		
38.)	Mystikal		Arron Davis		
39.)	Kurupt		Rasheed Wallace		
40.)	Slick Rick		Earl Monroe		
41.)	Big Pun		Larry Johnson		
42.)	Lil' Kim		Charmique Holdsclaw		
43.)	MC Shan		Ralph Sampson		
44.)	Craig Mack		Penny Hardaway		
45.)	Jeru The Damaja		Charles Oakley		
46.)	Fat Joe		Anthony Mason		
47.)	Spoonie Gee		George Gervin		
48.)	Foxy Brown		Nicky McCrimmon		
49.)	Mack 10		Malik Rose		
50.)	Just-Ice		Moses Malone		

43

MC SHAN
THE UNSUNG LYRICIST

The way I shine I got splendor
I'm the real thing not a pretender
You got the nerve
To pop the fatal question
I'm takin the time to make
A small suggestion
Write a will for your family's conveniency
Rappers I'll serve
Without mercy or leniency
No frame of mind no heart I'm relentless
Step to me I'm knockin you senseless
I've planted my seed so don't try to uproot me
You'd do better tryin to straight up shoot me

MC SHAN IS ONE OF THE tightest lyricists ever to not be recognized for his lyrical prowess. It's very well known that LL Cool J's early rhyme style was a combination of Kool Moe Dee, T-LA Rock, and Run, but not many people are aware of the fourth element, MC Shan. The record "The Bridge" was the B-side hit to the record "Beat Biter." That record was directed at LL for his taking MC Shan's beat/style, according to Shan. Fortunately or unfortunately, depending on how you look at it, the B-side made all the noise, and only insiders in Hip-Hop even knew about the beef. Nonetheless, "The Bridge" put MC Shan on the map.

Ironically, this record launched him into another battle with the legendary KRS-One. From this point on it seems that Shan was only looked at as a battle emcee. Because of KRS-One's overwhelming battle skills, and solid reputation as one of the best emcees ever, it seems like Shan could never get out of the shadow of the battle. Part of this was because of his rhyme style. MC Shan is one of the most fearless emcees ever to pick up a mic. He literally will battle any emcee, anytime. The reason that I said fortunately or unfortunately in reference to "The Bridge" putting him on the map is because there are so many other aspects to Shan's game. He has messages in him like "Jane," an anti-drug song, "Left Me Lonely," an attempt at a love song, and songs with the Juice Crew, where he showed a humorous side. Shan also is a master of the witty metaphor punch line.

My name rings bells and makes
Rappers petro God help ya kid when I get upset yo
The boss starts roll
Bid ya fans farewell
Cause the chance of you winning is
Like snow in hell!

That's classic Hip-Hop rhymeness! MC Shan is a pioneer who rhymed like a classic boxer-puncher. He understood how to set up the rhyme by opening with lyrical jabs, and put words together like combinations. Then he would flurry at some point, and end with a great punch line to tie it all together. He was also a pretty good storyteller, and a very visual conceptual emcee. The battle with KRS put a dent in his reputation, but if you know your Hip-Hop history then you know MC Shan is one of the greats.

Strengths: Rhyme structure. Shan knows how to put a rhyme together.

Weakness: Voice. Because Shan has a very high-pitched voice, a lot of fans never took him seriously. This was partly because of the era. In the era of Shan's dominance, the deeper voices ruled, and people were conditioned to hear lyricists in a certain tone.

Favorite Record: "I Pioneered This," "Juice Crew Law"

Favorite LP: *Born to be Wild*

#43: MC SHAN

ORIGINALITY: 95
MC Shan is definitely one of the early pioneers. The only reason he doesn't get a 100 is that he came a little later than the actual first pioneers of the equation, who set the tone for what he was doing.

CONCEPTS: 80
A lot of his rhymes were straightforward but he had records like "Jane" and "Left Me Lonely," so he also had concepts in his game.

VERSATILITY: 70
Shan comes from the conventional style of emceeing where it's about bragging how dope you are, how many emcees you'll crush, and what you can do to people. Shan exaggerates as much as he possibly can about his greatness.

VOCABULARY: 85
Shan is like an early wordsmith. He comes from the era where T-LA Rock, Just-Ice, and I, and even early LL were using heavy levels of high vocabulary. Shan is in that time zone and that was where he was coming from with vocabulary.

SUBSTANCE: 70
Other than the "Jane" record, it didn't seem like he was too concerned with being substantive.

FLOW: 80
When you listen to Shan you can hear that he's always on pocket, he's always on beat. I don't think I ever heard him stray. His flow was stellar.

FLAVOR: 80
Shan would play a little bit, and once in a while you could hear bits of humor where he didn't take himself so seriously.

FREESTYLE ABILITY: 75
He would only do freestyle if we were on a bus and he'd rhyme off the top of the head. That's where he would put the joke in. A lot of people don't know that with the Juice Crew, you had to be on your game, because the jokes were going to be coming. Shan would freestyle in that zone.

VOCAL PRESENCE: 75
A lot of people said that they didn't like his voice, or felt his voice was too light, but I give him points on the fact that as soon as he opened his mouth, you did know who he was.

LIVE PERFORMANCE: 75

A lot of times with TJ Swan and Biz, Shan would be onstage on his own, and sometimes he would be caught up in having to do records. Because of the battle zone that people put him in he was looked at as a battle emcee. A lot of times he didn't get a chance to do his thing, as far as the show, without confronting some type of issue.

POETIC VALUE: 70

Similar to what I've been saying about most of the emcees already. Rhymes over poetry.

BODY OF WORK: 80

He comes from the era of making singles, but got a chance to make albums later in the game. He definitely has hits, some very popular hits. "The Bridge" is definitely one all-time Hip-Hop classic.

INDUSTRY IMPACT: 60

Partially because of the timing of the era that he came in, there was no industry for him to make the impact. On top of that, he never really made the types of records that the industry could latch on to.

SOCIAL IMPACT: 60

He didn't get a chance to have the national or global impact, more of a local impact, but he did put Queens on the map early in the game before a lot of emcees were able to do that. Run did it at the highest level, and Shan is an early emcee that put Queens in the game at a lyricist level.

LONGEVITY: 70

He was there from the early to mid-'80s and got to '89–'90. He put seven years in.

LYRICS: 85

He's an underrated lyricist, because of his voice. He's a lyrical emcee.

BATTLE SKILLS: 85

Shan was a battle emcee. The only thing that he loses points for in the battle was that his voice would create a zone where you didn't take him seriously. Unfairly, on some level, people wouldn't pay attention and judge the rhyme for the content. But I listened, so I understand it.

TOTAL SCORE: 1,295

AVERAGE SCORE: 76.1

42

LIL' KIM
FEMME FATALE

What the blood clot
You wanna rumble with the bee ha
BZZZZ throw a hex on the whole family
Dressed in all black like the Omen
have ya friends this is for my homey
And ya know me for making nukkas so sick
flossing my six with the Lex on the wrist
If it's murder
you know she wrote it
Germal Looga for yo ass
Miss deep throat it

PUT LIL' KIM ON YOUR RECORD, and you instantly upgrade your record, but beware—there is a very good chance she's gonna outshine you. In fact, I would be willing to say she's one of the few people who could follow Biggie on a song. Few emcees have the ability to explode right out of the gate, and sustain it past a couple of months. Lil' Kim not only exploded and sustained, but she heightened her reputation and became a straight-up star. In 1995, Lil' Kim was featured on the J.U.N.I.O.R. Mafia's "Players Anthem." Immediately, everyone wanted to know who Lil' Kim was.

Once the video dropped, it set off a lustful explosion. The anticipation for Kim was heightened. When the posters for Kim's long-awaited LP *Hard Core* showed her squatting against a wall with her legs open, wearing silk panties, I was caught up just like everybody else. This set the music industry off on a tirade. Like Foxy Brown, the attacks had nothing to do with her music, initially. Before the LP dropped, Kim was called a hooker, and there were even rumors of her making a porno movie.

At first I felt angry and sorry for Kim. I thought she was being manipulated by the worst of sexism in the industry. Then I heard the album. Suddenly I realized Kim was the architect. She exploited the worst of sexism and materialism in America. Like Madonna, Lil' Kim approached her lyrical sexual prowess with an in-your-face attitude. Unlike Madonna, or any current pop star, Lil' Kim used very explicit, raunchy, detailed descriptions of sex acts. This seemed to go too far for even the so-called liberal music press. In my opinion this was sexism again, because by this point in Hip-Hop some very highly acclaimed male rappers and emcees had proven to be straight-up misogynistic, and they were not only accepted, they were revered. The climate was right. It was time for a gangsta female, with a sexy twist, who could really rhyme.

As I said Foxy Brown was like a female version of Jay-Z. Lil' Kim was a female version of Biggie. Lil' Kim's delivery is stellar. Her flow is incredible. In fact, she's so good people immediately thought that Biggie was writing her rhymes for her. Not true. Although you could tell his influence was there, Kim writes her rhymes. Another unfortunate comparison was made to Foxy Brown. This is because they came into prominence around the same time, filling the same void, using the same content. However, to the trained ear listening to the emcee instead of the records, you'll hear very distinct differences. One of the main differences is their approach to sex, lyrically. While both sound very confident, and make it very clear how they want to be pleased, Lil' Kim does a more masterful job on talking about pleasing a man. She talks about the taboo aspects of sex. She takes what's supposed to be degrading to women sexually, and boasts of being a champion at it.

> *You the best dada*
> *Now watch mama*
> *Go up and down di** to jaw crazy*
> *Say my name baby*
> *Before you nut*
> *I'ma dribble down ya but,*
> *Cheeks make you wiggle*
> *Then giggle just a little*
> *I'm drinkin babies*
> *Then crack for the Mercedes*
> *Act shady then feel my 380*

I could go on, but I'm sure you get the point. What I'm not sure of is how many people really understand the level of rhyme skills being displayed. Understand that in this era of music, the visual aspects of a rapper/MC has superseded the importance of the skills level, and as sexy as Lil' Kim is, it's very easy to loose focus on the rhymes, and focus only on the sex appeal and fantasy-inducing content. Speaking as a man, even if you're totally repulsed by her content and what she represents, you can still miss what's important as an emcee. Lil' Kim is putting in work. Not only the flow and delivery, but her flavor, inflections, and rhyme structure. Lil' Kim is rhyming her ASS OFF! She is a female wordsmith. You can rarely ever predict where she's going to go with a rhyme, from line to line. She is also a lyrically visual emcee, as she displayed on the songs "Drugs and Queen B**$h." On her latest LP, *Bella Mafia*, she went in a couple of different directions, but the lyrical game is still on point. Now the word is, Kim is adding acting to her résumé. If her acting is anywhere near her rhyming, she will be one of Hip-Hop's greatest artists, in addition to one of HIP-HOP'S GREATEST EMCEES.

Strength: Flow, flavor, and delivery. She adds life to her rhymes and makes it fun to listen to.

Weakness: Not enough diversity—even sex needs different positions to keep it interesting. Sex has an orgasm as the payoff.

Favorite Record: "No Time for Fake," "Queen B***$h"

Favorite LP: *Hard Core*

#42: LIL' KIM

ORIGINALITY: 80
Timing. Coming out in the mid-'90s. The subject matter, she was bringing it in a way we hadn't seen before. The only difference is the rhyme style and the cadences. We had already

seen that from Biggie, but she still brought who she was into the equation.

CONCEPTS: 75

Kim was a slightly conceptual "Queen Bee"— my favorite record that she made. I could see that she had the conceptual zone in her, and for the most part you knew what note she was on and what vibe she was coming from, and she brought it straight across.

VERSATILITY: 70

She played with flows and she played with different tempos and records, but she was very straight ahead. You knew exactly what you were going to get from Kim. It was just going to be a matter of when you were going to take your clothes off to listen to it.

VOCABULARY: 70

Kept it very simple, did a lot of name-brand rhyming.

SUBSTANCE: 70

It's hard to quantify the subject matter that she deals with, with the sex and violence. But there's still something to be said for it because if it's keeping it real, and it's what people are doing, and it's where people are coming from, she's giving you another side of life.

FLOW: 95

Ridiculous. Incredible. Lil' Kim is definitely one of the best female flow-ers I've ever heard. The way she brings it across, she has almost perfect inflections. She knows where to drop the voice, where to raise the voice, where to stretch the vowels. She's excellent in her flow.

FLAVOR: 95

Incredible. Colorful and enjoyable. You can follow her easily because she takes you on a ride. She knows exactly how to deliver what she's trying to deliver. She knows exactly what's humorous; she knows exactly what's being sexual.

FREESTYLE ABILITY: 80!

The subject matter and what she talks about seems like that's what she'd be about. That doesn't mean she doesn't have more stuff in her arsenal, but the indication on the freestyle side is she probably could do it off the top of her head, but at some point it's still going to be sexual and it's still going to bust you up.

VOCAL PRESENCE: 80

Anybody into Hip-Hop, when you hear Kim, you know it's her. As soon as she comes on a record, you know when you hear her voice. A lot of people outside of Hip-Hop might not know, but her voice still has a presence.

LIVE PERFORMANCE: 75

Lil' Kim is energetic, over the top; as soon as she walks out, the response is crazy. A lot of times artists have to find their stride onstage, and I think she's in the process of getting all of that together and mastering it. But she got so popular so quickly that she had to do whatever she could do with her hit records. The tour that she was on with Puffy definitely showed she put work into the stage show, but when you're doing shows at a certain level, the hit records basically make the show. Sometimes that limits the emcee from being able to do more. Kim does her thing in spite of all of that.

POETIC VALUE: 60

More rhyme over poetry.

BODY OF WORK: 70

Kim does have hits, but she also has a lot of things on the album that you wouldn't know about unless you were an avid fan. I think she's putting the albums together quite nicely. The first album *Hard Core*, was the best album to me. *Notorious K.I.M.*, after the passing of

Biggie, I'm sure through the pain of all of that, there was some kind of emotional letdown, and based on what she said about how much she had to go through to even get back in the studio, that's why I think the album suffered on some level there. It felt like she was going through something personally.

INDUSTRY IMPACT: 75

Even though the industry didn't give her accolades, they still took notice of her as a Hip-Hop superstar. For Kim this is more about her presence than the industry accolades.

SOCIAL IMPACT: 75

There was a lot of bad press about her. There was a lot of name-calling and mudslinging about her, but at the same time she stood up in the middle of the fire and spoke out and kind of represented for the opposite side of the equation, based on all of the misogyny that was going on with male rappers toward female rappers. Kim represented on the other side of that equation.

LONGEVITY: 75

Coming out in early '95, still here in 2003 with *Bella Mafia*.

LYRICS: 80

Most people still don't get it. Lil' Kim is an emcee. She is a rhyming emcee. She's not just what you think she is based on her subject matter. She is a rhymer; she's a lyricist.

BATTLE SKILLS: 80

It may have something to do with sex, or breaking you off, but I do believe based on what I hear from her lyrically that she definitely has the battle zone in her.

TOTAL SCORE: 1,305

AVERAGE SCORE: 76.7

41

BIG PUN
LATIN LYRICAL KING

Ay yo my murderous rap
Verbal attack is actual fact
Tactical tracks matched
Perfectly with graphical stats
Half of you lack
The magical gap of tragical rap
It tackles you back
And shackles and laughs at you that's
The mathematical madness I'm on
The savage the strong
The marriage and bond
Of having hit songs
This massacres on as if Picasso laced you
Disguised as hateful
Skeletons locked in my closet of grace

GIVE ME A LATE PASS!!! AND I'll give Big Pun a posthumous apology. I did not know how lyrical this emcee was. I saw him live a couple of times, and he didn't give me any indications of his lyrical level. A lot of today's emcees have twenty people onstage with them, and fifteen of them have mics, and many times this is done to hide some weakness in the emcees' game. I'm exaggerating the numbers to make the point, but Pun did have some other kids on the mic backing him up. I thought that this was because of his weight, and the breath control issue caused by it. The biggest mistake I made was not realizing that at a live show most artists only have a limited time and can only do their popular songs and the hits. This combined with Fat Joe not being there to sing the hook on his biggest hit "Still Not A Player" left me totally underwhelmed, so much so that I didn't pick up the LP.

A year and a half later, Pun passed away. I immediately called Mick Benzo to give my condolences, and find out about funeral arrangements. Later that day I went and picked up his LP/CD *Capital Punishment*, out of respect. As I listen to song after song, I was not only pleasantly surprised, I was absolutely blown away. From 1994–1999, I had not heard anyone outside of Lauryn Hill who was as lyrical as Biggie. In 2000, thanks to Big Pun, I finally heard somebody who was. I could not believe how he put his words together. He put words together like drummers doing drum rolls in patterns that sounded like a trumpet player doing a horn run.

Dead in the middle
Of Little Italy
Little did we know that we
Riddled some middle men
Who didn't do diddly

Trust me, that's one of many like it that you would have to hear in order to do it justice. Fat Joe has said on many occasions that Big Pun was the greatest lyricist of all time. That may be debatable, but if you ever really listen to Big Pun, you'll know that Fat Joe is not crazy. There are so many lines of Pun's that I could quote but that would turn into a book about Pun. He made references to battling Jesus. He said that he had Jesus and the devil on the same chorus. In the conservative world, that may be considered crossing the line. In the religious world, that may be called blasphemous. But in the world of Hip-Hop that's one of the illest lines ever. I'm sure that like Biggie and Tupac, if Big Pun were still here we'd probably hear some incredible works. Based on the work he's already done, he's definitely one of the true fifty greatest emcees.

Strength: Rapid-fire flow. He spits in tongue-twisting patterns and he's extremely lyrical.

Weakness: Live performance. The weight made it hard for him to deliver on stage.

Favorite Record: "Still Not A Player"

Favorite LP: *Capital Punishment*

#41: BIG PUN

ORIGINALITY: 80

Fat Joe set the table; Pun came in and capitalized, brought his own energy, brought his own flavor. He brought who he was into the equation. It wasn't anything brand new in terms of the rhyme itself, but he did contribute in different areas.

CONCEPTS: 80

Like Joe, Pun approached things differently. On the record they did together, you can hear that Pun approached the rhyme conceptually.

VERSATILITY: 75

He was almost like a lyricist that focused on being a lyricist more than making songs. Versatility has more to do with how many different things you bring into the arsenal, and I think he was more lyrical than anything else;

therefore, he wasn't as versatile as he could be because he focused on just being a lyricist.

VOCABULARY: 90

If you just listened to his records and listened to some of the words he used, you'd be surprised. Sometimes you can lose them in the flow, because he can triple up on the speed side of the equation, and you might not know where he's coming from or what he's saying. But if you pay attention and catch it, he's utilizing vocabulary at a high level.

SUBSTANCE: 75

The same enigmatic problem with all hardcore rappers—it's street, it's gutter, it's gulley—but it's hard to give more points in this category.

FLOW: 90

Pun will shift gears on you in a minute, rhyme at high speeds then break it down, back up to a high speed, and break it back down.

FLAVOR: 75

Pun is straight at you and it seems he's not really concerned with being colorful or flavorful. He's just bringing his type of flavor and it's basically straight at you.

FREESTYLE ABILITY: 80

A lot of people don't know that Pun had a crazy sense of humor, and he's too skilled out to not be able to freestyle. There are so many rhymes that he's written, and the way he's written them he could patchwork any of those rhymes together and it would be a crazy freestyle.

VOCAL PRESENCE: 80

As soon as he came on, you knew exactly who he was. He was very identifiable.

LIVE PERFORMANCE: 60

This was the weakest part of his game to me. I guess the weight issues made it difficult for him to bring it off on the live side.

POETIC VALUE: 70

More rhymes over poetry.

BODY OF WORK: 80

Even though he had a very short run, the level of lyrical prowess that he brought on these records, and how he put them together, is just incredible. One major hit with "Still Not A Player," but in this case it's not just about the hit, it's about how much work he put in on the rest of those records.

INDUSTRY IMPACT: 70

The industry basically fronted. They don't acknowledge emcees that break it down that way. He did make a little noise on the "Still Not A Player" record.

SOCIAL IMPACT: 80

I don't think people understand that when it comes to things that are outside the norm or when they make an impression in Hip-Hop, that impression is very significant. I think what Big Pun did in conjunction with Fat Joe, but even a little more as the time went on. He put Latinos on the map in Hip-Hop on a lyrical level where they were respected.

LONGEVITY: 40

Of course with his tragic death, he was gone too soon. He was just getting started before he passed away.

LYRICS: 100

He's one of my all-time favorite lyricists because I loved the way Pun put the lyrics down. He put so much work in the lyrics. I appreciate that. He's one of the more lyrical emcees I've ever heard.

BATTLE SKILLS: 85

Based on the lyrical prowess and the vocabulary, and based on the challenges and the way he put the rhymes together, you could tell he already was a battle emcee—he just didn't have any popular battles. I'm sure he could have been slaying people in his neighborhood somewhere, but based on his style and what he was working with, you could see that he was a battle emcee, too.

TOTAL SCORE: 1,310

AVERAGE SCORE: 77.0

40

SLICK
RICK
MASTER STORYTELLER

Well I'm sittin on my lunch break
Grittin my teeth
It's the last day of the week boy what a relief
My muscles kind of ache
They felt rigid and stiff
So I looked around
Then I looked I looked around
Then I smoked this big fat spliff
Now I'm happy as can be
I'm in this pothead spell
I put some visine in my eyes
so that no one can tell
It's 12:55 almost time for the bell
Put the breath mints, so that the mouth don't smell
Now back on the job, I don't bother no one
I keep strictly to myself, and all my work gets done
Now the jobs finally over, it's time to have fun
And I'm hangin out with Jack,
But pass the kid name John
They got me drunker than a skunk
And happy as can be
We went to the Latin Quarters, and we got in free
Scoopin' all the girls like nothin'
With my truck jewelry
Cause I'm a fly brown brother
And you can't school me
Boogie Down was performin', hey they ain't no joke
And a bunch of Brooklyn kids
Was lookin' all down my throat
Was it my big chains
With the big plates on 'em
Then they rolled on me and told me run 'em

LADIES AND GENTLEMEN AND LOWLIFES, IT is with outstanding pleasure that we are here to present Slick Rick, the Ruler, MC Ricky Dee, and the art of storytelling! Slick Rick raised the lost art of Hip-Hop storytelling to a level never seen again. Using multi-voices to portray multiple characters, moods, and feelings, Slick Rick and his alter ego, MC Rickey Dee, broke all the conventional rules of rhyming that preceded him. Rick added a comedic, dramatic flair to the game. Formerly in the Kangol Crew with MC Dana Dane, Rick was the first emcee I ever heard use somewhat of a Victorian English accent with his rhyme flow. This alone would have been enough to separate Rick from the pack. But in conjunction with him referring to his competition as lowlifes and crumbs, and wearing more truck jewelry than anyone in the history of Hip-Hop with the exception of Eric B, Slick Rick separated himself from the pack and came off like straight royalty.

Although Rick's first LP *The Adventures of Slick Rick* was released in 1988, Slick Rick had a huge underground following in New York since 1984. In 1985, he joined Doug E Fresh and the Get Fresh Crew and they produced two all-time classics, "The Show" and "La Di Da Di." This combination was so powerful and flavorful that most people thought that they were going to be an even bigger super-group than Run-DMC. Unfortunately the duo parted in 1986. It took two years, but when Rick emerged he had one of Hip-Hop's classic albums, four classic singles, and a reputation on the streets as one of the emcee greats.

One of the most significant things that Rick accomplished was being totally original at a time when most emcees were using very similar cadences. That's not to say that emcees were not original. In fact, this was what is known as Hip-Hop's golden era. The diversity, individuality, style, and substance in Hip-Hop from 1985 to 1990 was at an all-time high. Almost every imaginable subject matter was artistically covered at a high level. Emcees were the lyrical vanguards of Hip-Hop's budding cultural dominance, and Slick Rick was the most unique emcee of the bunch at the time. Creating an alter ego, and then using the duel personas to bounce off of each other as if they were two different people on the same song was simply genius!

One of the other things that made Slick Rick unique was that he was the only emcee at the time, other than Will Smith, "The Fresh Prince," that would tell a story with himself in the vulnerable loser's position. Plain and simple, there is nothing conventional about Slick Rick. He could also push the envelope with songs like "Treat Her Like A Prostitute," where he tells men to never respect women until you're sure she's worth it. Under normal circumstances, this would be an outrage. However, Rick always managed to keep these types of messages under the radar. Because of his masterful comedic delivery and hard-core track selection, songs like these were limited to being cult classics. Ultimately, Slick Rick hit Hip-Hop like a supernova. He had some legal problems, spent time in prison, and although he continued to record, he never had the same impact on Hip-Hop that he had in '85 and '88. With that said, when you hit like Slick Rick, your greatness can't be questioned.

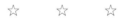

Strength: Storytelling with colorful flows. In this area, Rick is untouchable.

Weakness: A lack of substantive lyrics. Rick wasn't heavy on the positive messages.

Favorite Record: "The Moment I Feared," "Mona Lisa"

Favorite LP: *The Adventures of Slick Rick*

#40: SLICK RICK

ORIGINALITY: 100

Rick innovated the flows, upgraded the storytelling, and took on double personalities. Nobody did that before him, and no one has done it since, and if they did they didn't do it as well.

CONCEPTS: 90

The first album was simply a classic. "Behind

Bars" and "The Art of Storytelling" didn't capture the same level of magic that he had, but the first album was conceptual. Based on it being a classic with songs like "The Moment I Feared," "Mona Lisa," and "The Kit," record where the car was talking back to him, that was all concept.

VERSATILITY: 80

He's versatile in his flow and in his storytelling, but he loses some points on the versatility of the subject matter.

VOCABULARY: 60

Rick keeps it real simple. Because of his rhyme style, he couldn't get too intricate on the rhymes or he would have lost people.

SUBSTANCE: 65

Rick is about having fun. Rocking the party with fun stories and having a good time as a conceptual emcee.

FLOW: 100

It's self-explanatory.

FLAVOR: 100

The flavor is crazy.

FREESTYLE ABILITY: 60

Rick is too conceptual. You can tell he's a writer. He writes his rhymes and puts a lot of thought into it. He can do it, but it's not his focus.

VOCAL PRESENCE: 90

Rick's voice is very distinctive. Once in a while, people would confuse him with Dana Dane, but that's because they were in the same crew.

LIVE PERFORMANCE: 70

He's a lot better when it's Rick and Doug together than when Rick's by himself. Since his rhyme style is so conceptual, you have to get

into listening to the stories and it doesn't leave room for a lot of live theatrics, but he still brings it across pretty cool.

POETIC VALUE: 65

It's about fun storytelling, not about being poetic.

BODY OF WORK: 80*

We don't know what would have happened. He had a stint in prison that took a lot of his momentum. The *Behind Bars* album showed that he had other things on his mind. It didn't come off too well. When he came out he had *The Art of Storytelling* which is fine, but the classic alone brings his score up.

INDUSTRY IMPACT: 65

He was like a supernova. He was in and over real quickly. He came back and did his thing on the level that he could, but he didn't get a chance to make the impact on the industry because of the time away.

SOCIAL IMPACT: 65

Same as the industry impact.

LONGEVITY: 90

Even though he took time off, he came right back on stride. He's still making records right now with *The Art of Storytelling* at the end of '99. That's still fifteen years with a couple of interruptions.

LYRICS: 70

Rick is not about being a lyricist, but rather about telling stories and rocking you with the concepts, the inflections, and the verbal attack.

BATTLE SKILLS: 60

Rick is not a battle emcee, he's not in it for that. Doesn't mean he can't do it, doesn't mean he wouldn't be able to turn it on if he had to, but for the most part Rick is a conceptual, party, fun type of emcee, and people wouldn't even think about battling Rick.

TOTAL SCORE: 1,310

AVERAGE SCORE: 77.0

* The classic album is regarded by most as one of the best albums in Hip-Hop that alone gets a 100.

39

KURUPT
LYRICAL GANGSTA

Scadaddle
Emcees move these terrain
Terrorist teradactile
Over looking the plains
Off of propane planes
Stickin nukkas parapeutic
Poetically therapeutic
Emcees pulverized punished and executed
Don't say I shoot homeboy shoot it
You up against the grizzly cuz Mckenzy
I'm on a frenzy ain't nuttin fun or friendly
I'm headed to where ya friend be

YOU CAN CALL HIM A GANGSTA rapper. You can call him a thug. You can call him misogynistic. You might even call him an underground emcee without any mainstream hits. WHATEVER! What you can't say is he's not a great lyricist. Kurupt is one of the dopest lyrical emcees in the last ten years. Introduced to the lyrical landscape in 1994 by Snoop Dogg as a member of the Dogg Pound, Kurupt was the instant standout for the lyrical lovers. Other than the Lady of Rage, Kurupt was one of the first true gangsta emcees that warranted respect on the elusive lyrical level. As I have pointed out before, many times the listening audience gets caught up in the subject matter and misses the levels of expertise being displayed. The flip side of that issue is that when an emcee, especially a gangsta emcee, gets a hit record, everyone's too busy dancing or singing the hook to notice that the lyrics may not be up to par. This is exactly the case with Kurupt. The people that don't know how lyrical he is are probably paying attention to the singles, and not going into the albums. On *Kuruption*, where he does some of his best work, he tailor-makes two CDs, one for the East Coast and one for the West Coast. On this double CD/LP, there are at least four tracks that are not made for the radio where he absolutely does his thing.

How long could the war last
On the war path
I'm still heat nukku
Signing autographs
Still hittin the stash
And pullin pistols out the dash
The poetical poltergeist
Verbal Jerry Rice
*F*** the ice*
Gimme the mic
And let's see who's the nicest
*I'll f*** around and cause a crises*

I've never been a fan of gangsta rap, but I have always been a fan of lyrical emcees. Kurupt is of the highest order of lyrical emcees. One of the major complaints about gangsta rap is that most of the rappers use violent content to mask their minimal use of vocabulary and poetic prowess. Kurupt is the antithesis of this. He uses his vocabulary and poetic prowess masterfully. When you hear him use a word like *telekinesis* you can tell it's not thrown in for shock value, or to impress the high-brow audience. Kurupt is using his vocabulary to upgrade the flow and enhance the rhyme. Furthermore, it never feels like he just looked up a word to slap it in. Usually the words he chooses come in a succession of words tied together to create a cohesive rhyme. And he never compromises. He always keeps it gangsta! TRULY ONE OF THE BEST.

Strength: Wordplay. Sometimes he can milk the same word in all of its tenses.

Weakness: Song structure. Like many lyricists, he's so good lyrically the song seems to be a secondary afterthought.

Favorite Record: "Fresh," "Change the Game"

Favorite LP: *Kuruption*

#39: KURUPT

ORIGINALITY: 80
This is more about timing than anything else. By the time he came on the scene, gangsta rap was already in full effect. However, he did bring his lyrical side to the gangsta rap.

CONCEPTS: 75
He came straight at you, straightforward gangsta theme with lyrics.

VERSATILITY: 70
He doesn't sway, he doesn't stray from the gangsta rap formula, ever. He's still versatile within his style, because he'll switch tempos and flows, but he basically does the same thing.

VOCABULARY: 90
He upgraded gangsta rap with the vocabulary. He's one of the first emcees that I've heard do that.

SUBSTANCE: 70
Just like I give all the gangsta rappers across the board, it is substantive to talk about your life, but at the end of the day you have to offer some kind of solutions.

FLOW: 85
Kurupt definitely plays with the flow. He shifts gears nicely, and brings the rhymes back home. He doesn't leave any loose ends. He ties up all of the rhymes with the flow. He's tight with the flow.

FLAVOR: 70
He doesn't do too much with the vocal inflections or too much with the funny side of the equation.

FREESTYLE ABILITY: 85
Without even being around him, I've seen him on little shows and clips, heard him flow on a couple of video shows, and heard him do his thing live a couple of times. The key with his freestyle is he freestyles at a high level because of his vocabulary. A lot of brothers get credit for freestyling just because they

finish the rhyme, but Kurupt actually freestyles at a high level. He usually drops some jewels in there. There's usually some vocabulary in there, too.

VOCAL PRESENCE: 70

He doesn't do too much with the dynamics of his voice. He seems to be more concerned with keeping it straight ahead and blowing you away with the lyrical content of how he's bringing it.

LIVE PERFORMANCE: 75

It's hard for the show to have a lot of dynamics when most of the records are downbeat records. A lot of times that's a problem gangsta rap shows run into.

POETIC VALUE: 75

More rhyme than poetry.

BODY OF WORK: 75

The problem with Hip-Hop is you make your music for a tailor-made audience, and a lot of times, without the big radio-hit records, it's hard to move a lot of units, even though Kurupt has definitely sold some units.

INDUSTRY IMPACT: 70

Gangsta rap was already in full stride by the time he came around and it's harder to make an impact if you came after the fact, especially with gangsta rap. Quite frankly, when he came on the scene it was looking like it was getting ready to die out, but he still was able to maintain on his own.

SOCIAL IMPACT: 65

It's real hard to give gangsta rappers a lot of points on social impact, especially if it's not one of the first things you heard. He came a little too late in the game to make that much of a social impact.

LONGEVITY: 80

From 1994 to 2002, that's a nice little run.

LYRICS: 90

He is the first gangsta rapper that I thought brought the lyrical skills to a high level, outside of Rage, as far as that whole posse went.

BATTLE SKILLS: 90!

Based on his freestyle ability and his lyrical prowess, you can just tell that he's an emcee that has the battle skills in him. He hasn't been in any popular battles, but Kurupt definitely has the tools. You can see it on him. You can see he's a battle emcee.

TOTAL SCORE: 1,315

AVERAGE SCORE: 77.3

38

MYSTIKAL

You'll be tackled by the style I'm using
Got all my adversaries
Cruising for a bruisin
With contusions
Cuts and lacerations
Broken bones and open soles
Rippled spline sprained ankles
And broken noses
First the microphone'll drip on
I step on the stage and get my grip on
that's when you get the stiff arm
It's on I'm the sh** homes

AND THE DIRTY SOUTH, NEW ORLEANS—STYLE is officially on the Hip-Hop map. With a tongue-twisting, gear-shifting rhyme style, combined with vocal gymnastic inflections and James Brown–like screams, Mystikal has been one of the true, authentic, original emcees in the last decade. Like Craig Mack and Slick Rick, Mystikal created his own unique flow. He had his first breakthrough hit with "Shake Ya Ass" in 1999. With a Neptunes track seemingly tailor-made for him backing him up, Mystikal struck a chord with the mainstream and underground Hip-Hop sects. However, Mystikal is no rookie. Before the Neptunes version, there was the No Limit Soldier version. Before that, he had a little record called "Y'all Ain't Ready." This was one of my favorite records in 1995. More than the rhymes, it was a series of comical, sexual punch lines, delivered with his classic screeching screams that made this one of the most hilariously enjoyable records I've ever heard.

"Standin' five foot eleven d*** crooked like a roach leg"
"I'm harder than a nukka watching Janet Jackson in draws"
"You nukkas didn't think that I could swing mine, bitch I'm doing bad n singin rhymes at time"
"I ain't got no love for no b-ach-e-ach
matter of fact I've been that way
since I was wearin Osh Kosh be gosh"

It was like listening to a Hip-Hop version of a young Redd Foxx. But don't get it twisted, Mystikal is a true emcee in every sense of the definition. In fact, this was part of what took him so long to find his niche. In his short stint with his fellow New Orleans No Limit Soldiers, I got the feeling that the audience didn't know what to make of Mystikal. By the mid- to late '90s No Limit and the Cash Money Millionaires made such an impact on Hip-Hop that when you said "New Orleans rapper," you gave a clear picture of lots of bling-bling, truncated tracks with catchy hooks, and not a lot going on lyrically. Quite frankly Mystikal didn't fit. Mystikal is too explosive to be a part of an ensemble of a large camp. And musically, he comes off better on energetic bouncy, dance tracks. His hyped delivery and comedic inflections on party tracks make his overtly rated-X content much more palatable for the listener, and it goes almost unnoticed. What also goes unnoticed amidst the hype is how much is going on lyrically. His wordplay is incredible. Sometimes he'll cram twenty-five syllables into five seconds, followed by a screaming punch line, and then follow that with a slow procession of words, while masterfully conveying his message without losing any of the rhymes' metaphoric value. He's got so much style that it can overwhelm every other aspect of his game. After you finish dancing and enjoying him, go back, sit down, and focus on his rhymes. Listen closely and you'll hear how good he is. MYSTIKAL IS ONE OF THE GREATS.

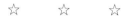

Strength: Always exciting because of his energy and unique delivery; he's never boring.

Weakness: Sometimes he's too hard to follow. The energy is enough to handle, but sometimes he'll add Cajun slang to the equation and make it impossible to understand.

Favorite Record: "Y'all Ain't Ready," "Shake Ya Ass"

Favorite LP: *Let's Get Ready*

#38: MYSTIKAL

ORIGINALITY: 100

I don't think people understand how hard it is to come up with something new in Hip-Hop at this point in the game, because so much has been done. We've been there, done that, seen it all. But Mystikal came with his own original style. There is no style like his, and I don't think there's going to be another style like his. He's the original.

CONCEPTS: 80

A lot of times he's being conceptual, but because of the New Orleans slang, people may not catch it. He does, believe it or not, have a couple of messages in his songs too.

VERSATILITY: 70

He basically does the same delivery in every

single song. He's not the most versatile, but he does play around with the subject matter.

VOCABULARY: 70

Mystikal's thing is more about flow and flavor, bringing it across with energy and making sure you enjoy it.

SUBSTANCE: 70

He's more about partying, sex, and women. Ninety percent of his records are about that.

FLOW: 90

His flow is incredible. To come up with something new with an original flow, and the way he shifts gears in his rhyme flow, is crazy.

FLAVOR: 90

This is not the conventional flavor, but with his James Brown yells, Mystikal is one of the most flavorful, period.

FREESTYLE ABILITY: 80

I've seen him do freestyle a couple of times, and he does it pretty well. He's better than a lot of cats that get credit for freestyling. He has fun with it and even brings his flavor across when he's freestyling.

VOCAL PRESENCE: 100

You know exactly who he is as soon as he starts rhyming.

LIVE PERFORMANCE: 75

It's real, real hard to bring that kind of energy

across when you're live, based on the type of flows he's doing. If he had a simpler flow, I'm sure it would come off a little differently.

POETIC VALUE: 60

He's basically having fun. He's not really trying to drop poetry on you. He's basically rhyming and doing his thing in the rhyme sense.

BODY OF WORK: 80

Even though it's a short time for a lot of people, most don't know about the old album, the very first album, *The Mind of Mystikal*. He's been doing his thing since 1994 or '95. He comes up with nice hit singles every time out.

INDUSTRY IMPACT: 60

He's going below the radar because of the timing in the equation. He came in very late in the game. It's hard to make a real industry impact, especially depending on what label you're on or what kind of record you make. He hasn't gotten a lot of accolades in terms of nominations, etc. He made a little bit of noise with the "Shake Ya Ass" record, but for the most part the industry impact wasn't that profound.

SOCIAL IMPACT: 60

Same as industry impact. Didn't get a chance to really make much of a social impact. However on some level, he represented for New Orleans very early before Master P and the Hot Boys and the Cash Money Millionaire Crew. Mystikal was one of the first from New Orleans to get down and make a name for himself and put New Orleans on the map.

LONGEVITY: 80

Whether you know it or not, he's been doing it for seven to eight years.

LYRICS: 80

You might not catch what he's doing because of the way he flows and how he yells a lot of times, but he definitely is a lyrical cat.

BATTLE SKILLS: 75

Usually when your content is sexual, about having fun, and colorful flows, that's usually not really the battle emcee zone. That doesn't mean he can't turn it on if he had to, but we don't know what he can really do as far as the battle skills go.

TOTAL SCORE: 1,320

AVERAGE SCORE: 77.6

37

KEITH
MURRAY
THE
RHYMOLOGIST

You seem to believe
All you need is a rhyme and a dream
To defeat the
All time great microphone supreme
But wake up
Cause you playin with the game of death
I'll smoke ya body ashes in a blunt
And leave no evidence left
Ashes to ashes dust to dust
I got you in my clutch
It's nothing furthermore to discuss
And it's scary though
When the eeriest voice on the radio
Is in ya hometown doin a show
With the technique that I'm using
Choosing abusing
Got more flows than D'angelos Cruisin'
Wit poisonous venom
Oh my God I get in 'em
Turn 'em out
Give 'em somethin' good to talk about

KEITH MURRAY IS A LYRICAL MAD SCIENTIST. It's like he's sitting in a laboratory with test tubes filled with words and he's mixing them together in combinations just to mess with our minds. He'll take a simple word like *beautiful*, add a suffix that doesn't belong, and turn it into *beautifulest*. Then on top of that he put it in the title of a song, which he also named the album, and then made it the hook of the lead single, so he could repetitiously beat us in the head with it. "The most beautifulest thing in the world." That's what makes Keith Murray hot. He just doesn't care about what you think!

Keith Murray is somewhat of a throwback to the era of Kool Moe Dee, T-LA Rock, and the young LL Cool J, when emcees prided themselves on their vocabulary usage. Keith Murray kills this area of emceeing. Record after record, rhyme after rhyme, he keeps the word heat on. The only emcees in the game that are there right now are Canibus, Rass Kass, and Kurupt. The difference with Keith Murray is he'll play with more. You get the sense that he's having fun, while he's blazing you with lyrics. His energy level is incredible, and when he hooks up with his Def Squad partner, Redman, it's an explosion. When those two are on a record or stage it's almost too much energy. Eric Sermon provides the perfect balance for the trio with his downbeat tracks and smooth delivery. This is also the formula for Keith's solo projects.

The other thing that's unique about Keith is there is no lyrical drop-off from his album cuts to the songs tailor-made for radio success. Only true industry heads and emcees that go through this understand how hard this is to accomplish. Most truly lyrical emcees water down their lyrical content to make their songs catchy. Everyone knows that a fan's love is partially narcissistic, so in order to make hit records, songs usually need to be constructed in a more simplified sing-along manner. Not so for Keith Murray.

Y'all mythological nukkas is comical
The astronomical is comin through
Like the flu bombing you
And embalming ya crew too
With the musical, mystical, magical
You know how I do
With word attack skills
And vocabulary too

Keith Murray just does his thing. His authenticity has created a fan base and respect from his peers. Had it not been for what many insiders call an unfair prison stint, I think Keith Murray would have been among the major impact emcees in the late '90s. However, he's out now and picking right back up where he left off. He made a quick guest appearance on Fubu Records "Phatty Girl" and within weeks the streets were calling women's big butts "Ba-dunk-ka-dunks." Whether it's the energy, the flow, the animation, or the lyrics, KEITH MURRAY IS ONE OF THE TRUE GREATS!

Strength: Animated energy. Because of his vocabulary, he uses his energy perfectly so the listener can follow.

Weakness: Vocal pitch/tone is the same on every record. In solo increments this works, but on an album, listening to the same pitch back-to-back can be tedious.

Favorite Record: "Psychosymatic," "Herb Is Pumpin"

Favorite LP: *Enigma*

#37: KEITH MURRAY

ORIGINALITY: 90
Keith Murray brought his own flavor, style, and energy to the game, and brought it across in a very unique way.

CONCEPTS: 80
Keith Murray is conceptual in his rhymes, not as much as the albums or songs, but his rhymes are concepts in themselves from hook to hook, like in the "Psychosymatic" record.

VERSATILITY: 70
He basically does the same pitch on every record and he gives you straight, raw, lyrical prowess every single time. It doesn't matter if it's a ballad, a club song, or a radio song, he's giving you the same thing.

VOCABULARY: 90
He's a rhymologist. He basically will take words, make new words out of those words, and still convey the message he's trying to get across, which is a testament to his vocabulary strength and how he uses it. He's a throwback emcee, in that sense.

SUBSTANCE: 75

Keith Murray is the throwback emcee, back to the days of how we rhymed with all of the vocabulary. It wasn't really about anything other than how dope we were and how much we could do with the mic.

FLOW: 85

Keith Murray has his own unique flow, shifting gears and stretching things out. He stretches words and changes words up. He plays with it quite nicely.

FLAVOR: 85

It's not the conventional flavor, it's the Keith Murray flavor. You can hear how he's delivering the rhymes, you can tell he's having fun while he's doing it.

FREESTYLE ABILITY: 85

When Keith Murray freestyles, because his vocabulary is so sick, his freestyle always comes off like perfection. Sometimes you would accuse him of writing the rhymes and that's just because of his vocabulary and he's recalling what he's doing and pulling up words. Some people would say, "How could he think of that so quickly," well, his vocabulary is crazy so his freestyle is crazy.

VOCAL PRESENCE: 80

The Hip-Hop fans that know what's going on definitely know who he is. A lot of people outside of Hip-Hop might not know, but his voice is distinctive enough.

LIVE PERFORMANCE: 80

He definitely has a lot of fun and translates the energy well. The only problem is his body of work. He doesn't have a lot of records the crowd can sing along with and party, jump, and dance with, but if you're coming to hear some lyrics, his shows come off well, if you know what you're going in there for.

POETIC VALUE: 70

More rhyme less poetry, just like most emcees.

BODY OF WORK: 70*

He didn't get a chance to really do his thing. A lot of people slept on the "Enigma" album and his first album. He came out the gate and they did well for him, but whether it's label problems, or the prison stint, he didn't get a chance to do his thing on the body of work. But I imagine we're going to be seeing a lot more as far as his body of work, because the albums he did do are still tight.

INDUSTRY IMPACT: 60

Timing. He spent too much time away because of prison, and didn't get a chance to make that much of an industry impact. There are no Grammys, no awards. He hasn't even made those type of records. His presence was still felt in spite of all of that.

SOCIAL IMPACT: 60

He's gotten a lot of negative press based on the incidents that happened in the club, which ultimately led to what a lot of people call an unfair prison stint. He hasn't had a chance to make a positive social impact yet.

LONGEVITY: 60*

He came right out when he was released and did his thing immediately with Fubu. His new single is banging right now. He came out in '94, had a couple of years off in between, but he's back and he's still relevant, doing his thing right now.

LYRICS: 90

Without question, one of the most lyrical emcees in the game period.

BATTLE SKILLS: 90

The way he rhymes, what he's working with,

and how he puts words together, he definitely has the battle thing. A lot of his rhymes are already written as challenges.

TOTAL SCORE: 1,320

AVERAGE SCORE: 77.6

* The score may seem low because the albums didn't have a big impact even though the work was tight.

36

DOUG E FRESH
MASTER ENTERTAINER

Rhymin is a skill that I perfected
And all around the world
I'm much respected
For all the dope beats
That's been selected
You tape 'em on your tape
And then eject it
From your box, and run down the block
And now the whole neighborhood's
In a state of shock
Feel elec-tricity
You wonder who is he
The rhyme seems to change
And it varies in different forms and
Different sizes
it paralyzes
And energizes
and it surprises me
I thought you knew
You don't know who it is
Guess who?

BEFORE I EVEN GET STARTED! DOUG E Fresh created the beat box! Doug E Fresh created the beat box! There was no such thing as the human beat box until Doug E Fresh created it! Just think about that for a minute! Keep thinking! OK! Do you understand how significant that is? The human beat box was to Hip-Hop what cable was to television. It started out as a small niche addition to the game that only Doug, Buff from the Fat Boys, and Biz Markie could do at a high level. Doug, however, being the creator, has always done it at the highest. He rhymed while beat-boxing simultaneously. He played the harmonica, he emulated records, he emulated scratching and cutting records, and much like cable TV, the beat box grew from a niche market into a phenomenon, and ultimately, into what's seen as commonplace. Doug E Fresh is also the first emcee to introduce two DJs playing onstage at the same time. Afrika Bambaattaa had Jazzy Jay, Grandmaster Flash had Disco Bee, Breakout had Barron, and the Cold Crush Brothers had Charlie Chase and Tony Tone, but Doug E Fresh is the only one that had two DJs onstage with four turntables, playing simultaneously as he rhymed.

Now let's talk about the rhymes. Doug is not known to the Hip-Hop world as a lyricist. This is not to say that he can't rhyme, because he really can! However, Doug made a choice to be a party emcee. He told me that he saw how people respected Melle Mel, Grandmaster Caz, and Kool Moe Dee but the respect didn't elicit the same level of excitement that the call-and-response did from the party emcee. Keith Murray is a throwback, but Doug E Fresh is a throwback's throwback. Doug uses the styles of the original DJ/emcees like DJ Hollywood and Love Bug Starsky. They were master party rockers before we recorded our own rap records. Doug took what they did and combined it with what we did, and created a style of balance. He understood that a crowd could easily get bored with an emcee just rhyming, so he mastered the techniques of the party emcee, implemented the storytelling aspects of the rhyme masters, and interwove the beat box to ultimately become the greatest entertainer.

Doug also used this formula to make his records. I don't know if people are aware of how much is going on in his hit record "The Show." It's like a reality TV show of a Hip-Hop performance, with a commercial break. The rhyme is constructed as if he and Slick Rick are getting dressed before the show, a stage manager tells them it's almost time to perform, Doug gets on, there's a commercial beat-box break, and then Rick joins him in a quick routine. True to the Doug E Fresh form, the record is not rhyme heavy, insuring that the listener gets to focus on partying. On the B-side, Doug shows his beat-box mastery by subtly providing the beat at the appropriate times in the song to heighten the listeners' interest in Rick's stellar delivery of "La Di Da Di." This is the most unique aspect of Doug's game. His approach to making records always has the party people in mind. Songs always have room for some form of call-and-response. Doug has had a series of label and management problems. This in turn slowed down his momentum and, ultimately, his legacy isn't as clear as it should be. However, Doug is a true fighter, and his perseverance is unquestionable. Most rap artists that go through what Doug went through would have quit. At the ("Show") pinnacle of his heat, he wasn't allowed to make an album. The follow-up single ("All The Way to Heaven") was not received well. After a two-year long legal battle, he changed labels and finally made an album, but didn't move too many units. He changed labels again, had his character assassinated, was falsely accused of trying to sound like Hammer, and ultimately, fought to get off of that label too. That's just the business side of things. He also had personal problems and, after all of that, he still came up with another hit "Uptown Anthem I-Ight" in the mid-90's. Doug has been making records since 1983, and although he has some major hits and an all-time Hip-Hop classic, that is not why he has longevity and success. Doug's greatest weapon is his live performances. Doug E Fresh is unanimously one of, if not the very best live performers in the history of Hip-Hop. He is a master of a lost art, and he is one of the only emcees that can tour and perform without a hit record. Because his performance is so high, rappers with hit records don't like to follow him. Many times Doug comes off as the guy with the hit record. His contributions to Hip-Hop are extremely significant, but his performance alone makes him one of the greatest emcees ever. DOUG E FRESH, MASTER ENTERTAINER.

Strength: Live performance. Doesn't need hit records to win.

Weakness: Records. Because he's so good live, he doesn't focus enough on making hits. Sometimes records are too gimmicky.

Favorite Record: "The Show," "Keep Rising to the Top"

Favorite LP: *D.E.F.*

#36: DOUG E FRESH

ORIGINALITY: 100

He created the beat box. That alone gets him a perfect score. I don't have to say anything else about anything he did. He is definitely an original.

CONCEPTS: 85

A lot of people are not really that familiar with Doug's work because he was on a small label, but if you get a chance to get your hands on his albums, you'll see that he's definitely a conceptual emcee. If you listen to "The Show" and "La Di Da Di" he and Slick Rick did their thing. Slick Rick's album was a little more conceptual than Doug's, but is still a conceptual emcee. His whole style is about concepts. He thinks of how to make a party record in a conceptual record by not making it just a party.

VERSATILITY: 80

He could do anything. Versatility as an emcee is one thing, but versatility as an artist is over-the-top. He'll add the beat box, the harmonica, but lyrically he doesn't do as much. He's focusing on entertaining you, but he's still a versatile emcee.

VOCABULARY: 70

Even though I know he has a high vocabulary, he doesn't really utilize vocabulary in his lyrical delivery. He keeps it very simplified and party style.

SUBSTANCE: 75

Other than the abortion and the Africa record, for the most part, his whole style is about partying. He tries to keep it on the positive side at the very least. He'll sprinkle little things in there, but not too heavy.

FLOW: 75

Doug's whole thing is he doesn't get crazy with the flow because in his mind I guess he feels it might get in the way or take away from the entertainment value on the party side. His whole purpose is to rock you.

FLAVOR: 80

He's one of the first emcees that took the edge off. He came from an era when everybody was using deep voices and attacking the mic. He lightened it up, loosened it up, and made it fun and party style.

FREESTYLE ABILITY: 70

His freestyle is very simplistic, because even if he's going to freestyle, he's still going to think of how he can involve the listener. His freestyle would be more about call-and-response than just actually freestyling.

VOCAL PRESENCE: 80

He doesn't have a real dominant voice but he definitely has a definable voice. When you hear Doug E Fresh, for those of us who are inside the game we understand, I don't know how many people outside of Hip-Hop wouldn't recognize his voice.

LIVE PERFORMANCE: 100

This doesn't even need to be explained. The best in the game.

POETIC VALUE: 65

There's not too much poetry going on in parties.

BODY OF WORK: 80

He's been grinding, has a couple of albums. He always seems to come up with some kind of single that makes some kind of impact. From the party side of the equation, whether it was with Biz Markie and DJ Kool on the "Let Me Clear My Throat" or "The Show" or "La Di Da Do" with him and Rick, the "I-Ight" record for New York's anthem, Doug always comes up with something that keeps the crowd rocking.

INDUSTRY IMPACT: 60

He's one of the few old school artists that's been able to last into the later eras. Because he doesn't really focus on making records, he doesn't get nominations, awards, and accolades. It's hard for him to make a real industry impact, even though the beat box basically changed the Hip-Hop industry.

SOCIAL IMPACT: 70

That's a little more to do with the creation of the beat box and how it involved a lot more people into Hip-Hop that might not have been able to be involved in it. It's very commonplace now, but a lot of people don't realize how significant that is.

LONGEVITY: 100

His first record was made in 1983. The Show was in 1985. He's still performing now and it's 2003.

LYRICS: 75

Doug is not a quintessential lyricist, he's a party emcee. Even though he does study enough to bring enough lyrics into the game so that when he's making his records he still has little jewels of lyrics within them, he just doesn't do it consistently.

BATTLE SKILLS: 60

Doug is definitely not a battle emcee. If he was going to battle you, he would battle you show for show instead of rhyme for rhyme. He would battle you on a different level psychologically.

TOTAL SCORE: 1,325

AVERAGE SCORE: 77.9

35

ICE-T
U. G. PLAYER

Six in the morning
Police at my door
Fresh Adidas squeek
Across the bathroom floor
Out my back window
I make my escape
Didn't even get a chance
To grab my old school tape
Mad with no music but happy cause free
And the streets to a player
Is the place to be
Got a knot in my pocket weighin least a grand
Gold on my neck my pistols close at hand

AND THE WEST COAST IS OFFICIALLY on the map. Of course there were other Hip-Hop artists already doing their thing on the West Coast, but with "Six In The Morning," Ice-T became the first impact player. This song was originally released as a B-side to a record called "Dog N The Wax." On that record Ice-T used a Run-DMC influenced yelling style of rap where he talked about partying, cutting, and scratching. However, as it is well documented this wasn't really what Ice-T liked to talk about. And what's now known to be very commonplace with Hip-Hop, once the audience got a taste of the authentic O.G. player style of Ice-T, there was no turning back. A new style of rap music was born, "Gangsta Rap." It's well known that Ice-T is the true Godfather of this genre. NWA, much like what Run-DMC did for conventional rap, exploded and made gangsta rap mainstream. This is all too well documented for me to spend time on. Instead, I want you to have a better picture of Ice-T, the emcee, and how the hype and sensationalism of gangsta rap does an injustice to what he's done lyrically. The cliché, gangsta rapper, is all about how hard he is, how hard life is, how close death is, and how quick he'll kill you etc. What makes Ice stand out is he's the only truly classified gangsta rapper who consistently offers some sort of positive messages. I believe as an emcee in order to be truly great you have to at least give back artistically to your fan base. Of course there are great emcees who don't do this, and most gangsta rappers only highlight and sometimes exacerbate problems. Ice-T has done this. He has a body of work where he constantly gives back artistically. On every album he has at least two songs with positive, substantive messages. Ice-T is an emcee that doesn't just rhyme. He approaches the microphone like a street poet. Pundits that accuse him of glamorizing the 'player,' 'gangsta' lifestyle miss the subtlety. Many times Ice-T will paint a picture with a rhyme. When he speaks on the street life, he starts it off with the flashy, colorful, flossy aspects because like street life, the floss is what catches the kids' eyes first. And like street life, the songs final verse is where he usually brings home the messages of how unglamorous street life actually is. I guess the critics seem to miss this, because Ice-T speaks/rhymes in first person. When he rhymes about the hustlers, he becomes the hustler. When he rhymes about the killer, he becomes the killer. This is not only artistic, it's extremely poetic. On top of that it adds authenticity because he can speak from experience in many cases. For the most part, he doesn't glamorize, he serves warnings of the pitfalls.

Ice-T is an example of why rappers in many cases are more effective than teachers, politicians, and some parents. He cleverly masks the messages with artistic idioms that usually go beyond the mainstream's radar. This is why he appeals to youth. The other thing that Ice-T does excellently is make political statements by showing the parallels between street life and the government.

> *I'll just walk like a giant*
> *police defiant*
> *you'll say to stop*
> *but I'll say that I can't*
> *my gangs my family all that I have*
> *I'm a star on the walls my autograph*
> *you don't like it so*
> *you know where you can go*
> *cause the streets are my stage*
> *and terror's my show*
> *Psycho analyze try and*
> *Diagnose me why*
> *It wasn't your brother*
> *To brutally die*
> *But it was mine*
> *So let me define my territory don't cross the line*
> *Don't try to act crazy*
> *Cause that s*** don't phase me*
> *If you ran like a punk it wouldn't amaze me*
> *Cause my colors death*
> *Though we all want peace*
> *But our war won't end*
> *Till all wars cease*

This is just one rhyme of hundreds. On "High Rollers," he breaks down the so-called "ballers." On "You Played Your Self" he breaks down fake rappers, male tricks, and groupies. On "I'm Your Pusher" he tells fans to get high on Hip-Hop instead of drugs. He even made a record about the gang truce. He also made a record called "Lethal Weapon," where he noted that his mind was more powerful than a gun. He went further to reinforce the point by shooting a video where he's breaking into a library to load up on books as a metaphor for weapons. Ice-T once made reference to pimping the music industry, because he believes he's not the greatest rapper. That might be true! But there's no pimpin' involved. Ice-T has put in a lot of work, and from what I've heard, Ice-T is DEFINITELY ONE OF THE GREATEST EMCEES.

☆   ☆   ☆

Strength: Essence. Ice-T is the embodiment of "represent." Who he is as an emcee persona is power. Instant credibility!!!

Weakness: Flow. Sometimes his flow is a little herky-jerky.

Favorite Record: "Lethal Weapon," "Original Gangsta"

Favorite LP: *Power*

#35: ICE-T

ORIGINALITY: 95

Everyone knows Ice-T as the O.G., the Original Gangsta. I call him "the O.G. Player," because he was the original gangsta player. He had the player style with the gangsta rap and created a whole new genre. The only reason he didn't get a hundred is because when he first came out, he started off rhyming in the same cadence, the same way that Run-DMC was doing, like New York rappers and party emcees.

CONCEPTS: 90

He's a storyteller and he's always conceptual. He has some kind of theme in 95 percent of his records. He's never just rhyming.

VERSATILITY: 80

He'll go back and forth from the positive message into the gangsta thing, into the player thing. He'll go back and forth and stay consistent with giving you some kind of message nine times out of ten.

VOCABULARY: 70

He doesn't get too wordy. He doesn't like to bog it down with vocabulary, just keeps it simple so that the message is heard loud and clear.

SUBSTANCE: 85

A lot of people try to paint him as just a gangsta rapper, but he's much more than that. He's absolutely one of the more substantive emcees in the equation because he's always offering solutions, as opposed to just posing the problems.

FLOW: 65

When he said he wasn't one of the greatest rappers, I think he's focusing on what his flow was like. The flow is a little rigid, a little uneven in places, but it doesn't really matter when you're coming with the substance that he's coming with.

FLAVOR: 70

Ice is straight at you. Doesn't really care about putting the emcee playful flavor on it. He still does what he does in his own style, and it's a different style of flavor, but it's still directly at you.

FREESTYLE ABILITY: 60

Ice-T definitely is not one of those emcees that's going to be in a circle freestyling and rhyming. He has a purpose when he's writing, and he has a purpose when he's doing songs, as opposed to just freestyling.

VOCAL PRESENCE: 80

Ice-T's voice, as they say, "cuts to tape." His energy, his voice and vocal pitch, and tone are very clear and distinct.

LIVE PERFORMANCE: 80

Ice-T is an energetic emcee. As you can see not only from his Hip-Hop side, but from his work with *Body Count*, Ice-T is like an emcee who's a rock star at the same time.

POETIC VALUE: 75

He approaches it more poetically than most people. He doesn't actually do poetry, but he approaches it poetically.

BODY OF WORK: 80

I don't think people understand how Ice-T was consistently going gold over and over and over, hit record after hit record. Even without having lots of radio records. In the late '80s and early '90s he started to have a little bit of radio success and then after whatever happened with the label dropping him and *Body Count*, and him doing his independent thing, he still has a lot of hit records. If you get his greatest hits, you'll see exactly what I'm talking about.

INDUSTRY IMPACT: 80

Ice-T has definitely got gold and platinum plaques without question, and he's been doing it for a long time. His bringing gangsta rap into the question, in and of itself, is enough to make an industry impact even without all of the Grammy nominations.

SOCIAL IMPACT: 90

There would be no gangsta rap without Ice-T. You have to give him credit for that. Not only for originality, but also for the social impact of creating a way of living for a lot of brothers who might not have anything else to do.

LONGEVITY: 100

A lot of people don't know that Ice-T is the emcee in the movie *Breakin'*, and that was in 1984. That's how far he goes back. *Body Count* happened in '92 and '95. "The Truth" record and now he's doing his own independent thing. He's done it, put his work in, done his time.

LYRICS: 70

Ice-T is not really a lyricist, but he's an excellent message maker. He uses lyrics to get there, even though it's not the quintessential emcee lyrical style. He brings his lyrics across the way.

BATTLE SKILLS: 60

Ice-T definitely is not a battler. As a matter of fact, when the thing was going down between him and LL, he basically said that the next time, instead of putting a rhyme down, he was going to put his address out on wax and then pay somebody off if they got to him. That's the way he was going to battle. He's not trying to be the battle emcee. He could do it, but he's not a battle emcee.

TOTAL SCORE: 1,330

AVERAGE SCORE: 78.2

34

GURU
THE QUIET STORM

One of the meanest and the cleanest
and still I'm kind of fiendish
when I'm at this
Been doing this for eons pions
bets'ta catch this
visions of excellence
precise raping ability
bout to make some dead presidents
mackin a million gee
the money thought got people acting funny
yo as soon as some nukkas get some light
they be like dummies yo
products and puppets and pawns
getting played out
when authentic nukkas step up
Respect be laid out

AUTHENTICITY IS IN THE HOUSE! AS quiet as it's kept, Guru has been putting together a stellar body of work for more than ten years. He's one of the handful of emcees that has been able to maintain longevity in spite of breaking every so-called rule to success in the music business. I mentioned earlier how Puffy created a masterful formula for success by using a combination of radio and hard-core street records to help showcase and propel Biggie and his talent to the top of the industry. Guru with DJ Premier, together known as Gangstarr, stuck to a formula that only the great Rakim and KRS-One were able to maintain success with: high level lyrics with fat doses of consciousness and stripped-down street beats. Guru used this formula masterfully. Right out of the gate, in 1988, I first heard him on the song "Words I Manifest." Because of my own shortsightedness I immediately thought he was one of the many new emcees who were trying to sound like Rakim. I enjoyed the record, but the jury was still out. The next year I picked up the LP *No More Mr. Nice Guy*, and I didn't understand why they chose to produce an album with no radio hit. This was unheard of in 1989. Even the greats at the time, Big Daddy Kane, Heavy D, LL Cool J, Public Enemy, and Kool Moe Dee all had albums with the obvious one or two radio hits on them. So I immediately thought, this guy is small potatoes, and he has a small limited vision and doesn't understand the game. HOW WRONG WAS I!

By 1990, MC Hammer explodes and the whole climate of Hip-Hop changes. The fans are aware but no longer have a tolerance for the radio-polished rap records. Yes, these records sold more, but they weren't selling to the Hip-Hop fan base. The fan base wanted a more "authentic" sound. Guru was right! Gangstarr's next LP was 1990's *Step In The Arena*, and it gained instant street credibility. I made a complete U-turn. First I heard the brother talk and realized that his speaking voice was the same voice he rhymed in. Believe me, some rappers were fakin' it on the voice. So I retracted my thoughts of the Rakim emulation. Second, I realized the brother's intellect. Ironically, that was the second song on the LP. What he was talking about was full of thoughtful, positive, mental, and spiritual uplift. This alone won my ultimate respect. The final stroke was he was rhyming his ass off!!!

Guru is the kind of emcee that I live for. A positive lyricist who can flow and bring it across effectively! As I went deeper into his work I went back to check the first album again and I had a much better understanding and appreciation for it. Guru has an elite level of respect from me because he always, always, always brings so much substance.

You can't tell me life was meant to be like this
A Black man in a world dominated by whiteness
Ever since the Declaration of Independence
We've been easily brainwashed
By just one sentence it goes
All men are created equal
That's why corrupt governments
Kill innocent people
With chemical warfare they created crack
And AIDS/Got the public thinking
These were things that black folks made
And every time violence shown in the media
Usually it's a black thing so where
Are they leading ya

Guru is an emcee on a mission with a purpose. Besides inspiring the audience to think, he also seems to have a desire to expand the boundaries of conventional Hip-Hop. He's done projects where he mixes Hip-Hop and jazz, working with legends such as Donald Byrd and Roy Ayers. He's done collabs with Chaka Khan and the Brand New Heavies, and he's also given back to the community artistically by helping young kids from a group home aka Group Home get a record deal.

Ultimately, because of his low profile, all of these things pretty much go under the pop culture radar. However, by staying true to who he is, and consistently trying to uplift blacks in America, Guru/Gangstarr has a loyal fan base. I make it a point not to play favoritism or pitch sales for artists, but I have every Gangstarr album/CD. If you want to hear some of the best Hip-Hop work ever done, pick up their LPs. ALL OF THEM!!! Pop America might not know, and some of urban America might not know, but I know, and I'm telling you, Gifted Unlimited Rhymes Universal, GURU, IS ONE OF THE GREATEST EMCEES EVER.

Strength: Substance. Multi-layered messages.

Weakness: Monotonic cadence and delivery. Sometimes his messages are missed because people are conditioned for excitement.

Favorite record: "Royalty," "Just To Get A Rep"

Favorite LP: *Moment of Truth*

#34: GURU

ORIGINALITY: 80

Brought his own style to the game. Based on the timing, he was reminiscent of some of Rakim's flavor on the down-beat, low, laid-back style.

CONCEPTS: 90

Guru is one of the more conceptual emcees. Street knowledge, spirituality, the way he brings the lyrics across, the way he puts his records together. Very conceptual.

VERSATILITY: 80

For the most part, he doesn't stray away from his natural formula or natural flow. But you can't overlook the fact that he absolutely delves into Jazz music, and he's done Jazzamatazz albums as well as his own albums. The only reason he didn't get a higher score in this category is that he still uses the same flow and cadence on most of his stuff, but on music selection and how he approaches it, he's versatile.

VOCABULARY: 80

Guru is not an emcee who's going to hit you in the head with vocabulary, but he definitely uses vocabulary in ways that you don't necessarily know what the next rhyme is going to be.

SUBSTANCE: 85

Spirituality, street knowledge, and you can also tell there's a high level of intellect going on. You can tell he's an intelligent brother just by what he's talking about and the way he's bringing it.

FLOW: 80

He's a consistent flow-er. He keeps his flow where he's not trying to lose you, or be too intricate, or doing any tricks, just coming straight at you.

FLAVOR: 60

Guru, like a lot of the substance emcees, doesn't seem to want to focus on the flavor in the equation because it's more about the message.

FREESTYLE ABILITY: 80

There are two types of freestyle. There's an old-school freestyle that's basically rhymes that you've written that may not have anything to do with any subject or that goes all over the place. Then there's freestyle where you come off the top of the head.

VOCAL PRESENCE: 70

His voice is not a really, really aggressive voice that's bombastic. It's laid back and monotonic, but you still know it's him when you hear him, so it's still recognizable in that sense.

LIVE PERFORMANCE: 80

This is interesting because as laid back as his energy and music are, when he comes off live, he brings it across very well.

POETIC VALUE: 80

He doesn't just structure rhymes all the time in rhyme cadence. Sometimes he approaches it very poetically, posing questions and answering them, and asking you to think.

BODY OF WORK: 85

Not a lot of radio hits, but very consistent on the type of underground and street hits that they make. You can tell he's an artist with a purpose.

INDUSTRY IMPACT: 60

The industry is very fickle. Certain records sell based on airplay and all the other political intangibles. In that sense, he hasn't made a big industry impact, even though he's been very consistent in lasting as long as he did with the kind of records that he did.

SOCIAL IMPACT: 70

Besides reaching back and working with jazz legends, he came up with the Group Home project, and literally put kids from a group home on the map. He has to get some points for that.

LONGEVITY: 100

From 1989 until now.

LYRICS: 85

Guru is definitely a lyricist. As laid back as he is, the lyrical content and prowess is still there.

BATTLE SKILLS: 70

Not that I don't think he can do it, I basically think Guru is an emcee who seems like he'd rather spend the energy and time on building something. That doesn't mean he wouldn't take it if you brought it to him, but I think a battle for him would have to be more purposeful than just battling for the sake of battling.

TOTAL SCORE: 1,335

AVERAGE SCORE: 78.5

33

SNOOP
DOGG
THE
SMOOTHEST
EVER

Creep wit' me
As I crawl through the hood
maniac, lunatic call 'em Snoop Eastwood
Kickin' dust as I bust f*** peace
And the muthaf***in' f*** police
You know I give a f*** about a cop
So why would you think
That it would stop plot
Yeah that's what we about to do
Take yo ass on a mission with
The boys in blue Dre
Yo I got the feeling tonights the
Night like Betty Wright and I'm chillin'
Killing, feeling no remorse
Yeah so let's go straight to the mfn source

AND THE EAST COAST'S DOMINANCE WAS officially over. Ice-T pioneered it, and NWA exploded it, but Snoop Dogg was the first gangsta rap superstar. With an ultra-smooth, laid-back delivery, and Dr. Dre's corpulent G-funk tracks, Snoop Dogg was an instant impact player. In 1992, the song "Deep Cover" was the title track to the film of the same name, featuring Dr. Dre and a young Snoop Dogg making his debut. For my money, Dre sounded like the professional. But the public voted and Snoop was the breakout star. The hype was incredible. For the first time in New York, an elitist Hip-Hop city at the time, cars and jeeps on the streets were bumping a West Coast artist. Hip-Hop radio in New York was even harder to crack, and "Deep Cover" broke those doors down too.

I, on the other hand, wasn't sold. The first time I heard the term "hater" was right after I told somebody how whack I thought Snoop was. The fan quickly called me a hater, and told me I was old school and out of touch. I went on to explain how Snoop wasn't lyrical, how his rhymes were novice-like and simplistic, and I explained how his profanity-laden lyrics were implemented to present the illusion of being hard-core, in the place of substance. The fan looked at me in disgust and said, "Whatever! I still like him." So now I'm saying to myself, I just recently missed the G.U.R.U. mastery, what could I be missing about Snoop? Later that year "The Chronic" comes out. Once again every car, jeep, and Hip-Hop radio station is booming it. I admitted that the music was hot, but I couldn't figure out why everybody liked, or I should say *loved* Snoop Dogg. I couldn't figure it out. He was too smooth to be a gangsta rapper, and he wasn't lyrical enough to be that classic emcee! Finally the next year *Doggy Style* drops. The first single is "Who Am I." It's another instant hit that I'm not feeling. I gave up. I figured that this was just one emcee I'm not gonna feel. WRONG AGAIN!

With so much drama in the LBC
It's kinda hard being Snoop D-O Double G
But I some how some way

I keep coming up with
Funky ass s*** like every single day
May—I—kick a little somethin' for the G's
And—make a few ends
As I breeze through 2 in the mornin'
And the party still jumpin'
Cause my momma ain't home
I got bitches in the living room
Gettin' it on
And they ain't leaving till 6 in the morning

Then it hit me! Right after I heard "Gin-N-Juice" I had a triple epiphany. First, Snoop is one of the smoothest, funkiest flow-ers in the game. Second, he's not a gangsta rapper. He's a player, approaching the rhyme from a partying point of view, and that's what's gangsta. Third, and most importantly, Snoop is an excellent songwriter. He, along with Dr. Dre, figured out how to do what New York emcees were trying to figure out for about a decade: how to make radio records while keeping the records street. Ever since "Deep Cover," Snoop understood that the most important element to a song, after the melody, is the hook. New York's Hip-Hop approach was beats and rhymes. Snoop and Dre took over with melodies and hooks. Not only was Dre's music more melodious, Snoop's lyrical approach was flavor-filled, melodic rhyming. Snoop was able to do this without compromising who he was. This opened the doors for many of today's emcees to be able to express themselves in a raw, uncut, uncensored, unabridged manner.

Snoop by no means is the first raw rapper, but he is the first to achieve such a high level of success. Many people attribute this to Dre's musical mastery, and of course Dre's contribution is unquestionable. I think Snoop's contribution is equally important. Songwriting and hook writing is a very underrated aspect of the emcee's job description. Other than Naughty By Nature, Snoop Dogg might be the all-time crowd-pleasing, singalong hook maker.

As he grew as an artist, his songs stayed up to par for the most part. He had a few missteps when he and Dre weren't working together due to business issues. However, his talent persevered. He made hits with Tupac, Nate Dogg, and Charlie Wilson to name a few. Although many people felt the music missed Dre's magic, to me it proved Snoop's talent. His hooks were still on point. You might not realize how extensive and hot Snoop's body of work is until you go to a concert and start hearing all of those hits back-to-back. In concert he's one of the few emcees that can turn the music down on almost every record and the crowd would sing damn near the whole song.

From 1992 to 2002 Snoop has been, without question, one of the most consistent Hip-Hop artists in the game. His last album was once again a well-put together piece. With collabs like Jay-Z, Redman, Charlie Wilson, and Pharrel, their involvement is a testament to how he's respected in the game. He also has an appearance from the Lady of Rage, one of the tightest emcees in the game, and that's a testament to his integrity. It's always cool to reach back for your peoples!

In conclusion, I went from not respecting Snoop to him becoming one of my favorite emcees. After listening to him for ten years, I can now see how much of a Hip-Hop student he is. He's done remakes or tributes to Slick Rick's "La Di Da Di," and Biz Markie's "Vapors," and he's made references in rhyme to D-Nice and other old school artists. Snoop Dogg is both a student and master of this game, and you gotta give him respect. SNOOP DOGG, ONE OF THE GREATEST EMCEES.

Strength: Melodic, smooth vocal tone and hook writing.

Weakness: Lyrical content. Sometimes it's just too simple.

Favorite Records: "Gin N' Juice," "B Please"

Favorite LP: *Doggystyle*

#33: SNOOP DOGG

ORIGINALITY: 95

Not that he was so new, but what he brought to the equation at the time was rhyming the way he rhymed.

CONCEPTS: 70

For the most part he's a party emcee, and the concept is, he's a party player.

VERSATILITY: 70

Snoop is not really going to change up the game on you too much. He's going to be consistent. It's about having a good time, being laid back, and smoking, drinking, and partying.

VOCABULARY: 60

Snoop is definitely a "non-vocabularic" emcee, if that is even a word. He keeps it real simple. He simplifies it and he's effective in his simplicity.

SUBSTANCE: 60

It's not about saving or changing the world, it's about having a good time and partying.

FLOW: 85

Even though his flow is not as intricate or technical as flow-ers who change or fluctuate cadence, he definitely is consistent with his flow, and his flow grabs you and makes you want to listen to his record.

FLAVOR: 100

Snoop is one of the most flavorful emcees out there. Just the way he brings it across is almost comical sometimes.

FREESTYLE ABILITY: 85

From way back, even seeing him on *Arsenio* before he was hot. They had him do a freestyle live. He came off the top of his head. Snoop is incredible on the freestyle side.

VOCAL PRESENCE: 90

One of the most recognizable voices in the game, without question. He's just one of those emcees whose voice people know immediately when they hear him.

LIVE PERFORMANCE: 75

Because his energy is so laid back, sometimes people want to party harder because of all the hits that he has. When you see Snoop live, you'll enjoy his presentation.

POETIC VALUE: 60

Not poetry, more about rhymes, and more simplistic rhymes.

BODY OF WORK: 95

From "Deep Cover" all the way through, he

hits you every single time with hot singles and hot records and very, very strong hooks. His body of work is stellar.

INDUSTRY IMPACT: 90

He gets a lot of accolades. He does MTV performances and he's all over the place in the industry. He's one of those people that's an icon in Hip-Hop and can't be overlooked.

SOCIAL IMPACT: 70

Because of the gang association and the way they do West Coast emcees, the social impact usually takes more of a negative hit, but he still is an impact player.

LONGEVITY: 100

Ten years without question, 1992 to 2002. Snoop has done it consistently with records almost every year.

LYRICS: 60

Snoop is not a lyricist, but he does tell his stories and brings his songs across in a way that's like making music as opposed to making rhymes. He approaches it from a songwriter's standpoint.

BATTLE SKILLS: 70!

Nobody even sees Snoop as a battler. Doesn't mean he can't do it, but nobody's battling Snoop. He said one time, nobody steps up to him to challenge him because everybody loves Snoop. Snoop won't have any battles because nobody is going to battle him.

TOTAL SCORE: 1,335

AVERAGE SCORE: 78.5

32

RUN
THE KING

Two years ago a friend of mine
Asked me to say some MC rhymes
So I said the rhyme I'm about to say
The rhyme was def n then it went this way
Took a test to become an MC
And Orange Crush became amazed at me
So Larry put me inside his Cadillac
The chauffer drove off
And we never came back
Dave cut the record down to the bone
And now they got me rockin' on the
Microphone, and then we talkin autographs
-n- tears and laughs, champaign caviar and
bubble baths
you see that the life
that I lead
and you sucker mc's
it's you I feed

HIP-HOP HAS HAD SOME MAJOR EXPLOSIONS. We've had the Grandmaster Flash Explosions in '78, '80, and '82. We've had the Hammer explosion in 1990. We've had the Sugar Hill explosion in 1979, Eminem in 2000, Kris Kross in 1992, Lauryn Hill in 1998, and Afrika Bambaataa in 1982, but Hip-Hop has never had an explosion like Run-DMC in 1986. Up to this point I've been very careful not to include any emcees from duos or groups, because as emcees in groups know, we work as a unit. Emcees with other emcees in their group usually write together, and feed off each other.

However, up until 1984, when Hip-Hop groups were still dominant, the artist and his fans would always pick the stand-out emcee of the group. Although most people thought that DMC was the more lyrical of the two, Run was the more dynamic. I break this down more in the book, *The True 50 Greatest Groups in Hip-Hop.* Run was the stand-out emcee, and the emcee of the year in 1983. Besides that, Run's impact and contribution to Hip-Hop is so huge that he has to be in any list talking about emcees. If you think I missed the boat on Guru, and didn't respect Snoop lyrically, multiply that by ten and then you know how I felt about Run. It was bordering on pure HATE! In 1983 the lyrical God Kings, Melle Mel, Grand Master Caz, and Kool Mo Dee were all at poetic pinnacles. Run-DMC, and Run in particular, came along with the arrogance and pomposity of a rhyme supremacist. What was crazy to us at the time was he was about the least lyrical emcee outside of a party emcee that we had ever heard. It just didn't make sense.

What also didn't make sense was the fans loved him. It was like he simplistically prophesied greatness and it came. By 1986 Run-DMC was the benchmark for everything in Hip-Hop. This began the trend in Hip-Hop where emcees started becoming musically gimmicky. We started trying to figure out how to make records that would get radio play. Ironically, Run started his string of successes by being as raw and ungimmicky as possible. Run is a series of ironies and dichotomies. He was a dope emcee, but he wasn't lyrical. He said he was hard-core Hip-Hop, but he mixed it with rock music. He made the best records with the worst rhymes.

So what made it work? What made Run great? Once again, AUTHENTICITY! Run was always real. He also had a belief in himself that came through in his voice. This combined with his obvious passion for Hip-Hop made him a true force to be reckoned with. Rule one in Hip-Hop: love what you do, and the audience will feel your love. Run is the only emcee outside of LL Cool J and Tupac who could say a simple, juvenile rhyme and make you feel like it was Shakespeare. On top of that, his energy while he rhymed live was like an explosion. Run was the opposite of many emcees of the time. Most emcees tried to be lyrical on records to rock the audience, and then couldn't bring it across live. Run seemed to have figured out that lyrics can get in the way in a live performance. The audience wants to participate with the emcee in a concert. This alone would have been enough to make Run one of the best live emcees, but combined with the hard-core Hip-Hop tracks, and bouncing back and forth off of DMC, an ice-cold persona, and Jam Master Jay's well-timed cuts, Run wasn't only great, he became KING.

My love, understanding, and appreciation for Run-DMC came after the heat and the hype was over. In retrospect I understood how important they were as emcees. The musical impact was obvious. As a group they set the tone for Hip-Hop to be the multi-billion dollar industry that it is today. Lyrically, they were as instrumentally important. I didn't know it then, but like the Sugar Hill Gang, lyrics had to be toned down if Hip-Hop was ever going to grow. If you had told me that the rapper who made the song perfection and rhymed,

> I got a dog, a cat
> A mouse, a rat
> A fly, he won't die
> And a little gnat

If you had told me that I would be singing his praises as one of the greatest emcees ever, I would have laughed you out! But in 2003, that's exactly what I'm saying. What I once called PURE SONIC FRIVOLITY, I now call MASTERY OF SIMPLICITY and an ARTISTIC NECESSITY. What might we be doing in Hip-Hop had it not been for Run-DMC. TRUE GREATNESS.

Strength: Energy and live performance.

Weakness: Lyrical content. Never did much with the same rhyme skills.

Favorite Record: "Down With the King," "Together Forever"

Favorite LP: *Raising Hell*

#32: RUN

ORIGINALITY: 90
It was hard to give him 100 because he'd come

after so many emcees and he was rhyming in the same manner, but his energy and the yelling on the mic—nobody was doing that before him.

CONCEPTS: 80

They did do a few records like "Mary, Mary" and "You be Illin' "

VERSATILITY: 80

They shifted gears on you and talked about a few different things, even though they didn't really, really stray too far from just the party vibe.

VOCABULARY: 55

Run was notorious for having the absolute most simplistic rhymes probably in the history of Hip-Hop.

SUBSTANCE: 60

They started out and had the records "Hard Times" and "It's Like That" on the first album, but other than that everything else seemed to be strictly about having a good time or just doing Hip-Hop on the fun level.

FLOW: 80!

His early flow is really simplistic, and what a lot of people don't know is Run is a better flow-er now than he ever was before.

FLAVOR: 70

Run does have a flavor; he has his own flavor. But for the most part, he has the yelling thing. Run does sprinkle his own type of flavor in there, depending on what type of record he's doing.

FREESTYLE ABILITY: 70

Run did do some freestyling back in the day, but because of the rhyme content the freestyle level would be high, but the content would not.

VOCAL PRESENCE: 100

One of the most recognizable voices in the history of Hip-Hop. Part of those Rock 'n Roll records would not have worked without Run's vocal energy.

LIVE PERFORMANCE: 100

One of the best live groups you'll ever see. It's like a rock band onstage.

POETIC VALUE: 55

Minimal, if any poetry at all. Very simplistic rhymes.

BODY OF WORK: 100

They've been putting it down for so long, and each album was like an event

INDUSTRY IMPACT: 100

Without question they are one of the pivotal points in Hip-Hop in turning the business around. The Hip-Hop industry became an industry almost single-handedly by Run. There were some building blocks ahead of time, but they took it over the top.

SOCIAL IMPACT: 90

Because of what they did for Hip-Hop, putting Hip-Hop on the landscape and crossing over, they had a major social impact.

LONGEVITY: 100

Starting in 1983, they did their ten-year anniversary record "Down With the King" in 1993.

LYRICS: 55

Run never was a lyricist. One of the more simplistic emcees ever.

BATTLE SKILLS: 55

Nobody wants to battle Run. Everybody in Hip-Hop loves him, so he won't have any battles. Based on his rhyme content, it's not battle-oriented for the most part.

TOTAL SCORE: 1,340

AVERAGE SCORE: 78.8

31

KURTIS
BLOW
THE ORIGINAL

If I ruled the world
And was a king on a throne
I'd make peace in every country
Build the homeless a home
I'm not running a conference
On the president
I'm just here to tell the world
How my story went
Ya see first I was a dream
I was living in Rome
And then I moved to London
Bought a brand new home
And everywhere I went
I drew lots of attention
Like a stretch limousine
Or a new invention.

KURTIS BLOW IS HIP-HOP'S FIRST SUPERSTAR. He is the archetype for Will Smith, MC Hammer, Puffy, Jah Rule, and Nelly. At a time when emcees were neophytes to the music industry, Kurtis Blow made the records most emcees wouldn't make, partially because we didn't know how, but more importantly, because we didn't want to take the chance. Kurtis Blow is the first time that Hip-Hop crystallized.

In 1979, Kurtis made a record titled "Christmas Rappin." It was a commercial success, and of the handful of records out at that time, only "Rappers Delight" achieved more success. The record also was a favorite in the clubs, and that set the table for his 1980 release "The Breaks." Kurtis Blow had an across-the-board hit. The record was a pop, R&B, and Hip-Hop smash. And for the first time, Hip-Hop was divided. It was adult vs. teenager, radio vs. street, rap vs. Hip-Hop, and Kurtis Blow was suddenly categorized as adult radio rap! This is one of the most frustrating aspects of Hip-Hop music for me. It's not the definitions that bother me, it's the connotation behind the definitions that are problematic. The implication was if you weren't street Hip-Hop, you weren't authentic. This was not true of Kurtis Blow. The only way someone is not authentic is if he or she steps away from who they really are artistically. Kurtis Blow was more authentic than some so-called gangsta rappers. Before there was ever a thing called a rap record, there were only deejays and emcees. There were deejays that played break beats, and there were deejays that played club disco and/or radio songs. At the time, the emcees would rhyme off of the music that they were most comfortable with. Some emcees did both. Grand Master Caz was one of the few that could do both. The most prominent club deejays were DJ Hollywood and Love Bug Starsky. Kurtis Blow was an emcee cut from that cloth. He was a party emcee. So when it came time to make records Kurtis did what he did best. He created very radio-playable, dance songs that the crowd could sing along with. In fact, if you listen to all of the records that came before Kurtis Blows' "The Breaks," you would notice that there was a very important element missing. The hook! Kurtis Blow is the inventor of the hook for rap songs. All of the significant records at the time had emcees rhyming continuously with a music break to break the monotony. So in a sense, Kurtis Blow showed us how to write songs, because if there's no hook, there's no song.

The other thing that Kurtis Blow brought to the game was original music. This is still lacking in Hip-Hop today. However, what's most significant about this is Kurtis was criticized for having radio records, when most so-called street emcees used popular radio/club records to try to achieve success. This is what's wrong with the enigmatically subjective connotations behind the defining of who's real or not. The other contribution that's overlooked from Kurtis Blow's game is the way he took chances with the subject matter, and helped change the lyrical landscape. In 1980 just about every respected emcee, other than Spoonie Gee and Kurtis Blow, was talking about how incredible they were. Kurtis dabbled into this lyrical bluster, but he made what I think was the first message record, "Hard Times." In the following years he made a record about "Basketball," he made a go-go record, "Party Time," he even made the first true Hip-Hop, R&B record "Day Dreamin," where he actually sings the record.

Are you getting the picture? Kurtis Blow is a true pioneer on so many levels. I'm only focusing on Kurtis Blow the emcee. If I were talking about all of his contributions I would have to break down his production credits on the albums of Hip-Hop icons Fearless 4, Dr. Jeckyll and Mr. Hyde, Love Bug Starsk, and the Fat Boys, to name a few. Kurtis Blow is one of the emcees that's ahead of the curve. He set the template for how to achieve success with simple dance records, catchy hooks, and a clean image. If Kurtis Blow had been born in this new era of Hip-Hop, he very well might have been the biggest rapper Hip-Hop has ever seen. ALAS, HE'S JUST ONE OF THE GREATEST!

Strength: Song writing and highly diverse subject matters.

Weakness: Flow and cadence. He never really upgraded his delivery.

Favorite Record: "If I Ruled The World," "AJ Scratch"

Favorite LP: *Ego Trip*

#31: KURTIS BLOW

ORIGINALITY: 100

Kurtis Blow was the original. He's the template for a lot of what's going on right now in Hip-Hop. The original guy that brought the hook into the equation.

CONCEPTS: 90

Kurtis' whole style was conceptual. Everything he did. He was one of the first emcees to go all over the place in the subject matter. The fact that he made a record called "Basketball" is conceptual enough.

VERSATILITY: 90

Because he would go all over the place and he would take those shots. It's like a basketball player taking a shot from half court, then from the other side of the court. Kurtis Blow would just take a shot from anywhere.

VOCABULARY: 60

Another one of the simplistic emcees that didn't get too diverse with the vocabulary.

SUBSTANCE: 80

I think Kurtis made the first message record with "Hard Times," and even on "Party Time" he was talking about records and people dissing females.

FLOW: 70

Kurtis is simplistic in his flow style.

FLAVOR: 75

Other than toning his voice down and whispering every now and then, we used to call it the "Kurtis Blow whisper," he didn't play with his voice too much.

FREESTYLE ABILITY: 65

I heard Kurtis freestyle recently and like a lot of old-school artists, when you freestyle the way they freestyle today, a lot of times it's not our forte.

VOCAL PRESENCE: 85

Kurtis Blow still has one of the more recognizable voices, and the way he attacked records, especially at the time of his heat, he made his voice stand out.

LIVE PERFORMANCE: 95

Even to this day, Kurtis is one of the best live performers. He has breakers, and he approaches it from a showmanship standpoint. He's never just standing onstage rhyming.

POETIC VALUE: 65

Kurtis wasn't doing a lot of poetry. It was songs structured for simplistic rhymes.

BODY OF WORK: 90

You would have to really go back to understand how important and how much work Kurtis Blow did. He's got a lot of hit records and a lot of albums too.

INDUSTRY IMPACT: 85

He's one of the first people to bring attention to Hip-Hop. After "Rapper's Delight" the next big record was his "The Breaks," which was also one of the first radio records.

SOCIAL IMPACT: 85

Kurtis made a social impact because he was the first breakthrough/crossover artist, and without these artists, the industry wouldn't be what it is.

LONGEVITY: 90

He was rhyming before we were making records so you have to give him points on that. Even though he made his first hit in 1979, Kurtis got all the way up to 1987 on the quiet tip with "Back By Popular Demand."

LYRICS: 60

Kurtis wasn't a true lyricist. He put songs together pretty well.

BATTLE SKILLS: 60

Who wants to battle Kurtis Blow? There's no reason to. So Kurtis doesn't get a chance to do the battles, and he's not that type of emcee anyway.

TOTAL SCORE: 1,345

AVERAGE SCORE: 79.1

COMIC HEAT

1) Flava Flav	Bombastic Hype
2) Biz Markie	Free Style Fanatic
3) O.D.B.	Wu Tang Jester
4) Busta Rhymes	Animated Delivery
5) J.D.L.	The Legend (Live Heat)
6) Slick Rick	Slickly Comedic
7) Dana Dane	Comedic Constant
8) Will Smith	Versatility—(Girls of the World…"
	"Parents Just Don't Understand")
9) Chubb Rock	Party Heat – Comedic References
10) Grand Puba	Pre Nubian – (First Song "Sexy")

These emcees bring comedy in the flow with skills, storytelling, and delivery.

30

SCARFACE

Imagine life at it's full peak
Then imagine lying dead
In the arms of your enemy
Imagine peace on this earth
When there's no grief
Imagine grief on this earth
When there's no peace
Everybody's got a different way of ending it
And when your number comes for souls
Then they send it in
Now your time has arrived
For your final test
I see the fear in your eyes
And hear your final breath
How much longer will it be till it's done
Total darkness at ease be it all one
I watch him dying when he dies
Let us celebrate
You took his life but your memory
He'll never take
You'll be headed to another place
And the life you use to live
Will reflect in your mother's face
I still gotta wonder why
I never seen a man cry
till I seen a man die

WHETHER YOU KNOW IT OR NOT, Scarface was the precursor to Tupac. If you listen to the early work of Scarface, when he was with the Geto Boys, you'll see that he fathered the cadence that Tupac made famous. Scarface is like the Godfather of Dirty South Hip-Hop. Before Scarface, the South was known for the Miami bass and Atlanta Krunk sounds. These were musically dominated dance sounds that never focused on lyrics beyond call-and-response chants. Scarface changed all of that. He was the stand-out emcee in the Geto Boys, and when the 1991 breakthrough hit, "Mind Playin Tricks On Me" hit the streets, Scarface was one of the most talked-about emcees of that year. He was beginning to be mentioned in the same breath as Ice Cube and the D.O.C.

Like with Ice Cube, the word on the streets was Scarface was the writer behind the concepts. This gave him another level of credibility. Although the group was seen by many as a Texas version of NWA, Scarface seemed to show a little more than just the hard-core street lyrics. He seemed to have a knack for storytelling. When he went solo, the other group members also had solo projects. Like the Wu-Tang, but pre–Wu-Tang, they still made albums together while doing their solo projects. Although the group had some success together, Scarface ultimately had the most success, and neither of the other members succeeded like Scarface. This was due, in part, to Scarface's solid street following. Scarface was viewed as a hustler turned rapper. In the ghetto, that's considered a true success story. The streets love to see people get out of the game, and they'll always support the artists that can make that happen. To me, the background is neither here nor there; what matters is talent, and Scarface had it. I knew he had hard-core rhyme capabilities but I didn't know how clever he was until I heard the song, "Cereal Killer." Based on the precedent he set, I was waiting to hear a lyrical bloodbath. Instead I got,

> *Once upon a time*
> *At the Honeycomb hideout*
> *Sugar Bear and Mikey*
> *Sat alone getting fried out*
> *Lucky walked in wit this nukka named*
> *Rice grain*
> *Pulled out a knot*
> *And conjured up a dice game*
> *Lucky looked at Mikey and he said with a smile*
> *Where's the silly rabbit*
> *I ain't seen 'em in a while*
> *Mikey turned to Lucky*
> *Shook his head cause he ain't know*
> *Probably trickin wit this bitch*
> *From rocky road named Cheerio*

This is exactly why I call Scarface the south paw. In boxing, a south paw is very hard for most fighters to fight because he fights left-handed. This gives the conventional fighter much harder angles to figure out. Scarface is a hard-core emcee that gives you many angles, which makes him hard to figure out. Sometimes he's ruthless and sometimes he's compassionate. This also was a precursor for Tupac. In 1994, Scarface hit what to me is his apex, "I Seen A Man Die." This was what I call melancholy mastery! It showed Scarface's poetic prowess, and solidified him as one of the best storytellers in Hip-Hop. Scarface is like a gully, ghetto, griot, telling stories from the streets to the streets. He's been able to maintain his respected status for over ten years. He's sold millions of records without much radio play, and he was also a pioneer as one of the first emcee, CEO/co-owners of his own label. Scarface has impacted the game in many ways, but primarily as an emcee. And as far as that goes, HE'S DEFINITELY ONE OF THE GREATS.

Strength: Rhyme cadence. His cadence is perfect for the street style of storytelling he does.

Weakness: Limited subject matter, fails to really stray outside of the elements of 'hood life.

Favorite Record: "I Seen A Man Die," "Crooked Officer" (Geto Boys)

Favorite LP: *The Diary*

#30: SCARFACE

ORIGINALITY: 80

Just a matter of timing. Scarface came at a time when he was immediately being compared to N.W.A., but I do think he set the tone for the cadence that Tupac used.

CONCEPTS: 85

"Never Seen A Man Cry"—that says it all.

VERSATILITY: 70

For the most part, Scarface comes at you and does the same thing and you know what you're getting nine times out of ten. He keeps it straight at you and he keeps it gangsta.

VOCABULARY: 70

Doesn't beat you up with vocabulary. Tones the lyrics down. Comes at you, conveys the message.

SUBSTANCE: 85

Scarface seems to always ride for the 'hood. He makes records from the streets for the streets. He adds a little more than just the gangsta rap to the equation.

FLOW: 80

He keeps it consistent and at you at a level where you can follow what he's saying. He's not trying to lose you, he's trying to convey his point.

FLAVOR: 75

It's not about playing games; he adds his own flavor to it. He does put his own stamp on it, but he's not doing a lot with his voice.

FREESTYLE ABILITY: 70

Scarface seems like an emcee who's not in it for the fun of the game. He's in it to make money and he's in it for a purpose. Freestyling is not his forte.

VOCAL PRESENCE: 80

You know his voice when you hear him, the Southern slang without being too Southern within the equation.

LIVE PERFORMANCE: 80

He comes across pretty cool with his records. His records are not really designed for the show, yet he brings them across in a cool manner.

POETIC VALUE: 80

He's a little more poetic than the average gangsta emcee.

BODY OF WORK: 85

Even without a lot of radio hits, stuff from the Geto Boys on through, you can't take away the work he did in the Geto Boys.

INDUSTRY IMPACT: 75

He sells records, doesn't get the big pop records or accolades.

SOCIAL IMPACT: 80

He all but put Houston and Southern rap on the map. That has to be recognized because it's definitely a force in the game, and Scarface is the father of that.

LONGEVITY: 100

Ten years and counting.

LYRICS: 85

He's not a conventional lyricist, he's more of a storyteller, but he's a proficient storyteller in a lyrical sense. He has substance and purpose behind what he's saying.

BATTLE SKILLS: 70

Scarface seems like he'd rather get violent with you before he battled you. A lot of his rhymes are geared towards battle, but you can hear, based on what he's bringing on the emcee side,

it doesn't seem to be his thing . . . but he could
if he had to.

TOTAL SCORE: 1,350

AVERAGE SCORE: 79.4

29

BLACK THOUGHT

SUBSTANCE SPITTER

We realized it's a planet of cream
To obtain, when the predominate rap
Conglomerate sparked a flame
Hark the name, the fifth from the ill
Power hill, at that he dropped me of within
The streets of South Phil
Where nukkus think the kill
Is livin' real
Shorties is getting wetted
Fulfillin their fantasies to set it
We don't sweat it, by the 5th ya get
Beheaded, I pivot through my borough
Givin' pounds to the dreaded
At the live spots, I got credit
Could run 'em down in alphabetic-
Al order it's sort of pathetic
Yo I'm livin' life within
A labyrinth of nonsense
This is a consequence
Of being Philly residents
Trying to get it on
The rhythm getting' sh**ed on
The exquisite I exhibit the shine

IF YOU'RE A SUCKER FOR SUBSTANCE, like I am, then this is your man. I won't spend a lot of time on him because like Run of Run-DMC, Black Thought is in a group, and I will go more into depth on the groups in the book *The True 50 Greatest Groups* (and of course the Roots are one of them). However, like Guru, Treach, and Chuck D, Black Thought is the preeminent voice of the group, and with the talent level he exhibits, it would be sacrilege to not have him mentioned amongst the greats.

First of all, Black Thought is the illest, dopest, bestest emcee's name I've ever heard. And when you hear him spit, you realize how appropriate the name actually is. Well known in Philadelphia's underground Hip-Hop and spoken-word sects for being one of the best rhymers, Black Thought had a buzz before he had a deal. He is one of the very best live rhyming emcees as a result of honing his craft with a live band, literally on the streets of Philadelphia. This translated well into his career with the Roots, one of the best live acts in Hip-Hop today.

Another thing that Black Thought possesses, as a result of his background, is the rare ability to be an excellent freestyler and an excellent rhyme writer. Once again I have to stress how rare this is in Hip-Hop. Some emcees would be highly offended if you truly broke down their freestyles, and assessed how low-brow the content actually was. Many emcees use freestyle as a crutch, because they can't write truly coherent high-level poetic rhymes. Black Thought is a coherent rhyme writer, songwriter, and live rhymer who freestyles well. I guess this confirms the old adage, "The master can play the fool, but the fool can't play the master." In Hip-Hop, Black Thought is the example of the master writer/rhymer who can also be a freestyler, but a freestyler can't fake being a writer/rhymer. Black Thought has been consistently lyrically pertinent. Each of the Roots' albums have gotten better, or at the very least have been artistically enhanced. Much of that has to do with Black Thought's rhyme skills. His vernacular early in the game was tight, but in 1996 it hit a poetic crest.

> *Lost generation*
> *fast pace nation*
> *World population confront they*
> *Frustration, the principles of true*
> *Hip-Hop have been forsaken*
> *It's all contractual and about money makin'*
> *pretend to be cats*
> *Don't seem to know they limitations*
> *Exact replication and false representation*
> *You wanna be a man then stand ya own*
> *To emcee require skills*
> *I demand some shown*
> *I let the frauds keep frontin'*
> *And roam like a cellular phone*
> *Far from home and givin' crowds*
> *What they wantin'*
> *Official Hip-Hop consumption*
> *The 5th thumpin', keeping ya party jumpin'*
> *With an original somethin'*
> *Yo I dedicate this to the one*
> *Dimension-al no imagination*
> *Excuse for perpetration*

That was an excerpt from the lyrical balance he was able to find on the hit single "What They Do." Of course, as with most lyricists, the most lyrically inclined work is found deeper on the album. However, Black Thought is so substantive he never loses much lyrically or substantively on any record. In 2000, the rare occasion of the industry awarding substance over style occurred, and The Roots received a Grammy for their 1999 song "You Got Me" featuring Erika Badu. In 2002, they released "Phrenology" and as usual Black Thought delivered, although the group seems to have taken some musical chances. All in all, Black Thought is one of the most prolific emcees ever, and should always be mentioned with the greats.

Strength: Substantive lyrical skills. Some emcees with substance lack in the skill department. Black has both.

Weakness: Vocal dynamics and enunciation. When you're as lyrically wordy as Black, you have to use vocal inflections and clearly articulate words, or you'll lose the listener. It becomes purposeful poetry without navigation.

Favorite Record: "What They Do," "The Next Movement"

Favorite LP: *Things Fall Apart*

#29: BLACK THOUGHT

ORIGINALITY: 80

For a lot of the newer artists, it's really about timing. They come out at a time when what they're doing doesn't really stand out because of who's out. But they're still being original in their own sense. It's not like Black Thought was doing anything that somebody else did, it's just that it wasn't anything as new as some of the things we've already heard from earlier artists.

CONCEPTS: 90

Black Thought is very conceptual. All you have to do is listen to his music and you know he puts songs together very conceptually.

VERSATILITY: 70

For the most part, he comes with the same kind of energy each time. He's a little diverse in the subject matter. He approaches it like a spoken-word artist on some level.

VOCABULARY: 85

He definitely will throw words in there, and if you're not up on your vocabulary, sometimes you may not be able to keep up.

SUBSTANCE: 95

Damn near his whole game is substance. It's all a purpose and it seems like it's about not only breaking down 'hood life, black life, but with the purpose of uplift.

FLOW: 85

Black Thought is one of the "pocket kids." He finds a pocket and he rides with it. He'll shift gears, be around the beat, and come back to wherever he started. He flips the flow quite nicely.

FLAVOR: 60

He doesn't play with his voice as much as he could. Still, you do know it's him when you hear him.

FREESTYLE ABILITY: 85

After all those years doing it on the corner, in the streets, literally, in the clubs, Black Thought can definitely come off the top of the head.

VOCAL PRESENCE: 70

He's not using his voice to draw you in, even though he's aware and does have a voice that does that on some level.

LIVE PERFORMANCE: 95

Without question, it's hard to separate him from the Roots, but he does his thing. The Roots does their thing and they're one of the best live groups ever.

POETIC VALUE: 90

Black Thought puts thought into the rhyme and the poetry, and the poetic aspect of the rhyme. Sometimes there's a very poetic flavor to the rhyme.

BODY OF WORK: 80

For the most part, they tailor-make their stuff for whatever they want to do, and it doesn't seem to be very concerned with radio play. However, the later albums seem to have had some success in radio play.

INDUSTRY IMPACT: 75

They finally got the Grammy. As far as the industry is concerned, it's one of those groups that's looked at as one of those underground, neo-soul, spoken-word kind of groups. It's very hard for the cliché world to define it.

SOCIAL IMPACT: 65

This also has to do with the timing. They came out around the same time that Arrested Development and other groups were hitting. A lot of times they seemed to have been in the background consistently grinding, and then finally coming into prominence.

LONGEVITY: 70!

The Roots made albums that were almost unrecognized in the first two years. Once '95 hit, they came to fruition and from that point on they've been consistent. On the one hand, can't just take points away, but can't add them. They could be, technically, ten years, but they weren't prominent until '95.

LYRICS: 90

Black Thought is definitely a lyricist. Besides having positive messages, he's an emcee, and you can hear the emcee all in his rhymes.

BATTLE SKILLS: 70

You can tell that he can absolutely do the battle without question. Again, who's going to battle Black Thought?

TOTAL SCORE: 1,355

AVERAGE SCORE: 79.7

28

COMMON

POETRY IN MOTION

I stagger in the gathering
Possessed by a pattern that be scatterin
Over the global my vocals be travelin
Unravelin my abdomen is lime that's
Babbling gramatics that are masculine
I grab the men verbally badgering
Broads I wish that Madalyn
Was back on video LP
I went against all odds
And got it even Steven
Proceeded reading not believing
Everything I'm reading
But my brain was bleeding
Needing feeding
And exercise I didn't seek the best of buys
It's a lot of text lies I analyze
Where I rest my eyes an chastise
The best of guys with punch lines
I'm Nestle's when it's crunch time
For ya mind like one time
If poetry was pus** I'd be sunshine
Cause I deliver like the Sun Times
Confined and once mines
I done rhymes I combine
I'm hyped like I'm unsigned
My diet unswine

COMMON SENSE, AKA, COMMON IS A case study on perseverance persevering for perfection. Sometimes you can feel an emcee's energy so clearly you can almost prognosticate his future work. This was the immediate feeling I had upon listening to Common for the first time. In 1992 I purchased the LP/CD *Can I Borrow A Dollar*. My first impression was he sounded too gimmicky! It felt like he was influenced by Das EFX and Kriss Kross, who were both blazing in '92. I also thought his voice made him seem like he was unsure of himself. The flow, cadence, and delivery selections didn't help matters either!

So he's wack! Right? Not so fast. If you have a masterful emcee ear, you can hear what the emcee is going for. You can also hear how production, or the lack thereof, can add to or take away from an emcee. In this case, the production was not enhancing Common's essence. Upon a closer listen, you could hear two things clearly. First, Common was an extremely clever, conceptual emcee. Almost every song had a theme and some form of double entendre. Second, his voice and delivery. He was more like a jazz poet, and not really a conventional emcee. At this point in the game it felt like Common needed to find his voice. I remember feeling like the first album was the project he used to get in the door, but he had much more to offer.

Two years later he proved me right. The album, *Resurrection,* was not only better, it was a quantum leap. His voice was clearer. His delivery was defined and became signature. His concepts were heightened, and his lyrics upgraded. Suddenly everybody in the lyrical know understood what he was doing. Everything was crystallized on the Hip-Hop classic "I Used To Love Her," where he compares classic Hip-Hop to a girl he used to love, who is now being exploited. The record is genius. However, his more conventional lyrical skills were showcased on the songs "Resurrection, Watermelon, and Some Sh*t I Wrote." Although more commercially successful than the first LP, as with all of Common's LP/CDs, it received much more critical acclaim than commercial success.

He's also seemed to hit a pattern of hitting commercial success on every other LP. The follow-up *One Day It Will All Make Sense* didn't catch on like *Resurrection*. It was, however, still critically acclaimed. In 2000, true to form, Common brought us into the millennium with his most critically acclaimed, commercially successful LP of all. *Like Water for Chocalate* was musically and poetically pertinent. It was like the capstone of his work. He seemed to be the older version of the budding poet that could now be viewed as an emissary. In my opinion, Common is at his artistic best when he's speaking universally rather than myopically. He's the opposite of the quintessential emcee. Common is actually more poetically inclined than lyrically inclined. Yet he's still very lyrical.

> Let the truth be told
> From young souls that become old
> From days spent in the jungle
> Where must one go to find it
> Time is real we can't rewind it
> Out of everybody I met
> Who told the truth? Time did
> We find kids speakin' cause
> It's naturally in us
> But the false prophets by telling us
> We born sinners vendors of hate
> Got me battling my own mind state
> At a divine rate
> I ain't in this to rhyme great
> See the truth in the thighs of a stripper
> The eye of my nukka
> If it's only one then why should it
> Differ! So constantly I seek it
> Wondering why I gotta drink a 6-pack to speak it!
> Took the picture of the truth
> And tried to develop it
> Had proof, it was only recognized
> By the intelligent
> Took the negative and positive
> Cause nukkas gots to live

Said I got to give more than I'm
Giving
Cause truth will never be heard
In religion
After searchin the world
On the inside
What was hidden—it was the truth

This is an example of poetic excellence. When people ask me about the category of poetic value, sometimes I tell them to just go pick up a Common LP/CD. He's absolutely the most poetic emcee in the game today. His last LP/CD, *Electric Circus*, wasn't my cup of tea, but I can understand that when you're an artist like Common you have to take chances. He seems to artistically want to move into many directions and does not want to be pigeonholed. All true artists can relate. However, as I said in the opening of this book, I'm focusing on the emcee, and in that regard, Common is still at the top of his game. His poetic poignancy and lyrical substance is almost unmatched on the Hip-Hop lyrical landscape today. He's been consistently doing this for close to a decade, and that makes him one of the great ones among emcees!

Strength: Poetic prose. He makes the rhyme sound like a conversation.

Weakness: Lyrical elision. Sometimes he gets on a roll and leaves out essential syllables or sounds, important to the rhyme. Sounds like he's out of breath.

Favorite Record: "I Used to Love H.E.R.," "Water Melon"

Favorite LP: *Resurrection*

#28: COMMON

ORIGINALITY: 80
When he came, he brought his own style to the equation on one hand, but on the other hand he seemed to be guided in the direction that was falling in line with whatever was going on at the time (Das EFX and Kriss Kross), but he put his own spin to that.

CONCEPTS: 95
"I Used to Love Her" says it all. One of the most conceptual records ever.

VERSATILITY: 80
Common will take some chances and do different types of things in music, but his voice is basically the same, his energy is basically the same.

VOCABULARY: 80
You can tell that he has an extensive vocabulary, but he seems like he tries to keep it at a level where the audience can follow him.

SUBSTANCE: 95
One of the more substantive emcees in the game. Rhyming with a purpose is what I call it.

FLOW: 80
Common's flow is very direct, straight, and in-your-face. It's a matter of conveying his messages, not a matter of being tricky and colorful with the flows, even though he can flow.

FLAVOR: 70

He does a little more inflections than the average "conscious" rapper, but not that much.

FREESTYLE ABILITY: 85

Common's an emcee that loves the game and freestyle is a part of it. Even in warm-ups before the show, sometimes he'll just freestyle, and he does it very well.

VOCAL PRESENCE: 70

His voice is very light and it showcases itself better on the mellow tracks.

LIVE PERFORMANCE: 70

The only problem that happens with Common live is that sometimes he performs with a lot of R&B acts. It seems when you're a poetic lyricist like he is, your show has to be packaged a certain way for it to be appreciated. I've seen people take the wrong thing out the show just based on the packaging.

POETIC VALUE: 95

He is poetry in motion.

BODY OF WORK: 70

He seems to be successful or making an impact on every other album. Nonetheless, he's still consistent in the work that he does within the albums, even if they don't make a lot of noise.

INDUSTRY IMPACT: 60

Strictly because Common does not get a lot of the accolades from the industry—the nominations, platinum plaques, etc.—but he perseveres in spite of that.

SOCIAL IMPACT: 75

He winds up being the magnet in spite of whatever the business is. People know him more than they actually know his music, which is a testament to him making a social impact.

LONGEVITY: 90

In the early '90s he still came, didn't have a real strong presence, but by the time "I Used To Love Her" hit, it was all over.

LYRICS: 90

Common is definitely a lyricist. He knows how to spit it. The quintessential emcee using his own style.

BATTLE SKILLS: 75

He had a little early run-in with Ice Cube, but even though he did OK on the battle side and he broke some real nice rhymes, to me it felt out of place like that's not what he would be doing. He did it because he could do it, he did it because he wanted to respond and was a little offended at Ice Cube's comment. That was a quick battle that didn't last, didn't make an indent in people's mentality. He can do it if he has to, but it feels like Common is an emcee who would rather not waste his time in the battle zone.

TOTAL SCORE: 1,360

AVERAGE SCORE: 80

27

XZIBIT

THE

HARDCORE

RHYMER

What an event we hard-core 100 percent
Makin' it stick Los Angeles
Proudly presents
The real deal how does it feel
No special effects
Take the chain off ya neck
Demand the respect
Now all ya conversations sound
Strange to me
Seems like everybody around me
Done changed but me
I stand alone on my own two feet
Stab a track strangle a beat
Restless no time for sleep
Nuggas be weak I'm concrete
Like Benjamin—E GRIMM
It's a very thin line between
A foe and a friend
Straight to the chin
Not these nukkas again
Call
His spot and slide right in
I ain't tryin to see nothing but progress
Regardless home of the heartless
Move right remain cautious
Represent nothing but the hustle and struggle
Hennessy rocks plenty of ice make it a double

HE'S NOT NECESSARILY GANGSTA, HE'S NOT necessarily playa, he's not necessarily pimped out or thugged out, and he's definitely not giggy. Xzibit is just purely hardcore lyrical. Xzibit is one of those emcees that you can tell was waiting a long time to get his chance to rhmye and show the world he's got skills. And that is exactly how he is felt! Some emcees are known for their hits, flows, or hooks, etc. Xzibit's reputation is strictly for his lyrics. There is a myth in Hip-Hop about L.A. rappers and emcees not being lyrical. For years, Hip-Hop heads on the West Coast have known that the problem was with the business. The deals were given to the more commercially polished rappers and emcees. However, the truly lyrical emcees in L.A. were always in the underground. It wasn't until the mid-1990s that these artists started to get some light from the industry.

Xzibit comes from that breed of underground emcees that built followings with lyrical command. Around 1995, I first heard him on a tape of a friend and I thought his voice was incredible. The only problem was he sounded like Craig Mack. A few months later, I saw a video with him rhyming to a violin-led orchestra. I thought, *This kid needs some direction*. But his reputation was so solid, people kept his name prominent in Hip-Hop circles. I finally picked up the LP/CD *Paparazzi* and I thought he was trying too hard to be different. I could, however, tell that lyrically he was no joke, and like Mike Tyson, if he got the right trainer/producers, he was gonna make some real noise.

A couple of years later he drops "40 Days and 40 Nights." This is where you could see he was more than just an emcee. I could clearly see his growth as an artist. He was able to display supreme lyrical skills while keeping it underground and gutter. He dropped some clever hard-core sexual innuendos, and some of his classic shocking metamorphic comparisons, including one that wasn't too cool referring to killing an emcee's "big plans" at Wilshire and Fairfax (Biggie's murder site). But he hit pay dirt with the single, "What U See Is What U Get." Not only was the song incredible, but it was, in my opinion, the best video of the year. This was when Xzibit reached the unique balance of representing lyrically on a hard-core track that was critically acclaimed and commercially successful. Most hard-core emcees never get a chance to experience this. Other than Xzibit, DMX is the only hard-core emcee that consistently hits a high level of success without compromising his formula for it. I think Xzibit is successful because for the hard-core Hip-Hop fan. It's rare to have someone of the lyrical order spittin' fire. Many hard-core emcees use the content and subject matter to carry them through. When a lyricist like Xzibit spits, the fans can appreciate the work he puts in. All emcees know that no matter how many records you sell, the respect always comes from the lyrical work. Xzibit exhibits the work.

The final level was reached when Dr. Dre exec-produced his 2000 release *Restless*. Of course that was the best music he's ever had, but lyrically Xzibit shined even better than he previously did. Collabs with Dr. Dre, Snoop Dogg, Eminem, and DJ Quick brought out another side to Xzibit. He made the song "Sorry I'm Away So Much," where he talked about missing his son.

> *My son was born 4 1/2 years ago*
> *loved and protected him*
> *amazing how fast they grow*
> *I came to know about his likes and dislikes*
> *Video Games*
> *Taught him how to ride his first bike*
> *This is the life my li'l nukka*
> *I see you getting all upset*
> *When I'm leaving the house*
> *Now let me tell you about*
> *Tryin to make it in this world*
> *To provide for you*
> *All them overseas plane rides*
> *I miss you too*
> *Never knew I'd have to be away so much*
> *$5000 dollar phone bills keeping in touch*
> *We Starsky and Hutch*
> *We partners for life*

I rock mic's
So I'm sorry when I hug you
If I squeeze too tight
Long nights in the studio take me away
Getting mad cause I'm tired
And you want me to play
Money can't replace time
I'm just tryin to get you
Out of the firing line
And expand ya mind

At this point Xzibit has become more than just a hard-core emcee. He's now entering the realm of becoming a complete artist. Nonetheless, he's definitely made his mark as a lyrical spitter, and I'm sure nobody's mad about putting Xzibit's name among the GREATEST EMCEES IN THE GAME.

Strength: Track Attack. He aggressively attacks the beat like a street fight. No holds barred.

Weakness: Songwriting. Sometimes the metaphors are scattered and have nothing to do with the continuity of the song.

Favorite Record: "What U See Is What U Get," "LA Times"

Favorite LP: *Restless*

#27: XZIBIT

ORIGINALITY: 80
Timing. He came out in the early to mid-'90s, his voice was very reminiscent of Craig Mack's, but he definitely brought his own flavor to it and brought his groove.

CONCEPTS: 90
One of the first emcees, if not the first emcee I've ever heard to rhyme over a string quartet, classical music, and Pavorotti.

VERSATILITY: 75
Xzibit is pretty much the same cat, album after album. He's coming at you with lyrical energy and trying to make hit records.

VOCABULARY: 95
He's one of those emcees that is a lyricist and will use his vocabulary like another weapon.

SUBSTANCE: 75
A lot of times his content is very West Coast gang-related. There's still some substance in that.

FLOW: 85
A flow-er as well as being a rhymer.

FLAVOR: 75
Doesn't play with his voice that much. Keeps it simple and plain.

FREESTYLE ABILITY: 80
Feels to me like he's a rhymer who has the ability to freestyle too. The piece he did with Eminem in the movie *8 Mile*, I don't know how much that was written or rehearsed in the

movie, but you can tell he has that presence where he can definitely freestyle.

VOCAL PRESENCE: 95

One of the more definable voices in the game.

LIVE PERFORMANCE: 85

He got a chance to show what he could do on the "Up In Smoke" tour. Lots of energy.

POETIC VALUE: 80

Still more rhyme over poetry, but he throws poetical things in his rhymes.

BODY OF WORK: 80

Each album has gotten better. On the last album with Dre, he seems to have found his groove on the track side and knowing what kind of musical pocket works best for him.

INDUSTRY IMPACT: 70

He's finally starting to be recognized on the industry side. Cats in Hip-Hop know him, and his lyrical reputation is sound, but there's still some more to come on the accolade side as far as the industry is concerned.

SOCIAL IMPACT: 65

Outside of Hip-Hop, not too many people know about him. I think he may be starting to try to make his mark on the Hollywood side.

LONGEVITY: 65

Mid-'90s to now. Still working, still in progress.

LYRICS: 90

Comes at it, keeps it raw and hard-core, and you can tell he loves spitting.

BATTLE SKILLS: 80

Because his rhyme style is so aggressive, even though he hasn't had a popular, public battle that we know about, for the most part you can

hear how his rhymes are designed and that he has the battle instincts.

TOTAL SCORE: 1,365

AVERAGE SCORE: 80.2

26

PHAROAHE MONCH

UNORTHODOX MASTER

Basically y'all could get ate twice
Like Lynn Swann plus get ate like pus**
Get ate like Mickey Dee's
After the hydro when you push me
Get ate like cannibalism
And sliced surgical
In an extremity
Y'all get infinity vertical
Every line a word of mine'll be verbally
Placed to murder you
The master, flippin' convertible flows
Irreversible
Unobtainable to the brain
It's unexplainable what the verse'll do
Pharoahe's the from ya mind's the egg
I'm breakin through

PHAROAHE MONCH IS LIKE AN ELOQUENT LINGUISTICS professor moonlighting as a rhyme serial killer terrorist, challenging the listeners' I.Q. while daring him or her to keep up. He's pound for pound the most lyrical emcee I've ever heard!!! The reason I call him the unorthodox master is because he will use metaphors in the opposite context. He's the type of emcee that will brag about being broke, while comparing himself to money. On top of that he'd break money down lyrically on the basis of the number systems (binary, decimal, etc.). Pharoahe Monch is a lyrical savant who seems to be unable to turn off the lyrical idiolect. He puts the emphasis on skillfully using his word stock in clever metaphors and concepts, and instead of dumbing it down, he forces you to raise your thought process if you're not on par. Pharoahe Monch has been doing his lyrical thing since 1991, when he debuted in the group Organized Konfusion. The self-titled album showed signs of lyrical excellence, and help set the tone for what Pharoahe Monch would ultimately become. On the song "Releasing Hypnotical Gases," Pharoahe and his partner, Prince Poetry, took listeners on an intellectual lyrical odyssey. It's always unclear who's behind concepts in groups, but what was clear was Pharoahe's lyrical command.

As you look from whence forth I come
Riding the wind thus eliminating
Competition from bird's eye view I'm
descending in helicopters
In a village raid
Flesh will burn when exposed
To the poetical germ grenade
I'm highly intoxicating your mind
When I'm operating on cell walls
To membranes cytoplasms and
Protoplasms disintegrate I'll

Eliminate 'em now no one has 'em in battle
I display a nuclear ray
That'll destroy bone marrow and cattle
Thereby destroying the entire food supply
that's crawling with AIDS
Maggots, flies, it's ironic
When a demonic
government utilizes
Bionics in a 6 million dollar man
To capture me, clever however you could
Never even begin to apprehend a
Hologram

His skill level was obvious, his cadence seemed to be reminiscent of Chill Rob G, Large Professor, and Snap, but his subject matter was much more eclectic. Although Organized Konfusion made two more LPs/CDs *Stress* and *Equinox*, Pharoahe didn't break through the industry's musical quagmire until the 1999 street banger "Simon Says" hit the streets. This was not only his strongest work, but it was, in my opinion, the best underground Hip-Hop album of the year. It was his solo debut, and he shone like it was the moment he'd been waiting for. The album had two of the best concept records I've ever heard: "Official," a song where he made a cohesive series of metaphors relating to sports teams, athletes, and sports activities; and the darkly witty, "Rape." This song was the inverse of Common's "I Used to Love H.E.R." Instead of loving the music, Pharoahe wanted to rape the music. He made reference to musical loops being similar to clitorises exposed in a vicious cycle of sin. This is what I meant by using metaphors in an unbecoming context. Nonetheless, as always, Pharoahe Monch did what he does best. He hit you with a lyrical firestorm, and concepts out of left field. His vocabulary usage is stellar, and his style is signature. As I've already stated he's pound for pound the most lyrical emcee I've ever heard. In my book THAT MAKES PHAROAHE MONCH ONE OF THE GREATS.

Strength: Vocabulary and concepts. Most of his rhymes can be conceptually self contained, verse to verse.

Weakness: Lyrical overkill. Sometimes it feels like the rhymes are disjointed and grammatically incorrect just so he can force-feed you more lyrics. It's like being lyrical for the sake of being lyrical.

Favorite Record: "Simon Says"

Favorite LP: *Internal Affairs*

#26: PHAROAHE MONCH

ORIGINALITY: 80
When he first came, there was a wave of Queens emcees, and he sounded very similar to the same cadence. He found his stride later in the game.

CONCEPTS: 90

He's one of the more conceptual emcees I've ever heard. On his solo debut, "Internal Affairs," he got extremely conceptual there.

VERSATILITY: 75

Even though he's conceptual and he will make different types of records, for the most part his energy is the same on all of the records, and I don't know if I've heard him do certain types of songs yet.

VOCABULARY: 100

He's a throwback type of emcee that uses vocabulary at the same level of Kool Moe Dee and T-LA Rock from back in the days.

SUBSTANCE: 85

You can tell he's an educated brother that likes to talk about things. He doesn't want to just rhyme, he likes to talk about issues.

FLOW: 85

His flow is much better than it was earlier. He plays with the energy and shifts gears on the flow better than most.

FLAVOR: 80

He will use his voice as a tool or an instrument. He fluctuates his energy nicely.

FREESTYLE ABILITY: 85

His wordplay is so crazy that you can tell, coming off the top of the head, the level of his vocabulary alone will take him over the top in the freestyle category.

VOCAL PRESENCE: 80

He's finally found a groove. His vocals are much more definable than they ever were.

LIVE PERFORMANCE: 70

That's only because he doesn't have the body of work yet that can come across and translate well live. He still does his thing in spite of that.

POETIC VALUE: 85

His vocabulary is so crazy, the way he approaches the rhyme in some cases just winds up being poetical.

BODY OF WORK: 75

The albums with Organized Konfusion were cool, didn't have a lot of radio hits or just tailor-made hits for anything other than rhyming.

INDUSTRY IMPACT: 60

It's just a matter of Pharoah getting a deal where he can do things at a certain level, because right now the industry hasn't been able to give him any of the accolades.

SOCIAL IMPACT: 60

Same as above.

LONGEVITY: 80

He was in a group Organized Konfusion and they had two albums in the early nineties. You can't penalize him for the albums or the group for not being popular because his presence was still felt.

LYRICS: 100

Pound for pound, one of the most lyrical emcees I've ever heard.

BATTLE SKILLS: 80

I know he's so lyrical that he could definitely do something on the battle side if he had to. He's got concepts and he's definitely got skills on the lyrical side, so that combination usually makes for a good battle emcee. He hasn't had a public one yet, so we don't know.

TOTAL SCORE: 1,370

AVERAGE SCORE: 80.5

THE 10 BEST HIP-HOP ARTISTS TODAY (ARTISTICALLY SPEAKING)

1) **Eminem**   Most Well Rounded Emcee
2) **Missy Elliott**   Most Entertaining
3) **Ja Rule**   Best Song Writer
4) **Jay-Z**   King of the Streets
5) **Nas**   Most Prolific
6) **DMX**   The Rawest Ever
7) **Eve**   Sexy and Skilled
8) **Baby**   All About the Money
9) **Nelly**   Hit Maker
10) **Puffy**   Master Marketer

These are the best overall Hip-Hop artists for 2002–2003

25

HEAVY D
THE ALL PURPOSE MC

Sittin' in my room
With my smoker's jacket on
The fireplace is burning
And the girly is warm
Time to make my move
So gently I kiss her
Twist her in her ear
And tell her that I miss her
She might try to pop that boyfriend junk
But I don't really care
Because I know he's a punk
I'll stomp 'em like a roach
If he tries to approach
He can't get close cause I'm the one who wrote
The book of romance
So come on take a chance
You don't need a long look
All you need is a glance
If wanna get warm
In my arms you belong
You have a problem Hev'll solve 'em
Nothin' can go wrong cause
The overweight lovers in the house

HEAVY D IS THE ALL-TIME GO-TO GUY. He's one of the only emcees that sounds almost tailor-made for any type of record. His flavor is supremely flexible, thus, whenever he's flowing on a track, no matter what tempo it is, he's naturally a complement to the music. In fact, Heavy D is one of the few emcees that uses his voice like an instrument. He has some of the most enjoyable inflections I've ever heard. When you listen to a Heavy D song, you'll hear an exemplary, inviting voice. Like Spoonie Gee, Heavy D is mainly associated with being a ladies', "lover type" of emcee. His body of work, although predominantly geared towards the ladies, is very diverse within the lover's template. He comes hard-core, ballad-style, dance, R&B, humorously, sincerely, Afrocentric, and sometimes he even comes in a vulnerable manner. His flow is impeccable. Combine that with his flavorful delivery, and you have one of the most enjoyable emcees ever.

Whenever you hear Heavy D, you get the sense that he's having fun. This is the main element in his charisma. I would venture to say other than Doug E Fresh and Spoonie Gee, Heavy D is the most well-liked emcee ever. I have never heard anybody say they didn't like him. Some hard-core fans may have a problem with his musical approach and subject matter, but they're never mad at Heavy D the emcee. This can also be attributed to the fact that Heavy's never been the type of emcee that bragged about being better than anybody. He never flaunted his talent, success, or money in anyone's face. He kept his lyrics simple, and his songs focused on evoking a good time. However, sometimes Heavy's upbeat approach can be a double-edged sword. Sometimes Hip-Hop's talking heads stereotypically create the impression that hard-core emcees are somehow more relevant than the other emcees. As a result, emcees like Heavy D get categorized as upbeat and fun-loving, and wear a connotation that they are not serious emcees. This has been the case with Heavy, and should shed some light on how it's been possible for Heavy D not to be on every and any Fifty Greatest Emcee/Rapper lists. This is absurd. Heavy D's rap faculty is still tighter than 90 percent of the hottest emcees today. This argument shouldn't even have to be made.

If you honestly look at Heavy's body of work you would see that from 1986's "Mr. Big Stuff" through 1999's "Heavy," Heavy D has put out hit singles, albums, and superstar guest appearances almost every year. In fact he stood out so much from the pack of rappers in 1989 to 1993 that he was sought out for Levert's "Just Coolin," Janet Jackson's "Alright," and Michael Jackson's "Jam." That didn't happen by accident. He also did the title songs to TV's *In Living Color* and *Mad TV*.

Simply put, Hev's the man. He's one of the most underrated emcees in the game, and he has many elements within his game that got overlooked. In 1990, he lost his best friend and backup dancer T-Roy. The following year, he showed his poignant side with the *Peaceful Journey* album. This shouldn't have been a surprise to anyone because in 1989 we made a record for the Stop The Violence Movement, "Self Destruction," and Heavy D spit one of the more poignant verses on that record. All in all, in the final analysis, Heavy D is one of the more well-rounded, positive emcees ever to pick up a microphone. If you don't have the LPs/CDs just pick up his greatest hits. I challenge you to tell me you don't hear the greatness! HEAVY D IS BY FAR, WITHOUT A DOUBT, ONE OF THE GREATS.

Strength: Flow/flavor. He's a verbal track enhancer.

Weakness: Lyrical simplicity. Sometimes his mastery is unrecognized because of the simplicity in the rhyme content.

Favorite Record: "The Overweight Lover's In The House," "Nuttin' But Love"

Favorite LP: *Big Tyme*

#25: HEAVY D

ORIGINALITY: 90

At the time he came in, he brought a different kind of energy to his flow. He was slightly reminiscent of the Fat Boys and Run with the energy, but Heavy had more flavor with his.

CONCEPTS: 85

Heavy was conceptual, most of it was in the love zone, but he was conceptual on how he approached it and how he approached the hooks.

VERSATILITY: 90

Heavy was able to bring in it many different ways within the same style. A lot of emcees don't know how to do that.

VOCABULARY: 65

He keeps it simple. Heavy is not one of the emcees that will hit you in the head with a lot of vocabulary.

SUBSTANCE: 80

Not trying to save and change the world, just trying to party and have everybody love each other.

FLOW: 95

Heavy D is one of the most incredible flow-ers. Fast, slow, whatever tempo, he rides the beat perfectly.

FLAVOR: 95

Over the top. He uses his voice like an instrument. Perfect inflections, flavor's crazy, plays with the voice, plays with the vocal tones.

FREESTYLE ABILITY: 70

Heavy's not that lyrical guy, so if it's coming off of the top of the head or even coming with scattered rhymes, he could do it because he has enough flavor and energy to do it.

VOCAL PRESENCE: 85

Heavy's voice is one of the main things in his arsenal.

LIVE PERFORMANCE: 95

One of the best emcees live you'll ever see. He understands how to work a stage and put a show on. From the moment he starts dancing, people are yelling, "Go Heavy."

POETIC VALUE: 60

Simplistic rhyme style instead of poetry.

BODY OF WORK: 100

Heavy's body of work is stellar. He has an arsenal of hits, and he's the king of the R&B/Hip-Hop zone.

INDUSTRY IMPACT: 70

He was able to maintain as long as he did and sell as many records, even though he didn't get the accolades and awards.

SOCIAL IMPACT: 65

Outside of being an emcee, most people never associated Heavy with anything other than having fun.

LONGEVITY: 100

He's done it from 1986 until very late 1999, and he's still going.

LYRICS: 70

Not really a lyricist, but he was effective in the simplicity of how he brought his lyrics across.

BATTLE SKILLS: 60

Heavy D is a lover, not a fighter. I'm sure if Heavy wanted to bring it there he could, but he seemed to be the emcee that's much more concerned with having a good time and partying. Heavy seems like the emcee who feels a battle would be a waste of time.

TOTAL SCORE: 1,375

AVERAGE SCORE: 80.8

BATTLE MASTERS

1) **Kool Mo Dee**   Battle Master

2) **KRS-One**   Weapons Master

3) **Grand Master Caz**   Untouchable

4) **Big Daddy Kane**   Ko Master Punch Line

5) **Eminem**   Untested, but you can smell it!

6) **Chino XL**   Unlimited Dis Master

7) **Canibus**   Scientific Spitter

8) **Nas**   Master Counter Puncher

9) **Mc Lyte**   Nasty

10) **Ice Cube**   Fearless

24

BUSTA RHYMES
MASTER ENERGY

Team select please collect
G's connect these nukkas direct
The trees to the smoke fest
Wanna take a toat (yes)
The newest zone I'm in
I'm like Smithsonian, nukka
Fu** it call Napolean
Wave the torch
Cut the head off the Leviathan
The terminology I'm rhymin' in
Caused a frenzy up in I-reland
Hit ya I'm gone get ya
And drop the bomb scripture
At ya barmitzvah

BUSTA RHYMES IS THE ONLY EMCEE in the game whose verbal animation is matched perfectly with his visual presentation and his live performance. He hits one of the most important trifectas in entertainment. Many emcees don't understand how important it is to have an exciting presentation. This is why emcees like Busta Rhymes, who are not particularly lyrical, can usually outshine the more conventionally intricate lyricist. Busta Rhymes seems to approach the game with an energy and intensity unmatched in the game today. There are other emcees that have high levels of energy, but none are at Busta's level. He is at a level of energetic supremacy reminiscent only of the Great J.D.L. of the Cold Crush Brothers.

Busta's energy translates through language and cultural barriers, because it is as visually and vocally entertaining. If you ever see him perform, you'll see a crowd that feeds off of his intensity, and then they send it back to him. Within five minutes, it's an inertia of frenetic pandemonium. As far as live performers go, Busta belongs in the Hip-Hop pantheon with Public Enemy, Run-DMC and KRS-One. There are, of course, other great live emcees, but these emcees create a frenzied type of atmosphere in concert. Busta, Public Enemy, and Run-DMC, in particular, separate themselves from the pack because they can do this at an arena level as well as at the club and theater levels.

Busta Rhymes is also instant energy on wax. Whenever he's guest appearing on another artist's record, he heightens their energy. A perfect example of this was when he made a guest appearance on the remix of M.O.P.'s "Anti-Up." "Anti-Up" was one of the highest high-energy records in Hip-Hop history. Busta added his furor and the record turned into hypersonic delirium. Pure insanity!!! Busta has been cultivating and perfecting this craft since the early '90s. As a member of the Leaders of The New School, you could hear the young Busta spitting rhymes with an intensity and explosiveness that seemed to be somewhat tempered. However, even early on you could see in his live performance that he had an uncontainable type of hype. Busta was an explosion waiting to happen. The explosion finally happened when,

As I combined all the juice from the mind
Powerful impact (BOOM)

From the cannon not braggin
Trying to read my mind just imagine
Vo-Cab-U-Lary's necessary
When diggin' into my library
Oh my gosh Oh my gosh
Eat it I do do?
Like the one Peter Tosh
Ugh Ugh Ugh all over the track
Man ugh pardon me ugh
As I come back
As I
I had to beg ya pardon
When I grow with the squadron
Rah Rah like a dungeon dragon

By the time listeners finished listening to Busta's highly entertaining, inaudible verse, the separation in the group was clear, and a rap force was born. From that point Busta became one of the most sought-after emcees for guest appearances. This whet the appetite of the fans and set the table for his inevitable solo project. Finally, in 1996 he delivered the LP/CD *The Coming*; it was the first among a succession of hit albums and singles to follow. His debut single "Whoo Hah" was a comedic, energetic, musical foray that hit the streets like a hostile takeover. The video was groundbreaking, a trendsetter that instantly upped the ante for the level of the creative quality of all future Hip-Hop videos. In this area Busta is also king. The only other rap artist in the game that is as consistently excellent with her videos is Missy Elliott.

Finally, one of the most important elements to any emcee's game is his flow. Busta Rhymes' flow is impeccable. Sometimes the audibility is questionable based on some enunciation issues, but the way he spits, especially in his classic, rapid-fire cadence, displays a fluidity that's analogous to an auctioneer. He also changes the dynamics of his flow by adding or taking away intensity levels, depending on the record. Heavy D uses his voice like an instrument, but Busta Rhymes uses his voice like an amplifier. When it's all said and done, Busta Rhymes is one of the most innovative, creative, and entertaining emcees in the game. He's made an indelible impression on Hip-Hop musically and visually. And he's definitely one of my personal favorites. BUSTA RHYMES IS ONE OF THE GREATS!

Strength: Vocals. The energy in his voice sets the tone for everything else.

Favorite Record: "Put Your Hands Where My Eyes Can See," "Whoo Hah"

Weakness: Scattered lyrics. Many times his rhymes seem to have no focus. It seems like the rhyme is only concerned with rhyming and not with being coherent.

Favorite LP: *When Disaster Strikes*

#24: BUSTA RHYMES

ORIGINALITY: 100

Busta came in with a whole new style. Nobody was rhymin' the way he was rhymin', nobody has rhymed like him since. That was even harder to do in the '90s than it was in the '80s because so many styles had already come.

CONCEPTS: 80

His albums are usually conceptual more than the rhymes or the songs. Each album started off with the apocalyptic warnings.

VERSATILITY: 90

People don't realize that he started off with one voice, then he would go back to the soft voice. The flow and cadence are crazy. He shifts gears crazy. His versatility is stellar.

VOCABULARY: 60

He'll sprinkle vocabulary in there once in a while, but for the most part he keeps it really simplistic.

SUBSTANCE: 60

For the most part, it's about partying and having a good time. The apocalyptic warnings on the albums are cool, but for the most part, Busta's not here to save the world, but to party and have a good time.

FLOW: 100

Stellar, incredible, ridiculous flows.

FLAVOR: 100

Let's repeat. Stellar, incredible, ridiculous flavor.

FREESTYLE ABILITY: 70

Busta definitely can freestyle, but the higher points in freestyle come from the content of the freestyle, not the fact that you can do it well. Busta does it well.

VOCAL PRESENCE: 100

Busta's voice is like a weapon or an amplifier. It takes the music to the next level.

LIVE PERFORMANCE: 100

Busta is one of the best performers to ever touch a stage. I don't mean that from the club level, but at the concert/arena level. His energy is incredible.

POETIC VALUE: 55

Busta does the scattered connecting rhyme where the rhyme is all over the place, and it's not really poetry in that sense.

BODY OF WORK: 100

Busta's body of work is incredible. Just listen from album to album and see how much he's doing on those albums. He's always got some kind of crazy single to lead the album off and set it up, or he has some kind of crazy follow-up single, and when you get the album, you won't be let down.

INDUSTRY IMPACT: 70

As of late, he's started to get more recognition and accolades, but it's been a longtime coming for him to get the Grammy and Soul Train award nominations.

SOCIAL IMPACT: 60

Outside of Hip-Hop, most people just associate Busta Rhymes with having fun, other than the fact that he does come across as one of the most unique emcees in the game.

LONGEVITY: 100

Leaders of the New School's work cannot be overlooked. He's been doing it at least ten years, '91 to '92 with LONS and all the way through on the solo tip to 2002.

LYRICS: 65

Busta Rhymes is not known as a lyricist; he's more of a party animal emcee.

BATTLE SKILLS: 70

Just recently, he's had a little conflict with Ja Rule, but I haven't really heard him in battle style yet. Busta is the party emcee and the all-time energy king. I don't know if the energy translates into battle.

TOTAL SCORE: 1,380

AVERAGE SCORE: 81.1

23

WILL SMITH

THE UNSUNG HERO

Here it is, a groove, slightly transformed
Just a bit of a break from the norm
Just a little bit some'n to break the monotony
Of all that hardcore dance that has gotten to be
A little bit out of control
It's cool to dance
But what about a groove that soothes
And moves romance
Gimme a soft subtle mix
And if it ain't broke
Then don't try to fix it
And think of the summers of the past
Adjust the bass and let the alpine blast
Pop in my c.d. and let me run a rhyme
And put your car on cruise
And lay back cause this is summertime

WILL SMITH, AKA, THE FRESH PRINCE, is probably the most underrated emcee in Hip-Hop history! Outside of Hammer, one of the greatest entertainers in Hip-Hop history, Will Smith was one of the most verbally ridiculed emcees of the late '80s to the early '90s. He was called soft, corny, weak, unskilled, and most inaccurately unreal. Ironically, it's his sincerity that pushed his career over the top. (That plus a couple of hit movies!) It was always amazing to me how the Hip-Hop climate picked and chose who they would deem cool or uncool, real or unreal, slick or corny, etc.

Will hit the scene in 1986 with the record "Girls of the World Ain't Nothing But Trouble." It was a happy-go-lucky, upbeat song about a teenage boy having problems dating. The approach was humorous and innocent. The record made an impact, and Will sold a lot of records. As the industry goes, he began to do some moderate touring because of the heat generated by the song. His live show was stellar for that time. He had a human beat box, Ready Rock C, who was famous for simulating, doing the beat box under water; he had back-up dancers; and for the coup de grace, D.J. Jazzy Jeff, one of, if not the greatest DJ of all time. Everything was great until they came to New York, and for whatever reason, the audience was non-responsive. In fact, they cheered Jeff and booed Will. The backlash of criticism began.

What was most ironic to me at the time was Run-DMC was king, and Will and Jeff were better than them. That's when we figured out how subjective the audience was. Kid Rock was cool until Vanilla Ice came; Hammer was reviled and Puffy was revered for doing basically the same thing; and Jazzy Jeff and the Fresh Prince made more simplistic, less fantastical records than most rappers at the time, yet they were called unreal. A couple of years later, using the template by Will, Special Ed dropped "I Got It Made" and was loved for it. Once again, Ed's song was much more obviously unreal, but the audience loved it. However, Will persevered and by the mid-'90s, he had numerous Grammys, music awards, a hit TV show, and a couple of hit movies under his belt. By the late '90s he'd become the absolute biggest Hip-Hop star in Hip-Hop history.

At this point everybody got a late pass. Will was now not only understood, but he was respected and appreciated for his ability to stick to his authenticity and weather the critical storm. However, what's still overlooked is his skill level as an emcee. Contrary to popular belief, Will's success in music is not driven by his stardom, it's because of his skills. Of course, being a star helps him in the marketing and promotion of his music, but he sustained his career by being an excellent songwriter.

Will Smith is the example I use when I'm talking about song structure. Every single record that Will makes is always thematically solid. Every rhyme is cohesively connected to the hook, and sometimes from rhyme to rhyme and verse to verse there is a continuity that's like a continuum. One verse picks up where the other leaves off. Another one of Will's strengths, which was ironically looked at as a weakness, was his ability to create and become different characters. This, to me, enhanced his storytelling ability. He was able to paint visual pictures with his stories by using his vocal inflections as an array of characters. In this regard Will is second only to Slick Rick and Notorious B.I.G. I think this was viewed as a weakness because of the climate of Hip-Hop when Will first hit. He took chances on conveying a lighter, fun-loving energy at a time where Hip-Hop was just being introduced to N.W.A.

This brings me to my final point. I call Will the "unsung hero" because in 1988, I don't think the average Hip-Hop fan understood the climate for Hip-Hop, especially with regard to rap music. The industry had been prophesying the downfall of rap music since its inception, due to what they deemed to be a fad with no mass appeal. In 1988, Run-DMC were fading and we had no presence on the pop charts. While Hip-Hop artists were yelling, "Stay true to the game," and "Make records for the streets," no one understood how important it was to have a Hip-Hop pop record. The only record that made a dent in this area was KMD's "Wild Wild West," but it was viewed more as an R&B record, and although it helped bring the urban adult crowd into Hip-Hop, we still needed "middle white America." LL Cool J dropped "Going Back to Cali" but it seemed a little too avant garde. However in April, Will came through with "Parents Just Don't Understand" and struck the perfect chord. It grabbed the attention of the kids in suburbia, and began to outsell major pop records. This record, plus Kool Moe Dee's "Wild Wild West," which I'll explain later, led to a chain of events that basically saved Hip-Hop/rap music. First it got massive pop radio airplay, which led to him getting his perfectly crafted cartoon-like video on MTV. Remember MTV didn't play rap videos, and Run-DMC only got some play because of their rock element. Shortly after Will's successful video run, Yo! MTV Raps was created, and rap videos now had a mainstream outlet. Finally, the Grammy committee announced that there would be a rap category to the awards ceremony. The year ended with Will having a double platinum album, and the following February he was the first rapper ever to receive a Grammy! Without these events, I very seriously doubt that Hip-Hop/rap music would have turned into the billion-dollar industry that we see today.

What's really crazy is as significant as all of these events were to the survival of Hip-Hop, they were the very things Will was being criticized for. What's equally incredible is how he took it with style and grace. He never took public shots at any of his critics. He humbly defended himself and continued to make hits. However, in 1988, he finally got some of this off of his chest on his "Big Willie Style."

Take ya place, allow me to flex a taste
As my accomplishments
Sprayin' my comp like mace
A' face me the star of stature TV
My face be seen in almost every country
Grammy winner soon to be Oscar nominee
Who he that dress giggy
Straight from West Philly
Thought I was wack
cause I wanted to act
now every brotha-n-his mother
That rap be tryin' to do that
The ill kid hundred million dollar bill kid
the one you love to chill wit'
come on keep it real kid
Don't try to act like this summer at the Greek
You won't be bumpin' Big Willie
In ya jeep
I know y'all still feel me
Really don't act silly
Thought I fell off
Just because I left Philly
Took a break from the rap thing
Went on hiatus
I picked up the art of acting
To multiply papers
I chilled on sick sofa's
Chatten with Oprah
She asked me if it's true
That me and Jeff broke up
While y'all kids busy playin'
Drug, pimp and playa
I was in my crib in Barbados
Chillin wit Jada
Today the vertex is me the magnanimous
Got you sayin', damn
I've always been a fan of his
Y'all know how it is
Oh wait, hold up y'all don't
Look here
y'all don't say nuttin
Then I won't

Ultimately, Will gets the last laugh. The bottom line is Will Smith is one of the more well-rounded emcees in the game, and he has a plethora of styles in his arsenal, complimented by an abundance of talent. His globally palatable, innocuous presentation of his brand of Hip-Hop, amidst the increasingly more dominant violent content in gangsta rap, showed the courage, resolve, and tenacity of an eventual Hip-Hop superstar. More importantly, the combination of his skill and integrity makes him ONE OF THE TRUE GREATS AMONG ALL EMCEES!

Strength: Acting. No accident he got an Oscar nod because he created characters in his music.

Weakness: Acting. His strength is his weakness. Sometimes his energy doesn't connect with the listener because it doesn't feel sincere. It comes off like he's playing a role, as opposed to coming from his heart.

Favorite Record: "Summer Time," "Getting Giggy Wit' It"

Favorite LP: *Big Willie Style*

#23: WILL SMITH

ORIGINALITY: 80

Will came at a time when he was telling stories, his energy was lighthearted and fun. It was right on the heels of Slick Rick and Doug E with "La Di Da Di" and a lot of people affiliated that kind of style with what was going on at the time (1986).

CONCEPTS: 80

Will is one of the more conceptual emcees. He made a record of a nightmare on his street, "Twilight Zone." He will go there on the concept side.

VERSATILITY: 90

Will is one of those emcees that can rhyme about anything. He definitely takes chances that a lot of emcees wouldn't in terms of the styles of rhymes and using his voice like an actor.

VOCABULARY: 80

This is unique because Will has an incredible vocabulary and he doesn't choose to use it within the rap. He'll sprinkle it in there now and then, but he's not one of those guys that will hit you with a bunch of high-level vocabulary words back to back.

SUBSTANCE: 80

Will kept it positive but he also kept it very light. He was always the alternative to what was going on in gangsta rap or hard-core rap.

FLOW: 80

Will kept his flow in a cadence that was easy to follow, which makes him one of the best storytellers. That's part and parcel of that type of success.

FLAVOR: 80

He's an actor. He can absolutely become characters within the rhyme and he uses it in a very flavorful manner.

FREESTYLE ABILITY: 80

I've seen Will at plenty of functions come off the top of the head and because his vocabulary is high, things that he uses you wouldn't expect him to use in his freestyle. His freestyle is kind of "nasty."

VOCAL PRESENCE: 80

He doesn't have a real deep dominating voice, but he has a voice that's recognizable, and he puts a lot of passion into it. Depending on whatever type of record he's trying to bring across, he usually understands how to use his voice.

LIVE PERFORMANCE: 90

One of the best performers. If you caught him older than later. He still does his thing on the live side, and now he understands how to put a show together. He does it more like a theatrical performance. That's been one of the consistent themes with him. His whole thing is about performance, and he doesn't let you down onstage either. It was really incredible when he had the beat box combined with Jazzy Jeff.

POETIC VALUE: 70

Will is one of the most underrated storytellers and he does approach it very poetically.

BODY OF WORK: 90

Will also does some of the best commercial albums as far as Hip-Hop is concerned. Because the albums are so commercia, a lot of Hip-Hop pundits don't give them their due credit. But, Will has definitely made some of the most well-rounded commercial hip-hop records ever.

INDUSTRY IMPACT: 100

The all-time industry impact king. There is nobody in the history of Hip-Hop that has made an impact in the industry as much as Will. Forget about the movies, forget about the TV show, just on the music alone he's probably the most well-rewarded emcee ever—Grammys, music awards, and Soul Train.

SOCIAL IMPACT: 70

Will is very much associated with having a good time and being positive in the positive role-model sense, but not being too heavy in the message sense.

LONGEVITY: 100

From 1986 till now, he has been at a high level in every single project he's been involved with.

LYRICS: 70

Will is not the conventional lyricist, but he is a great songwriter.

BATTLE SKILLS: 70

He's not associated with battle or conflicting energy, and for the most part he has been taking a lot of criticism a lot of the time and not responding. Based on the way his mind works, if you forced his hand I'm sure he could bring it across. He just never did it.

TOTAL SCORE: 1,390

AVERAGE SCORE: 81.7

10 BEST HIP-HOP POP KINGS

1) Will Smith	The Most Consistent
2) Hammer	The Most Explosive Ever
3) Kurtis Blow	The First True Songwriter (Hooks)
4) Puffy	Master Marketer
5) Tone Loc	The Platinum Voice
6) Wyclef	The Innovator
7) Coolio	Hardcore Pop Messenger
8) Young MC	Most Radio Friendly Intellectual
9) Sir Mix-a-Lot	Sex on Wax
10) Nelly	Hit Maker
10a) Vanilla Ice	Don't Act Like It Didn't Happen
10b) Ja Rule	True Songwriter

These MCs basically have been at the pinnacle levels of the pop charts, a feat unrecognized with the level of respect it warrants in Hip-Hop.

22

GZA
THE GENIUS

Heavy foot traffic jam
The hallway all day
adolescents working for small pay
world so little
he could never leave his block
his home bullet riddled
so he always need his glock
coast with his eye open
keep his metal smoking
young wastin minds
pheenin on dimes coping
B'got kids quick to break rules and
known to make fools
out of many
now the streets be more safe than schools
there's no diploma
that can break you from the coma
a bloody war in the country
the youth hungry,
on the corner,
hyena's amongst me
yapping about the stories they be
hearing always swearin'
can't even spell the sh**
that he be wearin'
Caught up in the silk web
of material
Superficial stained ya brain tissue
That's the issue
The young is lost
At their own cost dreamin'
Screamin' how they'll never
Hold positions that's demeanin'
Mothers of murder victims
Share the same grief
The elderly shake their head
In disbelief
But no relief came
until I aimed
And blast one shot
and left my name
The GZA

IF THE WU-TANG CLAN REPRESENTED the solar system, GZA would be Saturn. Why? Because Saturn is the sixth planet in the system, and it is lesser known than the Earth, Method Man; Mercury, Ghostface; Mars, Raekwon; and Jupiter, O.D.B.; yet, the way Saturn has rings around it, the GZA seems to have something extra around him. As I have already expressed in earlier chapters, I don't particularly care to separate groups, or pit their strengths and weaknesses against each other, so I'll just elaborate a little on the GZA's skills independently. GZA is an emcee that's a lyrical poet. His lyrical content always has some form of social commentary, mixed with the right balance of higher levels of vocabulary than the average emcee uses. Unlike some emcees who use their vocabulary as if it's a weapon being displayed in an arms showcase, GZA's words always seem to naturally fit the flow and subject matter succinctly. His lyrics resonate with a substance and wit that feels akin to a self-taught street scholar. He structures his rhymes with a phrasing that sometimes comes off sounding grammatically incorrect. However, many times when you get to the end of the rhyme, the feeling is that being grammatically incorrect was intentional in order to be ebonically correct. This is why, with an emcee like GZA, you have to really listen closely because you might miss the message he's delivering, due to the intricacies and the subtleties of the wordplay. In that regard, GZA is like a Shaolin architect building the rhyme from the roof down.

To say that he's an unconventional emcee is an understatement. Many times, because of the Wu-Tang's self-contained colloquialisms, the listeners can get lost in a myriad of slang-laden symbolism and pious mathematics. GZA, on the other hand, uses the most balance in his lyrical approach when it comes to the symbolic science and math of the Wu. His lyrical technique is superb at taking social issues, creating a poetic backdrop, and giving you just enough versified braggadocio to let you know there's a highly skilled emcee bringing you poetic social commentary. What's even more impressive about that is he never loses the potency of the commentary for the sake of the rhyme. The true rhyme masters in the game understand how hard it is to accomplish this. If you don't think or believe this is true just ask yourself how many times you have heard songs with positive messages that just seem to be missing something musically or rhythmically. Trust me, from the emcees point of view, when you're doing a song that has a positive message, artistically you're trying to save people, touch people, or help people, and when you're trying to save people, touch people, or help people, instinctively, the braggadocio bravado that's natural for an emcee feels out of place. This is why GZA is genius. He does this all the time and it never feels unnatural.

Finally, what I personally like most about the GZA is he's not one-note. He doesn't hit you in the head with message after message. He flips it up and gives you old-fashion beats and rhymes sometimes. And on top of that, he also is one of the more creatively conceptual emcees of the last decade. What's really enjoyable about GZA's concepts is the witty subliminations.

They was told not to ride I Patti Hearst
And stay out of Charles mansion
Took Abraham's Lincoln through

The Todd Bridge expansion
Willis Reid's the map
That mark spots showin
On his left George Burns a blunt
Williams holdin
Tyra Banks the money
That Chaka Kahned her for
Alicia keyed his car
For giving Melba Moore
For the Redd Foxx
She bought off the block
But thought twice as
Deborah Cox the gun
Cause she beat Kelly's Price
When Rosa Parks the truck
A farm of Kim Fields
Linda Tripp when tryin to walk Lauryn's Hill
Water dripped out of Farrah's Fawcett
In the glass, she was super fly
Curtis Mayfield her ass!

I could go on, but I'm sure you get the picture. All in all GZA is like a rhyme perfectionist. Although he may tie rhymes together in unconventional ways, he always ties them together. Within the Wu-Tang it's harder for him to shine, because there are nine hot energies, and GZA is more cerebral than the others. It really takes a masters ear to catch a lot of what he's dropping. So speaking from one master on behalf of another, GZA is one of the best lyricists in the game, and one of the TRUE, GREATEST EMCEES to ever do it!!!

Strength: Clever writing. With all the attention to freestyling, many people overlook the art of the written rhyme. GZA is supreme here.

Weakness: GZA's vocally undynamic at points in the rhymes where it would behoove him to be more emphatic. With his intricate style, the cleverness that he possesses is lost in the translation without highlighting key words!

Favorite Record: "Hip-Hop Fury," "Knock Knock"

Favorite LP: *Beneath the Surface*

#22: GZA

ORIGINALITY: 90

The Wu-Tang style was definitely new, and he stood out on the lyrical side.

CONCEPTS: 90

The whole Wu-Tang concept is original in itself.

VERSATILITY: 70

For the most part, he stays in the same zone, same cadence, and the same style of music.

VOCABULARY: 90

GZA brings the lyrical words into the equation. That's what the Liquid Swords are about, on one level.

SUBSTANCE: 85

He definitely made the social commentary for those who really listened and understood. He had a point of view and a purpose in his rhyme.

FLOW: 90

Unique style. Wu-Tang to a lot of people sounded like they were offbeat, but if you check it out, it's just a matter of a different cadence.

FLAVOR: 60

He's straight at you and doesn't play with his voice.

FREESTYLE ABILITY: 80

His lyrical content has so much in it automatically, you can tell that if he comes off of the top of the head. What he's going to recall and access is going to be high level. He's a writer more than a freestyler.

VOCAL PRESENCE: 70

His voice is not as distinctive as some of the other members in the crew. If you're not an avid fan, you might not know his voice, if you're not really paying attention.

LIVE PERFORMANCE: 90

The whole Clan, the energy is just crazy. Even when he's by himself, he feeds on that same kind of energy.

POETIC VALUE: 85

The key with him is you really have to listen to see what he's doing and see how poetical he actually is.

BODY OF WORK: 80

The two albums he did on his own weren't as potent as the first Wu-Tang projects, but for what it is worth, he is putting a lot of work into it.

INDUSTRY IMPACT: 90

You cannot overlook the impact he made within Wu-Tang, and standing out as one of the main lyrical persons.

SOCIAL IMPACT: 70

The one thing that Wu has had a problem with is being viewed as more than just a rap group. They've got Wu Wear and they did the marketing. What they did in the industry is bigger than what they did on the social side.

LONGEVITY: 80

From '93 or '94 till now. Eight years deep at least.

LYRICS: 100

GZA is definitely a top lyricist in the game.

BATTLE SKILLS: 75

Not that he can't battle, but you can tell that he could step it up there. It feels like that might be a waste of time, unless he's really breaking you down for a purpose.

TOTAL SCORE: 1,395

AVERAGE SCORE: 82

21

RAS KASS

THE PURE LYRICIST

Inside my mother's womb
doomed to return to the tomb
or was it from the dead I was raised
all too soon to pay, on judgment day.
Is this beginning or the ending
Died sinning still winning
Still grinning descending
Verdict still pending
Born pretending 300 billion
Men women and children cringing
DE-JA-VU could be I'm dreamin
But we all ask for divine reason
While still breathing and until leavin
Who What When Where How
But most of all why (why what)
Do we live just to die

OF ALL THE EMCEES IN THE history of the West Coast, Ras Kass has the most solid reputation as a lyricist. Kurupt's rep is unquestionable as a solid lyrical emcee, but he's viewed as a gangsta rapper first. Xzibit's rep as a lyrical emcee is also unquestionable; however, he is associated with being a hard-core artist that can bring it lyrically. But when you mention Ras Kass, the very first thing that comes to mind is he's a lyricist. In many cases, it's the only thing that comes to mind. Ras Kass is from the school of emcees who are strictly about the lyricals. His rhyme style is for the lyrical zealots and the rhyme junkies. For the average Hip-Hop fan that doesn't fall under this category, Ras Kass may be an acquired taste. However, if you're all about lyrics, then this is your man.

On his *Rassassination* LP/CD, he addresses this issue with a skit. In the skit, a fan tells him that they think his beats are delicate, and Ras responds telling him that he "don't give a F*** about a beat." As a lyricist, I understand the sentiment. However, as an emcee, this may not be the best strategy. As an emcee, at some point you have to spit it live onstage in front of an audience, and what the more lyrical emcee discovers is how hard it is to rock a crowd without music and other music-related production, i.e., DJ, live band, or beat box.

However, there is another place where the lyrical emcees really make their bones: the cipher. In the cipher (a circle of emcees rhyming round-robin), Ras Kass is literally a king. His reputation is straight legendary. To understand how and why this is so impressive just think about it this way. A man says a rhyme in a circle of friends on a playground in Los Angeles. The friends are so impressed with some of the one-liners and catchphrases, they recite them to others over and over. About one month later, people in New York are hearing about this cipher session. This is all done without a record, a staff, or any type of marketing and/or promotions. Ras Kass is like a lyrically self-contained human ripple effect. Without selling any gold or platinum records, and without having hit singles, and with only a couple of albums under his belt, Ras Kass' name still garners and warrants the respect of the streets and his industry peers, as if he were a multi-platinum selling artist. This is a true testament to his skill level lyrically.

Ras Kass is also, in my eyes, the most ambivalent emcee outside of Tupac and KRS-One. KRS-One would give you different messages from album to album. First, *Criminal Minded*, then *By Any Means Necessary,* and "Stop the Violence." Tupac would give you different messages from song to song: "Keep Your Head Up," "Dear Momma," and "How Do You Want It," songs geared towards women, respect, and love, and then follow it with "Hit Em Up," a song about violently killing other emcees, on the same album. But Ras Kass will do his in the same song and in the same verse. Sometimes, as close as four bars apart, he'll go from spiritual to sexual to violent.

I was lyrically Hip-Hop's top 5
Before two of my nukkas died
Syntax a deep impact
Bruce Willis couldn't survive
A'strange death
Cause nukkas wasn't loud
I'm throwin' monitors off the stage
Cause Rakim said "Move the crowd"
I'm one year older
Ten times more determined partner
A hairy situation
Like Chaka Fu**in Chewbacca
Connect the dots murder by design
Sh** on ya intellect and fertilize
Ya mind
Pull out ya cage
And we can face off like Nicholas Cage
Battle for the second coming of
Christ
And see who's soul gets saved
I got hoes around the globe
And one might be ya girl so don't trust her
I'll tell her like Usher
Girl I'll make you wanna leave the clown
The clown you with

In the very next verse, he sums it up accurately. He tells you that his style is sex and violence, vocabulary and science in an uneasy alliance. I would add to that and say, with a combination of spiritual and religious philosophical writings. This is evident in his song "Interview with a Vampire," which is also one of the illest high-concept records ever. Big Pun made reference to having Jesus and the devil on the same chorus, but Ras Kass took it one step further. Using an effect on his voice, he took on the conceptual personas of the voices of God and Lucifer, in a conversation with himself, asking them questions. This is the element of Ras Kass' arsenal that's personally my favorite. As a master lyricist, it's always refreshingly gratifying to hear an emcee that's highly skilled, taking chances on dealing with subject matters that are not commercially inclined.

In conclusion, Ras Kass has maintained a presence on Hip-Hop's lyrical landscape since he first came on the set in the early/mid-'90s. His album *Soul On Ice* was critically acclaimed lyrically and panned musically. In 1998, he fared a little better on the music, and lyrically stepped it up from superior to the superlative. I would venture to say that if Ras Kass had major hit records combined with what he does lyrically, it wouldn't be merely a hostile takeover, it would be a paradigm shift. It would force emcees to step their lyrical game up, and the music industry would be forced to look for skillful emcees, instead of commercially packageable rappers. Until he finds the musical complement to his rhyme mastery, the few who know will just have to enjoy knowing that he is one of the truly great emcees to ever touch a mic.

Strength: Metaphoric wordplay. He puts conceptual metaphors together cleverly and with comedy.

Weakness: Rhyme retardation. Sometimes you can feel him dumbing down his lyrical content in an attempt to touch the masses.

Favorite Record: "Interview with a Vampire"

Favorite LP: *Rassassination*

#21: RAS KASS

ORIGINALITY: 90
Ras Kass brought his own energy to the equation, though it wasn't anything new that we had ever heard before.

CONCEPTS: 90
Definitely a conceptual emcee. Just listen to his albums.

VERSATILITY: 75
He comes at you straight ahead and he gives you the same style, the same types of rhymes, and the same types of concepts for the most part—but he will flip it up on you every now and then.

VOCABULARY: 100
Absolutely one of the most well-worded emcees in the game.

SUBSTANCE: 80
The gangsta rap, the gangsta point of view, the West Coast lifestyle—since N.W.A. and Ice Cube have done it so well, it wasn't anything new, but it had substantive value to it.

FLOW: 85
Ras Kass will flow the way he flows and give little intricacies with his flow.

FLAVOR: 70
He comes straight at you and doesn't play with his voice.

FREESTYLE ABILITY: 100
He's one of the few emcees that, any time I saw him freestyle, whether it was on TV or in

situations with other emcees, he's always come with it at a very high level. It's not just getting through the rhyme, it's actually coming with something that has some potency.

VOCAL PRESENCE: 75

If you're not into him, you might not recognize his voice. For the emcee fans that follow, you can tell who he is on one level, but he doesn't really project that much.

LIVE PERFORMANCE: 75

He doesn't have enough of a body of work to go over that well onstage, but his energy and the fact that he commits to it gives him enough.

POETIC VALUE: 80

He's one of those emcees that you have to listen to, and once you listen, you can hear that he is poetical with his style.

BODY OF WORK: 75

Short on hits, but high on creativity.

INDUSTRY IMPACT: 75

Didn't have too much on the accolades or awards, but he has been able to sustain a high reputation as an emcee.

SOCIAL IMPACT: 60

Outside of Hip-Hop, you just might not know who he is.

LONGEVITY: 80

He was able to sustain without heat and hit records as long as he has with his reputation as tight as it is.

LYRICS: 100

He's one of the most lyrical emcees, period. I'm never let down when I hear him rhyme.

BATTLE SKILLS: 90

Because he is so lyrical and his vocabulary is so crazy, and his freestyle is crazy. You can hear he's basically a battle emcee, but a lot of people are going to challenge him.

TOTAL SCORE: 1,400

AVERAGE SCORE: 82.3

20

REDMAN

THE FIRESTARTER

I scored one point one
On my S.A.T.
And still push a whip
Wit' a right and LEFT A/C
Gorilla big dog
If my name get called
I'm behind a brick wall
Wit' arsenic jaws
Spit poison
Got a permit draw
Gunned down at sun down
You keep score
This trainin course
A'yall ain't fit
On my crew tombstone
Put we all ain't shit

WELCOME TO THE RED ZONE. ALL emcees from this point on are in scoring position, and appropriately Redman sets it off. I call Redman "the Fire Starter" because every time he starts rhyming it instantly feels like something is about to happen. He is the lyrical embodiment of "Set'n It Off." Other than Busta Rhymes, nobody in Hip-Hop displays more energy. Even when he's not being lyrical, he's still spitting fire. Take just about everything you've just read about GZA and Ras Kass and reverse it. When Redman hit the scene in 1992, he didn't have a reputation to build on. In fact, he wasn't taken that seriously amongst Hip-Hop heads. Everything Redman got, he earned it the hard way. He literally got on the Hip-Hop grind. First of all, the fickle nature of the Hip-Hop music industry always seems to start off skeptical. Even when someone starts off hot, the prognosticators are immediately questioning the sophomore project's potential. This was the case with Redman. He worked the underground, did a couple of shows with EPMD, and although he made some noise, people didn't know what to make of him. In '92 he dropped his debut album *What? Thee Album*, and he made enough noise to ultimately go gold. But the turning point for him as an emcee came when he collabed with EPMD on their single "Headbanger"—not necessarily because of the song, even though his verse was hot, but when people got to see him spit his verse in the video and mimic a man with cerebral palsy, suddenly everybody got it. Redman doesn't give a fu**!!! They now knew he would say anything and do anything. Of course many people were offended, but that was just like adding gasoline to the fire. It was like black comedy met hard-core Hip-Hop and tapped into the dark side of our psyche. To this day, people who remember that record don't really know the words, but everybody remembers the visual matching the lines,

Yes The Redman, that's what they call me
Wicked wit the style, you'd think
I had cerebal palsy like (aghllah)

Shamefully, I'm laughing hysterically right now! And that's what Redman does. He'll say anything, and make fun of anything. The reason this works for him is because Redman will also make fun of himself. He's like the lyrical anti-baller. Redman keeps it grimy, but he does it with flair and a flavor analogous to a court jester who's really a king. He brags about being broke, but it's like an inside joke, and the joke's on you. Redman's flow is uniquely colorful, and his delivery is perfect for creating the appropriate ambiance for his energy. It only takes about two bars of rhyming before you feel all of his fire. Redman is a master of the unexpected. You can never predict where his rhyme is going, his analogies are always crazy, and his energy is always high. He approaches the game lyrically with reckless abandon. He's more of a rhymer than a lyricist, and when he rhymes, you can feel him having fun with it. If most emcees are in the NBA, Redman is on the Harlem Globetrotters. He's having fun with his own brand of ball, and still entertaining you. And he's winning! Redman has figured out how to keep it gritty, and still make hit records. What's also crazy is that his energy is compatible with so many other types of rhyme styles. His work with the Def Squad is hot, and his work with Method Man is fire. He's done collabs with LL, EPMD, Keith Murray, DJ Kool, De La Soul, Scarface, and many others. And no matter what the heat level of the other artist, Redman always shines. Some emcees do records with other artists and they sound out of place. Redman just sounds like he's adding fire to the mix. In 1997, he was one of the five emcees on LL's "4, 3, 2, 1" with Method Man, Canibus, DMX, and LL. The heat on that record was crazy, and ultimately DMX was the star. But on the low, Redman's verse was his usual, unpredictable heat. True to form, two bars and he was turning "Christians into sinners."

I put it on a nukka, shi** on a nukka
Turn a Christian to a certified sinner
The bomb I release time ben' up
(explode) when you got sent up
I was hittin ya ex-ho
Sh** I kept low petro ya metro
Politic keep the chicken heads
Gob'el'n, sh** I'm driving in
Come wit funk halogen
Terrorize ya city
From the spliff committee
Kick ass till both Timbelands
Turn sh**y gritty
Smack the driver head in a gypsy
When I approach, rappers be takin notes
I drop like I should'a
Invented the rain coat
Absolute, I love to burn to the roots
I keep comin' til you
Pour sperm from your boots
Vigilante, hard-core to the penis
Tell you fu** you
My attitude is anemic

That ultimately sums it up. Redman, through Hip-Hop, is reminding us not to take ourselves too seriously. On one of his records "I'll Be That," he is being called names and being slurred, and his response is, "I'll be that." In today's climate, that's the last response you would expect. Most emcees would take that time to manifest their masculine machismo and display some form of physical threat. Once again, Redman goes against the grain. Compared to today's emcee, Redman is the consummate UNBALLER, UNTHUG, UNFACADE emcee. He keeps it more than real, he keeps it raw. The final testament to Redman's success is he's been doing his thing in the game for ten years at a very high level. He is affiliated with gold and platinum success, and that's without altering his rawness.

However, what's most impressive to me is that his last album is his best album. There have been many emcees who've had longevity, like Heavy D and LL, but none of their last albums were as potent as their earlier works. In that sense, Redman is once again one of a kind. From what I can tell, based on the humor he exhibits in his album skits and video clips, Redman could probably do his thing in Hollywood as a comedic actor. In the meantime, he's killin' 'em on the mic as an emcee. And without a doubt ONE OF THE GREATEST EMCEES! Redman.

Strength: Comedic wit and authentic rhyme bliss. Whatever he's saying, he conveys the energy of a true emcee having fun with it.

Weakness: Substance abuse. Lyrically he seems never to want to deal with any issues of a substantive nature. All rhymes seem to be geared towards DRUGS, PARTY, SEX, and anything of shock value.

Favorite Record: "Time For Some Action"

Favorite LP: *Where is Reggie Noble?*

#20: REDMAN

ORIGINALITY: 90

Timing. Coming in the early '90s, but it wasn't anything we had never heard.

CONCEPTS: 80

Redman is conceptual from rhyme to rhyme and even in his albums.

VERSATILITY: 80

He'll get into different flows and different types of energies, but he always comes across with the fire.

VOCABULARY: 70

Doesn't get too wordy with it. Keeps it simple, keeps it fun.

SUBSTANCE: 65

Redman's whole image is partying and getting high.

FLOW: 90

He has one of the more energetic flows in the game. He's one of the cats who is easy to follow on the rhyme flow, and it's effective.

FLAVOR: 100

His flavor is over the top. It's enjoyable energy when he's rhyming. He plays with his voice and he has fun with it.

FREESTYLE ABILITY: 85

Because he is having so much fun, it doesn't even make a difference. He's one of those emcees where the rhyme doesn't even have to make sense when he gets finished with it. He's having so much fun it's infectious.

VOCAL PRESENCE: 100

One of the most recognizable voices in the game, without question. His voice is very powerful.

LIVE PERFORMANCE: 95

Whether he's by himself or with the Hit Squad or Method Man, Redman always delivers on the live side. He's one of the best live emcees in the game.

POETIC VALUE: 65

He's so busy having fun, he's not thinking about poetry, he's just flowing and having a good time on the rhyme side.

BODY OF WORK: 90

If you check from album to album, you'll see each album got better, and his last album was his best.

INDUSTRY IMPACT: 70

Redman flies under the radar.

SOCIAL IMPACT: 65

He plays it down more than anything else. He's not even trying to make a social impact.

LONGEVITY: 100

He's done it ten years strong.

LYRICS: 85

Even though he's having fun, Redman does get lyrical.

BATTLE SKILLS: 80

He's busy having fun. He's the kind of emcee that will battle anyone if you have a problem with him, or you try to make, that way he'll definitely come with it. For the most part, he's not a battle emcee.

TOTAL SCORE: 1,410

AVERAGE SCORE: 82.9

19

MC LYTE

TIMELESS RHYMES

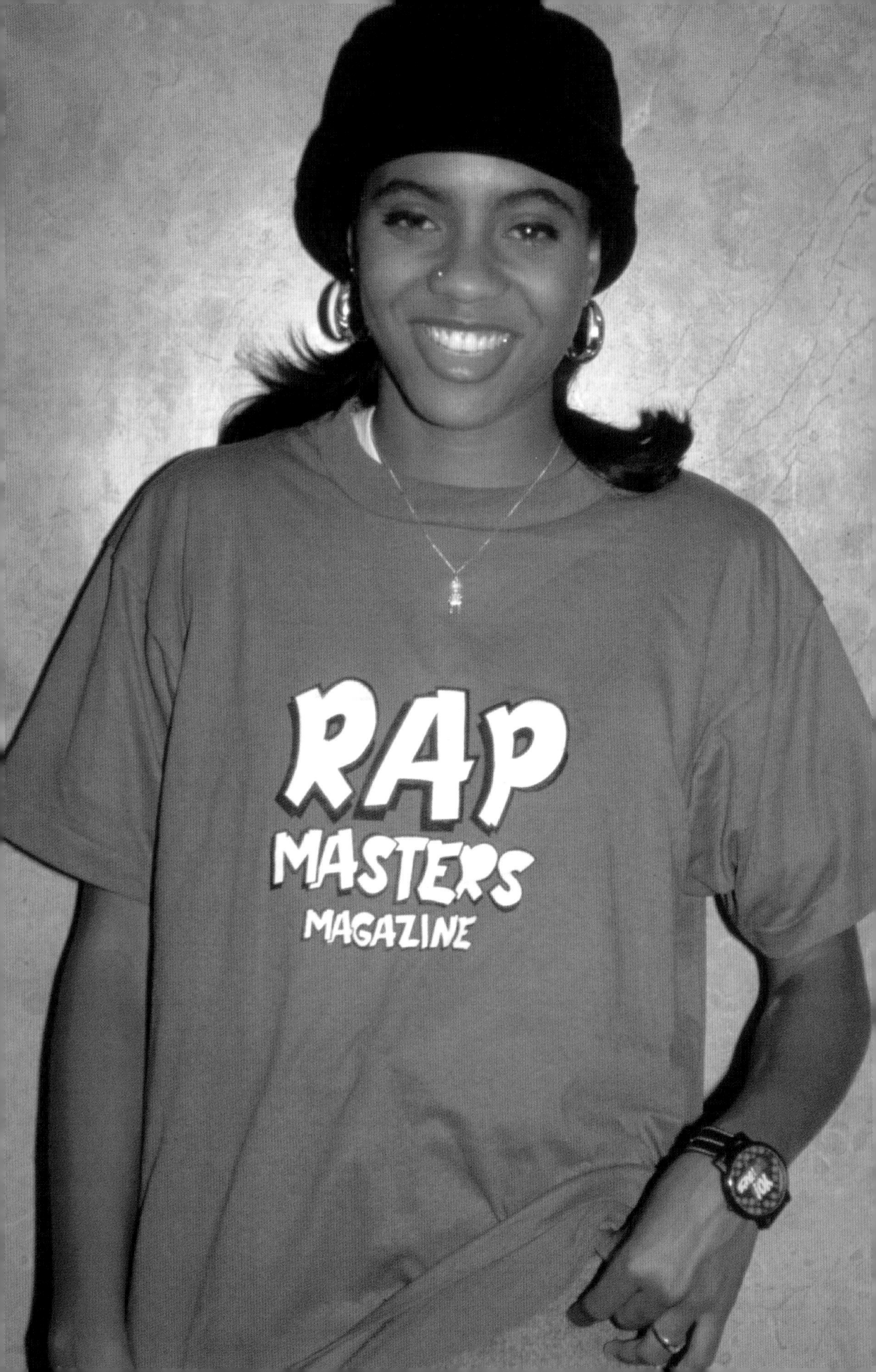
RAP
MASTERS
MAGAZINE

You can Cha Cha
To this Mardi Gras
I'm the dopest female
That you've heard thus far
And I do get better
The voice gets wetter
Nobody gets hurt
(as long as you let her)
do my thing with an 89 swing
the dope-ness I write
I guarantee de-Lyte
A to the Hip-Hop maniac
The uptown brainiac
In full effect MC Lyte is back
And better than before
As if that was possible
My competition you'll find them
In the hospital
Visiting time I think it's on a Sunday
but notice they only get one day
to shine the rest of the week is mine
And I'll blind you with the science
That the others have yet to find
So come along, and I'll lead you the
Right way, just clap ya hands
To the words I say

MC LYTE'S RHYME FLOW, COMBINED WITH her vocal pitch and flavor-packed delivery, is so flawless that no matter which time period or era she's rhyming in, she simultaneously sounds like a new artist and a veteran. Right out of the gate in 1988 with her song "I Cram to Understand U," she was a new jack that sounded like she was ready for battle. The song was about a guy she was in love with named Sam, who was cheating on her and doing crack. The way she told the story, and the level of confidence she showed in her delivery, you could tell she was going to be a force to be reckoned with in Hip-Hop. I, as a battle emcee, could tell that she had the gift of battle. You could tell that she would take no disrespect from anyone. And this is before I heard "10% Dis."

Shortly after that, she was in a battle zone with another hot female emcee at the time, "Antonette." At one point, Antonette came to me to write a dis record against Lyte. I understand that it was just business, and I really did like Antonette, but I was already loving Lyte. Besides that, I'm sure Lyte would have eventually found out about it, and ultimately, she would have dissed me, which means I would have had to come back, and so on and so on. I would never let this happen. MC Lyte is on that short list of emcees I'd never battle (too much love and respect).

As far as the rest of her skills, MC Lyte is also one of the most well-rounded emcees.

She's like a basketball player that has a wicked jump shot, an inside power game, and excellent defense. She has an exceptional flow, a diverse body of work and subject matter, hit radio and hit street records, and an impeccable delivery on top of her battle skills. She has managed to be ladylike and a thug-ette simultaneously, because of her amenable rhyme prowess. Her lyrical content is a complement to her persona which has been solidified as a female who's an intellectual, and sexy without being overtly sexual. She's a skilled out-class act that has represented females well during Hip-Hop's increasingly sexist and sexually exploitive climate. She keeps her skill level up, and she keeps her commentary current. But don't get it confused; Lyte is not POLLY PUREBREAD. When it's time to get gritty, she can get grimy. In 1993, she singlehandedly validated the thug love movement from the female side.

> I need a ruff neck
> I need a man that don't snitch
> Like a bitch shed tears or switch
> Doin whatever it takes
> To make ends meet
> But never meetin the end
> Cause he knows the street
> Eat sh** sh** fu** eat sleep sh**
> Then it's back to the streets
> To make a buck quick
> Quick to beg even though
> Gimmie got 'em here
> Hit 'em wit a bit a skins
> And he's outta there

Suddenly women were coming out of the woodworks claiming they wanted a roughneck and always had love for thugs. A year later, Tupac's a sex symbol. However, MC Lyte has shown that rare talent among emcees to be able to have success with almost any type of record. She was able to achieve some radio R&B and pop success with songs like "Poor Georgie" and "When Inn Love." Because of the divisive ignorance of the Hip-Hop climate at that time, Lyte got a little backlash for having a more radio-friendly commercial sound. I personally thought it was a natural progression. On top of that, I felt that she was on top of her game. Her storytelling was more subtle and more poignant, and lyrically she was as tight as ever. Nonetheless, I think the backlash on that project, *Act Like You Know,* led to her most rugged LP to date *Ain't No Other,* which produced the "Ruffneck" single, and earned her a Grammy nomination.

One more element to Lyte's game is her absolutely pristine enunciation. Every word she utters is absolutely crystal clear. She's the best in the game at this.

Finally, MC Lyte belongs in Hip-Hop's elite class of rap songwriters, along with Will Smith, Heavy D, and Kurtis Blow, just to name a few. In 2002, she dropped *Lytro Da Underground Heat,* her seventh album in fourteen years, and fourteen years after her debut she's still on point. Her songwriting is still hot, and her braggadocio is comfortably confrontational. She is like an empress who's been battle-tested, and is daring someone to challenge her throne. Lyrically she is a rap icon who sounds and feels as current today as she did fourteen years ago. MC Lyte is one of my personal favorites and definitely ONE OF HIP-HOP'S TRUE, GREATEST EMCEES.

Strength: Special delivery. She's the kind of emcee that could spit your rhyme and make it sound better. Her delivery is impeccable.

Weakness: The stage. The only place I've ever seen Lyte come off as shy was onstage. Earlier, more than now, she was a little stiff and had a hard time coming across in live performances.

Favorite Record: "Rough Neck," "Ride Wit Me"

Favorite LP: *Eyes On This*

#19: MC LYTE

ORIGINALITY: 90

Late '80s she came with her own flavor, a rhyme style that a lot of us were already using, but she brought her own essence into the equation.

CONCEPTS: 85

Lyte is a conceptual emcee and comes with a variety of concepts.

VERSATILITY: 85

Because she does come with a variety of styles, she's one of the more versatile emcees in the game.

VOCABULARY: 85

She doesn't beat you in the head with vocabulary, but she absolutely will throw words in there and you will need to be up on your vocabulary to stay with her.

SUBSTANCE: 80

Lyte has a lot of things to say about a lot of issues, and it's just a matter of what time and what state and what part of her life she's in at that point that determines what you'll get on the records. She'll come hard-core or she'll come fun-loving.

FLOW: 90

One of the more ridiculous flows in the game.

FLAVOR: 95

Probably the most flavorful female emcee ever in the game.

FREESTYLE ABILITY: 75

Lyte doesn't seem to have a passion for freestyle, but she has fun with it anyway.

VOCAL PRESENCE: 90

Voice is incredible. Cuts to tape, as we say. Without question, you recognize her voice from the instant she starts rhyming.

LIVE PERFORMANCE: 80

In the beginning, she struggled on the live side of the equation, but as time has gone on, she's definitely gotten better.

POETIC VALUE: 75

More rhymes as opposed to poetry, but she does bring it across, and she does sprinkle little levels of poetry in there.

BODY OF WORK: 90

Seven albums and the albums speak for themselves.

INDUSTRY IMPACT: 70

Although she got one Grammy nomination, Lyte also flies under the radar in the industry. She's very well known among her Hip-Hop peers, but the industry seems not to give her the accolades she's due.

SOCIAL IMPACT: 70

Lyte is viewed as an emcee that's having fun in the game.

LONGEVITY: 100

From 1987 to '88 on through.

LYRICS: 85

MC Lyte is definitely a lyricist. Lots of flavor, lots of energy, but on the lyrical side, she puts her words together very nicely.

BATTLE SKILLS: 85

The first half of her career was about battling. A lot of it was with Antonette, but a lot of it was open calls to anybody that wanted to bring it. She felt like she could battle anybody.

TOTAL SCORE: 1,430

AVERAGE SCORE: 84.1

18

ICE CUBE
THE UNSTOPPABLE FORCE

I heard paybacks a muthafu***in nukka
That's why I'm sick of gettin
Treated like god damned step child
Fu** a punk cause I ain't him
You gotta deal wit the 9 double-m
Na'there's something that ya all hate
Just think if nukkas
Decide to retaliate
They try to keep me from runnin up
I never tell you to get down
It's all about comin up
So what what the do, gone ban the AK
My sh** wasn't registered any f'n way
So you better duck away run-n-hide out
When I'm rollon real slow
And the lights out, cause I'm about
To fu** up the program
Shootin out the window
Of a drop top bro-ham
While I'm shootin, let's see who drops
The police the media
And suckers that went pop
And mutha fu***s who say they too black
Put'em overseas, and they'll be
Beggin to come back
They say keep'em on gangs and drugs
You wanna sweep a nukka like me
Up under the rug
Kickin sh** called street knowledge
Why are more nukkas in the pen
Than in college
Because of that line
I might be ya cell mate
That's from the nukka you love to hate.

IT IS SOLELY BECAUSE OF ICE CUBE that I understood and had to respect gangsta rap. I had respect for Ice-T because of how he approached it, and I hated N.W.A. because of how they approached it. With Eazy-E as the front man (a rapper who I thought had no skills), I thought that gangsta rap was the worst thing that ever happened to Hip-Hop. I thought it was crass, crude, uncouth, lyrical fodder posing as art. Ice Cube was in the group, and also known as the principal writer for the group. I could hear the quality in his voice, along with Ren, but I thought that the rhyme level was remedial. Combined with the subject matter of killing, drinking, getting high, and calling women bitches (in public), I was ready for battle. I did an interview in *Spin* magazine where I prophesied their doom. Although I believed that to be true, it was more of a tactic to lure them into battle. By 1990, Ice Cube left the group, and ironically both acts were better. N.W.A. started being a little more creative, and Ice Cube completely erupted and put a stamp on what was being called gangsta rap. Until Ice Cube's solo debut "Amerikkka's Most Wanted," the lines used to define gangsta rap were blurry. Most pundits couldn't decipher which elements really made it gangsta rap. Was it the language, the content, or the imagery? Furthermore, what separated gangsta rap from hard-core Hip-Hop? Better yet, was there a difference? Clearly Public Enemy and KRS-One were hard-core, but were we now to call them gangsta rappers also?

Ice Cube cleared it all up. He was the first West Coast emcee that the East Coast emcees couldn't say, "He can't rap." Ice Cube had skills. He also used excessive profanity much more cleverly than what the average gangsta rappers were doing at the time. You could tell it was his natural flow. Many gangsta rappers use profanity for shock value and for so-called street credibility. Ice Cube already had that. He was simply crystallizing how life in L.A. was simultaneously similar to all of urban America in poverty, and different in their gang ridden street life.

One might say, "So what's so different about him and the other gangsta rappers." Ice-T gave you positive messages, and N.W.A. expressed a violent nature caused by police brutality. Ice Cube was the first one to speak about it in an anti-American, Afrocentric, street militant manner. He stepped it up from shooting each other to shooting police. He talked about the black youth being viewed as animals in America, and because of that view we were an endangered species. He made it clear that America had a problem with what was being called gangsta rap, not because of the language or the violent content, but because of the threat of black youth being informed and inspired to rise against the government. The bottom line is, where Ice-T had a conscience, Ice Cube added a consciousness.

This is why in my book the two of them are the pinnacle of what gangsta rap is truly about. Ice Cube added the substance to the vulgar style. While I may personally not care for the levels of vulgarity, as an emcee I appreciate the way he, in particular, brings it across. What conservative America doesn't understand is when you are talking to people living in impoverished, hopeless environments, sometimes vulgarity is the only way to get them to listen. Ice Cube, like many other emcees, comes from and/or is surrounded by the results of the inequities of a racist American existence. We know that a large part of our audience doesn't want it sugar-coated, and Ice Cube never sugar-coats it. He brings it so real that sometimes he makes it uncomfortable for us by forcing us to look at ourselves on an ugly level. He did songs about the true feelings of a broke teenager in the ghetto that finds out that he may be a father to a child of a girl who's the neighborhood slut.

Now the taste of alcohol
Is fillin up my bladder
What's the date and time it don't matter
Had a pocket full of phone numbers
I was tryin to sort
To make a long story short
Ran into this girl named Carla

Knew her from the back seat
Of my homey's Impala
She said what's up, yeah what's the deal
Check the hair do, of course it ain't real
Then I looked down, she was fat
In the front
I asked how long, well about 7 months
Oh how time flies when ya havin fun
She said yeah but the damage is done
Where you been, on a little vacation
Oh by the way congratulations
Who's the lucky man, I don't have a clue
Then she said the lucky man is you
I dropped my brew
And everything looked fuzzy
Not a baby by you, the neighborhood hussy
She said yeah, remember that day
I thought back and tried to calculate
Then I said damn, are you sure it's mine
Cause I know you've been tossed
Plenty of times
She said that day, no I wasn't whorin
Yo ass is mine, that's when the sweat started pourin
Cause all I saw was Ice Cube in court
Payin a gang on child support
Then I thought deep about givin up the money
What I need to do is kick the bitch in the tummy
Naw cause then I'll really get faded
That's murder one
Cause it was premeditated
So what I'ma do, I don't have a clue
How many months left
Damn only two, I'm getting faded

This is one of the many ugly truths of adolescent ghetto life. What Ice Cube does is speak from the mind and thought process of many of our urban youth. And like it or not, these are very universal thoughts in many cases. As an emcee, he's been more of a cautionary storyteller than anything else. However, he has also had battles with Common, and his ex-partner Eazy-E. He showed his battle skills on the song "No Vaseline." He fearlessly and openly took shots at East Coast rappers during the time of the industry-hyped, publicity-hyped, East Coast/West Coast feud. As he grew as an artist, he began to figure out a formula for balance, and became less vulgar and less incendiary in his lyrical approach. Although he's been criticized for not being as hard-core as he was on his earlier work, I think Ice Cube's transition was more authentic. Many artists will make transitions to try to reach higher levels of record sales. But Ice Cube had already sold multi-platinum records without the radio play. His transition seems more like a boy that grew into a man, and his priorities changed. He's now a filmmaker, an actor, and a producer. Ice Cube's music is a reflection of how he's living. He's a hard-core, millionaire emcee. So why would he be rhyming about shooting or living in the 'hood. Wouldn't that be fake? Isn't that what keeping it real means?

Besides that, Ice Cube has always been of the ambivalent cloth of emcees. Many people tried to say he wasn't really a gangsta rapper because he was bused to school and didn't live in poverty. That, to me, sums it up perfectly for Ice Cube. The audience likes to be able to define us as rap artists according to what they can perceive and deem relevant to who we are. However, most emcees, and all true emcees are multi-dimensional, multilayered people. Ice Cube has been able to be gangsta, Muslim, battler, conscious, vulgar, profound, comical, misogynistic, poignant, ruthless, poetic, artistic, base, and educational. There are many dimensions to him and he displays many of those aspects in his music. He's always shown two sides to the story. On his album *Death Certificate* there was a "life side" and a "death side." He released a double CD, *War and Peace,* where one disc was upbeat and the other was dark. Ice Cube has been exemplary in demonstrating how there are mixed emotions in street life, vacillating from hope to hopelessness, frustration to motivation, and from fear to the fearlessness, all as a means of survival. He openly challenged the positively themed messages from prominent songs like "Self Destruction" with simplistic messages in one-liners like "Self Destruction don't pay the fu***n rent."

Although it seemed controversial and regressive at the time, it's now painfully obvious that those messages needed to be heard in conjunction with Ice Cube's simplicity, because all social struggles are part social and part economic. Economically speaking positive messages don't sound as good to a homeless person on an empty stomach. Ice Cube spoke for the listeners that couldn't hear us. He didn't offer much in terms of solutions, but he did enough to make an impact and change the focus of the conversations as an emcee. He stripped down all of the flashy, flossy, industry-driven political rhetoric, and gave us a much more socially relevant picture of what gangsta rap, and the poverty stricken L.A. gang culture that manifested it, was really about. That alone makes him a great emcee. The fact that he could grow into other areas of entertainment and sustain his rap career for over ten years from the gangsta rap template makes Ice Cube ONE OF THE GREATEST EMCEES EVER.

Strength: Social commentary at a layman's level. He kept it raw and simple for the consumption of the common man in the 'hood. Excellent storytelling.

Weakness: Prosaic instead of poetic. Part of his flack for gangsta rap was the lack of poetry. Rhymes seemed too simplistic and lacking metaphors.

Favorite Record: "Today Was a Good Day," "We Be Clubbin"

Favorite LP: *Amerikkka's Most Wanted*

#18: ICE CUBE

ORIGINALITY: 90

Came with his own energy. It wasn't too much that we hadn't heard already, but he brought his own flavor.

CONCEPTS: 80

Didn't get too intricate with the concepts, but he definitely brought concepts to the equation. He's one of the first West Coast emcees to put skits on his album.

VERSATILITY: 75

You basically knew what you were getting with Ice Cube every album out, for the most part. Changed it up a little bit at the end, and did a few different things with Westside Connection, but for the most part he kept it right at you in the zone and vein he was coming from.

VOCABULARY: 75

Ice Cube kept it simple, plain, and effective.

SUBSTANCE: 85

He's the one for me that put the face on gangsta rap and let you know that it was a lot deeper than just the robbing, stealing, and killing that people wanted to paint the picture of.

FLOW: 80

His cadence is incredible and his flow; he keeps it simple and keeps it effective. That's one of the running things with Ice Cube: make sure the rhymes make sense and keep it simple.

FLAVOR: 80

Ice Cube's flavor was more about the energy. As they say, he sounded like an angry Black man, but his cadence and flavor were cool.

FREESTYLE ABILITY: 80

Ice Cube seems to have much more of a purpose than just coming off of the top of the head.

Kind of like old-school artists, freestyle sometimes means being able to rhyme about whatever, and Ice Cube had that ability.

VOCAL PRESENCE: 95

One of the most recognizable voices in the history of the game, without question. Very strong and potent in his voice.

LIVE PERFORMANCE: 90

Ice Cube knows how to bring it across live. Ever since the days of N.W.A., then on his own, then with Westside Connection, then catching up with Snoop and the guys at the "Up In Smoke" tour. He brings it across well live.

POETIC VALUE: 75

Like most emcees, it's more rhyme than poetry.

BODY OF WORK: 95

Ice Cube's body of work is unquestionably stellar.

INDUSTRY IMPACT: 90

This is a rare case where he didn't get a lot of accolades from the industry on one side, but on the other side he made such an impact that the industry was always talking about him.

SOCIAL IMPACT: 85

It wasn't like he was trying to save lives or presented himself as a savior, but he served as an inspiration in a lot of cases, because of how he was able to articulate from his rhyme standpoint. Then, right after the rhyme in interviews, whenever you saw him, he represented well.

LONGEVITY: 100

Since '87 and still going.

LYRICS: 80

Ice Cube never really got that intricate on the lyrical side, but he was always lyrical enough to be effective.

BATTLE SKILLS: 80

Even though he had a couple of run-ins, the Eazy-E and Common situations, he's not really the battle-type emcee, but he's also so fearless that he'll battle anybody anyway.

TOTAL SCORE: 1,430

AVERAGE SCORE: 84.1

17

METHOD
MAN
MASTER
FLOW-ER

I came to bring the pain
Hardcore from the brain
Let's go inside my astro plane
Find out my mental
Based on instrumental
Records hey, so I can write monumental
Methods I'm not the king
But nukkas is decaf
I stick'em for the cream
Check it, just how deep can sh** get
Deep as the abyss
And brothers is mad fish accept it
In ya cross color
Clothes ya crossed over
Then got totally crossed out
And criss crossed
Who da boss, nukkas got tossed to
The side, and I'm the dark side
Of the force
The force is the Method Man
From the Wu-Tang Clan
And comin for that head piece
Protect it fu** it two tears
In a bucken nukkas want the ruckas
Bustin at me Ra' now bust it
Styles I gets buck wild
Method Man on some sh**
Pullin nukkas files, I'm sick
Insane crazy drivin' Miss Daisy
Out her fu***n mind
Now I got mine
I'm Swayze

METHOD MAN'S FLOW IS PURE-D HOT LIQUID!!! Like water takes the shape of whatever you put it in, Method Man's flow takes the form of whatever track he's spittin' on. What's really hard to explain is it's not like he's using any kind of gimmicks or tricks. It's just natural. It's like he's just smoothly sailing inside the pocket. His cadence is incredible. When the beat is up to standards, his rhymes almost instantly become like sing-alongs. This is an aspect of rap music that's usually reserved for the more simplified rhyme styles, or the song-like rhyme cadences. Other than Rakim, Big Daddy Kane, and Biggie, Method Man is the only emcee that makes this happen when he's being lyrical. However, he also uses the simplified song-like rhyme style cadences . In 1993, he debuted in the Wu-Tang Clan with the song "Method Man." He masterfully used the simplistic song-like rhyme cadence, and basically put the Wu on the map.

For the next two years, there was Wu-Tang mania. In New York at that time, outside of Naughty By Nature, the West Coast was dominating the Hip-Hop scene. The Wu-Tang Clan was a much needed, raw breath of fresh air. New York Hip-Hop had gotten gimmicky, and the Wu was purely beats and rhymes. Their style and musical approach was original, but what was most original was the fact that the group members all had their own solo record deals on other record labels. This unprecedented act paid off exceptionally well for Method Man. His solo deal was on Def Jam, Hip-Hop's premiere record label. That combined with all of the momentum created from the Wu-Tang mania helped solidify Method Man as one of Hip-Hop's true stars. However, there is a subtle dichotomy. At the peak of Wu-Tang's heat, Method Man, because of his flow, was the true break-out star in the group. However, as a solo act, even though he made hot records, he sounded like something was missing. His vocals seemed to be screaming for someone to bounce off of. Method Man's flow is so melodic it's almost like its own self-contained hook. This is what I think made him stand out so much in the group. When eight emcees are spitting with the rapidity that the Wu spits with, Method Man was like the calming force in the flow. He naturally felt like the hook, breaking the monotony when it was his turn to spit. This also worked well for him in his solo career. Many times he makes guest appearances on songs where he's only doing the hook.

Another part of his appeal is that, like Redman, Method Man just doesn't give a fu**!!! He'll say whatever, whenever, wherever. His energy is felt because behind the words, you can feel him enjoying his flow. This is probably why when Method Man and Redman partner up to make music feel like a perfect fit. Together they're like a rhythmic ebb and flow of hot and cool, fire and water, intensity and tranquility, manifest in the perfect balance of rhyme. Method Man, in particular, always sounds like he doesn't have a care in the world. I think he sounds better or is better appreciated when he's bouncing off of someone, because then you can hear the subtle difference between rhyming on beat and flowing in the beat. Method Man flows in the beat so effortlessly, he makes it look too easy.

Nonetheless, he's one of the emcees from the early to mid-'90s that ushered in the era of flow. Rakim invented it, Big Daddy Kane, KRS-One, and Cool G Rap expanded it, but Biggie and Method Man made flow the single most important aspect of an emcee's game to the listeners in the streets. From 1993 till now, what you say is not as important as how you say it, according to the new listeners. Your rhyme could be the cure for cancer, but if you can't flow, the streets will never hear it. Method Man is forefather of that movement. He's also been able to reach higher levels of success than most of his hard-core Hip-Hop peers, without changing his formula. In 1995, he released his Grammy-winning song "All I Need," featuring Mary J. Blige, and upon first listen, you might think it's the usual Hip-Hop, cliché-softened, R&B rap song, formulaically attempting to get radio play and cross a rap artist over. Not even close. If you listen to the original version on the album, you'd see that Meth never changed his verses.

Shorty I'm there for you
Anytime you need me
For real girl it's me in your world

Believe me
Nuttin make a man
Feel better than a woman
Queen wit a crown that be down
For whatever
There are few things that forever
My lady, we could make war or make babies
Back when I was nu'in
You made a brother feel like he was su'in
Das why I'm wit you till this day
Boo no frontin
Even when the skys were gray
You would rub me on my back
And say baby it'll be ok
Now that's real to a brotha
Like me bay-bay
Never ever give my pus** away
And keep it tight a'ight

This is the hardest Hip-Hop so-called love song ever. Meth kept it gutter. In closing, Method Man has put together a hot body of work ranging from work with the Wu-Tang to Redman to Limp Bizkit and many others. He's risen to Hip-Hop's elite status, and he's been on a run with heat since 1993. He's one of the all-time flow-ers in the history of the game and he has the uncanny ability to vacillate from being lyrical to coming with simplistic rhymes in catchy song cadences, without losing any validity. That's a testament to the authenticity felt in his delivery, and the purpose in his rhyme. He just wants you to have a good time. Undoubtedly, Method Man is one of the True greats among emcees.

Strength: Flow! Flow! Flow! Any beat is made to order.

Weakness: Secret codes. Sometimes his slang is just for him and his inner circle.

Favorite Record: "All I Need," "Judgment Day"

Favorite LP: *Tical 2000*

#17: METHOD MAN

ORIGINALITY: 90

In the middle of the Wu, he absolutely was the shining star of that crew. His flow was incredible so it caught on immediately, and he was original in the way he came.

CONCEPTS: 85

A lot of it was conceptual as far as Wu-Tang goes, and when he stepped out on his own, he kept similar concepts.

VERSATILITY: 80

With Method Man, you knew what you were

getting, but he also would take chances and do records in different styles with other people.

VOCABULARY: 70

He keeps it very simple.

SUBSTANCE: 75

Once in a while, he'll sprinkle a positive message in the equation, but for the most part it was about the rhymes.

FLOW: 100

Incredible. Melt into the beat.

FLAVOR: 90

He absolutely plays around with his voice and gives different inflections. Who would say nursery rhymes like he did in the hit single "Method Man" without having flavor?

FREESTYLE ABILITY: 90

He comes off the top of the head. Even if he loses his place in concert, he'll just go for it and keep the crowd going.

VOCAL PRESENCE: 90

His voice is one of the more recognizable, smooth voices. Even though it's laid back, he brings his voice with a little more presence and resonance than a lot of emcees with softer voices.

LIVE PERFORMANCE: 95

One of the best live performers in the game.

POETIC VALUE: 70

More rhyme over poetry.

BODY OF WORK: 90

Can't overlook the Wu-Tang work, and he's done hits, and he's making hits with other people.

INDUSTRY IMPACT: 85

His name is much more recognizable than a lot of emcees, and his name is more recognizable than his records. He also won a Grammy with Mary J.

SOCIAL IMPACT: 80

Meth looks like he's an emcee that's having fun, but then again his name is still out there and it resonates on another level beyond a lot of emcees. He seems to be more like a star than just an emcee.

LONGEVITY: 95

Very simple. Came in the game in '93 and he's still in the game.

LYRICS: 80

Method Man is a part-time lyricist, part-time fun/party emcee. He doesn't get too intricate on the lyrics.

BATTLE SKILLS: 75

Method Man doesn't seem like the battle type of emcee. Doesn't mean that he can't do it, but why would anybody want to battle Method Man?

TOTAL SCORE: 1,440

AVERAGE SCORE: 84.7

16

TREACH

MASTER RHYME STYLIST

It's time to erase efface
Enforce in'fact an inferno
Rise in my eyes'll make'em learn'no
You poppin' plottin' planin'
Half steppin' threatening
The streets clap loud
Like thunder clouds work the weapon
I'm stepping to clarify
Looking wit the hawk and the arrow eye
Turn the biggest part of yo
Ass into the narrow side
I'm that case yo place nukka
Tie yo bitch to the shi***r
Nukka throw yo stinkin ass
By the liver nukka
Me beef I rag fast
Repeats get dragged gagged
Getting' busy like Ra'sheed street
In bag dad
Have ya kids askin'
Why did they have to drag dad

TREACH IS THE AUTHOR OF THE anthem. Will Smith might be the best songwriter, and Snoop Dogg might be the best hook writer, but Treach takes the combination of the two to a whole "notha" level. The subtle difference is he uses big chants, over energetic upbeat tracks, directed at large audiences, in a call-and-response format. That's the science, but there's more to what meets the eye. The problem with these kinds of songs is they usually override the shine of the emcee. These types of songs are usually compatible only with the part emcee. DJ Hollywood, Keith Cowboy, Luke Skywalker, and Doug E Fresh have all used this formula with success. Tag Team's "Whoop There It Is" is one of the all-time great anthem chants. What makes Treach so unique is that none of these emcees are regarded as lyricists. On this level of the game, lyricists get swallowed up. Treach is not only a lyricist that doesn't get swallowed, he's a lyricist that shines.

What's even more unique is that the anthem chants he's made have had huge R&B and pop radio appeal, and for a hard-core emcee that can be the kiss of death. Treach's reputation as a hard-core lyricist has never been questioned. Naughty By Nature is somewhat of an enigmatic group. They were truly hard-core but constantly made sing-along radio records, and in the beginning Vinnie seemed to be more like a hype man. As of late, he's definitely doing more on the rhyme side, but Treach is still the lead emcee. Once again I don't separate groups, but based on the early work, and the amount of records Treach did by himself, he had to be on the list.

Besides that, he is also one of those emcees that just doesn't get enough props for his "lyricals," when it comes to these emcee countdowns. Treach is known for his signature cadence. Where Method Man is a natural flow master, Treach is a master flow flipper. He can downshift from his signature sonic, high-velocity flow into a melodic, smooth, songster's cadence, with a dexterity and flavor that makes it feel like it was all done in one breath. Which by the way is another secret to being a powerful rhymer. You can't rhyme if you don't have breath control. Treach has to have mastered this because the cadences he uses, and the energy and pitch he chooses to use, demand an extremely high level of breath control. An example of this is on the first two LL Cool J albums. If you listen closely, you can hear him gasping and taking deep breaths between lines. Treach doesn't have that problem. His flow is fluid. He brings an upbeat energy to the party jams, and an accurately darker energy to the more street songs.

Treach is an example and a study on balance. Everything in his game is properly offset by another aspect of his game. Where Ice Cube uses polarities, Treach uses increments of his multidimensions. In each of his songs, Treach uses combinations of hard-core, ghetto, sexuality, braggadocio, and poignancy in his rhymes. He does this with song themes as well as with visual imagery. His dress code never goes hard on the bling, and when he's performing in concert, he may take his shirt off for the ladies, but he never turns it into the R&B-type gyration-filled sex show. If he hits you with a party song first, he'll follow it with a gritty song. He is literally a balance of style, substance, party, and thug sexuality. Treach also feels like he's got the battle MC template, but I get the sense that he would rather mash a brother out, and dis him physically. His body of work is a collage of well written radio friendly songs with street edge. His lyrical content is always filled with raw street innuendos, no matter how musical the song may be. He's mastered keeping the Hip-Hop love/sex songs street, and when he recorded a tribute song, "Mourn You Till I Join You," dedicated to the memory of his good friend Tupac, he still kept it raw.

> *Dear God times are changing*
> *And the weather got hot*
> *Over the past year, a lot of*
> *Nukkas wit props dropped*
> *So I thank you for my life*
> *And all that I got*
> *I wanna praise you*
> *And drop off a message to Pac*
> *I was sittin here*
> *Looking at ya picture my nukka*
> *Putting hash wit the weed*
> *Wit a mixture of liquor*
> *We can't kick it you ain't wit us*
> *Is the sh** I can't figure*
> *Nukka I miss ya*
> *Just know I'm gone' mourn you*
> *Til I'm wit ya*

The song goes on to chronicle when they met as roadies, and how they got high, stole weed, and sexed groupies. Through it all and true to his form, the song is extremely well written. You can get a clear picture of how he and Tupac got down. In closing, Treach's work is an example of everything that's hot about Hip-Hop. While the gangsta rap of the West Coast was emerging to dominate the Hip-Hop landscape in the early '90s, Treach, via Naughty By Nature, was making upbeat party anthems, while simultaneously representing the ghetto and reminding us that there are two sides of the street. For his skill level and his anthem writing acumen, Treach definitely goes down as one of the ALL TIME GREATS AMONG EMCEES!

Strength: Balancing big anthem styled hooks with hard-core, and many times substantive lyrics.

Weakness: Rhyme pitch. Because he uses the same pitch on every song, people miss how truly diverse he actually is.

Favorite Record: "OPP"

Favorite LP: *Nature's Fury*

#16: TREACH

ORIGINALITY: 90
Treach came out the gate doing his own thing with the cadence he and Latifah made famous for the whole Flavor Unit.

CONCEPTS: 85
Actually, "OPP" is one of the highest profile concept records ever.

VERSATILITY: 85
Treach is very diverse in the levels of writing that he does and the styles of records that he comes with.

VOCABULARY: 75
He uses vocabulary occasionally, but for the most part he does keep it relatively simple. He

doesn't get too intricate, but he does flip it on you every now and then.

SUBSTANCE: 85
He definitely gets into the gritty side of urban America and brings that across on wax.

FLOW: 90
He's one of the more stellar flow-ers in the game. Shifting gears, rapid fire, the whole nine.

FLAVOR: 85
He plays with his voice a lot better than a lot of emcees, especially for an emcee that works with that high volume of rapidity in his flow.

FREESTYLE ABILITY: 80
Better in terms of writing rhymes, but I heard him freestyle a couple of times and he does a nice job there as well.

VOCAL PRESENCE: 100
Absolutely one of the most recognizable voices in the history of the game.

LIVE PERFORMANCE: 95
One of the best in the game ever.

POETIC VALUE: 75
More rhyme over poetry, as it is with most emcees.

BODY OF WORK: 90

Quite frankly, a lot of people slept on that last album that they did.

INDUSTRY IMPACT: 75

They came and did their thing. From '91 to '93, he was the only thing that the East Coast had to hold onto in terms of dominance in the music, because the West Coast was dominating. Even though he doesn't get a lot of the accolades from the industry itself with awards, he definitely made an impact on the other side of the equation.

SOCIAL IMPACT: 70

He deals with those issues in his music, but his imagery and how he's viewed is more like an emcee than a "social icon."

LONGEVITY: 100

From '91, and still going.

LYRICS: 85

Treach is a lyricist, a flow man, and a flavor man.

BATTLE SKILLS: 80

Treach is absolutely a battle emcee, but I can't imagine him having too many conflicts that may not get to the real physicality of the equation.

TOTAL SCORE: 1,445

AVERAGE SCORE: 85

15

JAY-Z

KING OF THE STREETS

Muthafu***s say that I'm foolish
I only talk about jewels
Do you fools listen to music
Or do you just skim through it
See I'm influenced
By the ghetto you ruined
That same dude you gave nothin
I made something doin
What I do through in through in
I give you the news
Wit a twist it just his ghetto
Point of view
The renegade you been afraid
I penetrate pop culture
Bring 'em a lot closer to the block
Where they pop toasters
And they live wit' they moms
Got dropped roasters from
Boched robberies nukkas crouched over
Mommy's knocked up
Cause she wasn't watched over
Knocked down by some clown
When child support knock
No he's not around
Now how that sound ya
Now jot it down
I bring you through the ghetto
Wit out ridin' round hidin' down
Duckin' straysfrom frustrated youths
Stuck in their ways
Just read a magazine that
Fu***d up my day
How you rate music
That thugs with nothin' relate to it
I help them see their
Way through it not you
Can step in my pants
Can't walk in my shoes
Bet everything you worth
You'll lose ya tie and ya shirt

NO ONE IN THE HISTORY OF the rap game has ever locked the street down like Jay-Z. From 1997 to 2002, he has been the absolute king of the streets. He dropped nonstop hits, back to back to back. The only reason he wasn't the king in '96 was because Biggie was still here. Due to Biggie's untimely death, his reign was only three years and two albums deep. What Jay-Z has done is unprecedented in Hip-Hop on many levels. First of all, he damn near dropped ten albums in six years. Most of us have a hard time droppin' one album per year. Second, every album is platinum or multi-platinum. That feat speaks for itself. Third, he debuted #1 on the charts on back-to-back albums. That also speaks for itself. Finally, although not unprecedented, he headlined the "Hard Knock Life" tour. It was the first successful all Hip-Hop tour since the 1988 "Dope Jam" tour. There have been rappers in the game that were hotter than Jay-Z: Hammer in 1990, Run-DMC in 1986, Biggie in 1994, Eminem in 2002, and Lauryn Hill in 1998. But for a sustained heat of five years, no one's even close. LL has had a longer reign overall, but even his heat wanes from project to project.

Jay-Z's body of work is incredible. His mastery as an emcee is displayed best in the one area that only Tupac and Biggie could match, the art of record making. The reason I usually don't acknowledge this side of the game that much is because most emcees do not make their own music. My feeling is, how are you gonna talk about being the best emcee and then base it on having better records, when you're not making your own beats. That doesn't make sense. However, when you come back to back to back, Biggie, Tupac, and Jay-Z, then you have to consider that it's more about them than the music. Of course music is always the key, but it's what Jay-Z is doing on top of the music that's drawing the people in. His ability to shift flows is incredible. He's spit some of the slickest one-liners in the game. He's one of the first and only New York emcees to touch the Dirty South style of music and flow, and sound completely at home on it. Even Biggie didn't sound as comfortable as Jay-Z did when he tried the dirty flow. Part of the reason for this is before Jay-Z blew up, he was spitting in a faster, triple-tongue style flow. This was early in the '90s.

Most of what little flack Jay-Z gets is about his content being dominated with materialism. Although I agree that this is true, it is somewhat an exaggerated truth. The problem is what I call "audience energy association." This means that once you become successful, the audience relates to the energy of that success, and unless you match or supersede that success with another energy, the affiliation will always be with the most successful first impression. This is why Eddie Murphy can't make the transition into singing, and why Will Smith is viewed as an actor before he's viewed as a rapper. Jay-Z's energy is viewed as a successful hustler turned rapper. Even though the classical, lyrical emcee braggadocio is there, he's made too many references to what his struggle in the streets was. Therefore, the undercurrent of who he is is bigger than what he's saying. This is also reinforced by the sentiments of rooting for the hustler as the underdog when he's broke, because everyone can sympathize with the hunger, and then rooting against the hustler when he's rich, because when you're not hungry anymore it turns into what's perceived as greed. Unfortunately, Jay-Z doesn't help his case much by dropping so many money, car, diamond, and name-brand references in his rhymes. But one thing he is right about is the fact that occasionally he does flip the subject matter.

Gather round hustlers
That's if ya still livin'
And get on down to that ol' jig rhythm
Here's a couple of jewels
To get through ya bid in prison
A ribbon in the sky
Keep ya head high
I youn Vito, voice of the young people
Mouthpiece for hustlers
I'm back mothafu***s
Ya reign on the top
Was shorter than leprocauns
Y'all can't fu** wit' Hove
What type of ex y'all on
I got great lawyers for cops
So dress warm
Charges don't stick to dude he Teflon
I'm too sexy for jail
Like I'm right said Fred
I'm not guilty, now gimmi Baly my bread
Mr. District Attorney
I'm not sure if they told you
I'm on TV everyday
Where the fu** could I go to
Plus Hove don't run
Hove stand and fight
Hove a soldier, Hove been fightin'
All his life, what could you do to me
It's not new to me, sue me fu** you
What's a couple dollars to me
But you will respect me
Simple as that, or I got no problem
Going back
I'm representin' for the seat
Where Rosa Parks sat
Where Malcolm X was shot
Where Martin Luther was popped

Like so many emcees, the substance in Jay-Z gets convoluted in the duality of the imagery. In this rhyme, he starts out talking to his fraternal order of hustlers, and by the end he's tapping into and connecting himself to the legacies of some of our civil rights icons. I, as an emcee, still have to put some of this on the audience, because our society has been conditioned by the imagery and characteristics of a person, as opposed to the character of a person. So I have to remind you again, Jay-Z, like most true emcees, is not a one-dimensional character. If you listen to how he puts his words together, and the things he makes reference to outside of the street colloquialisms, you hear an extremely high level of worldly intelligence. In fact, I would go as far as saying I think that Jay-Z is dumbing it down for dollars. He's one of those emcees that feels like he's smarter than his core audience. Just my opinion! In summation, because this is a book about the emcees' skill and his or her impact based on that, I only talked about Jay-Z's flow, body of work, and his rhyme content. However, as a businessman with Roc-A-Fella Records and Rocawear clothing, Jay-Z is also in elite company. He's one of the few emcees that have super-seded the limitations that the business inherently imposes on the emcee. His uncompromising style and his musical approach make him a vanguard and one of the main reasons that hard-core Hip-Hop artists can have a place in prime time, mainstream America. That alone would make him one of the greats, but that combined with his unprecedented run on the streets makes Jay-Z truly ONE OF THE GREATEST EMCEES EVER IN THE GAME!

Strength: Hit-making. He understands how to make that street/radio record better than anybody.

Weakness: Inflection connotation. Because he flips flows so much, it's of primary importance to put the proper emphasis on the right words so the meaning of the rhyme isn't lost. Many times he puts the wrong em-PHA-sis on the wrong sy-LLAB-le. This, combined with the materialism, makes him seem monotonically one note.

Favorite Record: "It's All Right," "Give It To Me"

Favorite LP: *Life and Times S. Carter 2*

#15: JAY-Z

ORIGINALITY: 90

He started out flowing one way early in the equation but didn't really hit, but when he actually broke through, defined his sound and got his definition of who he was, it was on.

CONCEPTS: 80

He vacillates. Many people think money, cash, hoes is his style for the most part, but he sprinkles ballad-type records and mixes it up a little.

VERSATILITY: 85

Jay-Z will bring a different type of record into the equation. You can't say you know what type of record he's going to bring, although you may know what the subject matter may be.

VOCABULARY: 75

Keeps it simple and plain, and comes straight at you.

SUBSTANCE: 80

Just like most of the street cats, there's substance in the equation without question. On the other hand, there's a lot of materialism in Jay-

Z's work, but he doesn't just come with the one subject like a lot of people accuse him of.

FLOW: 90

He plays with and flips the flows, and he's the first New York emcee to master the Dirty South flow.

FLAVOR: 85

There's more on his later work. He's a lot more confident and comfortable and you hear the flavor coming through in his voice now.

FREESTYLE ABILITY: 95

The legend is he doesn't write, and if he's putting a lot of that down in the studio like he's doing on wax, that's freestyle quality off the top.

VOCAL PRESENCE: 90

One of the more recognizable voices in the game. Doesn't really project as sonically as some of the emcees, but he has a presence in his voice that's quite palpable.

LIVE PERFORMANCE: 80

He's gotten better than he was before. He had a high volume of hits but didn't bring it across that well in the early part of his game, but he got better later.

POETIC VALUE: 75

More rhyme than poetry.

BODY OF WORK: 100

Pound for pound, the best body of work in the Hip-Hop game right now. Five years, eight albums, incredible work.

INDUSTRY IMPACT: 95

He's basically living on the charts these days. Whether or not he gets awards and accolades, which he's now starting to get, he has a huge industry impact.

SOCIAL IMPACT: 80

He's viewed as a hustler on wax, but there's a success story on another level, so there is some kind of inspiration behind the thought process.

LONGEVITY: 75

He hit in '95 to '96 and he's been going strong ever since, and he's still going. We'll see if he makes it to the ten-year mark.

LYRICS: 90

Jay-Z is a lyricist. You have to listen to him because he has a couple of problems on the inflection part of the game, but he is one of the more lyrical emcees in the game.

BATTLE SKILLS: 85

Did pretty cool on the "Takeover" record. I think he's got more personal than skill level, but you can tell he has the battle emcee template. On one level, it just doesn't seem to be his forte, but he's still hot with it anyway.

TOTAL SCORE: 1,450

AVERAGE SCORE: 85.2

THE 10 BEST HIP-HOP ARTISTS TODAY (ARTISTICALLY SPEAKING)

1) **Eminem**   Most Well-Rounded Emcee
2) **Missy Elliott**   Most Entertaining
3) **Ja Rule**   Best Songwriter
4) **Jay-Z**   King of the Streets
5) **Nas**   Most Prolific
6) **DMX**   The Rawest Ever
7) **Eve**   Sexy and Skilled
8) **Baby**   All About the Money
9) **Nelly**   Hit Maker
10) **Puffy**   Master Marketer

These are the best overall Hip-Hop artists for 2002–2003.

14

KOOL G RAP

LORD OF THE UNDERGROUND

I'm bad to the bone
Wit a style like Al Capone
I'm a smile while I give you
The dial tone
Eatin' shrimp and girls I be pimpin'
Walk like I'm limpin'
This brother ain't simpin'
Not to mention a winner of
Mack Daddy conventions
I get a lot of attention
Sleepin' in sheets
That's made of satin
Wit' one of my money makin' honey's
She's mixed Spanish and Latin
She's a fly type of swinger
20 karats on her fingers
minks on every coat hanger
in a high rise made for only fly guys
wit' a size that attracts the ladies eyes
keepin' a stash and a cash flow
profiles kept low
more Doe than Barry Mannilow
fly cars I got diamonds in jelly jars
to earn respect, collectin' bar fight scars
slick talkin' wit' a chick when I'm walkin'
midnight stalkin'
all those suckers be hawkin'
and I max while you be
waxin' your Cadillacs
smooth as a sax
but I can cut you like an axe
big spender cause I'm a winner
like Bruce Jenner, all beginners
and let'em simmer like a TV dinner
on a throne cause I'm hard like stone
holdin' my own
cause I'm bad to the bone

KOOL G RAP IS THE PROGENITOR and prototype for Biggie, Jay-Z, Treach, Nore, Fat Joe, Big Pun, and about twenty-five more hard-core emcees. And if you go back and listen, you'll see that he's truly the most lyrical of them all. Biggie's got the story-telling and the flow, others may have the record-making skills over him, but as far as straight-up lyrics, only Big Pun comes close. Kool G Rap murders hard-core tracks. If you just pick up his latest, greatest hits you'll hear hard-core metaphors back to back at such a high speed you'll have to keep rewinding just to appreciate and keep up with what he said.

Everything about Kool G Rap is hard-core: his voice, his energy, his cadence, his inflections, his subject matter, and his metaphors all sound like he's trying to commit a verbal homicide. The biggest difference between Kool G Rap and most of the other hard-core hustlers or gangsta rappers is Kool G Rap is a lyricist first. Many times the thug rhyme style uses violent content to hide the fact that there's not a whole lot going on in the lyrical department. With Kool G Rap, he's bustin' you up so much lyrically that the content is secondary. In that sense he's the exact opposite of Jay-Z. The perception of Kool G Rap is he's an emcee that turned hustler because the rap money wasn't enough. The other major difference between Kool G Rap and the street thug emcee is G Rap only referenced bodily harm in rhyme form, while many of today's hard-core rappers make threats of killing people between the verses, on interludes, and out of the context of a rhyme. Their focus is to let you know that they're serious about their threats. Although that may help their personas or sell records "It Ain't Got Nothin to Do Wit Rhymin."

Kool G Rap is also like the inverse of Jay-Z and Treach, because he has never been able to experience any of the high-level chart success. He made records for the streets, but because he was so lyrical, only future emcees and lyrical junkies could really appreciate what he was doing. He never chose the commercially musical tracks, or made the types of records that would have gotten him any type of airplay. Even when he made songs geared to women, they were sex songs like "Talk Like Sex" and the hook was "Rated X-X-X." In the song, he makes reference to breaking the bedpost, pounding like a jackhammer until her eyes pop out, and sending her home in a wheelchair, quite the romantic night on the town. However, by making these kinds of hard-core records exclusively, Kool G Rap built a reputation among true hard-core Hip-Hop fans that still resonates strongly today. His most popular songs are "Ill Street Blues," "Road To Riches," and one of the all-time Hip-Hop classic posse records, "The Symphony." However, pound for pound, the most lyrical record he ever made was "Men At Work." This record is an excellent example of what true freestyle really was. Before the '90s it was about how hard you could come with a written rhyme with no particular subject matter and no real purpose other than showing your lyrical prowess. Believe me, on this record Kool G Rap took it past the point of no return. One verse, the first, is actually sixty-eight bars. That alone obliterates the fundamentals of song structure. He took old-school freestyling to one of the highest levels I've ever heard. Also in his repertoire is a gritty, cautionary song, "Rikers Island," warning hustlers about the realities of jail life.

Listen to me ya young hoods
This is some advice
You do the crime
You payin' the price
Cause if you're in the drug stop
Sellin' crack on the block

Snatchin' chains bustin' brains
Like a real hard rock
If ya ever hear a cop
Say ya under arrest
Go out just like atrooper
Stick out ya chest
Cause ya might've been robbin'
Ya might've been wil'n
But you won't be smiling
On Rikers Island
Just to hear the name
It makes ya spine tingle
This is a jungle
Where the murders mingle
They say the place is crowded
But its room for you
Whether ya white or ya black
You'll be black and blue
Cause in every cell block
There is a hard rock
With a real nice device
That's called a sock lock
Don't ever get caught
In a crime my friend
Cause this bus trip is not
To adventures end

Kool G Rap was cool with storytelling, but his true shine was spittin' lyrical fire. All in all he did his thing at a low level commercially, and at the highest level lyrically. I think that if he could have figured out a way to make hit records with his street edge, he would be highly recognized in everybody's Top Ten rappers. Had he come out today with DMX, Jay-Z, and Eminem, with the way the lyrical landscape is, he would have been able to do the same types of records he always did, and he would have more intense production and would have shined with today's best. However, what he's already done is enough for those who know. Kool G Rap IS ONE OF THE TRUE, GREATEST EMCEES.

Strength: Lyrical terrorism. He always put lyrics first and music second.

Weakness: Hit formula-less. He never found the balance of how to pull back lyrically to get out of the way of the music. Without this he couldn't make bigger hits.

Favorite Record: "Men At Work," "Road to Riches"

Favorite LP: *Wanted Dead Or Alive*

#14: KOOL G RAP

ORIGINALITY: 95

The prototype for most of the hard-core, street, hustler, player-style rhymes that are going on today.

CONCEPTS: 85

He's definitely conceptual within that concept. He didn't stray too much from it, but he was one of the first urban, ghetto storytellers on the gritty side of the equation.

VERSATILITY: 75

He didn't fluctuate too much from the subject matter. He did his thing within the subject matter and could flip the flows.

VOCABULARY: 95

He just uses words at a high level.

SUBSTANCE: 80

Urban street rhymes, hustler mentality, put it into the equation.

FLOW: 95

His flow is incredible.

FLAVOR: 80

He doesn't do a lot with his voice, but he does change up depending on what type of record he's coming on.

FREESTYLE ABILITY: 85

"Men At Work" is a classic example of what an old-style freestyle is and it's one of the best I've ever heard. Don't know how well he comes off the top of the head, but his score is based on the real old-school freestyle.

VOCAL PRESENCE: 95

One of the absolutely most recognizable voices in the game. Cuts to tape harshly. You hear his voice sonically.

LIVE PERFORMANCE: 85

Even without a hot body of work, when Kool G Rap puts it down, live he comes with it. He's one of those energetic emcees, and he's one of the few lyricists that can pull off a live show well.

POETIC VALUE: 75

More rhymes than poetry. Even though he does sprinkle a little bit of poetic styles in there, he's more of a rhymer than a poet.

BODY OF WORK: 85

He doesn't have a whole lot of hits in his volume, but he absolutely does his thing by the way he brings it across. He puts work into it.

INDUSTRY IMPACT: 75

Not a lot of accolades, not a lot of recognition, but he influenced so many emcees that came out with the style that they patterned on his.

SOCIAL IMPACT: 70

Outside of Hip-Hop, he's not really recognized, but based on the people in Hip-Hop that do recognize him, he's respected.

LONGEVITY: 85

From late '87 he did his thing into the mid-'90s, did another album recorded with Nas. Eight-and-a-half years.

LYRICS: 100

He's one of the most lyrical emcees of all of the so-called gangsta emcees.

BATTLE SKILLS: 95

He's like a lyrical terrorist. Not too many people would want to even attempt to see Kool G Rap.

TOTAL SCORE: 1,455

AVERAGE SCORE: 85.5

13

TUPAC
THE TRUTH

Out on bail, fresh out of jail
California dreamin'
Soon as I step on the scene
I'm hearin' hoochies screamin'
Phenin for money and alcohol
The life of a Westside playa
Where cowards die and the strong ball
Only in Cali will we riot
Not rally to live and die
In LA we wearin' Chucks not Bally's
Just in Loc's and Khacky suits
And ride is what we do
Flossin' but have caution
With other crews
Famous because we programmed
Worldwide let 'em recognize
From Long Beach to Rosecrance
Bumpin' and grindin'
Like a slow jam
It's Westside so you know
The Row won't bow down to no man
Say what you say
But gimme that bomb beat from Dre
Let me serenade the streets of LA
From Oakland to Sac town
The Bay Area and back down
Cali is where they put they
Mack down
Gimme Love

TUPAC AMARU SHAKUR IS THE ALL-TIME, number one Hip-Hop artist. There are emcees, rappers, and Hip-Hop artists, when it comes to rockin' the microphone. Some of us are all three, and most of us are better in one aspect than the other. Tupac was a great emcee, and an even better rapper, but ultimately he was the greatest artist. He was the embodiment of unlimited artistry. Where Will Smith is in songwriting, and Jay-Z is in record making, Tupac is a master of both. Believe me, the two are not synonymous. There are great records that are not great songs, and there are great songs that are not great records. Tupac is such a good songwriter that even in death, all producers have to do is add music. The way he structures his lyrical content evokes a mood that tells you what type of music should accompany him.

Tupac's legacy is so multilayered that almost anything I say wouldn't be enough. The reason for that is he did the one thing that makes an entertainer or public figure unbeatable. He connected. Not only did he connect, but he connected on a level so personal that he felt like he was representing the listeners that he was connecting to. There are many emcees that rhyme better and are better lyricists than Tupac, but none can touch listeners on a mass level like Tupac did. What was so unique about him was he was like the Hip-Hop everyman! He was sex symbol to the ladies, and thug homie to the fellas. Because he was more of an artist than just an emcee, he took chances on making the types of records most emcees wouldn't dare to. He exposed himself in ways that took the mystique out of whatever you might have thought it meant to be an emcee. Trust me, I was there from the beginning of the lyrical emcees. Part of your whole game was to be able to create an aura of awe. The whole point of being a lyricist was to be able to wow a crowd with your words and your essence. Why do you think we had such colorful names: Furious, Fearless, Grandmaster, Treacherous, Cold Crush, and Mean Machine, just to name a few. Tupac obliterated this; he was truly the "real" in keeping it real. Ice-T and Ice Cube were respected, but Tupac was the first West Coast rapper *loved* on both coasts. Most of the true Hip-Hop heads didn't think he was that tight lyrically, but the fact that this hard-core emcee would come out of the gate with a record like "Brenda's Got A Baby," a song about teenage pregnancy, the respect level for him was so high, we had to love him. It was like a curve ball of reality. The title of the album was *2pacalypse Now* and we thought, "Thug emcee gives a prophesy of Armaggedon." Instead, we got sensitivity. Then the next album drops, *Strictly 4 My N.I.G.G.A.Z.*, OK now we're gonna get the thug style, right? Wrong, he drops "Keep Ya Head Up," an inspirational song for single mothers. Once again we can all relate and we gotta love him. Finally, to complete the trilogy, he drops the album *Me Against The World*, and for the coup de grace he drops the single "Dear Mama."

When I was young
Me and my mama had beef
17 years old kicked out on the streets
though back at the time
I never thought I'd see her face
Ain't no woman alive
That could take my mommas place
Suspended from school
I'm scared to go home
I was a fool wit' the big boys
Breakin' all the rules
I shed tears wit' my baby sister
Over the years we was
Poorer than other little kids
And even though we had
Different daddies
The same drama
When things went wrong
We blamed mama
I reminisce on the stress I caused
It was hell huggin' on my mama

From a jail cell
And who'd think in elementary
Hey, I'd see the penitentiary
One day, runnin' from the police
That's right, mamma catch me
Put a whippin' to my backside
And even as a crack fiend momma
Ya always was a Black Queen momma
I finally understand, for a woman
It ain't easy tryin' to raise a man
You always was committed
A porr single mother on welfare
Tell me how you did it
There's no way I could pay you back
But the plan is to show you that I understand
You are appreciated

At that point I realized we had a genius on our hands. Tupac took the one-dimensional, one-note, syrupy Hip-Hop love song and went deeper. Most emcees only dealt with the love or sexual aspects of a woman in a romantic context. Tupac ingeniously dealt with their maternal side. By the time we figured out what was going on, Tupac was literally a Hip-Hop superstar. His turbulent life outside of his music career heightened his stardom. The fan base that he built with women was unprecedented. It went beyond the usual teenage appeal. His songs touched a chord in older women because of their universal messages. He built just as much of a solid base of male fans that appreciated and related to the struggles he went through as a young black man in America. Outside of the maternally designed songs for women, Tupac also showed a high level of caring, concern, and consciousness for life in ghetto America. He felt like one of us, articulately speaking for all of us. His willingness to vulnerably tell you about his life to the extent of exposing his mother's crack problem, and then apologizing for not understanding, made it almost impossible not to root for him. This was a man baring his soul, and because nothing was contrived, he became more touchable and more tangible than any other emcee in the game.

Of course being as ambivalent as he was, there was a dark side. He constantly made references to his own death, and in his feud with his one-time friend, Notorious B.I.G., Tupac could show a venom that was the antithetical equivalent of his impassioned songs for women. In fact, when he made the song "Hit 'em Up," a song calling for the death of Biggie and Mobb Deep, it was the first time I heard some of his fans turn on him. It wasn't about picking a side; it was just that it was more hate than they had ever heard from the rapper they most revered. Many of the people that I talked to at the time said that the record had an eerie feeling to it. Frankly, it felt like death.

However, ending on a positive note, Tupac was that next level emcee. He had a depth and honesty to him that came across so clearly that he was the most revered emcee in the history of the game. His rhyme style was melodic, and the doubling of his voice gave him a chanting-type quality to his songs. He probably has the most diverse body of work in the history of the game, and pound for pound he might be the most substantive emcee in the history of the game. Other than Chuck D, and maybe Melle Mel, I don't know of another emcee that hit with the intensity that Tupac hit regarding social commentary. KRS-One also did this well, but Tupac was more selfless, and made much more universally commercial records. The bottom line is Tupac is one of a kind, and his contributions to the game make him, without a doubt, ONE OF THE TRUE GREATEST EMCEES EVER.

Strength: Diverse work. The only emcee that sounds just about perfect speaking on any subject.

Weakness: Death talk. I'll never be able to prove it, but I think because he made so many references to his death, he brought the energy to him, and manifested his own death. He could have put the energy into being more lyrical.

Favorite Record: "California Love," "Keep Ya Head Up"

Favorite LP: *All Eyes On Me*

#13: TUPAC

ORIGINALITY: 85

Based on the timing, as usual, it was a lot harder for the next level artist in the '90s to get a lot of originality points unless they came with something extremely original, and Tupac was a mixture and amalgamation of gangsta rap and social rap, kind of like Public Enemy and N.W.A. I gave him an 85 because he brought his own essence to the equation anyway.

CONCEPTS: 95

He is definitely one of the most conceptual emcees in the game.

VERSATILITY: 100

Probably the most versatile emcee, based on the types of records he made and the types of subjects he's talked about.

VOCABULARY: 70

He kept it pretty much straightforward. He didn't really get intricate with the vocabulary.

SUBSTANCE: 95

Tupac was damn near all substance. The only reason I didn't give him a 100 is because on "Hit 'em Up" he was talking about killing people and people dying from sickle cell. But he is definitely one of the most substantive emcees in the game.

FLOW: 80

Basically, he kept it simple, kept it plain and effective, but he definitely could flow.

FLAVOR: 85

The double that he added to his voice in his vocal inflections on his records was unique.

FREESTYLE: 85

He gets 85. With his energy and the way he rhymes, and how he brought it and put it down, he definitely could freestyle pretty good.

VOCAL PRESENCE: 95

Without question, one of the most recognizable voices in the game, and again, doubling his records on wax made it sound even more powerful.

LIVE PERFORMANCE: 90

Tupac definitely had a lot of energy onstage. He had a lot of hit records, too. They say the hit records do the heavy lifting, but he definitely carried it over well. He translated his energy well.

POETIC VALUE: 85

A lot of his rhymes were straight poetry, just in terms of the subject matter and how he approached it.

BODY OF WORK: 100!

I put an exclamation point next to this because he sold more records in death than he did alive. That is a testament to what he did lyrically. The body of work has to count on some level for the music, but what he did lyrically people were able to use enough to actually put on tracks after he passed.

INDUSTRY IMPACT: 100

Like I said, I don't think there has been an emcee in the game that has been as revered as Tupac, ever! That just says it all.

SOCIAL IMPACT: 95

He is also one of the few emcees that connected on such a level that he crossed into the pop side as well as the R&B and Hip-Hop world. He connected with a lot of people. He felt like he was representing urban America.

LONGEVITY: 75!

He got five to six years out of himself alive, an unfortunate untimely death did what it did, but his records are still selling today. So I put an exclamation point next to it, because he is still selling records to this day.

LYRICS: 75

Tupac wasn't really that lyrical, but he was lyrical enough to get the point across. Just not that intricate. More simplistic in the lyrical side.

BATTLE SKILLS: 70

Again, based on the song "Hit 'em Up" it didn't seem like he really, really had the energy to do the battle. He seemed more mad than skilled.

TOTAL SCORE: 1,480

AVERAGE SCORE: 87

THE 10 FUTURE HALL OF FAMERS

1) DMX   My Personal Favorite/The Rawest Ever

2) Eminem   The Most Well Rounded In The Game

3) Canibus   The Deadliest Lyricist Today

4) Mos Def   The Most Depth

5) Eve   The Triple Threat—Lyrics, Flow, Sexy As Hell

6) Jadakiss   Air To The Street Throne

7) Lady of Rage The Ruggedest Female I've Ever Heard

8) Talib Kweli Only For The True Listener

9) Rah Digga   The Rawness (Rawhiness)

10) Ludacris   MC For The Records

(Too Early To Tell)

50 Cent

G-Dep

Camron

Beanie Sigel

Memphis Bleek

Nore

Dra-Gon

These emcees are already among the greats, but they haven't got the time under their belts for the longevity.

12

QUEEN
LATIFAH

It's time to broaden your thought
The king and queen is on the set the
Competitions petty and ready to step
To the first one go 'head rehearse one
I hope ya don't know
You sound like the worse one
Rhymes are smokin'
Concentration can't be broken
Queen Latifah's out spoken
Use your imagination picture this
Any male or female rapper
Tryin to dis
Kill for excitement and enticement
When my competitors killed
I go build with my enlightment
Teach the youth feed the needy
Confident a descendant
Of Queen Nefertiti
The mother of civilization
Will rise like the cream
And still build a strong foundation
Secondary but necessary to
Reproduce, acknowledge the fact
That I'm Black and I don't lack
Queen Latifah's givin you a piece of
My mind, a rhyme spoken
By a feminine teacher

NEVER HAS A NAME BEFIT A person so well as "Queen" befits Latifah. Run-DMC *became* kings, Latifah was *born* Queen. From the very first time I heard her, she felt like royalty. Her braggadocio sounded more confident and truthful than arrogant and fantastical. Her vocal presence was deeper than any female emcee I'd ever heard. This automatically gave her an edge that female rappers hadn't been able to achieve. She was instantly viewed as someone that you had to take seriously, and she felt like she could do some damage in a battle. Her delivery was flavorful and threatening. Her attitude came across as if she didn't really care whether or not you loved her or hated her, because ultimately, you were going to respect her. She made it clear that no disrespect would be tolerated. This was all done musically and lyrically before any visual impression had been made. The buzz on the street created a curiosity about who this new female force was, and what she looked like. Finally the album *All Hail the Queen* came out and the videos dropped. Latifah superseded all expectations. She wasn't only a queen, she was an Egyptian goddess. She wore head wraps and African crowns that made her look like the deified, regal head of a new Hip-Hop army. The album was filled with a diverse range of Hip-Hop sounds that combined reggae, house, classic soul, R&B, funk, and hard-core

Hip-Hop tracks. However, the one thing that was consistent with just about every song on the album was that it had some level of consciousness. This only added to the regal, royal air. With song titles like "Queen of Royal Badness" and "Wrath of My Madness" there was a connotation that the force of god was behind her royalty. Her album cover was also a statement. An image in the shape of the continent of Africa in black was circled by her name and the album title in red and green, representing the colors of the Black American flag. While Latifah, dressed in a black and bronze military styled outfit, complete with a queen-like head wrap and knee high boots, struck a pose reminiscent of Marcus Garvey. It looked as if she intended for you to salute her if you even looked at the album.

Latifah let it be known from the beginning that she was here on a mission. She instantly upgraded the lyrical landscape perception of what a female emcee was about. Sha-Rock was the first female emcee truly respected for her skills; Salt-'N-Pepa were respected for being skilled, sexy, and classy; MC Lyte was respected for her skills, flavor, and battle ability; but Queen Latifah was the only female emcee at the time who was viewed as a social/political figure. Much like Chuck D and KRS-One, Latifah had lots of political and social commentary in her music. Her song "Evil That Men Do" was part social and part political. She also was able to deal with sexist issues in a seemingly more intellectual, rather than emotional, manner. This caused her to be viewed as an anti-sexist rather than a feminist. I can clearly remember some very conservative women who didn't care for rap music that completely reversed their opinions because of Latifah. Even those who never came around on the music still loved her and what she represented.

By 1991, Latifah was a solid Hip-Hop mainstay with a reputation as strong as any of the icons of the time. When she released her second album, *Nature of a Sister* the album wasn't received as well as the first. Latifah took chances creatively, and many of the fans seemed confused. I got the sense that they were looking for a more hard-core, edgy sound. Instead what they got was a more artistic, adult slice of Latifah's energy. The common mistake that was made by the fans was they had her pigeonholed as a certain type of artist based on her first works. However, like many Hip-Hop artists, there were too many levels to Latifah's creativity for her to ever be pigeonholed. She sang, wrote, acted, and started her own management company, Flavor Unit. Little did we know at the time, but 1991 to 1993 was a harbinger of things to come for the Queen. She starred in her own sitcom, made appearances in movies, and in 1993 she released her third album *Black Reign*, with the inspirational hit "U.N.I.T.Y." where she called for unity between men and women based on women demanding respect and men giving respect.

Instinct leads me to another flow
Everytime I hear a brother
Call a girl a bitch or a hoe
Tryin to make a sister feel low
You know all of that's gots to go
Now everybody knows there's
Exceptions to this rule
I don't be getting mad
When we playin it's cool

But don't you be callin me
Out my name
I bring wrath to those
Who disrespect me like a dame
That's why I'm talking
One day I was walkin down the block
I had my cut off shorts on
Right cause it was crazy hot
I walk past these dudes
When they passed me
One of 'em felt my booty
He was nasty
I turned around red
Somebody was catchin the rag
Then the little one said
"yeah me bitch" and laughed
since he was wit his boys
he tried to break fly
huh, I punched him dead in
his eye and said
who you callin a bitch!

Latifah struck the perfect balance using examples of first-hand stories to convey the message without being preachy. Ultimately, she was rewarded with a Grammy for the song. Suddenly the fans got it: Latifah, like Tupac, Will Smith, and a few others, was more than rap music. She wasn't limited to the invisible boundaries of Hip-Hop perception. She was purely an artist, and Hip-Hop was her core.

In the final analysis, Queen Latifah's impact on Hip-Hop is unquestionable. She is one of only two artists in Hip-Hop history (Will Smith is the other) to acquire both a Grammy and an Oscar nomination. That alone puts her over the top. But it's her consciousness and her lyrical skill level that makes Queen Latifah ONE OF THE TRUE GREATEST EMCEES EVER.

Strength: Duality. She's part singer and part rapper. She can actually sing her own hooks on key!

Favorite Record: "Wrath of my Madness"

Favorite LP: *All Hail the Queen*

Weakness: Talent excess. Because she was so good at things outside of rapping, fans were left unfulfilled with her rhyme output. After the first album, we never got to hear her spit it at that level again.

#12: QUEEN LATIFAH

ORIGINALITY: 90

Latifah definitely came and brought her own

style to the equation. She basically was doing the style of rhymes that was at the landscape at the time and she brought her own energy to it.

CONCEPTS: 90

Latifah absolutely was trying to make bigger records than just rap records. If you just listen all the way back through her whole career, right from the beginning she was mixing reggae and jazz. She was all over the place on the conceptual side.

VERSATILITY: 95

The fact that she sings and raps, and everybody knows that she is acting now, she set the template for Lauryn Hill to follow.

VOCABULARY: 70

Latifah basically kept it simple. You can tell that she does have a vocabulary, but she seems to be one of those emcees that doesn't choose to utilize excess vocabulary in her rhyme style.

SUBSTANCE: 95

Without question, Latifah is absolutely one of the most substantive emcees in the game. Period. It's just who she is.

FLOW: 90

She was just incredible. Her cadence, her energy, the way she flows and flips it is incredible.

FLAVOR: 90

She plays with her voice, using it like an instrument or a tool. She definitely has lots of flavor.

FREESTYLE: 80

Queen Latifah freestyled a couple of times off the top of the head. She doesn't really take it that seriously, but she could do it in her sleep because that's just how good she is.

VOCAL PRESENCE: 90

One of the most recognizable voices without question. That why she's on the Greatest list.

LIVE PERFORMANCE: 90

Once again, Latifah definitely comes and stomps the show out when she does it live.

POETIC VALUE: 80

She does more rhyme than poetry. However, she got very, very poetical when she was doing the singing thing. So it's kind of like a mixture in the way she would approach the poetic value.

BODY OF WORK: 80

The first album was absolutely, to me, her apex. The following two albums felt more like she was trying to find a voice. She had a voice, but she was trying to find a flow to do what she wanted to do, because again, I could feel her pressing to expand beyond just what people thought conventional Hip-Hop was. She still got the job done pretty well, and she got a Grammy for it on the third album.

INDUSTRY IMPACT: 90

She is the first female emcee that was really, really taken seriously and respected on another level. So she impacted the industry just on that alone. And like I said, winning a Grammy . . . that's enough to get you the points.

SOCIAL IMPACT: 100

She was absolutely affiliated with being the most positive female image in Hip-Hop history at the time. From this point on, she is looked at as a very, very classy queen.

LONGEVITY: 100!

Latifah is still going to this day. With the TV show, and doing the records, and the music for the TV show, and soundtracks, she is just all over the place, still doing her thing.

LYRICS: 90

Latifah is a straight lyricist. Whenever she chooses to do it, she does it. A lot of times she tones it down for the singing fad, but it is what it is.

BATTLE SKILLS: 80

Latifah definitely has had battle rhymes already. I don't think she's really been tested because nobody wants to test the Queen. Everybody loves her.

TOTAL SCORE: 1,500

AVERAGE SCORE: 88.2

10 BEST STORYTELLERS

1) **Slick Rick**	The Best
2) **Biggie**	Most Visual Ever
3) **Scarface**	Ghetto Griot
4) **Nas**	Prophetic Dreamer
5) **Ice Cube**	The News Breaker
6) **Will Smith**	Motivator
7) **LA Sunshine**	Shinin' On Stage
8) **Kid Creole**	The First Hype Man
9) **Dana Dane**	Comedic Wit
10) **Biz Markie**	Comedic Irony

This is one of the most important and most underrated aspects of emceeing.

11

NAS
THE GHETTO PROPHET

It's a thin line between
Paper and hate friends and snakes
Nine milli's and 38's
Hell or the pearly gates
I was destined to come
Predicted blame God
He blew breath in my lungs
Second to none
Wiked turn wives to widows
Shoot through satin pillows
The desolate one
Took a little time to claim my spot
Chairman of the board
Until this game stop
And I side with the Lord
Ride for the cause
While drivin nukkas
Shot at my doors
Plottin I'm sure to catch me
With they glocks to my jaws
Try stickin me up
But I flipped on these ducks
Instead of me ambulances
Were pick'n 'em up
Nukkas fear what they don't understand
Hate what they can't conquer
Guess it's just the fury of man
Became a monster
On top of the world
Never fallin
I'm as real as they come
From day one forever ballin

IF YOU WANT IT LYRICAL, STREET, and spiritual, Nas is your man. Nas is truly a ghetto griot. He is one of the best poignant storytellers in Hip-Hop. What's unique about Nas as a storyteller is that he does it as a lyricist. As most Hip-Hop aficionados know, most lyricists are not truly great storytellers, and most storytellers are not really lyrical. Although many emcees do both, Nas is one of the few that do both at an extremely high level. In 1994, he dropped his first album, *Illmatic*, and immediately the Hip-Hop press was calling him the next Rakim. This, in my opinion, was very unfortunate. It created an atmosphere of confusion and conflict that was unnecessary. The first problem was that Nas, although very good, was nowhere near the level of lyrical proficiency of Rakim at the time. The second problem was we didn't know if this was a marketing ploy to hype record sales, or if Nas was actually feeling like that himself. The final problem was, if it was a marketing play, the expectations would be too high, and the criticism would have been too hard.

However, none of it mattered. Nas had the goods. By his second and third albums everybody knew he wasn't the second coming of Rakim, he was the first coming of Nas. He had his own unique flow, which seemed to start the trend that we old-school emcees call the "off-beat conversational flow." Before Nas, every emcee focused on rhyming with a cadence that ultimately put the words that rhymed on beat with the snare drum. Nas created a style of rapping that was more conversational than ever before. Although KRS-One was one of the first truly conversational emcees, he still used an intensity and lyrical attack that was more conventional than what Nas was doing. Nas almost totally eliminated the intensity and changed the way most rappers that came after him would rhyme.

This was the beginning of the third generation of the three lyrical kings (Biggie, Jay-Z, and Nas). Of the three, Nas was truthfully the most cerebral. While Biggie was the potent intensity, and Jay-Z the flashy slick flavor, Nas seemed to be more spiritually inclined and more well read within that context. In 1999 he released his album *I Am*, and for me it confirmed what I thought about his spiritual inclinations. On the streets, however, the title seemed to have a different connotation. A few years back, Jay-Z made reference to the streets, asking who was the best among Biggie, Nas, and himself. Five years and many innuendos later, many fans thought that Nas was answering, "I Am." I think they totally missed the real meaning. I think that Nas was using a biblical reference to esoterically profess his connection to God. Nonetheless, on the streets, when it comes to Hip-Hop, sometimes the perception becomes the reality, and by the end of 2001 Nas and Jay-Z were in the second most popular battle in Hip-Hop history, the "King of the Streets" vs. "The Streets Prophet."

What was interesting to me was the fans showing their fickle nature. They overestimated, underestimated, and ultimately overreacted. First, because of Jay-Z's unprecedented five-year dominance, the fans overestimated his "touchability." They thought that he was untouchable. Second, because of Nas' seemingly cerebral, spiritual, lyrical calm, the fans underestimated his ability to get gritty. And finally, when it was all said and done, after hearing both emcee's records, the prevailing consensus was, "Nas killed Jay-Z." This is an exaggeration, also based on perception. Most fans had prejudged this contest so wrongly that they overreacted.

When you go back and listen to those records back to back, you'll see it was a little closer than you might have originally thought. In my opinion, Jay-Z had the better record, "Take Over," and Nas had the sharper lyrics. Even Nas' title, "Ether," was more esoteric than the average one might expect for a battle record. Ultimately, because a battle is about the emcee and the lyrics and not the music, Nas was the winner! Although Jay-Z came back with another answer, because he made a reference to a child in the song, many fans thought he stepped out of bounds, and it made him look momentarily weak. This heightened the perception of what Nas had done to him through battle. Nas seemed to have the psychological edge.

This goes back to something I always said about battles. Never underestimate a true lyricist, because in a battle, it's more about the lyrics than anything else. Furthermore, Nas is a true lyricist that's also spiritual lyrically. Spiritual energy usually heightens your lyrical ability, and that is almost an unbeatable combo in battle. This is why KRS-One is virtually invincible! Nas is like a Kung Fu master. By that I mean he's like a teacher that really knows how to fight, but he'd rather teach the art. This is very evident in the work on his last album, *God's Son*. The title once again says it all. You can almost tell just what you're going to get in the album just by reading the title.

> They can't break me or shake me
> They too fake to come kill me
> Think their faith is with Satan
> They mistake me I'm filthy
> Rich off the ghetto medleys
> So now they wanna dead me
> It's gonna be a murder
> Confront me them burners are empty
> Middle passage I made it
> I'm from the land of David
> The Nazarene of Bethlehem
> They had me wrapped in blankets
> Y'all bunch of backward gangsters
> Y'all signin' affidavits
> Snitches and smiling faces
> Got you blowin trial I hate this
> Hopin my child can see through this
> Tryin to be a good daddy
> I was there when she was born
> She'll be there when I'm buried
> Kind of weird and it's scary
> All my years have prepared me
> What I fear is my temper
> I see clear to the center
> Right through a mans soul
> Straight through his eyes
> Straight to his heart
> I'm still alvive
> How did I make it this far
> Cause I've been high I've been low
> Searchin for a way to go
> Every single night I pray
> And Lord I'm on this battle ground
> Lost just waiting to be found
> I guess it's the warriors way

Right now, Nas is somewhere else. He's on another level. Although his body of work has been solid for nine years, he has never done an album as diverse as *God's Son*. The subject matter and the lyrical content is definitely more thought-provoking than ever before. He has slipped into that rare zone that Tupac, Latifah, and few others have slipped into. He's now starting to be viewed as a voice for the culture, rather than a voice of the culture. His lyrical game was always tight, but he even stepped up the flow. For the first time other than on the songs "Ether," and "Hate Me Now," you can feel the passion coming out of him throughout the whole album.

In conclusion, there are a lot of hot emcees right now that are finally enjoying high levels of success and making lots of money. Unfortunately, too many of them don't have anything to say of any value. Nas is the antithesis of those emcees. He has a lot to say, and he says it well, and I'm glad that he's lasted long enough to see the real money in the game. Right now, Nas is at the top of his game, and as far as emcees go today, Nas is the best emcee. And the rule is, if you are ever the best emcees in this game at any point, you are automatically one of the greats. NAS IS ONE OF THE GREATEST.

Strength: Street level lyrics. Nas always keeps his lyrics at a street level, so it never feels like he's talking down to people.

Weakness: Undynamic. Many fans don't catch the lyrical nuances he brings because there's no vocal explosion in the inflections of the cadence. Combine that with his unorthodox flow, and many times he loses listeners, because his rhymes can become inconspicuous.

Favorite Record: "Hate Me Now," "They Shootin'"

Favorite LP: *Stillmatic*

#11: NAS

ORIGINALITY: 90

Nas brought his own style to the equation. Basically he was not too far outside of the scope of what was already being done, but he brought his own energy.

CONCEPTS: 95

He definitely got much more conceptual as he went along in his career. Nas, the conceptual MC. Storytelling is a part of the conceptual mastery thing.

VERSATILITY: 85

He also makes records in a variety of styles. He will throw R&B acts on the hook. And it's not just the R&B acts in the hook. With "If I Ruled the World" with Lauryn Hill there was a social commentary in there.

VOCABULARY: 85

You can just hear him. He sprinkles the vocabulary. He sprinkles it in with a lot of the street vocabulary. So he keeps it street and intelligent at the same time. He definitely uses the vocabulary card tight.

SUBSTANCE: 100

Without question, other than mixing in the street references, the murders, and telling stories, Nas is just one of the most substantive emcees period.

FLOW: 90

He invented a new flow. It's what we old-schoolers called the "off-beat flow" in the beginning. Now it's kind of taken over and every-body's adopted that flow, but he is kind of a pro-totype for what we were calling off-beat.

FLAVOR: 75

Nas is straight at you. He doesn't play around with his voice too much. It's direct, efficient, potent emceeing.

FREESTYLE: 90

Because of his rhyming acumen, there is too much going on inside of him for him not to be able to freestyle.

VOCAL PRESENCE: 80

His voice is very laid back. Although there are other emcees who have laid back, less energetic voices, Nas' voice doesn't compel the dynamics of a lot of emcees now, but it is still enough when he projects himself, especially when you get him mad in battle time. You can feel his energy go up.

LIVE PERFORMANCE: 85

In the beginning, when he started out, he really wasn't that good live, but as he moved along, he got a lot better. By the time he got to the one-mic stage, he had an anthem, and it clicked. He then started to perform on another level.

POETIC VALUE: 90

He is basically a street poet. A ghetto griot!

BODY OF WORK: 90

If you go back and listen to all of the stuff that he's done, a lot of times his best stuff is not on his hit records. So I've just got to give him a 90 because he is really putting it down and putting a lot of work into it.

INDUSTRY IMPACT: 80

Nas is one of the more underrated emcees as far as the industry is concerned. He doesn't get

a lot of accolades, Grammys, nominations, or what have you, but he still does enough to keep his presence there.

SOCIAL IMPACT: 85

He, like Tupac, connects to the street cats, but not to the same extent. The street-heads feel him. That is socially relevant.

LONGEVITY: 90

Without question, Nas has ten years in, '93 to 2003. His ten years are in the books. His album came in '94, but he had a single before that.

LYRICS: 100

Without question, he is just one of the most lyrical emcees, in the game. Period.

BATTLE SKILLS: 95

Based on the battle that we heard with him and Jay-Z, he definitely knows how to do the battle side of the equation.

TOTAL SCORE: 1,505

AVERAGE SCORE: 88.5

10 BEST CASUALTIES OF THE SUBSTANCE WARS

1) **Brother J**	The Best
2) **Kam**	Poetic Pundit
3) **King Sun**	Father of the Freestyle Battle
4) **CL Smooth**	Poignant Poet
5) **Paris**	Lyrical Activist
6) **Intelligent Hoodlum**	The Rhyme Paradox
7) **Chill Rob G**	Poetic Street Politics
8) **Lin Q**	Aggressive Spitter
9) **Lakim Shabazz**	Afrocentric Spitter
10) **Nonchalant**	Wisdom in Words

Because of the superficial nature of capitalism in hip-hop, emcees usually have a harder time getting a record deal than their less substantive peers. These are the best emcees (outside of Chuck D & KRS-1) in this category.

10

LAURYN HILL

ANGELIC WARRIOR PRINCESS OF POETRY

I'm the L
Won't you pull it
Straight to the head
With the speed of a bullet
Cutting, nukkas off at the
Meeky freaky gullet
Lyrical sedative
Keep nukkas meditive head rushers I give to
Creative kids and friends
Dreams of euphoria
Aurora to
Another galaxy phallic—see
Be this microphone
But get lifted
Lyrically I'm gifted
Burn on in without the roach
Clip it hinders
Mind bender
Pleasure sender
So frequently your nerve endings
Be long to me
you put me down
not receiving the full capacity
of my smoke
wack nukkas choke
from the fumes that I emote
or emit sh** see even I feel
the mahogany L
natural hallucinogen runnin boys to men again
with estrogen dreams
release blues yellows and greens
from Brownsville to Queens

LAURYN HILL IS LIKE AN EMCEE that's been sent from heaven to motivate us spiritually through her inspirational motivational poetry. She is by far the most poetic emcee in the game. Only Common and Tupac really come close. Although Common might be the most poetic, pound for pound, Lauryn Hill takes it to another level with her flavor, flow, vocal dynamics, and her higher levels of Biblical and spiritual references. Lauryn Hill, like Nas and Tupac, feels like a savior. The difference with Lauryn, besides the obvious feminine energy, is she's like a combination of the two. She is more vocally dynamic than Nas, and more lyrical than Tupac. Lauryn Hill is the only MC I ever heard that had no real weaknesses. It's more like a case of which of her strengths are not as strong as the others. She spent the first half of her career with the Fugees, and no disrespect to Wyclef or Pras, but Lauryn was the star of the group. I used to constantly catch myself listening and waiting for her part to come on almost every one of their records. What's most incredible about this to me is I think Wyclef is one of the most creative Hip-Hop artists ever. Lauryn seemed to take things to another level lyrically every time. In 1996 the Fugees dropped what I think is one of the top five Hip-Hop albums of all time *The Score*. On that album in particular, I think Lauryn was in some kind of lyrical zone. Almost every single rhyme was profound, colorful, or just plain lyrically skilled to the max.

Her impact was so profound that the industry wasn't only calling, they were just about demanding a solo project from Lauryn. And in 1998, oh boy, did they get it. Lauryn released *The Miseducation of Lauryn Hill*, and literally turned the industry upside down. She owned the charts for six months, and by 1999 it was the most nominated, awarded, and critically acclaimed album in the history of any Hip-Hop artist. It was the equivalent of winning a tennis or golf grand slam. She won the Grammy, American Music Award, Soul Train Award, and the NAACP Image Award. For one year she might have been the hottest Hip-Hop artist ever. And that's only talking about her heat and her accolades. The album itself is probably the most eclectically, well-balanced poetic Hip-Hop, pop, and R&B album ever. One again, lyrically Hill was in the zone. There were, however, some critics early on who were upset that Lauryn didn't do enough straight rhyming. While I understand the sentiment, as an artist I can always appreciate an artist expanding on their skills. On the other hand, Lauryn is so skillful as an emcee, I also wanted to hear more rhymes. Nonetheless, what she did in song was so poetic and profound I didn't see how anyone could be mad.

I'm about to change the focus
From the richest to the brokest
I write this opus
To reverse the hypnosis
Whoever's closest
To the thin lines gonna win it
You gonna fall tryin to ball
While my team win the pennant
I'm about to be in it
For a minute
Then run for Senate
Make a slum lord be the tenant
Give his money to kids and spend it
And then amend it
Every law that ever prevented
Our survival since our arrival
Documented in the Bible
Like Moses and Aaron
Things gon change
It's apparent
And all the transparent

Gonna be seen through
Let God redeem you
Keep your deen true
You can get
The green too
Watch out who you cling to
Observe how a queen do and
I remain calm reading the 73 Psalm
Cause wit all this goin on
I got the world in my palm

Lauryn Hill is a perfect example of a recurring theme in Hip-Hop. No matter how many emcees shine through stylish materialism, the lyricist with the substance always gets more shine, because that shine comes with respect. In 1998, Hip-Hop was probably in its most materialistic, frivolous, watered-down, lyrical stage ever. Very few emcees had anything of substance to say. Lauryn, with her lyrical mastery and her substantive rhymes, took over. Like Sha-Rock, Salt-'N-Pepa, MC Lyte, and Queen Latifah before her, Lauryn built on the combinations of all of their respect, class, sex appeal, flavor, and social commentary. She combined that with her spirituality and, ultimately, represented women in a most respectable, positive light. As Tupac became the accessible everyman, Lauryn Hill became the everywoman. She felt like she was talking from a point of experience, and was on a mission to help other women avoid the similar, yet common pitfalls of female adolescence and young adulthood. Men loved her, and women and young girls admired her.

In the end, Lauryn Hill is that rare triple-threat. She rhymes, sings, and performs at extremely high levels. Her days with the Fugees served her well; as that group was one of the best live performing groups in Hip-Hop history. Lauryn, in her live solo efforts, had very little drop off. Her live shows were very hot; as an emcee she is a lyricist with relevance and flavor. When she's at the top of her game, one can only hope to match her, because none can supersede her. Without question, Lauryn Hill is ONE OF THE MOST LYRICAL EMCEES, AND TRULY ONE OF THE GREATS!

Strengths: Songwriting and rhyme spitting. Almost every song has meaning, combined with her fluid flow; her rhymes are never in the way of the messages. She balances the braggadocio.

Weakness: None. The only thing she doesn't do as well as everything else is she loses levels of articulation in her flavorful inflections. This can sometimes take away from the rhyme endings from verse to verse.

Favorite Record: "Everything Is Everything," "The Vocab" (Fugees)
Favorite LP: *The Miseducation of Lauryn Hill*

#10: LAURYN HILL

ORIGINALITY: 90
Timing: She brought her own flavor to the equation. It wasn't too far outside of the realm of what was being done at the time.

CONCEPTS: 90

Lauryn Hill is absolutely a concept emcee. Her album, *The Miseducation of Lauryn Hill*, was basically a concept album.

VERSATILITY: 100

One of the most versatile emcees, period. She has all kinds of records. You can't pigeonhole her other then the fact that you know she is coming with substance. You just don't know how she is going to bring it across.

VOCABULARY: 90

Lauryn definitely makes references that you don't commonly hear in Hip-Hop. Her vocals, her rhymes, and her word selection are of the higher vocabulary ilk.

SUBSTANCE: 100

100! Period. Move on. End of story. Substantive emcee.

FLOW: 95

Lauryn is one of the best flow-ers period, male or female.

FLAVOR: 90

She uses her voice, and fluctuates as far as the rhyme side goes.

FREESTYLE: 85

The only time she seems to lighten up or loosen up a bit is when she's doing the freestyle, but even that still comes off with heat. Her vocabulary is high, her references are tight, so when she freestyles it's not going to be just finishing the rhyme for the sake of finishing the rhyme.

VOCAL PRESENCE: 90

One of the most recognizable, melodic voices on the singing side, and as an emcee you recognize her immediately. You know exactly who she is. She didn't get a 100 only because her voice is not as powerful as some of the more powerful voices out there, but it's absolutely one of the more prominently present voices in the game.

LIVE PERFORMANCE: 90

With the Fugees it was one level, and with her solo stuff she still brings it across excellently onstage.

POETIC VALUE: 90

Lauryn Hill is absolutely one of the more poetic emcees. If you listen to *The Miseducation of Lauryn Hill*, you find that damn near the whole album is poetry.

BODY OF WORK: 90

The album that she did on her own was absolutely stellar. I don't know how much Wyclef was putting in on the Fugee side, but you can't take points away from it. You just have to acknowledge it for being great. It was one of the top five albums, period. The first Fugees album didn't really click as well. It set them up for what happened with "The Score." And then her *Live Unplugged* album, even though that was a live show and they just put it out, it was unfortunate for her because fans got a misleading representation of what an album is for her, because it sounded like she was doing her thing live and they tried to capitalize on something that she was doing. It's almost like recording a comedian while he is working his jokes out and then releasing it.

INDUSTRY IMPACT: 100

Come on, when you look at what happened in '98 and how she basically was the most nominated Hip-Hop artist, she did the grand slam tour as far as '98 went. She was honored on all of the award shows, everything.

SOCIAL IMPACT: 90

She, like Latifah, although after Latifah, represented females in such a positive light you just couldn't deny her.

LONGEVITY: 70

She is still doing her thing. She hasn't done anything in a couple of years since *Unplugged*. With the Fugees, they did their thing from '94 until. So you've got to give her points for her years in the game.

LYRICS: 100

Lauryn is that lyricist. She is definitely that lyrical person, period.

BATTLE SKILLS: 70!

On the battle side, it feels like she can do it, but it also feels like she is more of a humanitarian and why waste time battling people when you can be uplifting people? So I put an exclamation next to 70, meaning I think she can do it but she is not going to be tested because nobody will test Lauryn Hill.

TOTAL SCORE: 1,530

AVERAGE SCORE: 90

11 BEST KEPT LYRICAL SECRETS

1) T-LA Rock	Vocabulary Extraordinaire
2) Rahiem	Royalty
3) Special K	Supreme Rhymer
4) Tito	The Flavor
5) Twista	High Speed Hear
6) Craig G	True Spitter
7) Lord Finess	Punchline Finesser
8) DLB	The Writer
9) Def Jef	Purposeful Poet
10) Tracey Lee	Philly Flower
11) Del The Funky Homosapien	Unknown Quality

There are so many old-school emcees that were truly great lyricists, but for a number of business-related reasons (and in some cases, because there was no business at the time), these emcees do not get documented. Their lyrical prowess earns the right to be among the greats.

9

NOTORIOUS
B.I.G.
THE POWER

If I wasn't in the rap game
I'd probably have a key
Knee deep in the crack game
Because the streets is a short stop
either you slingin' crack rock
Or you got a wicked jump shot
Sh** it's hard being young
From the slums eatin 5 cent gums
Not knowin where ya meals comin from
And now the sh**s getting
Crazier and major
Kids younger than me
They got the sky grand pager
Goin out of town blowin up
Six months later all the dead
Bodies showin up
It made me wanna grab
The nine and the shottie
But I gotta go identify the body
Damn what happened to the
Summertime cook outs
Everythime I turn around
A nukka getting took out
Sh** my mother got cancer
In her breast
Don't ask me why I'm muthafu**n stressed
Things done changed

NOTORIOUS B.I.G. IS THE ALL TIME greatest hard-core Hip-Hop storyteller ever. Slick Rick is the overall king of storytelling, but for the rated-R, violent type of story, Biggie is the man. As with many of the great emcees, I wasn't as quick as the general public to give B.I.G. his props. I was spending more time in Los Angeles than in New York in 1993 and '94, so a lot of what I was hearing was coming through the grapevine. Before his album dropped, the hype and anticipation was incredible. I thought Puffy had done an excellent marketing and promotions job. However, I thought it was just hype. I had only heard Biggie on two songs. One, the remix of Supercats' "Dolly My Baby," Biggie rhymed behind Third Eye and Puffy, and although he shone, I thought Third Eye had the most shine. The other song was his single, "Party and Bullshit." On that song I was totally unimpressed. By the summer of '94, Biggie's lead single, "Juicy," was to set the tone for his upcoming album release, *Ready to Die*. Although he had some heat, his label-mate Craig Mack had the single of the summer, "Flava In Ya Ear." Still, the hype was about Biggie. It was especially high for Hip-Hop fans in Brooklyn. The day the album dropped, I was with two Brooklynites, comedian Reggie McFadden and director Matty Rich. While Matty and I were debating whether or not Biggie was really the next great emcee, Reg was driving around looking for a store that had the CD/LP. For whatever reason, no stores had it. Reg was telling us that we had to hear the album. Somehow he'd gotten an advanced copy, and left it in New York. He was driving us crazy. I was convinced that Biggie was just hype and that Reg didn't know what he was talking about. Finally we get the CD/LP, and immediately I could tell that he was creative from the album's intro, but I was still cynical. Then, as the first song played, "Things Done Changed," I'm still pontificating on how I think he's got a great voice and a great attack, but I still don't hear any real rhyme acumen. And then it happened! Song number three, "Gimmie The Loot" comes on, and everything changed. I was literally sitting in the backseat trying not to rock, but Biggie was too powerful. The record went off and we were all sitting in silence, staring at each other. Reg was smugly waiting for a response. All I could say was, "Play that again."

After playing the song ten more times and screaming and laughing and high five'n, and singing along, Matty got out of the car and bought his own copy. By the time we got to song number five, "Warning," I got out to buy my own copy. From that day on I think I listened to that album every day for about two months straight. Biggie's CD never came out of my player. Biggie was the first emcee that made me rethink my lyrical approach. For the first time, I was wondering could I do more than I was doing rhythmically. Of course lyrically, I was god, but Biggie's flow and phrasing was something that had never been done before. He was truly a wordsmith. Of the third generation, of the three lyrical kings, Jay-Z is the slickest, Nas is the most cerebral, but Biggie is the most explosive. His flow was so tight and his delivery was so powerful that he could talk about robbing and killing women and children and nobody even blinked. I know Hip-Hop has its problems with misogyny and violent content, but believe me, anybody else of a lower skill level in rhyme saying the things that he said would have been run out of the business. This is why I call Biggie "the power." He was so potent as an emcee he could rhyme about anything and sometimes he would say anything. He himself said that his flow was potent because he would literally say anything.

Another testament to Biggie's power was at this stage in the game, people were buying records based on hits, singles, and music. Biggie is the first emcee since Rakim and Chuck D that had people buying product just to hear what he was going to say. Of course, ultimately, music always wins in the end, but it's a testament to his skills as an emcee that the initial focus was on him.

Another testament to Biggie's power was he was anything but your prototypical ladies man, and yet he made songs geared towards women, and had a huge female following. As Tupac was the father of the thug movement, Biggie was the father of the jiggy movement. Amid the dressed-down, Timberland, hoodie, sagging, baggy-pants dress code for the hard-core thug emcee, Biggie ventured where no hard-core emcee would go. He actually dressed in Versace suits. The urban legend of the time was you couldn't be hard-core if you dressed up. Once again, the power of Biggie made dressing jiggy hot. He was the beginning of the flossed out, iced out, domination in Hip-Hop.

The final testament to the power of Biggie is the types of songs he made. He single-handedly shifted the musical dominance back to the East Coast. From 1991 to 1994, the West Coast style of rap was the dominant force in Hip-Hop. Biggie, with the guidance of Puffy, used familiar melodic R&B loops, combined with his voice texture and rhyme skills, and caused a Hip-Hop paradigm shift. The shift was so powerful it affected R&B as well as Hip-Hop. Adding Biggie to your track gave it automatic cachet. By 1995, because of a serious reason, Biggie was in an all-out rivalry with his one-time friend Tupac. Instead of expanding on that, I'll focus on the emcee aspect of the rivalry. There seems to be a lot of confusion about who was better than who and for whatever reasons. To me there is no confusion. It breaks down the same way it has for the most popular battles in Hip-Hop history. Basically, Tupac is to Biggie as Jay-Z is to Nas and LL is to Moe Dee. Tupac, Jay-Z, and LL are the tighter artists, and Biggie, Nas, and Moe Dee are the tighter emcees. Tupac definitely had a more diverse body of work; he took more chances musically and lyrically, but for just straight-up rhyming, flowin', wordplaying, and spittin' fire, Biggie was untouchable in his time. Unfortunately, both of those masters met untimely deaths, and I think we missed out on the next level of what Hip-Hop was to become.

As far as Biggie goes, there have only been three significant, life altering Hip-Hop moments for me. One in 1978, seeing Grandmaster Flash introduce the backspin, and hearing Melle Mel give us the template for how to rhyme. Two, in 1986 hearing Rakim when I was at the top of my game, and realizing I had to pass the baton. And three, in 1994, hearing Biggie when I was out of the game and being forced to totally rethink my flow while being inspired to get back in the game. Bad Boy released two more albums posthumously, and even in death you could see the remnants of Biggie's impact and influence. On the *Life After Death* project, you can clearly hear the jiggy, bling, name-brand rhyme style so many rappers use today.

I put hoes in NY onto DKNY
Miami DC prefer Versace
All Philly hoes
Dough and Moschino
Every cutie wit a booty bought a Coogi
Now who's the reall dookie
Meanin who's really the shi*
Them nukkas ride di**s
Frank White push the six
Or the Lexus
Lx four and a half
Bulletproof glass tints
If I want some ass
Gon' blast squeeze first
Ask questions last
That's how most of these so-called
Gangstas pass
At last
A nukka rappin bout blunts-n-broads
Tits-n-bras

Ménage-a-tois
Sex in expensive cars

Overall, Notorious B.I.G. hit the game like a supernova. His shine was intense but short. His impact is legendary, and for the short run, nobody had the streets on lock like he did. Ultimately, *Ready To Die* was the second greatest Hip-Hop album ever made. He upgraded the way emcees would have to flow to shine, and to this day no one has matched his combination of flow intensity and efficiency. Notorious B.I.G. is by far ONE OF THE GREATEST TRUE EMCEES EVER.

Strengths: Story flow. He's so masterful that you can see his rhyme. The most visual emcee ever.

Weakness: Scattered rhyme. Many times his rhymes have no continuity. He sometimes jumps from subject to subject like a high-level freestyle.

Favorite Record: "Hypnotize," "Warning," "Gimme The Loot," "Kick In the Door"

Favorite LP: *Ready To Die*

#9: NOTORIOUS B.I.G.

ORIGINALITY: 95

He too, in the third generation of the three kings, like Nas and Jay-Z who came and brought their own energy, took over the streets and became known as the best on the streets. Biggie was bringing the intensity with it that was different than the other two and nobody was rhyming like him.

CONCEPTS: 90

His storytelling abilities were incredible and the stories themselves were very conceptual.

VERSATILITY: 85

You really don't know what he is going to come with but you do know what the content is going to be. You know what you're getting from Biggie and his energy. It's the big smooth guy or the attack and violent guy for the most part, but he is still rather versatile within that.

VOCABULARY: 80

Biggie did not really come at you with a lot of intricate vocabulary, but you could tell he had a great vocabulary because he would throw words in there every now and then and surprise you.

SUBSTANCE: 80

Just like any of the street emcees, it's automatically substantive on one level but then the content and the one-note-ness of it take away from it.

FLOW: 100

Biggie's flow was absolutely one of the more profound elements to his game and one of the more profound elements to the Hip-Hop game, period.

FLAVOR: 100

Once again, his flavor was incredible. That's part of what made it work for him. His delivery was just impeccable.

FREESTYLE: 95

He is legendary for being a freestyle artist. You

don't even have to hear him. Just ask other people who have been around him and they will tell you. A lot of times he would just walk into the studio and not write but just come up with a record right there. He and Jay-Z are famous for that.

VOCAL PRESENCE: 100

Without question, a dominant, powerful voice.

LIVE PERFORMANCE: 90

Biggie also knew how to bring it across live. He had Puffy onstage helping him in most cases, actually in all of the shows that I've seen, but he held his own and he knew how to get a crowd rallied up damn near just from rhyming. His energy was there in his live performance.

POETIC VALUE: 80

More rhymes than poetry, but there was a slight level of poetry in Biggie's game.

BODY OF WORK: 90

This could have easily been a 100, but with his untimely death he didn't get a chance to do his thing. The third album they released, a lot of people were mad at some of the content, but he did what he could do while he was here. *Ready to Die* was the second best Hip-Hop album ever. That alone got him points.

INDUSTRY IMPACT: 100

He set the industry on fire. He came in, exploded, supernova, undeniable.

SOCIAL IMPACT: 90

He got a 90 only because of the way that the marketing/promotion side of the equation went. Who he was and where he came from on the street basically set it up for a lot of kids in the 'hood to really feel like if he could do it they could do it. So he did have a wave of following, especially in Brooklyn.

LONGEVITY: 70

Speaks for itself. He got his five to six years in, unfortunate death a couple of years. After he passed, they still put out his music and his presence has been felt and still is felt to this day.

LYRICS: 95

Biggie was a lyricist. Not to the same level as Nas or Pun, because he was not really going at it that hard, but he was definitely a wordsmith and the way he put his words together alone makes him a lyricist.

BATTLE SKILLS: 95

He was also legendary for this, coming off the top of the head and cutting up whoever, whenever. You could just tell that he was fearless and rumor has it that "Kickin' the Door" was for Nas.

TOTAL SCORE: 1,535

AVERAGE SCORE: 90.2

THE PARTY PANTHEON
(10 of the Best Party Emcees)

1) **Doug E Fresh**	Greatest Entertainer
2) **Busy Bee Chief Rocker**	Master Of Call/Response
3) **DJ Hollywood**	The Original Party Rocker
4) **Love Bug Starsky**	The Crowd Pleaser
5) **Luke Skywalker**	The King of the Long Call
6) **Keith Cowboy**	The Coolest Ever
7) **DJ Kool**	All Party Energy
8) **Grand Master Caz**	MC + DJ Master
9) **Master P**	Party on Wax
10) **Rob Base**	Fundamentalist

This is a lost art. Most emcees don't have a clue of how to rock a party, concert, or show outside of having their hit records doing half the work for them. These emcees understand how important the crowd is and how to make them rock.

8

CHUCK D
THE VOICE

I got a letter from the government
The other day
I opened and read it
It said they were suckers
They wanted me for their army or whatever
Picture me givin a damn
I said never
Here is a land that never gave a damn
About a brother like me an myself
Because they never did
I wasn't wit it
But just that very minute
It occurred to me the suckers had authority
Cold sweatin as I dwell in my cell
How longg has it been
They got me sittin in a state pen
I gotta get out but that thought
Was thought before
I contemplated a plan
On the cell florr
Another fugitive on the run
But a brother like me begun
To be another one
Public Enemy serving time
They drew the line y'all
To criticize me for some crime
Nevertheless they could not understand
That I'm a Black man
And I could never be a veteran

CHUCK D IS THE GREATEST VOICE in Hip-Hop history. There has never been a greater voice in Hip-Hop, figuratively or literally. Only Melle Mel is in the same league. The difference is that Melle Mel is more of a classic emcee than Chuck. However, as far as social commentary, and rhymes for the upliftment of black people, Chuck D is in a league of his own. He is by far the most potent, lyrical, substantive, poetic emcee ever in the game. He is the absolute benchmark of relevant Hip-Hop social commentary. His voice and his delivery are the equivalent of an explosion. Combined with his passion and positive messages, he's like an explosion that's going to blow you up and save your life. He chose to rhyme over loud, chaotic, hard-core Hip-Hop tracks with multi-sample combinations that gave the songs a loud rock edge. This stylistic approach let it be known that dancing was not the prerequisite. Chuck D was trying to start the revolution on wax. He made it seem like it was God's plan all along to bring a music to the black youth, from the black youth, under the guise of partying and dancing, so he could have our undivided attention when Chuck came with the salvation.

Chuck D was like a master of smoke and mirrors. He was politics under the guise of art. He was public speaking under the guise of music. He was a social leader under the guise of an emcee, and he was even a soloist under the guise of the group Public Enemy. There are basically two divisions of Hip-Hop time. There's Hip-Hop B.C. (Before Chuck) and Hip-Hop A.D. (After D). Before Chuck, Hip-Hop was more self-centered in its rhyme structure. Almost every rhyme started off with "I." Once in a while after Melle Mel made the song "The Message," groups like the Treacherous Three, Fearless Four, and other old-school legends would do more socially conscious messages, but that was not their norm. The emcees' purpose was to show skills, and musically, it was almost exclusively about partying.

In 1987, Chuck D, through Public Enemy, began to challenge all of that. Their first album *Yo Bum Rush the Show* didn't really catch on. Fans didn't really know what to make of this new sound, on top of which, no one other than true old-school Hip-Hop aficionados even knew what a hype man was. I was on tour with Public Enemy that summer. They were the opening act for LL. It was brutal. Some nights they actually wouldn't get booed. However, midway through the summer, the soundtrack to a movie *Less Than Zero* dropped. P.E. had the song "Bring The Noise" on the soundtrack. Slowly but surely people began to understand what was going on. By the time the tour ended in N.Y.C.'s Madison Square Garden, Public Enemy was a hit. One month later, in October 1987, Public Enemy dropped the greatest Hip-Hop album ever made, *It Takes a Nation of Millions to Hold Us Back*. The album exploded.

From 1988 to 1991, there wasn't a more significant impacting force in Hip-Hop. N.W.A. did come at this time also, but P.E. was clearly the most dominant force. In '92, Snoop, building on the momentum of Ice Cube, N.W.A., and eventually combined with the force of Tupac, made gangsta rap the dominant force. Nonetheless, Chuck D was viewed as a cultural iconic figure. His flow was the most unorthodox to that point, and his subject matter was unfamiliar territory in Hip-Hop. What was also unfamiliar to the trained Hip-Hop ear was the fact that Chuck used none of the clichéd, familiar, conventional braggadocio emceeisms! He never talked about being the best, and he never criticized another emcee. He never even compared himself to another emcee. This only enhanced his image as a true lyrical leader, and he never even professed to be that. He was focused on one thing: bringin' the noise.

Never badder than bad
Cause the brother is madder than mad
At the fact that's corrupt as a senator
Soul on a roll
But you treat it like soap on a rope
Cause the beats and the lines
Are so dope
Listen for lessons I'm saying
Inside music that the critics
All are blasting me for
They'll never care for the

Brothers and sisters
Wide 'cross the country
Has us up for the war
We got to demonstrate (Come on)
They're gonna have to wait
Till we get it right
Radio stations I question their blackness
They call themselves black
But we'll see if they play this

Chuck D does it the way it's supposed to be done. He is truly hard-core. I would listen to his records and then listen to some of the so-called hard-core, gangsta/street rap records, and wonder how these other acts could call themselves hard-core. In my opinion, if your songs or rhymes are not challenging information, the establishment, or at the very least stereotypical mindsets, you're not hard-core, you're just profane. Chuck D is truly the hardest hard-core emcee. At the end of the day, he's done much more than I've talked about in this chapter. He is very much involved in trying to make moves so that artists can gain control of their music, as opposed to the standing arrangement that basically makes the artist a slave to the labels. As always, Chuck D is at the forefront of the artistic curve. As an emcee he laid the groundwork for many of Hip-Hop's future heavyweights by changing the way we approached the mic. He has given us a new template, and ultimately the biggest paradigm shift in the game so far. Lyrically, he's been poignant and poetically profound, and for all he's done for the game, and after all of the success he's had, he's probably the most humble icon in Hip-Hop. His flow and delivery are stellar, but his voice, combined with his messages, makes him one of the true greats among the greatest emcees ever!

Strength: Delivery. He uses his voice like a weapon! Any rhyme he says sounds like he means business.

Weakness: Clarity. Sometimes he's so intense you can't understand certain words in the rhymes.

Favorite Record: "Don't Believe The Hype," "Fight the Power"

Favorite LP: *It Takes a Nation of Millions To Hold Us Back*

#8: CHUCK D

ORIGINALITY: 100
Without question, there was nobody ever doing straight, political, Afrocentric, black power urban ghetto rap.

CONCEPTS: 95
The whole movement of Public Enemy was conceptual.

VERSATILITY: 75
He didn't stray from that subject matter for the most part. He stayed in the space that he was in, but within that, he was able to

fluctuate and use different tempos to "Can't Truss It" and "Don't Believe the Hype," and then the chaotic, anarchy-type records like "Bring Da Noise" and "Rebel Without a Pause."

VOCABULARY: 85

Chuck is not beating you in the head with the vocabulary, but he sprinkles it in there within the concepts. He sprinkles some words in there and you can just tell that by his vocabulary. He is a well-read brother, easily.

SUBSTANCE: 100

That's not even questionable. You know what they stand for. Black Power.

FLOW: 90

Chuck has what I call one of the more unorthodox interesting flows in the game. It stops and starts, it pauses, it influxes, it goes up and down. His flow is just crazy.

FLAVOR: 100

As popular as his voice is, he uses it like an instrument and a weapon combined. With all of the rock-star sonic samples and all of the sonic booming behind him musically, as loud and chaotic as that music is, his voice is still the most prevalent thing within that music. He uses his voice like a weapon.

FREESTYLE: 70

That is not really his thing. Chuck is not the freestyle emcee to just get in the cipher. He's rhyming for a purpose, with a purpose. I know that he can do it, based on where he comes from and how he can rhyme.

VOCAL PRESENCE: 100

This builds on the same thing as flavor. The flavor he uses, the inflections of his voice up and down, the vocal presence is a 100 because,

like I said, his voice is the main thing within the chaotic, loud, sonic music, and the music can't drown him out. He is never behind the beat, which is incredible because he's probably got the loudest music ever in the history of the game.

LIVE PERFORMANCE: 100

One of those few acts that you just don't want to get on after. You don't want to get on the stage after Chuck and Public Enemy.

POETIC VALUE: 90

He approaches it like a poet. That's probably why his flow is the way it is because he has to stop and marinate and give you different syncopations.

BODY OF WORK: 100

The work speaks for itself. P.E. is one of the few acts that can get on and do an hour and a half straight and you forget how many hits and how many records they have, and this is all done damn near without any radio play. Body of work is stellar!

INDUSTRY IMPACT: 100

They came and they set the industry on fire. They did it from the underground side and exploded into the pop culture. Not the R&B, not the Hip-Hop, they exploded into the pop culture. Very few artists can do that or make that claim.

SOCIAL IMPACT: 100

Absolutely the most uplifting group ever in the history of Hip-Hop. Chuck rhymes, and his ability to rhyme the way he does and bring it across—he's literally like a Black Leader on wax.

LONGEVITY: 85

By the time it got to '94, people—just because

of the way that the industry turns and does what it does—that was it for P.E. Even though Chuck still makes his presence known and does things, as far as musically, it's an 85 on longevity.

LYRICS: 90

Chuck is not the quintessential lyricist, but he is absolutely the relevant lyricist, so his lyrics are geared toward something totally different, and the way he puts it together is integral within that. If you hear him, if you go back and pay attention to the rhyme styles and the flow, once you get past the voice and the flow of the cadence, you realize he is putting lyrics together.

BATTLE SKILLS: 60

Chuck is absolutely not wasting any time battling anybody. Like I said, he is the only emcee that has never made reference to criticizing an emcee, comparing himself to an emcee, or saying anything about himself being the best. So with those being the fundamental elements to battling and him not doing any battling, 60 on the battle side.

TOTAL SCORE: 1,540

AVERAGE SCORE: 90.5

7

LL
COOL J
UNBREAKABLE
MASTER

I excel they fell
I said well hell
I signed the contracts
The bills were stacked
Play the wall or fall
I stand tall
Y'all small in fact
Step aside you might get fried
By this super technique
That the rapper applied
As a matter of fact the impact
Ill distract your attention away
From the rest who say
They could mess wit Cool J
The best of today
Ya fessed cause the rhymes
Are so funky fresh
I'm attack smack and make'm
Stand back black strong as cognac
I got the knack
To rhyme to the rhythm of this
And give'm a gift a swift
Other rappers are stiff
And don't riff with Mr. Smith
Cause that ain't safe
I get you wide open
Like a uncut 8th
I write to fight
Don't bite
To reach heights
Might makes right
Give me the spotlight
So I can prove the pen
Is mightier than the sword
LL hard as hell the lyrical Lord
The counterfeit misfits mid rap
Had to admit that my rhymes are so
Dangerous I need a permit to
Rap solo on the microphone
Emcees don't let me catch you alone

NEVER UNDERESTIMATE THE POWER OF WOMEN. LL Cool J is the first lyrical superstar emcee. Kurtis Blow was the first solo emcee superstar, but he wasn't lyrical. And there were many lyricist in groups at the time, but none of us were superstars. LL was able to pull off what none of us at the time could, for one reason or another. Women. He was the first lyricist that was a sex symbol. In the Hip-Hop climate of 1984, the lyrical emcees were basically playing to a predominantly male audience. It seemed like once an emcee got too intricate lyrically, women would disengage. When it was time to party with the call-and-response and shake their butts, they were in full force. However, the rules would change if they thought you were sexy. There were a handful of ladies men early in the game, like Kevie Kev, Master Rob, EZ-AD, The Devastating Tito, and even Kurtis Blow. But by 1984, those groups from the first generation of emcees were fading. That year LL hit the scene like thunder with "I Need A Beat." The record had a strong street buzz, but no one could really foresee what would happen just a year later. In 1985, the movie *Crush Groove* comes out, and even though LL had a small cameo, his scene was absolutely one of the true high points in the film. I went to see the movie five times, and each time LL's scene ended with the crowd erupting. As the cliché goes about black people in movie theatres, they talked about LL's scene through the next two scenes, especially the women. This is when I knew a star was born.

Shortly after that he released his album *Radio* and all hell broke loose. At this time the three lyrical kings of the first generation Melle Mel, Grandmaster Caz, and Kool Moe Dee were still of pharaoh-like status. The fact that LL would dare to use his heat and his platform to proclaim his greatness without acknowledging his predecessors planted the seeds for what would turn out to be the greatest battle in Hip-Hop history. In 1986, Run-DMC blew the doors open for the next level of Hip-Hop success, "Walk This Way." They also had the biggest Hip-Hop tour of all time, "Raising Hell." LL was one of the opening acts for the tour, and this set the LL craze into overdrive. Not only was he one of the premiere lyricists of the time, he was also one of the best emcees live in concert. He was sending crowds of twenty-thousand into pandemonium. One might argue that the other lyricists at that time didn't have the same opportunity, but I was there; even in the smaller crowds in clubs, most of the really lyrical emcees would lose the crowd with their live performance. LL understood the stage. He seemed to understand the laws of the energy. His show was short and powerful. This left the audience wanting more of him.

By 1987, he released his second album "Bad." If I'm not mistaken, the album went double platinum before the summer was over, and he released it in June. That summer he headlined his own tour, "The Def Jam Tour." Although the single "I'm Bad" led the charge for the album, midway through the summer LL released "I Need Love." This record took LL over the top, and solidified his position with women as a sex symbol. Whodini was co-headlining the tour with LL, and they were also seen as sex symbols, but after "I Need Love" took off, LL began to create separation as the lone sex symbol. He pushed this into overdrive by bringing a couch out on his stage, and every night he would take his shirt off, get on the couch, and simulate having sex on it while singing "I Need Love." PANDEMONIUM is not a strong enough word to describe how the ladies in the audience were reacting. In a couple of markets I joined the tour, and everything was cool until one night in Boston. LL missed his plane and the show's promoter asked if Rakim and I could just go up onstage and rhyme for a while and hold the crowd over with some impromptu freestyle. We agreed, and within fifteen minutes along with Grandmaster Dee cutting, Rakim, Jalil, Extacy, Mike C, and myself absolutely wrecked the crowd. We got the word that LL was in the house and we shut it down. Finally, when LL took the stage he turned the music down, walked over to a speaker and stood over all of the emcees that just saved the show, and began to explain to the crowd why he got on last, and why his name is the biggest on the marquee. He ranted on about how he was a bigger star than all of us. After the show his crew came to me and said they heard about the dis record I made for him so the battle was officially on. After he heard "How Ya Like Me Now" he said he wasn't impressed. LL was subscribing to the industry's rules of engagement. Until someone makes money, nothing he or she does is significant. Shortly after that "How Ya Like Me Now" was clearly a hit, and in route to being a gold album and single. LL responded with,

> *How ya like me now*
> *I'm getting busier*
> *I'm double platinum*
> *I'm watchin you get dizzier*
> *Check out the way I say my*
> *Display my play my J on the back*
> *Behind the cool without the ay*
> *I love to ride the groove*
> *Because the groove is smooth*
> *And makes me move*
> *And I'll improve*
> *As it goes on as it flows on*
> *When ya see me*
> *Don't ask me if the shows on*
> *How that sound don't come around*
> *Playin me close clown*
> *Pullin my jock to be down*
> *You need to stay down*
> *Way down*
> *Because ya low down*
> *Do that dance the prince of rap*
> *Is gonna throwdown*
> *Hearin the breeze*
> *While I'm killin emcees*
> *I'ma keep on hittin you*
> *Wit rough LP's*
> *day after day after day*
> *ya smacked in the face*
> *by the bass of Cool J*

This is why I call LL "The Unbreakable Master." He has never won a single battle, yet he just keeps on coming. He was still answering this battle eight years later on "I Shot Ya." However, battling was never LL's strength. But when it comes to making love songs he is untouchable. Spoonie Gee did it the smoothest, Heavy D did it the most energetic, and Tupac did it the most poignant, but LL did it the most romantic. He had the look and the charisma to pull it off. He was like a straight-up lady's man. But let's not forget that the early LL Cool J is almost the total opposite of the LL of today. He was truly one of the more lyrical emcees of the '80s. His albums were always diverse and he knew and still knows how to make hit records. He wasn't a one-note emcee. He would take chances on making the kinds of records that no hard-core rapper would make. This is still the formula for the superstar emcee today. Although many fans criticize him for making predominantly love songs now, I think it was the smartest thing he ever did. I think LL's longevity is a testament to the change. The women who loved LL didn't love him for the same reasons that the fellas did. The young boys loved the cocky, sonic, hard as hell lyrical LL. The young ladies loved the softer, "I Need Love" LL. They were coming to see him perform and take off his shirt so they could fantasize. If you study his track record it's always been the love songs that made the album sales. "I Need Love," "Around The Way Girl," "Hey Lover," and most recently "Paradise." If you follow the pattern from "I'm Bad" every other album is a hit. On those albums, he follows the formula. On the misses, the love songs are not strong, and he's trying to use more of the hard-core edge.

Ultimately, LL has nothing to prove. His reign of success in terms of his longevity is untouchable. He has the largest body of work in the history of the game. Only KRS-One has more albums, but LL has more hits. He's been able to change with the times musically better than anybody in the game, and he still gets called on to make high-level, high-profile guest appearances. He's been attacked lyrically by more emcees than any other emcee, ever. And, although he's never won any battles, he's never lost any momentum for any sustained period of time. He always bounces back with a hit record in the face of the battle aftermath. He's one of the most dynamic emcees ever in the game. His voice and energy can go from the purely sonic to the calm and alluring. With his record selection, he's been a master craftsman. He's built his career like a master builder, and he's in prime position to basically do whatever he wants. He's been the face of Def Jam since the beginning. Every album he's ever made has gone gold, platinum, or double platinum. As an emcee, he's been one of the most intense, passionate rhymers ever. Ultimately, he's been a Hip-Hop luminary with heat for over fifteen years. He's been at a high level in the game with very little drop-off, and now with his film career kicking in, he's just as popular as he was in 1987. It's been said that a great actor can read the phone book and make it sound good. As the rap equivalent, LL is the emcee that can make the alphabet sound like a hot rhyme (he actually did that on his song "It Gets No Tougher"). Without question LL's résumé makes it impossible for him to be anything less than one of the top ten among the greatest emcees of all time!

Strength: Charisma. More than the rhyme itself, his energy and charismatic vocal presence make you listen to him.

Weakness: Battle. He has absolutely said some of the weakest rhymes in battle. Part of the reason for that is he's one of the most arrogant emcees ever, and he's much more comfortable talking about himself. He's too busy on himself to focus on anybody else.

Favorite Record: "Nitro," "Jingling Baby"

Favorite LP: *Radio*

#7: LL COOL J

ORIGINALITY: 80

Everybody that knows the story about the time he came with the combination of T-LA Rock, Run, and myself, basically he just wasn't that original. What was original about him was the way he approached it with his energy lyrically.

CONCEPTS: 95

LL is definitely a conceptual emcee. A lot of people don't really realize because they look at him as the love-song guy now. But if you go back and listen, he put some concepts together, especially on the *Bad* album, the "Bristol Hotel," and the "357."

VERSATILITY: 100

One of the most versatile emcees, although Tupac is viewed that way more than everybody else. If you look at LL's work, he would go from hard-core into love songs and vacillate back and forth. He is a versatile emcee with a lot of weapons in his arsenal.

VOCABULARY: 100

Got to go to the old stuff once again to realize how incredible his vocabulary is. He stopped doing it later on in his career, but he has done enough of it for me to give him a 100 on the vocabulary side.

SUBSTANCE: 80

Most of LL's whole deal is me, myself, and I, but even in that you've got to give him points on the love songs. There is space for love to be considered substantive. It is what it is.

FLOW: 90

Especially when you hear the braggadocio records like "Nitro" and "It Gets No Rougher," and when you hear him at what I call the top of his game.

FLAVOR: 90

Even though he was sonic and was yelling when he was doing his thing early on, he still had flavor in his voice. You could just tell he was feeling himself, and he definitely would play with his vocals.

FREESTYLE: 80

His arrogance alone makes that possible.

VOCAL PRESENCE: 100

One of the more powerful voices in the game, a different type of voice outside of the Chuck D type, but definitely his voice was one of the things that grabbed your ear to make you listen to him.

LIVE PERFORMANCE: 100

POETIC VALUE: 80

Not that much poetry, more rhyme than poetry. He would do it with the "I Need Love" type of records. His poetic value comes in with the love songs.

BODY OF WORK: 100

His work speaks for itself. Album after album,

thirteen, fourteen, fifteen songs all over the place, he is diverse. Body of work is stellar.

INDUSTRY IMPACT: 100

Much later than earlier, at the later end of the career. First he came in with the hype and the heat, and then in the latter part of his career he's gotten the accolades with Grammys and nominations.

SOCIAL IMPACT: 80

Outside of being viewed as a sex symbol, for a Hip-Hop icon he didn't really, really have anything that anybody would grab onto in terms of what he represented for them, other than being a superstar.

LONGEVITY: 100!

He should be able to get two hundred on this because he is the longest-lasting emcee at the level that he's been doing it. His longevity speaks for itself.

LYRICS: 90

He is definitely a lyricist. The problem with the lyrics is, once in a while, he will throw in very, very low simplicity within the intricate rhyme, and you wonder why he would do that. More earlier than now.

BATTLE SKILLS: 80

This is the weakest part of his game to me. He seems to not know how to approach a battle. However, with the fact that he still brings the energy and the charisma into the equation, and he does not back down from any battle, he's got to get an 80.

TOTAL SCORE: 1,545

AVERAGE SCORE: 90.8

6

GRAND MASTER CAZ

LIVE RHYME MASTER

Each and every time
We put the music low
Or turn it down for a second to make you say ho
Somebody somewhere
Deep inside the crowd
Has to make a comment or snap out loud
No matter where we are
No matter where we play
There's always a knuckle head
With something to say
Since I'm on the subject
I thought I'd mention
A little somthin to ya
Since you want attention
Paid 5 or 6 dollars to get inside
No girl wants your ugly ass
So ya sit and hide
Wait for an opportunity
To scream out boo
Then leave like a sucker
When the jam is through
Go home and tell ya friends
That the party was wack
Next week we got ya money
Cause you came right back
But this time you brought ya
Girlfriend too
But the bit**
Is stink and ugly even worse than you
So you step up to the front
To watch us rap
Not knowin all along
That I set a trap
An no soon as you open
Ya mouth to speak
I'll be snappin all over you
And ya freak
First of all you're a duck
With wings and a tail
And every stitch of your clothes
Is from a fire sale
None of ya clothes match
Not even ya socks
And your shoes are so cheap

You can feel every rock
Don't try to play high post
It ain't ya station
Got ya coat from the army
They cal salvation
Piss'd on ya self
That's why ya slacks are damp
And when it comes to cash
You ain't got a stamp
Don't mean to hurt ya feelings
But I know cus you ain't had no
Pus** since you knew what it was
If ya don't want me snappin
I'll tell you what
Next time you're at my party
Keep ya big mouth shut

IF YOU KNOW YOUR HIP-HOP HISTORY and you know what a real emcee is, then this ranking will not shock you. However, if you weren't there, or you weren't born, or you just don't know, then look, listen, and learn. Grandmaster Caz is the grandfather of Jay-Z's style. CALM DOWN! Jigga is not biting, copying, or following Caz. Grandmaster Caz is the first emcee that was truly a lyricist, but had that extra slick, player-style, street edge to his game. His original name was Cassanova Fly. That was Big Pimpin' way before Big Pimpin'. He was the first all-purpose emcee. As Cassanova Fly he was actually a DJ and an emcee. He was one of the best party emcees, and could hold a party down with just party rhymes if necessary. He was also one of the best storytellers ever in the game. He had comedic elements to his live rhyme style, and could damage a heckler like he was a stand-up comedian. He had more vocal charisma than most emcees from 1978 to 1984. By 1982, as a member of the legendary Cold Crush Brothers, Caz was the stand-out in the group and definitely the streets' favorite emcee.

Because he was in a group, and the group didn't get a record deal until too late in the game for the style of rhyming they'd mastered, many people are not really familiar with Caz as a soloist, or the group as a force in Hip-Hop. It's really almost impossible to talk about Caz without talking about the Cold Crush. However, he is the final and most significant exemption of all, because without Caz, the predominant writer for the Cold Crush Brothers, groups like Run-DMC wouldn't know how to do a routine. This is a significant point because when you look to score Caz's body of work, you have to go into his group to understand where his true greatness lies. It was because of the groups' routines that they were able to be kings on a street level in Hip-Hop. Caz as the captain, creator, and anchor of the four emcees created song-like chants that helped separate the Cold Crush from all other groups at the time. What's also of major significance is the fact that from 1979 to 1983, when Hip-Hop was in its infancy in the record industry, the only way an emcee could get heat and separation from the pack was to have a hot record. The Cold Crush maintained heat and separation without any records, and Caz was seen as a true lyrical king.

The final testament to Caz's heat is that because of the routines he wrote, the group was able to sell cassette tapes of their live shows, and sometimes the tapes would outsell the hottest records at the time. I break this down in more detail in my book *The True 50 Greatest Groups in Hip-Hop.* As for now, in summarizing, Grandmaster Caz is one of the most complete emcees in the game. He's been one of the best lyricists for over two decades. He's one of the best live emcees ever, and he's also one of the best battle emcees ever. He's one of the many first generation emcees that didn't have the opportunity to make the transition from the streets to wax, but he still has maintained his skill level. He was also nice with the storytelling:

It was a long time ago
But I'll never forget
I got caught in the bed
With a girl named Yvette
I was scared like hell
But I got away
That's why I'm here
Talking to you today
I was outside of my school
Sniffin up the rock
A crowd of people all around
Listening to my box
Just me and my fam
And some guys from the crew
Chillin hard cause we had
Nothing better to do
It was me the L the A and the All
And then I slipped away
To make a phone call
To this very day
It was a move I regret
But I didn't know then
So I called Yvette
I said hello pretty mama
It's your lover man
She said baby come on over
As quick as you can
I said I can't come now
Someone's comin to get me
Then she said I'm all alone
There's nobody wit me
I thought for a second
Oh sh** she's alone
I was knockin at her door

Before she hung up the phone
Then she let me in the house
And gave me a kiss
She said gimmie that thang
That you know I miss
So we went into her room
And we got high
But she couldn't keep her hands
From off my fly
So I made her lock the door
And went to check it
And when I came back in
The girl was naked
That was my cue to do the do
I took my clothes off
And started on the brew
I started tearin sh** up
About a quarter to 3
She said Caz somebody's comin
I said yeah me!
The door busted open
And there was her folks
I said damn they could'a waited
Till I finished my stroke
Her mother was in shock
Her father reached for the shelf
Pulled down a 45
I almost sh** on myself
I said please don't shoot
And plead my case
You'da done the same thing
If you was in my case!
If you spare my life
Believe me friend
You'll never see me around
Your daughter again
Don't ask me why
But he let me leave
I ran 26 blocks
Then I stopped to breathe
Gave thanks to god
He wasn't too upset
And went home and thought about poor Yvette
He must'av beat her ass

Wit everything I assume
I could hear the girl screamin
All the way in my room
And even though I don't see Yvette no more
II know she ain't as fine as she was before

Stories like that are why to this day his reputation is solid. He's also contributed to the game as the writer of the rhymes that Big Bank Hank uses on the first rap classic, "Rappers Delight." Without a doubt, he is an icon, a legend, and a forefather of the slick player street styles of rhymes many emcees use today. By far, Grandmaster Caz is truly one of the greatest emcees ever.

Strength: Lyrical flavor. Most emcees with his level of flavor don't have the lyrical prowess. Caz is skilled out!

Weakness: Wax. Never was able to come across on wax the same way he did live.

Favorite Record: "The Gigantor Routine"

Favorite Tape: *The Harlem World Anniversary '82*

#6: GRANDMASTER CAZ

ORIGINALITY: 100

That goes without saying. He is one of the first of the three original lyrical kings. He is one of the originals.

CONCEPTS: 95

Definitely one of the most conceptual emcees of the game. He went back to the old Cold Crush tapes to listen to the routines, all of the pop-type music that they were doing in all of the songs and the chants . . . he wrote all of the stuff.

VERSATILITY: 100

Caz is a DJ, an emcee, a battle emcee, a party emcee; he was the all-purpose emcee from the very beginning. He was one of the most versatile emcees before records and without records. I know LL and Tupac are the most versatile emcees, and Lauryn Hill when it comes to having records, but I don't know what they would do without records. Caz is one of those emcees who's versatile without the records.

VOCABULARY: 90

Caz doesn't beat you in the head with the vocabulary. You can tell that he is well-read and when it's time to get vocal and vocabularyesque he can definitely bring it that way, but for the most part he tones it down, keeps it a little more street. But he definitely has a nice vocabulary and he uses the words well.

SUBSTANCE: 80

Again, original player heat, kept it street. His substance goes in the same vein of what the gangster rappers would do. It's urban, it's ghetto, and it's gutter.

FLOW: 90

He didn't get too intricate with the flow but he was very, very effective, always on beat, always in pocket, and knew how to grab onto any record that you played.

FLAVOR: 100

Caz is definitely one of the most flavorful, versatile emcees in the game. He's a lyricist with flavor and usually the rule of thumb is if you have flavor you aren't a lyricist, or if you are a lyricist you don't have flavor, but Caz is the perfect balance of both.

FREESTYLE: 80

Freestyle in the old school is not the same as freestyle now. Coming off the top of the head definitely wasn't our forte from back in those days, but Caz is one of those emcees who would definitely get in it live if you brought it that way. But for what freestyle was back then, it was really about writing rhymes outside of your records, about any subject just for the specific point of blowing up the crowd, and Caz was definitely one of the best at doing that.

VOCAL PRESENCE: 100

Without question one of the more recognizable voices. For those that only reference rap records for their history, you have to go deeper than that to understand who he is. A lot of people weren't there but I was and he gets 100 on the vocal presence.

LIVE PERFORMANCE: 100

One of the most legendary things about the Cold Crush was their live performance. Caz is the captain of that, without question. One of the best live emcees ever!

POETIC VALUE: 80

More rhyme then poetry, but he absolutely would use poetic styles when he was doing his storytelling.

BODY OF WORK: 85

Those of you who only reference records for your body of work don't understand that there were tapes being made. Before we made records, we played records and we rhymed on them. Cold Crush is legendary for their tape sales. There was a guy named Tape Master who damn near made his career off of Cold Crush tapes. They were selling like they were selling records. This is before wax, during wax, and they were keeping up with brothers that had wax.

INDUSTRY IMPACT: 90*

With those tapes, 90 percent of the emcees that came from the mid '80s, early '90s studied the Cold Crush. They studied the old-school emcees. Caz definitely, without question, being the lead man and the point man in the equation, was like the prototype for all of the studying that was going on. Some of the emcees today will admit it and some won't. But without question, his industry impact is a 90, with an asterisk next to it because its industry was where it was. He set the early side of the industry off, which basically helped to make an industry.

SOCIAL IMPACT: 80

We did a lot of work to put Hip-Hop on the map. Caz was instrumental in making that happen.

LONGEVITY: 80

1977 to '85, that's eight years, all day long. That's basically the run of the Cold Crush. The run of the Cold Crush is more from '81, but Caz himself as a DJ and an emcee gives him an 80 in longevity.

LYRICS: 100

Come on, he's a lyricist. It is what it is. That is self-explanatory.

BATTLE SKILLS: 100!

One of the best battle emcees ever in the pantheon of battle emcees.

TOTAL SCORE: 1,550

AVERAGE SCORE: 91.1

5

KOOL MO DEE

MASTER TECHNICIAN

I go to work like an architect
I build a rhyme sometimes
It climbs so erect
Skyscrapers look like atoms
Cars electrons
Rollin in patterns
Writing out word after word
With each letter
It becomes visibly better
Cause my foundation
Built a nation
Of rappers and after
I came off vacation
I came to Rome the land I own
And stand alone
On the microphone Daddy's home
So open the door
Play time is over
Time to go to work
Work and show the
Suckers in the place
Who run their face
A taste of the bass
And who's the ace
Start the race
I'm comin in first
With each verse I build a curse
So rappers can't capture
Mo Dee's rapture
And after I have ya
Senseless with endless
Rhymes don't pretend this
Is anything short of stupendous
And when this
Rhyme is done
Your mind will become
So trapped in the rap
You'll lust another one
But you gotta wait
It takes time
I don't write I build a rhyme
Draw the plans
Draft the diagrams
An architect and it slams

And if it's weak when I'm done
Renovate and build another one

WELCOME TO THE PANTHEON! THIS ECHELON of emcees, including Caz, have done things for the game that far supersede making money. I, Kool Mo Dee, am the beginning of the intricate lyrical content. I'm the creator of more wordplay rhyme formulas than anybody in the game. From restructuring sentences, to breaking words down and rhyming them syllabically, to bringing two words together to rhyme with one, to introducing and upgrading high levels of uncommon vocabulary, to creating the high-speed fast rhyme style. What's funny to me is I see many popular emcees today who don't hold me in high regard using most of my techniques. What's even more ironic is many of these same emcees are extremely flawed in the technical aspects of the rhyme. With this I mean many emcees don't match subject to verb properly. They'll sometimes rhyme vowels and lose the enunciation. Many times they rhyme three-syllable words with a one-syllable word, and only the last syllable will rhyme. These are just a few of the many mistakes that Kool Mo Dee never makes. The only emcees that I've ever heard take it to the intricate, meticulous levels that I do are Rakim and Eminem. If you go back and listen to the old Treacherous Three records and listen to how intricate those routines were, you'd get a better picture of what I'm talking about.

Speaking of the Treacherous Three, Special K and LA Sunshine wrote their own rhymes, but I wrote most of the routines. On "The New Rap Language" you get an example of the fast rhyming style I created. On "The Body Rock" you get an example of the chanting-song hook style I brought to the game. Also, "Body Rock," where I literally mouthed out (wrote) the music, is the first rap record with a rock guitar riff on it. In 1981 we had our biggest hit, "Feel the Heartbeat." At that point we began to be viewed in comparison to Flash and the Furious 5. The Cold Crush unequivocally became the kings of the streets. What was most unique about the Treacherous Three was we had very similar skill levels. Although I was the dominant emcee, unlike Melle Mel and Grandmaster Caz, who were viewed as infinitely better than their group members, the separation from me to Special K, and K to LA Sunshine was not that far.

However, the separation began after my 1981 battle with Busy Bee Starsky. Contrary to popular myth, I never had any conflicts with Busy Bee, and I never intended to battle him. That organically, spontaneously happened, because I was hosting the emcee contest that Busy Bee was in. Before the contest began, in front of a packed Harlem World crowd, Busy ran up onstage and began ranting like Ali, about how he was the best emcee because he was undefeated in every contest he'd been in. He jokingly took a picture with the trophy and was ready to leave when a fan yelled out, "Busy Bee can't beat Kool Mo Dee." Busy defended himself, and offended me at the same time by stating that he could. Later on that night I got on after Busy Bee and ended his two-year winning streak. Two weeks later, a tape of the battle began to circulate, and by three months time the city was saturated. The battle was all anyone on the streets was talking about. What was ironic to me was that I didn't like the tape because the rhyme was spontaneous, and thrown together, and I could hear the flaws in my performance. However, battle rule number ten was in effect (take the crowd).

Six years after that, in 1988, I was in the most popular battle of all Hip-Hop history. LL Cool J had been dropping innuendos in his rhymes, making references to washed-up, old-school rappers, and proclaiming to be the "Greatest Rapper in the History of Rap Itself." I respected his skill level, but I knew he didn't have an understanding or mastery of battle. So in 1987, I threw a light jab on "How Ya Like Me Now," just to engage him. He responded with "Jack the Ripper," and just as I suspected he didn't know what he was doing. He committed three cardinal sins: weak rhymes, bragging about record sales, and no references to my skill level.

Here are ten of the thirteen battle laws:

1. On wax, the best rhyme wins. Many emcees forget that a battle, first and foremost, is about lyrical skills.

2. Record and beats cannot save you. The producer is not battling for you! Hot beats and hot records may please the fan, but it doesn't win the battle.

3. Focus on the opponent, not on yourself. The battle is not about how great you are, it's about how great he or she isn't. Crystallize their weakness.

4. Never put simplistic rhymes on wax. Only the likes of KRS-One can do this because he can destroy you live onstage, so it doesn't matter. For anybody else, simplistic rhymes are setting you up for failure!

5. Your money, reputation, and heat cannot win the battle for you. So many emcees make reference to how much money, how many records, and how many accolades they get! It means nothing in battle. You still gotta rhyme, and the rhymes must stand on their own.

6. Mothers, girlfriends, and babies have nothing to do with the battle. For shock dis value, sometimes it's cool to make an occasional family reference, but it can't be the sole focus of the rhyme. You can't shock your way to victory.

7. Freestyles usually lose. It may work for a while, but that's only if you're an incredible freestyler. However, freestyle almost never beats the prepared written battle rhymes. It usually wins in spontaneous scenarios.

8. Personal disses only work live. Jokes about people's appearance, unless masterfully done, only work live because people need to see the visual. If you're talking about someone looking bad on wax, and the person shows up looking good, game over.

9. Assume the underdog position. If you're perceived as the bully or the favorite, subconsciously people are rooting against you.

10. Play to the crowd to take the crowd. This is for the few emcees that still have the heart to battle live—the audience responding usually throws the opponent off their game. Cheers for you are boos for him. Design rhymes for crowd interaction.

The final three rules are Mo Dee's ancient Egyptian secrets, just in case one of you nukkas wanna try me. Ultimately, I am undefeated in battle because I always bring something unexpected to the table. I couldn't believe that one of the inept writers in ego trips "Book of Lists" actually said that LL won the battle. WHAT FIGHT WERE YOU WATCHIN??? Show me one rhyme that LL ever said tighter than this:

I roll hard
Run the rap yard
I don't get even I get odd Todd
Always one up on ya
And I tried to warn ya
You slept you took a bad step
Ruined your rep and wept
You should'a kept
Your mouth shut you know what
You gotta say you're sorry (I'm sorry)
So what
You called me a punk
You wanna see who's soft
Put the microphone down
Let's square off
You need a hand
You got hands for
Tryin to be me
Now LL stands for
Lower Level Lack Luster
Last Least Limp Lover
Lousy Lame Late Lethargic
Lazy Lemon Little Logic
Lucky Leach Liver Lip
Laborious Louse on the
Losers List
Livin Limbo
Lyrical Laps
Low Life
With this loud raps boy
You can't win huh
I don't bend
Look what you got ya self in
Just using your name
I took those L's
Hung 'em on your head
And rocked your bells
Now here we go blow for blow
Let's throw rhyme for rhyme
Yours and mine ay yo

To battle rhyme I know
How to make it flow
So let's go to the ring
Rap or sing and swing
Words and verbs see who deserves
To be king
Serve a blow to that ego
As if you didn't know
Let's go

Any questions? All anybody has to do is go back and listen to "Let's Go" vs. his "Jack the Ripper." It's not even close!

The battle was cool, but there were bigger fish to fry. Many people don't remember what the climate was like for Hip-Hop in 1988, but it was in a very perilous position. Radio was all but boycotting the music. They were forcing the most prominent emcees in the game to conform to making certain types of records in order to get airplay. The formula was: no airplay, no sales, no sales, no deal, no deal, art form dead. This is why I call Will Smith, Heavy D, and myself "unsung heroes of Hip-Hop." Without the radio records we created, Hip-Hop was being systematically shut down. Will got the young kids, but I was the first emcee that the adults really connected with. Because of the mature sound of my voice, and the musical sound of "How Ya Like Me Now" and "Wild Wild West," the older audience began to separate me from the pack. The final stroke was when I was able to do interviews on BET and *Arsenio Hall*. The black adult market was finally paying attention. Believe it or not, as condescending as it sounds, they never thought emcees or rappers could speak proper English. I don't speak of this with any high regard, I'm just pointing out the significance of the timing. Because of my popularity, I became somewhat of an ambassador for Hip-Hop. I was able to get into areas where we weren't allowed. I was able to get people who didn't listen to listen. When I articulated our struggles as poverty-stricken black kids, the elders were able to connect. As an emcee, I was able to make more of a social impact, because of the types of records I made.

Ironically I took a lot of flack from the very industry I was fighting for. Fans wanted the edge, but by sacrificing a little of the edge, I damn near saved Hip-Hop. Of course, there were other elements to the saving of Hip-Hop, but my contribution was very significant as the face of educated Hip-Hop. By 1989, I was confirmed as a Hip-Hop star. At that time I was the longest reigning, successful rap artist in Hip-Hop's short history. The album *Knowledge Is King* was what I think was my best work. That same year I had an epiphany-like transition. I began to see the music industry for what it really was. I only wanted to make music to inspire and help people. Unfortunately, the music industry basically only wants to make money. I began to get industry pressure to make gangster-style rap records, and this was, in my opinion, the ultimate hypocrisy. The very industry that was fighting not to play rap records, touting its potential negative influence on society, was now finding ways to play edited versions of violence-laden gangsta rap because it was hot, and they wanted ratings. I began to battle the industry and silently got black balled. However, in 1990, I worked on the ultimate project of my career, Quincy Jones' *Back On The Block*. I learned more from one album with Quincy than twelve years in the music industry. In 1991 I released my worst album, *Funke Wisdom*, focused on battling the industry instead of making an album. Ironically, I still received a Grammy that year, and by 1992 I induced my release from Jive Records. I figured from 1978 to 1992 was not a bad run.

At the end of the day, when you look at the body of work from upgrading the lyrical intricacies, writing, performing, and producing hit records with the Treacherous Three, going solo, reinventing and creating more hits, introducing the world to high-level Hip-Hop battles, going undefeated in battle from 1978 to 1992, I would have to say that's an impeccable résumé. As far as the skills go, I'm probably one of the most underrated champions in the game. It's like Sugar Ray Robinson. Most of his best fights aren't on tape, but what is on tape is still good enough for you to see greatness. I invite everyone to go back and listen to my arsenal now that the hype is over. Listen to the lyrics and tell me what you think. In 1978, Melle Mel gave emcees a template. In 1978, I innovated it. Emcees, do your history, check your lyrical bloodline. Nine times out of ten I'm somewhere in your lyrical DNA. Kool Mo Dee, ONE OF THE TRUE GREATEST EMCEES EVER!!!

Strength: Rhyme craftsmanship—a true rhyme technician. No one in hip-hop builds a rhyme as intricately as Kool Mo Dee. If you listen to most of my rhymes, they are usually rhymes within a rhyme and they rhyme right down to the syllable.

Weakness: Too invulnerable—never taking position of weakness. Everything always came under the guise of the King, the Master, the best, and when Hip-Hop transitioned into a more personal, vulnerable space, fans were left feeling like they couldn't connect because I (KMD) was never willing to show vulnerability.

Favorite Record: "I Go to Work," "Feel the Heart Beat" (The Treacherous Three)

Favorite LP: Knowledge is King

#5: KOOL MO DEE

ORIGINALITY: 100

The God himself on the mic. One of the three original kings. The prototype for the intricate emcee. The intricate lyrical emcee.

CONCEPTS: 85

Pretty cool in the concepts, not really that conceptual, but then the "Wild Wild West" and the dean records I was doing were very conceptual.

VERSATILITY: 85

I would definitely take chances on doing certain types of records, but for the most part it was more braggadocio than anything else, but would definitely go into the message world on the positive energy without question on the substance side.

VOCABULARY: 100

I would venture to say that there is not an emcee in the game who has shown that he has a deeper vocabulary than Kool Mo Dee.

SUBSTANCE: 100

The records are not hit records, but still have the meaning and the impact in terms of what the subject matter is about. In the same mind of KRS-One and Chuck D, records like "Knowledge Is King" and "Pump Your Fist" and "God Made Me Funky." Absolutely one of the most substantive emcees, period.

FLOW: 90

Didn't get too intricate with the flow. Created many flows that people don't even know about. There are many flows that people are using that are based on what I created.

FLAVOR: 75

Weakest part of the game is absolutely the flavor. I didn't really play with the voice too much, just stayed in attack mode and didn't really use the voice like a weapon. Once in a while I'd take the energy off with the "Wild, Wild, West" song or the "Go See the Doctor," to use my voice instrumentally there, but for the most part it was not really my forte.

FREESTYLE: 80

Once again, for what freestyle was, just rhyming at parties, rhyming about subjects outside of your records, not really coming off the top of your head, even though I do that on an average level.

VOCAL PRESENCE: 100

Without question, the vocal attack was impeccable. One of the more recognizable voices, used as a weapon, especially in battle.

LIVE PERFORMANCE: 90

Could absolutely bring it across on a live stage. One of the first emcees, if not the first, to actually have dancers and do routines.

POETIC VALUE: 80

More rhyme than poem. Would get poetical in spurts, but for the most part was more rhyme than poetry.

BODY OF WORK: 90

You can't overlook the work done with the Treacherous Three with hits like "Heartbeat" and "Body Rock," which basically set the template for everybody using chant-type rhymes and chant-type songs in wax. On wax, a lot of people didn't know how to do that until I came into the equation. Then in 1987, when you got to "How You Like Me Now" and "Wild Wild West" and "I Go To Work," the records basically speak for themselves. The Grammy, Quincy Jones, it is what it is.

INDUSTRY IMPACT: 95

First emcee to get the NAACP Image Award. First emcee nominated for a Grammy, also working with Quincy Jones on the Grammy side.

SOCIAL IMPACT: 85

Not as impactful as Tupac on one level, but what people might not realize is that until I started talking in the late '80s, there was a stereotype about emcees, and nobody even knew that they could talk and put sentences together. I absolutely was the leader in that sense.

LONGEVITY: 100!

Fourteen years is what my run was. So it is second only to LL, quite frankly. 1978 to 1992, and if I really, really wanted to be technical, it was '94. I say '92 just on the humble side. So that's fourteen years without question.

LYRICS: 100

Without question, one of the more technical lyricists in the game. One of the few people who absolutely makes sure that things are grammatically correct, things are articulated properly, energy and voice control is definitely in effect. My lyrical prowess is one of my claims of fame.

BATTLE SKILLS: 100

I am absolutely the battle master in the game outside of KRS-One, Big Daddy Kane, and Grandmaster Caz. Basically battling is my domain. That's what I do.

TOTAL SCORE: 1,555

AVERAGE SCORE: 91.4

4

BIG
DADDY
KANE

MASTER OF
METAPHOR

The kiss of death on a rap pick
And you get a slap quick
So guard it with chapstick
In other words, protect and hold ya
Own, it only takes one punch
To get the head flown
Fists-of-fury suckers get weary
Cause the kane got more
Spice than curry
I add the flavor down on paper
And nothin can save'ya
From catch'n the vapors
Rhymes that'll sting ya face
Like a quick jab
And I'm rubbin'em in
Just like vicks salve
Captivatin, dominatin, innovatin,
Illustratin, fascinatin,
Motivatin, elevatin, terminatin,
Mutilatin, rhymes are worth
They're weight in gold, bold
Never sold to a bidder
They gleam and glitter
Yours are bitter like kitty litter
As for damage, don't tell me
What I'll never do
Cause I quote that I'm r-a-w
So make room, cause fighters are doomed
Try to consume, and make your own tomb
A grave or a casket, a tisket a tasket
Your rhymes out a basket
Boy you'll get ya ass kicked
For frontin like ya hittin hard
When your arms are too short
To box with god

THE MACK IS OFFICIALLY ON WAX! BIG DADDY KANE is like a poetic player pimp with deadly lyrics. On his first album, *Long Live the Kane*, he announced in no uncertain terms who he was. On his album cover, he's sitting in a gold chair (throne), dressed in a purple, gold, and white Roman robe, draped in truck jewelry, with three women around him, feeding him wine and fruit from gold cups and platters. Metaphor: Black Caesar is here.

Kane approached the game with an attitude like we were all wasting time rhyming until he came. His rhyme style was inherently challenging. He was a natural battle emcee, with a lyrical flare for the ladies. He was one of the most polarized emcees of the late '80s. His lyrics had the fury of fire, but his persona was as cool as ice. His rhymes were designed for battle, but he had no beefs with any emcees. He had the spiritual essence of the 5 percent nation, while simultaneously feeling like the player of the year. The combination of these aspects made Kane the hottest emcee in the streets. Before Biggie, Kane was that lyrical ladies' man that put Brooklyn on the map. Kane was so highly regarded for his lyrical prowess that he could come onstage dressed like a 1980s gangster in a three-piece suit and tie and never receive any flak from his dressed-down peers. The school of thought at the time was, a truly hard-core emcee dressed down, never up. This was normal for Kane; he usually broke all of the so-called unwritten rules.

In 1987, Whodini and LL had set the template for what came to be known as the Hip-Hop love song. In 1988, when Kane got his turn at it, he pushed it to the next level. Kane actually sang his own hook! Kane can't sing! Once again, his respect level was so high, fans just acted like that didn't happen. He was so hot that his album went gold without any real radio play. His rhyme style was so infectious he became one of the most imitated emcees ever in the game. I think this is because, in my opinion, Big Daddy Kane has the most perfect rhyme inflections ever! He always puts the emphasis on the more important part of the word, sentence, or syllable. He never leaves any part of the rhyme hanging. Every single word is always tied to another. The other thing that he does masterfully is the rhyme dismount. Few emcees know how to do it, and even fewer know how important it is to end your rhyme with a potent punch line, or a profound statement. In rhyme song structure, the final line in your verse should set up your hook. The reason the line is important is because the hook is the first time that the listener is really getting a chance to participate with you. The punch line should incite this. Big Daddy Kane is the king of this. What really makes him special is he fills the rhyme with punch lines, and then dismounts the rhyme with something colorful and usually perfectly inflected. Kane also had the rare combination of being a battle emcee and a supreme lyricist, with the flavor of sarcasm.

Kane took over where Caz left off. As a member of the second generation of the three lyrical kings, Rakim, KRS-One, and Big Daddy Kane, Kane was the only one that made music geared towards women. His status as a Hip-Hop sex symbol reached an all-time high in 1989. Kane, in keeping with breaking the rules, threw an all-women, ladies only concert at the Apollo Theatre. They really would not sell tickets to any men, and if a man scalped a ticket, he wasn't let in. The show was sold out, and the reports were Kane opened the show in a bathtub onstage. I don't think there is another level past that. Kane pushed the player image strictly from authenticity. He never needed it as a gimmick because he was already a lyrical king on the street. Many pundits however, look at this aspect as something that backfired on Kane. The feeling was, people began paying attention to the image more than his skills. In any case, what Kane has contributed to the game can never be denied. One of his most overlooked contributions is how he set the trend to change the terms of freestyle. Until 1986, all freestyles were written. Any emcee coming off the top of the head wasn't really respected. The sentiment was emcees only did that if they couldn't write. The coming off the top of the head rhymer had a built-in excuse to not be critiqued as hard. That all changed when Kane and Biz Markie recorded "Just Rhymin with Biz."

"Well it's the Kane in the flesh
Of course I'm fresh
Oh you thought that I was rotten
Huh I beg your pardon
To be gettin paid, and gettin busy
Fall together so
A man of my ambiance? Never
Could I be weak, why I'm rather unique
That I be usin and not many
Can manage, so a brother
Like me I do damage,
Just by pickin up the mic
To go solo, I cold turn a party
On out and oh yo,
I get physical mystical very artistical
Givin party people somethin
Funky to listen to
That's why the other emcees
Can't swing long
I stomp'em out just like
I was king kong
Steppin on roaches, I get ferocious
Super cala frajalistic expyaladocious
I go on and on and on and
Until the bright Shirley Murdox
Morning,
Cause I'm a pimp, here to primp
Yes the emp-eror, bringin much
Terror in ya era
I'm ready willin and i'm able
So bust the move
Never use a barber shop
I got my home boy smooth
Coolin out with the clippers
Right around the way
To keep my fresh cameo cut
Everyday"

The word on the street was that was a tape of Biz Markie and this new emcee named Big Daddy Kane and they were just fooling around, rhyming off the top of the head. That tape turned into a hot single and changed the perception of what freestyle was, and simultaneously made Kane one of the most anticipated emcees of 1987. As a member of the Juice Crew, Kane was known to write for Biz Markie and Roxanne Shanté. As a soloist, he was one of the most flavorful, most charismatic lyricists ever. His delivery is impeccable. One of the best battle emcees ever to not have a battle. This is a testament to the level of respect and fear that other emcees had for Kane. Other than KRS-One, no emcee has been as feared.

Which brings me to my conclusion of this chapter. In 1982, I'd just come off of destroying Busy Bee in a battle. From that time until 1987, I was the most feared emcee in the game. One day, as I stood in front of a high school "Printing," three students came up to me and challenged me to battle their leader. I looked to see which youngster would dare challenge me. I laughed and said "Don't do it to yourself" and walked away. For some reason the teenager smiled and he and his friends all slapped hands and acted as if I'd made their day. Five years later Big Daddy Kane introduced himself to me as that teenager. He said he didn't think he was ready but he wanted to take the chance and battle me to see where he stood and what he could learn. That kind of heart and insight is what made him shine. He was a student of the game and he approached it like a warrior. Big Daddy Kane is one of the few emcees on this list that could be about top rhymes and rhyme style alone. The fact that he's done more just ensures his place among the top ten. Big Daddy Kane is absolutely one of the true greatest emcees ever.

Strength: Metaphor delivery—the best in the business at delivering the metaphor punch line. Perfect inflections.

Weakness: Too much pimpin'—lost momentum when people started focusing on pimpin' instead of skill.

Favorite Record: "Mortal Combat," "Warm It Up"

Favorite LP: *Long Live the Kane*

#4: BIG DADDY KANE

ORIGINALITY: 95

Second wave of the second three kings. Big Daddy Kane came after the first three. He brought his own flavor to the equation, without question.

CONCEPTS: 85

Actually, he would get more conceptual within his rhymes more than on the albums.

VERSATILITY: 90

He was one of the first emcees taking chances, doing the types of records that people were scoffing at, at the time, but everybody is doing it now. He was doing records with Barry White and Blue Magic way before everybody else.

VOCABULARY: 90

He doesn't go crazy with the vocabulary, but Kane is absolutely notorious for getting on rolls and throwing in word, after word, after word, after word, syllabically matched.

SUBSTANCE: 80

Same line as Caz, Jigga, that's the family. The trinity is actually Caz to Kane to Jay-Z. They just rolled street flavor. The flavor, street hustler, mack, pimp style.

FLOW: 100

Kane is absolutely one of the best flow-ers ever in the game. He kind of changed the way people were flowing based on when he came.

FLAVOR: 100

One of the most flavorful lyricists. Again, he is like Caz, in that same bloodline. Jay-Z has it also, where they are lyricists and they have flavor. That is an unheard-of skill.

FREESTYLE: 90

That's just what he does. He's got the gift of gab and his freestyle is incredible.

VOCAL PRESENCE: 100

He absolutely understands how to project and use his voice articulately. His vocal presence is crazy.

LIVE PERFORMANCE: 100

Again, one of the best emcees live. Absolutely. If you go back, whether you've got tape or whatever, you can see Big Daddy Kane and even to this day he is still one of the best emcees performing live.

POETIC VALUE: 80

More rhyme then poetry. That is just the common formula that a lot of emcees are using now, and Kane is in the same vain.

BODY OF WORK: 90

His first album came out blazing. Second album, same thing. Lost a little momentum on the third and fourth, but you can't just look at it as sales and heat, you've got to look at what he's doing within the album, and he still stayed on point, especially lyrically.

INDUSTRY IMPACT: 90

He has a 90 on the industry impact, not from the recognition of the Grammys and the awards; his industry impact is a little more unique. In that trinity with Kane, Rakim, and KRS-One, more emcees imitated Kane than any of the three. It was more like when Prince came. There was a difference between Prince and Michael Jackson. When Prince came, he

had a lot of followers like the Jesse Johns Antra Crew/Review and Morris Day and the Time, that Minneapolis sound. Prince actually created a sound and a lot of people came out doing that sound. Big Daddy Kane is that guy in the Hip-Hop world. A lot of emcees emulated what he was doing more than anybody else, so I gave him a 90 on the industry impact on that alone.

SOCIAL IMPACT: 80

Outside of the Hip-Hop world, he wasn't really that well known. He is more popular now than he was then, even though he was hotter then. Right now, he is being affiliated with being the pimp in the game.

LONGEVITY: 90

He's got the nine years in, actually he did eight and came back, took some time off, and he is actually doing things right now. I think he is getting ready to drop something shortly. He did drop something in '98. It didn't talk over too well, but he still did his thing and he was on point lyrically.

LYRICS: 100

Self-explanatory. Listen to the records. You can tell that Big Daddy Kane is that lyricist.

BATTLE SKILLS: 100

One of the best battlers in the game, ever.

TOTAL SCORE: 1560

AVERAGE SCORE: 91.7

3

KRS-ONE

MASTER OF CEREMONIES

Everybodies bad
And everybodies tough
But how many people
Are intelligent enough
To open up their eyes
And see through the lies
Discipline themselves yourself
To stay alive not many
That's why the universe sent me
Today on this stage with this to say
The rich will get richer
And the poor will get poorer
In the final hour
Many heads will lose power
What does the rich vs poor
Really mean psychologically
It means you gotta pick your team
When someone says the rich gets richer
Visualize wealth and put
Yourselves in the picture
The rich get richer
Because they work towards rich
The poor get poorer because
Their mind can't switch
From the ghetto let go
It's not a novelty
You could love your neighborhood
Without lovin poverty follow me
Every mother father son daughter
There's no reason to fear the
New world order
We must order the whole new world to pay us
The new world order and the
Old state chaos
The big brother watchin over you
Is a lie you see
Hip-Hop could build its own
Secret society
But first you and i got to unify
Stop the niggativity and
Control your creativity
The rich is gettin richer
So why we ain't richer
Could it be we still thinkin

Like niggas
Educate yourself
Make your world view bigger
Visualize wealth
And put yourselves in the picture

A DOPE EMCEE IS A DOPE EMCEE! With or without a record deal, all can see! And that's who KRS is son, he's not your run of the mill, cause for the mill$ he don't run. KRS-One is the most feared emcee in the game ever! When other emcees talk about KRS, it's always with a tinge of awe. If there is ever any criticism expressed, the selection of words is so carefully chosen you'd think they were under the Spanish inquisition. Only the fearless, MC Shan and the masterful, Melle Mel would even battle KRS. However, that was well before anyone knew what he would evolve into. Nelly made an attempt to challenge him, but like many of the new artists, he only talked about selling records and making money. He never talked about his skills. Furthermore, by 2000 KRS was much more Spiritually Minded than battle oriented. This was obvious by his more toned-down cerebral rebuttals. The younger KRS would have gone for the jugular.

In 1987, KRS-One was positioned to be the final piece to the second trinity of lyrical kings. I'd already gracefully passed the baton to Rakim, and Caz passed it to Big Daddy Kane. But Melle Mel wouldn't relinquish his position. In fact, Melle Mel never concedes anything. One night in the Latin Quarters, Hip-Hop's hottest club at the time, Mel was in an argument with Biz Markie about lack of real lyrical skills coming from the next generation of emcees. Mel was referencing Biz as an example of the problem. Biz, on the other hand, conceded that he himself wasn't a lyricist but he was willing to bet all he had on Big Daddy Kane defeating Mel in a battle. Mel immediately pulled out one thousand dollars and dared anyone to battle him for it. Out of respect, not fear, Kane didn't accept the battle. The argument continued for a few minutes until a voice from the crowd yelled, "I'll battle you." Standing on top of the staircase was KRS-One; he was the voice accepting the challenge. They made their way to the stage and Mel rhymed first. Honestly, Mel's rhyme was better than KRS'. However, battle rule number one is, the best rhyme only wins on wax. As KRS displayed, battle rule number ten, he who wins the crowd wins the war (live)! There was one line that KRS said that shifted the crowd in his favor:

Old school artist don't always
Burn
Your just another artist that
Had his turn
But now it's my turn!

The crowd went ballistic. KRS took them into overdrive by using one of the top-secret methods of battle. From that day on, he was viewed as the third lyrical king in the second lyrical trinity of Hip-Hop. What was interestingly ironic to me was that I never saw KRS as a better emcee than Melle Mel. And truthfully, in the beginning stages of the battle with MC Shan, Shan was more technically sound than KRS. Frankly, early in the game, I thought KRS was rather remedial. However, I really liked him and I couldn't put my finger on why. He was christened by the streets and by Brooklyn in particular. This was significant because Brooklyn was the tone setter for Hip-Hop at that time. The Bronx was about your pedigree, and whether or not you knew your history. Harlem was about how fly your presentation was and whether or not you could be hard-core and still vibe with the ladies. Queens was more about the beats and whether or not you were making money. But Brooklyn just wanted you to be skilled and feel real! So when Brooklyn co-signed you, it meant you had a chance to make some noise. KRS-One had the Bronx pedigree, and the Brooklyn feel. Basically, he was official. The stripped-down, hard-core style of music he rhymed on was so different and so potent, that while he was battling MC Shan, in Shan's hometown (Queens), KRS had the whole place singing "South Bronx."

KRS made himself more than a force to be reckoned with, he was a force to beware of. You knew that he would battle and disrespect anybody. He was even going to battle Kane, solely based on his Juice Crew affiliation, and his inadvertent connection to Shan. I actually didn't know if he and I were on a collision course or not. In the spring of 1988, I got my answer. I got a call from Barry Weise at Jive Records, telling me that they'd signed KRS and my name was on his upcoming album. KRS had made such an impact as a battle emcee, I thought sure he was dissing me to call me out. I got an advanced copy of the song "Still Number One" and I couldn't believe my ears. He used the same rhyme that he battled Melle Mel with in the last verse, and as the record goes into its vamp he says, "Kool Moe Dee is down with us." This was more mind-blowing than the dis I was anticipating. Then it hit me. KRS was a student of the game that wasn't only studying the skills of emcees, he was also studying their personalities. Years later he expressed that he thought I was the only emcee from the earlier era that really got it. I was the only one that actually connected with the next generation. I don't know if I was the only one, but I definitely loved the new masters. And after hearing what I think is his hallmark album, *By Any Means Necessary*, I became a fan. Everything crystallized when I realized he was much more than a battle rapper. His consciousness was evident in the album-cover photo. He paid homage to Malcolm X, and sent a visual message to the Hip-Hop community. The cadence I once thought was simplistically pedantic I now understood was masterfully sonnetized. This was also very fundamental in him becoming one of the best live emcees ever. His cadence is perfect for people to sing along with and there's very little room for them to listen without participation. He, more than any other emcee, mastered the balance of polarity, and like Lauryn Hill, almost has no weaknesses. He's the party emcee with lyrics. He's the conscious emcee that delivers the positive messages with the same fury as the violent messages. He's the emcee that's extremely poetic without losing the edge of the lyrical spitter. He's a battle emcee that would stage a battle with his opponent so that the opponent could make money off of it. Remember he's very cool with MC Shan. He's the emcee that would make a love song and direct it towards materialism instead of women. He did everything that the gangsta rapper did lyrically without the lower levels of profane, mundanely executed rhyme styles. He was second only to Chuck D in being considered a black leader from the ranks of Hip-Hop.

He went into a zone in 1990 that propelled and sustained him from then through the turn of the new millennium. On every album he began to drop conscious poems that would cause people to think about things in alternate ways. In 1989, he hinted at things to come on the *Ghetto Music: The Blueprint of Hip-Hop* album. Now known in Hip-Hop circles as the original "Blueprint." He took on the persona of the teacher; the album was like a compartmentalized history lesson. The album was significantly more profound than any of his previous work, but as all emcees find out, the music industry is about music and not messages. It's about labels and not artists. It's about money and not people. Critics panned the album and on the surface, he lost momentum. But beneath the surface he solidified his core underground audience. He returned the following year and came even harder with more messages and even less radio-oriented music. He was literally battling the music industry, and he simultaneously coined a term that is now part of Americana: "Edutainment." If the word was around before him, I know most Hip-Hoppers didn't hear it until he dropped his album with that title. On that album he has excerpts of himself at a speaking engagement, confirming his position as Hip-Hop leader and not just a rapper! His aggression was higher and his poetic social commentary was at an apex.

> *You can call a man a bum*
> *With disgust on your morning run*
> *Casue he lives outside on the street*
> *You don't notice*
> *But you fail to realize*
> *That the one you so despise*
> *Reflects yourself*
> *Cause every black man is homeless*
> *You can take your alka seltzer*
> *While you talk about shelter*
> *You might even wanna talk*
> *About a little loan*
> *Cause no matter how rich you become*
> *You'll always be 2 not 1*
> *Cause believe it or not*
> *America ain't your home*
> *We've been taught to say our name*
> *Afro-american all the same*
> *Not fully american*
> *But getting there very slowly*
> *Cause to fully be american ya know*
> *You gotta take out the word afro*
> *Now they've relaxed our hair*
> *They might as well call us toby*
> *See afro and black are african*
> *While theft is american*

So how can afro-american make
Much sense
Your ancestor came from africa
By stealing them
Now you're born in america
So the black man is homeless
Even though he pays rent
Some black people say
We built this place
So we are american
But of the black race
Well let me make this
Little topic known
The japanese also built this place
In technology and they're
Winning the race
But at the end of the day
The japanese can go home!

KRS is always dropping messages to evoke alternative thoughts and many times his messages are misconstrued. This is why one of the biggest criticisms of him is "he's contradictory." I understand why people feel that way but I totally disagree. I think he is as ambivalent as Tupac but with a sarcastic edge. Sometimes he mocks the culture by taking on characteristics of it. This was the case on his album *Sex and Violence*. He was sarcastically saying, "This is what America is about." And since they wouldn't give his more conscious records any radio play, he was offering them what they wanted in sarcasm! Believe it or not, many people took him literally and thought he was selling out.

Ultimately, KRS is one of the most enigmatic emcees ever. He has fathered the Stop the Violence movement and the H.E.A.L. movements. He's been an emcee dedicated to uplifting civilization. He once called himself a humanist and even got flak for that by some of the more radical black groups who thought his humanist vibe was contrived to take the edge off of black consciousness. No matter what you think of how he does it, everybody knows that there is a deep level of conscious concern and effort to help the culture. His newest project is the "Temple of Hip-Hop" an institution dedicated to the preservation of Hip-Hop culture.

As far as his skills are concerned, from album to album, he didn't only get better, he quantum leaped in ways that no other emcee ever did. He went from criminal-minded to spiritual-minded. He went from battle rapper to philosopher, to teacher, to leader, to visionary, to missionary. And no matter what anybody ever says about KRS the philosopher, the teacher, or the visionary, you never hear an utterance questioning his skills. Without question, he's one of the fiercest emcees ever. Any list that doesn't have him in the top five is bogus. KRS-One is one of the true greatest emcees ever.

Strength: Potency—his delivery, flow, voice, cadence, and messages always come from a place of power. That power translates to the stage like a commando leading an army of followers. He never comes off looking weak.

Weakness: Women. With all of the jewels he dropped, he never geared songs to the ladies or focused on male-female relations from a feminine point of view.

Favorite Record: "Rapture," "Sound Of tha Police"

Favorite LP: *By Any Means Necessary*

#3: KRS-ONE

ORIGINALITY: 95

Part two of the trinity. The second-wave trinity, I should say. KRS-One coming down from the bloodline. Melle Mel to KRS to Biggie.

CONCEPTS: 85

The sound of the police, black cop . . . KRS is one of the more conceptual emcees in the game. The only difference with him is he is more of a quintessential emcee, so he absolutely will be doing the rhymes about how dope he is within that. But he definitely gets very, very conceptual and very socially relevant.

VERSATILITY: 95

One of the more versatile emcees in the game. I think he has more styles than anybody, period, so his versatility is based on his styles alone.

VOCABULARY: 90

He doesn't hit you in the head with the vocabulary, he sprinkles it in and uses it in strategic places.

SUBSTANCE: 100

Don't even ask. You know what he represents. He is the first guy with the heart to say on wax that Jesus is black. His substance is just over the top, period.

FLOW: 100

More flows than anybody I have ever heard. You have to listen to more of his latest stuff then his earlier stuff to really understand how tight and how upgraded his flows are.

FLAVOR: 90

Uses his voice excellently. One of the best conversational emcees. He is definitely one of the first and one of the best conversational emcees.

FREESTYLE: 100

The highest level of freestyle I have ever heard. KRS-One, 100!

VOCAL PRESENCE: 100

Potent, powerful voice.

LIVE PERFORMANCE: 100

Without question, the strong point in his equation is that he is one of the best emcees live ever. He might be the best. Doug E Fresh is a party emcee but in this realm, KRS-One is virtually untouchable.

POETIC VALUE: 90

Slightly more rhyme then poetry, but he absolutely approaches it poetically, especially when he is bringing you a message.

BODY OF WORK: 100

A lot of people don't know, but I think KRS-One has more albums than anybody in the history of Hip-Hop, including LL.

INDUSTRY IMPACT: 70

KRS basically flew below the radar, partially of his own doing. He never wanted to make records for radio so he basically said F@#$ the industry and it looks like the industry basically fronted on him.

SOCIAL IMPACT: 80

He still connected to people on the street level and even though he didn't really have a lot of the pop success, or a lot of the crossover success, he does a lot of things on the underground side that a lot of people don't know about. Like right now he is trying to do the Temple of Hip-Hop and the basis of that is to preserve Hip-Hop in its organic form. On that alone you've got to give him points.

LONGEVITY: 100

Speaks for itself. From '86 to still making records. It is what it is.

LYRICS: 100

Come on. Do I need to even say? He is the lyricist. He tones it down when he want to tone it down but he amps it up whenever he wants to amp it up.

BATTLE SKILLS: 100

Without question another straight battle master. KRS-One along with Big Daddy Kane and Grandmaster Caz, are basically three of the six or seven emcees that I would never battle.

TOTAL SCORE: 1,595

AVERAGE SCORE: 93.8

2

RAKIM

MASTER RHYMER

I learned to relax in my room
And escape from New York
And return through the womb
Of the world as a thought
Thinkin how hard it was
To be born
Me being cream
With no physical form
Millions of cells
With one destination
To reach the best part
That's lifes creation
Nine months later a job well done
Make way cause here I come
Since I made it this far
I can't stop now
There's a will and a way
And I got the know how
To be all I can be and more
And see all there is to see before
I'm called to go back to the essence
It's a lot to learn
So I study my lessons
I thought the ghetto
Was the worst that could happen to me
I'm glad I listened
When my father was rappin to me
Cause back in the days
They lived in caves
Exiled from the original
Man astray away
Now that's what I call hard times
I'd rather be here
To exercise the mind
Then I take a thought
Around the world twice
From knowledge to born
Back to knowledge precise
Across the desert
That's hot as the Arabian
But they couldn't cave me in
Cause I'm the as-i-an
Reachin for the city of Mecca
Visit Medina

Visions of Nefertiti
Then I see her
mind keeps traveling
I'll be back after I
Stop and think about
The brothers and sisters in Africa
Return the thought
Through the eye of a needle
For miles I fought
And i just bought the people
Under the dark skies
On the dark side
Not only there
But right here's an apartheid
So now is the time
For us to react
Take a trip through the mind
And when you get back
Understand your third eye
Seen all of that, it ain't
Where ya from, it's where ya at!

"Ladies and gentleman
You're about to see, a past time
Hobby about to be,
Taken to the maximum"!

RAKIM IS THE GREATEST RAPPER OF ALL TIME!!! There are other emcees that have certain elements that Rakim doesn't. Biggie's explosive delivery, KRS's live performance, Kane's condescension, Kool Moe Dee's craftsmanship, Melle Mel's bombast or Slick Rick's storytelling acumen. However, no other rapper emcee or Hip-Hop artist has ever been so potent lyrically, that fans would buy and listen to his records solely for the purpose of hearing the rhymes. In urban America, music is one of the most important cultural influences in our lives. If we don't like the music, we don't listen to the song. Rakim had many records that people didn't like musically, but because he was rhyming on them, we would listen to them again and again. I would venture to say that Rakim is the most studied emcee ever. Any emcee that came after 1986 had to study Rakim just to know what to be able to do. Rakim is the author of "flow." Before him there was no such thing as flow. While he didn't invent the word, the importance of how you said your rhyme and it being defined as flow started with Rakim. In 1986, Rakim was the second eight-year Hip-Hop paradigm shift. Remember, music works on the number eight. Eight notes, eight bars, eight-part harmony, etc. This is also true if you get into the mathematical science yearly. Hip-Hop has two-year, three-year, five-year, seven-, eight- and nine-year cycles. The eight-year cycle is the paradigm shift. That's when some emcee comes or creates something that changes the way we interpret a great emcee. In other words, from 1970 to 1978 we rhymed one way, Melle Mel, in 1978, gave us the new cadence we would use from 1978 to 1986. Then Rakim, in 1986, gave us flow, and that was the rhyme style from 1986 to 1994. Then Biggie came with a newer flow which dominated from 1994 to 2002. In 2002, Eminem created the song that got the first Oscar in Hip-Hop history. And, I would have to say that his flow is the most dominant right now. Rakim is one of the only emcees that is openly revered by other emcees to a level of conceding his superiority. As Michael Jordan is the basketball player's basketball player, Rakim is the emcee's emcee! He is referenced as the standard of lyrical greatness. Rakim was able to get props from other emcees at a time when it wasn't commonplace. His skill level was so evident no one ever even questioned whether or not he needed hot music to help or carry him.

When I first heard him I was in my car listening to the A-side of his two-side cassette single. On the song "Eric-B for President" I could tell something was special about him. His rhyme style was the opposite of the yelling, energetic cadences of Run and LL. Little did I know at the time, but the sonic cadences that Run and LL used, which were the heightened volume versions of Melle Mel's cadence, was on its death bed. Rakim's laid-back flow was the death of the yelling style. However, the song "Eric B" was a party jam and Rakim was a complementary element to the record. I had no idea what I was in for when I turned the tape over. The song "My Melody" was the official coronation of the paradigm shift, and the changing of the guard. I literally had to pull over and stop driving to fully take in what was happening. You have to remember, I was one of the first generations three lyrical god kings at this time, and everything in me is saying that there is a new king here.

I listened to the record ten times in a row, looking for flaws, but I had to be honest with myself: this was one of the best emcees I'd ever heard. I settled myself with the thought that this might just be a one-time thing. In addition to that, I would have to see him perform before I could really give him props. He had a couple of shows at the Roof Top and the Latin Quarters. The crowd didn't respond well, and at the Roof Top he actually got booed. I remember having mixed emotions. On the one hand, my fears of losing my spot as top-dog lyrical emcee were quelled. On the other hand, he was still the best new emcee I'd heard and I wasn't comfortable with people not responding to him. Finally, in December 1986, Rakim released what I think is the perfect Hip-Hop record, "I Know You Got Soul." The record was the perfect balance of lyrics, hook, and hardcore dance beat. And the first verse has one of the best rhyme dismounts ever!

> *It's been a long time*
> *I shouldn't've left you*
> *Without a strong rhyme to step to*
> *Think of how many weak shows*
> *You slept through? Times up*
> *I'm sorry i kept you*
> *Think'n of this you keep*
> *Repeat'n you miss*

The rhymes of the microphone
Soloist, so you sit by the
Radio hand on the dial soon
As you hear it pump up the volume
Dance wit ya speaker
Till you hear it blow
Then plug in the head phone
Cause here it go
It's a four letter word
When it's heard it'll control
Your body to dance (you got it) soul
Detects a tempo like a red alert
Reaches ya reflex and let it work
When this is playing
You can't get stuck with
A step so get set
And i'm'a still come up with
A gift to be swift
Follow the leader the rhyme'll go
Def wit the record
That was mixed a long time ago
It could be done
But only i could do it
For those that can dance and
Clap ya hands to it
I start to think and then i sink
Into the paper, like it was ink
When i'm writtin i'm trapped
In between the lines
I escape when i finish
The rhyme—i got soul

When this record hit the streets, it was confirmed I was no longer king, I was now a legend. From that point on, anybody emceeing was forced to focus on their flow. It wasn't to the extent of being more important than your rhyme like the Biggie era of 1994, but it was the beginning of the end for the lyrical masters without flavorful flows. Rakim set the tone alone for about a year before people realized that Kane and KRS-One were in the same league. However, from 1986 through most of 1987, Rakim was the man. When his album *Paid in Full* came, in June 1987, the anticipation was like waiting for a Prince album. That same month, LL was to drop *Bad*, his second album, and believe me there was nothing hotter than the two of them in terms of Hip-Hop's anticipation. It was like Michael Jackson and Prince coming out at the same time. The difference was Rakim was the new kid on the block with the new flow. Ultimately, LL's double-platinum LP out sold Rakim's four to one, but Rakim's album goes down in history as the classic. In my book, it's the third best Hip-Hop album ever! That album alone reshaped Hip-Hop on so many levels. Firstly, it put Rakim at rhyme-god status. Secondly, it elevated Marly Marl's status as a Hip-Hop producer to one of the best ever. Thirdly, it put lyricist back on the map. Fans were now listening for rhymes again. And finally, it killed the Run-DMC era, and redefined what would be perceived as hard-core. Snoop may be the smoothest rapper ever, but Rakim is the smoothest lyricist ever. His flow is godly. Other than Method Man, there hasn't been anyone in Hip-Hop's storied history that synchs with, or sinks into a track like Rakim. He is never off beat. Thematically, he's about as precise as you can get. For a laid-back voice, he has the most vocal presence ever. He comes at the game poetically and lyrically. In 1988, he solidified his rhyme-god status with the release of "Follow the Leader." That summer, DJ Jazzy Jeff and the Fresh Prince, Public Enemy, J.J. Fad, and I were on tour opening for Run-DMC. We were all standing around Will's tour bus waiting for Russell Simmons. The word was Russell had just signed Eric-B and Rakim, and he had the advanced copy of the album. I'm telling you, we were waiting for Russell like he was bringing us checks. That was the power of Rakim. Nobody moved for about a half hour because we couldn't wait to hear what Rakim had to say. After we heard the single "Follow the Leader," there was an orgasmic silence. Russell took the tape and left smiling like a proud father. He knew he had gold.

Rakim's body of work, more than any emcee, has been about his rhyme ability. His music and his messages were secondary. It was like going to a dunk contest. You don't want to see anything but dunks. Rakim's rhyming was always like a dunk. We were in awe of how he put his words together. This is what sets up the unfair backlash he gets for his live performance. When Rakim rhymes, people listen, they don't dance. However, he does have two killer all-time Hip-Hop dance tracks, "President" and "Soul," and this convolutes the matter when he's in concert. Rakim is more like a rhyming spoken-word artist with a musical backdrop. His music is not reflective of a party, it's reflective of a rhymer. There is no other emcee that has that level of rhyming acumen (Ras Kass and Pharoahe Monch are close).

In the final tally, Rakim is by far one of the greatest rhyme gods ever. He's impacted the game on a level that few emcees can claim. He's responsible for major transitions in the art of emceeing. His record "Lyrics of Fury" is one of the last examples of the high-level old-school freestyle. His song "No Omega" is an eighty-eight bar, one-verse masterpiece! Only Cool G Rap's "Men At Work" is longer in total rhyme time. Nonetheless, Rakim is synonymous with LYRICAL EXCELLENCE. He's the one emcee that other emcees revel in being compared to. When you're being compared to Rakim you are being considered in a realm of mastery. Without question, Rakim is so masterful lyrically the the music seems to be in the way! Like I said before, any list that has Rakim less than top five is absolutely bogus. Rakim is the GREATEST RAPPER, and one of the TRUE GREATEST EMCEES of all time!

Strength: Rhymes—the greatest rapper ever!

Weakness: Live lexicon. It's hard for him to translate live because the rhymes are not designed for you to sing along, they're designed to blow your mind.

Favorite Record: "I Know You Got Soul," "Follow the Leader"

Favorite LP: *Paid in Full*

#2: RAKIM

ORIGINALITY: 95

The final chapter to the second wave of the lyrical trinity. Rakim is absolutely in the lyrical bloodline. Kool Moe Dee to Rakim to Nas. The cerebral lyrical intricate emcee.

CONCEPTS: 90

Once you start to get into "Teach The Children" and "No Omega" and "Casualties of War," forget it. Rakim is absolutely one of the most conceptual emcees, period.

VERSATILITY: 90

He will shift gears in subject matter. He can give you the party side, but he is still lyrical. He can give you the social commentary, but he is still lyrical. He can give you relevance; he can go metaphysical on you and still give you lyrical. He can go spiritual, give you a 5 percent doctrine and still be lyrical. He is always lyrical within it.

VOCABULARY: 90

Within the lyrics, he is always bringing certain levels of vocabulary, especially when he decides to get spiritual and metaphysical with it. Just listen to "Who Is God" and you will get it.

SUBSTANCE: 95

On the substance equation, a lot of people don't know, but it's almost like Rakim meant all business on the mic. He got a little bit of the classic emcee braggadocio on one hand, but you could just feel that when you listen to the albums, he had a lot to say. He really, really kept it very substantive.

FLOW: 100!

Rakim is basically the inventor of flow. We were not even using the word flow until Rakim came along. It was called rhyming, it was call cadence, it was called whatever it was, but it wasn't called flow. Rakim created flow!

FLAVOR: 90

Laid-back energy with flavor. One of the hardest things on the planet to pull off. It's like the smoothest basketball you'll ever see. It's like a brother dribbling through his legs and behind his back and it looks like it's going in slow motion, but nobody can steal the ball from him. His flavor is ridiculous.

FREESTYLE: 90

A furified freestyle. Just listen to the lyrics of "Fury" and you will get it. Freestyle in the old-school style rather then in the new-school style.

VOCAL PRESENCE: 100

I don't know if anybody realized how hard it is to have a laid-back energy and still have the presence to really, really capture people with your voice. There are a lot of people who have laid-back energy, but they don't have the presence and the voice of capture. Rakim has the presence and the voice, even though it is laid-back, and that gives him 100 right off the top.

LIVE PERFORMANCE: 85

This is the most overblown, underrated scenario in the equation about Rakim. It's hype and it's a myth that he doesn't know how to perform. Well, he can perform. The problem, again, is you have big arenas and cerebral rhymes. He doesn't make a lot of party jams. So the illusion is the party is not happening. Well, that's because he is not doing party jams. He is a lot better then he was earlier but the rumors are just not true. People are just not analytical enough and they are not seeing it the way it's going down. People are actually listening to him as opposed to dancing. So the concert is still going the way it is supposed to go. They are enjoying Rakim for the way he is to be enjoyed.

POETIC VALUE: 100

His whole style is basically poetry. Just listen to the end of the first verse alone on "Follow the Leader."

BODY OF WORK: 100

Record, after record, after record, the rhyme level is so crazy, it is just stellar. It can't even be denied.

INDUSTRY IMPACT: 90

He, like Kane, basically took the industry by storm, even though he didn't have the same amount of imitators—but that was because his style basically couldn't be imitated, it was too unique. He definitely impacted the industry in terms of changing how people flowed and how people thought about rhymes, and what flow actually became. He is the inventor of that.

SOCIAL IMPACT: 90

He was the first emcee to really bring across the 5 percent doctrine. And within the 5 percent doctrine, whether you agreed with it or not, it got people thinking about putting spirituality in Hip-Hop.

LONGEVITY: 100

In 1997, when he came back with the single "Guess Who's Back," it just was what it was. It was almost like the anticipation of the king returning. So that goes from '86 to '97. So it is what it is.

LYRICS: 100

Come on. He is probably the most well-known lyricist for his lyrics alone than anybody in the history of the game. When you hear a lyricist, nine times out of ten you are being compared to Rakim. He became the benchmark.

BATTLE SKILLS: 95

Rakim is basically untested, but that is because no one dares test the R. The reverence and the love is too high on the lyrical side, but I have actually heard some of his stuff. There was a moment in time when people were trying to get him and Big Daddy Kane to battle each other, and I am probably the only person who heard both rhymes. Rakim is definitely a battler.

TOTAL SCORE: 1,600

AVERAGE SCORE: 94.1

1

MELLE MEL

THE GODFATHER OF RHYME

A child is born
With no state of mind
Blind to the ways of mankind
God is smiling on you
But he's frowning too
Because only god knows
What you'll go through
You'll gron in the ghetto
In the second rate
And your eyes will sing a song deep hate
The places you play
And where you stay
Look like one great big alleyway
You'll admire all the
Number book rakers
Thugs pimps and pushers
And the big money makers
Driving big cars
Spending 20's and 10's
And you'll wanna grow up
To be just like them
Smuggleers scramblers
Burglars gamblers pick pocket
Peddlers even pan handlers
You say i'm cool huh i'm no fool
But then you wind up droppin
Out of high school
Now you're unemployed all non-void
Walkin round like ya pretty boy floyd
Turned stick up kid
But look what you done did
Got sent up for a eight year bid
Now ya manhood is took
And you're a may tag
Spent the next two years
As an undercover fag
Being used and abused
And served like hell
Till one day you was found
Hung dead in ya cell
It was plain to see
That ya life was lost
You was cold and ya body
Swung back and forth

> *But now ya eyes sing*
> *The sad sad song*
> *Of how you live so fast*
> *And die so young*

POUND FOR POUND, "A CHILD IS BORN" is the greatest rhyme ever! When you talk about Melle Mel, you're talking about a plethora of superlatives, and a series of firsts. First of all, he's the first emcee to explode in a new rhyme cadence, and change the way every emcee rhymed forever. Rakim, Biggie, and Eminem have flipped the flow, but Melle Mel's downbeat on the two, four, kick to snare cadence is still the rhyme foundation all emcees are building on. With his brother Kid Creole, and Keith Cowboy, Grandmaster Flash's first emcee, Mel flipped the cadence from the simplistic call-and-response style, and added a rhythmic rhyme punch line style. Creole was known as the storyteller and the true first hype man for Flash, and Cowboy was the party emcee. The three of them had very similar cadences, and unlike most emcees at that time, they used their natural voices. But by 1978, they put two more emcees down, Mr Ness and Rahiem. The group became Grandmaster Flash and the Furious 5, and Melle Mel seized control as the dominant emcee. He began taking the rhymes into a poetic braggadocio, unparalleled at the time.

Along with Flash's innovations in DJ'ing (see *True 50 Greatest Groups*) Hip-Hop's first paradigm shift was complete. Hip-Hop had a whole new look and sound. It was all about beats and rhymes, and Melle Mel was at the forefront of the rhyme movement. He made everybody change their game and step up their lyrics. Anybody who started a group needed to have a lead emcee with skills as the anchor (Fearless Four, DLB, Cold Crush, Caz, Treacherous Three, Kool Moe Dee). The Funky Four recruited two emcees, Rodney C and Jazzy Jeff. Everybody was attempting to keep up with Melle Mel and the Furious Five's formula. And this is all done on a street level, before there were any rap records.

However, in 1979, after Sugar Hill dropped "Rappers Delight," Melle Mel went into a zone where he was basically untouchable. Without question Melle Mel was the best Hip-Hop songwriter from a lyricist's standpoint. I was the best intricate routine writer, Caz was the best song routine writer and DLB was the best theme routine writer, but none of us could touch Mel's consistent songwriting ability. Kurtis Blow was about as good, but Melle Mel was more lyrical, which gave him more of an edge than Kurtis. At the time, emcees weren't really allowed to make albums, but from 1989 to 1984 every single year Mel had some kind of hit on the streets. Although the records were by Grandmaster Flash and the Furious 5, everyone knew that Mel was the principal writer. In 1979, they had the marathon hit "Super Rappin," one of those eight-minute rhyme-athons with no hook. In 1980, they took over the summer with "Freedom." A party record, where Mel actually put the party on wax, with classic old-school call-and-response. In 1981, Birthday Party made a lot of noise, but this other great group The Treacherous Three, sewed up the year with "Feel the Heartbeat." Nonetheless, Mel's songwriting was still in full effect.

But in 1982, Melle Mel caused another paradigm shift, within a paradigm shift. Hip-Hop has a built-in three-year hit record paradigm shift. Every three years, since '79, a record comes out that shifts the way record-making is approached. However, the secret is the copycats can never duplicate it because it's a one-shot deal. In 1982, Afrika Bambaattaa shifted the planet with "Planet Rock" and Melle Mel shifted lyrical content with "The Message." This record is second only to Run-DMC'S "Walk This Way," in terms of what it did for Hip-Hop. Up until this point, there had only been party hits with lighthearted lyrical content. Kurtis Blow's "The Breaks," and "Hard Times" were messages, but "The Breaks" was more of a dance record, and Kurtis' execution was happy-go-lucky. The song "Hardtimes" just didn't hit. When "The Message" hit, Melle Mel began his separation from the pack of emcees. If Rakim was Michael Jordan, Melle Mel was Bill Russell (the first dominant champ). "The Message" caused a series of events that turned Hip-Hop on its head. The reason I called it a paradigm shift within a paradigm shift was because many things changed, but the cadence stayed the same. Change one, the record established Melle Mel as the official voice of the group. Ultimately, it broke the group up and he began his career as a soloist. Change two, it changed the routine formulas that groups were using on wax. It was the beginning of the end for the round-robin "Temptations"-like back-and-forth rhyming styles of the three-, four- and five-man groups. Suddenly, there were only soloists and duos. Even the Fat Boys were two emcees and a human beat box. Change three, almost every emcee tried to include some type of positive message in their music. Run-DMC'S "It's Like That," Fat Boys' "In Jail," Treacherous Three's "Yes We Can Can" and the Fearless Four's "Problems of the World" are just a few examples of the many groups that changed their party-style records.

The final and most significant change, in my opinion, was the record reported to have gone gold in twenty-one days. Within six months, the group was in court suing the label for royalties. This got everybody thinking about money and restructuring contracts. This also led to the breakup of the five-man groups because it wasn't enough money at that time to split five ways. After lawyers, managers, and taxes, the money from hit singles was merely a pittance. The contract issues and questionable business practices of record labels would resonate to this day. However, the creative changes lasted for four more years and Melle Mel rode the wave at the highest level. In 1983, he made his first true solo debut with "White Lines" where he masterfully slowed his cadence down to match the dark intensity of the track and the lyrical content. The song was the first record in Hip-Hop totally dedicated to the anti-drug movement. At this point, Mel was more associated with being an urban poetic messenger than he was an emcee. However, in 1984, he maximized the combination of the two energies and went into a lyrical zenith zone with the title song to the movie *Beat Street*. Mel's song, "Beat Street Breakdown," to this day has more poetic value than 95 percent of any Hip-Hop songs ever made.

> *A newspaper burns in the sand*
> *And the headlines say*
> *Man destroys man*
> *Extra extra read all the bad news*
> *On the war of peace*
> *Then everybody would lose*
> *The rise and fall, the last great empire*

The sound of the whole world
Caught on fire
The ruthless struggle
The desperate gamble
The game that left the whole world
In shambles
The cheats the lies the alibis
And the foolish attempts
To conquer the skies
Lost in space and what is it worth
The president just forgot about earth
Spending multi billions and
Maybe even trillions, the cost of
Weapons ran into zillions
There's gold in the street
And there's diamonds under feet
And the children in Africa
Don't even eat,
Flies on their faces
They're living like mice
And the house even make
The ghetto look nice huh
The water taste funny
It's forever too sunny
And they work all month
And don't make no money
A fight for power
A nuclear shower
A people shout out in the darkest hour
A sight unseen, and voices unheard
And finally the bomb
Gets the last word
Christians killed Muslims
And Germans killed Jews
And everybodies bodies
Were used and abused huh
Minds are poisoned
And souls are polluted
Superiority complex is deep rooted
Allegiance and license
And people got prices
Ego maniacs control
The self righteous
Nothin is sacred

And nothin is pure

So the revelation of death

Is our cure

Hitler and Caesar

Custer and Reagan

Napoleon Castro Mussolini-n

Gangus Kahn and the Shah of Iran

Men spill the blood

Of the weaker maaan

The peoples in terror

The leaders made an error

And now they can't even

Look in the mirror

Cause we gotta suffer

While things get rougher

And that's the reason why

We got to get tougher

So learn from the past

And work for the future

And don't be a slave

To no computer

Cause the children of man

Inherits the land

And future of the world

Is in your hand!

That's the best lyrical performance I have ever heard. If you look at my emcee scoring system, you'll see that Mel's execution of this song scores 100's in originality, substance, poetic value, vocal presence, social impact, industry impact, concept, and lyrics. This is an example of the highest level of the game. Ironically, it was also the song that locked Mel into a zone where he was no longer perceived as an emcee. His potency was too high. So when he tried to come with the classic emcee braggadocio demonstrated on "King of the Streets," he wasn't received well. He preceded that song with one of the darkest, poetically proficient records ever, "World War II" where he talked about the end of the world. Fans felt like it was too much. It made people think instead of dance. It was like Melle Mel was showing them that they were in the Matrix, and people don't want to hear or do anything about it. They just wanted to party. In the final analysis, Melle Mel laid the groundwork for the lyrical greats in the game. From 1978 to 1986, he did it at the highest level possible for the time. He showed the Hip-Hop world that we could use the music for more than dance. We could actually communicate our social, political, and spiritual views to try to help each other shed light on major issues.

As far as his skills go, they're unquestionable. He exuded a passion and attack that was literally a combination of Biggie and Tupac. He delivered powerful commentary with a reverence and cadence that was almost preacher-like. He rhymed in French on "It's

Nasty," he gave Chaka Kahn a street edge on "I Feel for You," and in 1990 he, along with myself, were hand-picked by Quincy Jones for his "Back on the Block" album. Ice-T and Big Daddy Kane were on WEA's distribution channels. (Warner Bros./Cold Chillin and Quincy's label "Q-West," distributed by WEA.) Ice-T and Kane were also two of the hottest emcees at the time, so this was a no-brainer for Quincy. However, I was old school and on Jive Records and Quincy hand-picked me anyway. But Melle Mel, arguably, was the only one selected strictly for his skills. Even I still had some heat on me in 1990, so one might say that was what my selection was based on. However, Mel hadn't had a hit since 1984. His impact and excellently profound lyrics is what sustained his energy and a master producer like Quincy Jones can't be fooled by heat or the lack there of. However, in the United States of Amnesia, fans seem to forget about whatever is not hot currently. I, on the other hand, am a fan and an expert analyst. Melle Mel is arguably the TRUE GREATEST EMCEE!

Strength: Vocals. Nobody comes across with the combination of vocal presence, intensity, substance, poetic value, and lyrical mastery like Mel.

Weakness: Transition. He never respected change enough to be able to make the transition to the newer styles of rhyming.

Favorite Record: "White Lines," "Beat Street Breakdown"

Favorite LP: *The Best of Grandmaster Flash, Melle Mel and the Furious Five*

#1: MELLE MEL

ORIGINALITY: 100

The original emcee who set the template for whatever we were going to be doing. Until Melle Mel, people rhymed completely in the party style. He is the first one to come with analogy, antonym, simile . . . he is the first emcee to bring all of that into the equation and in his regular voice. He is the original. He should be able to get 200 for originality.

CONCEPTS: 85

You've just got to go back and listen. He did not have the opportunity to do albums, but basically doing the singles that he did at the time, in the group Furious Five and then when he got out of it, just "White Lines" alone was a concept that was ridiculous.

VERSATILITY: 90

Mel can give you the braggadocio, he can give you the message, he can give you street commentary, he can break records about the president, records on Jesse Jackson, the concept about World War III . . . he was a versatile emcee, without question.

VOCABULARY: 95

With just the references that he makes, even in newer stuff that people haven't heard that isn't on wax, it is just ridiculous in terms of what he does with vocabulary.

SUBSTANCE: 100

The message says it all. "A Child Is Born With No State of Mind" in my opinion is the best rhyme ever heard in the history of the game.